Praise for David Poyer's Hemlock County Novels

"David Poyer knows the smell of Pennsylvania gas wells, the creak of pumps coaxing underground oil to the surface. He knows the northeastern woods, and the small-town isolation they engender. Most of all, he knows the people who live in the shadows of the Allegheny Forest . . . dark and gritty as a gravel road."
—Pittsburgh *Tribune-Review* on *As the Wolf Loves Winter*

"A grim, moving thriller from the prolific Poyer . . . a subtle, highly original blend of eco-thriller and novel of character."
—*Kirkus Reviews* on *As the Wolf Loves Winter*

"Poyer enlivens this courtroom thriller with vividly imagined and deftly rendered characters. . . . Careful pacing and colorful prose will keep readers swiftly turning pages."
—*Publishers Weekly* on *Winter in the Heart*

"Poyer's depictions . . . continue to be unequalled for authenticity."
—*Kirkus Reviews*

"Poyer creates characters who breathe."
—*Wilmington News-Journal*

"Poyer knows what he is writing about."
—*The New York Times Book Review*

"An assured and gifted storyteller."
—*Library Journal*

WINTER LIGHT

THE HEMLOCK COUNTY NOVELS

Thunder on the Mountain
As the Wolf Loves Winter
Winter in the Heart
The Dead of Winter

OTHER NOVELS BY DAVID POYER

China Sea
Tomahawk
Down to a Sunless Sea
The Only Thing to Fear
The Passage
Louisiana Blue
The Circle
Bahamas Blue
The Gulf
Hatteras Blue
The Med
Stepfather Bank
The Return of Philo T. McGiffin
The Shiloh Project
White Continent

David Poyer

WINTER LIGHT

A TOM DOHERTY ASSOCIATES BOOK
NEW YORK

WINTER LIGHT

This book is an omnibus edition consisting of the novels *Winter in the Heart*, copyright © 1993
by David Poyer, and *As the Wolf Loves Winter,* copyright © 1996 by David Poyer.

Chapter Nine of *Winter in the Heart* appeared in an early form in the *State Street Review*
as "Jaysine."

This book is printed on acid-free paper.

A Forge Book
Published by Tom Doherty Associates, LLC
175 Fifth Avenue
New York, NY 10010

www.tor.com

Forge® is a registered trademark of Tom Doherty Associates, LLC.

ISBN 0-312-87904-0

First Trade Paperback Edition: January 2001

Printed in the United States of America

0 9 8 7 6 5 4 3 2 1

Contents

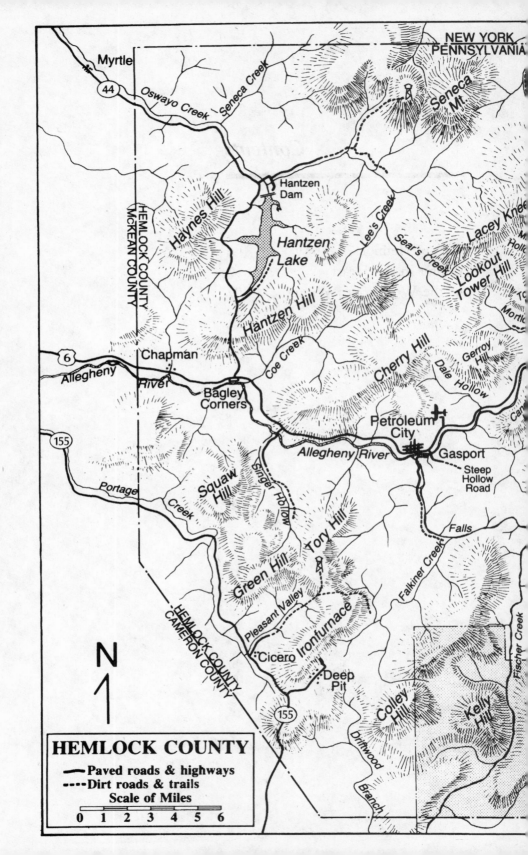

NEW YORK
PENNSYLVANIA

Myrtle

44

Oswayo Creek

Seneca Creek

Seneca Mt.

Hantzen Dam

Haynes Hill

Hantzen Lake

Lee's Creek

Sear's Creek

Lacey Knee

Lookout Tower Hill

HEMLOCK COUNTY
McKEAN COUNTY

Hantzen Hill

Coe Creek

Cherry Hill

Gerroy Hill

Dale Hollow

Chapman

6

Allegheny   River

Bagley Corners

155

Petroleum City

Allegheny River

Gasport

Steep Hollow Road

Portage   Creek

Squaw Hill

Singer Hollow

Falkiner Creek

Falls

Green Hill

Tory Hill

Pleasant Valley

Cicero   Ironfurnace

Deep Pit

HEMLOCK COUNTY
CAMERON COUNTY

155

Colley Hill

Kely Hill

Fischer Creek

Driftwood   Branch

N

HEMLOCK COUNTY
—— Paved roads & highways
----- Dirt roads & trails
Scale of Miles
0 1 2 3 4 5 6

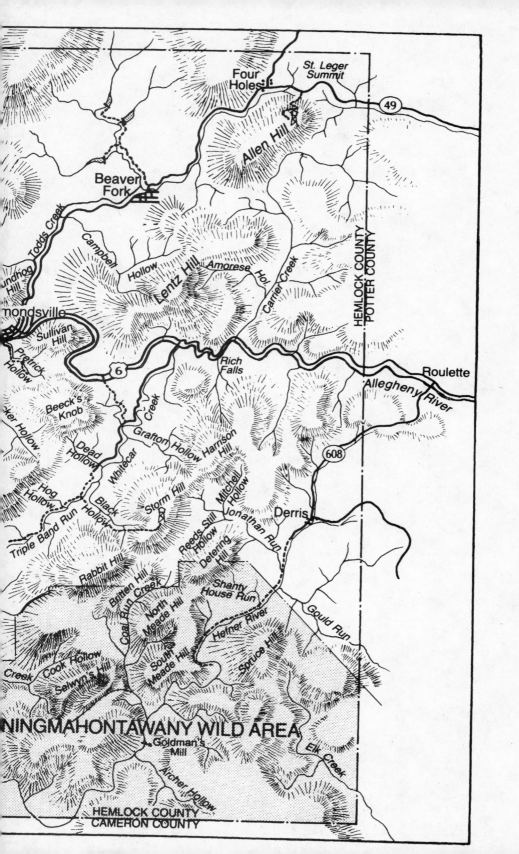

WINTER
IN
THE
HEART

For John,
Who left too soon
1933-1982

Acknowledgments

Ex nihilo nihil fit. For this book I owe much to James Allen, Laura Benton, Robert Chapman, Phyllis Cook, Tom Doherty, Candy S. Ekdahl, Donald Ekdahl, Kelly Fisher, Doris Peterson Galen, Frank Green, Robert Gleason, Lenore Hart, Frederick Hillyer, Russ Jaffe, Tim Jenkins, Mary Ann Johnston, Anna Magee, John Ordover, Jay Parini, Rick Peroginelli, Martin Pesaresi, Lin Poyer, Gary J. Richards, Howard Troutman, George Witte, J. M. Zias, Robert Legault, and others who preferred anonymity, though generously giving of their time. All errors and deficiencies are my own.

Acknowledgments

Prologue

The guards woke the old man early, slamming the barred door open with a jangling bang that echoed down the corridor of the cell block. Earlier than he'd expected; he hadn't thought judges and lawyers went to work that soon. They waited as he washed his face and dried it with the thin jailhouse towel and thought about shaving. He'd shaved yesterday, he decided, that should be good enough.

He moved around the cell, slowly pulling on faded green work pants, suspenders, a white shirt his daughter had brought, an old green work cap with ear-flaps. He favored his shoulder, which was still tender where they'd taken the bullet out. Then he sat on the bunk to lace up his boots. The lawyer woman, Quintero, she'd told him to wear a tie, but he drew the line at that.

If I'd of been the kind of fellow owned a tie, I wouldn't of ended up here in the first place, Halvorsen thought.

The breakfast tray came, the same meal as the last three days: oatmeal with raisins, toast, coffee. He wasn't hungry, but he made himself eat the oatmeal.

He was standing at the narrow window looking out at the hills when the U.S. federal marshal came for him. A big friendly-looking fella in a gray suit, but you could tell he was a cop. Another marshal stood behind him. "Morning, Racks," he said. "Ready for the grand jury?"

"Question is, they ready for me?"

The marshal chuckled and jerked a thumb at his deputy. Halvorsen held his hands out without saying anything. The heavy cuffs dragged them down.

"Leg irons too. And waist chains."

"Hell, give me a break, fellas. I got a good thirty years on anybody else around here."

"Everybody gets the same jewelry, old-timer. Had a eighty-six-year-old man assault a guard in Montana last year."

When they were done with him he could hardly walk, but he shuffled and jingled out into the corridor after them.

They went out the back of the jail, the marshal holding the door for him. Halvorsen stopped for a minute in the parking lot, sucking in the cold snow-smelling air and looking up at a glazed sky. He hadn't seen much of it for the last couple of weeks. The snowflakes fell toward them between the dark buildings in perfect beautiful silence, glittering fragments chipped from the white glacier of winter cloud. He sighed as one needled his upturned face.

It was winter. The seasons of sun, of green, were gone. Now each thing that lived had to endure. Or die.

"You ready? We got about five blocks."

He cleared his throat and nodded, recalled to the present. Snow crunched and squealed under their boots as the marshals led him to an unmarked car. Another plainclothesman sat in the front seat. The engine was running. "No squad car?" he asked.

"Attracts too much attention. Last year we had that guy who was testifying against the Colombians, maybe you read about him in the paper. We took him over in a bakery truck."

The marshal laughed and they got into the back seat. A steel screen separated them from the front. He leaned over Halvorsen to fasten the belt as the driver put the car into gear. As they turned into the street Halvorsen got his hands on the crank after a couple of tries and wound the window down. The fresh air felt good after the closed, overheated, man-thick atmosphere of the Allegheny County Jail.

They drove through the heart of town and turned at the Federal Reserve Bank. The car juddered suddenly over cobblestones. Grant Street, he remembered now. He hadn't ever gotten to Pittsburgh much, not for years now, and hardly ever downtown. The last time he'd looked up at this granite building the Depression had been on, and brown-uniformed National Guard with doughboy helmets and bayoneted Springfields had surrounded it, holding back a sullen crowd.

"You know," he said, "last time I was here, Roosevelt was president."

"Roosevelt, huh? Which one?"

He was about to answer, angry—how old did they think he was, anyway?—when the marshal said, "Just kidding. You mean FDR, right? Over there, Bill. Damn, there's a bunch of 'em this time. Okay, here we go."

The car doors opened into a sudden boil of faces, open mouths, a shouting wall of granite-echoed sound. Strobe lights detonated blinding-bright, pinning them with focused lenses. Two or three dozen jostling, elbowing people were shouting at him at once in an unintelligible gabble that let no word through. It sounded to him like a pack of hounds baying after a deer, the way they hunted down South. He kept his face blank, moving with the marshals, who surrounded him now. He caught a glimpse of himself on some kind of electronic screen they'd set up: a slightly stooped, thin old man with a jailhouse pallor, stalking stiffly through the mob in faded old clothes, the too-long chains dragging on the sidewalk.

Then the marshal had his arm, was half leading him, half lifting him up broad granite steps toward brass-edged doors. The snow fell harder now, whirling out of the white sky.

The revolving doors hissed closed on the pandemonium outside. Halvorsen glanced back to see faces and cameras pressed to the glass. Then he stumbled, the chains catching on the step of some kind of walk-through machine. An impassive black woman waved a wand over him, then nodded to the marshal.

At the far end of a low marbled corridor he saw the others. Boulton was sitting on a wooden bench with two men in overcoats. His attorneys, if that's what they were, looked confident, as if they'd just had big break-fasts and a shot of something to set them up. But something had changed in Boulton's eyes. He looked straight ahead, as if blind to anything or anyone around him. There was the Farmer girl, too, an older woman with her, sitting quietly in a corner. Halvorsen tried to catch her eye but failed.

He wondered if somehow the boy could see them too.

Quintero was waiting for him at the door to the grand jury room, her briefcase between her galoshes on the green and white tile floor. She was his court-appointed lawyer, a small woman with a scarred-up face. He'd wondered what had happened to her. It looked like she'd had a run-in with some mean dogs. But he hadn't asked, and she hadn't said. As they neared her the marshals slowed.

The first thing she said was, "You didn't shave."

"You goin' in with me?" he asked her.

"I told you, Mr. Halvorsen, persons called before a federal grand jury testify alone. You're the first witness today. So please, just listen. Are you listening?"

"Yeah, I'm listenin'."

"When you're in there, don't answer any questions about your actions or even your intentions. Just your name—that's enough to establish co-operation. You can answer anything that reflects on Boulton. Gibson will probably start with that to soften you up, make you feel he's on your side. Cooperate with that part if you like, but stay alert. Because after that, when you've set Boulton up, he'll go after you. Understand?"

"I get it."

"When you're asked anything pertaining to your own actions, excuse yourself, leave the stand, and come out here. Tell me what the question is, I'll tell you what to say, you go back in. *Don't say anything without asking me first.* Tell me you understand that."

"It's a pack of foolishness. *You* can't come in—"

"But you can come out and consult with me. That's right."

"Who made up that rule? No, forget it." Halvorsen swallowed. He wished he had a chew, his mouth was dry.

"If you don't want to come out, then take the fifth amendment. Just say, 'I refuse to answer on the grounds that it may tend to incriminate me.' This guy's smart. And whatever he says, he's not on your side. First he'll try to scare you. Then he'll mention immunity, but it won't be a real offer. If he was serious he'd have come to me. Don't try to match wits with him. If you don't watch yourself he'll have a full confession by the time you step down."

"Thought you said this wasn't a trial."

"It's not. But whatever you say before a grand jury can be used against you later, if you *are* put on trial. Understand?"

"I guess."

"Calling William T. Halvorsen," said a bailiff.

The marshal said, "You about done with him, counselor?"

"Remember what I said," said Quintero, taking a fold of his shirt between her fingertips. "Don't say a word about anything you did without coming out and talking to me first. And good luck."

Halvorsen blew out, grimaced, and said to the bailiff, "Let's go."

The courtroom reminded him of a church. Same worn wooden pews. The same let's-get-started murmur from the flock. The tall man waiting up there for him looked like the preacher. Only instead of a congregation, the jury. Ordinary-looking people, middle-aged, mostly women, one colored fella almost as old as he was. More of them than he'd expected. He felt their eyes follow him as they led him down front and took off the cuffs and chains and irons. There was a chair for him at a little table. Halvorsen sighed as he let himself down into it, rubbing his wrists and looking around. A little man in a bow tie sat a few feet behind him, limbering up his fingers, then tapping on a funny-looking kind of telegraph key. Taking down what they said, most likely, because he tapped some when Halvorsen had to get up again and swear on a Bible.

As soon as he sat down again the preacher-looking fella started in. Halvorsen squinted up at him as he began, no smile or word of welcome, just: "Please state your name."

He said slowly, "My name's W. T. Halvorsen."

"The W stands for William."

"That's right."

"Resident of?"

"Hemlock County, state of Pennsylvania. Live outside of Raymondsville."

"Mr. Halvorsen, let me introduce myself. I'm Gregory Gibson, the assistant U.S. attorney for the Western District."

Halvorsen cleared his throat, wondering if he should say he was glad to meet him. Finally he just said, "Uh huh."

"I understand you've been able to consult with a court-appointed attorney. Is that correct?"

"That's right."

"Good. However, just to be sure you're clear in your mind what's going on, let me explain what you're doing here.

"These men and women constitute a federal grand jury. If they think there's evidence you committed a crime, they'll vote an indictment against you. Then the real trial takes place, where the jury decides guilt and innocence, and the judge hands down a sentence. The grand jury has no power to punish. However, false or misleading statements before it are punishable as perjury. Do you understand?"

He nodded, muttered, "I understand." Was it just that he was old, that made everybody want to explain everything to him three times? Hell, he understood what was going on. Understood all too well.

They were going to try to pin it all on him.

Gibson nodded. He strolled a few paces away, as if collecting his thoughts, then came back. Now his voice changed, acquired a threatening edge.

"Mr. Halvorsen, I don't mind telling you we're dealing with a confused situation here, about the events that took place on December nineteenth of last year. And the events that led up to it.

"But first, I want to make sure you understand the gravity of what happened. We're talking about major damages, major impacts on the whole Allegheny watershed. Over seven hundred and fifty thousand people, in seven counties, draw drinking water from the river. For the past weeks they've had to depend on bottled water or emergency supplies for their drinking and cooking needs." Gibson glanced at the jury. "This includes most of Pittsburgh, by the way. A cleanup effort is under way, but it's going to be slow. Estimates vary as to how long it will be before the river is usable again, but even the shortest is in months.

"Mr. Halvorsen, someone is liable for damages. Not just for the expense of cleanup, not even just for fines, but for the dozens of civil suits already filed along the route that poison took.

"I also don't mind telling you that my office is drawing up federal charges against you and your co-conspirators. To make it brief, we're drawing up indictments on federal explosive charges and on dumping of hazardous substances. The knowing-endangerment charge alone carries maximum penalties of a quarter of a million dollars, fifteen years in prison, or both. And then there are the costs of cleanup, which it's quite possible will run into the millions."

Halvorsen took his green cap with the thunderbolt insignia off and put it on his lap. He wished he'd brought a handkerchief, it sure was hot in here. The talk about millions didn't scare him. He just didn't have it, that was all. But to spend the rest of his life walled in, never to see woods again . . .

"Those are the federal charges. I can't speak for the state charges, but they'll be at least as serious. Subject to the decision of a Pennsylvania grand jury, you may be charged with conspiracy, destruction of state property, a separate state explosives charge, reckless endangerment, brandishing of firearms, manslaughter, attempted murder, and murder. You and the others involved will stand trial for those separately from the federal charges. Do you understand that?"

He grunted, "Yeah."

Gibson nodded slowly. "Good. Now let's return to the federal charges, and your testimony.

"Mr. Halvorsen, I personally believe that if you testify fully and fairly about the events of that night, it may be possible to offer you immunity on some or all of the above charges, in exchange for your testimony against others involved in the violation of the Toxic Substances Control Act—those being the primary federal charges in this case. We're counting on you to clarify the reasons for your actions, and to clarify the reasons behind the actions of others. Are you willing to help us do this?"

He thought about Quintero's advice, and his mouth twisted. "You mean, make some kind of a deal? I say what you want, you let me off?"

"Not exactly like that, Mr. Halvorsen—"

"Because W. T. Halvorsen don't make deals like that. I'm goin' to tell the truth, y'see? Tell you what I done, and why. And I don't need you, or that lady lawyer they give me, or nobody else to tell me what to say."

He watched the prosecutor's face change; watched it take on the likeness of a man he could trust, a fellow who wanted to help him. "Let me see if I understand you, Mr. Halvorsen. As a concerned citizen, you're willing to tell us the full and complete story about events leading up to your actions on the night of last December nineteenth, without reservations, guarantees, or any promises on the part of the government as to immunity on any charge that may result?"

He caught a motion from the back pew, and half expected to see Quintero, her scarred face red and white now, waving frantically at him. He turned his head away, just in case she'd got in somehow, and said firmly to the preacherlike man, to the silent jury: "Yeah. I'll tell you folks ever'thin' I know."

"All right, Mr. Halvorsen. When you—"

"Long's I can tell it m'self, in my own words, without you interrupting me."

The prosecutor looked as if he was eating something he hated. But finally he nodded. "You have the floor, Mr. Halvorsen."

Halvorsen looked at the ceiling, at the lazily turning fans, trying to get his thoughts organized. Too damn hot to think. Had so much to tell. About Barry Fox, and the Farmer girl, and the doctor woman. About Ainslee Thunner and old Dan and the smooth-faced man who'd taken his place . . . about the little girl . . . the black trucks . . . the men who'd come to Mortlock Hollow with guns and cans of gasoline . . .

But how could he tell it all? Tell it so they'd understand? He felt sweat slide down his back under the stiff white shirt. Goddamnit, he'd told Alma he hated starch in his shirts. Maybe this wasn't smart. Maybe he was just sticking his head in the noose. No business for a man old as he was. Man who couldn't remember right, either forgot things or else remembered too damn much, saw everything, like it was happening in front of his eyes. He didn't want to be here. He hadn't wanted to do what he'd done. All he'd wanted was to be left alone.

But they'd never put it together if he clammed up. Quintero meant well. She wanted to protect him. But if they didn't get everything out in the open now, it'd never get told. Boulton and his pals and politicians would twist and shred and bury it, like cats covering their dirt, till no one knew what was hidden where. And the rottenness would go on, and spread . . . This was what the boy had died for. A chance to tell the truth, the whole truth, and nothing but.

The ceiling was white. At first it looked white as snow, until you stared a while. Then you noticed the brown stains seeping through.

Yeah, Halvorsen thought. A grim faint smile of memory took his white-stubbled jaw. Yeah, that'd been the beginning, far as he knew.

The day it had started to snow.

One

When dawn had come that day he'd been on the road for two hours, hiking downhill through the storm. He had his old-style floppy cap, earflaps tied down. Heavy army-surplus melton pants. Plaid wool coat, the kind not even hunters wore anymore. At each step his boots plunged lace-deep into new snow. And it was still whirling down steadily out of the darkness, lashing his numbed and downbent face.

An invisible pothole made him stumble. This stretch had been bad all winter, and now it was worse. There were springs above it, on the south face of Town Hill, and when they froze the macadam heaved and buckled like a slow earthquake. A few more years and Mortlock Run would be impassable to wheels, relapsed to the foot trail it had been two centuries before, when the names of this land were Seneca.

Well, Halvorsen thought, there's not many use it these days. There wasn't another house from here all the way back up to Mortlock Hollow.

He was resigned to hiking all the way out to Route Six, when he caught an orange flicker deep in the storm. He rubbed ice from his eyelashes.

A snarl of diesels, a creaking rumble of axles, the grating scream of steel on stone.

The lights rose like twin suns, blinding him like a jacklighted deer. The snowplow leaped from the blowing snow as if created from it, huge as a locomotive, yellow and black, the colors of peril and death. Halvorsen stood half facing it, as if waiting to be run down. A horn blatted, the warning echoing from the hills. Then was succeeded by a rush of braking air.

The plow rumbled to a halt. The driver stretched across the bench seat, and the passenger door swung open.

Halvorsen hauled himself stiffly up steel steps into the cab. He untied his hat and flirted snow onto the floor. The interior light showed a pepper of stubble on his cheeks, a rime of snow on his collar. Pale blue eyes closed briefly in the blast from the heater.

"Morning there, Racks," said the driver.

"Hullo, Barry."

Barry Fox eased the truck back into gear. The blade rumbled and boomed, snow hissing off it as they picked up speed.

"Goin' into town?"

Halvorsen nodded.

"Almost didn't see you. Guess winter's here for sure now."

Fox waited, then went on. "Ever ride the plow before?"

The old man shook his head.

"State's got newer now, but these old Loadstars just keep rollin'. Half-ton plow"—he gestured expansively, like a captain at his new vessel—"carbide steel, lasts the whole season. Carry eight ton of three-to-one in the bed. Lever here runs the spinner. Don't need a guy with a shovel like in your day. Say, she's glassy this morning, isn't she?"

Halvorsen sat silent, head nodding as the truck jolted and roared.

Fox said, "Saw a big old buck out here last week. Just caught a glimpse of him before he lined out for the brush, but looked to be a ten, twelve-pointer. Funny, looked like he had a heavier rack on the right side, you know? Ever see a deer like that?"

"Think I know the one you mean."

"Must be pretty crafty, takes 'em a while to grow antlers like that. Got to wonder if he'll make it through the season. Scary thought, you know? Wonder how we'd do, out in them woods, people after us . . . So, you still livin' way the hell up back of nowhere?"

"Uh huh."

"Takes all kinds, I guess. Me, I like people around. We just bought us a house out Finney Parkway. Solid oak floors. Get a paycheck ahead, we'll get some throw rugs from the Big Wheel—"

Halvorsen said, "On Finney? What number?"

"One-twenty-two."

"That was Dick Myers's house."

"Yeah, Myers, that was the name on the title."

"I worked a lease with Dick back in forty-eight. Dottie sold the place, huh? How's she doing?"

"She died six months ago. No, eight."

Fox shifted and the plow began snarling uphill. The headlights transmuted falling snow into spinning cones of gold, the whirly lights flicked

The details, then. He squinted. Pickard's Drug. Same gold-leafed sign. Only the displays had changed since his boyhood. No longer Save the Baby, Castoria, Black-Draught, but some new hemorrhoid preparation; inside no longer elixirs, paregoric, but antibiotics and stress vitamins . . . Beyond it the railroad embankment, that too the same, the rusty switches, the glass globes of the crossing guard round and red as candied apples.

But then a void, a vacancy in the world as it once was and thus to him somehow still ought to be. He stood blinking in the falling snow, wondering if his next blink would make the old Erie Lackawanna stationhouse reappear. Would retrieve from time's memory its rose-petal brick, the arched portico of sooty gilt and lace-metal, the porcelain drinking-fountain, the solid iron wheels of the baggage-wagons. If another blink would bring back the vanished blocks beyond. In his boyhood they'd been banks, producers' offices, machine shops, beer joints. From his manhood he remembered them as thrift shops, relief offices, and from middle age abandoned storefronts.

Then one day the bulldozers came. The *Century's* editorials had talked brightly of an assembly plant; then of a shopping center; at last, in a kind of Rotarian despair, of low-income housing.

Halvorsen squinted into the wind till the world wavered in tears. But nothing returned. The town's heart was still. Dead. He wondered what would spring next from that razed ground, sowed with sharded glass as with the teeth of dragons.

He shuddered suddenly, and forced his legs into motion. The snow fell like soot from burning icebergs. The Christmas decorations were already up. They hung shabby, decades old, from the lightposts. Abreast of Pickard's he turned for the Raymondsville Hotel. He remembered only when confronted by blank plywood that it too was gone, shot, kaput.

He stood for a moment shivering, brain empty as a jug. Then recognized the door next to it. It jingled gaily as he pulled it open.

"Morning, Racks." As he stamped snow from his boots a short man, fiftyish, came out from behind a stack of secondhand records. His hands trembled as he adjusted his glasses; his eyes, magnified to golf balls, focused somewhere to Halvorsen's left.

"Hullo, Les. How's business?"

"You're first one today. Help you with something?"

"Just come in to get warm, thanks."

Les Rosen, the owner, busied himself behind the counter while Halvorsen presented his backside to a nickeled Amherst. He looked around absently. Worn washboards, a thirdhand dresser with curling veneer. A Kelsey handpress, a bronze lamp without a shade. Engravings of Jesus and locomotives, sepia-toned men in handlebar mustaches with watch chains, grim busty women in black, all either faded or darkened to a contrastlessness that made it hard for him to tell in the gloom what he was look-ing at.

He strolled over to a wooden ice chest. On it, beneath a photo of the 1937 St. Rocco's women's basketball team, were three Nancy Drew novels, a glass rolling-pin, and a dented metal can a foot long.

"Bet you know what that is," said Rosen, puttering up behind him. His fingers never left the tables, the walls, as if he were hauling himself through the past by handholds.

"Nitro can."

"Yeah, picked up a bunch of those when the blasting company went out of business."

"Sell any?"

The owner shrugged. "They'll move. It's not like I got to worry about overhead. Say, I got one nice thing out of that sale."

"What?"

Rosen opened the ice chest. In it was a wooden box, mitered at the corners, with a walnut handle at the top. Halvorsen took it with both hands—it looked heavy, and was—and turned it over. The letters were burned into the wood. *Hercules Powder Company, 50 Cap Blasting Machine, Connect Wires Only After Charge Is Set.*

"Spark box," said Halvorsen. He lowered it to the floor and drew up the plunger. It came smoothly and he saw that the toothed metal was oiled and rustless. He licked his little finger and then his index. He bridged that hand between the brass screw-posts, then with the other drove sud-denly down. Within the box the armature whirred.

He smiled faintly and straightened, massaging shock-tingling fingers.

"Probably seventy, eighty years old. But she works, don't she? What you think it's worth?"

"No idea."

"I'd take fifty for it."

Halvorsen hefted it again, then slid it back into its copper-lined coffin. "Thanks, Les. But I got no use. Now, a bolt for a .30 Krag—that I might scratch up a buck for."

"Sorry."

Rosen puttered his way back behind the counter. Halvorsen lingered for a few more minutes, then drifted toward the door. A loose board gave him away.

"Leavin' already?"

"Got some errands to do. Then I'll probably head over't' the Brown Bear, see if anybody's around."

"Stop back anytime."

The door jangled behind him with ominous gaiety, returning him from the safe past to whatever year this was. He'd felt okay with Rosen. But the strangeness had waited outside for him all this time, like a stray dog hoping for a master. Again it stopped him, made him look vacantly down the street.

What in the hell was wrong?

His mind found no answer. Only the snow, the wind, the loneliness of a blighted and dying town.

Halvorsen shivered suddenly. Was it judgment? Over and over greedy men had torn fortunes from these blasted hills. They'd laughed at the future. Now it was here.

But whatever was coming, whatever he was dreading, he didn't want to meet it. He'd fought hard all his life. He was old now. Tired. He wanted to be left alone.

Closing his eyes, he lifted his face to the sky. To the icy death-kisses of snowflakes on his forehead, on his neck, on his bare still-tingling hands.

Another tremor shook him, of cold but also of something not far from terror. His hands slapped his pockets, then fell back helplessly to his sides. Only now, too late, did he remember that his scarf and gloves still lay on the seat of a snowplow, headed west.

Two

And the snow fell without cease. It whispered down on silent hills; on an old man's upturned face; on the cab of a snowplow rumbling toward the county line. Soft, heavy, endless, it hissed down past the windows of the high school like congealed silence.

Phil Romanelli was sealed off from it by grimy glass into a steamy class-room on the second floor. He sat at one of three dozen identical desks. His face was too thin and his hair too long, and his left leg was twisted like a climbing plant.

At last he lowered his eyes to the note that had reached him a moment before, announced by a pencil-prod from fat Alice Saunters behind him. Miss Marzeau had missed the pass. He held it unopened, trembling a little.

He was savoring the possibility that it might be from Alexandrine Ryun. His explanation, a few minutes before, of why Jim had accepted the chal-lenge of the island might have done the trick. An excited twitch made his leg knock rapidly against the desk.

With infinite care, shielding his hand behind Ed Masters's broad obliv-ious back, he peeled the palm-dampened paper apart.

KNOCK IT OFF SMART MOUTH read pencilscrawl. OR ILL TEACH YOU TO SUCK MY DICK INSTEAD OF MARZEAUS ASS.

Phil stared at it as the teacher droned on. Lozenge-shaped iron walls were closing on him, glowing-hot. Though half the seats in the room were vacant, depopulated by the first snowfall, the very air seemed suddenly solid with hatred.

He didn't know which of them had sent the note. But he knew the type. They sprawled in the back row with their arms folded, sniggering to each other. They made farting noises with their hands. Technically they were his peers, but Phil had realized long ago they were of separate species. *Jockus americanus*, the common musclebrain, resisted learning as the Dutch resist the sea. While he sat near the front in every class; could not let an idea pass without challenge; could not accept an assertion without subjecting it to the proof of argument.

And could never, ever, be a jock.

His eyes caught snow again, and drifted down with it. Till they found Alex. Two rows over she sat with chin propped on fist, a faint smile touching her lips. Her lips . . . he stared, unaware that his clenched jaw had loosened, his mouth had fallen open slightly. Rounded softnesses shifted beneath her sweater as she tossed back her head, sending that long, long hair back to break in fatal shining surf . . .

The teacher's voice faded to a dull ache. His eyeballs, sandpapered by the dry heat, centered and fixed. A more absorbing drama had taken center stage, with himself—edited here and there, but himself as everyone is most himself in dream—in the title role.

He and Alex had spent the evening at the Dirty Shirt, but neither liquor nor lateness slowed the Stag. He'd parked the Firebird off the road, across a disused spur, and they were screened from midnight travelers by brush and the solid dark mass of the hills.

The first kiss. She moaned. Soon she was panting.

Moonlight gleamed tangled in red-gold hair. His fingers polished soft flesh, slow, maddening. She leaned back, shuddering, and the moon silvered her eyelids. His fingers considered the curve of her breast as he bent his lips to her panting mouth, her long white throat. When his hand dropped she tensed, then gave in with a helpless cry. Her arms came up, round his neck, and drew him downward.

The bucket seats changed magically to a bed. Beyond the window snowflakes fell like cold manna from an opaque sky. She wore a nightgown the texture of fog. His hand explored beneath it, then dipped within. Her flesh was hot and smooth, like incandescent petals.

"Phil, I want you. I need you inside me." Her burning eyes locked with his in the near-darkness. Her hungry mouth demanded him. His fist gathered gauzy material, and suddenly ripped it apart. Beneath was wanton alabaster, smooth and hairless as Aphrodite in the art books.

He took her almost violently. Not because it was what she wanted. But because it was his desire.

Alex Ryun, the real one, stretched up her hand. Recalled by the motion, Phil wrenched himself back from cool sheets and scented moonlight.

Here the air was dull with carbon dioxide, suffused with a high earnest drone of literature, permeated by a glow of hatred like the dry heat from the rusting radiators.

"That's right, Alexandrine. The most interesting thing here is Conrad's use of what's called a 'frame.' The opening and closing scenes are set pieces within which a narrator tells a story. Now, why is it done that way? Who is Marlow, really? Yes—Bethany, go ahead."

The thin eager voice faded, leaving no mark or echo in his hormone-driven consciousness. The crippled boy's eyes glazed over again. Helplessly libidinous as a male mantis, they bored through the shadows that surrounded him to his inmost desire, the fantasy, the lubricious, impossible dream.

Yes, the disease still existed. To the surprise of people he met. It seemed they always had to know exactly what was wrong with his leg, his hip, his arm.

He didn't remember the onset. But the first images he could retrieve of life were of bed, doctors, stainless steel, and pain.

At Strong Memorial in Rochester the specialists hadn't encouraged his parents. There were operations, they said, that might straighten the twisted leg. But there was little chance of the boy's walking. It was Joe Romanelli who'd insisted on surgery. Regardless of cost, regardless of the pain.

The worst operation had been the third, when Phil was seven. Most of his leg muscles were gone, atrophied and resorbed. The surgeon, a quiet balding man, brought hand puppets on his rounds. He pretended they were biting the children's withered limbs and chests. He'd spent six hours teasing out smaller muscles from the undamaged ones in Phil's legs, and connecting them with ligaments cannibalized from the left arm.

After that came endless months of excruciating therapy. Nurses and therapists, pulling like devils in a Boschian hell, till it seemed the gleaming machines would tear his joints apart. Endless drill to retain muscle tissue, to reprogram his brain. A hundred thousand calf-builders, quad-builders, and stretches. Always stretches. He still did them every morning. If he neglected them, even for a day, those painfully rebuilt muscles would tighten back toward uselessness.

In a way, his father had been proved right. Phil was strong. He could walk for miles. But one thigh would always be too weak for him to move without a limp. He had to aid it with his lower torso, hitching it forward from the hip at each step.

Now the boy who'd outlasted the knife was seventeen. He dreamed, and knew bitterly that what he dreamed could never happen. In his fantasies he saw himself as the Stag. Awake, as a virgin, a cripple, and a nerd.

Which of the two did those around him see? Did Alex Ryun see?

It was an important question. He'd thought about it a lot. Because if he'd never be anything more, he'd decided it might be better not to live.

Alex had only panties on now, and was daring him to reach across the aisle by caressing her sweat-slicked belly, when he became aware of a change around him. He returned unwillingly to the other universe, the one outside his head. At least, nude or not, whether she knew he was alive or not, Alexandrine Ryun was in it with him.

Reality, he thought. Chipmunk shit.

"And that will be due next week," Marzeau's voice, at once dust-dry and breathless with excitement, concluded. "Any questions?"

Despite the total inattention of what passed for his conscious mind, Phil found that some obscure part of his brain had retained the words before that. They were "Four pages, typewritten, double-spaced." He raised his hand, conscious as he did so of the cessation of normal class-room sounds—belches, sniggers, undertones—from the back.

"Philip?"

"Ma'am, I caught everything about that except the subject."

"The subject of your composition is to be an older person, preferably over seventy. Interview the individual and record his life story in his or her own words. This is to show you how to bring out character through dialogue—something Mr. Hemingway was good at."

He nodded, lowered his head. The awareness behind him relaxed. But a flame had ignited inside him. His glance had crossed hers, just for a moment.

Had he imagined it, or had Alex Ryun smiled at him?

The next class was social studies, taught by Mr. Maxwell, a slight man with restless eyes who smoked a pipe in the teacher's lounge. Today's subject was socialism. Phil had been looking forward to it. He'd found the dusty tomes by Wells and Bellamy in the back stacks of the Carnegie. If socialism meant an even start for everybody, justice and equality, he was for it. When Maxwell asked for comments on the reading his hand lofted itself before he was well aware of it. It stalled halfway as he recalled the note, then continued up. He doubted whoever had passed it was in this class too. Anyway it was too late now. I may be a mouse, he thought. But I'm gonna squeak.

"Romanelli, enlighten us."

"Uh, I thought the reading was kind of slanted."

"Interesting. Meaning what?"

"Well, first all that stuff about Utopia. Then the Communist Manifesto;

then the thing by Lenin about how terror is great. Isn't that too simple? Like, you can choose capitalism and get freedom, or socialism and get prison camps. According to the book, there's nothing in between."

"You don't think the textbook's right?" said Maxwell. "Well, a hand from the hinterland! Yes—there in back."

"Horse puckey. Socialism, communism, it's the same thing."

"No, it isn't," said Phil, half-turning in his seat. "Communism, the government owns everything, socialism, just the industry and airlines and stuff. But then the country gets run to benefit everybody. Not just people with money, like now."

A different voice. "What's wrong with capitalism?"

"It doesn't do anything for the people on the bottom. Ayn Rand, I read her stuff, she's like the capitalist prophet. But she only writes about rich, super-talented people. How about the ones who aren't geniuses with megabucks? Who'll never have anything, unless somebody helps them?"

"They should get a job."

"Sure, but what if they can't? Like here, the casket factory, it's shut down. And Thunder Oil laid off tons of people. Is it their fault there aren't jobs?" Phil knew he was in too deep now. But he was getting mad. "The Gerroys, the Whites, the Thunners—why do they have so much, and old people who worked all their lives got nothing to eat? Why, if somebody gets sick, why's their family got to be poor from then on? Is that the way it ought to be?"

The kids around him were silent. "Look, I don't want to start an argument," he said, twisting in his chair. A fence of hostile or bored-out faces stared back. "But just because it's in a book doesn't mean it's true."

"You might have a point," said Maxwell. "But we have only a limited amount of time. Phil, can I ask a personal question?"

"Uh, sure."

"You're getting hot under the collar there. Do you just like to argue? Or is that what you really think?"

Some instinctive caution quelled his first attempt to speak; it made him stutter before he said, "I don't know. 'From each according to his ability, to each according to his need'—that don't sound too bad to me. But I guess it didn't work too good in Russia, did it?"

He forced himself to grin at the end of that. Foolishly.

Maxwell waited; then, when there were no more comments, gave a weary smile. "All right—ten minutes before lunch. Just long enough for a little pop quiz. Take out your crayons, kids."

The class groaned.

After lunch the school authorities surrendered to the snow. It had kept coming all morning, in bursts and flurries, and when Phil came out it was drifted to his knees. The wind bit at his face, pushed its icy muzzle down his neck. He zipped it out of his jacket, hugging his books under his left arm. Ahead of him kids hurried toward their parents' pickups or four-wheel-drives, some toward cars of their own. He didn't bother to look. It made him too depressed. His dad's car had a cracked block, hadn't run for years, just sat in the yard rusting.

Christ, he thought, Haven't we taken enough? Why do I got to be poor too?

He was looking at the way the snow had bleached Candler Hill to a faded, ominous gray when he heard the door clack open again behind him. He turned; slower than the rest, he'd thought himself last to leave the locker-lined corridor.

"Well, hell, if it ain't Professor Crip," said "Bubba" Detrick, grinning down at him.

Behind Detrick's red-and-gold bulk was another boy, a senior. Mooney, the bullet-headed shotputter, also in varsity colors.

"Let's go over behind the gym, buds."

"What for, Bubba?"

"What do you think for?" Detrick looked left and right, then gave him a shove that looked effortless but that sent Phil flying. Books hit the snow chuff, chuff, chuff, burrowing from sight like frightened woodchucks. "Come on, jerk, we got deep international issues to discuss."

Behind him, not speaking, the senior stood huge and immobile, screening them from the other students. "Move out. Behind el gym-o, Roma-nellito."

"Look, I don't want to fight you guys."

"Whoa! That's a relief. I told the Brick here, you sure we want to mix up with that guy? We piss him off, he'll hand us our assholes on a plate."

Behind the school the wind came hard and cold across the buried expanse of the football field, the goal posts like abandoned colossi in a white desert. When they were no longer visible from the lot Detrick moved close. He lifted Phil by the collar and breathed Juicy Fruit into his face.

"We had enough a' your wiseassin', Romo. Romo the Homo. I warned you in comp, but you done it again in Maxwell's class. You got no right to criticize America, buds. Not around us."

"I wasn't criticizing America."

"Shit you weren't! No, don't *explain*. We don't need to suffer through it again." Detrick shook his head wearily. "Okay, like I said, we already warned you."

The punch blasted low into his gut. He gasped and dropped the last book. The ball player hit him again, a careful backhand to the nose, then just below the breastbone. A sheet of light leaped up between him and his body. He dropped to his knees, unable to breathe or see. Mooney pulled him up and held him while Detrick took a few more shots.

Phil was dangling from the shotputter's arm when Detrick said something. "What?" he mumbled, through something slick and salty on his lips.

"I said, got 'nything smart to say now?"

"Yeah, I do. My dad—"

He stopped.

"Yeah, your dad, what? He's gonna come after us for roughin' you up? Hey, I doubt it, jerkoff. We know Pop the Cop. We know he's a lousy drunk too. You send him around anytime."

"Fuck both of you guys," Phil said. He hated it when he started to cry.

Pain ripped through his head like a bullet. He tried to scream, but before he could Detrick slammed a ball of snow into his open mouth.

"Listen up, Crip. There ain't no reason you're here. People like you, they oughta put them all away someplace so we don't have to look at them. So do the rest of the world a favor. Keep your fuckin' teeth zipped and stay out of my sight. There's a lot worse shit can happen to you than getting slapped around a little."

"Bubba?" A girl's voice, calling from the lot. For a moment Phil thought he recognized it.

Detrick turned his head. "Gotta go," he said to Mooney. "Think that'll give us a little peace and quiet?"

The shotputter jerked his shoulders. Detrick released Phil's ears and he fell into the snow, face down.

"Wait a minute. He breathin'?"

"You breathin', Crip? Say something."

A boot probed for his kidneys; he tried blindly to roll away.

"He's okay."

Bubba, shouting: "Comin', darlin'!"

"Anytime you want to talk more of that shit in class, have a ball," he heard Detrick toss back over his shoulder. "You want to be a troublemaker, hey, that's fine with us. It's a free country. Just remember, we'll be right behind you."

He lay there for a long time, watching his blood melt slowly into the perfect cleanness of the snow. Perfect cleanness. Perfect cold. Cold as steel. He closed his eyes, but it seemed like his mind went no further than that.

Than the cold blue steel of his father's service .38.

Three

O
h, *there* you are, dear!"

Jaysine flinched, jerked from reverie. At the door of her station Marybelle Acolino cocked her head, watchful as a crow. She realized she'd been
daydreaming in her chair.

"Your two o'clock's here, dear. Don't you think you should be out front
to greet her?"

"Yes, Marybelle," she said, but inside she thought an ugly word.

Her two o'clock looked pale and scared. When she closed the door on
the wind she stood waiting-still, one gloved hand to her mouth. Her eyes
darted like a trapped sparrow's about the busy hot interior of the Style
Shoppe.

Jaysine moved toward her, fitting a smile to her lips. Beyond the
swagged curtains the day was sliding toward dusk. She felt a spurt of anxiety about the storm, icy roads. Brad had said he'd be over tonight. Lord,
let him get here safe, she thought.

"Karen?"

The girl turned, startled. Her eyes fixed whitely on Jaysine's; her smile
was tremulous. "That's me. Are you the—?"

"Yes. Come on, let's talk in back."

As they passed the other customers Jaysine saw her glance fearfully at
them. Toweled, awaiting rejuvenation under the whining dryers, they ignored her. Most were three times her age. They're always so frightened,
she thought. What do they think I'm going to do to them?

Still smiling, she closed the door to her station. "Now, why don't you just sit down, Karen? And we'll discuss your little problem and how I can help."

Jaysine Farmer saw herself as too short, not blond enough, and too involved with chocolate and crullers. Her face was full behind Anne Klein glasses; her hips were what the magazines called "generous."

She'd grown up in Four Holes, a mile from the New York state line. Her grandfather had started a dairy store there in the twenties. Till she was sixteen she'd expected to spend her youth behind its counter, mining out Rocky Road and Mint Chocolate Chip with the aluminum scoop, making change, and flirting not too obviously with the customers, until Someone came to take her away.

Then business fell off. When the store failed, her father, a silent man, shot himself one night out in the barn.

After they sold the farm the family split up. Brothers and sisters gone to Richmond and Atlanta, two into the navy. Now only she and her mother were left, her mother still practicing Science in the old house and the store itself bulldozed into oblivion when they widened the road going north.

She'd used her share of the money for a year at Johnstown College of Cosmetology. All the courses were interesting: Personal Hygiene, Hairdressing, Dermatology, History of Beauty. But halfway through she'd read a book on Permanent Hair Removal. About how electrolysis was not just a job but one of the healing arts. And curled up that night in her rented room, looking at the awful before and miraculous after pictures, she'd suddenly known that there, not in fixing hair or doing manicures, was her profession, her calling, and her fate.

As the girl laid her purse and coat aside Jaysine noted the growth on her upper lip; the shoulder-length hairdo, swept forward to hide her face; the dark, slightly oily complexion.

She gave her a moment to look around the station. The only private one in the Shoppe, it was paneled with imitation walnut, dark, professional, rather than the frantic pink of the main salon. She'd decorated it too: a vase with silk nasturtiums, pictures of a covered bridge and of Jesus at Gethsemane, and a cypress plaque, Gothic-lettered with *Today is the first day of the rest of your life.*

And best of all, Eterni-Sealed on woodgrain plaques in front of the operating chair, her diploma from Johnstown and her R.E. certification from the Pennsylvania Society of Electrologists.

"Is this your first experience with permanent hair removal, Karen?"

"That's right."

"Well, let me tell you a bit about our procedure," Jaysine began, leaning forward. *Eye contact.* "Now, there are four things everyone asks. So to save us both time, I'll answer them up front! First of all, it doesn't hurt. Second, hair removed by electrolysis will not come back. It's not like waxing or tweezing or shaving. The root will be dead, you'll never see it again.

"Third, how long will it take? I can't answer that before we talk about your specific needs, but by the time you leave today we should have a timetable for your treatments. The same applies to the cost."

The girl nodded submissively. "Now," said Jaysine, lowering her voice, "How can I help you, Karen?"

"I'm kind of hairy all over, I mean my arms and things. So is my mother."

"I think you look very attractive," said Jaysine, though of course she'd noticed the upper lip right away.

"It's my bikini line."

"The lower abdomen?"

"Yes."

"How high does it extend?"

"Higher than it should." She colored. "I've been taking it off. But when I'm . . . intimate with someone, you can tell. My boyfriend used to say he liked it. But now he doesn't . . . say nice things anymore."

Oh Lord, Jaysine thought. She loved her work, but it dismayed her sometimes, the emotional freight her customers dragged in with them. It was funny. If you had an ugly behind or lousy fingernails you didn't waste time on shame. You fixed them, or diverted attention with accessories. But hair, body hair, seemed to be different.

"It's natural, Karen. Unfortunately, what's natural isn't always what's beautiful. Why don't we take a look at what we're dealing with."

She made her voice businesslike and the girl responded to it, straightening and stopping her sniffle. Jaysine tilted the chair. Karen lifted her skirt, peeled down her panty hose, and gazed without any trace of expression at the ceiling.

"Would you move your legs apart, please? Just an inch, please."

This was no bikini line problem. The pubic hair formed not a triangle but a diamond, with heavy centerline growth all the way up to the navel. Heavy growth on the thighs too. She pulled up a pinch of skin. Fortunately Karen had shaved rather than tweezing or waxing.

When Jaysine looked up her two o'clock was weeping silently. "Can you do anything?" she whispered.

"Look here," said Jaysine. "Sit up. See where my finger is? We're going to take away the hair from here up. Plus all this on the inside of your legs. Make it go away forever. How's that sound?"

Karen nodded. Jaysine turned briskly away and began opening drawers, laying out her equipment.

"This here is the electrolysis machine. I place this tiny needle right into the hair root and press the pedal down with my foot. When we're finished the hair slides right out. I'd like to have you come in twice a week. Karen, I'd say in about three months we'll have your problem down to nothing."

"That would be good," the girl whispered, and for the first time hope showed in her eyes. "I'd like that very much."

Later Jaysine stood outside her station, wiping her hands. The astringencies of alcohol and aloe vera sliced the perfumed air. Marybelle wasn't there. She dabbed at her nose; she'd felt a little feverish for the last week; but it hadn't developed into a cold or anything. Sighing, she perched the tissue on an overflowing wastebasket. Letting her hand fall to her side, she looked down the double row of chairs.

The salon was twice the size of a living room, five stations, with the sixth partitioned off for her. In the infinite multiplication of mirrored walls hundreds of ample women in white smocks bent over shrouded bodies. Hanging plants stretched off into a curving jungle, leaves swaying beneath the overhead fans. At each chair the operator had taped pictures of her children and inspirational knickknacks from Hallmark. The stands overflowed with brushes, curlers, nail polish, pumice stones. Tall glass jars held combs angrily erect in bluegreen Barbicide.

"You want this frosted, just a bit? Here on the side or down the middle? That's very stylish, yes?"

"So then he said, my son, he said a bad word. And I don't care how old he is, I taught him not to talk that way around his mother. And I took and hauled off on him. I tell you it taught him some respect."

"This strand here's the final color. Does that look like what you want, dear?"

Jaysine walked toward the front. Her feet hurt. She felt hot, and wondered for a moment if she was getting sick. She wondered how the older women, Marguerite for instance, could stand it. At least she could sit when she was working. But Marguerite, tan support stockings bulging like sausage casings, stood chattering bright-eyed as a jay from eight A.M. till six and seven at night; and her sixty-eight years old. It was a wonder, that was for sure.

"Hello, Mrs. Teach."

"Hello, Jaysine. I was telling Marguerite here, I told her to go right to the hospital with it."

"What's that, Mrs. Teach?"

"My daughter. She's been getting bad eczema . . . she breaks out all the time. On her face, on her arms. I don't know why, when she was a teenager her skin was flawless, just flawless."

Jaysine murmured something consoling and slid past toward the waiting area. She'd just let herself down, sliding the weight down with a sigh, when the door jingled open. She jumped up, but it was too late; Mrs. Acolino came in, carrying two lidded cups.

"*Jaysine*, dear. Don't you have any more customers? Why aren't you helping the others? How about this lady. Miss, what can we do for you?"

"I'm here for your special pedicure. See, I got the coupon out of the paper." The old woman looked up through cunning eyes, offering the scrap.

"Miss Farmer here will take care of you. Give Alison a break, Jaysine. Trud-*ee*! Here's your coffee!"

Jaysine hated doing pedicures, but Marybelle made her do them every chance she got. She knew why. It was the profits from the electrolysis booth. Marybelle had promised her half after six months, but here it was nearly a year and she was still only getting thirty-three percent.

Jaysine pried the customer's boots off, then peeled free torn knee-highs with black soles of rigid dirt. The feet were a mess. The cuticles sheathed the brown-ridged toenails almost to the ends. Worse, it was all too obvious she hadn't washed her feet in ages.

"What are you doing?" the woman snapped.

"This is a bath for your feet."

"I come for the pedicure. I want the pedicure."

"You get a foot bath first. There's no extra charge."

At the corner of her eye she sensed Mrs. Acolino's blue smock. "Is there a problem, Jaysine?"

"No. No problem, Marybelle." The old woman looked unpleasant, but didn't contradict her. Marybelle went in back, carrying her coffee.

Hot soapy water and an antiseptic bath improved the atmosphere somewhat. Jaysine eyed a splendid set of varicose veins while waiting for the cuticle softener to work. At last she tossed her hair back and got down to work, humming, pushing dead skin back with the orange stick.

The old woman muttered.

"What did you say, ma'am?"

"I said, it's a wonder a pretty girl like you isn't married."

She could hardly believe her ears. "What do you mean by that?"

"You know, no ring and all. How old are you, girl?"

"I believe that's my business," she said, thinking, Shave the corn down? Forget it. These feet weren't going to any cocktail parties. She selected a fresh stick and began working under the nail. That hadn't been done for a long time either.

The old woman shifted, then suddenly cried out.

"What's wrong, Miss?" Marybelle was there instantly, glaring sideways at Jaysine while she bent over the customer.

"She *hurt* me. She's diggin' in with that stick—"

"Jaysine, can't you be gentle! You know you can cause infection if you get too far up under the nail. I know you don't like to do pedicure, darling, you think you're above it."

"No, I don't, Marybelle, I—"

"Miss, I'm sorry, I don't know what's on her mind today. Some man, probably. Would you like another operator?"

"She'll do, but she got to take it easy. I'm an old lady," said the customer, humbly; but Jaysine saw the tyrannous spark in her eyes. She glared after Marybelle. What did she mean, that crack about men?

Two hours later she stood outside, inhaling the icy wind with relief as she pulled on her mittens.

The Style Shoppe, her workday universe, shrank to one door out of thirteen between Main and the creek. Her apartment was a block away. She stepped up onto the embanked snow, piled waist-high by the plow, but it was too soft to support her. Her flat Red Cross whites disappeared, numbing her ankles through the hose. She muttered an ugly word. Well, she'd have to change anyway, before *he* got here—

Thinking about Brad made the air suddenly warm. Humming, she swung along as above her the streetlights flickered, buzzed, then detonated copper light into the dusk.

After a hot bath and a half hour in front of her vanity, she perched on the window seat and looked down at the sidewalk. Then lifted her nails, scrutinizing them like a diamond cutter. She wasn't sure she liked Revlon Sunset Russet. But her hair was perfect. Marguerite had bobbed it, highlighting where it lifted off the forehead and sweeping it to one side to lengthen her face. The earrings were two-inch hoops made of old demitasse spoons. Daring, but she liked the effect. She'd made them herself.

She glanced across the room to a small workbench. A vise and anvil, a buffing wheel. A pitch bowl and an annealing pan made from a wok. Above the bench were racked saws and files, various punches, her other silversmithing tools. Her latest project lay on it, half-finished. She got up and put it away, in a drawer. It was a pair of drop-cast cuff links, which she was setting with a banded gray agate.

The things we do for men, she thought.

She went back to the window, waving her hands slowly, reviewing the status of dinner.

She was looking at her watch when the midnight blue two-door emerged from darkness. It slid past half-buried cars toward her block, slowing as it breasted where a pickup had just pulled out. But went on. Turned the corner, its exhaust glowing like evaporating gold in the clear icy air of night on Main Street, Raymondsville, Pennsylvania.

A few minutes later she started at a buzz. Her heels clattered down the stairs. Watch that loose step . . . She swung the door wide, shivering at the blast of cold.

A sudden vacuum pulled their bodies together. Her skin tingled where his car coat, dewed with melted snow, crushed her breasts, her belly. Snow glittered on his hair. Her hands curled into his back. "Brad! I'm so glad . . . I was starting to worry."

"Hi, babe. How've you been? Jeez, let's get warmed up, here."

In the apartment he pulled a bottle from under his coat. "Dom Perignon. Ever tried it?"

"Who are you kidding? If we have a good week at the Shoppe I might drink a Straub's."

"You're not a beer woman, Jay. You're a champagne girl. Get us some glasses, babe."

As they came opposite the kitchen nook she detached herself and unwrapped the bottle. Started to put it into the fridge. He stopped her. "It's chilled enough. I'll open it in a minute. Come on, let's sit on the couch."

"Dinner first."

"I said, the couch." He mock-growled and she squealed as his arms took her off-balance.

The veal was overdone, warmed too long, but the rest of the meal turned out fine. The wine, too, was what she'd come to expect of Brad Boulton: nothing sweet, nothing cheap, just the best.

She watched fondly as he devoured apple crisp with hand-whipped cream.

Brad was the tallest man she'd ever dated. His face was square, with no softness at all in his jawline, no fat, like so many men his age. His eyes were light gray; she'd had to return three lots of agates before she was satisfied she'd matched them. With his dark hair the combination was striking. She hadn't known men's shirts could be tailormade. He wore nice suits all the time, or expensive soft Italian sweaters. He did all his shopping in New York.

She interlaced her fingers, prim now, though she was wearing nothing but her slip, and let flow through her like champagne and honey the knowledge that he was secretly hers.

"Why didn't you call me from Nevada? You said you would. I waited up all week."

"Nevada?" He stared at her, fork poised. "You mean Tucson? That's Arizona. Yeah, I'm sorry, we got bound down in the negotiations, they went late. We're about to close. Going to start interviewing for a manager pretty soon."

"Is Tucson nice?"

"Compared to this, it's heaven. This damn snow . . ." He waved its dismissal. She smiled; it wouldn't have surprised her to look out and see it gone. "It's warm there. Dry."

"I'd love to go out west. Did you go alone?"

"Oh . . . not really."

She was instantly sorry. They had a sort of rule, not to mention his wife when they were together. She appreciated how he'd told her everything straight out, on their first date. He worked in oil, something about marketing. His marriage was loveless, but his wife was emotionally ill. He felt he owed it to her to stay. He had to think of his daughter too. He loved her more than anything else, Jaysine knew that just from the way he talked about her.

She valued that, his openness. It made her the "other woman," but after a struggle with herself she'd accepted that. It was like he'd said once. This was his real life, with her, and what he did with his wife was a masquerade.

He set the wineglass aside. She saw at close range how the heavy dark hairs of his wrist curled as he tilted up her chin. "Hey, almost forgot. You like silver, right?"

"Oh, Brad." She turned it, examining the dull gleam, the tiny hammermarks. Turquoise, but not a good grade, and the mountings were badly soldered. It looked like something he'd bought at the airport. "It's so . . . heavy," she said. It was all she could think of to praise about it.

"That's Navaho work. Picked it up out west."

Well, it wasn't his fault he didn't know anything about jewelry. "It's lovely. Thank you." She slipped it on, held it out as if admiring it.

"Say, babe. About that bedroom of yours—"

"It's still in the same place."

"Let's just check, to make sure."

His face filled her sight like the sun. Oh, it could be better. His wife could . . . get well, so he wouldn't feel he had to stay with her. He could call her more often.

But she didn't think things like that very often. Jaysine knew how few decent men there were in a small town like this.

She knew when she was lucky.

Later, in the street, Boulton stood beside his car, retying his tie and staring with disbelief at the rocker panel.

Christ, he thought. It's rusting already. There, faint yet undeniable beneath midnight blue, was the bubbled ugliness of corrosion. Not a year old. It's the fucking salt they put on the roads, he thought. Remembering it, he lifted his shoe. They were ruined too, three-hundred-dollar Johnson & Murphys.

God, he hated this hole.

He tucked in his tie, evened the ends of the scarf, and finished buttoning his coat. He looked up and down the street, then stared blankly at the sailor hats the snow had put on the parking meters.

His thoughts went back to what they'd never, even with the woman, left far behind. To strategy, anxiety, and survival. These things never left his mind. That was why he thought sometimes that Thunder Oil ran him more than he did it.

Before he'd taken over it had been run like something out of a history book. Zero debt-load, encumbered with illiquid assets, pensions, and over-employment. After he'd married Ainslee he'd worked like he'd never worked in his life, streamlining, firing, cutting back, divesting.

It hadn't made him Mr. Popular. But it had paid off. He'd turned cash flow around just in time, saving the company when oil prices crashed.

But it was still undiversified. The board called it sticking to their lasts. He called it dangerous idiocy. Thunder was economically marginal, and it was touch and go whether he'd be able to save it.

His mouth tightened. The board. Old farts with a few shares each, fighting him every step of the way. He could smell death on them. For Ainslee, for himself, above all for Willie, he had to destroy them.

The butt of his cigarette hissed as the snow quenched it. The door slammed. The Jag purred into life. As it crunched over the fresh fall he glanced upward. A shadow at the window. Could she see him? Just in case, he mimed blowing a kiss through the windshield.

What a wonderful night, he thought, his hand dropping absently to scratch his crotch. A home-cooked dinner with a small-town hairdresser . . . He remembered New York, the last trip to brief the new ad agency. That PR girl had been wild . . . But Jaysine gave him what he needed. She'd do, at least till things settled with Ainslee, and he could think about what came next. As long as she didn't get possessive.

He pulled out onto Route Six, dropping back from his first burst of speed as the Michelins writhed on black ice, treacherous, invisible till you were on top of it. A moment later his mind was back on business.

Four

The bear towered above the old man like a falling redwood, claws like the poised blades of guillotines. Eight feet of chocolate-furred fury snarled down at him, baring two-inch fangs the color of abused piano keys. He was that close he could smell its rank wild odor, faint now, overlaid with the smells of tobacco and beer and cooking.

Yeah, Halvorsen thought, blinking up at it for the thousandth time, Sonny done a hell of a job on this one.

He stood just within the tavern, squinting past the mounted animal. As his eye penetrated the gloom his hand reached up absently to pat a worn patch of fur.

They'd shot it in the Cassiars just before the war. He and Lew Pearson had put four .375 belted magnum bullets into the huge brown before it had stopped, as Lew used to tell it in his Alabama drawl, "With hits paws on our feet, like it was aiming to untie our bootlaces and start eatin' on us toes first."

So many years ago, yet the bear remained, still upright, still fierce, still awesome as ever. Just as the mountains remained; just as W. T. Halvorsen remained. Though, the old man thought, the less said about his own condition the better.

But Lew Pearson had never come back from Kasserine Pass that disastrous summer of 1942.

Behind the bar a fat man in an apron was stacking pilsner glasses. "Well, look who's here!"

"Hello, Lucky. What you up to?"

"About five feet five."

"Business good?"

"Can't complain. Be a madhouse when them hunters start coming in next week, though. I put in more miles behind this bar than most of them do in the woods."

Halvorsen nodded, looking around. Not much of a crowd for lunchtime. From the street window red-orange neon buzzed STRAUB'S. Uncushioned pine booths divided the room. Two men in Penelec jackets nodded to him over stoneware mugs. He lifted his chin; thought he recognized one of them; raised a hand, just in case. He turned back to Lucky Rezk. "Anybody in back?"

"Couple'a your pals, yeah."

He threaded his way past the cigarette machine into an alcove separate from the eating area and bar. Three old men sat there, hidden from the other customers, beer-glasses and shots of whiskey in front of them. He nodded to Jack McKee, Mason Wilson, Len DeSantis.

"Hey, Racks."

"H'lo, W. T."

"Hullo, boys. Where's Charlie?"

"You know how it is over't that home," said Wilson heavily. "Goddamn nurses won't let 'em take a leak by themselves, much less let 'em out in a snowstorm."

"Coffee," said Halvorsen to Rezk, over the Marlboro ad on the machine. "Fatso, shove over. You're double-parked again."

"Up yours, with a stick," said DeSantis mildly.

Halvorsen wedged himself into the seat, a pine pew Rezk's dad had carried out on his back when the Kluxers burned St. Rocco's. They'd started early, by the smell. But so what? No harm to anyone if a few old has-beens sat tippling away their Social Security checks. No harm.

He sat in silence for a comfortable while, absorbing the warmth from Lucky's big gas-heat blower and looking at his cronies.

McKee had been a tool dresser for the Gerroy outfit. Halvorsen remembered Jack's coarse blond hair, his curt, angry speech, the way he shaped carbon steel like whittling pine. Now he was bald and his hands shook with Parkinson's. Only the harsh way he jerked out his words, as if paying off a bet, remained of the man Halvorsen had gone fifteen rounds with in 1936.

Mase Wilson had worked oil, teamstering, and lumber from the day he turned fourteen. In those days there was no such thing as accident insurance, no workmen's comp, and no guards on the White Timber Company's bandsaws. For twenty years after he lost the arm he'd sold the Buffalo *Evening News*, Prince Edward cigars, and Hershey bars from a tin-sided newsstand on Veterans Square.

DeSantis. Halvorsen had known Fatso for sixty years; had played sandlot with him through the long dusk after his first day of school. A ladies' man once, bulky but a dandy, cheeks talced like a baby's butt as he bent to fit a shoe in the Fren-Le Bootery. Now he was gross, belly bursting his shirt, jowls drooping like a lard-assed hound's beneath whiskey-glazed eyes.

Time, you bastard, Halvorsen thought, you've made fools of us all. We fought the cold, fought this hard land to make our bread. Whipped Krauts on one side of the world, Nips on the other. But who remembers? Those who loved us most are gone. Those who remain—they see us not as we were, but as we are.

His eyes burned; he rubbed at them with a finger, surreptitiously, surprised at himself. Getting sentimental. They said it happened when you got old.

A cup rattled down in front of him. He grabbed for it, then restrained himself, ashamed of his greed for heat. "How much is that these days?" he asked Rezk, turning—no, it was Roberta, his wife. Her merry dark eyes were lost in flesh, like lumps of anthracite tossed into a snowbank.

"Straight coffee, no Irish? For you a quarter, William. You know I like to keep you boys happy back here." She waited as he counted out two nickels, a dime, five pennies onto the wet-ringed wood. "Anything else? Sandwich? Lunch? A little late for it, but—"

"Thanks, I ate out home."

"You still living out in the woods, in that old basement? You ought to get yourself married again. I worry about you, all alone out there. What if you had a fire?"

There was silence around the table. Halvorsen kept his eyes down, stirring in the sugar. "Oh," she said then. "I'm sorry . . . but really, you ought to. Now, I got a friend, she's got a house in town. You like cherry cobbler? She makes the best—"

"Thanks anyway, Roberta."

"Say, I heard a good one the other day," said DeSantis, belching. "Naw, Bert, don't go 'way. There's this guy out drivin' one day, and he goes past the old homestead. There's a farmer out there on his tractor. Guy stops and says, Say, this is where I grew up. Let me plow for a while. So the farmer says okay, and he goes inside for a break.

"When he comes back the guy's plowed the field real nice. All except two places. He's just plowed around them. And the farmer says, Why didn't you plow those two places? And the guy says, Well, right in the middle there used to be a big old willow tree, and I got my first piece of stuff under it.

"And the farmer nods and says, Okay, I understand that. But what about the other place? And the guy says, Well, that's where her mother happened to be standing. Oh, not so good, says the farmer. What'd she say when she saw you? And the guy says, 'Moo.' "

Despite himself Halvorsen had to smile. Not at the aged joke. At

DeSantis. From beneath that mountain of fat, from behind the beer-filmed eyes, for just one moment an elbow-poking twelve-year-old had grinned out. And by extension McKee, and Wilson, and he too, were still somehow the same, each man's changeless self lurking and slouching like a night watchman through a vast decaying warehouse, recognizing here or there a shipment lost so long in inventory its destination had passed out of existence. *All else is turmoil'd by our master, Time.* Now where was his old-man's memory pulling that from, so many years before?

Halvorsen shook his head, still smiling, as the boys lifted their glasses in wry salute to the retreating insulted behind of Roberta Rezk.

Phil lay on the field for what seemed to him to be a long time. Long enough for the snow to frost his coat, trousers, gloves with translucent silver.

When he was able to move he got himself first to his knees, his body crimped on the ache in his gut, and then, finally, to his feet. He swayed there, looking down at the twisted, pink-splotched snow-angel his fallen, beaten body had made.

He shivered, and kicked fresh whiteness over the blood. Turning, hunting under the drifts, he gathered up his scattered books.

His hip hurt. He couldn't remember from which punch, or if it had happened when he fell. But it made it hard to walk. That and the snow. He headed down Main Street. He didn't think about what he looked like till an old woman, shoveling her walk, gave him a frightened glance.

Face must be a mess. He paused at the window of Capriccio's News to examine it. Bloody scabs had clotted or frozen to his lip. When he bent his nose with his fingers it hurt. He was a little disappointed it wasn't broken. It seemed a shame to be in a fight and have nothing permanent to show for it—a crooked nose, a scar.

To hell with them, he thought. Detrick and Mooney and all of them. I got a right to say what I think.

He didn't feel like deciding just then whether he was going to use that right again.

Aiming himself like a bent arrow down Main, he observed the street with cold slow hatred, memorizing its every line and flaw. As soon as he could manage, he'd see Raymondsville for the last time.

He limped rapidly past the old City Hall, a brick monstrosity whose cracked foundations bore a yellowing certificate of condemnation. Past an Italian bakery, its yeasty smells calling to him like his grandmother's kitchen; a Texaco station; the *Century* building, the Moose hall, a closed and boarded opera house. Once this town had glittered with the gaslit ostentation of the Gilded Age. Now the faded brick and peeling wood emanated poverty and abandonment. From the carved granite lintel of the Oilmen's Haberdashery, 1889, dangled the tarnished globes of a pawn-shop. He passed a plasma center, the Salvation Army store, the Raymonds-ville Club, where twice a month patient lines of shabby overcoated women waited for surplus cheese and rice and flour.

A sardonic smile twisting his mouth, he limped past it all with a bitter dogged persistence. Behind three-story buildings with false fronts, rows of shabby houses, peeling and gray, plodded up the slopes above the town like defeated and retreating soldiers. He'd climbed their wooden walks, stumbling as rot gave way under his boots. He knew the shrill women with filthy hair, the pale children who lived in those paintless wrecks. He knew the old who sat motionless and hopeless on foundering porches, or stared all day at the blue flicker of mass illusion. Like the dreaming Julian West he saw the faces of the defeated, the forgotten, pass before him.

The land of opportunity, he thought bitterly. Was this remote town part of it, the nation that boasted to the world of its ease, its plenty, and its freedom?

He was looking up at the bank—TIME 3:34 PM, TEMPERATURE 12 DE-GREES—SAVE AT FIRST RAYMONDSVILLE—when a door swung out a few feet ahead. He knew the place, a greasy spoon left over from the thirties. The kids called it Wrinkle City. An old man in a red and black coat came out, stood for a moment eyeing the sky, and then turned away, heading down the street.

Phil noted him absently. Then, a moment later, looked up again with renewed interest. The old guy looked familiar. Where had he seen him before?

He hesitated for a moment, then followed him.

"Mr. Anderson?"

Halvorsen plodded steadily on, head down. The wind whistled past his numbed ears, and his bare hands were tucked deep into his coat.

He was thinking again of the grizzly. How it had appeared suddenly around the edge of a rockfall. Like in the old poster, Remington Cart-ridges, where the miner on a mountain trail meets the she-bear. He and Pearson had been heading back to camp. Neither of their guns was loaded. The bear had reared from behind the rubble, not fifty feet away—

"Sir? Can I talk to you for a minute?" The voice startled him; it had moved up beside him. He stopped dead, staring blankly at a dark-haired kid with a bruised face and swollen lip.

"It's Mr. Anderson, isn't it?"

"No. Name's Halvorsen. D'I know you?"

"Well, sort of. Don't you remember me?"

The old man's slow blue eyes, blinking against a burning sensation, moved up and down. He saw a thin boy, in clothes too cheaply made for this wind. A stack of books on his hip. Italian, from the nose. "I don't think so," he said at last. "Who's your dad?"

"Joe Romanelli. He's on the force here."

"The force?"

"He's a policeman. My name's Philip."

"I don't seem to—"

"Yes, sir, we met last year."

"Where was that?" said Halvorsen, turning his head to look down the street. Lord, he thought, it's twenty below freezing. He didn't recollect this boy and he didn't know his family. Nor did he know the town police anymore, though he had in his drinking days.

Phil shuffled his feet in the snow, realizing that his pants and socks were wet through. He remembered now that Halvorsen had intimidated him at their previous meeting too. Embarrassed, not sure how to reach this aloof old man who seemed about to turn his back, his mind cast back to summer.

His mom had got a part-time job in "telephone solicitation." She sat in a rented room with other women and called people to sell them things. Notions, lotions, shoeshine in spray cans, cheap shampoos with French names. After her first day she'd asked him if he wanted to make some money too.

He'd ended up on his three-speed, delivering. He got a nickel for every dollar's worth they bought, and sometimes more, though tipping wasn't a custom in Hemlock County.

Halvorsen; sure, he remembered that run now. Seven miles out, seven back to town, for a nine-dollar order. There hadn't been much traffic and he'd cycled along in drowsy bee-buzzing heat. The road lifted and dropped as it unrolled along the valley. Here the river was smooth-flowing and green, bordered by old farms.

A ways out of town—he had the directions, penciled in his mother's sloppy hand—he took a turnoff to the right. The farms dropped behind. The road narrowed to one lane, crumbling at the edges back into soil, and started rising. It squirmed against the south slope of Town Hill like a climbing snake. The woods closed in as he moved into the welcome shadow, and abruptly his tires ground on gravel.

Even in low gear he was sweating when he got to the top. At the crest was an abandoned lease road, hard-packed and rutted. The trees met over it, and here and there saplings and bushes poked upward actually in the middle of the way.

He ground on, too far now to turn back, swerving occasionally to avoid puddles. Toads spat like watermelon seeds away into the grass. Now and then the trees thinned and he could look out across the hills. They stretched out green-blue, then blue, and beyond that a flat violet gray, ridge after ridge, all the same height as his whirring Ross. Far below a tiny truck had crawled along the valley, going away, away, into the world.

"Well, boy?"

Phil came back to winter, to the steady chill wind starching his wet pants and the old man studying him coldly. They were almost the same height.

"Yes, sir. You live out Mortlock Run. I was out your place last summer, deliverin' some stuff your daughter ordered for you. I think it was soap, shampoo—and boot sealer, yeah."

"Alma buys fool things like that," said the old man. "That boot sealer's no good. Got a can of bear grease does me fine."

"I just deliver it. Anyway I biked all the way out there. Uh—I got an assignment today in English. I have to interview somebody. I thought you might want to talk."

The old man's eyes narrowed. "Talk? What for?"

"Well, like I said, it's for school. Then I was walking home and I saw you and I thought, well, maybe you'd be willing to help me out."

"I don't think I got anything to tell you'd want to hear," said Halvorsen, looking again toward the bank. Was it really two o'clock?

"You're pretty well known in town, sir. Didn't you used to hunt? There's a picture of you with a lion in Fretz's window."

"Puma. Ain't no lions in Mexico."

"You used to hunt in Mexico?"

"Used to."

"I'd really like to hear about it. Sir."

Halvorsen stamped his feet. The itch in his eyes was increasing; he had half a mind to rub them with snow. He said, "I just ain't got the time, son. Got a long way to walk before nightfall."

"Maybe I could come out and talk to you there sometime?"

Halvorsen reached into his pants as he considered this, nipping off a thimble-sized chaw of Mail Pouch with his thumb. He almost offered the boy some before he remembered no youngster in this day and age knew what to do with a cheekful. He said reluctantly, "Well, if you got your heart set, guess I couldn't stop you comin' out. Might not be there, though. You'd do better to get somebody else, here in town."

He turned away then, nodding a curt farewell, and bent himself again into the wind. The boy vanished immediately from his mind, replaced by the prospect of seven miles in deep snow.

Phil watched him step stiffly over the piled-up banks, where the sidewalk ended, into the road. Was he really going to walk all the way back to Mortlock Hollow?

He turned too, shifting his books to the other hip, and set out in his own direction. Who else old could he interview? His grandmother was getting too spacy. Halvorsen was his best bet. No one else in class would think of him. And he'd said it was okay to come out.

Phil touched his nose and looked at the glove. The bleeding had stopped.

He decided to go tomorrow, Saturday, and see if he could get W. T. Halvorsen to talk.

Five

Willie was alone now. After she broke the bottle with the rainbows in it Miss Stern had given her a pill. Then put her here, in the big room, and told her to play while she and Ainslee had their talk.

And then she'd closed the door. But there was no one to play *with*. Except the animals. And she was afraid of them, afraid even to look at the fierce dead faces.

The little girl stood trembling in the white light from the tall window. After a while she leaned against the curtains. When you looked through them things looked grainy, like a picture on TV. Then she slipped behind them. Suddenly hidden, secret, safe, she smiled dreamily at her reflection in the glass.

She whispered, "Goodbye, Willie." Then leaned her nose against her image. Breathed out. And it was gone.

Outside it was getting to be night. The snow lay white and deep. She wished she could go out and play in it again. Inside here it was warm. There was a fire in the front room. But she wasn't supposed to go in there. There were too many pretty things. Ainslee was afraid she'd break them. Like the rainbow bottle. "I didn't mean to," she whispered. But then she thought: *But I did. And maybe I'll break some more.*

Standing on the polished floor, singing to herself behind the curtain, she suddenly had to go to the bathroom. But there was nowhere to go. Nanna had told her to stay here. And Ainslee wouldn't like it if she disobeyed.

She nudged back the lace and peeped out. But the animals were

waiting. Their eyes glittered at her from the walls. She sighed and re-
treated again to her covert.

Faintly now, through the walls, she could hear Ainslee and Miss Stern
shouting. It made her remember how mom and dad shouted at each
other. That was before they came to live with Ainslee and Grandaddy
Thunner.

She wished she had somebody to play with. In the mornings Miss Stern
gave her lessons. They were learning to make letters together. She smiled
a hidden smile, tracing her finger across the frost.

"This is an *R*, Williamina. Say it now—'R.' "

"R," she'd said, her mind only half on what she'd just scrawled, imitat-
ing the beautiful one Miss Stern had made. She let the crayon doodle,
making big curves at the bottom of the sheet.

"Do you like *R*s? Let's do another one. Look at this."

She watched the pen. It made another funny shape, loop, then a down-
stroke and a backwards loop. A snake. That was a 2, wasn't it? They just
did numbers, she'd done lots of them—

"That's not an R," she said.

"No, you're so smart. It's the next letter. Can you guess what it is?"

"No." Sullenly.

"What does it look like?"

"Like a snake."

"Yes! This is what it looks like, isn't it?"

She stared at the pen. In Miss Stern's thin fingers it made an elegant
curve, sinuous, then broadened suddenly. Suddenly there was a tongue
and two eyes, and looking at her was the snake, real, and suddenly she
was kind of scared.

"Doesn't that look like a snake? And how do snakes go, Willie? They
go s-s-s-s, don't they. So what letter is this?"

She thought of the one in the book, the apple, and the trees in the
yard. "S," she said, putting three fingers in her mouth.

"What a smart girl. Let's make some *S*es, and then I think we'll get
dressed and go outside and look at the snow. What letter does snow start
with? Can you guess?"

Snake letter, then zigzag N, round mouth O, then funny new letter,
down and up and down and up, S N O W sssnow—

She wished there were lessons now. Or something to do. Usually at
night she got to see her dad, if he was home. Or else she and Miss Stern
played a game or watched *Sesame Street* in the nursery.

But since lunch today things had been different. Bad different. Ever
since Ainslee had slapped her. Not *hard*; it hadn't hurt much. She
wouldn't have cried, she never cried when she was punished, if she understood why. But just from being so surprised she'd screamed and broken
the bottle before she could think.

But all since then things were bad and no matter how good she was Ainslee looked angry. From time to time all that afternoon Miss Stern would do something Willie had never seen her do before: She'd start crying. Not out loud, she'd just keep doing whatever she was doing. But all of a sudden Willie would feel her go rigid, her eyes staring off into a corner of the nursery. Finally, overcome by a dread she had no word for, Willie had asked Miss Stern why she was sad. She'd just looked at her, not speaking, and then a tear slipped down her cheek.

"What's wrong, Nanna?"

"It's all right, Willie," she'd said then. "It's time for your Ritalin now. Then we'll go downstairs. I think it's time I had a talk with your step-mother."

When Miss Stern came back it was long after dark and the animals were gone, their dead eyes and teeth eaten up by the dark. When she turned on the light Willie saw her face was all red and swollen. She stood in the door, looking at her. "Have you been good, Williamina?" she said at last.

"No. I've been bad today," she said remotely.

"What's this puddle on the floor, Willie?"

"It's been snowing," she said.

Her nanny laughed and came to her and hugged her. "Don't worry about that, I'll wipe it up. But why didn't you use the bathroom?"

"You said to stay here."

"Oh, dear, and you were too frightened to—I see. *Don't* say that about being bad, Williamina. It's not true, you're as good as gold and my precious girl. It's time for you to be in bed."

She knew it was past that because she knew what the big hand meant. She asked where her daddy was and Miss Stern said he was still at work, he'd be home late, but he'd be there in the morning when she woke up.

Miss Stern gave her a bath and shampooed and dried her hair. Willie didn't complain or fight as she helped her into her jammies, turned down the covers, and tucked her in. Maybe tomorrow would be better. The sooner she went to sleep, the sooner it'd be here. She stiffened, though, when she saw another face at the nursery door.

"Is she behaving now?" the woman said, looking in.

"Yes, Mrs. Boulton."

"Good. About your termination. I've talked to Jones. He'll drive you to the airport at noon. Your check will be ready then."

"All right, Mrs. Boulton."

"Good night, Williamina." The cool voice was like the bared teeth of the animals downstairs.

"Good night, Ainslee," she whispered.

Willie closed her eyes, wishing her stepmother would go away, but she could feel her watching them as Miss Stern moved about the bedroom. She tucked the blanket in and smoothed her hand over her hair. When Willie looked toward the door again her stepmother was gone.

Miss Stern sat down on the side of the bed. She looked tired, not like Ainslee, who was always beautiful. Her hair fell over her eyes and she looked sad. Willie still didn't know why. But suddenly she felt scared.

Miss Stern smiled. "You look very pretty in your new pageboy. Willie—"

"What?"

"When Ainslee hits you, that's wrong. No matter what you've done. I've tried to stop her. But I can't. I'm sorry but I can't."

Willie was silent. The thought of it made her scared more. She hadn't been Bad. She'd just wanted to move around, wanted to do something instead of just sitting at the table trying to be quiet and still and nice like Ainslee wanted. It was hard to be quiet all the time. She'd wanted to play with Lark or talk to Grandaddy. So she'd whined, she couldn't help it, and Ainslee had suddenly reached right across the table, and the next thing she knew she was on the floor and her ear hurt something awful. Then she was so mad that without thinking she'd reached for the glass thing and Ainslee had screamed—

"Williamina . . . your Nanna's going to have to go away."

She caught her breath. Her mother had *gone away*. To the hospital. And never come back. Was that what Miss Stern meant? She wanted her to stay. She didn't want to be left alone with Ainslee. But she was afraid to ask now. It was safer just to nod. To make her face blank, like it didn't matter, like she'd just taken a pill.

"You know I want you to grow up to be a good girl. That's why I want you to forgive your . . . to forgive Ainslee. She doesn't mean to do things like that. You'll understand someday."

Willie didn't answer. She turned her face away. Looked around the room, the familiar nursery, and saw that the walls were decorated with bunny rabbits. What did "go away" really mean?

"Where are you going?" she said, digging her fists into her eyes.

"Away, just away. But don't worry, you'll have a new nanny in a little while."

Suddenly, not understanding why, she began to cry. Miss Stern said swiftly, "Now what are you crying about? Don't be a baby. I'll play with you all tomorrow morning. We'll play castles and we'll watch your *Sleeping Beauty* tape. Then Mister Lark and your father and Ainslee will take care of you till you get a new Nanny. Don't you want to sleep now with your old Raggedy Ann?"

"I don't like her anymore. She's for babies, Ainslee says."

"Oh, Willie, not everything she says is right or true." Miss Stern started to cry again. "Oh, *shit* . . . I'm going to miss you, Williamina Boulton. Hey! I want some loving up. Hello! Hug me!"

Willie turned her face and made herself limp and heavy. Finally Miss Stern gave up and tucked her in again. She murmured the same words she always did—"Goodnight, sleep tight, don't let the bedbugs bite"—but Willie didn't say goodnight back or kiss her like she usually did.

When Miss Stern went away Willie lay in the dark for a long time without moving, breathing through her mouth, listening to the whisper of the snow and watching the shadows reach across the wall from the tree outside the window.

At last she got up, padding out of bed so quietly in her jammies.

The air was cold. The floor was cold too. Her closet was full of stuff, old toys, her old clothes, a lot of things. She pushed them aside and burrowed down. At last she found the doll, soft and warm and floppy, and took it back to bed, holding it tight against her chest.

The room was too dark. The pills made monsters come in her dreams. She lay in her bed, staring out at the blackness, panting a little in fear. The animals didn't scare her. She knew they were dead. Grandaddy had explained that. That was why their heads were hanging on the walls.

But the monsters weren't dead. There weren't any monster heads up there at all.

She ducked her head under the covers. It was warm there. She curled into a ball, holding the doll tight. Hurting slithered in her stomach like a sssnake. She curled around it, pressing her face close to the doll's, breathing the hot close air she knew she couldn't stand for long. Soon she'd have to come out, into the cold.

Without knowing why, Willie Boulton, five years old, began to cry.

Six

Dawn filtered down through an overcast sky, through several inches of new snow, to fall at last on the old man's pale blue eyes. Open, as they'd been half the night, laid like a poultice on the two high slits of dirty glass that were the only way the light could find him.

Halvorsen thought: *What the hell is wrong with me today?*

Getting no clear answer from his body, he laced his fingers atop the blanket, looking around in the growing radiance.

The hole he lay in was unfinished, walled with ripsawed planks over fieldstone. Behind that was earth. In the chill air his breath rose slowly, wraithlike, luminous. Opposite him a plank bench was covered with square cans, presses, other things still obscure in the gloom. Beyond it a wooden door was caulked with strips of blanket. To his right was another, heavier door. It gave onto a mud room, and thence up to the open air.

Lying there, he listened. To snow whispering beyond the already covered windows. To the far-off croak of a raven cursing the new day. To a sudden sneeze beneath him, under the bed.

But there was something else too, something unnatural: a huge and malevolent vibration like giant mill-wheels, so low and vast it might be the slowing rumble of a dying universe.

No, Halvorsen thought, that can't be. It's somethin' wrong with me, is all. In my ears, or in my head.

His mind labored slowly through possibilities that ended with the stove. He rolled his head to stare at it. The cold was intense. The pipe, the joint where it met the roof, all looked sound. And Jezebel, he thought, she sounds okay. No, ain't the stove.

Then why in hell did he feel like this?

His mind tired at last of unanswerable speculation. And drifted. What had they been talking about, there in the Brown Bear—yeah. The time he'd been running a rig on the Christen lease, and Lew Pearson come out with the news about the fire at Number One. Now, he remembered that as the beginning of the big strike, there in the winter of '36. But Wilson, he'd said it started later, out at Minard Run . . .

And then without cause or volition there was a picture in front of his eyes, like the instantaneous cycling of a projector: the image of an animal, off-white, suspended in space as if leaping into flight. He mused over it. Then had it, suddenly, the memory more vivid than yesterday or even now.

The Rockies, in '51. They'd spent days climbing, nearly dead from altitude and cold. The goats, the big Dall sheep, toyed with their hunters. Their vision was eight times better than a man's and they went up scree-covered fifty-degree slopes like they were rocket-powered.

Then late one afternoon he'd found himself, after a day spent working his way up a goddamn-near-vertical chimney, looking down at the grand-daddy of all goats.

He'd dropped immediately in the snow, focusing his glasses. The face of the mountain gave way, two hundred yards below, to a ledge no bigger than his front yard. The huge old male, with the nose of a Borgia pope and a magnificent curved rack, had been feeding. He could see that from the piled snow in front of its hooves, the dun bristle of forage. But now it was standing motionless, looking out over miles of canyon and beyond that mountains and then the setting sun as if it, the goat, had just created them all and was thinking, It is good.

While the ram ruminated, Halvorsen, on his belly, was inchworming toward a windswept ledge of granite. Only ten yards distant, but it took him fifteen minutes to reach. Twice the animal glanced around, but its motion-sensitive eyes must have detected nothing but snow and rock.

Once behind cover, he'd set the sights on the 7mm Winchester Magnum he was carrying that year, thinking not of the goat, nor of the cold, nor of the hundreds of square miles of desolate rock below them both; but of the shot. For mountain work he favored a Lyman adjustable peep over a scope. It was lighter, and there was no glass to break. But he couldn't make out in the fast-dying light how much drop he'd cranked in. With the 175-grain boattail he'd handloaded—

He lay freezing against gray gneiss, staring down. Not three feet from his face it had opened, blown apart, a hole leading down forever.

His father stood facing him on the far side of the pit. His face was set and white, his mother's negated by a black veil. Above them blue sky burned like a gas flame. Over the hole, between him and his parents, six soldiers slid a wooden box. The letters US were burned into it.

The man they called the Major finished folding the flag. Handed it, like something worth far more than what they had paid, to Thorvald Halvorsen.

The old man took it wordless and stood looking down, eyes empty as the sky, his gnarled farmer's hands clenched on it.

There was a thud as the box came to rest, and then the machine-gun rattle of stones.

Halvorsen closed his eyes, but he could still see it. The little Lutheran cemetery above town, the summer of 1918.

What had Mase Wilson been saying about the strike . . .

When he looked back up from the sights the goat was peering up at him, the wool blowing around its face like the beard of a patient patriarch. The golden eyes unfrightened, even weary . . .

Halvorsen stared up at the rough-hewn beams, breathing rapidly. Getting senile, he thought. That Altschuler's disease. This must be how it started. With this randomness of memory, more real than his empty room. This tremor and nausea, stabbing in the eyes, hammer-slam of pulse. And beneath and most disquieting of all, the deep unending rumble, like mountains being ground to powder.

He dragged back coverlet, quilt, and blanket, and tried to swing his legs out. On the third try he won and sat hunched, coughing and staring at the floor. His hugged arms covered where the union suit gaped.

"Time to rise 'n shine, Jez," he muttered.

The brown-and-black puppy squirmed out and attacked his ankles. He suffered it for a few seconds, then forced himself erect and staggered to the stove. Not even an ember. So it wasn't monoxide poisoning. He rattled the grate, sneezing as fine ash rose. He wadded a newspaper, rested; reached the kindling, rested; then stacked two chunks of beech.

An Ohio match sputtered across cast iron. The flame took paper, then curled under kindling like the fingers of a cautious lover. When the beech started to smoke he clanged the door shut and latched it.

Halvorsen nursed a yellow trickle into a coffee can. The door by the bench groaned open reluctantly. Solid earth-cold met his face. He stood shivering in baggy cotton, looking at the shelves. *Should of bought something when I was in town. Beans or something.* He looked for a time at a pint bottle on the top shelf. Then turned away. Instead he considered over several bundles of dried leaves and roots hanging from a water pipe, selected one, and closed the door.

The tea bubbled presently, sending up a resinous sharpness. He sat on the bed half-dressed, fondling the puppy's ears. At times his chin fell halfway to his chest; then he raised it again, angry at his weakness.

But I really ain't feeling any too good. . . .

A mile down the hollow, Phil prodded the body with his boot.

The raccoon lay belly up in the middle of the road. He'd thought at first, seeing from some distance off the crows worrying it, that it had been run over. Then he realized the snow was flawless, unrutted. Only wind-eroded footprints showed beneath it. The ones he'd followed all the way up Mortlock Run.

The coon's eyes were open. One was torn, beaked apart into jelly. The other was glossy-looking and probably, he thought bending slightly closer, frozen that way. It'd gotten down to five above that night. Strange, he thought. Well, even animals must die of disease or old age. Not all of them got eaten.

Phil straightened, circled it—it might have fleas or something—and trudged on up the hill. When he looked back a hundred yards on the crows were back at work.

A while later he came out on top of the ridge. He rested on a stump for a few minutes, then trudged on. His breath drifted ahead of him. It was very cold and he was starting to hurt. He hoped it wasn't much farther.

Half an hour later he paused again, in a clearing. Was this it? Last summer it had been pleasant, grassy, part of the Alleghenies' million-tinted green. Now it was wind-whipped and stark, a flat white nothingness with birches sere and vertical beyond. Only a stand of spruce gave this dead world color.

But smokesmell lurked under the evergreen sharpness, the ozone bite of new snow. He rotated slowly, sniffing. At last he smiled, making out a shimmer in the icy air. Shrugging the pack on again, he followed the all but invisible trail to the steps.

After he knocked he stood for a while looking at the stumpy stovepipe, at the lazily ascending smoke. Somebody was here, or had just been. He knocked again, louder.

The door jarred suddenly against its frame and he started back, staring into gloom. At first he saw nothing. Then something dim, as if it was drifting upward from beneath deep black water. A gaunt face, white hair, stubbled cheeks, bristly and gray as a porcupine. The eyes were red-rimmed.

"Who is it?"

"Hi, Mr. Halvorsen!"

"*Who're you?* I said."

He stepped back before the fiercely repeated question. The frozen earth of the stair-pit stopped him. "I'm Phil Romanelli. Remember, we talked yesterday? In town?"

"What do you want?"

"Well, you—you said it was okay if I come out and talked to you some-time."

The old man blinked, seemed as if about to speak; then disappeared. Phil stood there, uncertain what to do. He wondered if he should leave, then thought: I don't want to walk all the way back right now. I don't know if I *can*. He ought to let me get warm at least.

The old man reappeared. "Might as well come in, get warm."

"That's just what I was thinking."

"What's that?"

"Nothing, sir."

The darkness inside stank of urine. Searching with his hands, Phil found another door. "Close it," came a growl. He turned and shoved it shut. He went through the second and closed that too. Then he stood still and tried to see.

The only light came from two dirty, webbed apertures high on the walls. That, and a yellow flicker from an iron stove. Something was bubbling on it. It smelled vile. As his eyes adapted he saw the old man hunched over, buttoning his fly with uncertain, trembling hands. He was suddenly sorry he'd come, had intruded on this.

"Sit down, boy."

He was looking for a chair when something came at his legs out of the dark. He flinched back, then realized it was a dog. No, just a puppy. It pinned him against the wall, wriggling and whining, nosing his crotch. He put his glove over it.

"Jez, get off him. Chair behind you."

"Thanks."

"Take y' coat off. Want something hot?"

He dusted snow from his sleeves. It was warmer inside than out, but not much. "Uh . . . what you got there?"

"Feverwort tea."

"I think I'll pass, Mr. Halvorsen. But thanks. Thank you anyway."

The puppy came back to his knee and he patted it. It lowered its head and dug its muzzle under his glove.

At last he could see in the subterranean gloom. Opposite him was a bed, actually an old horsehair sofa under layers of grimy-looking blankets. Opened cans lay in and around a wooden box next to the stove. There were stacks of old magazines and newspapers; long cloth-wrapped bundles in racks on the wall; a bench crammed solid with junk. He looked back at the door to make sure he'd closed it and saw a lever-action rifle propped against the jamb.

The old man came back from the stove and let himself down slowly into an easy chair. A stoneware mug steamed in his hand. He had his pants buttoned and his suspenders braced. And old-fashioned half-moon spectacles on his nose. Phil thought he looked less intimidating wearing glasses.

"So, y'say you come out to see me."

"Yes, sir." He remembered the pack and unslung it. "I brought you some stuff. Cookies, some bacon—"

"Cookies, huh?"

"Yes, sir, oatmeal, my mom made 'em."

"Haven't been feeling too good this morning. But I might try one."

Fortunately the old guy seemed to like them. He ate three, sipping the fetid liquid between bites. Phil thought, *Christ, I hope I don't end up like this if I get old.*

"So, y'say you walked all the way up here from town?"

"Not all the way. Mr. Bauer gimme a lift part of the way."

"How's Ernie doing? All right?"

"Yes sir, I think so."

The old man seemed to lose interest after that. He stared into the stove. Phil played with the puppy. It was easier, somehow, to look at it than at Halvorsen. At last he made himself say, "Sir, did you mind if I interviewed you?"

"What?"

"Well, like we talked about back in town. I'd like to ask you some questions. About your life."

The old man shrugged.

Phil was proud of the recorder. He'd bought it for a dollar from the junk box at Ray's Gun and Pawn. The speaker wires had broken: he'd resoldered them, and now he had a working machine, practically free. Electronics, fixing things, he was good at stuff like that. The blue eyes followed him without curiosity as he uncoiled the cord and hunted around for an outlet. At last he found an old two-pronger under the bench. He plugged it in, then stared at the silent machine.

"I don't have no power out here, if that's what you want," said Halvorsen at last.

Feeling his face heat, Phil cursed himself. Of course there was no electricity. Not in this literal hole in the ground. He noticed only now the kerosene lamp hanging from a joist.

"That was pretty dumb, huh," he said. "Real dumb. Well, let's just forget it. I'll just get warm, and then I'll head back."

"This's somethin' for school, you said."

"For composition class." He flushed again, thinking how stupid he sounded. He wished he was lying outside in the snow, beyond it all. Like the raccoon.

Halvorsen sat silent for a moment, then cleared his throat grudgingly.

"Well. Long as you come all the way out here, might as well get what you come for."

"Sir?"

But the old man had already pulled himself up by his arms and disappeared back into another room. When he came back he had a pencil, very short, and a damp pad of yellow paper.

Phil swallowed. "Thanks, Mr. Halvorsen."

"So, let's get to 'er," said the old man, settling back into the chair and rubbing his eyes.

"Sure you don't mind? I can come back some other—"

"Let's get it done, boy. I ain't feelin' too good this morning and I'd like to just get it over with."

"All right. All right, sir. Well . . . were you born here?"

"Here?"

"I mean, well, in Raymondsville."

"A little ways outside." Halvorsen collected his thoughts. "Some ways south of here, down Racker Hollow."

Phil began to write.

"Yeah, I grew up on the farm there. There was eight of us, my ma and pa, and I had three brothers and two sisters. My older brother, he died in the Great War. That was what they called World War One then. I was just thinkin' about the day they brung him home.

"My pa was Thorvald Halvorsen. He come over from the old country when he was sixteen. Come over on a boat. They made him shovel coal into the furnace. He didn't mind, 'cause, he said, they gave him cake to eat. It was nothin' but white bread, was all . . . he never did learn to talk English too good.

"My ma's name was Alma. You know where Hantzen Lake is? Used to be a town down in that valley, before they built the dam. Probably still there, hundred, two hundred feet down under the water. That's where she was from.

"We grew potatoes and corn and truck, and on the weekends we'd come into town and sell it. First we had a buggy and then my dad he got himself a used Ford. I saw John D. himself once—"

"John who?"

"Rockefeller. Yeah, ridin' through Petroleum City in a black Packard. And he didn't look a bit prouder than my father looked that day, sittin' up in the cab of that old truck."

"When did you leave home?" Phil asked him.

"Well, first time I left the farm was when I was twelve. Went down to the Kinningmahontawany, trappin' with old Amos McKittrack."

Halvorsen had a sudden image of the old man, little and stocky, his white beard rusty with tobacco juice. He'd meant to look him up once.

But he had to be long dead. It was nearly sixty years ago they'd wintered together.

He caught the boy's paused pencil and recollected himself. "Anyway, we went down along Blue Creek, into what's the Wild Area now. We sawed down spruce for the cabin, then split out clapboards and puncheons. Built the chimney out of fieldstones. Then we chunked it up good with mud and moss from the spring.

"We trapped down in the Wilderness all that fall and on into winter. Got us fisher, marten, skunk, fox, once even a wildcat. We had a line of two hundred traps. Oneida Jumps, Victors, Newhouses . . . I still remember how to set a log deadfall."

He sat silent, fingering the worn memories again: remembering how the hemlocks, long gone now except in the deepest, most remote hollows, had stood shadowy and tall as the nave of a cathedral. He remembered McKittrack's hands, so tanned from salt and acid it looked like he was wearing leather gloves. And he remembered how he used to run up the hillsides, leaving the trapper laughing sadly, laboring along behind.

"What did you do all winter?" the boy asked him, and Halvorsen started, coming back again to the basement, to the chill slow realization that now it was he who was old.

"Well, you trap some in the winter too. And hunt. But mostly we'd lay up in the cabin and Amos'd tell stories. He had some good ones. When he was a kid he knew Ben Yeager."

"Uh . . . who's he?"

Halvorsen blinked. "Never heard of Benjamin Yeager? He was king hunter of all northwest Pennsylvania. Yeager was huntin' these woods back in 1820, 1830. Back then this was a howling wilderness. The woods was full of game—buffaloes, elk, wolves, panthers . . ."

"What did you do then?"

"When?"

"After you went trapping."

"Oh. Well, when I come back that spring I was thirteen, so I went to work."

"What jobs did you do?"

Halvorsen nodded approval of a reasonable question. "Like most guys around here then, went out in the oilfields. Slush boy, that's what I did first. Worked six and a half days a week, three dollars a week."

"What's a slush boy?"

"Well, you had your can of rod wax and motor oil, and every morning you'd dip your leather in it and grease the rod lines out to the jacks. You know the jacks, pump the oil out'a the ground? Now they're electrical powered, or natural gas, but when I started out they were steam. They had the boilers in houses, and the steam lines running all up and down the hill. We'd fix barkers—different lengths of pipe so you'd get a different pitch. You could tell that way when the well was pumped off. I packed stuffing boxes, cleaned out the tanks. Stuff like that.

"I made roustabout in nineteen and twenty-eight. I worked at that, then as a driller all over Hemlock and McKean and Potter and Cameron counties. Drilled wells, and put in the casings, and the power and the band wheels. That's what drives the rod lines, looks like a ferris wheel on its side.

"Then later on I was a shooter. You get these torpedoes, they call them, sheetmetal cylinders is all they are, that you pour the nitro into. I shot wells for Wolf's Head and Kendall. Then worked for Minard Run for a while, then for Thunder Oil the last thirty years. Worked my way on up with them, lease foreman, then field foreman—that was highest I ever got. Worked all over northern Pennsylvania, even some out in Oklahoma, showin' them how to drill."

Phil was writing hard. The pencil was blunt and the light was dim. But he'd resolved, after making a fool of himself with the recorder, to get it all down somehow, and make sense of it later.

"Uh . . . what'd you do during the war?"

"Worked. They didn't draft the skilled men, but they took the rest so we had to pull twelve-, fourteen-hour days. But we knew our boys needed that oil."

Phil decided he had enough about the oil business. "They say in town you used to hunt."

"In them days everybody did. Got your pot meat that way. Rabbits and squirrels when you're little, then you work up to your deer. You hunt, boy?"

"No sir. I don't think it's—"

"And wild turkeys—not like your store-bought ones, they're so dumb they drown in the rain. They look up at the clouds with their beaks hangin' open and they're too stupid to put their heads down again."

"Did you ever hunt raccoons?"

"What? Raccoons? Not since I was a kid. They used to pay good for the fur."

"I seen a dead one on the way up here."

"Dead coon?"

"Yeah. It was laying on the road, down the hill a ways."

"I've seen one or two there myself," said Halvorsen. "Not touched or anything. And possums, and a doe once. Mystery to me."

"You were saying, about hunting."

"Oh, yeah, it took hold of me when I got older. Shot my first deer with m'dad when I was eleven. Later on, when I was workin', I'd save up and go on trips. Mule deer and blacktail out west, Wyoming for the pronghorn, Colorado and Mexico, elk and moose and goat in the Cassiars."

He fell silent, rubbing his eyes, and to help him along Phil asked him where that was.

"Where's what? Oh. Canada."

"You shot that bear in the Tavern?"

"Me and Lew Pearson. Sonny done a nice job of taxidermy on that one, didn't he?"

"Tell me about one of your hunts."

Halvorsen laced his fingers over the nausea. He wished this was over with, so he could lie down.

"Well, I was just rememberin' this morning about one time when I was in the Rockies. Hunting goat. And one day I happened to come up behind one of them. He was just standing there lookin' out over the mountains. And I glanced down to adjust my sight. And when I looked up again he was looking right at me. Once those Dalls see you that's it. So I jerked the rifle up and snapped off a shot. I was aiming at his neck, but the bullet was heavier than I was used to. And so it hit him in the back instead. Made a *thunk*—like that. And a cloud of dust come off his hide, like when you beat a carpet.

"I found out later they do this sometimes, but it surprised the hell out of me that day. See, when he realized he was done for he took about three jumps, slow and graceful, and the last one took him right out off the edge of the cliff."

Phil felt sick. Killing helpless animals—that wasn't his idea of sport. "You said you quit. Why?"

Halvorsen sat silent, holding his belly surreptitiously. *Feel like a gut-shot deer*, he thought.

How could he explain it? Just that at each kill he'd felt more strongly a loss, not a gain. Had found himself looking down at his quarry and thinking not about the spread, how it would mount out, but things he could not admit even to himself. So he'd concentrated more and more on the technique, the tracking, passing up easy kills and taking only the canniest game, the hardest shots.

Not that he'd turned against hunting. He still thought it hardened a man, gave him the tenacity and self-denial without which you were no man at all but something house-kept by women. It was as natural for man to hunt as for the wolf. But man, though he was still mortal, had become something more. He had the power to destroy, and the power to save. And knowing that, he took on some of the responsibility of God.

"Can't tell you, not exactly," he said slowly. "All I know is, one day, after the house, I shot a buck. Plain old whitetail. And lookin' down at it, I knew I wasn't going to do it no more."

Phil kept his eyes on the tablet. There was more to it than that, he felt sure. But he didn't know how to go after it. Instead he said, "What do you mean, after the house?"

Halvorsen didn't answer for a long time. At last he said, "I always wanted a place out here in the woods. We built it together, Jennie and me. Two stories, lookin' out over the valley. Had a big living room, den, all that stuff."

"What happened to it?"

"There was a fire."

Phil waited. At last the old man, turning his face away so Phil could see the furrows in his neck, said, "I was drunk. I was tryin' to pour gas into the chain saw. I spilled some and went to the garage to get some rags. While I was out there, it—well all I can figure is the fumes must of got to the water heater. I tried to get up the stairs but the smoke got to me. I woke up outside, on the grass. She was so proud of that lawn. She was laying beside me."

"She got out?"

"No. Jennie was upstairs. She jumped. Broke her neck."

Phil stared at the pad. The stove muttered to itself, settling. After a moment his hand wrote, *Caused fire that killed his wife.*

"So since then—"

"Since then I been waitin' here to die. An' I think that's about the end of my story."

The old man got up abruptly and staggered toward the stove. Afterward Phil thought he might have been headed for the other room. But he never got to it. Instead he halted suddenly and put out a hand for support. Flesh hissed on red-hot metal.

Halvorsen felt his skin burning even through the sudden faintness, yet could not move. A dark behind his brain was lighting up, dancing in shimmering bands. The Northern Lights. He'd seen them only once in his life, in Alaska. He hunched for a moment, his other hand pressed to his stomach, watching the light and thinking how beautiful it was. Then he went toward it.

Phil stood up when he crumpled to the dirt. *Oh, shit*, he thought. "Mr. Halvorsen?"

The old man lay motionless, like a discarded rag. Scared now, Phil bent over him. Halvorsen was breathing, but so slow and slight it was hard to see. He rubbed his wrists for a few minutes, then slapped his cheek.

Neither seemed to help. Phil straightened and looked around the basement. Nothing offered itself. He fought against guilt and panic.

After a while he bent again. The old man wasn't heavy, but lifting him hurt his hip. He laid him in the chair and stared at the sagging, lined face, the silent eyelids.

At last he decided there was only one thing to do.

He moved rapidly around the basement. The blanket came off the sofa. He found rope and a hatchet, and went up the steps.

When he came back he bundled Halvorsen into his coat and put his cap on him. He looked for gloves, found none, but came up with a gray sweater. He knotted that around the old man's neck and pulled a pair of wool socks over his hands.

When he was dressed Phil staggered with him out the door, up the steps—pushing the door closed on the puppy's muzzle—and laid him on the blanket. After a moment's hesitation he went back down and got the puppy, carried it up whining and wriggling, and buttoned it inside the old man's coat.

Standing in the snow, he picked up the ends of the saplings he'd cut and lashed. A makeshift sling took the weight off his left arm. It was bearable. For the moment. But he wasn't at all sure his leg, his hip, could take it for four miles, even downhill.

He decided he had no choice but to try.

Seven

Brad was hanging his overcoat when his secretary brought in coffee. "Good morning, Mr. Boulton."

"Morning, Twyla. You look great today."

She left smiling. He hung up his suit jacket, straightened his tie, and glanced at his desk. Then crossed to the window, cradling the warm mug.

A new week, already scheduled full. But he was unwilling just yet to look at the appointment book. It was important, every morning, to take a few minutes to remember where he was, and who he was, and to plan what he'd accomplish with this day.

Petroleum City was the largest town in Hemlock County. Five stories below its streets shone like jet in the winter dawn. A yellow PennDOT truck was salting, and traffic was picking up. At the far end of Main the stop light glimmered like blood on the wet asphalt. It was snowing again; would continue on and off all day, the *Deputy-Republican* had said, though the trend was warming.

Beyond the two- and three-story office buildings, beyond the new brick branch campus of the University of Pittsburgh, he could make out dimly the real heart of town. It loomed like a tripled steel keep behind the snow: the three twelve-story catalytic cracking towers of Thunder Oil Refinery Number One.

Driving out of town on his way to Raymondsville he often slowed to look down on it. Number One looked as if some deranged deity of machines had torn apart the engine rooms of a hundred ocean liners and reassembled them on two hundred acres of once-fertile valley bottom.

One of the engineers had told him it contained forty thousand miles of pipe. By day it was a pillar of steam and smoke, boiling with tank trucks and rail cars. By night it was a twinkling carnival of lights, capped by fire. Three hundred feet above the valley the volatile waste gases were flared off in a roaring yellow-orange flame so bright you could read a newspaper by it anywhere in town.

From a thousand wells scattered through these hills the raw Pennsylvania crude, finest in the world, throbbed down to Number One; from it, by truck and rail, the refined products flowed out to the world. Everyone in America knew Thunder Gasoline, Thunderbolt Premium Racing Oil, Magick Penetrating Oil, Linette Paraffin. Less celebrated steady sellers were "#1" home heating oil and the expanding gamut of TBC Brand industrial chemicals, high-quality feedstocks for the dye, plastic, and drug industries of the U.S., Europe, and Japan.

Number One and the Company had taken a century to build, passed down from the legendary Beacham Berwick Thunner to his son Charles, and thence to his son Daniel.

Now they, and the house above the town, and Cherry Hill, were his. Because of Ainslee.

Boulton turned from the window. He stood for a moment gnawing at the tips of his fingers, then walked quickly across the room.

The cover sheet of the display chart was blank. He hesitated, then flipped to the first page.

On the fifth day of January, the Thunder Oil Company would become The Thunder Group, Incorporated.

The Company as he'd found it was an unlimited-liability, privately held corporation. Seventy percent of it was held in the name of Daniel Thunner. Ainslee voted that. The rest was owned by Thunner's prehistoric cronies on the Board. The financial structure assured family control. But in terms of flexibility, leverage, innovation, Thunder Oil was still nineteenth-century.

Slide two showed Thunder return on net assets over the last decade. It varied from four percent to minus two, and the trend was down. The company was economically marginal and had been for years. There was still oil in the hills, in the deep sands, but to get it out required pressurization or chemical treatments.

It was a classic case of diminishing marginal returns. Only OPEC and the succession of troubles in the Mideast kept crude prices high enough to make secondary extraction economical. He could cut costs only so far. Sooner or later prices would drop again. When they did Thunder was doomed.

He had to diversify. But to do that he needed capital. The company's captive bank had already been sucked dry and their lease lands mortgaged. For a privately held concern, that left only two ways to raise money.

He could borrow, issuing notes or bonds, but that meant SEC and bank interference. Or he could seek it in the venture capital market. But they'd want an equity kicker and a representative on the Board.

He flipped to slide three. His answer was to take Thunder public. A successful stock issue would provide a hundred million dollars in fresh capital. He could modernize Number One and replace the aging motor-oil plant. The biggest change, though, would be conversion of the cat towers to the new Hart-Havelange process for environmentally sensitive gasoline.

Slide four showed the four ways the new fuel, tentatively called "Thunder Green," outperformed conventional gasoline in reducing emissions. First, it was less volatile, reducing evaporation at the pump by lowering butane and isopentane content. That reduced the volume of hydrocarbon fumes released into the atmosphere. Second, it had a better detergent balance than Thunder's previous fuels, making it burn more efficiently in modern fuel-injected cars. Third, the sulfur content was lower, eliminating the rotten-egg smell you got sometimes in exhaust. And fourth, it was oxygenated, which lowered carbon monoxide emissions.

Boulton smiled tightly, sipping the coffee. They'd sent samples to Ford and GM, and their fuels engineering people loved it. With any luck at all, it would make Thunder competitive enough to survive a Mideast peace and a fall in crude prices of 20 percent. If peace didn't happen, then they'd be earning from 11 to 15 percent.

The last slide, five. The second major result of the restructure. The spinoff of Hemlock HealthCare, Thunder Oil, Thunder Petroleum Specialties, First Raymondsville Financial Services, and TBC Industrial Chemicals into independent divisions would wall off the old board within Thunder Oil. The old-line ownership would be diluted in over a million shares of new common stock.

He stared at it, biting his fingertips, going over for the ten thousandth time how it should happen. One-quarter of the new offer would go to holders of current Thunder preferred in a four-way split. They'd be happy; Merrill, Paine and Wheat had advised an initial tender at $135 a share. Since the last recorded sale of T.O. stock had been at sixteen and a quarter, that would instantly double their worth. But he'd also asked the issuing brokers, off the record, to estimate a buyer profile for new petrochemical issues. It went 45% institutional, 21% pensions/mutual funds, the rest small investor/miscellaneous.

Net effect: the board's proportional equity would be reduced to the point where he, Boulton, would become the sole decision-maker.

The new Group board would be his appointees.

He stared unseeing at the neat boxes and flowcharts. Only when the intercom beeped did he blink. He pressed the button, his eyes resting for a moment on twin malachite-framed portraits of a dark-haired woman and a blond child.

"Dr. Patel is in the reception area. Shall I send him in?"

"Who?—Oh, yeah. Ask him to wait, I'm in conference."

"Yes, sir."

He sat down, looking again at his daughter's picture. What chubby cute cheeks she had!

It had taken him a long time to get used to the idea of a family. Of people who'd always love you, who depended on you.

There hadn't been much happiness, or love, in his life till then.

To call his father a miner was a guess. He could still recall, if he cared to, the little apartment above Jackson Street in West Scranton where Marya Boldoronek took her friends. He'd played in the front room while she went in back with the men who smelled of sweat and coal dust even though they'd showered after coming out of the shafts of the Lackawanna Coal Company. They'd treated him kindly, rumpling his hair and tossing him a coin or a sparkly piece of mineral. Once his present had been a flat rock with the outline of a fish on it.

Then two grim women had come, a policeman with them, and the time when he'd been happy, or at least content, was over.

He remembered the Municipal Home with fear even now. He'd wake sometimes at Cherry Hill, his cock hard as a boy's in terror, believing himself in dream still there. Its cream-painted corridors and iron bunks still labyrinthed his brain. Its soulless parody of family had been at once blind and all-seeing. At the Home you were never alone. You fought, hated, and cried in common, one in a lonely multitude.

At first his mother had come for him at holidays. But then one Christmas—he'd been eight—he'd waited in his room, watching the snow fall, net bag packed with clothes he'd washed in the sink. The building emptied gradually until only he and the orphans were left. He'd never seen her again. When he was in junior high she'd sent him a rambling letter from Wilkes-Barre, in a County Jail envelope. He'd never answered.

Some of the counselors at the Home hadn't minded using the boys, those who had no relatives to complain to, and were too small to fight back.

He'd thought for a long time he'd be a miner when he grew up. He and the other boys dug elaborate tunnel systems in the slag heaps at the edge of town, heedless of frequent cave-ins. Miners were strong and happy. When he'd seen them with his mother they were always laughing. But when he quit school there was a strike on, it had lasted a hundred and twenty days already, and the only way he could hire on was as a scab. Everyone knew what happened to them after the union came back, down there in the dark. So he'd joined the army instead, marched in off the street into the recruiting station with his suitcase and told the sergeant to put him on the bus.

In Germany the Red Cross forwarded a telegram Mercy Hospital had sent to the Home. The chaplain had asked him how much furlough he'd be needing, and he'd said none. He was saving it to sell back when he got out.

He came back to his office to find his hands clamped white on the edge of the desk. He let go and reached for the first cigarette of the day. No use revisiting that. Marya Boldoronek had been a loser, and she was gone.

After Fort Dix he'd served two hitches in Europe. He was a combat equipment MOS in Schweinfurt, vehicle issue, and there wasn't much to do but drink and screw frauleins. His company commander let men off for classes, so he'd begun studying, at first purely to avoid field training.

He took it slow, a year to catch up to where he'd dropped out, and one day a teacher told him he had a good mind; he could be an officer; could be anything he wanted to.

No one had ever said this to him in Scranton. He passed his high school equivalency and kept on with the Armed Forces Institute, studying at night. When he left the Army he went to Carnegie-Mellon under the GI Bill. He'd worked nights and weekends, plant watchman, stacking vegetables, till finally one of his teachers steered him to a loan officer work-study with Manufacturers Hanover.

And ever since it had been sugar. Even his first marriage had worked out, in a way. She'd left him, but he'd won custody.

He smiled. Williamina. He'd been so sure she'd be a boy. Tricked again by inscrutable Fate. But this trick he didn't mind a bit.

And then the incredible luck of being sent out here, and meeting Ainslee—

It was almost eight. He finished the coffee—New Orleans style, between-roast—and glanced around the office. New furniture, new carpeting, on the wall the award from the Hemlock Recreation Association as Booster of the Year. Only the painting of Beacham Thunner with his first well remained of the antiques he'd inherited from Dan. He reached out.

"Yes, Mr. Boulton."

"Send Patel in now. Hold my calls. But say, when Weyandt comes in, tell him we got to talk about ethane before the meeting at nine."

"Yes, sir."

V. Chandreshar Patel turned out to be short and nearly spherical. In a blue suit he looked like a satellite photo of the earth. His smile was full-lipped below thinning hair and his cologne was sweeter than Twyla's.

Showing their teeth, the two men came together in the center of the floor, gripping and wringing each other's hands.

"Dr. Patel. Great to meet you. How was the flight?"

"Good, sir, very good."

"And the hotel? You're comfortable?"

"A Holiday Inn is not a Marriott, but I am not hard to please."

"Coffee?—Twyla, get the Doctor a cup. French roast today, you'll love it. Cream? Sugar?"

"Just call me Vinay, please. Sugar, plenty, yes. I have a weakness for it."

They laughed. "Let's sit here," he said, waving at the corner settee. They sat down, crossing their legs toward each other, and chatted for a few minutes until the secretary came back. When she left she closed the door quietly.

"Vinay, I'm glad you came. We badly need more medical talent at Hemlock HealthCare, Incorporated. That's our long-term caregiving division. Here, we just got these printed."

Patel fingered a glossy six-color brochure on coated paper. The cover was embossed silver. "Very nice," he said, nodding. He looked, Brad thought, like a sweaty little Buddha.

"Well, let me give you a brief outline of our organization here, and then we'll talk about how you might fit into it.

"HHC's a privately held company at the moment, fully owned by the parent corporation, Thunder Oil. I'm President and CEO. I started the HealthCare Division two years ago with the purchase of an old fifty-bed facility here in Hemlock County.

"To make a long story short, growth has been phenomenal. We have four facilities on line and two more will open next year. We're opening our first Hemlock Manor outside the tri-county area, in Tucson, Arizona. We have four hundred beds now and in the next two years we'll double that.

"Our policy is to provide the most efficient long-term residential care possible, bar none, period. We're well positioned for growth. This part of the country is aging rapidly and up to now the only long-term residential care facilities have been the church-owned old folks' homes."

"The local hospitals, they are municipal?"

"Yes. No for-profit hospitals up here."

"That's good."

"It is. Not only are we in an underserved market, but local conditions allow us to staff at minimum wage. Don't get me wrong, without us they'd be on welfare, but let's just say there's no union problem. Along with cost-effective management, that keeps rates low. We're seeing people coming in from New York already. So I feel confident that in four or five years HHC will outperform the parent corporation, maybe not in terms of gross, but in bottom-line return.

"The position we're interviewing for is staff physician. We have one M.D. with us now, but frankly Dr. Kopcik isn't what we need. He's an old-line physician. He doesn't understand the realities of modern caregiving."

"I hope we can come to an understanding," said Patel, nodding agreeably, but with dignity.

Boulton leaned to pull a letter off his desk. "Okay, let's see . . . we contacted you 1 September. At that time you indicated your expected salary would be in the neighborhood of seventy thousand, correct?"

"That's what I was making in my last position."

"Resident at the Veterans Administration hospital in Hampton, Virginia."

"That is right."

"Vinay, I believe in telling it like it is. We're a private company. We can't match government pay scales. In this growth phase, we've got to keep our belts tight. I'm prepared to offer forty, with a review after the first year."

The little man's eyes dropped. Boulton watched his hands. After a moment they lifted, as if to go to his mouth; but they didn't. Instead they took out a cigarette. "Do you mind?"

"Go right ahead."

". . . Just a moment . . . there. Well, Mr. Boulton—"

"Brad, please, Vinay."

"Brad, it would not be fair to my family to accept that. The average income for M.D.s of my experience is currently over a hundred and twenty-five thousand."

Boulton grinned boyishly. "Never sell yourself short! But that's in a major urban area, right? This is a small-town environment. Your expenses will be lower. I might also mention that there'll be ways to augment your salary."

"What ways?"

"Let's talk about that later, after we get to know each other. Vinay, let's not haggle. I just can't start you over forty. It sounds low but I think it'd work out for you. Better than things did in Virginia."

"I'm sorry, I don't understand."

"Hell, V. P.," he said, slapping the other man's knee, "like I said, let's talk straight, okay? I've never heard of a doc being fired by the VA before."

"I was not 'fired.' I resigned."

"What do I know? Just what the clipping service sends me. Mismedication, overmedication, something about mistaking a nerve for a blood vessel during surgery on some old guy's throat. What was all that about, anyway?"

Patel's cigarette trembled. "My assistant did that. We all make mistakes in training. He was a military officer, however. Air Force. It was more convenient for them to place the blame on a civilian."

"Well, that's good to know," said Boulton. He looked at the sweating fat man for a moment, then got up. "Can I get you something?"

"No. Nothing."

"I'm having one. Keep me company. Johnnie Walker?"

"A small one, then."

"Uh huh . . . Now, let's go back to before your employment at the VA."

"I think we can talk about salary now."

"Not just yet. You're without a position at the moment, isn't that right?"

"I'm in private practice."

"I see . . . you started out in private practice, in Charleston, wasn't it, after you came to this country? Your license was suspended for irregularities in pharmaceutical accounting."

Patel said nothing. He sipped at his drink stolidly.

"After that you worked for a mill in San Juan, the San Marco Clinic, you did what there?"

"Gynecology."

"Gynecology. Why did you leave Puerto Rico?"

"Personal reasons."

"Which personal reason was it? Codeine? Amphetamines? Or the fact you couldn't tell a nerve from a vein?"

Patel didn't answer.

Brad grinned. "Hey! Don't take it personally! We didn't have to go through this bullshit, Vinay, but you came in here gunning for top dollar. I just wanted to make it clear that what I'm offering is a lot more than you could rake off anyplace else. Can we agree on that?"

The fat man sighed. He put his hand over his eyes. After a moment Brad got up. He refilled Patel's glass, then pressed the intercom. "Twyla, call up our executive employment contract. No, make that the consultant's contract. Prepare it for Dr. Patel's signature, with the figures we discussed."

"Yes, sir."

He stared out the window, giving the other time to compose himself. The interview was going as expected. He felt light and aggressive, ready to finish this and charge on to the ethane price decision. Below him, at the corner of Mulholland and Main, a pickup had broken down. He made out the blaze-orange coats, Ohio plates. Hunters, in for the start of the season. He'd never hunted. He considered it a lower-class sport, like bowling.

When he turned the fat man had regained possession of himself. He said, "You hunt, Vinay?"

"No."

"Golf? No? Too bad, we're building a new course out by the club."

The Indian didn't respond. "Okay," Brad said. "Let's go over some other things while Twyla's typing the contract. Policy matters. Say, you feel like this? Want that freshened up?"

"Sure, go ahead."

"I'll leave the bottle . . . we'll discuss this in detail later, but I want you to know up front that I run HHC as a profit center. We hold staff to minimum federal standards. You'll be overseeing all four hundred beds in the county. Our nurse-to-bed ratio is one to thirty."

"R.N.s?"

"No, L.P.N.s."

"At night?"

"That's night and day both. Now, some of the things I'm going to talk about are the facility manager's business, but I don't want you to be surprised when you see them."

"I'm listening."

"We provide complete banking services within each facility, coordinated from here. What that means is the residents' Social Security and pension checks go into the till. That also lets us run FICA withholding for the employees through a revolving fund and pick up the interest on it."

"Go on."

"Cleaning supplies, medical supplies, we deal with a wholesaler in Erie. On durable goods, walkers, wheelchairs, restraints, blankets, we buy them, charge 'em off, then resell them from resident to resident as new. We figure on reselling things like that five to seven times.

"Same on food, laundry, so forth, we've got deals worked out with a single supplier. Oh, and a new line of portion-controlled nutrition stuff. We can feed at a dollar eighty a head a day.

"We'll be running you around every so often to churches and town councils to ask for donations. Cash, but food and supplies are okay too. We resell them to another chain down in the south of the state.

"We just had safety and fire inspection last month, so we're clear till next winter. Fortunately they don't check all our locations at the same time, so we can shift gear around to some extent. And once a year the state inspects training, staff qualifications, that kind of thing. Don't worry about them, I know the guy and he's reasonable." Boulton paused. "Any problems with anything I've said?"

Patel shrugged. He reached for the bottle again. "How often is doctor's call?"

"That's up to you."

The intercom interrupted them. "Mr. Boulton, Mrs. Boulton on four-three."

Brad got up. "Excuse me for a minute."

"Of course."

Behind the desk, he swiveled to face the window. He looked out, seeking the confidence he'd felt a moment before. But the towers were out of sight. He took three deep breaths and picked up the phone. "What can I do for you, darlin'?"

The voice was cool and deliberate and angry. "Brad, remember what we talked about last week? About your daughter?"

"Yes. I do. I called, and—"

"You'll have to take her today. I just can't handle her. We've got to get somebody, this is impossible, she's being annoying and destructive."

He closed his eyes. "Destructive?"

"She broke another piece. A beautiful Baccarat *millefiori*."

"Ainslee, she was probably playing."

"Play or not, it cost nine thousand dollars. And then she lied about it." Faintly, behind his wife's voice, he could hear Willie sobbing. "*Stop* your bawling! Brad, I don't know if you realize how sick she is. This child needs special attention. I don't think she belongs in this house."

Oh, Christ, he thought. "Ainslee, listen. You just fired Miss Stern. It takes time to find people like that. Can't you just tolerate it a little longer? I'm sure she's not being deliberately bad. She's only five—"

"I'm not here to *tolerate* things, Brad! She's your responsibility. I made that clear last time this happened. She's your daughter, not mine."

"Daddy?"

Her voice.

"Get off that extension, Williamina, I'm talking to your father."

"No. *Daddy!*" A cry of pain and fear so terrible he flinched.

"Bunny, now listen. Don't bother Ainslee, all right?"

"Daddy, are you going to send me away?"

"Who told you—Never mind." He closed his eyes again. "No one's going to send you away, Willie. Now listen, sweetheart. Be good, stay quiet, and I'll play Chutes and Ladders tonight with you. Yes, and then we can talk. All right? Good. Now let us grown-ups talk."

The rattle of the receiver. His sense of helpless anxiety grew, and with it anger. But he couldn't give way to it. Not with Ainslee Thunner Boulton. Carefully screening it out of his tone, he said, "Okay. Okay, darling, you're right. But I can't come in now. I'm in a meeting. Can't Lark watch her? Or the cook?"

"I can't leave her with him, Brad. You know why. And the cook has her own work to do. Dad will be up soon and I don't want her bothering him. You'll have to take her."

"Well, I can't come myself. I'll send the car."

"I can't believe you expect me to put up with this."

"I don't, I don't. I'll take her, darling, I'll bring her here. And I'll call the agency again. This afternoon." He remembered Patel, managed a wink. "Okay?"

"Do it now, Brad. I'm warning you."

"Soon as I hang up. We'll get somebody good, out of New York. Okay?" He breathed deep again. "How's Dad doing?"

"He's still in bed. Tell them at the agency we want somebody tomorrow. Fly her out. Charter. I don't care what it costs."

"Okay. Talk to you tonight, Ainslee."

The receiver clicked.

He hung up too. After a moment of silence he uncapped a pen and jotted NEW NANNY. URGENT on a Post-it note and tabbed it to the intercom.

"Family troubles?"

"Oh, my wife and daughter don't get along. Previous marriage. And Ainslee, she's . . . Look, I'm glad to have you aboard." Brad got up, trying to recall himself to business. "Let me tell you something, Vinay. You're coming to the county at an exciting time. The ground floor of a lot of things.

"Don't let the past hold you back. Anybody can make it in this country, if you're willing to sweat a little. Doesn't matter who your parents are. Doesn't matter where you're from. You invent yourself, market yourself. If they buy, it's real. When I was a kid I had nothing. I worked three jobs after school. Newspapers, mowing lawns, an Amway distributorship. Know what I learned?"

Patel shook his head.

"You've got to deliver the goods. Nobody asks you how. All they want is to have the job done. What matters at Thunder right now is a positive cash flow. Everything else is waste motion. I've operated on that philosophy since I took over and I've not only turned the company around, I'm building the Thunder Group."

The Indian nodded. Brad glanced at his watch. "Well, I guess that's about it . . . Twyla, you done with that contract?"

"Coming in, sir."

"Take a desk and look it over. If you have any questions I'll be here till noon." Brad almost asked him to the club, but stopped himself. He'd better prepare the older members first; Patel was pretty dark. Instead he said, "I've got a lunch meeting, but the Holiday Inn has a good buffet. Tell 'em to put it on my tab."

They shook hands again and the doctor left. He looked, Brad thought, even more like a loser than when he'd come in. He'd almost laughed in his face when he came up with that average income figure. Hell, he'd been ready to go up to fifty, but it hadn't been necessary.

He stared out. The snow was coming harder, each flake driving down as if competing with its fellows for the swiftest doom. Between him and the house on the hill a curtain was being drawn. Below him Main Street, plowed that night, was turning white again.

Suddenly he felt dread so deep it made him tremble.

Like a general in battle, he'd committed all his reserves. Now he had to hold everything together—the Board's support, Ainslee's, fourth-quarter profits—till the reorganization went through.

But if they held for another two months, through the sale, he'd be set for life.

He gazed out and down. Through Ainslee he owned the towers, lost now in the falling snow; owned the stone and steel around him; owned this town, this county, remote though it was.

Not too bad, he thought, for a whore's kid from Scranton.

He smiled angrily up at the cloud-sealed sky, remembering his wife's imperious voice. Ainslee didn't know it yet. But once he was in charge, he wouldn't need her anymore, either.

The intercom beeped. "Mr. Weyandt, sir."

He brought his palms down. Still smiling, he slid out a laptop computer and centered it on his desk. He booted up 1-2-3 and looked at the figures one more time.

Scratching himself absently, he said, "Okay, Twyla, send him in."

Eight

The snow blew straight into his face as Phil pushed himself the last five hundred yards up Mill Street. "God *damn*," he muttered. The wind froze his cheeks, jammed flakes between his eyelashes, turned his nose to wood despite the application of alternate gloves. His left leg dragged like a dead dog. When at last he reached the portico he had to stop, leaning against a pillar, and rest in its shelter.

Weak as he felt now, yesterday he hadn't even been able to get out of bed. The long haul down to the highway, pulling Halvorsen, had done him in. There'd been a scene with his mother about missing Mass. He hadn't felt like coming to school this morning, either, but he couldn't face another day at home.

Leaning there shivering after the two-mile walk from Paradise Lane, he looked up for a long time at the hills.

When he went in the clocks stood at seven-thirty and the halls were filled with kids. The blast of heat as the doors closed behind him was intense, close, instantaneously somniferous. The smells of wet wood, floor wax, perfume, and rubber filled the corridors. He unzipped his jacket and headed for his locker.

The fact that something had changed only gradually penetrated. The kids he passed didn't look at him. Their eyes slid aside. He said "Hi" to Fred Bisker—they were lab partners—but Bisker said nothing back, just looked away.

Oh, Jesus, Phil thought, something's happened. But he had no idea what it was. And of course no one would tell him. No one would talk to him at all. It made it hard to concentrate on class work. He found himself listening for whispers when he got up to put a problem on the board. He blew it, and Mrs. Brodie warned him she expected more in the way of attention than he'd shown that day.

The next class was Maxwell's. As Phil came in he saw Mooney and Detrick sitting together in the back, saw their eyes find him and their mouths grin suddenly, together. It was the first time anyone had acknowledged his existence all day, and he thought instantly *It's them*. Fear scurried in his stomach, disgusting him with his own cowardice.

He sat motionless for the next fifty minutes. Even Alex Ryun failed to distract him. He sat with his notebook closed, neither raising his hand nor even noticing Maxwell's puzzled look.

He was busy hating them all. He stared out the window, watching snow detach itself from a sky lightless as a gun barrel. From time to time people went by outside. An old woman waded through the drifts, burdened with groceries. Two little kids with a sled. A black dog, more intelligent-looking, he thought, than the brain-dead mutants around him, tail curled jauntily over its ass, its white breath piston-driven. The dog reminded him that the puppy was in the basement. He had to feed it . . . he ought to visit old Halvorsen at the hospital . . .

At last, long-awaited as summer, the bell rang. No one spoke to him in the lunch line. He lockstepped bitterly ahead, eyes stabbing about the seated students. He imagined how many he could get if he had an AK-47.

He was thinking this when an auburn flame ignited. For a moment his glance lingered on it.

Alex Ryun was sitting in a circle of girls. Her coterie, he thought; the beautiful, the socially accepted, in a word the rich, or those who passed for well-off in a small town. One of them, Sheila Hazouri, glanced his way. Their laughter rankled his ears. Only Ryun didn't laugh, looking speculatively at him for a moment.

Phil thought nothing of it. He was a cockroach who craved a goddess. He hated them all, without distinction of sex or race or class.

When he limped out with his tray he faced the problem of where to sit. Now, at last, people had something to say to him: all the seats were saved. He wound up with the commercial ed students. They chattered among themselves while he ate rapidly, eyes on his food.

I hate this fucking town, he thought. This state. This country. This race, human, but so seldom humane.

I hate this fucking life.

English too went badly that afternoon. He frankly didn't give a shit about point of view in fiction. When the last bell rang he shuddered with relief.

He slammed his books into his locker, and was limping grimly toward the cold, enjoying his bubble of solitude, when someone called his name.

When he turned he couldn't speak for a moment. Alexandrine Ryun was smiling up at him. He noted through shock that his fantasies had left out her fragrance. She came closer and closer, approaching more and more slowly, and finally stopped a foot away, leaning forward, her eyes raised to his.

"Hi."

"Well, uh, hi. Alex."

"Phil, you're getting an A in English, aren't you?"

He stared at her perfect teeth. "Uh, I'm okay, I guess."

"Can I ask you something? About that book she made us read?"

"Well, sure." The hallway opened to a lobby before the doors. She moved out of the press, and he followed, nudged close by the crowd. Eyes swung; he caught surprise on passing faces. She was saying something. He stared at her lips. Perfume eddied into his brain. The wiring connecting it to his gonads suddenly energized. He got a tremendous erection, and began to sweat.

His face was to her when Bubba Detrick turned the corner. He didn't see the ball player pause, eyes going hard; then shove his way between two kids walking together, ignoring their protests, and go on out of the building.

Alex paused and smiled. After a moment of enjoying this he came far enough out to say, "What?"

"I said, do you think that's the right interpretation?"

"Oh, sure, oh sure."

"Well, I see that now! I figured you'd be able to explain it better than Marzeau does."

"You really think so?"

"Sure. I mean, you're smart. I can tell by the questions you ask in class. Everybody says so."

"They do, huh? Say—" He searched his mind. "Say, do you know why nobody was talking to me today?"

"Oh, that. It was stupid. They say you were in a fight with Greg Detrick, that when you lost you threatened to have him arrested."

"*What?* You got to be kidding. What happened was—"

"I thought so too . . . Well, my folks like me home when it's snowing. Do you need a ride?"

"Uh, thanks, I like to walk." He cursed himself a heartbeat later. He could have ridden in her car, talked some more; but no, he'd blown it. He stared after her, thinking no more than a rock, or a male praying mantis at its final moment of self-immolative transcendence, then trailed her out into the lot. He could distinguish her scent, rare and distinctive,

from the schoolgirl dabbings of the others. He watched her unlock
her car.

A moment later slush spattered as its wheels spun, pushing her into
Mill Street. He ran forward, and a moment later stared down. He'd picked
up a handful of the grimy ice her tires had spurned.

Idiot, he thought. But still he smiled. For the snow was suddenly silver,
and damaged limbs the only anchor to his soaring heart. Smiling, squeez-
ing dirty water from his glove, he turned for home.

Paradise Lane was a dirt alley halfway up the flank of Sullivan Hill, on the
far side of tracks and river from town. You got to it after crossing an iron
footbridge, not by a sidewalk—the hill was too steep—but by plank steps
that led up from the pavement. In summer the boards were rickety. Now,
in winter, they didn't creak—the frozen mud and ice lent structural in-
tegrity—but the way was slippery.

He hauled himself upward by handfuls of rusty pipe, the same dreamy
smile playing about his lips. He stepped aside once to let an old woman
by. Fearing a fall on the glassy hill, she'd simply sat down and let herself
slide toward town.

Eleven was one of five identical houses on the lane, a shotgun with
broken aluminum siding and three naked posts holding up the porch
roof. Beneath it two rusty chairs squatted like freezing beggars. When he
opened the outer door the first thing he heard was the television. Then
his mother's voice, and then his father's. Only then did the trance lift,
suddenly and completely.

Inside, through the storm door, he could hear them shouting at each
other. His smile disappeared as he wiped his feet. The tiny front parlor
smelled of onions and Lemon Pledge and stale smoke. In the dining
room, through a bead curtain topped with a dried frond of palm, he saw
his mother. She was thin, gray early, mouth unhappy. She wore a brown
housedress and was eating Planter's peanuts from a can.

His dad was sitting across from her on the couch, smoking a Marlboro
and watching a cop show. He was wearing his uniform trousers and a
yellowing V-necked undershirt. The tinny blare of electronic dialogue
filled the house with false urgency. His parents had suspended the argument as he came in and now glanced up at him, their faces still set for
each other, so that it looked like they resented his coming. He took off
his coat without looking at them, already reinfected with the anxiety and
hopelessness that filled these close rooms like the greasy smell of old
cooking. He hoped he could get upstairs without a scene.

"What do you say?" said his mother.

"Hi, Ma. Hey, Pa."

"Cold out?" grunted his father.

"Yes, sir." He got his boots off, padded into the kitchen. Pots were simmering on the stove. He lifted the lids. Red cabbage soup, redolent with meat broth and olive oil and chopped garlic. Beside it was his grandmother's risotto. The steam came up fragrant with basil and tomatoes, rice and shallots and sausage, pepper and Parmesano and butter. At least he could look forward to dinner. "What's for dessert?" he called, but the crash of cars was louder than his father's reply.

"What?"

"Angel food cake," said his mother, her voice tight.

"What'd you say, Pa?"

His father was coughing, hacking away as if to expel some clawed animal lodged in his chest. At last he gasped, "Nothin'. See if there's any more beer in the fridge."

Phil got him a fresh Bud and went back into the kitchen.

"Your mother said you felt bad yesterday," Joe Romanelli shouted to him over the television. "You feel better now?"

"Yeah."

He waited, but that seemed to be all. He looked through the kitchen window. The chinaberry bushes were white humps, as if a battle had been fought there, and the snow draped frozen corpses. He remembered one Christmas he'd been building a snowman, balancing on his crutches, when the Roemer kids, real bastards like their old man, began throwing snowballs from their yard. He'd been unable to avoid the hard-packed projectiles, they came too fast from four arms to dodge; and when he'd lifted his face to curse them, one had hit him in the eye and knocked him down. He'd hated them for years afterward, till the old man died and they moved away. He felt an anachronistic fear even now, when he passed children, that they'd turn on him with jeers, snowballs in their hands.

He trudged up the creaky stair to his garret. It was a converted attic, too low to stand in; he had to crouch or kneel. The room held a bed, a dresser, and cardboard boxes filled with his electronic junk. A single window glowed, arabesqued with frost. He'd be cold with the door shut, the only heat was downstairs, but he shut it anyway.

He half lay on his bed, bracing his kidneys against the wall. Below him the voices began again, his mother's shrill, his father's growling. Two defeated, imprisoned animals, he thought. The same old sins and guilts returned to unendingly, the same old lines a hundred thousand times repeated. He could have chanted them from memory. His mother accusing his father of drunkenness, failure, lack of ambition. His father telling her she was frigid, stupid, to take it to the priest.

Phil mused bitterly on what they'd made of life.

His father had grown up in Raymondsville, his mother in Nanty Glo.

His father's family were stonecutters, and his uncle Tony still had a memorial business in town.

Joe, the youngest, had survived Vietnam and drifted into the police. He'd done all right at first, but as Phil's medical bills mounted he'd begun drinking. The old chief, Hodges, had cautioned and counseled without effect. The new one, Nolan, had simply suspended him. They'd nearly starved; suspended, you couldn't even draw unemployment. That, Joe had told his son bitterly, had taught him his place. Now he was on "night patrol," condemned like a ghost to wander the length of each darkness with an iron key round his neck, checking in at each city property. His pay grade after eighteen years was rock bottom.

Well, Phil thought, I better get some work done. He sighed, crossed himself sarcastically, and reached for the yellow pad old Halvorsen had given him.

He hunched over the nearly illegible scratching, then reached under the bed for the Underwood II that Mrs. Skinner, at the library, had given him for cleaning out the back room. He worked for a time, then paused to press a finger against the frost. Melting out a tiny peephole, he stared out, sifting his memory for words.

The old machine threw letters crazily. It ghosted the *T*s, and the bellies of the *P*s and *R*s were solid darkness. But gradually line by line it tapped the life of W. T. Halvorsen faint and hollow against the hiss of snow. Gradually Phil forgot the voices below, forgot his anger and pain. The hole healed with icy intaglio. He was lost in the magic of words.

. . . Can't tell you. All I can say is, one day, after the house, I shot a buck. Plain old whitetail. And looking down at it I knew I wasn't going to do it no more.

He wrestled for a long time over what Halvorsen had said about the fire. He didn't feel right leaving it out. It explained why Racks lived as he did, penitential, self-exiled, alone. But telling it, writing down the deepest secret Halvorsen had, felt wrong too. He'd been sick. Maybe he hadn't known what he was saying.

Phil asked himself why it mattered, and decided he didn't want to offend the old man.

That was interesting. Why? Because he'd saved his life? Or maybe that he identified with Halvorsen somehow. He gnawed his thumbnail. Then thought: Can't happen. I'll kill myself before I live like that.

At last he just put down that Jennie Halvorsen had died in a fire. He pulled the sheets out and clipped them together, feeling relieved.

Now that he was done he felt the cold. His breath hovered near the ceiling as if trying to escape. He covered himself with the blanket and stared up at a piece of plywood. He'd hammered it up that fall; he'd found nuts in his bed; squirrels had been coming in.

Finally he got up and unbuttoned his jeans. Kneeling on the bed he hesitated, listening, then reached up to slip out a magazine.

She was a dark-haired ballerina, posed with one leg extended on the bar. This was his favorite picture in the entire magazine, though he'd loved, in his way, each woman in it.

This time she was showering with him. He held her close in the carpeted bathroom and her perfume made him tremble. She smiled up at him as the Stag unbuttoned his shirt. Her blouse fell open and he kissed her neck as he slid it off.

Her freckles were the color of fawns. They were both naked as he stepped back in the steamy room. She raised her arms and pirouetted, her narrowed green eyes mirroring his lust. Her breasts were tiny but perfect, nipples pointed like Hershey's Kisses.

Beneath the blanket his hand moved and relaxed, moved and moved and moved.

Under the million hot needles she moaned as he soaped her breasts. His fingers slipped over her belly and then between her thighs, moistened with more than water. "Darling," he muttered, into the curve of her neck, into her flame-bright hair, holding her open while the strongest part of him slid upward, into delight. "I want you. Oh, my God, Alex—"

Behind his closed eyelids he saw again the golden explosion that had created the universe.

He was lying spent, the towel clutched to him, when steps creaked on the stairs. He half-rose, realized it was too late, and covered up in panicky haste.

"Philip, are you all right?"

"Yeah, Ma."

"What are you doing?"

"Studying."

"I lit the hot water. You want to take a bath?"

"Okay."

"Are you feeling all right today?"

"You asked me that already. I said I was."

The door came open an inch or two. "Don't leave this door closed, it'll get cold up here."

"I'm all right, I said! Leave me alone!"

His angry shout stopped her. After a moment he heard her sigh. The door clicked closed. He heard her shoes thud slowly back down, and then, a few minutes later, a clatter as she set out plates.

He looked for the magazine, and saw with horror that it had fallen face up. If she'd come in . . . but simultaneously came another thought. In his arms through the endless golden moment he'd held, not the dark dancer, but Alexandrine Ryun.

It occurred to him suddenly that he ought to ask her for a date.

She'd been friendly in the hall today. Even he'd known that was no routine question. But could he ask her out? He'd daydreamed rape and bondage, but he'd never considered a date. He knew she'd been going with Mike Barnes, then stopped seeing him for Detrick. He'd figured she liked winners, athletes, and guys with cars. They both had their own, Barnes a used but hot Datsun, Detrick a shiny new pickup. While the only car his family had ever owned, the old Fury, had lain for years now rusting in the back yard. His father had never made enough to replace it.

So even if he had the guts to ask her, and she said yes, where could he take her? He had a few bucks left from his summer job at Dopel's Donuts. A movie, then a Coke downtown? Not real exciting for a girl like her.

Anyway, she was terrific. Not just pretty—she was kind and good too. When he thought about how nice she'd been today, when the others were such bastards, he was ashamed of his fantasies. He was a nobody, Failure Son of Failure; she was only the most beautiful and popular girl in the whole class.

Well, all she could do was say no.

He pushed back the spread and buckled his jeans, suddenly sick of this room, this house, himself. He picked up the typescript again. He found two typos and corrected them with a ballpoint. It looked neat, a nice piece of work. In fact it looked so—so *professional*—that all at once he thought of showing it to somebody down at the *Century*.

"Phil-lip—"

"What?" he snarled.

"Dinner."

She sounded hurt and he was sorry again. He had to get control, Christ, he was going to pieces. His parents had done their best. He felt like howling aloud in rage and despair.

He tucked his shirt under his belt and slid down the stairs. His father called his name and without thinking he jerked another Bud from the fridge. His mother wouldn't touch alcohol, literally. He sat between them, blinking in the smoke; his father kept one going in a saucer, snatching puffs between bites. Crockery rattled and he set to work, only now realizing how little he'd eaten at lunchtime. It was good, but he was eager to leave. As soon as he was done he got up.

His mother called after him as he went into the parlor, "Philip—where—"

"Library," he lied, throwing on his coat, wet with snow-melt, his cap, lacing up his boots.

"Here. Take these scraps down to that dog. How long are we going to keep it? I don't want a dog. It whines all the time under there. It'll drive me crazy. I don't want a—"

"For Christ *sakes*, Ma, I told you, just till the guy gets better."

"Don't talk like that, the name of the Lord—"

"Want a ride?" said his father. "Wait half an hour, I'm about to go on duty."

Normally he would have but he was sick of his parents. Besides, he wanted to get there before the paper closed. "No thanks," he said, carefully demodulating his voice.

"Well, be back soon."

"G'night."

Outside it was already night. He folded the pages carefully and thrust them inside his jacket. Then he went around back. The puppy was glad to see him and he rubbed his ears as it ate, thinking again of the old man. As long as he was downtown he might as well drop by the hospital a minute, see how he was doing. The thought made him feel virtuous.

He locked the dog up again and went down the lane to the steps. Pointing his toes, he let gravity slide him down the edges of the ice-covered treads, bump-bumpbumpbump, down the hill toward the lightless snake-writhe of the river, and beyond it the glittering loom of town.

Nine

Seven blue plastic chairs. A wooden bench. Green tile floors, and a bite of wintergreen lingering in the overheated air. The chairs were the same, the tile the same, even the smell was familiar. But the Maple Street Hospital Emergency Room felt different from the plant-hung, magazine-strewn waiting area of the Style Shoppe.

Jaysine stood uncertainly, holding her warmth-fogged glasses. Beyond the translucent, swinging doors she could make out nothing but light.

She'd stopped at the front desk, holding her face rigid, and asked casually where was the Monday clinic. She knew it hadn't been her imagination, the look she got with the directions.

At last she chose the bench. She took off her coat and unwound her scarf. Then sat hunched, looking at her boots. She rubbed her glasses with a mitten, put them back on.

Through prescription lenses the room lost its neat astringency. The overhead lamp was one of the giant ice-cube trays she remembered from grade school. Rust bled down the walls, a grout of dirt edged the tile squares. The ashstand was a cemetery of burnt-out filters, some smeared with cerise or strawberry. The wall clock buzzed, hesitated, and jerked a minute farther into the present.

She'd sat waiting like this before. Through nights at the Cow Palace, for someone to need milk or chips or beer. At school, for her turn to do an aniline tint under the gimlet gaze of Mr. De Bree. And last, for him; at her apartment, or places where she felt as if the price tags on her clothes were showing, like at the parking lot at the We-Wan-Chu Motel.

She shivered. Remembering that night, the first time he said he loved her, she felt pressure behind her locked eyelids, straining at the cold around her heart. Like shouts in the distance, she recognized emotion, though she couldn't feel or name it yet.

This can't be happening, she thought for the hundredth time. It felt like the dream she had sometimes, where Marybelle demanded this awful finger wave and she couldn't find the waving lotion, and got it in a tangle, and finally wads of Mrs. Acolino's hair, brittle as uncooked vermicelli, came out in her hands . . . this couldn't be happening to her. *I'm a good person*, she thought. I *don't sleep around, I've never hurt anyone.*

She glanced around without turning her head. Like her, the others had spaced themselves as far apart as the room allowed. Beside each was a jumble of clothing, coats, hats, gloves, and sweaters, already beginning that process that would end with the ultimate nakedness.

A little boy crept toward her, eyes on her boots. She smiled and held out her hand. But his mother jumped to her feet, snatching the child up roughly, ignoring his screams. Jaysine watched him borne away, their eyes still locked over the rigid back.

The man across from her recrossed his legs, letting his grocery-store tabloid fall open. He wore a loose casual suit like the models in *GQ* and sunglasses and a kind of beret she'd never seen before in Raymondsville.

He glanced up and caught her examining him. "Big crowd tonight, ain't it? This your first time here?"

Jaysine put on her hard, not-interested face and looked away. Instead of answering she took out her compact. She powdered her pores, then searched her bag for lipstick. When she felt safe again she closed her purse with a sigh and pushed it under the chair.

She sighed again, feeling something thick in her throat. Marybelle would be angry. Sick time cost her money in lost appointments. Jaysine was losing money too. She began adding it up. Elizabeth had been scheduled at three, Lucille at three-thirty, then Frances—a third of that, divide by three—

"Jaysine Farmer."

"Here," she said quickly, standing up.

A woman stood in the open doors, the light so bright behind her no face was visible. "Come on back. Booth on the right."

The examining room was even brighter, even hotter than the waiting room. White partitions sectioned it. Her boots made vinyl sucking noises. She drew the curtain quickly. Chilly light glowed over stainless instruments, an examining chair, a steel dresser of medicines, ointments, bandages. A cartoon was taped on the wall, a monkey examining a human skull: *Constant change is here to stay.*

Jaysine didn't smile. She laid her purse on the chair, trying not to look at the stirrups. She'd hated Dr. Kopcik looking up her that afternoon, probing her with cold metal. Again she wondered: Had *he* been here? She imagined being a man, holding it out, the act of exposure no vulnerability but an assertion: "Here it is."

Voices approached, and the curtain that walled her off whiffed out. Beneath it appeared two sets of shoes. Black work boots, wet, cracked, salt petrified, confronted by new white cushion-soled running shoes.

"Do you have any discharge?" a woman said on the far side of the curtain.

"Say what?"

"Discharge. Do you have any bleeding? Does mucus come out of your penis?"

"Oh yeah . . . oh yeah, discharge. Yeah, I got me some of that."

"What color is it?"

"What?"

"What color is the discharge? Is it whitish?"

"Oh yeah. No, it kind of, kind of yellow. I thought I check this out, I might of got me a strain. Can you give me some pills?"

"Injections are more effective. Is it difficult for you to urinate?"

"Oh, when I go to the can . . . yeah. Just a little there, yeah."

"Let's see what we've got."

The boots were covered by brown trousers. They went to tiptoe as the Nikes approached, then sank down again.

"Hooeee . . . you shouldn't to put them gloves on, that plastic sure was cold."

The Nikes left the booth. Two minutes later they returned.

"Mr. Smith, you have gonorrhea. I'm going to give you a shot to take care of it."

"Oh, no. I don't need no shots. You could give me some pills, you want, but I don't take no shots."

"Turn around, Mr. Smith. Bend over, please."

Staring at the floor, Jaysine began to tremble.

She saw the Nikes first. Then blond hair. Lightened, but not properly. It looked like a cream, done at home. Last of all Jaysine made out the eyes: tired, brown, set too close. Her mind chattered professionally: *You could be pretty if your posture was better, if we let your hair grow and style it away from your face.* Instead she was all business, no makeup but a passé shade of lipstick, carrying a clipboard, stethoscope, pen.

"Ms. Farmer. How are we doing today."

"Hello. Is the doctor going to be in pretty soon?"

"I'm Dr. Friedman."

"Oh, I'm sorry—"

"I'm used to it. What's the trouble?"

She explained in a near-whisper. Friedman glanced over the clipboard. "Are you married, Jaysine?"

"No."

"Pregnant?"

"No."

"Are you on the street?"

"What?"

"Of course you aren't . . . Do you use needles?"

"Yes."

"I see. What are you on?"

She felt confused. "What am I on? I don't understand—"

"What do you put in the needles?" said Friedman patiently. "What are you on, what do you use in them?"

"I don't put anything in my needles. I'm an R.E., a registered electrologist, I remove hair with them. I work at the Style Shoppe, on Pine Street, by the Odd Fellows Building."

The doctor gave her a glance over the clipboard, as if seeing her for the first time, and then smiled and put it aside. "Let's skip the rest of these. Sit down, Jaysine. Is this your first occurrence?"

"Yes."

"How long have you had it?"

"I noticed something . . . Saturday. I think I, I've had kind of a low fever for quite a while. I thought it was a cold coming on."

"Does it itch?"

"It sure does."

"Sore throat?"

"Yes."

Rubber snapped as the doctor stretched on gloves. She made Jaysine say "Aah," then examined her palm. Finally she said, "Well, let's see what we've got. You've been in a chair before."

My turn now, she thought through the coldness, removing boots and peeling down hose and panties. As she fitted her arches to cold metal she remembered the women in her homey station, exposing guiltily to her what they concealed from the world. She stared up as a little sun came on above her and tilted up and down and centered itself hotly between her legs.

The doctor's head appeared between her knees. "Spread a little more, please. . . . Yep. Something going on here."

"That's what Dr. Kopcik said."

"You saw him? When?"

"This afternoon. He said I'd better come over here, tonight, to the Monday clinic."

The gleam of the other woman's hair, her lowered head, made her think of the way she lowered hers to Brad. He liked to do it other places than in bed. In his car, up at the abandoned lookout tower east of Four Holes; when it was warm, in the woods, on the picnics she packed for them. Once even in the stairwell of her apartment. She'd been scared, listening for someone coming up from the street. He wanted her on every date, sometimes the first thing. She didn't always feel like it then, so sudden, but because he loved her she let him.

She smiled, remembering, and then her lips stiffened as she came back to when and where she was now.

"Let's try for a scrape," the doctor was saying. "There's a place here that looks amenable. Be right back."

Jaysine let the cold light fill her while she waited. Guilt and shame ebbed, replaced by a numbed disgust and fear.

The doctor returned with a silvery shard of metal, eyed her privates critically, and began mining. She fixed her eyes on the light, feeling the tears rise again, a flood pressure behind a frozen dam.

"Okay up there?"

"It hurts."

"Sorry. Got to get some live stuff."

Steel clinked into glass. A silken thread of blood uncurled. Friedman was done with the scrape and was taking blood when the door opened and the attendant waddled in. She got something from a locker and left. "Privacy," said Dr. Friedman, inspecting the full tube, "is not our number-one concern here . . . okay. You can get dressed now. I'll be right back."

The doctor seemed to be gone a long time. Jaysine sat on the table, waiting, once she had dressed.

Friedman came back in. "Well, we'll do a blood test, just to be sure, but the dark-field's pretty trustworthy."

"What do you think it is?"

"This?" Friedman looked toward the curtain; her mind was somewhere away, Jaysine thought, perhaps on another patient, and she felt sudden jealous rage; not even here could she get attention just for herself. "I don't think there's much doubt it's syphilis. Secondary stage. The chancre's inside the cervix, that's why you missed it till the later symptoms appeared. We're probably looking at six to ten weeks after initial infection. I imagine Dr. Kopcik told you that."

"He said—that disease. Yes."

"You've read about it, I suppose."

"Oh, sure. In the magazines, at work."

"Once we have positive tests, we'll start your treatment. Are you allergic to penicillin?"

"I don't think so."

"All right, then. Do I have your number here? I'll call when we want you for the first course of shots. In the meanwhile, I'd advise discontinuing intercourse. If you can't, have the male wear a condom."

Jaysine nodded. "Tell me—"

"Yes, go ahead," said the doctor briskly, glancing toward the curtain.

"How did I get this? I mean, is there any other—"

"Sexual contact. That's it."

She stared at the floor, then took a deep breath. "Would he know he had it?"

"Not always. But usually. Nine times out of ten, at a guess."

Friedman snapped off the gloves and threw them into a bin. One finger caught, hung over the edge like, Jaysine thought, his penis, limp and small after he took it out and reached for his cigarettes. "If you're sure who it was, I'd tell him if I were you. Make sure he receives treatment. Otherwise you leave yourself open to reinfection. And you'll need to take some precautions in your work—I'll want to talk to your employer. Gloves should be enough, just for a few weeks." The doctor smiled, brief, weary, unexpected; then suddenly reached down and patted her with her bare hand. "Cheer up! It'll take a little while, but we can cure this. That's more than you can say about a lot of things."

"No problem," said Jaysine, sliding down and reaching for her clothes.

In the waiting room the seats had grown new people. Instead of leaving she sat down again. Reflected in the face of the clock, her own wore the hard look again. Her mouth was set wry and a little bored. She told herself she'd expected this, or something like it.

When her knees stopped shaking she got up. Pulled the scarf over her hair. Climbed the stairs to the lobby. Then stopped, wondering what to do, where to go next.

The outer door opened and a boy in a knit cap came in. Snow blew in with him from the darkness, lived for a whirling moment in the lobby heat, then vanished. She turned suddenly toward the invitation of night. He held the door for her and she went through it, not looking at him, feeling nothing yet, into the dark and the wind.

She didn't see the streetlights, haloed glows spaced away in the falling snow. She didn't see the icy road beneath her boots, or the headlights at the top of the hill. Only when a horn screamed out and the station wagon dipped, plowing toward her on locked wheels, did she flinch, then hurry forward. She didn't look back at the stalled car, the woman who stared after her from behind the wheel. All that was real was internal, the unanswerable dilemma that drummed in her brain:

He said he loved me.

Then how could he do this to me?

The lights faded behind her as she stumbled on, seeking solitude like a wounded animal. Past darkened, shabby houses, their only light the ghostly flicker of screens. Past an abandoned garage, into a vacant lot, junk and garbage drifted deep with snow. Here, in the darkness, she stopped, leaning against a shattered, roofless wall of icy brick. Sagged to her knees, then on down into the snow where she could smell dogs had been. She didn't care.

He said he loved me.

The whiteness built on her back, her shoulders, her calves. She laid her burning cheek against the icy ground.

I know I loved him.

Her eyes closed and the hard look slipped off her mouth. She lay without moving in the darkness, in the silence, beneath the slowly falling snow.

Ten

P hil wondered what *her* problem was. She hadn't said a word, or even looked at him. A little heavy, but not bad looking. He glanced after her, wondering who she was, but she was already gone.

He forgot her. Waiting for the elevator, he went back over his visit to the *Century* office.

It'd been brief. He'd had maybe sixty seconds with Jerry Newton, and the editor had been preoccupied by a rattling teletype and a screen of text. He'd nodded continually, hurrying Phil through his explanation; glanced at the typescript, then when a phone rang dropped it into the maelstrom that covered his desk.

Well, Phil thought, at least he said he'd look at it.

The elevator stopped. He nosed uncertainly down a hushed corridor. The hospital smell made him uneasy. Visiting hours were almost over. He'd already passed the double room when he realized the silhouette within had been W. T. Halvorsen, sitting up in the dark.

He had a weird sense of déjà vu as he felt his way in. He almost expected a puppy at his knees. When he got to the bed he hesitated. At last he decided, and whispered the old man's name.

Halvorsen had been sitting there, awake, for perhaps half an hour.

He'd napped through all that day, waking only when someone came to do something to him. And not wholly then. Though he remembered injections. But at last, not long before, he'd opened his eyes on a tangible world.

Lying there he touched, very lightly, a needle taped above his wrist. He turned his head, and made out an obese man who lay with his eyes closed, wheezing with every breath.

Funny, he couldn't for the life of him say how he got here. Last he remembered he'd been at home. The boy had come by, the Italian kid, and they'd been talking about the old days. After that he didn't remember anything. Yet here he was, obviously in a hospital, and a window told him it was night.

When he opened his eyes again he caught the shadow. He watched it hesitate, then approach. When it whispered his name he started.

"What are you doin' here, boy?"

"Hi, Mr. Halvorsen. Come by to see you. Uh, how you doing?"

"I don't rightly know. Where the heck are we?"

"This is Raymondsville Memorial."

"Uh huh. Figured so . . . but how'd I get here?"

"Oh. Nobody told you? Well, you remember, we were talkin'? You kind of passed out. I was pretty scared. You wouldn't wake up, so I dressed you and dragged you down to the road. A trucker gave us a ride. Actually, he drove us right up to the emergency room. He was from Texas, talked funny, but a real nice guy."

Halvorsen nodded. Now he remembered. He'd felt suddenly sick, sick to his guts, and had headed for the doorway to puke it up. And after that, nothing.

"What day's today?"

"It's Monday night."

He'd been out for two days. He thought about that. Then muttered, "Guess I owe you a thanks for packin' me out. Must not of been easy, that's a four-mile haul."

"It's okay," said Phil, and after a moment added, "Don't worry about your puppy. I brought her along too. She's up my house, on Paradise, I'm feeding her and everything."

"I thank ye. That's good to know."

They waited in the darkness for a while. At last Halvorsen said, grudgingly, "What was your name, again? Sammonelli, something?"

"Phil Romanelli."

"Uh huh. Well, ought to be a chair here someplace. Can you reach this light, here, up above me?"

The single bulb clicked on, showing them each to the other. The old man's face was drawn and his gray hair looked wet. There was some kind of rash on his cheek. His arms came out of the hospital gown thin and knobby-elbowed. A tube was taped to one of them. His eyes were cavernous in the glare, and shadows hid his mouth beneath a bony skull.

"You're looking better," Phil told him. "What do they say's wrong with you?"

"Well, I ain't talked to anybody yet. Ain't been in shape to. Feel like I just woke up after a bad drunk." Halvorsen reflected on this, didn't like the sound of it. "Though I ain't had a drop. Hey . . ."

"Phil."

"Yeah, would you mind findin' the doctor? I'd like to know how long they're planning on keepin' me here."

Phil found a nurse at the hall station. The doctor would be in on night rounds in an hour, and unless Mr. Halvorsen needed attention, he'd have to wait till then. He took that back and the old man nodded. "No hurry," he said.

"It doesn't hurt, does it?"

"Well, this needle stings some, but I don't dare pull it out. Another thing—" He lifted the coverlet, stared at himself under it. "By jiminy, here's another one."

Phil sat back. He thought, I'll stay another couple minutes, then head home.

"What's it doing outside?"

"Oh, still coming down."

"First snowfall don't usually last."

"Well, it's been cold for a long time. And it hasn't really stopped since Friday night."

The man in the corner muttered, wheezed, and tried to turn over once or twice before giving up.

Phil whispered, "By the way, I got that interview typed up."

"What interview?"

"You know, what you were telling me out at your place."

"Oh."

Halvorsen had been feeling for a while like he had to pee, but he didn't feel right just letting go in the bed. What if something leaked? But with the tube in him down there it didn't seem like he had much of a choice. He glanced at the boy's waiting face. "Oh, those. Just some old stories . . . Did I tell you 'bout Ben Yeager?"

"You mentioned him."

"Old Amos only told me about a hundred stories about him." Halvorsen remembered the sudden pop and sizzle as McKittrack would lean to aim into the fire, his beard swinging dangerously close, and then rear back and make a miser's-purse of his mouth before he went on with whatever tale was in train. He licked his lips. "You got anything on you to chew?"

"What?"

"Never mind." He should have known. He remembered how the trapper had started him in on Navy Cut out there in the Kinningmahontawany, and how his mother had a fit when he come home, thirteen years old, with a bulge in the side of his face like a chipmunk.

"Well, I better be goin'," he heard the boy say.

"Nah, sit down, let me tell you one of 'em." Halvorsen suddenly wanted to talk, maybe because he was alone and sick and maybe even a little scared. He felt weak, but talking didn't seem to tire him. "Did you ever hear about—"

"Just a minute," said Phil, getting up. When he came back he had a pen and a note pad. "Okay," he said, grinning shyly at the old man; and he saw Halvorsen's face move, just a bit, in what might have been meant for a smile.

"Now, I told you Yeager was king hunter all around here back in the old days. Amos—you remember Amos?"

"The trapper."

"Yeah. He knew Yeager just after the war, the Civil War, and Ben was seventy-one then, so that would born him around 1794, '95. His dad moved out here from the Amish country on the Purchase of 1784. He had the first still west of the mountains. This was wilderness, wasn't a dozen white men in northwest Pennsylvania back then."

"Uh huh."

"So he started huntin' around 1810. When Amos knew Ben he was kind of fat, but still tough as ironwood and fast as a thunderbolt. Used to wear a old-style huntin' shirt and buckskin breeches. Then he had a big leather belt, and stuck his mittens in that, his bullet-bag, and his big bowie. And squirrel-lined moccasins.

"Yeager was what they used to call a professional hunter. He told Amos he'd killed three hundred and fifty bears, probably three thousand deer, exactly sixty-four panthers and two thousand one hundred and five wolves, and then of course elks, and wildcats, fox, and so on. He knew the numbers 'cause in them days the state paid eight dollars for every wolf or panther scalp you turned in. That was real money then."

Phil's pen scratched. In the corner the other man shifted again, but his eyes stayed closed.

"Now, what are you? Sixteen?"

"Seventeen."

"When he was a year younger than you he was out huntin' with the Senecas. They adopted him into the Turtle clan, and he burned a white dog with 'em. I don't know what that means. But they taught him to call wolves. One time he called 'em so good a pack surrounded him. He got two with his old muzzle-loader and killed another one with his knife before the rest ran off over a hill.

"That same winter he was hunting down along Falkiner Creek, out where Ironfurnace is now, and he shot a deer with his last pinch of powder. Now in them days all they took was the pelts, they left the meat unless they wanted some right then. Well, he had it dressed out and was ready to head home when it commenced to snow.

"And it snowed so heavy he couldn't see. So he tore down some boughs and bedded down under a hemlock, there's always a dry place there, covered himself up with the hide and went to sleep.

"Well, he woke up around midnight, and felt around, and found that he had sticks and leaves all over him, and the hide he was under smelled of cat sign."

"Cat sign?"

"Cat piss. He knew in a minute what it was. Some mama panther had claimed him, and was gone to get her cubs for dinner."

Phil, listening to the old man's flat mutter, felt a sudden chill. He imagined himself huddled in darkness, half-buried in boughs and above that snow; around him the stink of the cat's staling. Beyond that only utter night, icy dark, black as blindness. Yet in it something moved, huge, powerful, night-eyed, and hungry.

"And he didn't have any more bullets?"

"No more powder. Anyway, he pulled that hide back over himself and gathered some of the dry needles and struck him his steel and got a fagot lit. And he hid that and waited.

"Pretty soon, sure enough, Ben hears her comin' over the snow, pad-pad-paddin' toward him. He waits till she's sniffin' the hide and then he suddenly throws it aside and pushes the fire into the cat's eyes. It gave a scream, its whiskers caught, an' it was gone. He nursed that fire all night, but she never came back."

Halvorsen smiled. Something in him felt completion, passing these tales along. He knew it was sentiment, telling this boy as he had been told, as McKittrack had heard them from Yeager himself a century or more before. But at his age, he figured he could afford a little sentiment.

And the boy deserved it. He'd come asking for stories, now hadn't he?

"Now, bears. There's still bears, but not like they used to be. I remember once when I was livin' in town one came down the street one night, killed two dogs that come out to chase it. I was on the porch loading my thirty-ought-six when Pete Riddick got it with two barrels of buckshot." He paused, frowning up at the light. "No, wasn't Pete—he dropped a can of nitro in '39. Anyway, yeah, these woods used to be full of them. Full-grown, yearling, cubs. Yeager took 'em all."

"He killed cubs too?"

"And skinned them. And sold 'em. Sure. It was his business."

Phil's initial admiration for this Yeager character was ebbing. "He sounds pretty rough."

"Oh, I imagine he was. There was a whiskey shanty out in Medicine Spring then, that's what they used to call Petroleum City. One night some fella from Philadelphia disagreed with him, said you couldn't call a wolf, they were too smart. So Ben grabs a jug of dew in one hand and the fella that mouthed off in the other and heads up Dale Hollow.

"So they're going through the woods in the middle of the night, up above Cherry Hill, and they hear a dog-wolf howl some distance off. Ben says, 'Stop, and be quiet.' And they hear a slut-wolf answer, closer to them.

"So they go in that direction, an' Ben he gives a bark every once in a while, and the bitch keeps answering. Finally after an hour they come to a blown-down oak. The she-wolf's under it. See, Ben knew that when the pups were small the dog-wolf would bring food back to the den. So he crawls under there and gets eight pups out from it and kills six and scalps them. The old wolf comes out showing her teeth, and the guy was going to shoot it with his pistol, but Ben stopped him. He said, 'I've got three litters out of this bitch, don't stop her now.' And he took the live pups back with him and sold 'em, and the city fella paid his whiskey the rest of that night."

"She let him take the pups?"

"They say a wolf won't fight for its young the way a bear will. I don't know, they've been gone here since Amos was a kid. They killed one over in Potter County in 1890, but they ain't been seen in Hemlock since the Civil War."

"Those panthers—painters—sounded like the meanest."

"Yeah, guess they was. Eleven, twelve feet long. A panther could kill a bear. Yeager shot the last one down in Reeds Still Hollow. They still call that Painter Rocks, where he got it."

"Yeah, I heard of that. Only they call it Painted Rocks now."

"No, it's 'Painter,' not 'Painted.' "

Phil made a note.

Halvorsen lay motionless for a time, staring down at his hands. "Yeah, they killed 'em," he said. "All the buffalo, all the wolves, all the painters and catamounts and wildcats. Just deer and a few bear now, what they can hunt with no trouble. And then they cut down the woods."

"What do you mean, cut them down? Who cut them down?"

He lifted his head. "My God, boy, don't you know that? The Campbells and the Gerroys and the Goodyears. Why, Christ, there was white pines here a hundred feet high and two hundred years old. Hemlock higher than that and thick as a man's tall. There was hardwood, chestnut and oak where the ground was good, and ash and hickory and maple and birch everywhere. On the hillsides you had poplar, and linnwood, and down low the butternut and sycamore and elm. That's what these old short-line railroads was for, that's how they hauled it out."

He closed his eyes as he spoke, and the picture came still terrible though it was sixty years gone. They'd been bumping southward along the rutted track in McKittrack's old Model T, and come round through Grafton Hollow and then the road dropped, the scrub pine dropped away, and he'd gone to stone in his seat.

Before them was desolation to the blue horizon, fold on fold of hills stripped like battlefield dead under the autumn sun. Their sides were littered with stumps and briars and slashed with the Shay engines' right-of-way. The old man, cursing in a whisper, told him how the timber companies had bought politicians, lied and cheated and forced Indians and small owners off their land; then in ten years whipsawed, toppled, and stripped for tanbark twenty-eight million acres of virgin forest. They'd never replanted, just moved on west, and now nothing was left, nothing.

McKittrack had told him then greed would be the ruin of the land. That where the ancient forests had fallen no tree might ever grow again, and for certain none as darkly and broodingly majestic.

Now, two generations later, Billy Halvorsen nodded slowly. "I seen them cut down those woods. And I seen what come back. Aspen and gray birch, maple and spruce and beech . . . it's woods, but it ain't the same. It'll never be the same."

They were sitting there together in silence when Dr. Leah Friedman came in. Behind her was a woman Phil recognized after a moment as Alma Pankow, Halvorsen's daughter.

"Hello, Racks." The doctor flicked on the room light and perched on the bed. "Is this your young friend? The one who brought you in?"

"That's right. Alma, want you to meet Phil."

The woman's round face was reddened by cold. She looked tired, older than she ought to be. At Halvorsen's introduction she looked at Phil, but said nothing.

"We met before," Phil told her. "You work there at the unemployment with my sister. And then last summer, you ordered some stuff for your dad over the phone, and I came by your house for the money—"

"Oh yes." She sat down, placing herself in the chair like a heavy bag of groceries.

Friedman took Halvorsen's wrist. "So you're back with us at last."

" 'Fraid so."

"How are you feeling?"

"Tired."

"Um hum. What have you been eating out there in the woods, Mr. Halvorsen?"

"I eat all right. Do a little garden. Alma brings me things in the winter, potatoes and canned stuff."

"Do you take vitamins?"

"Not out of no pill," said Halvorsen. "Start feeling slow, I'll brew me some hemlock tea, or feverwort, somethin' like that. I doctor myself."

"You'd get C and B complex from those." She switched her gaze to Phil. "You were with Mr. Halvorsen when he had his episode."

"Yes, ma'am. I'm Phil Romanelli."

"Leah Friedman, Phil. Have you felt faint or weak? Then or now? Skin troubles, rash anywhere on your body?"

"No."

"Have you two been spending a lot of time together?"

"I wouldn't say so," said Phil, and looked at Halvorsen. The old man shook his head. He looked back at the doctor. "Maybe two or three hours, all together."

"He ought to move into town," said Mrs. Pankow suddenly. They all looked at her. She was staring at the floor, at the muddy footprints from her boots. "I've tried to get him to move in for years. Fred's got a extra room over the garage we could fix up. It's warm, he could help out around the pumps. But he won't listen."

"That's not your fault." The doctor patted her twice, with a sort of professional compassion, then folded her hands on her clipboard. "So let's go on . . . You didn't eat anything that might have disagreed with you?"

"Can't think of nothing."

"Have you been around any pesticides, any recently sprayed areas, any chemical spills?"

"I been out at my place, that's all, mindin' my own business," said Halvorsen shortly. "What're you getting at? What's wrong with me? I figured it was my heart, or maybe I was goin' crazy."

"Your heart? They tell me how you go tramping through those woods, up and down those hills. I don't think it's that. And you're certainly not crazy. But I don't believe it's diet-related either."

"Then what?" said Alma.

"I don't know." The doctor pressed her lips together and looked toward the window. "Snowing like this, I hope people wear their seat belts . . . Okay, here's what I think. I only get traces from the urine, but they're pretty odd. It's a little like cases you read about in the shipbuilding industry, where workers are exposed to organotin paint. And yet it's like pesticide poisoning. That rash you've got is a chemical eczema. And last, I see signs of heavy metal toxicity."

"You're saying, some kind of poison?"

"That's right, Mr. Halvorsen. That's the diagnosis."

"Am I goin' to live?"

She smiled. "This time. What I want to know is, where did you pick this stuff up?"

Halvorsen lay quietly, reviewing the last few days. He'd puttered around in the basement, oiled his old .22 Hornet . . . Thursday he hadn't done much, gone for a walk down the hollow . . . Friday he'd walked into town, had a coffee at the Brown Bear, and got a ride back with Fatso. And Saturday he'd woke up sick. "Can't think of any place I might of got sprayed with any chemicals," he said slowly.

"Try."

"I *did*."

"All right, all right!" She smiled wearily. "Phil, can you contribute any-thing?"

"Well, not really. He didn't look too good when I got out there, and he just got worse and worse. But I don't know why."

"So, when can I get out of here?" Halvorsen asked her.

"I'd like to hold on to you a few more days. Let you get your strength back. That reminds me, are you hungry?"

"Still a little queasy, but funny, I ain't hungry." He lifted his arm; the tube followed it. "I figured that was what this was for."

"That's right, that's sugar solution, but you should get some solid food in you too. You don't look like you've got a lot in reserve. Maybe a milk-shake, would you like that?"

"I'll give 'er a try."

Friedman got up. She crossed the room and felt the sleeping man's pulse; touched his forehead gently; made a note on her clipboard. Hal-vorsen, growing tired of the light, covered his face with his free arm. All that talking had taken more out of him than he'd realized. When the doctor came back she murmured, "Mrs. Pankow, Mr. Romanelli, I'll tell the nurse you can stay past visiting time if you like. I've got to finish my rounds."

Alma nodded; Halvorsen whispered, "Thanks." Phil hesitated, then jumped up and followed her out into the corridor. She was leaning over the counter, talking to the nurse, and his eyes slid up her leg. Old as she was, she had a nice ass. She finished and turned to him, brows lifted, and he said, "Say, Doctor, I had a question—"

"Go ahead."

"What kind of chemicals are these? That you think he's been ex-posed to?"

"They're pretty dangerous. Toxic, mutagenic, carcinogenic. That means poisonous and cancer-causing. He's past having children, fortunately."

"What are they used for?"

"Pesticides, insecticides, nerve gas, and various industrial uses."

"*Nerve gas?*"

"Among other things."

"Well, how would he get any of that? He lives way out in Mortlock Run."

"That's what's puzzling me, Philip. I'd hoped one of you could help me find out, but no luck, I guess.

"The thing is"—she paused, tapping her foot and frowning—"this isn't the first case like this I've seen this year. There've been several eczemas and gastrointestinals with no clear-cut etiology. I mean, no obvious cause. There's only one case I've been able to trace. A family out in Chapman bought a load of cut-rate heating oil from somebody in a truck. The stuff was full of cadmium and lead."

"Mr. Halvorsen burns wood."

"Right, I know." Her wrist shot out and he jumped before he realized she was only checking her watch. "Well, look, gotta go."

"Wait—is he—I mean, what's going to happen to him?"

"He's pretty weak now, but he's in good shape for his age. I know he doesn't have much of a pension, and I don't want to eat up his savings, if he has any, but I don't want him to go back to that basement. I know he's the hermit type, but he should have somebody around to keep an eye on him." Friedman hesitated. "Alma would take him, but I don't know how Fred really feels about it. Anyway, he needs professional care. I'm going to recommend he be transferred to a long-term care facility."

"A what?"

"A nursing home. But that's up to his daughter, and to him." She patted him, the same quick double pat she'd given Mrs. Pankow. "Okay, really got to go now. Good night."

"Good night."

Head down, Phil retrieved his coat, said good-bye to the old man and his daughter, and walked thoughtfully out into the night.

Eleven

In the winter night the grimy snow glowed scarlet, as if dyed by the neon light with humming radiance. Beneath her boots cinders crunched like the dried husks of locusts. Slower, and slower. Then stopped, and she stood still, looking up.

By day Sherlock's looked abandoned. Its windows were dirty dark, ragged with the portraits of long-defeated politicians, and the brick-look siding had cracked away from rotting wood beneath. But by night it changed, spread its wings and lived and fed. It was open now, ready for whoever might need.

Jaysine shuddered involuntarily as the door sealed behind her. In the moment before vision fogged overhead fans peeled spirals off a slab of tobacco haze. Balls clicked, backed by a steady throb of Charley Pride. The men wore wool shirts and jeans, boots and hunting vests. She heard their voices as if through cotton. They were talking about their first day in the woods, about deer.

But none of them looked her way, and she moved forward, reassured. The moment she slid onto a sparkly plastic stool a huge round man in a red shirt was in front of her, hands like two rashers of bacon to either side of hers on the bar. "Evenin'. What can I get you, miss?"

"Straub's."

"What's that? Couldn't quite hear you."

"I said, Straub's."

"Are you all right?"

"What do you mean? I'm fine. Just bring me what I asked for, please."

The next thing she knew he had her hand. It took her a moment to snatch it back. A spark of anger flared through the numbness, like a match struck in a frozen forest. "What do you think you're doing?"

"Sorry. But you look froze through." He winked slowly. "Tell ya what. I'm bringin' you a ginger brandy first. After you drink that you can have your beer. And I want you to sit over here, okay?"

Close as he was, she could see him without her glasses. Big and old and bald, with a big wedding band with a cross cut into it on his thick fingers. He didn't seem threatening. So she moved obediently to where he pointed.

And gasped, blinking up into a blue hell. The heater above the bar was angled down, aimed right into her face. Its breath dried her eyeballs and scorched her neck as she unbuttoned her coat. When she looked down again, a long-stemmed glass gleamed in front of her. She tipped it and the fiery spirit stripped her throat.

After another sip she took off her kerchief, shaking out her hair to let it bake. She realized suddenly she'd nearly frozen to death. She rubbed her glasses with a damp paper napkin and put them back on.

To her left were foosball games and pool tables, surrounded by the hunters. She looked away, but not soon enough. One of them glanced up as he positioned his shot.

"How much is that?"

"Ladies, ninety-five cents. I were you, though, Miss, I'd stay here a little longer. Don't have to drink. But you ought to warm up some 'fore you go out again. You know they closed Route Six?"

"Closed it?"

"Uh huh. Pileup at the overpass. Four cars. It was on WRVL."

"Who was it? Was anybody hurt?"

"They didn't say."

She couldn't think of anything else to ask. She stared past the bottles of Carstairs and Bankers Special into the mirror. I'm too heavy, she thought. I need to lose some weight, maybe cut my hair different . . . Then her mind stopped.

None of that mattered now. She was different. Diseased. And cured or not, she'd never feel clean again.

Jaysine gripped the glass. She wanted to throw it. She wanted to shatter things, destroy, destroy. Instead, when the man came back, she said, turning the gleam of silver and turquoise around and around on her wrist, "That was so good. Give me another one of those, please."

Some time later she put down a five-dollar bill, straightened her skirt, and went out again.

Her face felt warm. I'm drunk, she thought, a little amazed. The street was dark and unfamiliar. The snow came down, snow she remembered from when it had tried to cover her up. Alone under it she had thought and thought and finally come to a decision. Only now she couldn't remember what it was.

She giggled. As if in sympathy, water chuckled to her left. She found herself on a little bridge and paused there, leaning over the iron rail.

The stream was frozen. The ice was opaque and white as frosted glass. But below it somewhere the creek still flowed. She could hear it.

Some time later she paused again, calf-deep in heaped snow. The plows had thrust it aside and left it, burying the parking meters. Main Street was deserted, silent, under a burnished hennaed light.

She lifted her eyes to the streetlamps, remembering all the times she'd stared down at them from her window.

They lit the descending snow in blurry halos. Blue nearest the bulbs, then green, and last and outermost a rose gold like the old bartender's ring. The endless snow came down out of the darkness, was lit for a moment, falling, and then passed as silently out of her sight. If you didn't look close it was just snow. But now, her vision slowed, she saw that each individual flake had its own path. Some were falling, some rising, some zigzagging as if undecided, or as if each had to guess or calculate its own way to the ground. From far off came the howl of a dog. That and the harsh pant of her breath were the only interruptions in the white silence.

Above the five and dime her window glowed welcome. She could see her dried flowers and beyond them on the wall a corner of the forest print. She stared up at it for a while, shivering, before she understood why the light was on. She walked a few paces on and looked down Pine Street.

The midnight car was parked in front of the Keynote.

She climbed the stair slowly, clinging to the handsmoothed rail. Then, with her key out she hesitated, listening through the door. She heard an argument, a shot . . . No, it was television. She unlocked the door awkwardly and pushed it open.

All her lights were on. He was sitting on the couch in his shirtsleeves, watching TV with his feet on the coffee table. His coat and scarf hung on her workbench. A bottle stood at his feet, foil scraps littering the floor. As she came in he turned his head and gave her an angry grin.

"Where've you been? I've been waiting for you for hours."

She didn't respond; couldn't think, through the ice, of anything to say. From the mist before her eyes his face emerged suddenly: gray irises flecked with blue, dark nostril-hairs, stubble on his jaw-line. He smelled of cologne and cigarettes and wine.

"So where were you, babe? I called the shop but they said you were out today. I been here since six. Left once, but the road's blocked, so I come back. Good thing I had a key. Where the hell you been?"

"Out."

"What do you mean, out? Monday night—that's what I said last week, right? When you say you'll be here I expect you to be here. I have to fix these things up in advance."

She didn't answer. After a moment he let go her shoulders. "You eat yet?"

"No."

"I could stand some spaghetti, or something. That veal last week was great." He reached for the bottle, then swung back. His eyes moved over her face. "Are you all right? You look like you're getting a cold."

"Should I be all right?"

"What?"

She stripped off her mittens and threw them on the couch.

"What did you say? Never mind. Mm, mm. I know what you need. Let's have a taste of those lips."

She closed her eyes and bent back her head obediently as his mouth fastened on hers. Her arms lifted, then stopped, hovering an inch from his back. After a moment his lips moved on. The room began spinning around her. His hands found the zipper of her dress.

"Brad—"

Before she could think or react he'd unhooked her bra. His fingers were cold. "Don't," she whispered. The couch came up beneath her. She tried to close her thighs but he was too strong.

His fingers left her suddenly and she lay limp. She felt dizzy and sick. The air was cold and she tried to cover herself with a hand. The other went to her mouth.

Through the numbness, slowly, like the outlines of the hills emerging from night, she was beginning to feel.

"Hey, babe, what's that I smell? Brandy? Well, you're already primed, let's have a party."

She opened her eyes. A foot away his member strained toward her, vein-shot like an old woman's legs, the head questing to and fro like a blind snake. Then his hand was pulling her forward. She felt warmth at her mouth, pushing back her lips.

"Ouch! God damn it!"

He'd jumped back, staring down at her. He looked huge and angry. Then, suddenly, started to laugh. His penis wilted, nodding disconsolately toward the carpet. His laughter filled the room, rattled the windows and the glasses on the shelf. She put her hands over her ears.

"You little bitch! Christ, you startled the hell out of me. Any harder and you'd have bit it off!"

She said thickly, "Brad . . . listen. We got to talk."

"Talk? Sure. Let's play first, though." His hands found his penis again; he pulled it upward, stroked it.

"*Get away from me!*"

She screamed it so loud her throat hurt. He paused, and something changed in his face.

"What the hell's wrong with you tonight?"

"Wrong with me. With *me*. It's always somebody else, isn't it? What's wrong with *you*?"

He stared around the room, his face little-boyishly puzzled. "What's going on here? I was looking forward to dinner, a little kissy-face, but suddenly it's very unfriendly."

"I wonder why."

"I wonder too. What's the story? There's nothing to eat; you've been drinking and you look like hell. You're all wet and there's some kind of dirt in your hair. Leaves, and dog shit, or something." Her hand moved to it automatically. "I'm not used to being treated like this. Let's get to the bottom of it, right now." He zipped himself and sat down.

"You poor man. I don't appreciate you."

"Wow. I've heard this before. You sound like my fucking wife."

"Do you? Fuck your wife?"

He said softly, "Jay, seriously, what the hell is going on?"

The hurt tone reached her even through her anger. She remembered suddenly how hard he worked, how many jobs depended on him, how much he gave up and suffered to have one night a week with her. No one else understood him; no one else, except of course his little daughter, loved him. A warmth ran through her chest, as if her heart were melting. She put out her hand to his hair. He put his over hers, and they sat like that for a moment, not speaking, just looking unhappily at each other.

"I'm sorry," she whispered. "I'm not acting very nice."

"I can see something's wrong. Tell you what, tell me about it, and then I'll fix it up."

Her eyes stung suddenly, her breath caught in a half-sob. "I was down to the doctor's this morning."

"Oh." He shook his head, looking, she thought, relieved. "What's the problem?"

"Dr. Kopcik sent me to the hospital. The Monday clinic."

She saw, then, something she'd never seen before. It was as if a little piece of steel slid across behind his eyes, like a man closing a peephole.

"What is it, Jay?" he said quietly.

She told him. He sat with his eyes on the carpet, swinging his shoe. It took all the courage she had to ask, at the end, "Did you know you had it?"

"Well, I felt kind of itchy now and then. And there were these little blisters. I didn't think it was anything."

"Where?"

"Well, you know."

"Brad . . ." She shook her head slowly. "Did you ask anybody about it? Did you go to the doctor?"

He shrugged. "What the hell, it went away. I wouldn't worry about it."

"Brad, this doesn't just 'go away.' I read, it's still there, you can give it to people, you can die from it, you've got to get it taken care of. I read—"

"Well, that's if it's not treated, right? But if they can take care of it, what's the problem? We'll just get it taken care of."

She stared at him. He didn't understand at all. "Brad—listen. People looked at me in the waiting room. There was a mother there, she wouldn't let her baby near me!" She felt herself losing control, and said in a rush, to get it all out at once before she did, "And you're saying . . . you knew you had something, you had, had these *blisters*, and you just went ahead and put it in me anyway. Without using anything. Without telling me."

Boulton shrugged. He glanced toward the kitchen.

"Anybody who thought he had something, maybe he might not tell people, but he, he'd go to the doctor. Or use something. Oh, God, Brad! Not keep right on exposing his girlfriend. Or whatever I am to you. What if it was something worse? Something they couldn't cure?"

"Calm *down*. Christ." He made a dismissing motion, a flip of the hand. "Look. This is not what you seem to think. Seriously. What do you say we have some dinner?"

"There's no place open this late," she said, and then realized what he meant. Her voice climbed again. It was bewildering; she hated him, then the next second it felt like love again, and then hate. "You want me to *cook* for you? *Now?* I don't believe this."

"Well, look, I'm sorry. Believe me, honey, the last thing I had in mind was hurting you. Do you need anything?"

"What?"

His suit jacket was beside him on the couch; he reached for it. "Two hundred, will that help? For the doctor." He put four fifty-dollar bills on the coffee table, then smiled across it at her, still holding the wallet. Something about that smile made her remember the blade Dr. Friedman had held up, glittering in the light. A thread of blood, uncurling in glass . . . After an endless moment during which she could not reply his hand moved again. "Two fifty. Okay?"

She whispered, "Brad, why are you giving me money?"

"Well, you had to take off work, right? This is to make up. I want you to be happy, Jay."

"Why do you want me to be happy?"

"I want everybody to be happy."

"But why do you want *me* to be happy?"

"Well, I told you before."

"Tell me again."

"I'm crazy about you. If it wasn't for my wife being the way she is I'd be here full time. You know that."

He smiled up at her, the gray eyes crinkling gently at the corners, the sincerity clear and pure and she saw, all in one killing moment, how very very false.

"If you loved me, you wouldn't have given me this."

"Let's not get into that again."

"Why not? That's what this whole, this whole *discussion* is about. If you cared about *me* at all, about my *happiness*, you'd have gotten it checked. You'd have used precautions, you'd have told me—" She felt, to her horror, the tears start. They'd make a mess of her mascara. She looked around for a Kleenex. There weren't any. She was about to ask him for a handkerchief when he sighed and got up, tightening his tie.

"What are you doing?"

"He didn't answer, only took the billfold out again. Another picture of Benjamin Franklin joined the others and he picked up his jacket.

"What are you doing," she said again, sniffling.

"I don't have to take this."

"What do you mean?"

"There's motels here. The Antler'll be full, but the Gerroy—"

"No, wait." She heaved herself up and stumbled toward the kitchen. "I got some lasagna frozen, I can—"

"Eat it yourself. You're not such a great cook, either."

She forced her lips into a frightened smile. "Don't get so mad. I'm sorry, Brad. I was upset, it was such bad news. I'm—I'm okay now."

"Forget it." He finished the glass and turned it in his hand. "This one I bought you?"

"Yes."

He balanced it for a moment more, as if deciding something, and then threw it against the stove. It burst heavily, fragments skittering along the floor, and she cried out before she could stop herself.

"You want to know something? You've got a little mind, Jaysine. You've never been anywhere or done anything and now you never will. Fat thighs and a little brain, like a chicken. Me, me, me, that's all that's in it."

Filled with sudden terror, she started toward him, forgetting she was half-naked. Her hose were tangled and she fell over the table. He was heading for the door. At it he turned, his hand moving in his slacks. She thought for a moment that he was about to undress, come back, make up. Then something glittered in the air between them. It hit the rug, bounced, vanished under the couch.

"There's your key. Give it to some shoe clerk. You had your shot, Jaysine. I was going to take you to Tucson. But I was wrong. I think you belong here."

Anger and terror fought in her. Why would he say that about her thighs—he said they rubbed him where it felt good, he—"Brad, no, don't leave me, not now! Take the money. I don't want it. I need *you*—"

She looked up to an open door. The room rolled suddenly, like a boat in a gale, and she hit the jamb hard and clung. Down the stair his shadow paused against the light from the street. She flattened herself at his shout like a rabbit at the hunter's approach. "Keep it. *Keep it!* That's what you wanted, isn't it? You're a cheap little cunt, you even smell cheap. A cheap little disease kind of fits."

The words hit her like a thrown glass, bursting into edges that cut inside her head. "Brad," she gasped, "I'm sorry, don't—"

The street door slammed, and glass shattered and tinkled on concrete. I'll have to pay for that too, some detached part of her mind said. The rest was numb again, numb and empty.

She sagged into the jamb. Cold rose toward her step by step. She sagged farther, mouth coming open, staring into the dark. Her stomach lurched then, at last, like a frozen river beginning to break.

Twelve

The kitchen window was still dark as Phil, sitting at the table in stocking feet, gulped the sugar-slush his mother called orange juice. He shivered; the linoleum floor was ice-cold, the air only slightly warmer. His leg jiggled nervously. He shook open the paper and frowned at the front page.

"Philip, you want some eggs?" His mother, from the bathroom.

"No thanks, Ma. I got cereal. We need new milk, this's goin' bad."

"Put a drop of vanilla in it and it'll taste all right. Scrambled, or sunny side up?"

He hated his mother's eggs. She drowned them in margarine and they tasted greasy and stale. He'd asked her not to a hundred times, but it was like there was only one way eggs could be done. And then her ultimate argument would follow: Joseph liked them that way.

The toilet flushed. She came in in her robe and went to the refrigerator. He glanced up. Sure enough, she was examining gray celled paperboard . . . "Mom, I said I don't want any eggs!"

"Don't shout at me, Philip. I'm making some for myself."

"Oh." He was suddenly filled with self-loathing. "I'm sorry."

She didn't answer and he felt even worse. He was trying to think of something nice to talk about with her when a headline caught his eye.

COUNTY EMPLOYEE FOUND ILL

Barry Fox, 29, of 122 Finney Street, Petroleum City, is reported in critical condition in Bradford Public Hospital with frostbite and exposure. Mr. Fox is employed as a road clearance operator with the Pennsylvania Department of Transportation, Hemlock County Division.

Fox was discovered Friday night in his stopped snowplow west of Bagley Corners. He has not yet regained consciousness. *Century* reporter Sarah Baransky has ascertained that hospital authorities suspect exposure to chemicals may be a contributing cause of his collapse.

In a possibly related case, Mrs. Molly Selwin was treated and released at Raymondsville Hospital for pesticide exposure. Mrs. Selwin had been treating her home with insect foggers from Fishers Big Wheel. Dr. Leah Friedman asked us to remind our readers to read the fine print on chemical products, and not to remain in the home while insecticides are being released.

Dr. Friedman also said that several other cases of toxic effects had recently come to her attention. Anyone knowing about possible sources of contamination or hazardous waste in the area should contact her or responsible city authorities immediately.

Phil stared at the print. There was a Jack Fox worked nights as a dispatcher, his father sometimes mentioned him.

"Say, do you know a Barry Fox?" he said to his mother, in the next room now.

"Not so loud, your father's asleep. Isn't that Jack Fox's brother?"

"Yeah, I thought that's who he was. It says here he's sick."

"Everybody's sick. It's this weather. What's he got?"

"They don't know."

"It's the weather. Do you want some more orange juice?"

"No, thanks."

When he turned to the second page he immediately saw something odd. There seemed to be space at the bottoms of the stories; in fact here and there were blanks, as if snow had fallen on the page. He was flipping toward the comics when he thought for a moment he'd seen his name. His eye went back. FORMER OILMAN AND HUNTER RECALLS OLD DAYS, it said.

Underneath it was his interview. He read it without breathing. They were the same words he'd typed upstairs, but in justified columns beside the pork prices they looked different. He noticed that some words were misspelled that he didn't think he had, but it still looked nice. His eyes went back to the cutline: *As Told to Philip J. Romanelli.*

He lifted the paper, not looking at the dish his mother slid in front of him. "Hey, they published my article."

"That's nice."

When he was finishing his third reading his mother said from the living room, "How are your eggs?"

He stared down at them. Yellow grease congealed like candle wax at the lowest point on the dish. He messed them up with his fork and dumped them into the garbage.

He picked his coat off the wall and carried it into the parlor. "What'd you say, about an article?" she said as he bent to buckle his galoshes.

"Nothing."

"I thought you said something. Were the eggs good?"

Phil took a deep breath, then let it out. "No, I didn't say anything. They were awful, Mom, can't you cook them without so much butter?"

"They stick to the pan."

"Don't we have a Teflon pan?"

"Your father likes them that way."

As it was in the beginning. So it is now and ever shall be. World without end amen, he thought. His elation drained away; the gray depression flooded back. At that moment there was a muffled whine directly beneath him, beneath the floor itself. "Oh—oh, the dog, I forgot, can you feed it for me?"

She sighed. "I knew I'd end up taking care of that thing."

"Never mind, then! I'll get it!"

"No, no, you go on to school, you'll be late."

Hearing her sigh again, he gave up. He had to get out, get out before he went nuts. He pulled the storm door shut behind him and stood for a moment on the porch, pulling on his gloves and taking a first cautious lungful of the icy air.

It was still dark. Across the valley Town Hill lay long and low, like a capsized ship. Above its barely visible prickle of leafless forest the sky was the color of spoiled salmon. The streetlights bounced light up from the snow, the sagging clouds reflected it down again. None of it can leave, he thought, none can leave nor can any new light come. . . .

The snow crunched and squeaked as he pushed his body gradually into motion, like some long-unused machine. His lips drew back from his teeth. The first hundred yards were straight agony. At night he'd wake sometimes, recalled from sleep by the tightening of his calves and thighs. Every morning he had to stretch them again, like woolen sweaters washed too hot. He was glad his day started with a downhill. Though he'd pay the price coming back.

By the time he got to the footbridge his legs were moving better. Boards rattled under his boots. In the spring Todds Creek rose to an ocher torrent, covering the planks, tumbling along saplings, stumps, floating trash. Now the ice was like cast iron. Leaves and sticks lay a few inches down, preserved like mobsters in concrete. He pulled his scarf over his mouth and nose, warming the icy dark air he drew in thirty times a minute and then pushed out, through the wet wool, back into the wind.

The side streets were empty. He pushed his way through ankle-deep powder on walks shoveled the day before. The plows had come through in the night, tossing up long ramparts, like the frozen bow waves of speed-boats. He vaulted one clumsily, sinking to his hips, then fought free and struck along through an inch of loose crystals above ash and salt, and under that hard asphalt, jarring him with every pace.

He paused at the corner of Main, and looked at Raymondsville on a dark winter morning. Down the street came the wind. A gelid, invisible glacier, pushing before it an occasional tardy flake. Through it the street-lights shone untwinkling. Through it, too, came a steady parade of shad-ows, like an army on the move.

He hiked along the side of the road, facing them as they rumbled past. Pickups, Scouts, Broncos, each packed with hunters. Headlights silhou-etted the racks of bolt-actions and lever-actions, pumps and over-under combinations.

Seven A.M. and Main Street was wide open, windows tossing out light like they had no use for it. He limped past Ray's Gun and Pawn, crowded with hunters buying maps and Jon-E warmers. Past the Brown Bear; past the Odd Fellows Building, with a sign, HUNTERS BREAKFAST 4–7; past Mama DeLucci's, the door as he came abreast of it pushing out on a hot rich breath of fried ham and buckwheat biscuits and then two men in blaze orange, carrying their weapons muzzle down. Past him without cease whined and jingled the heavy vehicles, taillights ruby and amber, stream-ing out of town east and west, north and south, aimed at the blank gray-ness of the predawn woods. None of the drivers noticed him, hunched over his books, dragging himself down the street under the first ominous foreglow of day.

Bastards, he thought. A couple of years before he'd picketed one of the gun stores with some of the other kids. When the black-and-white had dropped him off at home his dad had pulled off his cartridge belt, taken him into the back yard, and whipped him savagely, without a word of explanation. He hadn't understood then. Now he did.

They were all interlocked. The store owners, the ones who sold the guns, the ones who ran the town, they were who his father really worked for. He read their ads in the *Century,* in the Season Supplement that came in the Sunday sports section all November. Come to Hemlock County, home of good hunting. Buy in Hemlock County, home of friendly mer-chants. Kill your deer by aiming at the lungs and heart. Butcher your animal like this, but tie off its genitals first. Bank at First Raymondsville, use Thunder Gasoline, buy a Winchester at Ray's, a new snowmobile at Stan Rezk's. After you've bagged your stag dine at the Hudson Grill, at Nero's Villa. The Hemlock County Recreational Association spared no

effort to lure out-of-towners into the county. They were a resource. Like
the trees, the animals, like all this dark land. The exploiters' universe
consisted of what they could convert to money. Nothing else mattered.

He had a sudden image of the valley as the old man had described it;
the great trees, the great cats, the swarming of deer, elk, and bear. Down
it now streamed the glaring, jingling monsters, trampling the hills under-
foot, powered by the dark fluid sucked from beneath them; cabs crammed
with the race that had displaced the Indian, destroyed the forest and all
the beasts without speech, but whose greatest conquest had been the sub-
jugation and extinction of its own soul.

He turned the corner for the final stretch, and staggered as he met
the full force of a wind like an icicle crammed into his teeth. He recovered, bent, and stalked forward, gasping. It was too cold to breathe. He
pulled the cap lower over his deadened ears, and yanked his leaden legs
upward again and again.

The school loomed through the snow-pale dawning like a hostile for-
tress. The kids streamed past him. They chattered, but no word came to
him. He smiled bitterly; sure, he'd been silenced. How he hated these
fools, these shallow pricks, these happy blinded cretins, these willing stupid bourgeois victims.

But *she'd* spoken to him.

Suddenly he remembered that this was the day he was going to talk to
Alex Ryun. Then he thought: Why bother? He was crippled, ugly, poor.
Be real, Romanelli, he sneered at this dreams. Why ask for more humili-
ation?

Replenished with rage, he levered himself forward like a cartridge, and
was lost a moment later in the hurrying hundreds of Raymondsville Central High. He noticed as he struggled that the corridors were lined with
tile exactly like the bathroom walls.

He realized something else before the day was an hour older; that the
memory of man is imperfect, or maybe that in some hearts lies forgiveness. More likely, he thought, they just got bored with it. Still he was
grateful when Fred Bisker looked up in chem and said, "Hey, Phil," before
going back to his lab notes. Another boy complimented him on his newspaper article.

In Marzeau's class he glanced at Alex from the corners of his eyes,
yearning like a Zen monk toward a less tangible Good. She was wearing
a pale blue sweater; her legs were crossed back under her chair. His eyes
fastened themselves to her ankles. She looked wonderful, impossible. Yet
she'd seemed to like him . . . he felt like Cortez at the Pacific. Or was it
Balboa? Anyway, he realized then he was gonna try. Crazy as it sounded.
She'd probably say no. He expected that, actually he'd be relieved.

He just hoped she didn't laugh.

That left the question of timing. He considered this carefully. He'd never asked anyone out before and he wanted to minimize the chances of blowing it. He could ask her between classes, in the hall. No, too public, and they'd both be in a hurry. At last he decided lunchtime would be best. Then too it was comfortably distant, two hours away.

But two hours later, when he picked up the wet tray in the lunch line, he felt as he had in the final minutes before an operation. Scared shitless, the way little kids get scared when they put the mask over your face, smile, and tell you to breathe deep. And you know that when you come up, you'll be screaming.

He loaded his tray with some crap or other and wandered out into the seating area.

The noise was deafening, as usual. He saw them right away, Alex and Sheila and the rest. Their table grew slowly before him, like a rogue meteor just before it smashes into the starship *Enterprise*. His tray wavered, trying to deflect him. He gritted his teeth and swung it back on course. *Warp speed.* Ahead of him one of the girls, Cindy something, saw him. She squeaked and put her fist over her mouth. The way the tables were arranged he couldn't face Alex directly, so he stopped behind her, presenting his right side. His tray was in his right hand, and he had it supported unobtrusively with his left, the one he couldn't lift.

"Hi, Alex."

The girls were deadly silent. After a moment Ryun twisted. She looked surprised. He felt his face flush and had to look away.

"Why, Phil. What a surprise. Are you going to eat with us?"

A sibilance passed around the table, a sigh or whisper without words.

"Well, no, thanks. One of the . . . guys is waitin' for me. I was just wondering, uh, if you'd like to see a movie sometime. Like maybe Friday night."

He'd hoped to keep this private, but they were all listening. He glared at Cindy and she dropped her eyes; two of them turned their heads as if to say something to the others; but none of them spoke. He turned his attention back to Alex. Those lovely green eyes, close up . . .

"Why, Phil, I'd love to." She was drawling out the words, a little louder, he thought, than necessary. She glanced around; the other girls stiffened, their eyes flickered. Then the tension broke, and they all stared openmouthed up at him. He realized he'd missed something. He jerked and said guiltily, "I'm sorry, what'd you say?"

"I said I'd love to. Friday'll be fine."

"Alex!"

"*What*, Sheila?"

"Oh . . . well. Nothing."

The other girls looked dismayed and uncomprehending, though they tried to dissemble it by a sudden interest in their food. "I'll pick you up at seven," he said, preparing to move off.

"Oh, we'll still be at dinner then. Could you make it seven-thirty?"

"Sure. Seven, uh, seven-thirty. Right."

"Thanks, Phil. See you then."

"See you, Alex." He got a new grip on his tray, smiled nastily at the other girls, and headed for the Commercial Ed table. He glanced back once, and saw them all staring at him; all except Alex and the one called Sheila. Ryun was smiling down at her tray, beatific and mysterious as a plaster Virgin. Hazouri was getting up, dark eyes slashed narrow.

He was sitting with the geeks, listening to one explaining the fine points of his after-school job at the Pik 'n' Pak, when he saw a familiar bulk rise from the training tables.

Bubba Detrick moved through the press like a bear through low brush, jaws still chomping. His eyes roved over the bent heads, the busy forks and mouths. Phil dropped his attention to his carrots but Detrick bulled over to him, pushing kids into the edges of their tables. Bubba leaned over and put his elbows beside him.

Phil noticed then that the sound level had dropped. He could actually hear Detrick when he said to the others, not very loud, "Ain't you jerks got the word?"

"Hi, Bubba. What word?"

"Shithead here, nobody sits with him. Pound sand."

The other boys got up at once and took their trays toward the scullery, eating with their fingers on the way. The fattest one tripped over a chair and there was a clatter of metalware and plastic.

The ballplayer pulled out one of the vacated seats. He studied Phil's tray. At last he selected a slice of carrot. He placed it and then several more in a row on Phil's shoulders, like stars on a general, then took a fingerful of mashed potato and smeared it into his ears. "Turn your head," he said, and filled the other too.

Christ, Phil thought, can she see us? No, thank God.

"Can you still hear me?"

"Yeah."

"Good. Look, Crip, you and me we got a kind of a personality conflict going. That means I find your personality a royal pain in the ass. Right?"

Phil nodded.

"Now, we already discussed your steady stream of useless bullshit in class. Brick and me we got our views across last week, I think, 'cause you ain't wisin' off the way you used to. So that's good."

"Thanks."

"Shut your fuckin' lip! But somebody just told me you asked Alex for a date. Is this real, or am I dreaming?" He picked up the mystery meat and put it on Phil's head. Phil took it off.

"Put it back on."

He put it back and sat there, feeling numb. Grease ran down his neck and into his shirt.

"Yeah, I asked her."

"Well, I guess you ain't no homo. But you're stupid as shit, Romo, stupid as a box a' rocks." He shook his head slowly. "You got this attitude that somebody else got something, and you don't got any, they oughta share it with you. Life don't work that way. The way it is, guys like me got it, and guys like you don't. Period. And it ain't ever gonna be any different, so you might as well get used to it.

"Now, you know we're goin' together, me and her. So why you annoyin' her? And how do you expect to breathe after I tear your stupid fucking lungs out, Romanelli?"

He didn't know where he got the guts to say it. Maybe just because she liked him. But he said now, "You're not going steady with her."

"I'm not?"

"No. She's going out with me Friday."

Detrick had had something ready to say, it looked like, but now he didn't. He sat there a moment, then took out a pack of Wrigley's and offered Phil one. Phil shook his head. Detrick was thoughtfully unwrapping his stick when one of the monitors, a senior named Berenger, came over. Detrick scowled up at him. Berenger said, avoiding the ball player's eyes, "Romanelli, take that shit off or you're getting detention."

Phil took it off. "Put it on," grunted Detrick.

Phil put it on. "Last chance," said Berenger.

He didn't move. "Okay," said the senior. "Playing with food in cafeteria, one period of detention." He moved off, looking relieved.

Bubba regarded him moodily, chewing gum and picking his nose. "Romo, you got balls. But it ain't gonna help you. You probably figure I'm gonna trash your face for sniffing around Ryun, right?"

"Yeah."

"Well, I'm not." Detrick belched. "Hell, let the best man win! This is entirely, you know, separate.

"See, Phil, it ain't that you're crippled I got a problem with, or being a certified spaz. It ain't the way you jerk when you're happy, or the weird way you hug yourself. Lots of guys, they overcome handicaps like that. It's that you're stupid. And I told you why.

"Now, that can hurt you in life. So I'm gonna do you a favor, I'm gonna teach you how stupid you really are. You're a meathead. So you'll be wearin' that meat from now on. For the rest of the day, and after that tomorrow, no, tomorrow you can put on fresh. But I see you without a piece of meat on your head, you're fucked. Your little lesson last week'll be nothing compared to what I'll do for you. Got that?"

Phil nodded. His tongue was too thick to answer.

Detrick flicked his ear painfully with a finger. Potato flew, spattering a boy and girl at the next table; they wiped it off silently. He heaved himself up and left. Back at the training tables he and Mooney bent their heads together. Copper glinted as the shotputter's shaven skull turned and they both grinned at Phil across the cafeteria.

He sat alone, unable to decide whether to be happy or terrified. At last the bell rang and he drank his milk quick and turned in his tray.

He wore the meat to the next class, but Maxwell made him throw it in the wastebasket. As he walked back to his desk Mooney shook his head sadly, and Bubba kissed his fingers, patted his rump with them, and waved Phil a regretful good-bye.

Thirteen

Jaysine jerked awake, instantly angry at the hateful buzz. She rolled over, lids glued shut, and thrust out an arm. The crash as the clock's cord took the bedside lamp down with it made her moan.

She opened her eyes, wincing at daylight. For a moment her mind wobbled forward to routine: tea, weigh herself, breakfast, off to work . . . instead she lay back, blotting out morning with her wrist. She had to pee, but she couldn't get up. She had a sick headache, an awful sour dryness in her mouth.

Then she remembered, and struggled up onto an elbow.

Her bedroom was tiny and dark. Through the door she could see the front room, the couch, where beer bottles lay in a litter of magazines and wadded-up potato-chip bags. The shiny paper flickered, an electronic glow. She stared at it for a long time before she realized it was reflecting the television. Her clothes lay piled in the doorway; underclothes too; under the sheet she was naked.

She saw, then, the little pile of money on the coffee table, and everything came back at once, the night before and the day before and the night before that. Her head hammered and she sank back. Her arms crept out to the empty side of the bed. When they found the other pillow they pulled it to her, holding it tight.

When she woke again an hour later she thought immediately of work. She rolled over with a grunt and pulled the phone toward her across the floor by its cord. A nearly empty wine bottle and the crumpled foil of a half-pound Nestlé's Crunch came with it. As she listened to the brrrr she hoped Mrs. Acolino wasn't in yet.

"Style Shoppe, Marguerite speaking."

She spoke slowly, trying not to sound hung over. "Margie, this is Jaysine. Would you please tell Marybelle I can't come in? I'm still sick today."

"Jaysine, honey, I'm sorry to hear that. But you know, Marybelle's awful upset you been out two days already. She wanted Trudi to try doing one of your appointments but she wouldn't, she's afraid of electricity."

"Well, I'm not feeling good," she said, thinking, *It's true, too.*

"Why, what have you got, Jaysine?"

"A cold. A real bad one."

"You don't sound bad."

"Well, I feel awful. Maybe I'll be in tomorrow. Will you tell her?"

"Yes, I'll tell her."

"Thanks a lot. You be good now. Good-bye, Margie."

Next she dialed again the same number she'd tried a dozen times the day before. She didn't have to look anymore. Her finger went 362-3650 without search or hesitation. The line clicked, making the connection between Raymondsville and Petroleum City. When it began to ring, a modern electronic-sounding note, she reached for the wine bottle. The dregs tasted warm and flat, like someone else's saliva.

"Good *morning*, The Thunder Group."

"Hello. This is Jaysine Farmer, calling for Mr. Boulton."

"Oh, Miss *Farmer*. I *don't* think Mr. Boulton will be available today either . . . let me check. Can you hold?"

"Yes."

She held for fifteen minutes, then hung up and called back. The same woman answered. "Good *morning*, The Thunder Group."

"This is Miss Farmer. You put me on hold but nothing happened. Is Brad there?"

"Oh, I am *so* sorry, Miss Farmer. Mr. Boulton won't be in today, I'm sorry."

"Do you know when he'll be back?"

"No, I really don't. But if you'll leave your name and number I'm sure he'll get back to you."

She slammed down the receiver. She got up slowly, holding her face like a fragile, unset opal, and staggered into the bathroom. When she turned on the light she saw she was crying again. Her face was puffy, her eyes hopeless and swollen, hair straggled down in limp rat's-tails. She glanced at the scale by the bathtub, looked quickly away.

She took a deep breath. Her eyes caught a little plaque over the commode: *Today is the tomorrow you worried about yesterday.*

"Shit," she said. It felt so good she said it again.

She forced herself into motion. After emptying her bladder she brushed her hair and washed her face. She bathed her eyes in the icy stream from the faucet, then dripped Visine in them. She took aspirin and vitamins. She felt both hungry and ready to throw up.

She wandered out to the couch and lay down, pulling his overcoat off the rack to pillow her head. He'd forgotten the coat when he left, just stormed out in his suit jacket. She stared out at the overcast sky, at the television antennas on the buildings opposite. At last she decided she might be able to keep down something sweet.

Fortunately there was a quart of pistachio Sealtest in the freezer. The color was nauseating but she covered it with semi-sweet bits and sliced almonds and that helped. Till she was done. As soon as she put the bowl in the sink she felt bloated.

I ought to clean up, she thought, wandering into the front room again, looking emptily at her workbench. I ought to wash all those dishes . . . pick up, vacuum . . . ought to put my finger down my throat and barf up all that beer and wine, chocolate and ice cream.

He wasn't taking her calls. She wasn't surprised. She'd handled this whole thing wrong, she realized that now. God, she felt so small when she remembered the scene she'd made. No, no more crying, Jaysine.

She stopped, looking at the cuff links. They were almost finished. She'd looked forward to surprising him with them . . .

Suddenly she had a plan. She put water on for tea and went back into the bathroom. When she came out, showered and her hair washed and blow-dried, it was whistling. She made dark strong Earl Grey and drank a cup and then put her work apron on and pulled her stool up to the bench.

She finished setting the agates, then turned the links over. She'd already built the swivel frames out of 18-gauge sheet silver. Now she soldered them on carefully and then attached the swivel. She drank another cup of tea while she waited for the metal to cool.

You didn't want to do too much finishing on drop-cast jewelry—form-lessness was its charm—but she buffed it down with Tripoli compound, then switched to low speed and highlighted the front and findings with rouge on a muslin wheel. Then tucked a loupe into her eye.

She smiled to herself. The frosty surface of the silver set off the deep gray sheen of the agate. No one could resist anything this beautiful. It was the best thing she'd ever done. She packed cotton wool into a little box and dropped them in.

All right, now for herself. She went through her wardrobe. Nothing clean, nothing new.

She looked at the money on the table.

She got back from LaMode at ten and showered again and did her hair in a braid. Then she took that apart and did a quick roller set, brushing up from her forehead and then down, into a whirlpool of ringlets. She gave it a spritz of sculpting spray, then froze it with ultrahold. She did her face carefully, torn between holding down the powder and the need to cover; finally she shrugged and covered. On the eyes, dark shadow. She found her alligator heels and rubbed them with a rag.

She slipped into the new dress in front of the mirror, glad she'd allowed an extra size. Her eye clicked critically from crown to toes. She tilted her chin, raised an eyebrow; shook her head violently, and watched her hair settle back on her shoulders.

At last she nodded. She pulled on boots and picked up her coat. Carrying the jewelry box and her heels, she hurried down the stairs. Her car was almost buried; she hadn't driven in days. While she was scraping the windshield she remembered his overcoat.

She smiled. He'd be back.

She rammed the little Toyota back and forth till she had space to turn. It was a used two-door her brother had bought in Florida for her. There was rust now on the hood, and lining hung from the ceiling like flypaper. But it ran, as long as she asked the man to put in oil every other time she got gas. She left the snow tires on all year and now when she put it in Drive it jumped forward just like, she thought, a little snowplow.

She left Main behind, slowed for the overpass, then accelerated to pass a car full of hunters. As the town dropped away she turned on WRVL for music and then news. From time to time she saw more hunters, their pickups turning back onto the highway from side roads. Route Six curved and recurved along the Allegheny. From time to time black rock thrust itself up from the level, snow-covered ice, but aside from that there wasn't much to see. The road writhed between the hills, the ridges constant and reassuring on either side, as if her little car was a white marble rolling peacefully and inevitably along a track.

She saw a dead deer by the side of the road, just lying there.

In Petroleum City she stopped at a Thunder station to ask directions. She'd been to P.C., as people called it in Raymondsville, a few times, but she'd never been to his office.

She was unprepared for its size. The Thunner building dominated the west end of town like the refinery did the east. She found a parking space, refreshed her perfume, and checked her face one last time, feeling nervous but eager. She slipped on the heels and clicked over the steaming pavement toward the door.

The lobby was vast, with mirrors and a huge modern chandelier of hundreds of glass rods. She felt intimidated, till one of the mirrors gave her back herself. She smiled again, and went on.

There was no one at the fifth floor desk when she came out of the elevator. She followed her instincts down a corridor. A dark little fat man was sitting in a side office reading a magazine. She put her head in. "Excuse me. Where's Mr. Boulton?"

"End of the hall, ma'am."

"Thanks." She continued, emboldened by the smell of fresh-brewed coffee.

He was sitting at a table with other men in suits. She looked through the open door, rapped, and when he looked up, smiled sweetly.

The office he showed her to was larger than she'd expected. There was a vase in the corner as big as she was. The rest of the room matched it, all light wood and polished things, spotlessly clean. It impressed her. His face looked different too. "All right," he said, closing the door. "What is it?"

"Aren't you going to ask me to sit down?"

"Sure, sure, make yourself at home. You've already interrupted my re-insurance meeting."

She sat slowly, crossing her legs. She felt cool and self-possessed. The men with him had glanced at her coming out. She'd seen the interest in their eyes.

"It was rude, the way you wouldn't talk to me on the phone."

"I was out yesterday."

"Your secretary said you were out today, too. But I had something for you."

He stood behind the desk, looking stolid and, she thought, rather defensive. "What?" he said.

She brought out the little box, then, when he made no move to take it, opened it and set them out facing him. They gleamed dully in the white light from the window. "I made them," she said. "For you."

But when she lifted her gaze she saw with a shock that she'd erred. His eyes were much darker than the stones she'd picked with such care. Dark as oxidized silver.

He shook his head slowly, glancing out the window; then sat down. Pressed the intercom. "Twyla."

"Yes, Mr. Boulton."

"There's a woman in my office. Without an appointment. How'd she get here?"

"I was away from my station for just a moment, sir. I'm sorry, she must have come in then."

"In the future call the floor guard if you have to leave the elevator area."

"Yes, sir."

He let go the button. "Okay, Jaysine. Make it quick, I've got a lot to do. You didn't come up here to give me the damn cuff links. What do you want?"

She was hurt, he hadn't even touched them, but she put that aside and said, "All right. I came to say I'm sorry."

He picked up a gold pen and started to play with it. He didn't look at her. She had to make him meet her eyes. Then he'd be halfway back. She took a deep breath and made her hands stop fidgeting. "I've been thinking about it, what we argued about. I decided you're right. I know things like this happen. It's not really anybody's fault, is it?

"Anyway, I wasn't very nice. So I'm sorry I shouted at you, and I brought the money back—except for what I spent on this dress." She slid it onto the corner of his desk.

He flicked his eyes to it, then away. But he still hadn't looked at her. She wanted to keep talking. But he had to say something first.

"That it?" he said.

"That's it. Oh, and—I thought I'd make some fettucine Monday night." She managed a smile. "So. Can we make peace?"

"I don't think so."

"Brad, lovers quarrel, that happens. It'll be even better, once we make up."

He got up suddenly, but kept the desk between them. He shoved the cash back toward her, pushing one of the links off the desk. "Let's make this short and sweet. I'm dropping you. Or however you want to put it. Go back to Raymondsville. Do whatever you want, but don't bother me again. Don't call and don't come here again. Understand?"

She looked at the carpet. At the silver gleam down there, almost lost. Unwanted.

"Don't cry, for Christ's sake!" He came around the desk, toward her, but stopped a step away. That close she knew he could smell her perfume. He'd always said it made him lose control . . . but he looked so cold now, so angry, she couldn't believe it was the same man. "Another thing. We had our laughs. Some women would try to use that against me. I expect you to keep quiet about it. If you don't you'll be sorry. That's pretty clear, isn't it?"

"It's perfectly clear," she said through frozen lips. The numbness had come back, but this time it was more fragile, thinner; only a thin sheet of ice between her and the world. Not solid, like before.

"Then why are you still here?"

"Because I don't think you mean it."

"What are you talking about?"

"You aren't treating me like you should. As soon as we get close, you look for a way out, a way that hurts me. Why is that, Brad? Is it because I'm a woman"—she thought suddenly about what he'd told her once—"and your mother, she—"

She could see that hit something. He leaned forward. "Get out of here."

"I'm not going anywhere till you apologize."

He reached back to the desk, pressed something, and a moment later a black man filled the doorway. He looked at Boulton, who said, "Lark, escort this lady out of here. And take her dime-store jewelry with her."

A moment later she was out of the room, her arm held so tight she thought it would break. She was so surprised she couldn't speak till they were in the corridor. Then she shouted, "Brad, wait! I'm not through talking to you!"

She fought him, dragged back, but the black man didn't say anything, didn't hurt her, just held her off as if she was a pet dog with a fit. He marched her out a back way, instead of through the lobby, out into the flat scarred concrete of a loading dock. He thrust the box at her, and the door closed. She whirled, and scratched at it till she broke a nail. But there was no handle or knob from the outside; no way in to him, no way in at all.

Five stories up he sat silently, swiveling back and forth, and watched the bedraggled little figure move slowly up the street. She got into her car, pulled out into traffic, went north, disappeared.

It was over. He felt relieved. A nasty little scene, right in his office too. But he'd done the right thing. She'd gained weight already, God knew how she'd packed herself into that cheap dress. It had just gotten too hard to pretend he was interested in her TV programs and her magazines and the latest news items about the girls at the shop. He'd toyed with the idea of setting her up, introducing her to some other fellows at the club, older guys whose wives no longer satisfied. But that wouldn't be a good idea now.

He looked at the money and thought, I'll wait a couple of days and then send it to her. With a couple hundred more. She'd cool off. It was the best thing for her too.

Still he sat thinking. What she'd said . . . no. It didn't make any sense. Take his first wife. He'd been fair to her, a generous settlement, more than enough for her pills and psychiatrists. More than she deserved, she'd betrayed him and left him. Bitches! They all left sooner or later.

Gradually his anger ebbed and his thoughts moved on. He didn't like the way things were trending in the county. The *Deputy-Republican* understood his position on alarmist reporting, but he hadn't gotten the story wrapped yet in the *Century*. And Raymondsville was the county seat. Over time he'd bring them around, though, through the ad department if not more directly, through Pete Gerroy.

He sat staring at the distant towers, thinking one by one of people who might have a reason to interfere with the disposal deal, and how well set up his firebreaks were. Finally he decided there was no point in getting worried. Not yet.

But it might be wise to let things cool for a while.

He closed his eyes, tapping his fingers, then reached for the phone. He patted his pockets as he waited for the connection, then slid open his desk and went through it, frowning. Where was his book? Then Twyla said "Newark, sir," and he waited for her to click off and said briskly, lifting his head, "Hello, John! Brad here, at Thunder Oil."

The distant voice said, "Hold on a second. Who's that? Boulton? Okay, go ahead."

"Hi. John, look, we need to hold your shipments up for a few days."

"What do you mean?"

"The natives are getting restless." He glanced at the closed door. "Not to worry, but I think it'd be best to take it easy for a while. Let it die down."

"How long you talking?"

"A few weeks should be enough. There's a lot of hunters out in the woods now, roads are traveled a lot more."

The voice dropped. "You trying to back out, Brad?"

"No. I'm acting in good faith. You'd let me know if there was a problem at your end. I'm doing the same. Our arrangement's good for both of us. I'm trying to keep it going."

After a pause the voice said, "I don't think so."

"John—"

"Listen. We're paying you the money, we expect the service. Every business works like that, don't it? Don't yours?"

"Sure."

"Let's see, you're scheduled for a payment on account pretty soon. Do you want to hold that up too?"

Boulton felt himself start to sweat. "Well," he said. "Well, no."

"If it's serious, now, I guess maybe we could reroute," the deliberate voice went on. "Or slow down for a while. But I got no place to put this stuff. I can't keep it here. Tell you what, I'll look at it and get back to you."

"Thanks."

"But till then things go as scheduled. I appreciate the call, but it's got to be something major for us to stop shipping. Local shit you take care of. That was how I understood it."

"Yeah, sure, I understand. See what you can do."

The voice changed. "No. *You* see what *you* can do, Mr. B. Control the situation. That's what we're paying for. Transport we can get anywhere. If you can't cope, let me know. Don't use the phone, no fax, send the details overnight mail. I'll send a guy out, he'll figure what to do on the spot. Understand?"

"That's good advice. I'll think about it."

"Yeah, you do that. So long."

He was sitting with the receiver in his hand, muttering, "Shit, shit, shit," when the intercom said, "Mr. Boulton, your wife and daughter are here."

"I'll be right out." He jumped up, brushing at the shoulders of his suit, and was out of the office in three strides.

"Willie!"

"Daddy!"

At the elevator a dark-haired woman hung back, smiling coolly within gilded steel as the little girl hurled herself forward like a blond comet toward the sun. She hit his arms and he swung her up, up, both of them laughing, and then dropped her and her doll tumbling and shrieking through space before he caught her again and snuggled her up. He felt his heart move, felt it physically contract within his chest with sheer love like he'd never felt for another human being. Her hair, fine as angora, tickled his nose. He burrowed into it. Nothing else smelled as good . . . "You'll never go away, will you?" he whispered into her ear.

"You're silly! Go where, Daddy?"

"No place. Just kidding." He cleared a sudden thickness from his throat and, still holding her, turned back to the elevator. "Hi, darling. Everything okay out at the Hill?"

In the middle of the reception area Mrs. Ainslee Thunner Boulton had stepped out of her coat. She glanced in the mirror, touching her hair and straightening her sleeves as the secretary hung the fur. Then crossed her arms as she watched father and daughter, that same cool distant curve bending her lips once again.

"Better," she said.

"Dan doing all right today?"

"Dad's—as usual."

"Anybody call yet about the nanny?"

"I was going to ask *you* that, Brad. I can't believe it's taking them this long. Perhaps you ought to think about calling another agency. The cook's had her since breakfast. So I brought her in. You can take her for the rest of the day."

"Sure, sure, no problem." He hugged the child again; she squeaked. He pulled back, his mouth an O of surprise. "What does *that* mean?"

"It's mouse talk."

"Is that right! And what mouses have you been—"

His wife said, "I hate to interrupt such a charming scene, but are you ready to talk?"

"To talk? About what?"

"About our plans for Thunder Oil, Brad. Or have you forgotten about those too?"

He flushed, but his voice was still hearty as he said, "No, they're going real well. We'll talk about them, sure. Maybe you can give me some ideas on a couple sticky points. Just let me get somebody to look after Pooh

Bear—*how* you been? And how's Annie?" He ruffled the fringe on the doll's lolling head, but he couldn't take his eyes from his daughter's. They were bluer than anything in the world.

"Oh, okay."

"You say hi to Twyla? You remember Twyla."

"Uh huh. What's the matter, Daddy? You sound funny!"

"Well, so do you, so do you, punkin!—Twyla, take charge of this bundle of beauty, will you?"

"Anytime, Mr. Boulton." His secretary came forward smiling and Brad offloaded the child into her arms.

The turn of the corridor cut off sight of the tall man, the dark-haired woman, from the little girl's suddenly thoughtful eyes. She sat on the big sofa beside Twyla's desk, holding a grown-up magazine and looking at ladies in pretty clothes. Twyla was pretty. She looked like one of the ladies in the magazine.

On impulse she said, "Twyla, do you like my daddy?"

"I like him fine, Williamina. Why do you ask?"

"Ainslee doesn't. They fight."

"I'm sure you're wrong, Willie. Grown-ups fight sometimes, but it doesn't mean anything bad."

Willie Boulton put her fingers on one of the ladies in the magazine. She had dark hair, like Ainslee. She hoped Twyla was right. She pushed her finger, and it went right through the lady's middle. She shrank on the big sofa, suddenly frightened. *Destructive*, she thought. That was the word Ainslee used. *Destructive. Hyperactive. Going to send you away.*

But no one said anything, and she turned the page, hiding the ugly tear. A moment later she was prattling to herself, not even hearing, over the sudden rattle of the typewriter, the raised and angry voices from the inner office.

Fourteen

Halvorsen patted the bear's muzzle, peering past it into the gloom. Five days into the season the Brown Bear was packed. The coatracks were buried under hunting caps and jackets. The air smelled of wet wool, gas heat, frying meat, and whiskey. A throbbing roar of voices warmed his cold-numbed ears.

The door hissed shut and he sidled in, tugging his cap over the bandage on the left side of his face. He was halfway to the back when a jolly voice called, "Well, look who's here!" It was Roberta, puffing under a tray of fries, burgers, and the shots of White Seal that with a bottle of Straub's made a boilermaker.

"Mornin', Berta. Business good?"

"You kidding? Look at this crowd. You're spending a lot of time in town these days, ain't you?"

He grunted; she laughed and went on. He recollected the plug in his cheek—first thing he'd done was stop at Capriccio's for a pack of Top—and got rid of it in the men's room. At last he gained the alcove and sank gratefully into the pew. He was the only one there. Probably still too early, he thought. But it was sure nice to be out.

The nurses had cleaned his clothes and hung them in his room, but they'd locked his wallet and watch up somewhere. When he'd discharged himself of course he couldn't ask for them, so all he had was what change had been in his pockets.

As it was he'd had to sneak out, watching the corridor till it was empty, then shuffling quickly round the corner to the fire door. The steel steps

were slick, unshoveled and unsalted, and he'd nearly fallen, saving himself
with his burned hand. But at last he'd reached the ground, panting into
the cold air, and immediately swung into a stride that said, *Mind your own
business; I'm minding mine.* Only when the hospital was out of sight did he
slow, tilt back his cap, and aim himself downhill toward Main Street.

Nursing home, like hell, he thought. W. T. Halvorsen wasn't going to
no old folks' home to die. He thought of the wolves they'd had over to
Kane, years ago. Wild wolves penned up like pigs, yellow eyes burning
crazy through the wire mesh. No thanks, he'd draw his last dollar out in
the woods, just like he'd lived.

After buying the chew he had fifty-six cents in his pants.

"What'll it be, Racks?"

He didn't open his eyes. "How much is coffee?"

"Short today? Guess we can spare a cup. Got to make new anyway.
Cream an' sugar, right?"

"Well . . . okay. Yeah, thanks."

She brought it in a stoneware mug. He sipped at it cautiously, then
tipped more sugar over it. The little flap lifted and a white stream poured
out. He didn't like the way it wavered. Whatever he'd met up with, it'd
taken something out of him. He felt every year of his age and then some.
He felt bad, weak, chilly even though he knew it was hot in the tavern. I
should of waited till after breakfast to leave, he thought. Least I'd of had
a full belly then.

The question was, how had he gotten sick?

Sitting there, pondering, his mind cast back over sixty years in the
county. He knew every foot of it from trapping, hunting, oil-drilling,
gas work.

He concluded at last that there was one man he ought to talk to.

"Hey, W. T.," Fatso DeSantis grunted as he let himself down.

"Hello, Len."

DeSantis stank of whiskey, even—Halvorsen glanced toward the bar,
missing his watch—at eight in the morning. His eyes blinked deep in an
unshaven face. Dirt showed at his collar and his belly bulged between his
suspenders. Lucky showed his face over the machine; DeSantis grunted,
"Beer," and licked his lips. He took an envelope out of his shirt. Unfolded
it slowly, examined what was inside, then put it back and rebuttoned the
pocket.

"How you holdin' up, Billy Boy?"

"Okay, Fatso."

"Been doin' any hiking?"

"I try to stay out of the woods this time of year. Too many crazy flat-
landers out there shootin' at anything that moves."

DeSantis jiggled his jowls quietly, then frowned. "Say, didn't somebody
said you was in the hospital?"

"Few days, yeah."

"Guess you must be all right now."

"Well, I ain't ready for no knockdown dragouts. Starting to feel my age, I guess."

"About time," said DeSantis. "Want a beer? No, I forgot. Well. Anythin' else new?"

"No, how about with you?"

"Not much."

They sat there for a while. DeSantis drank a Black Label and then another. At last Halvorsen said, "Say, you still driving that Willys of yours?"

"Sure. An' I still got the spotlight on it, too. Remember when your grandson told me to get rid of it. He used to get on my nerves. But don't get me wrong, I'm sorry he's gone."

"Uh huh," said Halvorsen. "Well, look, think you could give me a lift?"

"I don't know, s' gettin' pretty deep. Might not be able to get you all the way up Mortlock. Guess I could try, though."

"I ain't going straight home. Goin' out to Cherry Hill first."

The filmy eyes blinked. "What for?"

"Got to see me a man. See old Dan."

"Dan Thunner?"

"Yeah."

"Old Dan," mused DeSantis. "I remember once he come in to the Bootery, wanted me to fit him to a pair of half Wellingtons . . . That was, Jesus, that was before the war and he was old then. Size ten. He ain't still alive, is he?"

"I don't know what shape he's in, but I ain't heard nothing about him dying."

"He's old as Charley if he is. Well, hell, even if he's still kicking he ain't gonna see you."

"Just drive me out there," said Halvorsen.

"Say please."

"I'll buy you a beer."

"The way to my heart." DeSantis belched. "I guess so, okay. Can't say I got nothing else much pressing to do today."

"Loan me a five," said Halvorsen.

"What?"

"I'm busted. You want me to buy you a beer, loan me a five."

"You always was the generous sort," said DeSantis.

The yellowed side curtains of the old quarter-ton flapped and roared as DeSantis shifted again and again, flogging it toward a desperate thirty-five miles an hour. Halvorsen, sitting stiffly in the passenger seat, looked into the back. Empty bottles, rusty tools, empty Quaker State cans shifted sides at each curve. He couldn't watch when DeSantis drove. Fatso liked the crown of the road, moving maybe a foot for oncoming trucks. Cars came up rapidly behind them, swerved suddenly when they realized how slow he was going, then skidded around them on the left or right, sending snow drumming on the torn fabric top.

"Can't you go no faster, Len?"

"We'll get there. Way these young puppies is ramroddin' it, only place they're goin' to beat us is to hell."

He gave up and looked out through cracked plastic at an aged world. Young puppies . . . he'd have to remember to get Jezebel back from the boy . . . had to get dog food too somehow. Gerroy Hill rose to its triple peak on the right of the moving truck, and to their left he looked down on the frozen river. Back in that direction, way back of Candler Hill, he remembered one winter they'd drilled twenty holes, all dry, twenty wells in two frozen months, all because of some foulup the attorneys had made; mineral rights reverted to the landowners in February if it wasn't developed; Thunder had to pump crude or lose the lease. So he and Steve Popovich and the other guys on the rig had busted their tails working round the clock.

Halvorsen remembered that winter in his hands. Fisher Fifty was out on the clearout rump of an unnamed hill and the wind came straight down the valley like, Popovich said once, the whole Boche Army with fixed bayonets. There was no road so they'd bulldozed one up Hog Hollow. The grade was too steep to haul rotary equipment, so they'd told Halvorsen to break out one of the old cable-tools.

A cable-tool didn't rotate; it pounded its way down into the ground like a giant chisel. For each well they had to bolt together seventy feet of derrick. The stem assembly was hoisted with cable by a bull-wheel driven off a twenty-horse steam engine. It swung in the wind high above the crew; sometimes when it snowed it was invisible. The bit worked like a whip, the walking-beam nodding up and down, the spring in the line cracking it against the bottom. At first you could hear it under your feet, smashing its way through shale and sand and limestone, but gradually the impact grew fainter, till at last the bit plunged downward into bottomless silence.

It was a hard way to make a hole even in good weather but in winter it was hell. The shaft was full of water, and when the bailer came up it spewed it all over the rig and the men and it froze; they slipped and slid over the muddy ice, and the sludge froze and their faces froze and their fingers froze to the temper screws and gudgeons, the clutch levers and pipe tongs. The off-shift men slept in a trailer heated only by their bodies; the cook quit, taking the cookbook, and they had to live off corned beef sandwiches, cold; the only place you could get warm was if you stood right beside the boiler, but you didn't get much work done that way.

Rothenberg, their geologist, had been number two on the Music

Mountain strike. Halvorsen always figured finding three and a half miles of oil had gone to his head. On Fisher Fifty, he predicted a trap along the corner of the hill at about a thousand feet. They'd drilled the first four holes on this assumption, but there hadn't been one showing. Under good conditions a cable-tool could make ninety feet a day, but six hundred feet beneath the frozen blackberry snarls they hit a conglomerate that dulled and jammed the bits and slowed them to three and sometimes only two feet a shift.

Halvorsen had looked at that, and concluded they weren't going to make deadline. So the next time Rothenberg came up he'd suggested they start another rig at the top of the hill. If there was oil down there they'd get to it quicker. They could bust through the conglomerate with a jack-squib and nitro.

Rothenberg had laughed. Said there was crude there all right, sure as there was gold in Fort Knox, and they wouldn't need to blast if Halvorsen, the foreman, would get his lazy bastards to put their backs to it.

He'd asked the geologist quietly if he wanted to take back what he'd said about his crew.

Now, clinging to the dash with one hand, he worked his fingers as a grin etched his lips.

A high, square silhouette loomed ahead, a slush-caked tractor-trailer. He stiffened, waiting for DeSantis to give way. But he didn't, not an inch, and at the last instant the wide-eyed teamster wrenched his wheel right. The cab turned but the trailer didn't, and a steel wall slid sideways toward them.

"Christ, Len!"

The Willys missed the taillights of the trailer by a foot. They skidded off the cleared road along the berm, slamming and slowing as the flat nose threw snow. The windshield went white. Then it cleared suddenly, showing them a miraculously empty road ahead. DeSantis giggled. Halvorsen, looking back, saw the trailer switching like a cat's tail. At last the driver got it straightened out and back on the road.

"You almost killed us!"

"Teach him to crowd a man."

"You go off the right-of-way here, Fatso, we're done for. There's slime pits along here ten foot deep."

DeSantis shrugged. Halvorsen stared at him a moment, then faced front. He was sweating, even in the icy wind.

A few miles past Petroleum City he pointed DeSantis onto a cleared but unmarked road that struck off up a hollow. The quarter-ton downshifted. A mile on it left behind a snow-drifted field, abandoned farm buildings. Then the woods closed in. He made out white oak; beech; farther up on the hill, the blue prickle of spruce. Snow lay still on them and on the slopes, and the only mar on the white silence was their own motor growling back from the hillside. The road narrowed, curved left and then right. Above them Cherry Knob was a bulbous mass of rock and earth, a massive nipple on the hill's breast.

"Wow," said DeSantis.

"Watch the *road*, Len."

"Man, look out there. You can see all the way to the lake."

Below, as they whined along the contour line, a stream lay rigid among rocks and fallen boles and the pale polished trunks of birches. Brows of hemlock and spruce suspended white masses above rock-choked ravines. Ideal snake country, and he'd put money on trout in those pools. Beyond that, as Halvorsen lifted his eyes, the valley sloped down till the gray bare treetops turned blue. No town, no curl of smoke nor sign of man interrupted that rolling sea till far off, maybe twenty miles distant, a white patch marked where Hantzen Lake had backed up behind the dam.

Every hundred feet, on either side of the road, the woods were posted.

"I never been out here."

"Slow down," said Halvorsen. "I think this is it comin' up."

DeSantis put the truck in neutral and coasted the last few yards uphill to the gate. Black-painted iron, twice the height of a man, it extended across the road from two piers of mortared fieldstone. On either side barbed wire stretched away into the woods. Its only marking was a bronze plaque that said PRIVATE DRIVE.

"Man," said DeSantis after a moment. "You know, I was in Germany in forty-five. Quartermasters. That's the only time I ever seen anything like this. One of the Krupp estates down in Bavaria. What do they call this again?"

"Cherry Hill."

"So what now? You gonna climb it?" DeSantis snickered. He groped grunting under his seat and at last came up with a bottle. He unscrewed the cap and sat back as Halvorsen got out.

He found a little grille and a button underneath it. When he pressed it a voice said, "Yes?"

"Dan Thunner, please."

"Mr. Thunner's not receiving."

"Tell him W. T. Halvorsen's here to see him."

"W. T.—"

"Halvorsen. I'll wait."

The grille went silent. He went back to the jeep and leaned against the mudguard. DeSantis had turned on a gas-fired heater. The fat man cut his eyes at him but said nothing. At last a buzz came from the grille, and the gate clicked. He strolled over and leaned against the bars. When they swung wide so did DeSantis's eyes. He almost flooded the motor getting it started.

They drove slowly up a circuitous road toward the top of the hill. The trees got bigger and farther apart as they climbed. At last they saw lit windows, then the house. Four or five buildings set close together. De-Santis pulled over at a carriage entrance. He set the brake, then aimed the bottom of the vodka bottle at the overcast sky.

"Want to go in, get warm?" said Halvorsen.

"No way. Say, Bill, you don't really want to go in there."

"Why not?"

"Ain't our kind of place. Nor our kinda people. Why do I get the feeling you're mixin' in things ain't your business?"

"Maybe you're right," he said. "Guess I'll find out, though."

"Well, I'll jus' wait out here."

Halvorsen slowly climbed the steps. When he got to the door someone opened it from inside. He looked up.

And up. The man was about seven feet high and as wide as the hallway behind him. His neck was thick as a well casing. His teeth looked like they could drill rock. He was black as asphalt-base crude.

"Mr. Halvorsen?"

"Hullo there. Where you folks keeping Dan?"

"I'll take you to him. Just follow me."

"Ought to take these boots off, get this nice floor wet—"

"Don't worry about that."

He followed the man down a long hallway. The floor was little pieces of wood fit together in a pattern, so shiny he could see his face. I don't look real good, he thought. Should of shaved. He stared at a mounted cat's head, slipping his cap off.

"Through here."

Beyond was a sun room, all glass, and Halvorsen skirted the tiled edge of a pool. A row of lamps, some bright, some deep red, glowed down from the transparent ceiling; the sky looked dim beyond their incandescent glare. Potted palms in terra-cotta tubs circled the shallow end. He unbuttoned his coat as he walked and at last had to take it off. On the far side of the palms, in a ten-foot-wide spot of light and heat where the lamps focused, an old man sat in a wheelchair by the pool.

"You can sit down here," the black man said, moving a lawn chair a little closer. "I'll take your coat."

Halvorsen eased himself down. Piano music was playing somewhere. He blinked in the glare and looked at the man in the chair.

"Red?"

It took him a moment to recognize Dan Thunner. The bones of his jaw had grown out but his face had fallen in, cheeks and eyes sunken as if everything vital had been pumped out from under them. His shoulders were hunched forward and his legs were just wrinkles under the plaid comforter.

"Hullo, Dan."

"You're the last person I expected to see today."

"Been a while, ain't it?" Halvorsen blotted his face. A finger inched out along the arm of the chair; touched a button; several of the lights died. "Thanks. That's pretty hot when you come in from outside."

"So," said Thunner, and his head came forward an inch or two. "How do I look? Pretty good for ninety-two, eh?"

"You look bad, Dan."

"Ain't that the truth . . . Let's see, when was the last time we were together? That hunt up in Katahdin. Remember the moose I got?"

"Sure was a beauty." Halvorsen smiled slowly. "Them things take gettin' used to just for size. Eight foot at the shoulder. How big were the racks, again?"

"Sixty inches."

"Holy smoke."

"Yeah, that made Boone & Crockett easy. Say, you never saw my heads, did you?"

"That's all right."

"You never would go out to Africa with me."

"Too rich for my blood."

"You could've afforded it. See that leopard in the hallway? Got her in Kenya." Thunner raised his jaw slightly. "I see you met Jones . . . Lark, get Red somethin' to drink."

Halvorsen turned his head; the black man had stayed, standing just behind his chair. "No, nothing for me, thanks," he told him.

"Not drinking? You were antifreezed up good in Katahdin, I remember."

"I quit." Halvorsen remembered the Top in his pocket. "I'll have a chew, though, if you don't mind."

"Be my guest . . . I'll have a short one. The single malt." Jones left them.

"So." Thunner studied him. "You been doin' any hunting?"

Halvorsen put the plug back in his pants. Around the fresh stiff tobacco he said, "I quit that too."

"Quit *hunting?* You'd be the last one I'd guess that of. What happened? Heart?"

"It ain't that. I just got tired of it."

"Haven't turned into one of those anti-hunters, have you, Red?"

"Don't know any so I can't say. I just don't do it no more."

The man came back, and held a brandy glass to Thunner's nose. The old man's nostrils hovered over it for several breaths; then his eyes sank closed, and he nodded. Jones carried the glass to the pool. The ripples chased each other across the blue water, glittering in the hot light.

"It's hell being old," mumbled Thunner, "as you'll find out . . . Can't believe it, Red Halvorsen off the sauce, off hunting. You quit fighting too?"

"I try not to anymore," said Halvorsen. "Unless somebody don't leave me the choice."

"I remember the time you knocked that rock-guesser down . . . What was his . . ."

"Rothenberg."

"Yeah, that stuffed-shirt Jew. I felt like knockin' him down myself when I saw how he was spotting those holes. You were right, we should of started from the top and blasted through that shale."

Halvorsen emptied his cheek into one of the potted plants. "Then why'd you fire me?"

"Hell, I couldn't let my foreman go around knocking down the salaried. Especially you, with your Bolshie reputation. And you got to admit, I hired you back next day." Thunner chuckled. "What was that? Second time?"

"Third."

"I remember once in '36—and then—"

"Washington field."

"You deserved it that time. Goddamnit! Still makes me mad. What made you go down in that well?"

"Only way to get the tool out."

"But hell, Red, to go down on the line—eight hundred feet—"

Halvorsen didn't like to think about it. He'd been a young fool, and realized it halfway down: jammed so tight in the eighteen-inch pipe he could barely expand his lungs to breathe; the dead dark, the clammy smell of mud and oil. He'd had nightmares about it for years. But he'd got the bit free, saved two weeks of work. "You were right."

"Course I was. We had our differences. But we always fought fair. Didn't we?"

They looked at each other. At last Halvorsen shifted a little in the chair and said, "I think *you* always did, Dan. Some of your boys, though, they must of thought different."

"Well, we had a good time." Thunner turned his head slightly; Jones came around behind and pivoted the chair. Halvorsen realized he could only move head and fingers. The old man stared out at the quadrangle, the smooth plane of snow, and beyond it the rise of hemlock-dotted hill. "I miss it. I miss the drillin', the gamble there was something down there nobody'd found before. Business was fun then. Now it ain't. No oil left, hardly, got to squeeze it out. It's lawyer crap, sales meetings, tryin' to shave a hundredth of a penny a barrel off your refinin' costs." He sighed. "I'm glad I'm out of it, Red."

Halvorsen said, "I remember all that. And them picnics the company used to have. You used to welcome us, make a speech, then we'd have games for the kids, softball, all the beer you could drink . . . Why'd they stop havin' those, Dan? All the guys, they loved those picnics."

"Ah, my son-in-law said it cost too much. Said it was old-fashioned."

The two old men sat silent for a while. Beyond the glass a few flakes zigzagged down. The fingers crept out and the lamps blazed on again. "Well, anyway . . . say, what's that bandage for, Red?"

Halvorsen straightened from spitting. "That's what brung me up here, Dan."

"Got something to get off your chest? Shoot."

Halvorsen told him about his collapse and hospitalization. He told him what the doctor had said. Midway through the explanation Thunner began shaking his head. When Halvorsen was done he said, "I don't know nothing about that. Why'd you think I would?"

"They make a lot of strange stuff out of oil these days. Not saying the company's responsible, but it's a place to start."

"What'd you say it was called?"

"They ain't sure. PCB was one of them."

"We don't make it, I'm pretty sure. Just gas and oil and feed-stocks, your basic fractions, fluid catalytic products, and some polymerization. But, see, I ain't really in charge of T.O. anymore, Red. I passed it on to the board about ten years back, then my daughter got married, and now she and my son-in-law, they run it."

"Who's he? Maybe he's the fella I ought to ask."

"His name's Boulton, Brad Boulton. Comes from Scranton, his family was in coal there. He's a hardnose. Done a lot for the company. Not all of it I like, but like I say I'm out of the business now. I doubt he's here, he spends most of this time in the office, or at the house in town." Thunner paused. "But he might be back tonight. And like I say, my daughter, she's pretty well up on things. You might want to talk to her. Lark?"

"Yes, Mr. Thunner?"

"Is Ainslee here?"

"Yes, sir, unless she's left in the last hour. She and Miss Williamina are over in the West Wing."

"You won't join me in a little snifter?" Thunner asked him.

"No, thanks."

"Another single malt, Lark. Then I think I'm 'bout ready for my nap."

"Yes, sir."

As Jones wheeled Thunner away from the pool Halvorsen went to the window. He pressed his forehead to the glass and looked out at the hills.

Jones came back. "Did you want to see Mrs. Boulton?"

"If she's here."

"This way."

They went back down the corridor, through several rooms, then through a glassed-in walkway to another building. Halvorsen, looking out, saw a white plume drifting from the Willys's tailpipe. He hoped DeSantis wasn't hitting the vodka too hard. Headlights flickered between the tree trunks, coming up the drive.

"Mrs. Boulton? A Mr. Halvorsen to see you," said Jones, and stood aside.

A fire snapped in a fieldstone hearth. In the corner a twelve-foot Norwegian pine glittered with gold tinsel. The paneling was burled walnut, nice enough, Halvorsen thought, for gunstocks. Along the walls were glass things, vases, cups, glowing and glittering under little ceiling lights like jewels. He didn't know a thing about glass but it looked like an expensive setup. The woman on the sofa was expensive-looking too. No more than forty, but as hard-looking a one as he'd seen in his life. He could see Dan in her, sure enough.

He realized too late he should have gotten rid of his chew.

"So who are you, and why were you annoying my father?"

"No, ma'am, he seemed to enjoy seein' me again. I'm W. T. Halvorsen. We hunted together, and I worked for him back on the—"

"Jones tells me you have a question. What is it?"

"Yeah. It's about some chemicals I got sick from. Seems like there's a lot of it going around."

"See our public relations staff." She got up. "Thank you for coming by. Jones will show you out."

Halvorsen stood his ground, trying to work the chaw around so he didn't need to spit so bad. "Well, I thought maybe you could help me figure out where this stuff's coming from, Mrs. Boulton. I come up to see Dan because I put in all these years with Thunder Oil, I figure I got a right to ask—"

"Maybe you don't understand where you are, Mr. Halvorsen. This is our home. Not our office. I don't know why my father let you in here. Since his stroke his behavior is erratic. But whatever impression he gave you, we don't keep open house at Cherry Hill for our pensioners. Do you understand me?"

Halvorsen's pale blue eyes studied her. "I guess I do now."

"Show him out, Jones."

He turned for the door, and stopped. A dark-haired man stood unzipping a leather car coat. He raised his eyebrows at Halvorsen, glanced at the woman. "Hi, darlin'," he said. "Who's this?"

"I'm W. T. Halvorsen. You must be Mr. Boulton. Dan told me about you."

Boulton looked him up and down, not offering to shake hands. Halvorsen was abruptly conscious of his grizzled whiskers, his suspenders over worn green cotton shirt; most of all of that he was shaking like a kitten, not from nervousness or anything like that, but because he was still so weak.

"Don't bother, he was just leaving," he heard the woman say behind him.

"What was he here for?"

"Something about some chemicals, he got sick."

The man looked at him, Halvorsen thought, a little strangely. "Tell me about it."

He said awkwardly around the tobacco, "Well, what your wife said just now, that's about it. I got put down for a week." He held out his wrist, showing the hospital bracelet. "Doc said it was a reaction to a chemical of some kind."

"What kind? How'd you get it?"

"They don't know. Whatever it is it's gettin' around the county, other people than me's gettin' sick from it."

"What'd you say your name was?"

"W. T. Halvorsen. Thirty years with Thunder Oil."

Boulton seemed to relax. "I see. Well, Mr. Halvorsen, if you have any complaints just have your lawyer get in touch with us. Lark, see him out."

"Yes, sir, Mr. Boulton."

Halvorsen felt the colored man's hand heavy on his shoulder. It helped him pivot around and he nearly slipped on the polished floor. Jones walked behind him on the way back. When they got to the entrance he held out his coat. "Sorry if I was rough, old-timer. But let me give you a piece of advice. Whatever your problem is, don't come back here with it. These people don't like to be bothered."

"I noticed," said Halvorsen.

He paused on the steps and unloaded his cheek into the bushes. The Willys shuddered as it idled. DeSantis's alcohol-glazed eyes peered out at him through the curtains like the puppy's when she played hide-and-seek. Then he fumbled them apart, thrusting his reddened face out. "How'd she go?" he mumbled.

"Not so good."

"Talk to Thunner?"

"Little bit. And his daughter. Jesus."

"What you gonna do?"

"I don't know," said Halvorsen slowly, looking up at the house. "I just don't know."

He spat one last time, as much for luck as anything, and climbed in.

Fifteen

F or the two days since he'd made the date with Alex, Phil hadn't been able to think of anything else. Or only one thing. He still had a couple of brain cells left over to dread his next meeting with Bubba Detrick.

He wasn't proud of how he'd avoided him so far. After Maxwell had made him take the meat off his head the ball player had come up behind him in the hall. "Out back, Romo, same time, same station." But instead of going to the field after the last bell he'd gone out the front, as fast as he could limp, and cut this way and that through side streets till he felt sure Detrick couldn't find him, even driving his truck. So that had been one evening safe. The next day he'd cut the last class and left early. Today—Friday—he hadn't gone to school at all, just faked a sore throat till his mother called the office.

No, he wasn't proud, but as far as he could see getting beaten up tomorrow was better than getting beaten up today. There was always the chance Detrick would choke to death on a fishbone, or be born again and stop beating on people. Or something.

He spent the day in bed studying and came down around four. His mother was humming as she ironed. He looked at her face closely; she looked happy.

"What's wrong, Ma?"

"I'll let your dad tell you about it. Are you feeling better?"

"Yeah, lots."

"You'd better gargle again."

He sniffled a little, for effect. "It really feels better. The salt water helped. When's supper?"

"Soon as your father gets home."

"Gets home? Where is he?" Joe usually worked from six P.M. to three in the morning, then slept till dinnertime.

"I'll let him tell you."

He thought about that for a minute. Then dismissed it as another family mystery. "I got a date tonight. Going to the movies. I got any clean shirts?"

"Look in your drawer," said his mother, humming to herself.

When his dad came home they sat down to supper. Phil kept checking his Timex. "Is it still going?" said his father at last, holding his cigarette away from his plate as he helped himself to scalloped potatoes.

"What?"

"Your watch."

"Oh. Yeah. I got a date tonight."

"A date?" said his mother. "What kind of date? Where are you going?"

"I told you about it, Ma."

"Well, I didn't hear you. And you're not going to enjoy your evening very much if you eat so fast. You're going to get a cramp."

"Ah, I could eat anything when I was his age," said Joe.

"I'm not that hungry," said Phil.

"I didn't say to eat more, I said not to eat so fast."

"Okay, okay!"

"Raise your voice to your mother again, you won't be going anywhere."

"Sorry." He finished his pie and jumped up. " 'Scuse me. Got to get ready."

Behind him he heard his father say, "Get ready? What's he got to do? Kids don't dress up for dates anymore. Is it mental preparation, or what?"

"I don't like him going out with the girls from that public school. He's only seventeen."

"I had a talk with him. He knows what to do."

"That's not funny, Joseph. He's not that kind of a boy. But I don't trust those girls."

In the bathroom Phil examined his chin. Was that the beginning of a beard? He decided it was. His father's razor was on the sink. He lathered his face and began scraping.

Even getting ready for a date with a girl like Alex Ryun was scary. He still couldn't quite figure why she was going out with him. Then he thought, Who cares *why*? Even a one-timer would help his social stock at school. Which so far was zip.

He nicked himself on the upper lip, then on the neck. Not good. He tore out little squares of toilet paper and stuck them over the blood, like his dad did when his hand shook after a hard night at the bar.

Upstairs, crouching in the too-low space, he pulled off jeans and sweatshirt and threw them on the typewriter. He looked through his closet, shivering as the air goosebumped his arms. What would she like? He tried on several combinations before deciding on brown slacks, a pale yellow shirt, and a red patterned sweater. The bulky sleeves would hide his arm. He evaluated the result in the dresser mirror, then took everything off and changed his undershirt and put it back on again.

When he was satisfied he checked his watch again. Two after six. Closing his door and moving to the bed, he reached up and felt around guiltily. He doubted he'd need them, but it was best to be prepared. He tucked the foil pack into his wallet.

He checked his watch again, thinking he'd have to call the cab pretty soon, but it was still only three minutes after six.

"Phil!" From below.

"Yeah, Dad."

"Come down here."

"I'm busy."

"Get down here! I want to talk to you."

He went down unwillingly. His mother had cleared the table. His father was sitting in his T-shirt, a just-opened Bud smoking in front of him. "Yeah?" Phil said.

"Sit down. Here's to your first date. You're pretty young for it, though."

"I thought it was kind of late."

"Maybe . . . guess I just didn't think you were interested in that kind of stuff. When you picking her up? What's her name, anyway?"

"Look, I got to get moving—"

"What's her *name*," said his father.

"Alex Ryun."

"Alex?"

"Short for Alexandrine. She's beautiful."

"You're sure she's a girl," said his father, in the voice he used when he was trying to make a joke.

He didn't answer and after a moment Joe went on, "Well, say, how are you going to get her there? Gonna walk?"

"She has a car, but I figured I'd pick her up in a taxi."

"That's not too cool."

Phil shrugged. His father sucked down half the bottle and gazed at the bubbles. "Cancel it," he said. "Take the black and white. Here's the keys."

"C'mon, Dad, that's city property. I don't want to get you in trouble."

"I been in it before." His father narrowed his eyes at the window. "But things are turnin' around a little. Nolan's puttin' me in for day shift, and I might get my stripe back. So don't argue. Just be careful, for Christ's sake. Just to the movie and her house and back."

"Well . . . okay." He weighed the keys in his hand. "That's great news, Dad. And thanks."

"Don't mention it. Say, see if there's another pack in my shirt, by the TV, would you?"

Outside it was crisp and clear. It had stopped snowing and the wind was light. The patrol car was parked down on State. He started it and let it warm up, checking the controls to make sure he knew where everything was. He'd barely passed driver's ed; they wanted two hands on the wheel.

He thought about where he was going then, and though he was nervous about driving he hugged himself with anticipation. Then sobered. Better not do that around her. She'd think he was a geeko for sure.

At seven-twenty he was parked across town, listening to the ticking of the block as it cooled. When his watch said seven-twenty-six he turned off the courtesy light and got out. Number 263 was a two-story ranch with attached garage. An illuminated Santa waved from the lawn and colored lights blinked along the eaves. When he pressed the bell a chime tolled far off. A middle-aged woman with faded auburn hair came to the storm door.

"Uh, Mrs. Ryun? Hi, I'm Phil."

"What did you want?"

"Well, Alex and I got a date tonight," he said, thinking, She must still be getting ready. "Are you her mom?"

"Yes." The woman examined him through the glass. "A date, you said?"

"That's right."

"She didn't mention anything to me. But come on in." She disappeared, leaving him standing on one foot and then the other in the living room. He noted the depth of the carpet, the heavy oak furniture, all matching, all polished; he strolled around to examine books ranked on shelves built into the wall, a grandfather clock in a recess. Its indolent tick made him realize how quiet the house was. The air had a cedar freshness.

Mrs. Ryun came back with a glass of milk and a plate of imported butter cookies. "She'll be down in a few minutes, Bill. Please sit down. Won't you have something while you wait?"

"It's Phil. Sure, thanks."

"What was your last name, Phil?"

"Romanelli."

"And where did you say you were going?"

"Just to the movie downtown."

"That sounds good."

"Yeah, thanks." He looked at the clock and then at his Timex. "Is she coming down pretty soon?"

"I imagine so."

"Hi, Phil."

She stood on the stairs, pulling on her mittens. He got up. She was wearing green, with a cream cashmere pullover and a kind of matching hat. "Wow. You look great," he said.

"Thanks." She was giving him the same frown her mother had. "What's that on your lip?"

"What?"

"On your neck, too."

He realized then what she was talking about. He jerked the paper off and felt the cuts sting and start to bleed again. Oh, Jesus, he thought. Her mother left the room and came back with a Wet One while Alex stared in silence at the blank television.

At last it clotted. Alex let him help with her coat. She kissed her mother.

"Now don't stay out too late. Bring her home early, Phil. And have fun, both of you."

She laughed when she saw the squad car. "What's this? Are we going in *this*?"

"Sure. My dad let me have it for the evening."

"Weird. I never rode in one before. Not sober, anyway."

He laughed and held the door. As she got in her hair brushed his arm, sending a funny thrill up it. He saw a flash of her knees, slim and hollowed beneath, by the courtesy light. "Watch the nightstick rack," he said.

"Where're we going, Phil? You told me, but I forgot."

"Oh. The movie."

"What's playing?"

He told her. She said, "Oh, I saw that already. We rented it. Wouldn't you rather go to Cresson?"

"Gee, I don't know. My dad—"

"That's where everybody goes Friday night. The Heathen Creeps are playing, and FKU might do a late set. What do you say, let's go to the Shirt."

He glanced over at her. She was so beautiful; the smell of orange blossoms and of her hair easily put to flight the squad-car funk of Camels, sweat, old vomit, and leather. He wondered again why she was with him. Then thought: That's just your problem, Romanelli. You don't think you're good enough. While obviously she did.

So maybe it could be that he was wrong and she was right, and maybe he deserved love, deserved happiness, after all.

He felt the same sudden joy he'd felt on Sullivan Hill, releasing the brake on this magical night. As for taking her to Cresson, he didn't want to, but he couldn't say no. Not to her. He wanted their first time to be perfect. She reached across and hugged his arm, lifting her eyebrows, and somebody else, maybe the Stag, grinned suddenly and gunned the engine. "Okay," he said. "Sure."

"Great! Now, show me how to put the siren on."

"Christ, Alex! Wait till we're out of town, at least."

Cresson wasn't a town. It was just a crossroads a mile across the state line from Four Holes. But the cops looked the other way when kids drank there, as long as it didn't get out of hand. So tonight, despite cold and snow, the lot by the low log building was full, and cars and trucks lined the side road too. He found a place and locked up; that was the last thing he needed, to have somebody rip the car off. They waded through tracked-up snow to the door.

"So, what would you like?"

"Michelob Light."

The place was wall to wall. Phil got her seated at a table at the far end from the band and pushed his way toward the bar. It took him a while but at last he got two bottles and shoved his way back through groups, between couples, bumping, apologizing. He hoped she didn't want more. After the cover and the beer he had six bucks left. The band was rattling the glasses above the bar with a bass beat he could feel in his guts. The air, solid with smoke, was just like home.

When he got back two other girls were talking to Alex and he had to stand around until they saw him and shoved their chairs over. She'd gotten a cigarette somewhere and was lighting it off one of theirs. He saw right away they weren't going to do much talking here. Well, maybe they could get away, park someplace quiet.

He tilted the bottle and let his tongue pickle for a while before he swallowed. Alex's lips moved and he leaned toward her. "What?"

Something inaudible. *"What?"* he shouted, leaning in front of the other girls.

"Dance," she screamed directly into his ear, deafening him. He grinned and bobbed his head. She took a last drag and handed the cigarette to her friend.

There was an excuse to take her hand as they moved through the crowd, and he used it. Her palm was sweaty. When they reached the floor she let go and spun. Her hair came out in a firework wheel and he saw, with mingled pride and pain he'd never felt before, that she, and he with her, were instantly the cynosure of a hundred eyes.

For the first time he tasted what it might be like, to be a man.

When the number started the strobes cut on and suddenly her body reappeared as sculpture, melted by hot darkness and then refrozen from inchoate black a dozen times a second. Each pose was graceful, abandoned, and different. He stared at her as he danced, conscious as always of his withered arm and faulty legs, but not caring anymore.

A bolt of joy burst up from his feet into his heart, and he lifted his face and danced.

They stayed on the floor through the whole set and when they walked off he was wringing wet. Someone had cleared or stolen their drinks and he bought two more. Her girlfriends, he noted with relief, were gone. It was just possible to talk over the canned rock and he leaned over and shouted, "You dance great."

"Thanks." She upended the beer and looked past him. She didn't seem to like looking directly into his eyes. He shouted, "You look really terrific tonight."

"Thanks."

"You know," he shouted, "I was really looking forward to this. Maybe after this we could go someplace and talk."

"Oh, I got to get home early."

"What?"

"I got to go home. Maybe one more beer. We're all going out to Hantzen tomorrow, to the lodge. Skiing."

"Oh. Well, anyway, I think you dance really great. And you look beautiful."

"Thanks," she said, looking past him.

He tried to see what or who she was staring at, but couldn't; there were maybe two hundred people in the Shirt, and its far end was impenetrable with smoke. He got up and she looked at him then. "Where are you going?"

"Find the can. Be right back."

She nodded. "Bring me another one, okay?"

"Uh, yeah."

He was filtering through the crowd, heading for where he figured the john ought to be, when he came face to face with Bubba Detrick and Brick Mooney. They were leaning back with their elbows on the bar, holding bottles of Killian's Red and looking bored. Their faces lighted when they saw him and Mooney said, "Whoa. Look who's here."

"It's our pal."

Emboldened by beer and the crowd, Phil said, "Get out of my face, Bubba."

"You little prick, you played your mouth to me once too often," said Detrick, and came off the bar at him. Phil was trying to get his sweater-front unwadded from his fist when a just slightly less massive body than Mooney's slid itself through the club sandwich of people toward, then between them. "What you want, Stein?" Detrick asked him.

"Take it outside, Bubba. Them's the rules here."

"You heard the man," said Detrick, shoving him toward the door. "Let's go, Romanelli. I'm through fuckin' with you. This time you're dead."

Outside the wind was bitter and the stars were a thousand pinpricks in a black tent. Engines vroomed and a group of boys staggered by, arms linked. One fell down, screaming, and all the rest did too. The snow squeaked under their boots as Detrick propelled him along the wall, out of the light.

"So, Crip, what the hell're you doing here?"

"Having a few beers."

"That's great, I like to see the retarded have a good time. How come you been avoiding me?"

"I been sick."

Detrick shook his head sadly. "Nah, don't *lie*, Romo. It might come true. Lemme ask you something, you ever have fits?"

"What?"

"Fits. You know, fall down, kick around, shit like that."

"No."

"Good," said Detrick. " 'Cause you have seriously pissed me off, and I'd hate to do this to somebody who might throw a fit on me."

He hit him in the mouth. But Phil was ready this time. He got his head out of the way, then, surprising himself more than Detrick, he punched back. But even as his fist thumped on the other's chest he felt how weak the blow was. Detrick grinned and jabbed him twice in the face with his left, then put him on the ground with something so low and fast he never saw it, just folded over like a jackknife. He writhed around in the snow, seeing nothing but slow red flashes.

When he got his legs under him he went for Detrick's waist. He had his good arm around him and was hanging on to the back of his belt when he heard the ballplayer laugh and then his knee came up and smashed into his mouth.

"Thought you said no fits," said Detrick. "Come on, Wop, get up. We ain't even started yet."

"What's going on out here? Is that you, Bubba?"

Headlights swept across them as Detrick turned, a black cutout with clenched fists. They went on, wheeling across the tops of the trees, and into the returned darkness the ballplayer said, "Who's that?"

"Me. Alex."

"What are you doin' here—no, *wait* a minute, now I know. You're with wimpy-dick, ain't you?"

Coldly: "He brought me out here."

"Yeah, well, what about that? I heard it but I didn't quite believe it. What is this shit?"

"There's no shit involved. He asked me to come here with him and here I am."

"But Romanelli . . . Christ, Alex, I thought we were steady."

"I thought so too, till Sheila passed on a little item about you and this sophomore. What a bastard you are! What's her name, Greg? Does she put out for you?"

Phil found that he was bleeding from the mouth and that two of his incisors were wobbly. He dragged himself backward through the snow. When he hit logs he pushed his upper body into a sitting posture. He could hear dimly through the wood kids screaming and laughing. The beat of the band tickled his loose teeth.

"You know you're it, Alex, you're the one I want. But you don't come through, a man's gotta get it where he can. She's nothin' to me, it was just for fun."

"And you're nothing to me. Not if you're going to humiliate me in front of the school for some little bitch who's probably taking guys on for lunch money."

"Yeah, but . . . I don't get it, Alex. From first string to the ugliest little cripple in school." Detrick made a helpless gesture with his hands. "Don't you *care*?"

"Why not? It was just for fun."

Slowly, Bubba grinned. "Wait a minute. *Wait* a minute. Why do I get the idea you wanted me to see you with him? And he's the only one who's far enough out of it to go out with you when I'm on the scene. Right?"

"Maybe. Something like that."

Suddenly Phil saw the two shadows melt together. "Greg . . . why are we playing these games? Why are we hurting each other?"

"I don't know, babe. People like us, we belong together. C'mere, you little slut. Pull this up. Rub those against me."

"It's cold out here. Warm me up."

"Sweet Alex."

"My Wolf."

"What a touching scene," said Phil thickly.

"Shut up down there, Crip, or I'll kick your fucking teeth in."

"Let go of her, Detrick. She's with me."

"Greg! Don't hit him anymore. He can't fight you. He can hardly dance."

"Make up your frigging mind! Are you with me or him? I got the truck, I got knobbies on it, I got a case of Stroh's. Let's see if we can make it up to the lookout tower."

"Just a minute." He heard the crunch of her boots; caught his breath; but though she leaned over him she said nothing, just put her hand on his hair for a second, then turned away.

Alone again, he stared at the stars for a while, breathing shallow and touching his front teeth gently with the tip of his tongue. At last he wadded snow and packed it under his lip.

When he could move without crying out he got up and staggered across the lot. His shame and rage had passed, gone like mists burned away by summer sun. He had nothing again. In a way it felt better. He wanted nothing. No pain, no longing, no tears.

There was a way he could never be hurt again.

He had the keys. He had a car to get home. He knew where his father kept his service .38.

He started the motor, floored it, and pulled blindly out onto the road.

Sixteen

——————————

Hand over hand, Halvorsen hauled himself up the ice-slicked hillside stairs. He moved slowly, but without cease. Only when he reached a temporary leveling did he stop, pulling in the cold air over and over, and look around him.

It had seem warmer to him that day, but as soon as the sun set the air whetted itself again to a tungsten edge. Below him the town was a rhinestone glitter. But up here night was relieved only feebly by the clear bulbs under white tin reflectors that had been the latest thing in outdoor lighting in 1931.

Wonder why they don't answer their phone, he thought, clinging to the handrail to stay erect.

An engine yowled and a moment later a police car shot past. His head jerked round after it. It skidded from side to side on the ice, but kept on climbing, until at last it swerved out of sight.

Fifty steps on was another landing. He paused there too, breathing hard. He was hungry and from time to time the hill tried to spin away beneath him. But he still had a way to go that night. A long way, in the cold.

He spat onto the snow-slick bricks, and forced himself again into the immense lean of the earth.

A few hundred yards above him, Phil touched the gun.

His father's Smith & Wesson, hanging behind the bedroom door. He listened again to the empty house, then pulled it out of the patent leather holster.

It was heavy and old. The blued barrel was gray at the muzzle and the grips were worn checkerless. His father had carried it for sixteen years. But Phil knew it worked. Joe had taken him out in the woods when he was thirteen, and with great solemnity shown him how to use it.

Standing in his parents' bedroom, he pressed the latch and swung the cylinder out. He slid six nickeled cartridges out of their loops, loaded the gun, and closed it. Then held it for a moment, looking around the house for the last time.

His mom and dad had left a note; they'd gone out too, to the same movie. Shit; they'd give him grief about not seeing him there. The next moment he smiled bitterly. No, they wouldn't.

The woods started two hundred feet above Paradise Lane.

He considered leaving a note himself. But even his hatred had dimmed, melted like everything else he'd ever felt into the gray despair. Even writing a note would keep him here longer than he wanted to stay.

Let's do it, he thought. He dropped the gun into his jacket and went out, closing the door carefully behind him. He dropped the car keys in the mailbox and turned up the hill. For a moment he thought he saw someone at the bottom of the lane. But when he looked again, no one was there.

The climb pulled anew at his legs. His mouth hurt and he could wiggle his front teeth with his tongue. The revolver dragged at his side. Woodsmoke filled the dark air. It smelled good.

Upward, upward . . . the last house. Yellow rectangles of light lay quietly on smooth snow. He waded through them and left them behind. He climbed a cut bank and was in the woods.

The sky was no longer completely overcast; here and there stars burned down from a frigid sky. He recognized Jupiter, brighter than the rest. Around him as he labored upward the planet's light showed him the winter-stripped trunks as black verticals. Snow crunched and moaned beneath his feet. First a thin crust; then, under that, softness; last, the yielding resilience of dead leaves. He sucked the freezing air through his teeth. It's a ways to the top, he thought. Why go any farther? He could have done it at home, but he didn't want to cause his parents problems. Out here the end would be clean.

Thinking this, that he'd come far enough, he stopped and turned, panting a thin warm stream back into the icy river of night.

Below him, between the black trunks, the valley was a pit of darkness among the hills. At its bottom, lapping up the slopes, the parti-colored sparkle of town surged and glittered. He could see the parallels of lights on Main Street; the on-and-off glow of the time/temperature sign in front of the bank; the blue-lit cross atop the Baptist church; here and there the red-orange flicker of a bar. Like planets among the fixed stars crept the twin white flares of automobiles, red as they receded. Above it all low clouds, trembling with a yellow reflection, passed slowly between him and heaven.

For a moment he wondered if it could be true, if there was a life beyond this one. Then his mouth twisted. That was a joke, a cruel fable the governing classes had made up to numb the weak to injustice, insult, and pain.

But he'd had enough. He looked around. The silence of the trees, the soundless passing of the clouds mirrored the emptiness of his heart. People moved below him in the glitter, like angels the corridors of the stars, with smiles and money and straight strong bodies. They laughed and danced and said, *This is happiness. Be like us and you'll be happy too.*

But he couldn't. It wasn't just that he believed in different things, in justice and equality and truth. It wasn't even that he was crippled. The thing he couldn't change was the one thing they would never forgive: his conviction that, no matter what they thought, he was better than they were.

The hammer caught on the lining as he drew it out. He freed it carefully, not wanting to tear his coat. Muzzle-down, the revolver's weight drew his arm to the ground, like a dowsing rod pointing to where he would fall. The butt was cold and hard through his glove.

For a moment, looking down, he wondered if the town itself might be the root of it. He'd always planned to leave as soon as he could. Maybe what he needed lay elsewhere.

Then he thought, It's not Raymondsville. It was he who was different, who was unhappy, who was so poisoned with rage and inferiority he could no longer bear to see or speak to another human being. The problem was not below him. It was within.

Oh, Christ, he thought. If only she hadn't patted my head. He could live with pain, he could live full of hate. But he couldn't live with pity.

He cocked the gun awkwardly and lifted it to his ear. "Good-bye, you bastards," he said aloud, staring down at the town that had seen his birth, his struggle, seventeen years of a life he now judged not worth the breathing for. He closed his eyes.

"Yo!"

The voice came from below him, not far distant. He opened his eyes and crouched, instinctively merging with the earth. Amid the trees a shadow moved, hesitated, moved again. Someone was climbing toward him between the naked trees, under the glowing sky.

He didn't answer. The shadow stopped a few feet away. He couldn't see a face, but it seemed to be looking at him.

Phil brought the gun, still cocked, around in front of him and extended it, feeling the trigger creep inward.

Halvorsen was so tired he could hardly stand. "Who's that?" he said doubt-fully, thinking about the click he'd just heard. The shadow ahead was bulkier than the tree boles, but it didn't move. Then after a moment it did; stood up, and became a human form.

"What're you doing, boy?"

"Nothing! Is . . . Mr. Halvorsen—is that you?"

"Yeah, it's me."

"What are you doing out of the hospital? What are you doing up here?"

"Lookin' for you."

"How'd you find me?"

"People leave tracks," said Halvorsen. "Say, don't you folks ever answer your phone? I been callin' from my daughter's since suppertime."

"I wasn't there."

The boy's voice was high, quavering; he was afraid, or angry, or maybe near panic. The click, Halvorsen thought, had sounded an awful lot like a hammer going back to cock. Cautiously he moved up a step and said again, "What you doing up here, anyway?"

"Just thinking. I got a right to go off and think, be by myself—"

"Don't get upset! Sure you do. I just wanted to talk to you."

"What about?"

He took another step up the hill, feeling with fear the weakness in his legs, the shallow patter of his heart. The kid sounded hostile now. What the hell was going on? He glanced quickly around, thinking he wasn't sure what. But they were alone, just the two of them high above the town. "I got me a problem. But sounds to me like you got one too."

"What's that mean?"

"Sorry, couldn't hear you." Halvorsen took another step up the hill.

"I said, what does—"

He took one last step, and the stick he'd picked up to help him in the climb whipped down. A sudden flash and report shattered the night; fire leaped past his cheek. He lurched forward and got the boy in a bear hug, locking his hands behind him. "Just take it easy a minute 'fore you hit me," he muttered into his ear. "You can knock me over with a feather, but then you'd have to carry me back down to the hospital all over again. What you doin' up here with a gun, all alone at night? I didn't know better, I'd think you were fixing to do some silly-ass thing like shoot y'self."

Halvorsen felt the thin body go rigid; tightened his grip; then heard a short, choked exhalation. The boy's face burrowed into his shoulder. He held him close, in the darkness, and said after a moment, "Go on and cry, boy. I done it myself lots of times. Just go on an' get rid of it for a while."

The sudden flare of yellow phosphorus pulled pines toward them out of
the darkness, then swayed them back. A slip of flame grew hissing from
the pyramid of twigs, then winked out; but beneath it blue tongues licked
with increasing hunger at the heavier sticks.

"Seems to be goin' now," said the old man. He slid the match-box
closed and put it in his pocket. "You'll find them lowest branches on your
pitch pines, they'll stay good tinder all through the winter. Just feather
'em up with your knife like I showed you."

Phil sat on the rock. He felt empty. Crying had embarrassed him, but
only for the first moment. Then he'd given way and bawled. The old man
had held him stiffly against his doggy-smelling coat the whole time, and
the shame had disappeared, then the rage, and last of all the hurt.

Now he felt like a Thermos bottle. A brittle skin of self, wrapped around
a vacuum.

His eyes followed the firelight over the old man's face. He squatted
stiffly by a scooped-bare patch of forest floor, feeding in a stick now and
then. The fire ate them greedily, snapping and popping, and steadily grew.
In its leaping light his face looked emaciated and evil, like a skull with
gray stiff whiskers and a bandage. The curved butt of the revolver poked
out of his pocket.

Halvorsen fed the fire another pine twig, feeling awkward. At last he
cleared his throat and said, "You ready to talk?"

"It's nothing. It was stupid."

"Maybe stupid, but couldn't'a been nothing. Only fella I ever knew to
shoot himself, on purpose I mean, had just lost title to fifty producing
wells in a poker game. Was it somethin' like that?"

"Not exactly."

"Couldn't be women."

"Sort of." He flinched.

"That's about the dumbest thing I ever heard of," Halvorsen told him.
"Shoot yourself over a woman. My advice'd be to find another one. A nice
fat one, they're best when it's cold."

Phil thought of Alice Saunters and had to smile. "Maybe you're right."

"Anyway, pull yourself together. I need some help."

"Is that why you came after me?" He flinched again.

"Told you it was. What's the matter with your mouth?"

"I was in a fight. It hurts when I say 'f'."

"What, your teeth loose?"

He nodded.

"Well, quit playing with them, your mouth'll swell up and hold 'em in.
You was in a fight, huh? Over the girl?"

"Sort of."

"You lost?"

He nodded.

"You land one?"

"One."

"Ain't no shame losing, long as you can dish out a couple 'fore you go down."

Phil stared into the fire. Thinking of it as a fight over a girl made it better somehow. After a moment Halvorsen went on, "Anyway, you want to hear about this? Why I come up here after you?"

"I guess so."

"Reason I need help is I'm still some feeble." He hesitated. "I don't know, my mind don't seem to be as good some ways as it used to—fact is, I remember you told me a couple of times, but I can't recall your name."

"It's Phil. Phil Romanelli."

"Okay, Romanelli, you remember what that doctor lady was telling me about what made me sick. What gave me this rash, and knocked me out the other day when you were out at my place."

"Yeah."

"Well, it made me mad when I figured out what she was sayin'. What it means is, somebody's using this county as a dump. Bringing things in here they don't want and spreadin' 'em all over where we live. Now, I don't like that, 'specially since I—well, if you hadn't of been there, I'd probably froze to death by now."

The old man turned his pale eyes to Phil's. "Now, I don't like to mess with people much. Just as soon leave them alone, have them leave me alone. But this kind of stuff gets under my hide. Fact is, I wouldn't mind getting my hands on the sonsabitches who did it."

"Yeah, I can see that," said Phil. "Look, talking about that, I read—"

"So I was sittin' down at the Bear this evening, warming up before I started for home, and I started going back over everything I done before I got sick. My mind's clearer now than it was Monday." Halvorsen pondered. "Anyway, I remembered one funny thing. Friday, day before you come out to the Run. You remember, we had that heavy fall that morning?"

"Yeah. But look, Mr. Halvorsen, I saw—"

"Don't interrupt. Like I was saying, I was sitting there thinking, and it just come to me that I got a lift in that morning from a guy in one of the snowplows. He took me from the foot of the run right down to Rosen's.

"Now, I remember him telling me about this oily stuff under the snow. I looked and seen it too. Didn't think anything of it then, but some of it must of come blowing in the window. With the snow. I recollect having to take out my handkerchief and wipe it off. Had to wipe it off"—the old man's hand came up to the bandage—"right here, off the left side."

Phil couldn't contain himself any longer. "That was Barry Fox," he said.

"Drivin' the plow? Yeah, Fox, that's who it was. Now if we look him up—"

"He's in Bradford Hospital. With the same thing you had, sounds like, only worse. They found him out by the county line, passed out in the plow. He'd of frozen if somebody hadn't stopped."

"Is that so?"

"I read it in the *Century*."

Halvorsen nodded reflectively. After a moment he reached into his opposite pocket. Bit off a piece of tobacco. "Makes sense," he said. "Dump it on the road. That'd be easy to get away with. The way the old cars leak around here there's always that oily line down the center of the lane. Warm weather, you'd never notice. Only see it when they made a mistake, tried to dump it on top of fresh snow."

"So who's doing it?"

Halvorsen looked up at the stars. "You got me . . . I figured the place to start was out Cherry Hill. You know what that is?"

"Sure. That's the Thunner estate."

"Right. Anyway I went out there today."

"You went to Cherry Hill?"

"Uh huh."

"Wow. What was it like?" Phil blushed suddenly, glad for the dark. "I meant, who cares what it was like. It's all stolen from the workers. What did they say?"

"It ain't *stole*, old Dan put in a lot of years in the fields. But he's out of the business now. His daughter's got a swelled head. But it didn't sound like either of them had anything to do with it. Thunners got more money than's good for 'em now, can't see them doing something like this. They got to live here too. No, I figure it's somebody from out of the county."

"So what do you want to do?"

"Well, first I thought, what business is it of mine? And then I recalled all the animals dyin' out Mortlock; and how I got sick; and now you tell me that driver did too. Maybe there's more we don't know about. I don't mean to bother anybody, I just wanted to be let alone. But they aren't leaving me alone. So I figure I'm gonna try to find out where this stuff is coming from.

"Now I got some friends, but they're getting kind of long in the tooth. Even when they're sober. So I thought you might maybe want to help."

"Uh huh."

"Well, what do you say?"

"What would you want me to do?"

"Well, I figure we might post a lookout along one of the roads. Find someplace where we could stay warm, keep an eye on things, and sit out a couple nights."

"What would we do if we saw something going on?"

"Depends," said Halvorsen. "Get a license number and report it, I guess. Didn't you say your pop was a policeman?"

"Yeah, but he—"

"What?"

"Nothing. Yeah, he's a policeman."

"Well, there you go. I thought about calling Bill Sealey, over at the State Police barracks, but I'd like to have something better to give him than some old guy's suspicions."

Halvorsen dropped his eyes and Phil nodded slowly; seeing suddenly how the world might look to another human being. He's alone, he thought, lots more alone than I am. Maybe things aren't so good for me right now, but I can look forward. He can't even do that. He felt like saying something to cheer the old man up, but he couldn't think of anything that didn't sound stupid or patronizing. So he just said, "I guess I could help."

"Good, that's good."

"When do you want to start?"

"Oh, anytime. We could take every other night." Halvorsen squinted up at the stars. "Gettin' late . . . be warmer tomorrow. I need to head on home, but I wanted to talk to you, and oh yeah, get Jez. I hope she ain't been too much trouble."

"No, heck, it was fun playing with her."

"Good, well, thanks. I'll just take her off your hands then." Halvorsen stood up, brushed snow off his trousers.

"You're going to walk back to Mortlock?"

"Ain't got much of a choice."

Phil stood up too. "I can give you a ride. Down to the run and part way up it, anyway. That'll only leave you two or three miles to walk."

"That'd help," said the old man. He stood and looked down at the fire. After a moment he pulled the revolver out and handed it to the boy. Phil took it as silently and stuck it into his belt.

Halvorsen cleared his throat. "Say, don't feel right asking you this, you done so much for me already, but . . . well, I left my wallet at the hospital. Think you could let me have something to take out there with me? Something to eat?"

"How's frozen soup sound? And we got canned stuff."

"Yeah, that's the ticket. Till I can get out and get me a rabbit or something."

"I thought you didn't hunt," said Phil.

"Don't unless I got to, to eat."

"I guess that's okay . . . well, come on. I don't think my folks'll be back yet, I'll get you some tuna and beans and stuff. And your dog. Then we'll go."

"Sounds good." The old man dragged snow over the fire with his boot. The flames hissed and steamed, fighting for a moment, then died beneath crystalline whiteness, knit of ice and cold beneath the glittering stars.

Together they turned, and headed down the hill.

Seventeen

FOUR WAYS TO FORGET THAT
MARRIED MAN YOU'VE BEEN SEEING

One: Do something NICE for yourself. Go away for a weekend somewhere you've always wanted to go. Give yourself a "new look" with a makeover and new outfit! Start a project you've been dreaming about for a long time. Do something absorbing and above all DIFFERENT from what you usually do with your time.

Two: Reinforce your "social web" by calling an old friend. Make a date for lunch or a movie. Talk about good times you had together—BEFORE you met Mr. Wrong.

Three: Begin the "uprooting process" by consciously not thinking about HIM. Throw out or at least put away out of sight all your old photographs, the gifts he gave you, mementos of places you went together.

Four: Most important, DON'T go right out looking for another man! You're too vulnerable at this stage. Give yourself time to heal!

Jaysine let the magazine sag to her lap. She stared past it, past the wineglass beside her on the window seat, down at the street.

The weather had definitely turned. A passing truck threw out a spray of dirty slush. The snowpiles were smaller and looked rotten soft. She sipped at the wine and reread the last paragraph.

Deep down, you have to admit you knew this day might come! It's part of the HIGH PRICE of loving a married man. However, it doesn't mean you're a failure, a "homewrecker," or any of those other names people used to throw at the "other woman." As clinical psychologist Ella M. Bernstein of Chicago told us, "Every 'failed' relationship has within it the seeds of regeneration. Each is, or should be, a learning experience that will lead to a fuller understanding of ourselves and our drives. Your life isn't over when a man leaves you. In a sense, it's just BEGINNING again!"

The sun came speckled through the glass and she thought vaguely, I ought to clean this window. Shadowed patterns fell through the peperomia and pothos, warming her thighs under the robe. She remembered how he used to pull it down over her shoulders and pin her arms . . . she shifted uncomfortably. She'd had her second shot yesterday . . .

She threw the magazine across the room and stood up and threw the wineglass after it. She threw the pothos next. Its pottery weight balanced in the air and then exploded in a scatter of leaves and dirt against the wall, next to her workbench. Next to the shattered agate, the chunks of silver that had been fashioned so lovingly for him, now mere flattened masses, hammer-marred, battered out of shape back to shapelessness.

She stood rigid, fingernails digging into her eyes. I don't want to forget him, she thought desperately.

You can't have him. He doesn't want you anymore, someone inside her head answered.

What can I do about it?

You can kill him.

She froze, horrified. Had *she* thought that? She didn't want to kill anyone. Did she?

Hesitantly, like a woman considering a drastic makeover, she let herself think it.

She found that she wanted his blood spilled on her carpet like dirt. She wanted to make him beg her to take him back, and then kill him. She remembered a movie about a woman who'd had an affair with a married man. He'd jilted her. She'd kept calling him up, then started threatening him, and at last murdered him with a butcher knife. She saw herself in violent fantasy, steel shining in her hand, plunging it again and again into his chest.

It was incredible, what she read in the magazines. Apparently men did this all the time. The advice columns were full of letters, no, screams of pain from women who'd been strung along for years by men with wives and families.

Oh, she thought, it's evil and it's wrong. How can they do that to other human beings? He'd said he loved her. Said when his wife got better he'd think about a divorce. But it was a lie. She wouldn't be surprised if the rest was lies too. What if his wife was fine, not mentally ill, if he was just . . . having her on the side, because he was bored?

She felt sick. She went to the bathroom and waited there on her knees. But nothing came up.

At last she got the dustpan and whisk broom. The pothos's pale-gleaming roots curled helplessly on the carpet. She remembered when she'd bought it, before she met him. She'd wanted something to brighten the apartment, something to take care of. And now she'd killed it. Well, maybe not. She repotted it as best she could, muttering apologies as she watered it and put in some Jobe's Spikes.

She wondered if she should go in to work. Saturday was a full day at the Shoppe. No, she couldn't go in now, with wine on her breath. Maybe that afternoon. If she felt better.

Jaysine, you have to do something, she told herself. You can't just sit around here reading magazines and swilling wine and thinking about killing him. But that part of her that had answered her back wasn't listening. She sat in the window and looked down at the people plodding up and down the street, and found herself plotting ways she could get back at him.

She could find his car and slash the tires. Break the windshield. But where did he park? Downtown P.C., in front of his office, probably. But there were always people there. She could go to the house, the one he talked about, Cherry Hill. They'd probably have guards there, though. She remembered the black man at the office. All of the things she thought of were too dangerous. They were physical things, what a man would do. She wished she had some poison, in a ring, like that Italian princess.

She wished she could think of some way to really hurt him, as much as he'd hurt her. It didn't seem right that he should just walk away.

Maybe, she thought then, If he lied about his wife . . .

He'd never given her his home number. But it occurred to her now that she might have it. She'd gone through his overcoat the night before, after she came home. The one thing she could think to do was burn it, and she had. Taken it down to the alley and poured strawberry-scented lamp oil over it and watched till it was a smoking tissue in the snow.

But she hadn't burned the little book.

She slid open the drawer by the sink. It was under the potholders. She hadn't looked at it close, but it had his card in a pocket in the front, and yes, his home number too. Without pausing to think—if she did her voice would start shaking—she dialed. Waiting, she thought: What if he answers? Then she'd just hang up. She remembered the woman in the movie again and smiled. Doing that a few times might be fun.

"Cherry Hill. Who's calling?"

It sounded like the black man. She said as coolly as she could, "Mrs. Boulton, please."

"Who's this?"

"It's about her, her styling appointment."

She was congratulating herself on her quick-wittedness when the line clicked and a soft voice said, "Ainslee Thunner Boulton."

"Mrs. Boulton?"

"Yes, who's this?"

"You don't know me, but I know your husband."

Mrs. Boulton didn't answer immediately. Then she said, "Wasn't this about my tinting appointment? Are you calling from Anthony's?"

"No."

"Can you hold a moment?" There was a click on the line. Then she was back. "All right. Who is this?"

The soft voice was businesslike now. Jaysine thought then: This is no helpless madwoman. She almost hung up. Then she remembered how *he* had thrown her out of his office, how he'd infected her, and never even said he was sorry; and she said quick and short, "Mrs. Boulton, I'm your husband's mistress."

"I see. Have we met?"

"No. No, we haven't."

"Why are you calling me?"

"Why? . . . Well, to tell you that Brad's been, he's been having an affair with me. For a long time, almost a year."

"I see. Was that all?"

For a moment she couldn't respond. Had she really said that? Was she crazy after all? "Maybe you didn't understand me, Mrs. Boulton. I said your husband has another woman."

"Oh, I understood you perfectly. What I should have said at first was—when you said you were his mistress—I should have asked, 'Which one?' " Laughter tinkled on the line. "*Esprit de l'escalier,* the French call it—the comeback you think of after the party, going down the stairs. Was that all you needed to tell me? I was getting ready to swim, I swim for an hour each morning, then—Well. I don't imagine you care about that. I should tell you, though, that if he hasn't paid you, you're wasting your time calling me about it."

Jaysine closed her eyes. She was being forced farther than she wanted to go. "Yes. Wait. Yes, there was something else." Maybe the woman already knew. Obvious, perhaps, but it hadn't occurred to her before. I'm a little tipsy, she thought. But then again, maybe she didn't know. In that case she'd be doing her a favor.

"It's about—this disease he gave me. I just found out about it."

"A disease."

"Yes."

"Do you mind telling me the name of it? Or do you know yet?"

Jaysine told her.

"How perfectly awful for you, dear! But you must have known something like that might happen. If he'd cheat on me with you, odds are he'd fuck anybody else who offered, too. Don't you think?"

Jaysine hiccoughed suddenly. She couldn't think of anything smart to say back to that. She heard the static again.

"But you say he gave it to you? Recently?"

"Yes."

"You're quite sure?" The voice was interested now.

"Oh, yes, I'm sure. I haven't been with anyone else for, for over a year."

"I see." The line hummed as Jaysine poured herself another glass of Gallo. Let her chew on that, she thought viciously. That should light a fire under his home life.

"Would you care to testify to that?"

"I'm sorry?"

"I'd make it worth your time. Look, Miss, I don't know your name—"

Jaysine didn't say anything. Suddenly, unaccountably, she felt frightened. Maybe it hadn't been such a good idea to call from her own phone.

"Well, you don't want to say right now. I understand. I don't blame you for the other either, he can be a heartbreaker when he wants to.

"Let me put it this way. Brad and I haven't been intimate for some time. I suspected he's been having his little amours, but I didn't have any details. So I'm glad you called, Miss X." The laugh was like icicles falling on concrete. "How would you like to make some money?"

Jaysine wavered, the glass in her hand. She set it carefully on top of the refrigerator. "I don't think I understand."

"You don't? Really?"

"No."

"Well, don't be offended, dear, but Brad does tend to avoid women who challenge him intellectually. I'll spell it out. I'm considering a suit for divorce. I haven't decided yet if I'm going through with it, or when. But if you'd be willing to repeat what you've just said, we could recompense you for it. You wouldn't have to appear in court, nothing public. All you'd have to do is sign an affidavit. My attorney will meet you. This week, if you like. Anywhere you say."

"Oh, no. I don't think so," she said. "I mean, I couldn't do that. My mother lives here. I couldn't let people know that."

"We could keep your identity secret."

"I can't risk it."

"As I said, I can make it pay for you. What do you do for a living? Was it hair styling, you said? You can't make much money there. Surely you could use a little something extra?"

Jaysine felt sweat roll down her nose. Something evil was creeping
through the telephone line, closer and closer to her.
"Hello?"
She hung up, rattled the receiver to make sure it was down, and backed
away. Her hand, groping among the cereal boxes, almost knocked the
wineglass to the floor. She held it in both hands and drank it down and
refilled it. *God*, she thought, staring at the phone, and shaking. *My God.*
She wished now, too late, she'd never touched it.

She managed to go back to sleep till noon, then got up and heated a can
of potato soup. She had a headache, but she felt stronger. Outside the
window workers were putting up more decorations. It looked dangerous,
high on a ladder with cars going by, and she watched while she spooned
up the soup. When she was done she washed the bowl and then took
down her old copy of *Science and Health.* She carried it to the couch and
opened the worn soft pages at random.

> *If you believe in and practice wrong knowingly, you can at once change your
> course and do right. Matter can make no opposition to right endeavors against
> sin and sickness, for matter is inert, mindless. Also, if you believe yourself
> diseased, you can alter this wrong belief and action without hindrance from
> the body.*

She sat for a long time staring at the repotted plant. Wasn't this just
what she'd done? Fallen away and sinned; believed in disease; and sure
enough it had come to her. She closed the book and opened it again,
and stared at the page.

> *I am wholly dishonest, and no man knoweth it. I can cheat, lie, commit
> adultery, rob, murder, and I elude detection by smooth-tongued villainy. An-
> imal in propensity, deceitful in sentiment, fraudulent in purpose, I mean to
> make my short span of life one gala day. What a nice thing is sin! How sin
> succeeds, where the good purpose waits!*

She shivered. Did she know someone like that?
Seen in *Science* it was easy to know what to do. I should forgive him,
she thought, then never see him again. I sinned, so I suffered. She saw it
all clear when the book gave her the answers. Hatred and revenge were
just new sins, and they didn't injure him. They only ate at her own heart.
She'd done wrong again in calling his wife, and in saying the name of
a "disease" aloud. She closed her eyes, trying to pray for the first time in
years.
But it was like talking into a phone with no one to accept the call.

The air outside was almost warm. She took a deep, thorough breath, losing herself in the antiseptic smell of melting snow. Unbuttoning her coat, she stepped carefully among piles of translucent slush. A little man in a coat longer than he was stood in front of the bank. He was always there, every day. He shuffled his feet as she approached and winked, as he winked at everyone who passed, his eyes secret and afraid. She looked away at first, then looked back and smiled at him. He smiled too.

On Pine Street the loudspeaker outside the Keynote was playing "God Rest Ye Merry, Gentlemen." She smiled again; it was time to start thinking of gifts. This year there was a new little baby to be auntie to, if only by mail.

The door of the Style Shoppe jingled shut behind her.

After her week away it looked dingy and crowded. She hung her coat and went down the aisle, through the close scented air, saying hello to the girls. Marguerite said, "Are you feeling better now, Jaysine?"

"Yes, thanks, a lot."

"We missed you."

"It's nice to be back," she said, and meant it; she was eager to get back to work. Making people beautiful, removing things they were ashamed of—that was good, that was helping in the work of the world. She remembered the dark girl, Karen. She'd made her appointments Saturdays at three, and it was almost three now. Jaysine opened the door to her cubicle and stopped.

Marybelle Acolino was sitting in the operator's chair, reading a book. She placed her finger in it to mark her place, then glanced up over her glasses.

"Why, if it isn't little Jaysine. Hello, dear."

"Hello, Marybelle."

"You're coming in to work?"

"Yes. I have a three o'clock. If you'll excuse me, I need to get cleaned up in here, get ready for her."

"Well, there's a problem with that, dear."

"What's that, Marybelle?" She was instantly on her guard. "There's no problem. I've been sick and now I'm back. You said we got ten sick days a year. I only used six so far."

Mrs. Acolino laid the book deliberately aside on the equipment stand. Jaysine saw the cover. It was her manual on the short-wave machine.

"The fact is, Jaysine, we got a call about you."

"What are you talking about?"

"Why, about what you were sick with. You know you never told any of us, dear, just exactly what it was."

She stood in the doorway, unable to wholly enter; she had a sense of not being wholly there. The shop was silent behind her. She heard herself say weakly, "I told you, it was a cold."

"Well. All I can say in response to that, Jaysine, is that's not what the doctor said it was."

"Doctor? What doctor?"

"I don't remember her name. The doctor from the hospital. But she felt that, since you were employed in a health-related profession, we should know as a matter of public responsibility. So we could take precautions." Mrs. Acolino pursed her lips. "I'm so sorry. But I know you'll understand, you always cared so highly for your clients' welfare."

"*What* are you talking about, Marybelle?"

"Why, just that we have to maintain our standards of sanitation, Jaysine, like anyplace that gives personal care. You can pay me the rest of what you owe on the renovations later. Till then, we'll just"—the older woman motioned at her machine, the magnifier on its movable arm, the chair, the needles and lotions and powders—"just keep these, as security. And of course we'll need them to continue helping our customers who desire hair removal services."

"You can't do that. Look, Marybelle, I'm not going to give anybody . . . anything, doing the electrolysis. You can't just . . . *take* my equipment."

Mrs. Acolino's look went iron. Her voice rose too. "Yes, dear, I understand that, but the fact is that once they know just what you have, they'll stop coming in at all. You know how people are about . . . *those* kinds of diseases. And you owe me money, dear. I put four hundred dollars into this fancy paneling and so forth in here. But your income hasn't covered that yet. So really I can't let these other things go out of the shop." She got up from the chair. "Do you want to see the accounts? I have them right in the back."

"I don't want to see the accounts! I want to keep working. You have no right to fire me!"

"I'm not firing you, dear, don't take it that way." Mrs. Acolino's eyes glittered behind her spectacles. "You've always been one of my favorite girls. But really, wouldn't it be better if you resigned? We can't have you infecting our customers, can we?"

For an endless second Jaysine fought an impulse to slap her. Instead she turned her head, and saw with sudden horror that everyone in the shop was listening. They were all, girls and customers, all staring at her. She switched her attention back to Marybelle, lowering her voice, though she knew it was too late. "You old . . . *witch*. You're not going to get away with this. Give me my paycheck."

"I'm holding that too," said the owner inexorably. "You want to call names, do you? I knew what you were from the minute you walked in here. You can shout all you want to, Miss Farmer, but we're on to you now. No party girl is going to work in my shop. And no cheap little tart is going to jew me out of what's mine."

"Give me my book. Give me my diplomas!"

"Oh, no, we'll have to keep those as long as you're still officially employed here. Trudi, Trudi can—"

"No!" she screamed then, shocking even herself. "No! All right, I quit!"

"What was that, Jaysine?" The shop owner cocked her head, eyes glittering like a raven's.

"I said I *quit*! Give me my things!" She snatched the book from the old woman, making her gasp, then reached for the diplomas. The cord behind one snapped and it came down off the wall, smashing down onto the rack of instruments. She snatched it up and turned for the front door.

It was a hundred miles away. She moved past chair after chair in the hot silent waiting, past eyes that followed her, the whispers beginning already in the rear of the shop when she was halfway to the door. Only Marguerite said in a low voice as she went by, "Give us a call, Jaysine."

She couldn't respond, couldn't speak. It felt like someone had her by the throat. The sunlit window ahead, the pale faces of the waiting customers wavered as if they were underwater. One of them was the dark girl, Karen. She stared at Jaysine in horror.

Jaysine found her coat and fumbled her arm into it. She dropped the book, picked it up. No one spoke at all.

She found herself in the street. The loudspeaker was playing "Good King Wenceslaus." It was December, but the air felt as warm as her tears.

Eighteen

Below Brad the empty streets glistened like wet coal. Not a car moved; nothing moved the length of town. Above him the hills were just as still, slopes streaked with brown beneath the steady cold drizzle.

Sunday morning, he thought. They're crouched in their little churches, praying for their little souls, or home under the covers, waiting out the rain. The hunters snug in motels, recovering from a week of tramping the woods, no doubt cursing the steady erosion of their precious snow.

"Your turn," said Williamina, giving him an annoyed push. "Pay *attention*, Daddy."

"Sorry, Punkin." He swiveled from the window and leaned over the game. He was sorry now he'd bought the thing. It looked simpler than it was. Sixty-some little wooden blocks. First you piled them up into a tower two feet high. Then you started taking them away. The tower got shakier as its supports weakened. He selected a block near the bottom, poked it out and laid it aside. "Okay, kiddo, you're up."

While she studied it he leaned back in the Execuliner, tapping his pen against his teeth.

Behind them the office was empty; the whole building was shut down. The only lights that burned were here, in the suite of the president and chief executive officer. He liked to come in on Sundays. It was his time for reflection, the only opportunity he got to do long-term planning.

"There," the little girl said, triumph in her voice. He glanced at the tower, noted a sway to the left, and removed a block from the right, near the top.

Not that he felt much like planning at the moment. His mind kept going back to yesterday.

He'd come home after a liquid lunch to find Ainslee waiting for him like a hungry predator. He'd known from the first sentence out of her mouth what had happened. The Farmer cunt had done exactly what he'd told her not to. He couldn't get any details out of his wife, but that didn't surprise him. He'd find out what she knew only when she had the bag over his head and the wire around his throat.

He sighed and glanced at his watch. An hour till Patel arrived. He patted his pockets, wondering again where his notebook was. In the process his eyes met the flip chart. He looked at it for a time, then glanced at his daughter. She was still studying her next move, brow puckered intently. He got up, crossed to it, and flipped to the last graph.

The spinoff slide, showing the pyramidal structure Thunder would assume when it went public. Hemlock HealthCare, Thunder Oil, Thunder Petroleum Specialties, First Raymondsville Financial Services, TBC Industrial Chemicals.

It occurred to him that there was room for another block. Perhaps he might restructure one of his current relationships, rather than terminating it.

He recalled an article he'd read in *Forbes* about hazardous waste disposal. Very few of the industries in the East had anywhere to dispose of the toxic by-products of chemical manufacture, outdated stocks, medical wastes, and products withdrawn from the market. There wasn't any legal place to dump, or only a few very expensive ones, far to the south and west. That was why the people in New Jersey had stepped in.

A waste disposal company would fit beautifully within the Thunder Group. The local environment was ideal: rugged, distant, poor, with an aging, conservative population. The local chamber would give a party for Lucifer if he brought jobs with him. There'd be soreheads, but they could be dealt with.

As he'd dealt with the *Century*. Pulling ads hadn't worked, but he'd had a talk with Pete over martinis. Gerroy owned it, third generation. Owned WRVL too. Hadn't been a peep about mysterious illnesses since. That suited him. They could scream as loud as they wanted after this stock sale. It would be a fait accompli then.

He realized his daughter was staring up at him, her eyes blue and innocent. "How you doing there, Punkin?" he said.

"Daddy, what are you thinking about?"

"Business, honey, just business."

"What's business?"

"Just . . . business. What I have to do so we can live in Cherry Hill, in a pretty house, and have nice things." He smiled tenderly at her puzzled expression.

"We don't *have* to," she said.

"What's that, Punkin?"

"I don't *want* to live there. We don't need a big house. I don't like Ainslee and she hates me. I'm scared of her. Daddy, let's *go away*."

He chuckled and picked her up. "Sure, sure."

"Daddy, I mean it. Let's leave and go back to Pip-burg."

"Pip-burg! That's great. Go ahead, Punkin, move."

A sigh. "I already *did*. It's your turn, Daddy."

He set her down by the desk and studied the problem. The column was shaky now. It swayed perceptibly, all its weight balanced on one block near the bottom. He selected another near the top, began edging it out, but something went wrong. He tried to steady it, but the touch of his hand was too much. The tower twisted, tottered, broke, and fell apart, clattering across the polished oak and bouncing on the carpet.

"Okay, Willie, that's enough. No, not again. You take them out front and play quiet, build yourself a fort, okay? Daddy's got to do some work this morning."

When she was gone, carrying the box with her, he pulled a file folder toward him. A few minutes later he took the computer out and called up a spreadsheet.

The doctor came in at eleven. Brad got Willie bundled up and they went across the street for the buffet. He'd promised Patel a look at the new facility in Beaver Fork, and after brunch he packed his daughter and her doll into the back seat and the Indian in front. He pulled the Jag into the street, flicked on lights and wipers, and aimed it north, noting with mild amusement Patel trying to fit the seat belt around his paunch.

"By the way, thanks for taking care of my little . . . medical problem, Vinay."

"My pleasure, sir."

He glanced sideways at the little man. Patel was wearing the same cheap suit he'd had on at the interview. Brad realized he'd worn it the whole week he'd been in P.C.; it must be the extent of his business wardrobe. Hell, he thought, if I'd known that I'd have offered him less. But he only said, "Don't call me sir. Or boss. This is America, right? Just call me Brad."

"You are right, there," said the Indian, looking out the window at the speeding hills. "It does not look like India, that is for sure . . . maybe a little like Patna. But not very much like that either."

"Did you say your family was due up from Hampton Roads?"

"They shall be here tomorrow."

"Flying in?"

"No. No, we rented a truck. My brothers decided it would be less expensive to move our possessions ourselves."

"Your *brothers*? How many people you bringing up here, Vinay?"

"Eleven. My wife, my brothers and their wives, and our children. I have two daughters. One of them is about the same age as yours, as a matter of fact."

"That right?"

"Your daughter, she's beautiful. You must be very proud of her. And it is nice that you spend so much time with her."

"Well, thanks, but that's sort of temporary, we're short a nanny." He cleared his throat, dismissing the subject of the Patel family. Below them as they climbed the refinery came into view, a maze of storage tanks, pipe stills, fractionating towers, condensers, percolators, holding tanks for finished fuels and lubes. Steam and smoke rose in lingering plumes, and above it all the flare-off flickered. Number One worked around the clock; letting those miles of pipe and equipment cool overnight, or over a weekend, would cost hundreds of thousands of dollars in fuels and repairs.

The valley dropped back and hid itself, and his mind moved on ahead. "Think you'll like the layout up at Beaver Fork."

"What kind of building is it?"

"An old mansion, built back in the boom days. Last time I was up the walls were ripped out and plumbing and wiring was going in. Should be pretty near complete by now. We're calling it Beaver Manor. It's already ninety percent booked."

"I look forward to seeing it."

He glanced into the back seat. Willie was playing with her doll, twisting its arms and singing to it. He couldn't make out the words. She wasn't listening to them, but just to be sure he found the Erie FM station and turned up the back speakers. He flicked Patel a man-to-man grin. "Only one thing: there's a girl out there I hired for food service, Gloria, don't get any ideas about her."

"Oh? I thought the woman who came up to see you, in your office— she looked very nice—"

"Who? Her? Well, I suppose you'd go for the well-padded ones, come to think of it. She's a loser, Vinny. Don't get mixed up with her."

When he glanced over again the Indian's head was going up and down, like one of those spring-necked toys he'd bought Willie when she started crawling. He seemed awfully jolly. Well, he was probably looking forward to his family's arrival.

Family . . . he didn't like the way Ainslee was acting. She'd never taken to Williamina, but now she was actively hostile. He didn't like to think of the effect it was having on Willie. When he'd asked Ainslee to marry him he'd figured it would be good for the kid. Replace a crazy female role model with somebody strong. He wanted her strong, she'd have to take over after him and hold what he'd won. Ainslee was that, all right. She was the only woman he'd ever met who scared him.

But he couldn't let this latest flareup worry him too much. Ainslee needed him and they both knew it. Not in any personal way, that hadn't lasted long after the ceremony, but to save Thunder Oil.

But though he told himself this he still couldn't shake the worry. Ainslee kept talking about sending Willie away. He'd never do that, he'd see Ainslee and everything she owned in hell first, and she knew it. And other things too disquieted him, things that had come up at meetings of the board . . .

He came back to Route Six to find his knuckles pale on the wheel. They were climbing the long shoulder of Gerroy Hill; on its far side was Raymondsville. The speedometer needle trembled at 25. Practically parked ahead of them was a truck, the bed full of what looked like crushed glass. Cars kept coming toward him on the two-laner. He couldn't pass. He leaned on the horn, a long blast just for the hell of it.

"Do you mind if I smoke?" said Patel.

"No, but crack the window. Smell gets in the sheepskin."

"By the way, Brad, you were going to tell me what you expected of me for the extra income you mentioned."

He nodded, recalled now firmly to the road, the present, and the destination. He checked in back again, but Willie was still deep in her fantasies. "Uh huh. You remember what I said about running HHC as a profit center?"

"Yes."

"Okay." Ahead of them the truck's brakelights glowed for a railroad crossing; Brad ticked up a finger from the wheel. "Number one. Our Medicare loading right now is seventy-three percent. That's guaranteed cash flow, there's noplace else they can stack 'em.

"So I want you to concentrate on the private bodies. Remember, they always get wheeled out for visitors. Don't let outsiders back of the desk. The ones out of their minds, we've got them double-bunked and the family thinks they're in private rooms.

"Number two, I don't know if you've run into this angle in the VA, but Medicare pays us according to what they call a DRG—diagnosis related group. No one goes into a HHC facility without a diagnosis. I'll get you a copy of the disease/reimbursement schedule so you can act accordingly."

"All right."

"Along with that, we've got deals with some professionals around the area. There's a diet therapist, a chiropractor, an acupuncture guy—you'll like Chao—and this real weird lady shrink who does a biofeedback thing. Anytime you refer a patient to them instead of the local AMA twenty percent of the billing comes back to us."

"How much of this is mine?"

"Half."

"Okay."

Brad saw an opening. The Jag accelerated smoothly, pressing them back in the seats, and he gave the truck driver the finger as he passed. At eighty he cut back in just in time to avoid a van. "Okay . . . next, we all know that despite our best efforts people die in nursing homes. I'll give you a number to call before you release the news to the family. The bodies go direct to Ron Whitecar's. Ron shoots us back ten percent of gross. His dad Charlie's county coroner, so if we scratch their backs that covers our butts on questionable death certs. Understand?"

"Sure."

"Next, I want you to liaison every week with Mrs. Suder, our accounts receivable person. We don't carry dead meat. If a resident can't pay, their insurance coverage is exhausted or their family's past due, dump 'em to the public hospital. Put makeup on them and ship them out."

Patel nodded.

"Now, we can make money in the facility pharmacies, but we've got a fairly tough state code here. I want you to keep the controlled substances books yourself."

"How do we shave it?"

"Couple ways. First, I've got a guy in New York who ships us expired pharmaceuticals from the city hospitals there. They write it off as destroyed. We use it and bill it as new."

"Who thought of that?" said Dr. Patel, lighting another Benson & Hedges.

"I did."

"Very nice."

"Thanks . . . oh, hell."

The rain came. It lashed suddenly against the windscreen, a storm, a deluge. Drops shattered and danced on the hood, and the wipers flailed like birds pinned against the glass. The car bored steadily through, steel and leather muting the water's roar. Brad hardly raised his voice. "Well, I guess that's about it . . . Oh, yeah, while we're on the subject. Once money loosens up, I'm thinking of putting in a hospice unit for the county. That'll get us PR points for social responsibility. Plus, the government's loosening up on some of the hard stuff for terminal patients. Figure an angle on how we can work with that. I know people, can sell whatever we can supply."

Patel inclined his head to the window. The slipstream sucked smoke from between his lips. The road began to climb. As they entered the woods the rain slacked off. After two miles he cleared his throat. "I understand that, and I can do it, Brad. But, do you mind if I ask you something?"

"Shoot."

"I need to know, I suppose you would say, where to stop."

"Stop what?"

"I am not saying I would not do something because it is wrong. I suppose that is bad karma . . . whatever." Patel shrugged. "But I work for you now. You tell me what I do. What should I not do?"

"Let's let the legal system define that, Vinny."

"The legal system?"

"That's right. Why are we in business? To make money, for our stockholders and ourselves. I don't recognize any other limitations on that than the legal system. You play by any other book, you're handicapping yourself, and a sharper operator will cut you down.

"Now, we got to pay these staff shysters anyway, why not use them to cover our butts? We comply with legal minimum requirements. Except, of course, when they're not enforced."

"And you are saying, in that case, what?"

Brad turned his head. The doctor was passive in his seat, looking down at the empty hollows, packed with fog like pill wadding, that stretched off into the hills. "Don't get sanctimonious on me, Jack. I don't respond well to that."

"Believe me, I had no thought of that, Brad. I just wanted to know if you would back me in any questionable situations with my patients."

"You want to know what I think of your patients? They're a profit opportunity. If we don't take their money somebody else will. I think of them as no different than I think of myself."

"How is that?"

"People are scum. All of them—us too. Only we're riding in a Jag while they're pissing in their sheets. If they were in my place they'd do exactly the same. Now, I hired you with the idea you share that view. Do you or don't you?"

"Yes, sir, I do."

"Then we're partners. And in that case yes, I'll back you, a thousand percent."

He downshifted. The car wound through patches of forest, curving down the long grade that brought Route 49 out of the hills to the Beaver Valley. Trees leaned over them; caught in their branches like Spanish moss, the fog trembled above the polished black glass of the road. Instead of slowing he flipped his lights to amber and held his speed.

"No, Vinny, I can't afford to get sentimental. Not now, with things coming up to crunch point.

"Maybe it sounds heartless, or cold-blooded, what I'm telling you. Well, I've been called that before. Doesn't bother me a bit. What I'm doing will help, down the line, everybody who lives in this county. It'll bring in money and jobs. That's not why I'm doing it, but that'll be the end result.

"So I'll tell you right now what makes Brad Boulton run. If push comes to shove I'll sell you, I'll sell myself, I'll sacrifice anything to keep Thunder Oil afloat. That's what I'm drawing my pay for and that's what I'm going to do."

Patel did not respond or answer. The world glowed orange as fog clamped suddenly down, dropped from the trees. Two silent men and a child engrossed in play hurtled in their metal shell through a world created moment by moment from nothing, and that was sucked back into nothing, into whirling mist and rain again, behind the speeding car.

Nineteen

T he rain fell invisibly from darkness into darkness, less water passing through air than a fog-sewn mist, trapped and floating between black velvet hills.

Phil hunched shuddering at the edge of the road. Above him a cheap poly tarp snapped in the wind. Occasionally, when it gathered enough water, it suddenly purged itself into the ground beside him. Below him a blanket oozed when he shifted his weight. Behind him was the forest, invisible, but alive with the drip and patter of a million raindrops through a million pine needles; and ahead of him, also dark except for a far-off glimmer from the Kendall station at the crest of the hill, was Route Six.

The main road through Hemlock County was two lanes of asphalt, not in good repair. Frost heaves took their toll every year, and the trucks that hauled out coal, stone, oil, lumber took theirs too. The Blue Star Highway meshed with the Allegheny's writhe like an ardent eel for seventy miles traversing the forty miles from east to west. The state legislature had postponed improving it for more years than Phil had lived. So it carried traffic all winter and was plowed, and then all summer and was patched, over and over until the patches were patched, and the county crews had repaired the same potholes so often they'd given them names.

He pulled his jacket tighter and wiggled his fingers. Since his talk with Halvorsen they'd stood watch here all through the night. He, Phil, was on from sundown to midnight. When the hands of his Timex pointed toward the treetops the old man would come swinging out of the darkness. They'd nod to each other and turn over the things—the flashlight and the pad and the shampoo bottle he'd scarfed from his sister's beauty junk—and then he'd climb back on his three-speed and head for home, geared down for the hill, but after that coasting the next three miles clear into town.

Tonight was their third night on guard. At first it'd been kind of exciting, like the late shows, where the hero was radioing in the position of the tank column. But now he was wet as well as freezing. Missing half his sleep was starting to get to him. Nor was he getting any homework done.

But he didn't mind. After what he'd nearly done up above Paradise—well, getting a C in chem didn't seem real earth-shaking anymore.

Headlights showed far at the end of the road. He waited, looking to the side so he wouldn't be dazzled. They came on fast and low and he made it as a car. Halvorsen said they didn't have to worry about cars, but Phil lifted the binoculars, old German things the old man had dragged out of some corner of his basement, just to make sure.

It hummed past and dwindled up the hill. He yawned, looking down at the yellow pad. Fifteen trucks so far tonight. Sunday night there'd only been five. Yeah, things picked up on weeknights. But nothing you'd call suspicious.

He sat in the rain and yawned again, hugely, and snapped his mouth shut like a weary dog.

Lights came up the road. Repair truck, Penelec, license Pennsylvania ALA-216. He took off his glove to log it and shivered again, this time so deeply his teeth clattered.

He didn't feel different, though. Which was funny. In school he said hello to the kids he knew and they said hello to him. Alex smiled at him once; he'd looked away. Detrick and his gang ignored him, as if their encounter on the far side of the border had erased his existence.

And he himself, that complex assemblage of molecules that thought it thought, sat shivering and alone, thinking:

I ought to be dead.

In the midst of night he lifted his hand before his eyes and saw nothing. Was this what they saw, the dead? Or did they wander the earth, like in that book by Aldous Huxley . . . No. Death was nothingness.

He looked at his watch for about the fiftieth time. The flashlight was getting dim. He wished he'd brought something hot, cocoa or something. But he'd had enough trouble getting out of the house. He'd padded the bed, the old dummy-sleeper trick, and snuck out the back door while his mom and dad were watching TV. They seemed to be getting along better, anyway. He figured it was his dad's promotion.

Headlights gnawed anew at the rain. He made it as another car. The lights dipped and swayed, first right, then left, lighting the dripping branches above his head. Suddenly they died, into ruddy sparks, into blackness. The car rolled off onto the berm and stopped.

The dome light came on. The driver sat there for a while, too far away for Phil to see much of him. Finally he got out. The light went out and the hollow slam of the door bounced off wet tree trunks.

Another roadside whizzer. Why did they all pick that spot, fifty yards up the road from him? Probably the same reason he was there: you could see a long ways both up and down the road. So people's headlights wouldn't catch them with their dick in their hand.

He sat and listened to the motor idling, an uneasy murmur beneath the cat's-feet patter of rain. After a while there was another *thunk*. The lights came on and accelerated up the hill toward town.

He shifted on the blanket as his mind went back to his interrupted death. What did it mean? That he'd been given a kind of reprieve?

Because he'd been ready to do it. His finger had been tightening on the trigger. He'd wanted it to end. But then old Halvorsen had showed up, just when out of all his life he'd needed somebody most.

Of course it was coincidence, but still he had a weird feeling of being somehow redevoted. Born again, though not into anything religious. The old man was right. No wonder, he'd been through some shit too. If they wouldn't leave you alone you had to fight back. His life, renounced, forfeited, was devoted now to a Cause.

A new set of lights. He was reaching for the binoculars again when the grinding clatter of gears changing down and then a hiss told him it was heavy, and it was slowing, just as the car had done.

A sixteen-wheel whizzer. He grinned sardonically in the darkness and raised the binoculars. He noted the number, then sat waiting for the truck to start up again.

A flashlight vanished and reappeared, swinging over the road around the back wheels. A black outline knelt, flicked the yellow circle over the axles. Diesels grumbled. Checking his tires, Phil thought. The shape stood, the light went off. Then came on again, just for a moment, showing him a gloved hand turning a valve.

He stopped breathing, steadying the binoculars.

The light moved forward, up to the cab, and went out. A door slammed. Then the motor bellowed, gears meshed, brakes hissed off. The headlights came on full bright and the tanker eased out onto the pavement, clumsily positioning itself for the pull up the hill.

The binoculars thudded onto the blanket. Two quick steps, hardly enough time to limp, and he snatched his Ross off where it was propped against a pine. His tires ground on gravel and then sizzled, gaining speed over wet asphalt.

Fifty yards ahead the tank truck, rumbling into the first rise of the hill, shifted gears. He pushed hard, standing on the pedals. Going to be close, catching up before it hit its pace. But the hill would help. He slacked for a moment, then steadied again, aiming between the taillights. Then thought, No, the valve's there, my tires will be going right over the stuff coming out; if it's slick . . . he bore left, just behind the taillight.

A gust of rainsoaked wind hit him as they emerged from the shelter of the woods, rocking him, peeling scarlet-lit veils of spray off the curved hull ahead. He bent his head, blinking, and drove on. The first pain shot through his hip. His open mouth sucked exhaust. The tires whined in his ears. They were beginning to kick up spray. The running lights, ringed with blurry haloes, showed him swaying mudguards decorated with girlie cutouts and there, right above the yellow Pennsylvania plate, a black thread coming down. Coming out slow, like a half-cracked kitchen faucet. But drive for a few hours, through woods, back roads, up hollows . . . that would empty it. Sure.

The vehicle ahead shifted and so did he. They were hitting the grade now. The gear-change slowed him but not as much as it did the truck, and he put everything into a last sprint. The final ten yards narrowed to one, and he grabbed for the big pressed-steel fender.

He missed, wobbled, dropped back into the spray. He gnashed his teeth in the roar of tires, pedaling savagely, and closed again inch by inch till he could make a second and, he knew, last lunge forward.

His hand closed on gritty steel. Beneath him huge tires whined in the dim light. The stack snorted and roared above him. His milling feet slowed, then relaxed as the truck, and his extended arm, took up the drag.

Now, too late, he realized he'd need two hands for this job. One to hold on, and one to manipulate the bottle. Instead he leaned forward. His chest on the handlebars locked the front wheel, and his chin hooked painfully over the fender. He fumbled at his jacket, then extended his arm.

This close he could see it clearly. Black, heavy, curling and drooling downward as its viscosity varied. His hand entered it. Warm and slick, like a heated bath oil. He could smell it too, under the odors of exhaust and rubber, rain and pine woods.

No time to analyze. He flipped up the bottle top and jammed the plastic rim right up under the valve. Held it there till his head felt like it was coming off, then let go the fender.

The bike wobbled wildly. He almost lost it, but managed to straighten. He dropped back, losing speed against the uphill, snapped the cap down and thrust the bottle into his jacket. The truck was drawing ahead steadily when he realized that all this time his generator-powered headlight had been on. Whoever was driving the tanker, if he happened to glance into the rearview—

A rushing hiss came from ahead and the truck slowed, too suddenly for him to react. The bike slammed steel, then went down so hard it threw sparks. His knees slammed into asphalt. He went down too, too fast to think, except that his hand snagged the fender, and that was all, probably, that saved him from going right on under the wheels after the Ross.

The truck dragged him about seventy feet. When it stopped he let go and lay there on the cold roadway, face down.

"What the *hell* ya think you're doing?"

He didn't look up, just kept trying to breathe through the pain and shock. Hard hands grabbed his jacket. They stood him, whirled him, and slammed him against metal. His bike lay like a stepped-on insect some yards down the hill.

"I *said*, what ya think ya doing, ya little asshole?"

Phil mumbled, "Just hitchin' a ride."

"What?"

"Goin' home . . . it's late."

"How long you been back there?"

"Take it easy, Mister. I just come around the bend. Saw you goin' up the hill. Thought I'd catch me a free ride."

The big pale face swung back; hard small eyes studied him out of it. Doubt and rage struggled in them for a moment. "Fucking kids . . . well, can't say I ain't done it myself. But god damn it, I hope this teaches you it's dangerous."

He nodded.

"You walk?"

He nodded.

"Get outta here."

He stumbled away as the trucker swaggered back to his cab. The truck fired up, then resumed its caterpillar climb. The taillights shrank to mist-smeared pinpoints, hung for a moment at the crest of the hill, then disappeared.

He tried a step, then another, and so crossed the road. His knees were scraped raw, hurt like hell, but he didn't think the damage was serious. Bending to the bike, he dragged it off the paving. He suddenly remembered the bottle and grabbed for his pocket. It was dented, but the plastic popped out again. The cap was secure.

Holy shit, he thought in dawning wonder. I did it. I got some!

He looked at his watch. In fifteen minutes the old man would be there. Limping, exultant, he moved toward the trees.

Halvorsen showed at midnight, striding down stiffly from the Run. He built a fire, examined Phil's legs, then wiped his hand off thoroughly with wet leaves. He gave Phil his down bag. When first light came they struck camp. They dragged the tarp, their wet gear, and the mangled bike back out of sight from the road.

They stood on the berm together in the drizzle, thumbs turned out in the dawn. At last a pair of middle-aged men in a Wagoneer pulled over. They looked curiously at the man and boy, but mentioned only the wretchedness of the weather.

They got out at the foot of Maple Street and hiked up to the hospital together. Neither of them spoke. At the desk Halvorsen asked for Dr. Friedman.

"She's not in yet," said the fat lady.

"Well, look, Doris, we need to see her—"

She frowned and extended her lower lip. "Do I know you?"

"Why, ain't you Doris Wiesel? Judge Bob's daughter?"

"It's Doris Hull now, but that's me. And—wait a minute—I know who you are!"

They began talking. Phil stared at the walls. He examined a colored print of some doctor scraping something off a cow. Next to it was one of a guy in a bow tie cutting somebody's tongue off. When the conversation got around to modern times he drifted back. The fat lady was saying, "Yes, sure, I'll let her know. And where will you be? Sure, Racks, I'll call you there as soon as she comes in."

They went out onto the street again. Phil looked at Halvorsen, shivering. Didn't the old man tire, didn't he feel cold, or hunger, or the rain? He didn't move fast but he never seemed to stop for long.

"Well, guess we got to wait around. Doris'll call me when she comes in. You look like you're ready for some breakfast, get warmed up a little?"

"Sounds good. Where do you want to go?"

"Well, I told her we'd be over to Mama DeLucci's."

The restaurant had five stools in front of a dark wooden counter. The deep fat fryers were caked with carbonized grease and so was the overhead fan. The two women behind the counter were both ancient, dark, and angular, with the same black hair-nets and identical noses. They greeted Halvorsen with shrieks. Phil smiled derisively. He'd seen Mama's from the street a dozen times, the old folks huddled in the steamy heat like tropical flowers, but he'd never come in; no more than one of them, probably, would go into the Pizza Den. But now he realized he didn't feel self-conscious, the way he would have before. He didn't care anymore if his classmates saw him sitting here, eating hash browns and bacon in the window opposite old Racks, in his boots and suspenders and his crazy-looking hat, with no one there under sixty.

"So which one is Mama?" he asked Halvorsen.

"What's that?"

"I said, which one of them is Mama?"

"Oh. No, the old lady, she died when I was a kid. These are her daughters." Halvorsen mopped at a yellow run of egg with a triangle of toasted

Sunbeam. "They was some lookers once, believe it or not . . . So, ain't it time for you to be gettin' to school?"

"Not today. You and me, we got things to do, right?"

"What time you supposed to be there?"

"Oh . . . eight."

"Finish your breakfast. Then you can head on over."

Phil thought, Well, guess I go to school today.

"What you grinning at, boy?"

"Nothing."

He reached for his pocket, but the old man said, sounding angry, "I got it. I got three bucks left out of my nickel jar, and I'll stop in the post office today, pick up my check. You just go on."

When the boy left, Halvorsen unbuttoned his shirt and sat back. The smells of onion and garlic opened up his head, and he blew his nose deliberately in a paper napkin, one nostril at a time. Skipping school . . . Kids nowadays had no idea what it was like breaking your back with a shovel. He'd done without an education, but the world wasn't what it was in his day. Maria came over and he counted her out the coins and asked for a refill. As it steamed in front of him he stared out at the street. Rain, rain . . . this was exactly the weather he'd choose if he was dumping waste oil on the roads.

He remembered dumping things. Hadn't been no environmental protection when he worked in the fields.

He sat in the heated air, warming his hands around the heavy mug, and remembered how it was, in the winter, back then.

At fourteen he'd been full time on Don Ekdahl's lease on Portage Creek. In those days you were on the job at seven, sunup or not, whether you had to ride or walk or crawl. In the icy dark the men would set about getting ready for the day's operations. With guttering torches, rags wrapped on sticks and dipped in the crude, they'd begin thawing out the rod lines to the jacks. And he remembered, so many long years before it seemed like a previous life, building the fire under the storage tank, scraps of wood, oil-soaked batting, whatever offered, to gently heat the inflammable crude to the seventy degrees it needed to flow . . .

He remembered when there was a hole at every well, and if you got paraffin out of the settling tank you dumped it into the hole. And there was a man come around with a horse and wagon and picked it up. Then later they didn't want it, but the gaugers wouldn't pump your oil unless the tank was clean on the bottom, so you had to climb down and shovel it out.

No, there was no such of a thing then as an environment, he thought. The paraffin and scum and dirt went down the hill and like as not right into the creek, just like everything else: used acid, salt water, washout water, and a good lot of crude too, and it didn't make no difference, nobody cared. The oil came out of the ground mixed with natural gas but they just let that evaporate, or it howled out of the well pure and colorless and they flared it or just blew it away in the air. In the woods the seepage from the wells and separator pits made the ground marshy and foul as a pigyard. And they built the refineries on the creeks so they could dump what they didn't want.

So in those days Whitecar Creek, and Falkiner Creek, and Todds and Cook and the Allegheny too were all covered inches thick with chocolate scum. It lay on the flat shale banks when the river fell and stank. Sometimes someone would burn it off, or it would catch fire on its own, and burn for days, sending a black cloud up behind the hills. Downstream of the refineries the rocks shone with bizarre colors, purplish red, silver, brass, weird metallic greens. The air was sweet with the oily tang of crude petroleum. It was a smell W. T. Halvorsen had always liked. It meant home.

He thought, But the woods was so big then. Oil was down in the ground; you brought it up on top, that was all, and if you didn't need something you threw it away and there was room for it, didn't seem to matter much whether you tossed it in the creek or burned it off into the clear sky. So much room. The world itself was bigger, seemed like.

Yeah, he thought then, but crude never hurt nobody. He remembered his mother rubbing it into his cropped scalp when he got lice. Some people drank it, hell, that was all mineral oil was. It didn't do the bushes much good when it got on them but the next year they were back same as before. Never hurt no deer, no animals. Course, the fish in the streams, yeah. Anybody who fished in Hemlock County in those days was crazy.

But this stuff in this little bottle was different. The doctor said it'd kill you. Give you cancer. Make women miscarry or worse. No, this was new, to the earth unnatural, to his mind monstrous.

But we shouldn't of done the other either, he thought. It was just like Mase Wilson losing his arm. In those days nobody made you put guards on bandsaws. So nobody did. It was pure ignorance, that and people crazy mad to make the money.

Probably the same reason those midnight trucks were rumbling through the county, too. Root of it didn't change, anyway.

Maria came by. "Phone for you in back."

"Thanks."

It was the woman doctor. She listened silently to his explanation, and said, "Come on over. I'll be in my office."

Friedman's office was on the second floor, down a part of the hospital he hadn't seen before. Young people in green cotton eyed him curiously. He rapped at the door of 233. When she looked up from a littered desk she smiled, looking tired already, though it was only nine in the morning.

"Our escapee returns. Come on in."

"Thanks."

"You gave me a scare, Mr. Halvorsen. But if you were in good enough shape to walk out, I guess it wasn't my place to keep you here."

He didn't say anything. She went on, "Anyway, you left this. Here it is. With both dollars still in it. And—oh—your watch."

He accepted his belongings gravely. "You mind if I close this here door?"

She nodded, and they sat. Halvorsen fumbled in his coat, then produced the bottle. He centered it on her desk. After a moment she flipped it open and waved a hand over it, pushing the smell toward her nose.

"Whoo. Some kind of aromatics in there."

"Powerful, ain't it?"

"The boy got this off a truck? Whose?"

"Tank truck," said Halvorsen. He leaned his chair back and glanced at the door again. "He couldn't see who owned it. Too dark, too rainy. But he got a tag number."

Dr. Friedman raised one eyebrow. He let his eyes dwell on her face as she poured some of it out into a little glass. Cool now—it must have been going through a heater before the valve—it was gelatinous. Dark, but when the light hit it right green tints gleamed. Its smell seeped into the room. A petroleum smell at first. He could pick out the heavy fraction, like a heating oil. Then a tang like acetone, but beyond that something else.

He'd smelled indigo once. This was something like it: a honeyed reek that warned you not to come too close; that here was something you might like too much for your own good. A smell like the smile of a whore.

He asked her, "Well, what you think it is?"

"No idea. But give the lab people a few hours and I should be able to tell you pretty accurately." She crossed to a file cabinet and slid out a paper. "Meanwhile you can start on this."

"What is it?"

"A reporting form."

Halvorsen laced his fingers over his stomach. "I guess you better do that. I've got about as far into this as I want to go, Doc."

"What? Why? Are you afraid?"

"That ain't it. I just don't care to get caught up in all this stuff."

"Whoever's dumping this almost killed you, Mr. Halvorsen. Do you want them to keep on? Maybe kill a child?"

"Well, no."

"Then I recommend you report it. *I* can't; I don't know where it came from. I didn't see your sample taken. And they'll need your assistance to

track it down. I'll help, and the hospital will too. But eventually somebody's got to put his name on the dotted line."

Halvorsen looked at her for a while. At last his hand dipped into his
pants. He fitted the glasses slowly to his face, slipping the wire rims over
one ear at a time. "All right," he said. "You got you a ink pen?"

He was sitting there still, thinking about a chew, when she came back.
"Jackpot," she said.

"How's that?"

Friedman picked up his form, clipped a printout to it, and tossed them
into a wire basket. "EDB, PBB, vinyl chloride and chlordane; trace mer-
cury, cadmium, arsenic; all in a heavy base, maybe used motor oil. The
boys tell me it'd burn in an oil furnace."

Halvorsen nodded. "So what do I do now?"

"Not a thing," she said. "I'll fax this in to the proper people. They may
want to call—I mean, go out and see you, to follow this up. You might
want to stay close to home. I have a feeling things will move fast once they
read this analysis. But basically you've done your duty as a citizen, and I
for one thank you."

"And the boy. I put him in the write-up too."

"Yes, him too." Friedman smiled and stood up. "By the way, your face
looks better."

"Thanks," said the old man. He had risen too, when she did, but when
he got to the door he paused and turned. "That reminds me. How much
I owe you? For the hospital?"

"Don't worry about it."

"Don't worry about it?"

"Don't worry about it."

"I don't take charity."

"This isn't charity."

"It isn't?"

"No."

Halvorsen stood in the doorway for a moment more. But he couldn't
think of anything else to say. So he put on his hat and went out again,
back into the rain.

Twenty

The old Thunner mansion stood alone above the town among massive oaks, granite-solid on what had once been a forest bench and was now terraced lawn. Buttresses of yellow light streamed from its windows, footed on the soaked grass. Through each golden slant darted the rain.

It was built in Gothic Romanesque of an intricately carved local stone. Two-storied, but a turret reached to four, and the clustered columns of a huge porch gave the effect of an arcade. Behind beveled glass and falls of damask, shadows moved, pausing now and then to lift glasses, to talk. Music came faintly across the lawn, but died in the misty air before it reached a spike-topped wall.

Brad stood at the window of the garden room, looking out. Security lighting picked out the walks and cold frames. Past that was the dim bulk of the arbor, and the pale glow of the fountain Colonel Charles Thunner had imported from Chioggia. But beyond and above them was only the blackness of the hill, bare at first, then forest.

He was remembering how three years before his father-in-law, still walking then, had taken him to the mountain. Not far above them was the long-abandoned site of the first producing well in the Seneca Sands, drilled in 1869 by the legendary Beacham B. Thunner and his hunchbacked partner Napoleon O'Connor at the very outset of the company's history. Back then it was the Sinnemahoning Seneca-Oil Company. After O'Connor was killed in a boiler explosion, it became Thunner Sinnemahoning; then Thunder Sinnemahoning; then, and for the last hundred years, just the Thunder Oil Company. Old Dan, leaning on Lark Jones's arm, had stood for a long time silent, looking out over valley and hills and the distant towers of Number One, before he'd said: "So you want to marry Ainslee."

He took an icy swallow of martini and turned back into the house.

In the study the quartet was finishing the last movement of Pachelbel's "Spring." Violin and bass viol penetrated century-old stone and timber like incense. Fires crackled in the bar, the living room, the dining room, the upstairs den. In the foyer hung steel engravings and oil portraits of Beacham Berwick Thunner, Colonel and Mrs. Charles Thunner, and Dan and Lutetia Thunner; the latest was of Ainslee, aged ten. In the dining room was a Bronzino portrait, a small Jean Clouet, and a Correggio Amazon.

Above, in the master bedroom, his wife lay under the valances with an arm over her eyes.

In the bar Dr. Patel, Peter Gerroy, and his third wife, Melizabeth, were listening to Vince Barnett, chairman of the Recreation Association, tell fishing stories. In the billiard room, where Charles's massive slate table had once stood, three people in their early twenties—sons and daughters of the older guests—were gaping up at the head of an African elephant. In the oak-paneled dining room, imported from a Tudor manor house in Kent, Rudolf Weyandt, Charlie Whitecar, and a Deep Pit businessman who was a member of the State Ethics Commission were discussing capital gains taxes with a real-estate woman and a young Frenchwoman visiting from Paris.

And rising now from their folding chairs in the study were the chamber group, from the University of Pittsburgh at Petroleum City, and the rest of the evening's guests, including Dr. Kopcik, Mayor White, several university department chairmen, the chairman of First Raymondsville Bank, Rogers McGehee, a former county Republican Party chairman, a visiting Episcopal bishop, the presidents or their representatives from most of the local manufacturing firms, and most of the other people worth saying one knew in Hemlock County.

As they moved past him into the dining hall Brad shook hands, inviting them to help themselves to after-dinner liqueurs, desserts and coffees, or to refresh themselves at the bar. He waved the mayor aside and told him smilingly that if he didn't want to cause a divorce he'd have to take his cigar into the garden room. White guffawed and headed for the rear of the house, trailing a tangible aroma.

He ran his eye over the fireplaces, the bar, the catered tables, the stolid women who stood behind them. Everything looked fine. Still he wished Ainslee was here. This was his third pre-Christmas party at The Sands, a traditional occasion for opening the house in town to a wider hospitality than the family's, but he still didn't feel entirely used to it, entirely at ease.

He chatted for a while with the banker and then some of the board

members' wives, then made a leisurely orbit through the house. The barman, borrowed from the club, was doing a brisk business. The French girl
was playing Gershwin on the Steinway. Through the window, out on the
lawn, he glimpsed the silver-sewn arc of the security guard's flashlight. He
put his head in the kitchen; the cooks and servers were having their own
late dinner.

He'd decided to have another martini when a round thirtyish man put
his hand on his arm and said, "Jack asked me to tell you, he's sorry he
couldn't make it. He hopes he can next year, but with the tax vote coming
up, he wanted to stay close to first base."

Brad nodded and smiled; DeSilva was Jack Mulholland's chief of staff.
"Well, I'm glad you could come, Andy."

He started to move away, gin still foremost in his mind, but the aide
touched his arm again. "Got somebody I want you to meet. Took the
liberty of bringing him along."

"Sure, hell, more the merrier. Who is it?"

"Name's Nicholas Leiter. He's from the executive side"—DeSilva
winked—"but he keeps in touch. Nick! C'mon over. Here he is, right
here."

Leiter was slim, young or young-looking. Brad thought it couldn't all
be the tortoiseshell glasses and bow tie. They shook hands warmly.

"Well, what brings you to P.C., Mr. Leiter?"

"I thought we might talk for a minute."

"Oh?"

"Mr. Leiter's from one of our alphabet-soup federal agencies," said
DeSilva, tapping his foot as the piano segued to the "Maple Leaf Rag."
"He just got in from Philly. Gave Jack a call before he arrived. Professional
courtesy."

"I see." He thought about that. "Looks like you could use a refill, my
friend. Join me?"

"I'm okay," said Leiter, examining his glass and then raising his eyes
quizzically.

"Well . . . let's go up to the den."

He'd had the turret room redecorated the year before. There was a
fireplace there now and a small bar by the curved window that looked
down on the terrace and the garden. The walls were covered in aubergine
suede. He'd left Dan's pictures, though: wildlife and Western studies by
Charles Deas, Stanley, Remington, and Russell. He hitched up his slacks
and sat on the corner of the desk, nodded to a wing chair. "Grab a seat.
What can I do for you, Mr. Leiter?"

"I thought I'd ask you that." The young man took out a pipe. "You
mind?"

"Go ahead," said Brad, watching him.

Leiter began stuffing the pipe; he touched the tobacco only with the tips of his fingers. "Mr. Boulton, I work for the Environmental Protection Agency."

"Is that so," Brad said after a moment.

"Yes. It's like this. We got a report that hazardous wastes are being dumped in this county. Not just once, appears there've been several instances. It might be an ongoing operation. We've seen the profile before. Often there's mob involvement."

"What kind of wastes?"

Leiter shot a glance up at him and said, a trifle louder, "Hazardous chemicals." He lit the pipe, waving the lighter over the bowl.

"Go on."

"I'm not a regular investigator. The agency's shorthanded. As usual. Anyway, on the flight up I happened to think of Andy. So I called him from the airport."

"DeSilva's a good man. Where do you know him from?"

"Friend of a friend. He suggested I stop in and see the Thunners. So I went over to your estate this afternoon to talk to your father."

"Father-in-law, actually."

"Uh huh. But your butler, or whoever he is, told me he wasn't in charge anymore. That you are. So I called Andy back and he laughed and said I was at the wrong house, that you had two places, and you'd be at this one today. He said to come over here and he'd introduce me."

He'd been wanting that drink more and more and now he crossed to the bar and poured a brandy. He listened to the distant piano. Below, in the garden, a flashlight came on, probed around, and went out. He said, keeping his voice casual, "You said something about having a question."

"Well, I'll make this brief, Mr. Thunner—"

"Boulton."

"Sorry. Mr. Boulton. Somebody's dumping waste on the roads up here. We've got a chemical analysis by a reputable source. Evil stuff, all right. It's apparently affected some of the local residents. Now, as I said, we've seen midnight dumping before. And dealt with it. The director regards it seriously. She's just put two men away in Georgia. They bought a warehouse, piled five thousand drums of banned pesticides, hexane, and paint sludge in it, and set it on fire. Fifteen years each."

"What's that got to do with me?"

"Exactly." Leiter blew smoke toward the track lighting. "What has it got to do with you? Seventy-one percent of toxic waste comes from the chemical and petroleum industries. In this county that's you, mister."

Brad grinned. He swallowed the rest of the brandy and set the snifter down. "Have you visited our plant, Mr. Leiter? Come by anytime. Thunder Oil's had an outflow monitor in place for five years. We employ a Ph.D. in chemistry to keep an eye on it. Monthly reports. On file.

"As to toxics, we don't make 'em, and use very little in our business.

We're a fuel, lube-oil, and feedstock company. I don't want to sound smug, but I'll match our environmental responsibility against any other small refinery in the United States."

Leiter nodded. He smoked his pipe for a while and then said, almost sadly, "We've got an eyewitness."

"To what?"

"A Thunder Oil truck doing the dumping."

"What? When?"

"A week ago. Monday night."

Brad reached for the bottle again, then withdrew his hand. He sat down behind the desk and looked at Leiter. "So," the young man said, "That's about it from my end, sir."

Brad put his fingers together. He looked out the dark square of window, conscious at the periphery of sight of the younger man, relaxed in the wing chair, looking blandly at him while he tamped his pipe. Okay, Mr. Philadelphia, he said to himself. Are we playing chess here, or poker? He decided it was chess.

He went over what he knew. The man was not a regular investigator. He knew Jack Mulholland. He also knew, or had taken the trouble to look up, the name of his home-office aide. When he added that up, he got a lower-level political appointee. Limited tenure. He'd be out next election, if not sooner.

Next, Leiter hadn't started the investigation yet. He didn't have the specifics. Nor did he give the impression of caring too much about them.

He sat for a minute more, going over everything again to make sure there were no gaps in his reasoning. Then he stretched in his chair and said, "Do you like saunas, Nick?"

Leiter looked surprised for just a moment. Then he smiled. "I love saunas, Brad."

Stripped, they sat opposite each other in the cedar-scented atmosphere. The electric grate ticked softly; he'd set the thermostat at eighty-five, comfortable in bare skin, but not high enough to make them sweat. He looked at Leiter again; slim, pale, bony legs, a long thin dick. His biggest handicap in whatever was coming off here was twofold. He didn't know exactly who Leiter was, and he wasn't sure Leiter knew who Brad Boulton was. He decided to start the ball rolling on the latter and see how the other reacted.

"I guess you know, Nick, I'm on the Committee to Re-elect Jack Mulholland."

"I didn't, but that's great. We need more fiscal conservatives like Jack on the Hill."

"I contributed to Senator Buterbaugh's campaign, too. And Thunder

Oil's a contributing member to several PACs and to the state victory committee."

Leiter nodded. Brad stared at his placid face, suddenly annoyed. "The point being, Mr. Leiter, that if you plan to come into this district with wild accusations against me or my company, you won't find yourself in very good standing with the Republican Party."

The other man smiled around the pipestem. "I'm not too worried about that. I'm not a Republican."

"Christ. Then what are you doing here? Put them on the table, Leiter, or get out of my house and do your goddamned snooping on somebody else's time."

"Okay. You know Richard Mill."

"The columnist? Of course."

"I'm his son."

"Mill?"

"He was married to Norma Leiter at one time. Actually it's Nick Leiter-Mill, but I dropped the hyphenation."

"Well, well, well." Brad nodded. "Any political ambitions?"

"Watch."

Brad thought for a while more, then turned the thermostat down. "Ready to get dressed?"

While they were buttoning their shirts he said, "I suppose I should thank you, then, for coming by here. It'd be good press for you to crucify me."

"It certainly would."

"I'm not saying whatever was reported to you has any foundation in fact."

"I understand that."

"But this isn't a good time even for rumors. Please treat this as confidential. The company's going into a major reorganization. As part of it there'll be a four-for-one split and a new floater of a million shares of stock. The initial price will be a hundred thirty-five." He paused. "Let's say a hundred shares of that goes into an account with a number I call you with next week."

Leiter chuckled. Brad felt his nose flare; the little snot was laughing at him. He was about to turn on his heel when the other man said, "This *is* back in the sticks, isn't it? I can't accept stock in your company! For Christ's sake, Brad, this isn't 1880!"

"Why not? If it's for a campaign contribution . . ."

Leiter just smiled and kept shaking his head.

"Well, I can't make it as much if it's cash."

"Now we're going *way* back. I don't want cash either."

"Well—I assumed . . ." He stopped, his sense of danger suddenly reactivated. Yet he'd seen the man naked; and he knew there was no possibility of bugging the house. "Look, maybe I'm off base here. Then what do you want?"

"First let's make sure we're straight on the main issue. Am I going to hear any more about this dumping?"

"No. You won't hear another word," said Brad. "I'll make that a personal guarantee."

"There you are. So why make a big deal of it? Investigations, litigation, that costs the government money too. But what I could use . . ." He paused. "Have you ever heard of something called soil remediation?"

"No."

"It's new. Promises to solve a lot of problems. You know we've got all these Superfund sites, a lot of contaminated soil around the country, they've got to be cleaned up. We thought once we could burn it, but nobody wants a huge incinerator in their back yard. The Agency's really on the spot for this one. But how are we going to do it?"

"I don't know. And I don't care."

"Genetically engineered bacteria, that's how, Brad. The contaminated soil's scraped up and trucked to remediation plants. They tailor the bacteria to the waste and turn them loose. Friendly little germs, eating up the bad chemicals and turning them into harmless dirt. Who pays? The government will be happy to pay. The federal government will be *overjoyed* to pay. The money is already in the budget. We can't figure a way to spend it fast enough."

"You're starting to interest me, Nick."

"I suspected I might. Well, some people have gotten in touch with me. One of them a friend, we went to school together, Yale. They've got the process. A fantastic new development. Their bugs multiply a hundred times faster than anything anyone else can show. As it happens, I'm in a position to award contracts for a pilot plant. All we need is a place to try it out."

"I see," said Brad, thinking it out. Remembering his own thoughts about how to expand in years to come. It was as if his own foresight had brought Leiter to him. "Well . . . I could talk to them. On one condition."

"Which is?"

"I'd like to reserve some of the stock in that partnership, or corporation, or whatever form it takes, for later distribution. You won't be at EPA forever, now, will you? And after you've started that political career you mentioned, campaign donations will be acceptable, won't they?"

"I think we understand each other, Brad. In broad, general terms. The specifics you can discuss with my friend."

They shook hands. "I'm glad I came out here to meet you. I thought we could help each other," Leiter said. "But now, I imagine you want to go back to your guests. So I'll just head back to the hotel."

"Well, it's been interesting. Oh. By the way."

"Yes?"

"You mind telling me who reported this? The dumping?"

"No problem, it's public record." Leiter pulled a folded paper from his sport coat. "Keep that, it's a copy."

"Thanks. Stop by the bar, take a bottle of Pinch with you."

"Can't do it. But thanks. Good night."

When Leiter left Brad poured himself another brandy. He was pondering the paper when there was a knock. He slid it into a drawer. "Yeah!"

"Mr. Boulton, somebody want to see you."

"Thanks, Melissa . . . Well, come on! Don't stand around out there, don't be a weluctant wabbit!"

It was Williamina, sleepy-looking and pouty in blue pajamas and her mouse slippers. He filled his arms with her, felt her hands warm on his neck. He lifted her and buried his nose and lips in her golden hair. She clung like a little monkey, and he laughed, forgetting everything but her.

"How's your new nursie, Bunny? You and Melissa getting along?"

"She's nice. She sings to me."

"Well, that's good. And what do you think of her, Melissa? She behaving herself?"

"She about the nicest child I ever did see, Mr. Boulton."

"Uh huh, between the two of us we'll spoil her good. Is it time for bed already?"

"Lord, Mr. Boulton, it's way past ten o'clock!"

"Is it? Well, Punkin, guess we got to say good night."

"No. No, Daddy!"

"Willie, darlin', come on now. Give us a kiss, then let's see the last of you till morning."

The child began to cry. "Oh, now. She excited," said the nurse, coming forward and holding out her arms. "It's the party and all, Mr. Boulton. Come on now, let go your daddy."

He kissed her one last time, feeling tears hot on his lips, then disentangled her from his neck. He was surprised to feel his eyes burning too. He said, "I'll look in after the party, see if she's asleep. Good night, now, Punkin. Daddy loves you."

Pouting, the little girl did not reply as her nurse carried her from the den.

After things wound down, a little before one, he went through the house. He found two of the young people in the guest bedroom, and closed the door on them quietly. Jones was sitting pensively in front of the dying embers in the Tudor fireplace. Brad asked him to check the rest of the rooms and the grounds, then he could turn in. He pulled his tie off, poured a nightcap, and hoisted himself slowly up the stairs again.

Ainslee was lying face down on the bed, almost as he'd left her at eight, but she'd taken off the dress. He stood uncertainly above her. "You awake?" he muttered.

"No."

"How's the headache?"

"Shitty. Go away."

He looked down at her for a while, noting the wide muscular shoulders, so unexpected on her small body; the smooth swell of her calves. She kept herself in shape, you had to say that. At last he sat down beside her and began tentatively rubbing her neck. Her skin was softer than the silk slip. She didn't say anything so he kept on rubbing, his mind moving to the way the French girl's eighteen-year-old breasts had swayed as she hammered out Scott Joplin. When his hands got to hers she said, into the pillow, "Don't bother."

"What's wrong now?"

"Nothing's wrong. I just feel rotten and I don't want a drunk in my room."

"Did you take your—"

"Go *away*. You smell like a distillery."

He took his hands off her and sat there for a while, wishing he knew what to do with her. Or just what to do. At last he went into the shared bathroom and brushed and flossed his teeth. When he came out he pulled the chair up to her bedside and said, "That new nurse seems to be working out."

"We'll see. I didn't expect her to be black. How did the party go?"

"All right. We had a problem surface, though."

After a moment she said, "What?"

"Andy DeSilva got me aside and introduced me to a guy he brought. He was from the EPA. Had a report about midnight dumping. I took him up to the den, we talked, and I resolved the situation, I think."

Ainslee Boulton rolled over and sat up. She put one hand to her left eye and dark hair whispered down over bare shoulders like an eclipse. "Oh my God. You paid him off?"

"Well, not in so many words."

"My God, you *idiot*! What if he was wired?"

"I made sure he wasn't."

"I don't see how. How much did it cost us?"

"Nothing. He wants me to talk to a friend of his. About some kind of government-funded chemical treatment plant. It sounded interesting. So I said, okay."

"That's all?"

"That's all. Oh, and to hold some of the stock for him."

"You know it won't stop there."

"Well, I don't know. Why shouldn't it?"

"Who reported it?"

"Apparently two people off the street, right here in the county."

"Did you get their names?"

"Yes."

"Well, that's a break, anyway."

Her tone was a little warmer. He hesitated, then moved onto the bed. She turned her shoulders, inviting his hands like a pampered cat. He rubbed her back for a while, then said, "I'm thinking of pulling out of that business. It's getting too dangerous. People reporting it . . . I promised Leiter I'd stop it."

"Stop dumping," she said, her voice muffled by the pillow, "or stop them reporting it?"

"I don't know . . ."

"You don't just 'pull out' with people like that. They'll never let go a sweet deal like this." She was silent a moment. "But you're right, once the reorganization's complete, we won't need them anymore. But then how do we get rid of them? Anyway, till the stock issue's sold, what would we use for cash?"

"I don't know. Borrow it."

"Brad, wake up. We can't borrow without losing control."

When he didn't say anything she pushed his hands off and got up. She rummaged through the drawers of an Art Deco dresser, found pills and swallowed two. "This goddamn migraine . . . Brad, one of these days my father is going to die. And then we'll have to fight for our lives. I don't know if you realize it, but Weyandt and those other jerks you keep around have all got their knives pointed in your direction."

"Rudy's our friend."

"Rudy makes fucking Machiavelli look like Pope Pius the Twelfth. Plus you've got Pennzoil, Quaker State, Kendall crowding us. If we lose any more market share in motor oil, K-Mart and Walgreen's will drop Thunder Premium. Our dealer network's crumbling away. We lost ten stations this year to the cut-rates and we only built three. If we falter they'll defect all at once. And we can't fall back to being a producer anymore. Our lease lands are security on what we've already borrowed."

"I know that, Ainslee."

"If a company stops growing it starts to rot. My father never realized that. He thought he could park Thunder Oil in 1949. I thought you'd see that things were different, that they had to change."

"I do." He looked around her room dully. "You got anything to drink in here?"

"You've had enough. Sometimes you scare me, Brad. This reorganization won't just happen, it's got to be rammed through. At the same time we've got to take the old-liners on the board with us. You're the rammer; I'm the legitimacy."

"I understand all that."

"Then I shouldn't have to tell you that we've got to keep dividends and net worth up so the offer sells. That means you've got to keep Newark, and the nursing homes, and the other cash cows on the line." Her tone had passed gradually into scorn. "Is it getting too rough for you? Is that it?"

"No."

"I wonder. Somebody reported you to the government. Get serious! My family didn't build this company by letting nobodies kick us around! If you can't find the guts to run a company you can go back where I found you, turning down high school boys for car loans."

Seeing her now, straight and proud and angry, he suddenly felt sad. He was tired of fighting. For a moment he wished he could tell her everything. To his surprise he heard himself mutter, "Well, sometimes I get scared."

"What?"

"I said, sometimes I'm not so sure I can handle this. It's getting too complicated."

"Are you serious? Is that why you got drunk?"

"Yeah."

She came over and stood above him, smoothed his hair, smiling distantly. "Well, it won't be for long. Once the divisions are in place we can get some decent middle management. Then you won't have to do everything yourself. We'll be able to sit back and kibitz from Cherry Hill, or New York if we want."

Somewhere in his drink-slowed brain he wondered if she could mean it. That was the trouble with Ainslee Thunner. You never knew. It sounded nice. Get decent executives. Sit back in Manhattan. But it wasn't him. Once he had his own board in place he wasn't going to let go. And Ainslee sure as hell wasn't either. After three years with her he knew that.

It didn't matter, he was too close now to worry about it. Once The Thunder Group was a reality he wouldn't need her fucking "legitimacy." He didn't even like the word . . . But even drunk he knew he couldn't say that, couldn't so much as hint it. If she ever suspected that she would truly become dangerous.

It occurred to him then, feeling her hand smooth his hair, that once the reorganization was over she wouldn't need him either. What was she thinking? What did that dark head contain, not two feet above his own, but inaccessible as the far side of the moon?

But the room was spinning, and he was so tired that the thought slipped away. Her hand paused; she was waiting for a response. He mumbled, "I hope we can do that, Ainslee. You and me and Willie."

"We will." Her hand patted him, once, then he heard her move away.

He took a deep shuddering breath. "I wish you and Williamina got along. I wish we still loved each other."

"It's kind of late for that, Brad. Let's just try to keep what we have."

He realized as he pulled the sheets back in his own room that he hadn't looked in on his daughter. But it was late, and he felt dizzy and sad and he thought, tomorrow morning. The huge old house was quiet around him; and outside, in the garden, the flashlight swung over the netted humps of the bushes, over the ancient fountain, and then winked out.

Twenty-one

The librarian looked at her, Jaysine thought, as if she'd proposed sharing the disease with her, instead of asking for a book on the subject. "If you have one," she finished, lowering her voice still more.

"I'll see. Something like that would not be in our open stacks, of course."

When she went away Jaysine straightened, sighing, and looked around, unbuttoning her coat.

The Raymondsville Public Library had been endowed ninety years before by a Scottish millionaire. Since then the busts of Ben Franklin and Chief Cornplanter, the models of clippers and locomotives in glass cases, the chromos of David's "Death of Socrates" and Rembrandt had aged. Even the librarians looked as if they could use a good meal. Or maybe, she thought, drinks all around.

"This way, Miss."

She followed the assistant's upswept hair out through the reading room—there was only one other person there, a boy reading magazines—and back into the stacks. The narrow dim aisles smelled of steam heat, book dust, and oxidizing paper. The woman reached up from time to time to pull strings that dangled from the ceiling. Finally she stopped.

"This is it. Our restricted collection. Anything we might have on, that kind of thing would be filed here."

Jaysine accepted the key and looked at the wire-mesh door. The footsteps tapped away into mortuary hush. At last she turned the key in the old-fashioned padlock and stepped inside.

Phil stared fascinated at the *National Geographic.*

A town near Detroit had discovered 33,000 drums of wastes from steel mills, chemical plants, and refineries, filled with millions of gallons of polychlorinated biphenyls, cyanide, and hydrochloric acid. It was leaching into the town's reservoirs with every rain.

The sewers had blown up in Louisville, Kentucky, when an animal-food plant used them to dispose of used hexane.

The government had bought a whole town in Missouri because a contractor sprayed dioxin-laced oil on the streets to control dust. It was evacuated and paved over, but former residents were still dying.

A company in Los Angeles had built a secret pipeline to discharge into the city's sewer system.

A pesticide called EDB had been banned because it caused mutations. But American companies still sold it overseas, and it came right back on imported fruits and vegetables.

Apparently anyone who wanted was free to make defoliants, herbicides, pesticides, DDT, PBP's, dioxin, chlordane, without any supervision at all. It was illegal to dispose of them without rigorous safeguards. But there were only thirty inspectors in the whole United States, and they were powerless to arrest dumpers even if they caught them in the act.

Toxic chemicals, he read, caused miscarriages, cancer, birth defects, liver damage, nervous disorders, brain damage, blood diseases, Hodgkin's disease, convulsions, seizures, nosebleeds, hyperthyroidism, and death. PCB persisted so long it would still be measurable in the great-great-grandchildren of those exposed. Dioxin was two hundred times more lethal than strychnine, and its first sign was a skin rash.

He thoughtfully examined the rash on the back of his hand.

Since there was no legal place to put it, organized crime had taken over. They accepted waste, got paid for disposing of it, then sprayed it over regular trash and shipped it to city dumps. They pumped it into abandoned mines. They rented warehouses, filled them, and torched them. They mixed it with heating oil and sold it; forty percent of the oil sold in New York City was laced with PCBs or benzene.

He read with a shock of recognition in the *Reader's Digest* about tank-truck dumping. The drivers opened their spigots along the Jersey Turnpike in rainy weather. Others had been caught doing it further north, in rural Connecticut.

He scratched his hand, wondering if he'd die. Probably not. But one article said sometimes chemical rashes never went away.

He leaned back in the deserted library and watched a lone fly wander among the light-globes. Only the one directly above him was lit.

His musings were interrupted by a woman who came out of the stacks carrying a book. He watched as she looked around, then came over to his table. She was short, blond, and wore glasses.

"Hi."

"Hi."

"This is the only light. Do you mind if I read here?"

"Sure, go ahead."

She sat down and he looked back at the article. She looked familiar. He glanced up from the page, but couldn't place her. She was older than he was, but not bad-looking. He tried to see what she was reading, but couldn't make it out.

There wasn't much in the special collection. Was syphilis really incurable? Why was she taking shots for it, then? She turned to the front of the book and saw that it had been published in 1920.

She put it aside, glanced at the boy, and turned it so he couldn't see the title. She looked around. There was no one else in the library. The wall clock said four-thirty.

She took the notebook out of her purse.

It looked expensive. Limp leather binding and snap-out, replaceable pages. She flipped through them. Each had a printed date at the top.

Apparently he used it to list things to do, meetings to go to, inspections, appointments. There were a lot of chemical names. One page had a rough drawing of some kind of equipment. She flipped past it. There were also figures. Money stuff. *Bond yield, Hanover Trust, 1,500,000, 7.24%* was typical. She couldn't make much out of it. She wondered if the book had any value. Whether he missed it. She hoped he did, hoped he was going crazy missing it.

Jaysine wondered what she was going to do.

She had fifty-nine dollars in her checking account and the rent was due next week. There were two other shops in town, both smaller than Marybelle's; she didn't think there'd be any openings there. Well, there were other jobs. She'd bussed tables at school. She could sell dresses— no, she couldn't do that either, she suddenly realized. The first thing every woman in the Shoppe would have done when she left was tell the first person she met how Marybelle had thrown her out. And why. It was all over town by now, of that she was sure.

What could she do? Where could she go? Back to Four Holes? She couldn't stay there. Her mother didn't make enough practicing to support them both.

No, she thought with dread, I'm going to have to leave. Go someplace they don't know me. Maybe Norfolk; her brother could put her up for a couple weeks, she could help with the new baby till she found a place in a salon. She'd have to start all over again, get relicensed, buy new equipment.

But even a bus ticket would cost more than she had.

That left drawing unemployment. She didn't want to do that. But it wasn't as if she had a choice. She thought, trying to steel herself: If you've got to, do it. Go over and put your name in. Now, before they close for the day. It wasn't her fault. It was his, when all was said and done.

She wished Brad Boulton would die.

She sat motionless, remembering her other alternative. Signing Ainslee Boulton's piece of paper. It felt wrong. Maybe she should have asked how much she was willing to give, to sign it.

She decided not to make up her mind just then, and looked at the notebook again. All this about chemicals. What did it mean? Then she thought, Who cares. She was looking around for a trash can when she noticed one of the boy's magazines was *Chemical Engineering.*

"Do you read that?"

"What?" He looked up.

"Do you read that magazine? Do you know much about chemistry?"

"I'm taking it in school," Phil said cautiously.

She shoved the notebook across the table. "Can you read this?"

He examined the open page, then the next one. "Well," he said, "I can't tell you what it all means, but it's about oil. Ethane, pentane, octane, those are things you make out of it."

"Like at Petroleum City? The refinery?"

"Sure. Like, it says here, under November 9, *Ad agency: campaign for Thunder steam turbine oil,* and over here it talks about cutting premium unleaded with methanol." He glanced up at her. "Where'd you get this?"

"Found it."

"Uh huh . . . Well, you could probably mail it back to Thunder Oil and they could find out whose it is."

"I know whose it is."

"Oh." He thought about that briefly, then dismissed it. He scratched his rash and riffled the pages. For November 14 there were notes about laundry contracts and about a drop and then something about electric power conservation. He was about to ask her where she'd found it when she looked at the clock, took it back, and stood up, reaching for her coat. "Thanks," she said.

"Sure," he said. When he looked up again she was gone.

Mrs. Skinner came back not long after and told him he had to leave, they were closing. He went reluctantly, limping out into a cold wet wind.

Someone had made new stars, or polished the old ones; they glared clear and brilliant down through a billion miles of space. He pulled his scarf up and headed up the street, pondering what he'd read.

Mr. Maxwell talked about interest aggregation, how political parties picked up what people wanted and if they got voted in they did it. But it didn't seem to work that way. Sometimes democracy got polluted.

That didn't surprise him, that special interests got their way. What surprised him was how nobody seemed to care. If they cared they'd get action eventually. Like on air pollution, or air bags. But on this they didn't. You couldn't exactly see increased cancer rates, or more miscarriages, the way you could bad air. That was pretty much what the magazines said, too.

Anyway, the question wasn't what other people were doing about it, but what he was going to do. He wondered what Dr. Friedman had found out about the sample. He wished there was something exciting he could do meanwhile. Check out the license number? He thought fleetingly of using the squad car radio, but his voice was too high to fool anyone.

He fantasized his way down the street, daydreaming holding his father's gun on the trucker who'd jerked him up off freezing asphalt and said, "Whaddya think you're doing?"

But after a while cold penetrated his boots, bit his toes, made his fingers and dick numb; and he saw lights on in the building where his sister worked. He decided to go in and say hi, warm up for a minute, then head home.

Jaysine moved slowly through the line. All the others were men. They smelled of old sweat, tobacco, liquor. She clutched her purse and when she came up to the little window said shyly, "Hello."

The woman behind it said, "Where's your card?"

"Card?"

"Are you here for the first time? Did you just lose your job?"

"Yes."

"You're in the wrong line, but you're lucky, the counselor's still in. Wait over there and I'll find her."

She was sitting in full view of the men when the swinging door opened and Karen came out from behind the counter. Jaysine saw her face go still, then flush. Her own cheeks heated, and she looked down at her purse. "Well," said the dark girl after a moment, "Jaysine. What are you doing here?"

"Applying for unemployment. What are you doing here?"

"I work here. Come on back."

The desk wasn't private. They sat down. "Well, you were there," Jaysine said after an awkward pause.

"Yes, and I thought it was terrible. I thought you were doing a wonderful job." Karen turned even redder and fussed in a drawer. She whispered, "I know you were helping me."

"I didn't know you worked here."

"It's only till I start school again."

"Oh. Well, I don't have any money saved. So I guess I thought, well, I'll apply for unemployment."

Karen's eyes went past her shoulder; she waved to someone. Jaysine didn't look because at the same time she asked, "How long had you been working at the Shoppe?"

"Almost a year."

"And why did your employment terminate?"

"You were there. Didn't you hear?"

"This is for the form."

"Oh. Well, I quit."

"Yes, but . . ." Karen's blush grew still deeper. "The thing is, if you . . . See, the rules say you have to be laid off to get unemployment assistance. If you leave voluntarily you're not eligible. And we have to verify that with the employer before we issue you a card, to draw benefits."

Jaysine sat still. Too late, she saw how cleverly the old woman had manipulated her into saying the very words that would hurt her most. How Marybelle must hate her!

Karen looked unhappy.

"I wish I could help some other way. A recommendation, or something. Let me know if I can."

"That's all right," said Jaysine again. Then, to her horror, she began to cry.

Phil stood uncertainly behind the woman, looking past her at his sister. He'd recognized her as the one from the library. From what little he'd heard it sounded like they knew each other, so he thought it was okay to come up to the desk. But now she was crying, and Kay looked flustered. "Hello, Philip," she said.

"Hi. What's going on?"

The woman twisted around. "Oh. It's you . . . I just lost my job."

"Oh. That's too bad. You'll pick something else up, though."

"I don't think so. Not around here."

"Did my sister help you?"

"Who?"

"Kay. She's the counselor here."

"Oh, Karen. Are you his sister? No, she couldn't help." She looked away from them both. "Doesn't seem like anyone can. I don't know what I'm going to do. I don't have any money to go anyplace else, or live on . . ."

On impulse he said, "Here."

"Phil!" said his sister, in a shocked voice.

"It's my money, Kay . . . It's not much. I was saving it, but I don't need it. Go ahead, take it."

"I don't want your money."

"Go on. You can pay me back when you get another job."

She wouldn't take money from a strange man, even if he was only a kid. She said, "No. But tell you what."

"What?"

"I'll let you buy me a drink."

"A drink?" He sounded stupid even to himself, and tried to recover with, "Oh sure. Sure, yeah, we can do that. Where you want to go?"

"Phil," said his sister.

"I don't care. Anywhere."

"We could go to the Brown Bear, or Sherlock's—"

"I like Sherlock's."

"Okay."

"Phil!" said his sister for the third time, in her *I am appalled* voice. He smiled at her and went out.

It felt strange, walking with an older woman. He wondered if any of the guys would see them. He wondered if she was a hooker. Then thought: Get serious. They don't apply for unemployment.

"So what did you do?" he asked her.

"What?"

"Before you got fired. What'd you use to do?"

"I was at the Style Shoppe. On Pine Street."

"Oh. Fixing hair?"

"Beauty culture. Yes."

Tuesday night, Sherlock's was almost empty. Phil looked around as he took her coat. Years of Catechism and his mother's warnings had given bars the same aura of seductive danger as women, or the Baptist Church. It seemed not too threatening now, just dim and scuzzy, smelling of old smoke and beer and chalk. He pulled out a chair for her, then stopped. He was standing there, unsure what to say, when she looked up.

"You aren't old enough, are you."

"Uh—no. Not in P.A."

"I'll get it. You sit down."

To his disappointment she brought him back a pop. They sat and looked at the silent old Wurlitzer. Finally he said, "My name's Phil. Phil Romanelli."

"Oh, sorry. I'm Jaysine Farmer."

"Uh huh . . . did you figure out what that stuff meant?"

"Stuff?"

"In your little book."

"Oh. No. What were you doing? Studying?"

"No. Something more important."

"What?"

He took a swallow of pop, thinking about it, and couldn't see any harm in boasting a little. "Well, me and another guy, an old guy, we're tracking down some criminals."

"Really?"

"Uh huh."

"What kind of criminals?"

"Midnight dumpers, they're called."

"What do they dump?"

"Toxic chemicals. Dangerous stuff nobody wants."

"They dump it in people's yards, or what?"

"No, no. On the roads. I caught one. We're reporting them to the state."

"Aren't you afraid they'll do something to you?"

"Like what?"

"Beat you up, or something—I don't know."

His tongue checked his loose front tooth. "I been beat up before. I'm not scared of that."

"You're pretty brave. You said you caught one? How?"

"Well, we took turns watching Route Six, down by Candler Hill. Finally saw one late at night, a tanker, just letting stuff run out the back out onto the road. I chased it on my bike and got a license number."

"You're pretty brave," she said again.

There was something strange in the way she said it and he looked quickly up at her. She'd taken her glasses off, coming in from the cold, and he realized again that she was kind of nice looking.

Now she got up and went to the bar and when she came back she was carrying another Coke. She pushed it over to him. It tasted funny. He realized it had rum in it. "Tell me some more."

He told her what he'd learned in the library. Halfway through it he pulled off his glove and showed her the rash. "Mr. Halvorsen got one like it, on his face. Must have breathed some, too, because he was in the hospital for a week. And there's a snowplow driver sick, and a family that bought some of the oil to burn in their furnace, and others, too, the doctor told me."

"What doctor?"

"Dr. Friedman, down at Maple Street. She's helping us on this."

"I know her." Jaysine sipped ginger brandy. She didn't feel angry at the doctor. She'd just done her job. It was Marybelle who'd decided that "taking precautions" meant humiliating and firing her. "Do you think they'll do anything about it?"

"Well, they've got to now we caught them. Racks—that's Mr. Halvorsen—

he's reporting it, like I said, so all we're doing now is waiting for them to get here and take charge."

"Well, I wish you luck," she said.

Phil asked her, "Have you decided what you're going to do?"

"My mom lives up in Four Holes. I might have to go back there. I don't want to."

"Jaysine, why'd you quit your job?"

She had been wondering when he'd ask that. She thought about telling him, but couldn't. "Oh, the owner tricked me into quitting. That way she got to keep my equipment."

"What kind of equipment?"

She caught herself just in time; the kid didn't need to know that about his sister. "Just hairdressing stuff. Anyway, thanks for the drink. I needed one. Maybe I'll see you around town."

She got up, hesitated. "Or you could come up sometime. To talk. I don't know many people in town. You know Gray's Drug? I'm in the apartment upstairs, next door, over the Woolworth's." She laughed softly. "I don't know for how long."

"Uh, thanks. Maybe sometime."

"Good night."

" 'Night."

He looked after her thoughtfully. What did that mean? He wondered how well she knew his sister. He wondered if—

"Hey!"

It was the bartender, a big old guy, coming down on him like a bear after garbage. Phil got up hastily. "I was just leavin'," he said.

"You better be. Don't come in here again till you're of age, kid. I'm not losin' my license over you."

Outside, he stood in the street for a moment, looking at the stars. Catching crooks, invited up by a blonde, and now he'd just been thrown out of a bar.

He had to admit it, things were looking up.

Twenty-two

The old man stood at the top of the steps, looking at the sky. Behind his contemplative stillness a stand of blue spruce consulted in whispers. Below him Town Hill fell away, dotted with the tarnished pewter of beech trunks. Above it all the clouds rushed past silent and swift and gray.

Jamming his numbing hands into his coat, shutting his eyes, Halvorsen squeezed the stale smells of the cellar from his lungs, then drew cold air like fine steel wire through his nostrils.

Snow.

He shivered—under the coat was only a sleeveless undershirt—and headed for the woodpile. Before he got there he stopped. Looked around again, frowning, though nothing moved and no sound came.

The spruces whispered, but gave no answer. He stayed alert as he selected five chunks of aged hardwood.

In the cellar, moving with the economy of old habit, he tapped his stove latch free and fed the embers. Then closed it, and looked around the dim interior of his home.

He'd found the basement rock-cold, coming back, and it had taken a couple of days to get back to living temperature. He'd cleaned up, not exactly energetically—he still felt washed-out—but now the cans were picked up and the floor swept and the trash burned. The fire was sputtering like oil in an iron skillet and he could hear the coffee starting to boil.

"Feel like breakfast, Jez?"

The puppy followed her nose out from under the couch. She sniffed and stopped by the door, looking at him and whining, and after a moment he bent. "You're goin' to be a big old dog, ain't you?" he said, rubbing her head.

By the time she was finished outside he'd found a handful of dry chow and replenished her water dish from the pump. He poured himself a mug of coffee and added sugar and slow-flowing Carnation. Then set to work, shuffling in and out of the cold room with his ingredients.

Cup of flour, pinch of soda, two tablespoons of shortening. No buttermilk, but a little vinegar in the condensed milk remedied that lack. He mixed it, dusting his hands with more flour. He cut the dough with absorbed deliberation, round as silver dollars, and slid the pan into the baking compartment.

After a time he let himself down into the chair and had hot biscuits and syrup. Gray morning edged slowly in to light the room, the reloading bench, old magazines, clothes hanging from ten-penny nails in the beams. Just as it had ever been, for years and years and years.

The puppy snarled in the corner, tussling with a deer skull Halvorsen had picked up on one of his treks. He cleaned the plate, carried it to the sideboard, and refreshed his mug. Then sat down again, chewing over the thought that had just occurred to him.

He was wondering if he ought not to go back into town.

Trouble with that was he didn't want to. He'd seen more people in the last few days than he cared to for a long time. He felt like laying up here for a couple weeks at least. Just thinking, maybe reading a western, or going for a walk before it snowed again.

On the other hand, balancing in his mind like a powder-scale, was his pension check. He didn't mind what he ate anymore, but a puppy should eat right when it was growing or it wouldn't have a nose. He'd got Jez the year before, after his old hound had got herself shot. Wasn't the same kind but he figured that didn't matter, not at this late date.

Yeah, his check, supplies . . . and there were other things he ought to be checking on too.

He sighed, resigning himself, and began hunting around for his boots.

Later, dressed, he stood in front of the gun rack. He took one of the bundles down and unwrapped a corner of the oilcloth.

His old single-shot .22 Hornet. His eyes crinkled as his mind gave him a sudden picture of a bird, wary, big, and beautiful.

He'd seen the flock as he worked on the lease; he'd come across their scratchings here and there, and at last realized where they were roosting, in a stand of white pine on the dark side of Lacey Knees Hill. That November he'd told Jennie not to buy a Thanksgiving bird and took the rifle out with him when he went to work that morning. A little after dawn he'd parked up the road, out of sight, and climbed up a ravine to a grove of chestnut oaks. He'd stopped a good distance off, but where he could see up into the grove, and settled behind a log, laying a broken-off brow over him and the rifle.

They'd come into sight half an hour later, hens and young toms, big this late in the year but still under the sway of the old male. Through the four-power Fecker he could see every feather. He heard their "prip, prip, prip" clearly, the scratching and fluttering, but he didn't move. Just rested the rifle-stock on dead wood and waited, so still that after a while he'd heard a stir above him and knew two squirrels were chasing each other.

When the old tom stepped out of the bushes it took his breath away. Its bronze-black was iridescent in the sunlight, and its beard dragged in the dry leaves. Facing him, still ninety yards distant, he knew it wasn't coming any closer. So he swayed the barrel, like a branch moved by the wind. To get decent meat off a turkey you had to place the bullet just right. The picket-post settled toward the wingbutt and he eased off the safety. The high-velocity crack scattered the feeding hens and bounced back from the hills.

They'd had all the folks over that year, and his mother had remarked on the nutlike sweetness of the flesh.

Smiling slightly, Halvorsen glanced toward the bench. He still had his molds for the old Loverin gas-check bullet. Now he thought about it there should be a box of loaded hulls someplace. Must be twenty years old, but powder didn't stale. He rooted them out and dropped a few into his pocket. He worked the action several times, then put some light oil on a rag.

He slung it over his shoulder and said to the dog, "I'll be back pretty soon. You be good now."

He went to the door, but couldn't get it closed. The bitch kept wedging her head into the crack and crying. At last he gave up. He stood at the top of the steps, watching his breath drift away on the wind, and adjusted the sling. "So," he said grimly, "you just got to come along."

The puppy frisked and barked ecstatically around his ankles.

Shaking his head, he set himself into motion, headed down along the side of the hill. The puppy hesitated for a moment, glancing at him and then into the woods, before she ran after him, flop ears flapping.

The old man marched steadily, grateful the snow wasn't too deep yet. He had a long way to go. He caught the last tang of woodsmoke, then lost it in the clear heavy wind that told him it was going to be cold, very cold, and soon.

Mortlock Run. He'd lived up here for more decades than he cared to remember, but there was always something new to see. After a while the road dipped sharply and the woods moved up to wall it in. The road turned left and followed the creek awhile, not as steep, but the descent good for a man who was getting on in years.

There was no hurry. He stopped three or four times, perching on the bank or on a stump, husbanding his strength. The puppy cast about ahead of him. Once she stopped to sniff at the remains of a raccoon, bare bone now, crow-picked, subliming. By next fall it would be earth again. Halvorsen called her sharply away, then went on.

He'd dressed warm but now he unbuttoned the coat and put his earflaps up. The woods were quiet, the only moving beings blackbirds and a late hawk cruising far off.

He was thinking about the raccoon, and the other dead animals he'd seen along this road.

Who would do a thing like that? Dump poison where people lived, for money? He thought about it as he rested, worked at it as he walked. After a while it occurred to him to wonder why he'd taken the rifle along. The only answer he could come up with was that same nameless apprehension he'd felt at the woodpile.

He didn't get far along Route Six, a straight old man in red and black walking erect and a little stiff along the gravel berm, before a sedan pulled over. The rifle went in the back seat. The puppy was excited at being in a car and he held her on his lap the last few miles into Raymondsville.

They got out near Rosen's. Halvorsen thought of going in, saying hello, but remembered his missing check. Settle that first. He headed up Main Street toward the post office. A boy whistled at the puppy, but no one looked twice at the old man with the slung rifle.

There were three letters for him, all ad junk or *You May Have Won Millions*, which he dropped into the can by the ranks of brass boxes without opening. Then stood there, puzzled and a little annoyed. He generally got the check by the tenth, and here it was the sixteenth and nothing.

At the station the gas jockey said Fred was over in Olean getting parts, but he was welcome to use the phone. He propped himself at Pankow's desk, staring out through dirty glass at the pumps, and put a call in to the pension office. A girl answered and he said, "Lemme talk to Mickey."

"I'm sorry?"

"Mickey Zacharias, the manager."

"I'm sorry, sir, Mr. Zacharias is no longer with the company."

"What's that?"

"He's no longer with us. Would you like to speak to Mrs. Bridger?"

"I guess," he said grumpily.

After a while a woman came on the line. "May I help you?"

"This's William T. Halvorsen, Thunder Oil, retired. I ain't got my check this month yet."

"Let me call up that record. How do you spell your last name, sir?"

He told her. There was a pause, during which something tapped faintly at the other end. A deafening clang came from back in the repair bay, steel on concrete, followed by curses. One of the mechanics came out and

looked at him, looked at the rifle, propped in the corner; then jumped
back as the puppy attacked his oil-stained boots. He laughed and went
out to the pumps.

"Mr. Halvorsen?"

"Yeah."

"We have no record of your being a pensionable employee, sir. There
was a W. T. Halvorsen who worked for Thunder Oil back in the thirties,
but he was discharged."

"That's right, I was, but Dan hired me back."

"Well, we have no record of a rehire. I'm sorry."

"Wait a minute," said Halvorsen. "I got thirty years in with T.O. I been
gettin' my checks regular since I retired. What's the trouble? Seems to me
you better ask that machine again."

"I've checked our records, sir, and you're not on the pension list."

"Well, just call Mickey—"

"I've told you, Mr. Zacharias is no longer with the company, sir."

"Oh." Halvorsen thought for a while. "Well, call Dan then, he remembers me."

"Who's that?"

"What do you mean, 'Who's that?' Dan *Thunner*, don't you—"

"Mr. Halvorsen," the voice interrupted, brittle and young. "Mr. Thunner has taken no active interest in the company for years. If you think
you deserve benefits, write us a letter setting forth your position and it
will be considered. Have a good day."

Halvorsen stared at the receiver. Very slowly, his eyebrows crept up.

"I want to talk to the lady doctor."

"Just a moment, please."

When she came on the line he told her who it was. "Oh, Mr. Halvorsen,"
she said. Her voice dropped at the end.

"What's wrong?"

"Nothing seems to be going right this week. How are things with you?"

"Fair to okay. Look, you remember that paper I wrote up for the government? Did you send that in yet?"

"I sent it in that same day. Bad news, Racks. The inspector called back
from Philadelphia."

"What inspector?"

"Apparently he stopped by the hospital, but I was out. He picked up
the sample, though, from my secretary. He called me yesterday. Said he'd
checked it out and there was nothing to report."

"What do you mean? He was here, you say?"

"That's right."

"I never seen him. And he said there wasn't nothing to it? Hell, I mean, heck, we got 'em dead to rights. And you did them tests. How can he say there ain't nothing to it?"

"I don't know. Something about the oil being residue, or something. I'm as puzzled as you are. But at the moment I don't know what else to do."

"Who's this inspector fella?"

"I have a number here . . . Hold on. Got a pen?"

Halvorsen found a ballpoint in the drawer. He tried it on the corner of a Champion flyer. "Yeah. Go ahead."

"His name's Nicholas Leiter, and the phone is (215)597-9370."

"That's a lot of numbers."

"A lot of . . . how long has it been since you made a long distance call, Racks?"

"I don't know. 1958?"

"I see. Well, are you going to call him?"

"Maybe."

"Let me know what you find out."

"Okay."

Halvorsen hung up. He looked out at the street for a while, scratching the dog's head. At last he tore a piece off the flyer. FRED I USED YR PHONE TO CALL PHILLY. WILL PAY YOU WHEN I GET CHECK. HALVORSEN. Then he dialed in the numbers and listened to it ring.

"Office of the assistant director."

"This the operator?"

"The what? This is the district office, EPA, assistant director's office."

"Oh. Got a Nicholas Leiter there?"

"Yes, Mr. Leiter's the assistant director."

"This here's W. T. Halvorsen, Thunder Oil. Want to talk to him."

"What was that company again, sir?"

Halvorsen told her. A moment later he heard a young man's voice on the line. "Who's this? Brad?"

"This is W. T. Halvorsen."

"Who?"

"W. T. Halvorsen."

"Ah—well, how are you?"

"Fine, just fine."

"Is there something I can do for you, Sir?"

"It's about a report was sent up to you fellas last week," Halvorsen said. He leaned back, propping a boot up on the desk. "About some stuff bein' dumped on the roads up here. I wanted to see if you'd got time to look into it yet."

The voice went eager. "Yes, sir, I did. I remember your name now, sir. I traced that plate number. Then I flew up there and checked it out with the company that owns the truck. Turns out, though, the sample's just residual oil. What's left in the bottom from a delivery. The driver left the valve open and a little of it dripped out on the road. Thanks for your alertness, but you don't have anything to worry about up there."

"What kind of oil?"

"Lubricating oil. SAE low-30, I believe it was."

"I put in fifty years in the oil business up here, Mister. That wasn't no lube stock. You could tell that with your eyes closed, by the smell."

"Well, I'm afraid that's not what our analysis shows."

"Then your analysis's a lie," said Halvorsen.

Leiter sounded annoyed. "Mr. Halvorsen, I don't really know who you are—"

"Told you twice. Say, who'd you talk to up here?"

"Thunder Oil."

"Why didn't you talk to me? I'm the one filed the report."

"I'm satisfied with the investigation, Mr. Halvorsen. Unless you have something new to add I'm closing out the file on it."

"What was it they gave you? Money?"

"No money changed hands, Mr. Halvorsen, and I'd be careful about making remarks like that if I were you. There are slander statutes that can be invoked. I've got the sample bottle in front of me. There's nothing in it but Thunder Premium Lube Oil."

"Now, maybe," said the old man. He tried to calm himself. "Look, Mister, there's people sick up here cause of this. It's only going to get worse if it ain't stopped. You ought to think about what you're doing. You might be sorry you done it when you're older."

There was a peep on the line, almost too high for him to hear. "We're recording now, Mr. Halvorsen," came Leiter's voice, triumphant. "Please repeat the threat you just made."

The old man sat motionless in the overheated office, looking out at the gray sky. He didn't say anything, just listened to the electronic beep every few seconds.

Later he sat in the kitchen of the little house behind the station. His daughter was carefully pouring scalding milk into a mug of cocoa and saying, "Well, it's 'cause I worry about you."

"What's Fred got to say?"

"He'd be glad to have you. He's always complaining he can't get nobody to make change, clean up, things like that."

Halvorsen looked out the kitchen window, across the trodden-down brown grass of the back yard, to the garage. A rickety stair led up to a second-story door. Beyond it was the upper curve of the Texaco sign. In a sudden frenzy of barking the brown-and-black pup came tearing across the dead grass, followed by a Border collie. He sighed and reached for the sugar bowl. Alma brought down some cookies. He selected one and dipped it in the cocoa.

"I don't think so," he said.

"I wish you would."

"Well, I ain't goin' to, and that's an end of it."

"What's wrong, Pa?"

"Nothin', Alma. Just gettin' tired of people trying to make me do what they want."

"Well," she said. Her rough red hands twisted together, her mouth unhappy. "Well . . ."

"Don't miss it till it runs dry."

She didn't smile; she'd heard the joke all through her childhood. He said, "Sorry. What was it you were goin' to say?"

"Well, there's other places you could go, than here." She looked past him into the living room, where the television set was telling them what to buy for Christmas. "I'd like you here in town with me, but just about anyplace would be better than out there in those woods."

"I'm happy where I am. Just need a loan, that's all."

"That's not the problem, Pa. You know I'll help with that. What worries me is, you aren't getting any younger. I worry since Ralph died. I dream about you falling down, getting sick, like you did last week—"

"That wasn't sick. That was poison."

"Whatever. I want you to get taken care of better."

He didn't say anything. She stared at him for a while, then got up and went into the front room. He heard the desk drawer. When she came back she put something white on the table in front of him.

"I didn't bring my glasses, Alma. You want to tell me what it is?"

"It's from a place here in the county. They got a special program for Thunder retirees. A doctor brought this by. We had a talk. It's for me, but it's about you."

"What's it *say*?"

"Don't get mad, Pa. You have to promise you won't."

Halvorsen nodded, but his mouth was tight.

"It's about a place they just built, real nice. Look at the picture. It's up in Beaver Fork. You get to go in free."

"Free? Food and everything?"

"That's what it says." She smiled slowly, lips quivering.

"What do we got to do?"

"Nothing."

"Alma." His voice was quiet. "Ain't nothin' free in this world. Just tell me what they want you to do."

Not looking at him, she whispered, "I got to say you ain't in your right

capacity. That's all. It don't have to be true. I just got to sign this paper.
There's a doctor there, and people to make sure you get good care and
good medicine."

He looked at his hands, curled round the chocolate like sleeping men
round a campfire; at the wrinkles and age spots and old scars. One of the
nails was missing. He'd been holding a spike on a deadman in East Texas
when the roustabout had missed with his sledge. Carried the mark of that
hammer for forty years, he thought. Carry it to my grave.

"You goin' to sign it?"

"Not unless you say to, Pa."

"Better give it here."

He tucked it into his pocket. Then selected another cookie and
munched it slowly.

"Why you carrying a rifle, Pa? Are you hunting again?"

"No."

"You ain't going to tell me what's going on?"

"Ain't nothing going on, Alma. I'm just trying to live my life, what's
left of it, without bothering anybody or having them bother me."

"I wish you'd move into town."

"That's enough," he said sharply. She sat quiet a moment longer, pushing her lips out, then got up. When she came back she held out money.
He nodded and took it.

"Want me to go down with you while you shop?"

"No need. Can I leave the dog? I'm too old to chase after a pup."

"Sure. Will you need a ride back? Fred's got the Dodge, but I can take
you out in the tow truck."

A few minutes later he stood still and alone on the pavement in front
of the garage. The wind came slow and cold and inevitable down the
street.

Fight it, he wondered, or give in?

If he gave in they'd let him alone. Maybe give his pension back. But if
he fought he'd lose not just his retirement but likely his freedom too.
Even if they couldn't break Alma they could probably find somebody to
put him away. He'd of trusted old Judge Wiesel with his life but there was
a new man on the county bench now. A young one. And all too often to
the young anyone who was old and set in their ways was senile, and anyone
who didn't live like the rest should be made to. Especially if there was a
way to come by a dollar doing it.

He figured he didn't have long to make his choice.

He wanted a chew. But when he put his hand in his pocket his fingers
found first the commitment papers and then lead-tipped brass. Narrowing
his eyes, jingling the cartridges, he began walking forward, into the wind.

Twenty-three

L ater, in town, the streetlights buzzed and flickered on one by one. In their sudden brassy brilliance a woman sat in a window above Main Street. From the sidewalk a late shopper might have seen her: a solitary figure crouched on a window seat, hair tumbled forward, covering her face.

Jaysine was eating chocolate cake. She didn't look down, at the fizzling short circuit in one of the decorations, or the creche on Veterans Square. Nor did she look up, at the clouds that had wrapped the stars and put them away. She kept her eyes on the plate.

At a quarter of eight she disappeared from the window. A few minutes later the stairwell light came on.

She stood on the pavement, looking up at last. Her gaze focused between herself and the sky, on the moving air become suddenly visible.

The first flakes were falling. Airy, twinkling, they drifted earthward, as if coming home to rest.

She shivered, lifted her collar, and set out.

She'd passed the Reading Room a hundred times since she came to Raymondsville. Sometimes she'd stop and read the Weekly Lesson through the window, the open Bible spread flat beside it, the matching passages highlighted. Once a gray-haired woman had smiled out at her. She'd smiled back, and walked quickly away.

Now an old man in a gray coat held the door for her as she approached. He said good evening and she said good evening, too.

The room itself was like all the others in all the other towns in America. Overstuffed chairs and reading lamps, shelves of *Sentinels* and *Journals* looking as if no one ever touched them except to dust. Through it was a larger room. She went in with her head down and sat in a left-hand pew. There were four others there, all old, seated near the stove. She felt better once she'd stolen enough glimpses to see she didn't know them.

The waiting silence was familiar. She sat in it for a long time with her eyes closed.

Her family had been Christian Scientists for four generations. The story as she'd heard it was that her great-grandfather had had some unspecified (and perhaps, she thought suddenly, in those days unmentionable) disease and had gone through the entire *materia medica* to no avail. Then one day he'd gone to Salamanca for a shay. He'd bought it, a Studebaker, and was looking for a saloon when he saw a practitioner's shingle.

He'd gone in, and been healed that very day and hour. And after that all her family had been Scientists. Right down to her.

Jaysine's mother was a practitioner, a devout dumpy woman who'd kept the house filled with the smells of canning and the lilt of hymns throughout her childhood. She remembered people coming to the porch, her mother taking them into the parlor and shutting the door. She'd peeped from outside, ankle-deep in the flowerbeds, hoping to catch her in the act of miracle. But all they'd ever seemed to do was talk.

She remembered her playmates at Sunday School singing around her, the circle of faces full of innocent confidence that her scrape would be healed or the glass would drop out of her finger. And it had seemed to her that often it had.

Till that spring night. Her father hadn't gone to service for years. And later there'd been long periods, weeks, when he wouldn't talk to her mother. He'd never said anything about the store, that he was sad or needed healing, or betrayed in any way what he was going to do. Till they heard the shot, and her mother, trembling, had sent her oldest son out to the barn alone.

Jaysine had stopped paying her Mother Church dues that fall. And gradually the whole idea of healing yourself through reliance on the Divine Mind seemed stranger and stranger, until now when people asked her what she was she just said Protestant, or sometimes that she wasn't really anything at all.

At a scrape at the front of the room the old people stirred. She opened her eyes to the hand-lettered gilt GOD IS LOVE and the quotations from Matthew and Mary Baker Eddy.

The reader was Marguerite, from the Shoppe. Jaysine felt herself redden and her head go down, too late. She saw the older woman glance at her, but she only smiled briefly, and began the service.

Wednesday night meetings were simple. No sermons, no ceremony. Just a few passages from Scripture and then the correlating ones from *Science and Health.* Someone played an organ, not very well, and they sang "Lead, Kindly Light." Then came the Lord's Prayer, said together slowly, and then a period of silence.

It seemed to go on forever; it could have been ten minutes. Jaysine began to tremble. At last one of the women stood, supporting herself on the back of the bench.

"I want to tell everyone here about a wonderful healing I experienced some years ago.

"It happened when I had my grandchildren with me. My grandson was ten, and one night he left his skates on the landing. I was coming down from the bedroom the next morning, and I stepped on one. My very next step took me onto the other, and I fell, not down the stairs, but over the banister.

"I remember while I was falling saying 'God is All.' It seemed to take so long that I think I said it twice. Then I came down across an end table near the bottom of the stairs.

"My husband and my daughter wanted to take me to the hospital. It was hard to refuse, the pain was so great. Yet I kept reasoning to myself, and at last late that day I was able to get up and walk about. The practitioner came over that evening and she began my treatment.

"I progressed for some weeks in this way, and the pain lessened. But my husband said there would be a question of insurance, so I let them drive me to the hospital, just to put their minds at rest.

"The doctor looked at the X-rays and said, 'This woman has a broken hip, and I will need to put a pin in it. Admit her today and we'll do the operation tomorrow.' Well, I was dismayed at this. But I didn't protest or argue. I just told him quietly that I was a Christian Scientist and asked if there was any other way to proceed.

"And he said, 'How long has it been since you fell?' And I told him, six weeks. He said, 'Have you broken your hip before?' I said no. Then he said, still looking at the X-ray, 'It's interesting, but I see here, looking more closely, that the bones are beginning to knit. I've not seen that before, hips don't do that without pinning. Let's leave it alone and see what happens. I want you back in a month for another picture.'

"I went home rejoicing and continued my treatment. When I went back he said nothing, only asked me to continue whatever I was doing. When I went back again, he came toward me, smiling and holding out both hands, and said 'Here she is, the woman who heals herself.' He told me there was nothing left on the X-rays, that it had healed perfectly and he was very happy for me.

"I am very grateful for Christian Science."

She sat down. They rested in silence, and then a man got up and told how Divine Mind had rescued his daughter from smoking cigarettes. Then another woman, very thin, told about waking up without the use of her arm and how it had come back after an earnest session of prayerful thought. Jaysine listened, her tension growing.

Part of her regretted now that she'd gone to the doctors. It wasn't evil, but it showed lack of faith.

She'd been told from her earliest years that man wasn't a material but a spiritual being. Deny what was false, and it could no longer cause sin or sickness. There were no such things as diseases. They existed only in the carnal mind.

The trouble was that although she partly still believed, enough to make her feel guilty, she no longer had her childhood faith. Even if the people around her were right, she was too steeped in error and sin for it to work for her.

And if evil did not exist then *he* was not evil, and she couldn't blame him for what had happened. If there was anything Scientists believed, it was that one had to forgive in order to be forgiven.

But she couldn't. Not after the things he'd done. Given her this sickness, abandoned her, taken away her job, shamed her.

But still she stayed, standing from the polished pew, not needing the hymnal to sing:

> I was not ever thus, nor prayed that Thou
> Shouldst lead me on; I loved to
> Choose, and see my path; but now . . .
> Lead Thou me on.

For one moment, singing, she was able to try. *Tell me what to do*, she prayed. *If you would just tell me what to do, then I'd do it. Just tell me, please, I'm so lost and confused.*

She didn't really expect an answer.

Marguerite hurried toward her after the service. Her eyes reminded Jaysine of her mother's. She mumbled, "Good night," and fled.

In the hour she'd been inside the town had turned white. When she got back to her apartment, cursing the cold, the blue car was parked across the street.

For a while, standing beside it, she watched the flakes sweep down out of the dark, smashing themselves apart on the metal hood, then changing suddenly and mysteriously into shimmering ovals of water that reflected the streetlights in their hearts. Then she climbed the stairs, slowly, looking up toward her landing. She was starting to sweat, and she felt nauseated.

But when she got there it was deserted. She unlocked the door and let herself in, feeling a strange conflict of relief and regret.

A moment later her buzzer went off.

She knew instantly he was drunk. The smell came through the chained gap in waves. When she just stood there, unable to either close the door or open it, he grunted something.

"What?"

"I said, you going to let me in?"

"No. Go away."

"C'mon, damn it. We need to talk."

"What have we got to talk about? You told me to go to hell."

She was trembling. He'd come back. A week before she'd have been overjoyed. She'd spent hours fantasizing it. Then it seemed her love had turned, like wine left out overnight.

"Let me in. Right now. Or I'm leavin'."

"Brad, did you drive here? You shouldn't drive when you're like this."

"Hell I will . . . last chance."

She closed her eyes and imagined letting him go. I don't love him anymore, she thought. I tried so hard, but he doesn't love me.

But she didn't want him to go yet, either. There was intimacy here, a strange bond between one who inflicted pain and one who was hurt. Was being with him, bitter and wretched though it made her, any worse than being alone?

Rattling slightly, the chain pendulumed to and fro.

He lurched past her and half-fell into the couch. Big as ever, but to-night he seemed to have sagged. His tie was loose and something had spilled on his shirt. She stood by the door, paralyzed with contradictory emotions.

He rolled over, looked blearily at her, then toward the kitchen. "How's the wine situation?"

"I don't have any. You don't need any more to drink. Look at you. Do you want some coffee?"

"No. What else you got?"

"Chocolate layer cake. I just bought it. Do you want some of that?"

"No." His eyes ran down her. "You ought to lay off that stuff, Jay, it's starting to show."

She laughed. "What's it to you? Listen. I'm going to make some coffee."

He didn't say anything. She went into the kitchen. Starting to show, she thought bitterly. She hadn't dared weigh herself for two weeks. It was his fault, where did he get the nerve to reproach her? She was measuring drip-ground into the filter when his arms slid around her.

"You still care about old Brad, don't you, babe."

She closed her eyes, the spoon held out stiffly in front of her. Coffee jittered out and danced on the counter. She wanted to turn around and take him back. She also wanted to smash the Pyrex pot and grind the jagged pieces into his eyes.

There seemed to be no one inside her skull to choose between the two. At last she said, her voice thick and strange, "I don't think it's good for me to care about you, Brad."

"Oh, listen to this. You used to think I was. Pretty damn good, in fact." His breath stirred the hairs of her neck. The whiskey smell was overpowering. Out of nowhere, she remembered her father had smelled like that sometimes, and she remembered just for a moment the ceiling of the barn, so far away it seemed like heaven . . .

The image, the memory, vanished as she grasped it. She was struggling with this, trying to regain it, when he took the pot out of her hands and began unbuttoning her blouse. She hit him, once, on the neck, but it was as if she struck underwater; her hand was empty of all power. She put her head down, feeling dizzy, so dizzy and empty that when his arms slid under her she could say nothing, neither in denial or desire, only turn her head away.

Lying beside him, exhausted, she eased her breath out with a ragged flutter. She was still pulsing down there, still tightening and loosening. No matter how she felt about him, the sex was still incredible. All that the magazines promised. Her lids sagged closed. This was all she wanted right now, to lie here with her arms around him, her head on his chest.

"You asleep?" she whispered, smiling to herself.

He grunted. Then swung his arm up. "Jesus!" he said, sitting up suddenly.

"What's wrong?"

"Hell." She heard him groping in the dark, and the bedside bulb came on. His belly sagged as he hoisted himself out. Water rattled in the toilet.

He came out zipping his fly. He didn't look at her. The springs creaked as he sat down. He smelled like sweat and whiskey and sex. "What's wrong?" she said again.

"Got to get home."

"You said you'd stay here tonight. With me," she said, hearing her voice gentle, sleepy.

"I can't do that. I didn't plan on this when I came over. Tell you what, I'll call you tomorrow at work, okay?"

She remembered he didn't know. "Brad, I lost my job. I don't work for Marybelle anymore."

"Is that right? That's too bad. Say, did you find my coat? Did I leave it here?"

"Yes."

"Where is it?"

"I burned it."

"You what? Burned it?" He peered down at her and she wondered how much you had to drink to make your eyes liquid and shiny like that. "You're different, babe, you know that? You even look different. I bet you did at that. And my appointment book? I hope you didn't burn that too?"

She came a little further awake. For a moment she thought about giving it back. Then she thought: Maybe that's why he's here. Through suddenly numb lips she said, "I didn't see anything else. Just your coat. I took it out into the alley and poured lamp oil on it and lit it."

He looked relieved and angry at the same time. But he didn't say anything, just started pulling on his shirt, getting the buttons wrong. She lay rigid, watching.

"You're pissed at me, aren't you."

"What a perceptive guy you are, Brad."

"Well, maybe you're right. Listen, I still got that money for you."

She almost told him what he could do with it, then remembered how much she needed it. Time to swallow your pride, Jaysine, she told herself. "All right," she said.

"Atta girl, now you're talking . . . Look, let's get something else cleared up. You calling Ainslee, that made me mad. Let me tell you a little something, the way I operate. People treat me right, I treat them right. They try to screw me, I give them one warning. They don't take the hint, the next one goes between their eyes. I don't want you talking to her again, ever. Understand? . . . Hey, you sure there's nothing to drink?"

"No. Nothing," said the part of her that hated him. But then the part that kept telling her to do what men wanted added, "But I could go down to the store."

"Never mind, I got booze at home . . . Anyway, wanted to ask you, there's people around this town who're trying to hurt me. Make me look bad, the company too. You know anything about that?"

She thought instantly of the boy. The old man he'd told her about. "No, I haven't heard about anything like that."

"You sure you don't got that notebook? Leather cover, gold-stamped? I'd sure like to get it back."

She put her hands on her belly under the covers. It felt as if she was being twisted around a stick, tighter and tighter. "Was that all you wanted? To get your book, and a . . . free fuck? Or just your book, and then you felt *sorry*—"

"Hold on, Jay. Hold on." He waggled his head. "Damn! Look, I'd like to fix things up between us. But I can go the other way, too."

"What does that mean?"

"Well, look, I'm sorry I said those things to you. You know what things. I just got mad. I'm sorry you got canned, too."

"Is that supposed to make me feel better?"

He patted her shoulder. "No, but maybe this will. You lost your job? Here's what I'm gonna do. I got some positions coming open, nursing assistant positions. Doesn't pay shit to start, but you work out, you'll go to supervisor in a few months." He reached for his tie.

"And you have plans for us, too, I suppose?"

He smiled again, but he was looking toward the door. "I might get by once in a while."

"When? How often?"

"I don't know. Don't try to pin me down."

She sat up, aware suddenly he was leaving. She swung her legs out into the chill. "So basically you're saying, you'll hire me, then maybe come by and screw me when you're in the mood."

"Only if you want, baby, only if you want."

"You know what I want!" The pain in her belly was like a huge hot needle. So bad she couldn't stand; she huddled naked in the cold air. "I want to love you, and have you love me back! You don't have to leave your wife. But you need me, Brad. Believe it or not, you need me."

She was crying and hiccoughing now, ashamed, terrified, but she had to say it all, get it all out. "I know I'm not pretty or smart. You think I'm . . . ordinary, and fat, and dumb. But I'd do anything for you. I could have hurt you and I didn't. Your wife wanted me to. I never told you that. Brad, they're going to stop you—"

"Who?" he said instantly. When she didn't answer he reached down and shook her. "I said, *who?*"

She said lamely, "Everybody. People around here. You can't keep treating them the way you do."

He gave a disgusted snort. "Okay. You've declared your scruples. Let's wrap it up, I got a headache. You taking my offer?"

"No."

"What?"

"I said no! I'm an electrologist, not a nurse, and not your whore!"

He looked so strangely at her that for a moment she forgot how to breathe. She was terrified at what she'd said. But she couldn't take it back. It was the truth.

He stood suddenly, huge, swaying. "Let's see. I apologized. I offered you bucks. A job. Chance to see me again sometimes. But no, you're like my fucking wife, you got to have everything your way.

"Well, you don't have a thing I can't get cheaper and better someplace else. And you don't scare me. These people are sheep.

"So fuck off, Jaysine Farmer, but listen to this: From now on, stay out of my way. And don't call my wife again, or I'll kill you."

"Brad, no!" she screamed. She lunged out for him as he turned, caught his legs, but he was already moving away. He dragged her from the bed, cursing and trying to free himself, but she gripped his suit with desperate strength. She was screaming incoherently. Till she heard the slap and then after a time, like thunder and lightning reversed, felt the pain.

She felt him kicking her off, like a dog. Then he was gone, leaving the door swinging above the windy blackness of the stair.

She crawled a few feet and then stopped, curling naked on the window-seat, holding her stomach and waiting, just waiting, filled with freezing despair. There was light below her, a bright copper glow. Somewhere in it red flared on, then dwindled away. But the snow was coming down too thick and hard for her to really see.

Twenty-four

P hil lay motionless in the room under the eaves, listening to the snow, staring up at the plywood sheet.

It'd be the fourth time today, but he was thinking of doing it again. The only thing that even transiently held his interest. For a few minutes he could forget this depression, this deadening nausea that had clamped down again, shorting out thought and emotion like a clamp over the poles of a battery. He no longer bothered to fantasize about girls he knew. Separating it from women, other than the ones in the photographs, made it somehow purer, less painful.

He sat up in bed, and reached for the thumbed damp pages.

When it was over he lay under the covers and stared at the darkened window for a long time. The last faint echo of desire ebbed back into the chill. His body was spent, his mind empty. He no longer wanted or cared for anything at all.

He thought, there's only one thing left to finish up. To make sure of or else to fail at finally and forever. Then he could go.

Take the gun, or the razor, and find the peace that would last forever.

Faintly, through the snow-hiss, the purr of a motor came to his ears. His father. Home early, he thought. He didn't wonder why. He stared at the ceiling, thinking already of doing it again.

Later someone called his name downstairs. He thought at first of ignoring it, pretending sleep. Then he identified the voice, and the tone. He threw back the covers and rolled out, ducking his head without thinking, pulled on pants and padded down the steep narrow stairs, sucking air through his teeth at the sudden cold laid against his skin.

Joe Romanelli stood in the living room in uniform. Brown striped trousers, uniform shirt, the lamb-lined bomber jacket with the stitched-on flag. The badge, the gun, the cuffs. He didn't say anything as Phil came down the stairs, just followed him with his eyes. When he saw his father's mouth his step slowed.

"What you doin' home, Dad?"

"Where's your mother?"

"I'm here," she said, coming out of the pantry. "Joe, what are you doing home?"

He said harshly, "Nolan put me back to night shift."

"Oh, Dad."

"Oh, no, Joe. Were you—you weren't drinking on duty again—"

"It wasn't me this time," said his father, jerking his head up at Phil where he stood on the stairs. Phil's feeling of nameless anxiety deepened into dread.

"Joseph—"

"Maybe you better stay in the kitchen, Mary."

His father reached out as he neared him. Phil hadn't felt for a long time how strong his father was. "Okay, living room."

The old dread was growing like a baby in his gut. Just like always. It was just the same, nothing was ever new in the world, maybe that was why there had to be new people all the time, so they'd think it was . . . He followed his father's back into the living room and stood waiting as he stripped off his jacket and threw it on the couch and turned, his eyes cop's-eyes, folding his arms over the badge.

"Let's have it, boy, I don't want to have to make you tell me. You and this crazy old guy, this Halvorsen, what do you think you're doin'?"

"I don't know—"

"I told you, don't *give* me that kiddie-crap." His father hit him, not real hard, but the way it landed made his eyes tear. He blinked, cursing himself and thinking *I hate that. I don't care if he hits me but I hate it when I cry.*

"Well?"

He didn't say anything. Couldn't think of anything, and didn't feel like saying it if he had.

Joe picked up the *TV Guide* and glanced at it, then dropped it back on the coffee table. He put his thumbs under his belt and said in his serious voice, "You're getting old enough to learn some sense. Learn about how things work. Now why don't we make this easy on both of us. What you up to with him?"

"We're on the track of some criminals."

The elder Romanelli laughed sudden and bitter, eyebrows climbing. "On the track! On the *track*! What the hey! Now he's a detective!"

"No, we—"

"You been reading too many books down in that library. I told your mother that, but she laughed." His father glanced hate toward the kitchen. "What kind of criminals? How come you ain't told me about it?"

"I didn't think you'd be interested. It's waste dumping, on the roads."

"Oh, Christ. You're right, I ain't."

Phil saw his mother's face, white and frightened, peering around the jamb at them. He tried to smile at her. Then switched his attention to his father, who was looking at the TV and slowly pulling his belt through the loops of his uniform.

"Nolan calls me in today, calls me into his office. Closes the door. Says: Romanelli, you keep an eye on your boy? I say, sure. He says, you know he's into something he got no business in? Stirring up trouble? Says, item one, teach me to keep tabs on what you're doing, I'm going back to night shift. Forget about the stripe. Can't supervise my kid, can't supervise a squad."

His father paused to light a cigarette, waved out the match, flicked it still hot to the floor. He looked at the ceiling, blinking in the smoke. "Item two, my pension. He hears about you again I won't have to worry about it. I'll be on the street. Reminds me I got three years to twenty. Seventeen years lickin' Hodges's shit, then Nolan's . . . See what we're talking?"

"Yeah."

"Yes sir."

"Yes sir."

His father coiled the belt, looking off to the side. "Get those pants down. You should be too big for this. But you don't got the sense of an adult, I can't treat you like one."

"I think I got enough sense."

"Shut up! Bend over!"

"No. You should be asking me who's doin' this—"

His voice went high then and broke and all at once he lost it. He knew it was stupid but he tried to slap his father back. Joe was inside his guard and had him doubled up in some kind of armlock before his hand reached where his father's face had been. His eyes bulged and he cried out; it felt like his arm was being torn off.

But then, distantly, he heard his mother say "Joe—here, take this—"

He looked at her. Mary Romanelli stood in the kitchen doorway, one hand holding a rosary, the other arm rigid as a statue's. In her outstretched hand trembled a bottle of beer.

"Get back in there!"

"Don't hit him, Joe. Don't, he's not well—"

His father shouted and she came out of the kitchen. Then he slapped her too. There was the usual crying and carrying on, and somehow that toughened him and he got his mouth shut again. Bent over, biting his lips under the repetitive sting of the heavy belt, he was abruptly sick and disgusted. His whole being recoiled from the leather-wool-tobacco smell of policeman. He opened his eyes to find the worn butt of the service revolver inches from them, bent as he was over his father's hip.

He was still staring at it when Joe released him, slamming him against the wall with the same motion. He leaned there, drooping his eyelids as if bored, to hide the shame and anger.

"Okay, tell me what you learned." It was the phrase he used whenever he whipped one of them.

"Nothin'."

"Philip, tell him what he wants to hear, for God's sake!"

"I learned you're a coward."

His father looked shocked and sad, grim, as if this hurt him too, though Phil knew it didn't. He slapped his son hard on both sides of the face. Phil leaned his head back against the dark brown wallpaper. Behind his eyes he saw for a moment the inside of a house. He didn't recollect where it had been, somewhere his mother had taken him when he was small and they'd tried to leave; neat rows of brown pottery crocks, each filled with cookies, nuts, ground-up leaves and roots and blossoms that smelled so sweetly they lived like everlasting flowers all over the house . . . He shook his head and was back. His voice shook when he let it out.

"I seen you learn your lesson, Dad. About crawlin' around for the ones with money. I'm not gonna do it."

"You think it's any different anyplace else? I did too, once. We got our place here, Phil, and it ain't a bad one, all told. It's a hell of a lot better than some I seen."

"It ought to be better."

"You think I like it? You think I enjoy this? Christ, you're my son. Crippled or not, I got to show you how to get along. I want you to make it through in one piece."

"It ought to be better," he said again, knowing how he must sound, like a child crying to be given the moon; pretending he was being proud and scornful, but knowing he was really just bawling. "There ought to be more than just making it through."

"Maybe. But just doin' that's hard enough. You better face up to it. I sure as shit had to."

His father's voice was harsh, Police Lecture tone, but just for a moment Phil heard something else there too. He squinted up, startled, and Joe said, "Ah, both of you, just shut the hell up." He turned, and the door slammed behind him.

His mother was on him, crying. He pushed her away, then gave up and let her wipe his face and cry on him. *What the hell*, he thought then, feeling his twisted vicious and enraged victory, over them, over life itself. *Let her, she won't be able to much longer.*

He remembered, from deep in his childhood, going fishing with his father. Or maybe being taken fishing was more accurate. Or maybe being dragged off, forced to go fishing was it. This was one of those dim memories that you knew had happened, but you hadn't understood how little you were even though you might have been able to say a number when somebody asked you, three or four or five. Anyway it was summer, incandescently hot. He didn't recall where they'd gone. It couldn't have been far, but when you were that little you couldn't see over the bushes so you had no idea where you were. Now as he remembered it the pictures brightened, like a bulb coming on behind them. He could see it clearly even now, but different, as if the light of the sun had been different then. So different that he knew even if he saw the same place, the same creek they'd hiked along, he wouldn't recognize it.

Anyway he'd stumbled and run after his father for what seemed like hours (this was before his illness) till his legs hurt and things had bitten and scratched him and he was exhausted and crying.

And his father, towering up to the trees, would look back and yell angrily, "You coming? Or am I gonna hafta leave you here?"

And he'd run, frantically, tripping over roots and rocks and clumps of grass trying to catch up. When he did he'd reach up for a hand but it never held his for long.

When they got to the pond he was afraid of it. More water than he'd ever seen. The edge was slippery but his father sat him right at the brink and began showing him how to push the hook through the worm's belly. Somehow that afternoon he got the hook in his ear and cried and cried while his father cut it out with his knife. But he hadn't been afraid. It was the pain that made him cry, not fear. He knew his father would get it out. Just as he knew how to fish, and drive the car, how to do everything.

He remembered the fish too. It was huge and silver and dreadfully alive. It kicked itself around on the grass without legs. It snapped at the air and thrashed and then lay gasping for a little while before fighting itself in the dirt some more. His father picked it up by the tail and handed it to him, grinning, telling him he'd caught it all by himself, his first fish, telling him to feel how heavy it was. And he'd dug his fingers breathlessly into the slippery cold silver, feeling it buck and strain desperately to escape.

Then suddenly, he couldn't say why, he'd pushed it away, back toward the silver water. It hit the mud and bucked and was instantly gone beneath a thousand spreading circles. The men at the pond had laughed. He could hear them laughing now. Then his father had taken him into the bushes and whipped him for throwing away good food. And he'd pooped his pants and his father called him a name, and hit him some more, and at last took him down and washed his underpants there in front of them all right where the fish had gone back . . .

He lay under the plywood patching, the covers packed tight as gun-wadding around him, and let tears slide slowly down his face.

It wouldn't be hard to die.

It wouldn't be hard at all.

Twenty-five

Damn, it's cold, Halvorsen thought, leaning into the hill. Damn! Cold as he remembered it ever being. The wind seared the few exposed inches of his face like hot iron. He blinked snow from his eyelashes, peering uphill, into the falling dusk.

Why do I feel this way? he thought. Like there's something out here with me. Somethin' that, when I meet it, I won't like.

Around him for miles the deserted, leafless woods lay hissing-silent. This was the hill's northern face, and north of it was only emptiness. Old maps showed names there. But now there were no roads, no houses, except deep in a hollow the tumbled silvery boards of a long-abandoned farm. Only a slow heave and dropping away, like a white, empty, forest-covered sea. From here to the New York border, as this day dimmed toward evening not another human soul moved or lived.

Just now he was plodding homeward, following his drifting breath up between darkening sycamores. Swinging in his gloved hand was the light single-shot. Beneath his snowshoes crunched six inches of fresh fall. The shoulders of his coat, the crown of his hat, were frosted with what had come down in the last hour.

I don't know, he concluded at last. Must just be tired. Hiked a ways today for a man who still ain't feeling himself.

A few minutes later he came over the lip of a bench, a slackening in the hill's ascent. He paused there, glancing around, more from long habit of the woods than anything else. Beside him a lightning-shivered oak leaned into the reluctant embrace of a middle-aged beech, their upper branches tangled and partially intergrown.

He was resting against its massive cold bole, listening to the slither of snowflakes through the twigs, when a whine came from under his ear.

The old man sighed. He unbuttoned his coat. Lifted the pup out and set her down. Watched, as she sniffed around and finally squatted, blinking up at him.

When she was done he bent slowly to scratch her head. "You little devil. Getting heavier ever' mile. I think you better walk the rest of the way."

The puppy whined again, looking up at the furry broken thing that swayed by its ears from the man's belt. "You just wait," he said sternly. "You just wait."

A few hundred feet across the bench and then uphill, but not too far after that to home. Yeah, she's coming down hard, Halvorsen thought, planting one boot in front of the other.

He couldn't honestly say he minded. Maybe in a few more years, though. It seemed like the cold sank another eighth of an inch into his bones every year, and edged out, each spring, more reluctantly. Each year the slopes got steeper, till he could swear the hills were buckling upward.

But he wasn't ready yet to find a warm place to die. This was where he belonged. In these empty, chill woods, free of man and anything conceived of or invented by him, free of his pride and greed and relentless self-obsession.

He thought of Man with neither sneer nor pity but a deep regret. What other creature would afflict its God with its own image? Could admit with a snigger its irremediable sinfulness, craziness, murderousness, and in the next breath vaunt its similitude with the Almighty?

As for me, he thought, give me a god whose image is the tree. Silently uniting rock and sky, light and soil into food and shade for all manner of creatures. Or the deer: fleet and graceful, melting and moving like shadow; gentle, killing nothing, free as the wind. Or even the wolf: bringing death, but only to those no longer capable of life; destroying, but without treachery, without hate, without the masks of patriotism or honor.

He looked at the puppy, trotting along self-importantly in the marks of his snowshoes. But not in the image of a dog, he thought. They been keeping bad company.

He discovered he'd stopped again, half-crouching in the lee of a tree. Shoot, he thought, what are you doing? Acting like a spooked doe. But nonetheless he respected the instinct and stood still, a shadow in the driving snow, looking patiently between each stroke of gray in the dying light for motion or silhouette, up and down the hill. When he was sure there was nothing there, no one watching or stalking him, he resumed his climb.

A quarter-hour later the cover lightened, letting a little more twilight seep down. That meant the top lay just ahead. He was ready. He'd had to stop and rest every hundred feet of the last slope. This was the steepest part of Town Hill, damn near impossible in summer, when it was choked so tight with scrub and bramble a weasel would have hard going.

But he knew his way through it. He'd hunted and hiked here for sixty years, and at the steepest cuts had trees picked out to haul himself up on hand after hand. He did this now just below the crest. Then he was up and the puppy scrambled panting up after him. They stood for a moment, looking back down into the valley. It was almost dark there now.

"Couple minutes, Jez, we'll be home," he muttered.

He was turning, getting ready to hike on down the ridge, when he heard a motor. He cocked his head, but lost it. He couldn't even tell what kind of a machine it had been; airplane, snowmobile, car; only that it was far off.

He moved forward again, even more cautiously now. And behind him scampered the hound, hopping from one to the next of the shallow depressions his snowshoes silently embossed like ancient seals into the blank and yielding snow.

Sometime later he stood motionless amid a copse of hemlocks, peering through their snow-loaded branches toward the clearing. Twice more, as he moved down the spine of the hill, the sound had come, swelled, then faded again behind the dancing veils. The last time he'd made it out: the growl of an approaching truck. Beside him the puppy keened once, low. "Quiet now, girl," he muttered.

It wasn't Alma's old Dodge. Wasn't DeSantis, he knew his Willys too. Beyond the stand of hemlock was a little space without trees. He bent stiffly, lowering his cap below the tops of the snow-covered bushes, and moved forward, cradling the old rifle.

He came to the edge of the woods. Past a vast old maple his land proper began. Twenty years before, a barbed-wire fence had marked this division. The open snow beyond it had covered sleeping flowers, when there'd been a woman to want flowers. On its far side, past the smooth white openness of the road, was his basement.

The sound came louder now, engine dropping into low gear for the last long climb up Mortlock from the base-valley of the river. Halvorsen fitted himself behind the maple, lowering the rifle so it wouldn't stick out. Behind him the pup dropped her belly to the snow.

When it came into view he did not so much as breathe. Only his faded blue eyes moved, following it. It dipped and swerved on the hidden road, throwing snow as a boat throws water. A four-wheel-drive, red, new, Japanese. It snarled up the last rise; then the back wheels spewed frozen mud and dead leaves as it left the road and swung out into the clearing at the top of the mountain. White vapor streamed from the tailpipe, hesitated, then was carried away in the chill steady wind.

Four men got out. One pulled a pump shotgun after him and leaned it against the bumper. They wore orange vests, heavy boots, flame-orange caps. Two lit cigarettes as soon as they were out of the cab. They were close enough he could make out the brands. Close enough, when one of them leaned back in and the engine snored down to silence, that he could hear.

"Christ, I got to piss."

"You sure this's it, Nickie? Looks like the ass end a' nowhere to me."

"That's what he said it was. Remote."

"Where's the house? Boulton said there was a house."

Silence for a few moments. One of the men, blunt-faced as the butt of a camp-axe, heavily bearded, floundered a little way off. After a moment steam rose from between his straddled legs.

Halvorsen watched it all intently, leaning against the cold black roughness of maple bark. The rifle hung motionless in his hand.

They looked like hunters. Or thought they did. But as they passed a flask, tossing back short hard nips while they waited for the bearded man, the faded blue eyes saw that their boots were new. All their clothes were new. And the license windows on the back of their coats were empty.

The blunt-faced man, apparently the leader, finished and came back to the truck. They stood around it, discussing something in voices too low to hear. Halvorsen's gray-stubbled mouth twitched. He'd been out long enough that the fire had burned down. Embered, there was no telltale of woodsmoke and very little smell. The basement lay so low beneath the snow it was indistinguishable.

The hatchet-faced man raised his voice. "Naw, goddamnit, it's gotta be up here. Tommy, you look over there. Mitch, down the hill. I'll go this way."

Cold blue eyes followed them as they trudged about the plateau. At last one shouted. The others turned and waded toward him. They gathered at the top of the steps, then went down, one after the other, into the ground.

When they disappeared Halvorsen looked down at the pup. "Well," he said slowly. "Guess you and me, Jez, we ought to get somethin' fixed for our visitors."

When they reappeared several minutes later, Halvorsen straightened. He edged himself slowly back into the woods. But they weren't looking in his direction. They were headed for the truck. He studied them with far-sighted eyes as the blunt-faced man lifted out two red cans with spouts, let them drop to the snow—they sank into it, heavy—and shut the gate with a hollow slam.

He was opening the door of the Toyota when a whine floated out from the woods. The old man bent instantly, clamping his glove over the pup's snout, but it was too late.

The men turned, reaching into vests, pockets. Ah, thought Halvorsen, through the cold alertness that had taken him. He'd wondered why these "hunters" had no rifles. And only one long gun, when they should have had four, racked in the mounts bolted in the back window.

He straightened. Across fifty yards of snow his eyes met theirs. Holding their pistols out and ready, they slogged forward, toward where the puppy keened again, shivering, too hungry and too cold to stay quiet.

He stepped out, dropping the stock of the rifle into his left glove. His breath came warm and rapid, puffing steam into the bitter wind. It was too bad, he thought then, facing them, that the old falling-block was empty. He'd fired the last handload an hour before at the rabbit that dangled now head down, sightless eyes glazed open, from his belt.

"My name's Racks Halvorsen," he said quietly, into the mouths of the waiting guns. "And I want you boys off my land."

They stopped, facing him in a semicircle. The one with the shotgun moved sideways. The others moved too, edging apart, glancing to where the bearded man stood.

He said, loud, "What d'you want up here?"

"You Halvorsen?" said the bearded one.

"Just said so. Who're you?"

"That don't matter."

"What're we talking for?" said the youngest suddenly. "Let's get it done and get outa here."

"He got a rifle."

"So? Four of us, one a' him."

"You take him, then."

"Shut up," said the bearded one. To Halvorsen he said, "Put your gun down and come on out."

"I was you fellers, I'd get in that nice shiny truck and head back to town. You want me, come in and get me. You ain't going to like it, though, if you do."

"Can you count, old man?" said the one called Mitch. "You'd better come with us peaceful."

"Don't think so," said Halvorsen. He took a step back from the maple.

"Get him!" shouted the bearded man suddenly, raising the shotgun and letting go, pumping the forestock. The others took a moment to react, two aiming their handguns clumsily, as if unused to them. The shot whipped above him, rattling off branches. He didn't see or hear where the bullets went.

He was already moving backward, crouched on the snowshoes, when they lowered their guns and began running toward him over the field. He scooped up the puppy and stuffed it down inside his coat. Then he had trees between him and them, and he turned and set his face downhill, into the deepening darkness. He didn't know if they'd follow. He wouldn't, if he were them.

He still felt weak. But for the moment at least his heart pulsed strong, he felt warm, ready for a fight. He didn't know how long it would last, but it felt good. They were city men, that was plain. Unused to the woods, and not armed for it; the short-barreled guns they carried were concealable, but not very accurate. He'd have to watch the fellow with the pump, though.

He thought he could make things interesting for them.

Turning, now, he glanced back up the rise. To see the first, the fleetest or most eager, loom suddenly into view framed by the two trees Halvorsen had been standing between. The man was running hard. He was almost between the trees, the gun coming up in his hand as he ran.

Halvorsen, just to keep his eyes on him, stopped, turned, and waved.

The first man's name was Tommy, but he was usually called "Tommy Del." He had shot people before, but in parked cars, not in the winter woods, and they hadn't carried guns themselves; in fact two of them had been tied up at the time.

So that now, running heavy-footed ahead of the others toward where the old man had disappeared, he felt a little fear that made him slow for a moment, just before he entered the woods. Then he came to where the land started to drop, and looking down it he saw the old man, turning, lifting his arm.

Got you, you old bastard, he thought. He was raising his automatic when he felt the tug at his foot.

Tommy Del looked down, the upper part of his body still running though his legs had abruptly stopped, to see the loop of barbed wire rip up from under the snow. His arms windmilled, the gun went flying, and then he fell. He wondered, as he went down, whether it was some kind of trap. It didn't seem to be. Just wire. He was still thinking this as his eyes flicked to where his upper body would land. He caught the yellow gleam of sharpwhittled wood just before his hands struck the snow on either side of it.

Halvorsen halted at the bottom of the first slope, breathing hard, and listened. There'd been a hoarse shout as the first of them entered the woods, suddenly cut off; and then silence. Between them, now, the snow had drawn itself dense and sound-deadening. So even if they were still on his trail, he might not be able to hear them.

Or they him. The puppy was squirming and scratching at his chest. He unbuttoned to give it more air, but it kept on whimpering.

He plunged his hand into his pockets, hoping for an overlooked cartridge. The little single-shot wasn't much for firepower, but a .22 Hornet would do more than startle a fellow. His groping fingers found his old Case, the knife he'd used to whittle the stake-trap. Matches, he always carried them. Tobacco. But other than that his hand came empty out of the last pocket.

So that was that. He thought of dropping the rifle; it'd be that much less to carry; but then he thought, it'll make them keep their distance. Till they realized he had no ammunition. The end would come quickly after that.

He lifted his snowshoes and turned at right angles, heading east along the bench. The puppy whimpered again and without stopping he plunged his hand into his coat. Her fur was warm and her breath was hot against his chest. "Just hold on there, girl," he muttered. "Just hold on. This won't take long, one way or t'other."

The second man was the one they called Mitch. He had a part interest in a junkyard. Mitch Burck didn't like guns much, though he used them when he was told to. In his opinion it made smaller men dangerously equal. He preferred an iron bar, or better yet, his hands.

He'd been the second to reach the woods, and he'd bent over Tommy Del where he fell. He'd hardly grasped the meaning of the pointed wood that grew so oddly out of his back before Nickie was on him. The bearded man had shoved him, and he'd turned, snarling, and said, "Hold on a fucking second! Tommy's hurt!"

"We'll take care of him. You get that fucking old man or you're next."

Now he was ahead of the others. Couldn't see them, but they must be back there someplace. And ahead of him, somewhere in the falling snow, was the old guy. Mitch thought, What was that animal with him? Something small. Maybe a dog? He hoped it wasn't. He had six at home. But then he thought, Maybe I can get the old guy without hurting it. Then Nickie might let him keep it.

Okay, the old man . . . He stared around at the trees as he stumbled down the hill, using his left hand to steady himself when he started to slip. Keeping a sharp lookout for wires or stakes. He held the .38 snub out in front of him. Christ, he thought, it's spooky back in here. He shivered. And cold; the wind cut like busted glass. They'd bought wool pants and coats for the job but all he had on under them was cotton underwear, thin socks, an Italian silk shirt.

When he came off the slope onto the flat he felt relieved. It was hard for a heavy man to go downhill. He bent; the old man's prints were clear. The tracks moved on fifty feet or so and then made a sharp left. He grinned tightly and fingered the trigger. Yeah. He'd get him.

Burck trudged through the darkening woods, glancing around alertly. Getting darker . . . too dark to aim anymore, he'd just have to get close and give him the four he had left from the hip. Then charge. He'd crushed bigger men with his hands than this Halvorsen.

He was moving along, squinting toward something bulky and dark up on the bench, when he heard from ahead of him, low but unmistakable, the moan of a puppy.

He hunched down a little and moved forward, using the trees for cover. Just like a Indian, he thought. Ain't too much to this. It was in the woods instead of the unlit piers and abandoned warehouses of the waterfront. That was all that was different.

The dark ahead of him became boulders, huge rounded rocks half-sunk in soil. Their tops were white, their sides still bare and black. He moved cautiously in among them. They were higher than his head, but not so close he felt cramped. The falling snow melted invisibly on his outstretched hand, and he shivered again, hard. Somewhere ahead, or behind, around him somewhere, he heard a chuckle of water. And above it, again, the low wailing. It sounded close.

He stepped around the boulder and made out dimly ahead of him something dark and man-sized, with the straight line of a barrel jutting off to the side. At that moment the whimper came again, from directly ahead.

He jerked the revolver up, eyes wide—the old guy had a rifle—and pulled the trigger. The muzzle flash showed him plainly the stump, the rifle hung on it by the sling, and the puppy, crying at its foot with a head-sized rock on its tail. But his finger pulled twice more before his brain deduced from what it saw that the old man wasn't there. Wasn't in front of him. Might be, in fact, *behind*—

A terrifyingly loud crunch inside his head. His fingers opened and he fell. No, only started to, because he hadn't been knocked out. The blow hadn't been powerful enough. Or his skull was too thick. It just knocked him sideways. He kept going that way, rolling, and started to come up, hands spread, ready to grip, to crush.

Instead the ground slipped out from under him. The earth opened and before he could think rocks smashed into his side, his back.

He hit water with a cracking splash. Its icy shock revived him instantly. He went under for a moment and panicked. He couldn't swim! His feet groped. He flailed his arm wildly.

Then he stopped. He raised his head and looked around, feeling suddenly stupid.

He'd fallen down a short, rocky bank into a little pool. The chuckle he'd heard was a spring, bubbling idly out of the hillside and gathering here. There'd been a sheet of ice over it, through which he'd plunged, but it wasn't very deep. He had his feet on solid bottom now, and it only came to his chest. Something was wrong with his arm, though. It didn't hurt yet, but he suspected it was broken.

Burck realized suddenly that the water he was standing in was freezing. He waded clumsily to the edge and hauled himself out. Water poured off his clothes. But out of the pool, in the wind, it seemed suddenly a hundred degrees colder. He crouched on the rocks and beat his fist on his legs. It was like beating logs with a hammer, he couldn't feel either the fist or the legs, just a distant impact.

He looked up at the empty woods. He didn't see the old man. He couldn't hear the puppy anymore. He wondered where the others were. Nicky and Nate. He opened his mouth and tried to call, but all he could get out was a whimper. He couldn't feel his face or his tongue. He tried to climb up, but now his legs wouldn't move, either.

Well, he couldn't say he felt bad. No pain. His arm didn't hurt anymore. In fact, he was starting to feel warm.

Dimly, all alone in the dark, Mitch Burck realized he was going to freeze to death.

The two men stopped, halfway down the hill, and listened to the *pop pop pop* of a handgun echo from the trees and then, lower-pitched, come back seconds later from the night-shrouded hills.

"Burck," said the blunt-faced man, tasting the icy air.

"Yeah," said the other, the youngest one. "Think he got him?"

"Sounds like."

"I don't think Tommy's gonna make it with that stake in his chest."

"I don't think so either. Unless we get this over with damn quick."

The bearded, blunt-faced man with the shotgun was Nicodemo Asaro, "Little Nickie," a wiseguy from Saratoga Avenue who'd come up through charge cards, loan-sharking, brokering stolen cars, and heroin. He'd drawn a stretch for contempt and when he came out his family's distribution had been wrecked by a federal narcotics task force. He was working his way up again now in a different racket.

Till a few minutes ago this had been routine. Take three men. Drive out to the sticks, see the guy, do a job for him, drive home. He hadn't been told specifics till that afternoon, but they rarely varied; break somebody's back, torch his business, kidnap his daughter; whatever the guy said. This hadn't been any different. Go to this old guy's house, shut him up, go home. He was eager to get home. Tomorrow was his son's thirteenth birthday.

The younger man, who was twenty, was Nate Diamond. Diamond hadn't had much experience yet. He'd had a year of college on an athletic scholarship and realized he needed three more like a pig needs the Talmud. He had some friends in retail coke and when he showed them he could use his size for something more constructive than wrestling they'd passed him up the line. He was fast and ambitious and he kept himself in shape.

He also, unlike the others, knew how to shoot. He'd spent quite a few hours on the indoor range with the .44 magnum automatic he gripped now muzzle-down alongside his right leg.

Diamond didn't care about getting home for the weekend. He liked to see people die.

They came to the rockpile and threaded their way slowly into it, alert and primed. A strange whimper came sporadically at first, as they moved deeper into the maze, then ebbed away to silence. It hadn't sounded like a dog or any other animal they could name. So they took their time. Neither of them wanted to run into any traps. At last, perhaps a quarter-hour later, they came out on a clearing. It was too dark to see now, but then there was a click, and Asaro flicked the beam of a key-chain flashlight over a stump, a rock, a torn-up spot of leaves and snow, and a chunk of wood lying to one side. That was it.

"What the hell?" said Diamond in a low voice.

Asaro moved to the side. They looked over a short drop. It wasn't far down, maybe five feet, and then there was a sheet of ice. Beside it, sitting on a rock, was Mitch Burck. His arms were in his lap and he was smiling dreamily. Asaro kept the flash on him for almost a minute, but he didn't move. His open eyes glittered in the light.

Halvorsen was some hundreds of yards ahead of them by then.

When the splashing and cursing from below stopped he'd dropped the length of wood and bent to free the dog. Then slung on the rifle again; and finally, bent to feel in the torn-up snow at the edge of the slope. At last his fingers touched the revolver. He broke the cylinder and took off a glove and rubbed his thumbnail over the primers. A five-shot, with one round left. He pressed the ejector, discarded the empties, and replaced the live round. He positioned it to the right of the forcing cone and snapped the gun closed.

Now he was trudging along the bench. He was tired now. The long hike down that afternoon, the long climb home again; the brief burst of fear-fed energy when he'd first seen the men; the swift pace since; they'd taken their toll. He felt his years on his shoulders now, each one like a pound of lead.

He consulted his mind. Though it was fuzzy on some things, like what he'd had for breakfast, or who the President was, he found his map of

the land he walked on etched sharp and clear as a surveyor's plat. He was
headed west along the slope of Town Hill, on the second bench. Half a
mile farther was a saddle, then a creek, then the start of Lookout Tower
Hill. No tower there anymore, hadn't been for years, but he remembered
it. That was perhaps three miles from here, in the dark.

Cold he outrun them? Go up the run, angle left down the valley, then
over Gerroy into Dale Hollow and back down to Route Six? It'd be a hike.
Eight miles at least. He figured if he had all night he could do it.

If he had all night. He paused and looked back. Under the overcast
sky, not far back on his trail, swayed a faint glow. His mouth tightened in
the darkness. They had a flashlight, then. They could track him. They
were on foot, not used to the land, but their youth and strength would
make up for that in a chase lasting several hours.

He thought then about foxing them. Red fox had a thousand tricks.
One was to circle back and get on the hunter's trail. Sooner or later the
man realized he was going in circles, and the fox, having more time on
his hands, generally won that game. Halvorsen slogged on for a few
minutes. He could circle back. Once behind, he could wait till the flashlight illuminated one of them, and then . . . No, that wouldn't work. He'd
get one, but the other could take him at his leisure thereafter.

He was thinking this when something caught him painfully across the
chest. His fingers explored iron, an inch thick, rough and cold. He recognized it as a rod line. So there was a powerhouse nearby . . . sure, he
remembered it; how could he forget? It was number six on the Dreiser
lease, a seven-spot pumping from second sand fifteen hundred feet down.
He couldn't remember if it was uphill or down from this bench, but made
sense it'd be uphill; power went down easier than it went up.

The next question was, was it still in operation? He felt his way hand
over hand up the line. It cut through a tree, or the tree had grown around
it; a few feet beyond that was a support post. His fingers found the slide
fitting. The grease was fresh.

He wasn't sure yet what was evolving, back behind his mind, but it had
something to do with the powerhouse. He felt his way up the line, stumbling through brush, barking his head on invisible limbs. He wished he
had a light. Then thought: Better I don't. Then I won't depend on it.

At last, a few hundred yards up the hill, corrugated iron drummed
faintly under his outstretched hand.

"Hold up," said the blunt-faced man, clicking off the light.

The younger one halted, blinking. Without the bright circle they'd
been following he couldn't see a thing. "What is it?" he whispered, his
fingers tightening on the .44.

"Listen."

Faintly, from somewhere ahead, came a thud. They stared up through the darkness. Asaro was thinking: Wasn't a gunshot. Too soft. Balanced there in the dark, fingering their weapons and straining their ears, they heard again, after a time, a second thud. A third.

Somewhere above them a great heart began beating; irregular and slow. And faintly too came to them through the falling snow a weird squeak and groan, like damp wood rubbed together, or ancient hinges turning.

"What the hell's that?"

"I don't know."

The older man scratched his beard. Thinking: Maybe we should go back. Somehow the mark had turned the job his way. Suckered them onto his turf and whacked Tommy and Mitch. He didn't like the feeling he was getting out here in the dark, in the cold, the weird metallic groaning getting steadily louder.

"Think we should give it a pass?" he muttered.

"D'I just hear Little Nickie Asaro pissing his pants?"

"Fuck you."

"Hey, fuck *you*, Nico-deemo. You ain't made yet. I'm going to get him. You coming?"

"Sure," said Asaro. He slowed, letting Diamond step out in front of him. He lifted the shotgun, pressed the safety off, and pointed it where the crunch, crunch of footsteps was. His finger came taut.

Then he thought: Let's get the old man first. Then I'll whack this mouth-off asshole. He pushed the safety back on and began to walk again, uphill, toward the thudding that he now recognized as some kind of engine.

The six-foot iron flywheel rumbled as it turned, filling the tin-walled, tin-roofed shed with slow thunder and the crying of cold bearings and the smells of oil and exhaust. In the darkness—there was a kerosene lamp, but Halvorsen didn't want to light it—the old gas engine shot a blue flare out the through-roof exhaust every time the cylinder fired. He could see it flicker over the snow outside the two windows. It flickered too over the bandwheel, marching around with slow deliberation, one step left, one step right, pulling the pump-jacks at the ends of the rod lines through their nodding cycle.

He'd had set them up by feel, hooking on whichever wells his hand came to first. He didn't know which the crew was pumping ten hours a day and which they pumped one. But he did know one thing, that he needed fresh crude in the stock tank.

Ain't got much time, he thought, sweating, though it was ice-cold in the shed. Not hard to figure this's where I went. It would take the men behind him a little while to find their way in the dark. A while, but maybe not enough. It depended on how long ago the day crew had left, and what lay in the sands below, deep in the earth.

Reaching inside his jacket, he fondled warm fur. "Just take it easy," he whispered, glancing out the window into the night. "It won't be long."

The younger man was sweating now. Not from fear. This was a good sweat, a workout sweat. Sure, he figured the old man was fixing something for them. Like he had for Tommy Del and Mitch. But he wasn't falling for it. They were coming round the back way. Uphill in a long loop, then casting around and coming downhill toward the noise.

It was spooky and dangerous on the slope. They weren't using the flash now. They'd take him by surprise. In the darkness they stumbled over stumps and rocks and ran into trees. The squeaking and groaning came from all around them, all up and down the hill, and they kept running into what seemed to be steel bars stretched across between the trees. He couldn't figure it. When he put his hand on one he jerked it back, as if it was hot. It was moving, going uphill two or three feet, then stopping with a jerk and then pulling itself back down again.

Weird, he thought. But not frightening. Not to a guy like Nate Diamond, two-twenty and in top condition, with a recoil-compensated .44 Auto Mag in his hand.

Behind him he heard the Italian stumble and curse. He wanted to snigger but it could wait. The big mobster. They'd said he was tough nuts. Wait till he told them how some old geezer had wadded Nickie's panties for him.

Behind him Asaro could barely keep going. The Jew kid moved too fast. It'd be a pleasure blowing him away. He had other worries too. The thin kidskin gloves, his car gloves actually, couldn't stop the cold. The steel of the shotgun sucked warmth out of his flesh. He couldn't get Burck out of his mind. He'd seen men die, he'd put two inches in their mouths and grinned into their eyes as he pulled the trigger. But for some reason the image of the frozen man stayed with him.

Maybe because it could be him next.

They made out a black angularity ahead at the same time. Some kind of building. There was a blue flicker above it . . . exhaust? . . . all these rods led to it like an iron spiderweb. Asaro didn't know what it was and he didn't care. He was freezing. He wanted a drink. Time to finish this up.

He aimed the pocket flash and pressed the button briefly. The momentarily lit circle showed them a door before the world was black again. "Take the back," he snapped.

"I got this side."

"Take the back!" Asaro hissed, swinging the pump toward him.

"Okay. Okay, goddamnit!"

Diamond jogged away, thinking *That prick's not gonna make it back to the truck*. The old man could take credit for three as well as for two. He reached the rear of the shed. Groping, he found a big iron tank and a batch of pipes going in through the wall. There was a window too. He crouched under it, the magnum held low, and over the irregular banging of the engine shouted, "Yo!"

"Take him!"

Up and over. The window burst inward. His feet hit hard and instantly scooted out from under him. He sprawled in something slippery, sucking in heavy, choking air, and scrabbled around in sudden panic until he found his gun again.

There was a heavy dull boom and the door at the far end blew inward. Asaro followed it, flashlight in one hand, the pump in the other. Their guns followed the beam as it swept the interior. It showed them machines, slowly revolving wheels, spokes, pipes, valves, and levers. But no old man. The light came back and down and steadied on him.

"What're you doing on the floor, Diamond?"

"I slipped."

"Christ," said Little Nickie. "Smells like a fucking gas station in here. Smells like—"

"Holy shit." Nate scrambled suddenly up, reaching for a pipe. It broke under his weight, and more of the slick darkness came pouring out of it.

"What?" said Asaro.

"We better get out of here."

They saw the face at the window at the same moment. It might have been there before, peering in at them from the night. But now it was suddenly and brilliantly illuminated, as if by a flare. Diamond jerked round instantly, bringing the pistol up. Asaro was turning too, lifting the shotgun. But neither of them had gotten close to aiming when the big wooden kitchen match, still sputtering in bright flashes of igniting phosphorus, came sailing lazily in to join them.

Halvorsen lay face down in the snow, waiting for burning things to stop falling out of the night. The initial eye-searing flash had been natural gas. The fireball that followed had been natural gasoline, the volatile fraction crude petroleum carried even before it was cracked. The major part of the thousand cubic feet of hell that now filled the roofless shed was the slower-igniting flammables: kerosene, naphtha, fuel oil, and paraffin. It was mixed, unrefined. But it was all there in the two or three hundred gallons of fresh-from-the-well, high-grade Pennsylvania crude he'd pumped out onto the concrete floor of the powerhouse.

He lifted his head. Something was staggering out where the door had been; something that resembled a pitch-pine branch on fire. It didn't stagger far.

When the cartridges stopped cooking off Halvorsen got up. The fire was good on his face and he stood for a little while in front of it, warming himself.

This wouldn't end it. These four thugs had been strangers to the county. From outside. They'd been hired by somebody and told where he lived and what to do to him. So this was just the beginning. There'd be more.

Got to clear out, he thought. Fill a pack with food, ammo, his old down bag, and clear out into the woods.

And after that? Well, he'd have to think.

At last he judged it was time to go. He retrieved the pup, her belly wet from the sudden noise, from inside an abandoned drum and put her back in his coat. He got the rifle from where he'd hung it on a tree.

He reached for his tobacco, but his fingers stopped instead at a hard curve. He held the revolver for a moment—he hadn't needed it after all—and then tossed it into the fire, on the far side of the glowing outline of the engine. After a few minutes it went off with a pop and a little shower of sparks.

Biting off a chew, blinking thoughtfully, Halvorsen trudged slowly back up the hill.

Twenty-six

She sat at the window, by the telephone, in her pink quilted robe. Her face was swollen and red and she hadn't put on any makeup when she got up.

She was past caring about makeup.

I tried my best, Jaysine thought. In that last savage moment she'd finally managed to say it. That *if he'd loved her* she'd have done anything for him. Lie, sin, give up her profession. Anything.

Now she knew the truth. Her shame and her renunciation meant nothing to him.

She'd never meant anything to Brad Boulton.

She sat quietly in the growing light, looking down at the street with empty eyes. It didn't seem right, it didn't seem how things should be, that it was so hard to find someone to love.

Finally it was seven. She hadn't wanted to call too early. She positioned the phone book beside the telephone and dialed.

A woman answered. When Jaysine asked for Phil she sounded first surprised, then disapproving. At last she said, "Just a moment." While she waited Jaysine carried the phone into the kitchen and poured coffee. There was one doughnut left. Coconut sprinkles.

When he said, "Yeah?" it sounded like his mouth was full too.

"Phil?"

"Uh, yeah. Who's this?"

"Jaysine Farmer."

"Oh. Oh, hi. How are you?"

"Can I come over and see you?"

"What, now? I got to leave for school pretty soon. What, uh, what's it about?"

"It's about what we talked about."

"Oh."

From the pause she could tell he still wasn't sure what she meant. "About the chemicals," she said.

"Oh. Yeah."

"Listen." She took a deep breath, closed her eyes. Said, all at once, "I know who's doing it."

There. She'd done it. Up till that moment, she hadn't been sure she could.

"Doing what?"

"What you were talking about in the bar. Dumping stuff. Here in the county."

He didn't say anything. She stirred sugar into her coffee, hesitated, added more. At last he said, "How do you know that?"

"Remember the notebook I showed you? In the library? I'm not *absolutely* sure, but I think it's got something to do with it. Unless—unless you got it all taken care of already."

Again he didn't respond immediately. She heard a distant thud, scratching on the far end, as if the phone were being moved. Then his voice came back, lowered. "We ought to tell Racks."

"Who?"

"Mr. Halvorsen. The guy I told you was working on it with me. Look, can you meet me at the Todds footbridge?"

"Well—okay. When? After school?"

"No. Right away. And look. Dress warm. Wear boots."

"Why?"

"We're going to do some climbing."

She put on light powder and lipstick, just for the street, and went out. Before she'd gone ten feet she was glad he'd warned her to dress warm.

The boy was waiting for her when she got there, leaning against rusty iron, staring into the creek as if contemplating a jump. His jacket was cheap and worn, and he looked thin and sad. For a moment she stepped outside her own misery, thinking: He's unhappy too. It made her feel like hugging him. She said, coming up beside him, "Here I am."

"Hi." He straightened, looked her up and down, and blushed a little. She thought it was cute.

"D'jou bring it?" he asked her. "The book?"

"Yes."

"Okay, let's go."

She hadn't really understood what he meant by "climbing"; she'd thought, maybe walk up a road. Instead they went straight up past the houses into the woods. She followed him through deep snow for half an hour. As the town dropped away below them snow filled her boots and brambles clawed at her coat. She had to stop and rest twice.

She wasn't used to this. She was thinking about giving up when at last he stopped, looked around, and pointed. She looked, but saw only a pretty little patch of Christmas trees. Not till they were standing over a dead fire between two logs did she realize how artfully concealed the lean-to was.

The boy bent and looked inside it. Then straightened, looking frightened. "He isn't here."

"You lookin' for me?"

They both stiffened, looking toward the voice.

An old and evil-looking man stood back in the trees, holding a rifle. His face was grizzled white as ashes and there was an open sore on it. Dead animals hung from his belt. He looked cadaverous and sick and insane. As she stared he came forward a few feet, and she saw a little dog behind him.

"Ain't good business sneakin' up on a camp, boy. Better to call out, when you're comin' up. So, who's this?"

"Somebody I thought you should see. She's got something to tell us."

"Yeah? Well, looks like you about froze her." The old man came forward, short shuffling steps, and bent to pull off snowshoes. He propped the rifle against a log and squatted.

She couldn't see how he did it, but in less time than it would have taken her to brush her hair he had a little blaze going, shimmering the air but giving up no smoke at all. She sat on a log and stretched her hands to the heat. The puppy came up to her. She petted it and it gamboled awkwardly, one eye on the old man.

"Had breakfast yet, Miss?"

"No, just a doughnut, but please don't—you don't have to . . ."

But he'd already produced a knife. Before she had time to catch her breath he had the animals opened, gutted, and reduced to strips of meat. They went into an aluminum pot with snow and handfuls of nuts and sliced-up roots. That went on the fire, followed by a smaller pan with more snow. She watched, fascinated, as he stirred and seasoned with pinches of dried herbs.

They looked out over the valley as they waited for the stew to cook. She'd never been up this high before. She was surprised at how big the land was, and how empty; how small Raymondsville looked, huddled along the frozen river.

At last the stew was ready. She took a wary spoonful, followed with a

sip of coffee. It was delicious. Meanwhile sourdough bread had been cooking on peeled sticks. Halvorsen broke it in his hands and they mopped
the pans with it.

When the meal was over and everything scrubbed out with snow the
old man adjusted himself against the lean-to, bending his gaze on her at
last. "All right," he said, "Now who are you? And why'd Mr. Romanelli
bring you up to see me? Go ahead, Miss. We're listenin'."

She remembered, then, why she was here. The brief sense of escape,
of wonder at the view and breakfast on the mountain, disappeared. "My
name's Jaysine Farmer," she started, nervous under the old man's intentness.
"I work—worked on Pine Street, at the Style Shoppe. I've been dating a man.
When we . . . split up, he left his appointment book at my place."

The old man nodded, pale eyes locked on hers.

"Anyway I ran into Phil down at the library a few days ago. He told me
what he was working on. Then I got to reading the notebook."

"You were readin' it when I met you," said the boy.

"I mean, I figured out what it meant. Actually I—It took a while to
decide to tell anybody this."

They both nodded. It was funny, they looked so solemn, like the Mor-
mons who came to town in the summer on their bicycles. She almost
laughed, then recalled herself. "Anyway, look," she said. "Right here, on
this page. Where it says, 'Drop #12, Gould Run, 536.' "

"Let me see." The old man took the book. After a moment his hand
moved to his coat for a pair of old-fashioned spectacles. He turned several
pages. Then flipped it closed and looked at the front. "Whose is this?"

"His name's Brad Boulton."

Halvorsen had been thinking about the entries, but the name made him
blink. What had the blunt-faced man said last night, the four of them
looking like hunters and yet not, at least not of deer—"Boulton said there
was a house."

It came to him now that yes, he'd met a man of that name, not long
before.

"Who's he?"

"He's with Thunder Oil, in Petroleum City. He's important, the president, I think."

Halvorsen nodded, slowly, slowly. Sure. That was the guy.

He didn't like it, but it made sense.

You saw the big T.O. tankers on the roads so often you didn't think
about them. They were part of the scenery, like the hills. The big black
trucks with a jagged thunderbolt in a red circle, same as on the peak of
his old green hat. No one looked twice at them around Hemlock County.

The ease of it suddenly came clear. They left the refinery full of gasoline for the stations. You saw them all the time, the big rigs pulled in close to the gas pumps, hoses snaking down to underground tanks, drivers standing talking to the owners or setting their valves. And the specialty products, fine grades of lube oil, feedstocks, headed east too in the same black rigs.

He'd never thought about it before, but they'd be coming back empty. He could see how a certain kind of a person might see that as an opportunity.

Holding that possibility suspended in his mind, he studied the pages again. He turned to a blank one and plucked a twig out of the fire.

Using the charred end and flipping back and forth, he noted each time the word "drop" appeared. Roughly twice a week, with the names of various roads or hollows, and the number—the truck, he thought suddenly. Sure, they had to have some kind of number so the dispatchers could route them.

He didn't like the idea of his company, he still thought of it that way, being mixed up in this. He smiled faintly. Oh, the old-line men were no plaster saints. They'd jump each other's leases, short-stick the pipeline companies, steal oil from each other with vacuum and crooked wells; they'd gamble and drink and fight like tomcats over a fancy girl; they might even, during Prohibition, smuggle in boxcars full of—well, he'd go back and think about all that later.

The smile faded. But they wouldn't have dumped poison in the county they lived in. Or any other. They just weren't made that way.

But Thunder, like the whole country, was in the hands of a new kind now.

"Lemme see," Phil said, leaning forward. It made sense; it made a lot of sense. "New Jersey."

"What's that?"

"That's where it's coming from. There's a lot of dumping there. Now they found a way to get rid of it out here."

Jaysine smiled at him. "Your face is getting red."

"Well, I'm excited!"

The old man handed him the book and leaned back, lips pursed, eyes musing behind half-moon lenses. Phil flipped the pages rapidly, thinking, What day was it Racks got sick? and remembered it was a Saturday. He looked at the twenty-eighth. Nothing. Then he looked at the page before it. The twenty-seventh. It said, halfway down the page amid the other jottings, *Drop #14, Mortlock, 950.*

"Holy shit," he said. "You're right. This's a dumping schedule."

"Course 'tis," said Halvorsen, sounding irritated. "See that soon's you open it."

Phil laid the notebook carefully on a dry spot on the log as Halvorsen fitted another slab of split maple into the fire. There was a brief silence, broken by the crackle as flames found the wood, and then, far and faint, the nasal drone of a train. They no longer stopped in Raymondsville, though the old man remembered when they had. They watched it wind through town and over the trestle over the river and creep off down the valley east, toward Coudersport, East Towanda, Scranton . . .

"Okay," said Jaysine. "Now you talk. Tell me what's going on. From the start."

Halvorsen and Romanelli looked at each other. Finally the old man cleared his throat. He told her about the snowplow, his hospitalization, and the diagnosis.

The boy broke in then with what the doctor had said about other cases in the county. He told about their stakeout of Route Six, their eventual success.

He stopped there and the old man took up the thread again. This time he told of going out to Cherry Hill, his reception, and the subsequent cutoff of his pension. He told about his call to the investigator, Leiter. Last he told them about the four men who'd come to burn him out the night before.

When they finished Jaysine sat silent. Part of her couldn't believe it. But she knew it was true.

"It's him," she said.

"You know him, you say?" said Halvorsen. "I've only seen him once. He's the type to do this?"

"Yes."

"He'd send out to kill somebody in this way?"

She thought about that one. She remembered his last words to her, when he was leaving, when he hit her. She took a deep breath. "Yes. I think he would."

Phil said, "What is this, a trial? He owns Thunder Oil. We know how he's been planning the runs. I'm convinced. The question is, what do we do about it?"

"Go to the police?" said Jaysine.

He told her about his father. "So that's worthless," he finished. "All that'll do is get this Boulton to send more thugs after you and me along with Mr. Halvorsen, if he hasn't already. No, there's only one thing to do."

"What's that?"

"Kill him."

Jaysine went cold inside. She thought suddenly, *They're crazy.* The old man looked it and the boy, with his hate-filled, bitter laugh, sounded like it. She felt sorry for them both, especially Phil. He didn't walk right and it was obvious just from looking that he'd never been loved. But talking about . . . what they were talking about, that was just crazy. "I don't think that would be a good idea," she said.

"Why not? It's the only way to stop it for good."

"It's wrong. That's why."

"What he's doing's worse. How many people are going to get sick, get cancer, die from that stuff? And there's no other way. We've tried."

"It's still wrong."

"No, *you're* wrong—"

"Hold your horses, boy. She's right."

Phil felt like shrieking at the treetops. "What? Mr. Halvorsen—he's the one sent those guys to kill you! Don't you want to—"

"Kill him? Not especially."

"But those crooks—you said you—"

The old man said coldly, "That was different. Right then it was them or me, boy. But if you're thinkin' to murder somebody, shoot him from ambush over at Cherry Hill or something, well, forget it. It could be done, sure. But W. T. Halvorsen won't do it."

"I'm sorry, I didn't mean that, exactly. I just thought—"

Meanwhile Halvorsen was sitting back, thinking. He reached for the book again. When the boy ran down he said, "Might be a way to make 'em listen to us, though."

"What's that?"

"We got to make it so this Boulton can't lay low any longer, or say he didn't do it and pay people to cover it up. We got to drag the whole stinking shebang right out in the open."

"How?"

"Stop one of the trucks. Hijack it, or force it off the road—something like that."

"Holy smoke," said Phil. He jerked slightly and started to smile. "Sure! That'd do it. That'd be great!"

"What do you think?" Halvorsen asked Farmer.

"I don't know. I guess if nobody got hurt."

"Can't guarantee it a hundred percent. Or wait, maybe we could . . . pretty close anyway." Halvorsen showed them the charcoaled page. "Look at this here. See what it says? On the nineteenth—that's tomorrow—truck number 223's going to be dumping out by Rich Falls. There's a dollar sign by it, too, I don't know what that means . . . Know where Rich Falls is?"

"Sure."

"I don't," said Jaysine.

Halvorsen swiveled to face her. "Nine, ten miles east of here, some rapids, used to be a dam. Iron bridge leaves the main road, crosses the river, and heads on up into the woods. There was a tavern-house and a planing mill and a tannery up there years ago, but all there is now's the oil leases and a gravel pit. That's Rich Falls. The next date after that, y'see, isn't till January."

The three sat around the fire, thinking.

Halvorsen hacked off another length of maple and added it to the fire. He was remembering another time he'd had to face up to Thunder, and to Forest, Kendall, Wolf's Head, and the rest of the Northwestern Producer's Association. That cold as shit, dangerous winter of '36. He remembered the florid faces of the hired thug-muscle, the line of brown-shirted National Guard. That time too they'd had no other recourse. No other place to turn.

Jaysine was thinking about her future. Once she'd dreamed of her own shop, a neat little place with a tanning salon, a counter with her own line of beauty products. That was the time to sell them, when women were feeling lovely and wanted to stay that way forever. Then for a while she'd let herself dream about being Brad's wife. If only she'd—No, she thought. It wasn't her fault. It wouldn't have happened, not ever. He's evil and he never loved me.

She didn't think about the future anymore, or if she did it was too dark to look at, like the sun in reverse. But she wanted the world to know what kind of rottenness was inside Brad Boulton.

Phil fingered his front teeth gingerly. Like the old man had said, they'd set again. He grinned bitterly inside. Funny how a guy who didn't care whether he lived or died could be glad he wasn't going to lose a tooth. He liked Halvorsen's idea. Hijacking a truck sounded exciting.

"More coffee?" said Halvorsen, reaching for the pot. They both nodded. "So. What do you think?"

"Isn't anything else *to* do," said Phil. "Except lie down and let him do what he wants. What he did to you . . . He'll kill us if he can't keep us quiet any other way. No, we got to stop him."

"It's me that's got to do that," said Halvorsen mildly. "I'm the one he's mainly after. I don't want you young people to get in any trouble. You got your lives ahead of you. All I might need's a little help. To get some things, since I can't go into town no more."

"Mr. Halvorsen?"

"Yes, Jay—Jaysine?"

"I'll help you any way you want."

"Me too," said Phil. "I got nothing to lose."

Halvorsen looked at them for a long time over the fire. They were so darn young. But maybe that was an advantage. Young people weren't afraid. They didn't believe in tragedy, loss, death. Whereas he'd seen it too many times to believe it couldn't, wouldn't, come to W. T. Halvorsen.

Well, if it came, he'd had a long, full life. And in some ways he was looking forward to Judgment.

"Okay, that's settled," he said. "Now the way I see it, we can't wait till January. We got to do her now, catch that truck tomorrow, or like as not he'll get us first. So we ain't got much time to put it all together."

"How do you want to do it?" said Jaysine, scratching the puppy's head.

They waited; the old man stared down the hill. At last he blinked. "If I done it right I could drop the bridge at Rich Falls, and the truck with it."

"Drop it? What do you mean, *drop* it?"

"Blow her up. Or at least fix it so's it goes down when the truck turns on to it."

"Yeah, but then what?" said Phil, unable to keep skepticism out of his voice.

"Once they got a truck sitting in the Allegheny River it'll be hard to pretend ain't nothing going on that oughtn't to be. Remember a couple years ago, when that tank collapsed at Ashland and a million gallons of diesel went down the Monongahela? They didn't have any drinking water in Pittsburgh for a week. I figure soon's it goes in, we call Bill Sealey, at the State Police barracks. I'm sure Bill's square, I've known him since he was a kid, but we got to give him a mouthful 'fore he can bite down.

"So here's the way I figure. Just tell me if you think of a problem, or of something better."

"Don't worry, we will," said Phil. He looked out over the hills, and pulled in a deep breath of icy wind. He felt as if the old man had offered him the world. He grinned boldly at Jaysine, and after a moment she smiled back.

"You listenin'?" said Halvorsen.

"I sure am."

And Jaysine said, taking her own deep breath, "We're ready. Just tell us what you want done."

Twenty-seven

Done, Boulton suddenly knew deep in his heart as the man across from him struggled to his feet, tugging at his tie, a lost, confused look in his eyes. It's a dodge. A fake. A bluff.

Because Luke Fleming was the biggest independent lease operator left in the state. A few years before he'd been next door to broke. Now, with tertiary recovery proving out, he held the key to millions of barrels of oil, locked like vaulted gold in the sandstone under the hills.

Their meeting had been good business. Thunder owned leases, but they no longer supplied all the crude Number One needed. This meant federal tax law put the company at a disadvantage. The depletion allowance let the majors, Exxon and Shell and Mobil, subtract revenue from domestic crude production from their pretax income. Since they lumped production and refining costs, they could charge themselves more for crude, and pay less tax on refinery profits than companies that had to buy on the open market.

That, with economies of scale, had gradually squeezed out their smaller competitors, and driven Thunder's margins down to where it couldn't afford to modernize.

Fleming, and five more men like him, were Boulton's answer. A few minutes before, Brad had offered him a directorship in The Thunder Group in return for exclusive marketing of his crude. This would let T.O. exercise the same pricing and tax policies as the majors. If the producers accepted, the Group would be born as a mini-major, instantly dominant in the specialty lubrication market. The only threat then would be technological, the new synthetic lubricants. But no oil company had much interest in pushing them, for obvious reasons: They increased gas mileage.

Now, standing, he shook the broad soft hand and thought: Business is war. And as in war, victory gave herself not to the most deserving, the wisest, nor even the most ruthless, but to whoever lasted longest. Whatever it took—battle, borrow, lie, steal, scam—you had to just keep going. Till your vision proved itself or the receivers walked in.

When Fleming left, Brad ordered another drink. He looked idly around the dining room.

The Petroleum Club had been built during the oil rush, a hundred years before. The atmosphere was late Victorian: carved-oak balustrades, carpets, Austrian crystal chandeliers. Above the walnut wainscoting hung age-freckled engravings. Hundreds of timber derricks sprouted like forests, horse-drawn wagons plowed through mud streets, tiny figures posed in stovepipe hats and bonnets. In paling sepia gushers leaped skyward, a governor clipped the ribbon to an opera house, Adah Isaacs Mencken posed nude on a white stallion.

Now, at the bar, a white-jacketed waiter poured Heineken for a lawyer. Other members, all male, local executives and professionals, sat reading the *WSJ* or *Business Week*.

He finished his martini and signed the chit. Pulling on his new overcoat, he cycled through the revolving door, and stood tucking in his scarf, looking down the main street of Petroleum City.

The air was keen after the steam-heated club, sharp as an accountant's pencil. On the far side of town, above the dull brick of the college, Cherry Hill rose like a granite skyrocket. From habit he looked for the soaring towers, but caught only a flicker against the overcast.

He was thinking again of the fencing over lunch. Fleming hadn't agreed. Wanted to have his lawyers go over it. Something about a counteroffer from Kendall—

He held his breath. The wind moved past his face like icy water past a swimming salmon's, seizing his ears with steel pincers, touching his cheeks with tingling anesthesia. He lifted his suddenly brimming eyes to the hill again.

Fleming would sign. That's what his confused look meant. He was old, ready to quit. He was stalling, that was all, trying to carve out leverage. Leverage that now, since he'd revealed his weakness, he wouldn't have.

Just that simply, he'd won.

Once the deal with Fleming was announced, the stock sale would be a pushover. The refinery would be rebuilt, and the new superclean fuel would reestablish Thunder as a leader in the gasoline market.

The Thunder Group was a reality.

The warmth of triumph, like the glow from a handball workout, faded after a block or two. His eyes fell gradually from sky to hill, to buildings, at last to the partially cleared sidewalk.

The reorganization would work, *if* nothing went off the rails in the next week.

But on another front, he had a major problem.

A car passed; he caught a waved hand; nodded back, recognizing Pretrick, from the Industrial Chemicals division . . . The phone call that morning had been upsetting. Of the four guys from Newark, only one was still alive, and he was badly hurt. Something about a stake in the chest. Remembering the shaking old geezer who'd come to Cherry Hill, Brad found it hard to believe.

He'd told John to send his best team this time. They'd flown in this morning, in his view not a day too soon. This had to be closed off quick.

Had to be sealed off . . . He wondered if he didn't need someone full time for this kind of thing. It wasn't smart for a CEO to deal with it himself. Best to have a cutout between him and the muscle. For just a moment it occurred to him how dangerous this whole thing was.

Not just legally but . . . His neck prickled suddenly under the cashmere scarf. He glanced quickly around, searching faces on the lunchtime street. Halvorsen was loose, unaccounted for. They said he was a hunter, a damn good one. Old, sure. But he'd just killed three of the men who'd gone after him.

It occurred to him suddenly that he was totally exposed. It was a new and intensely unpleasant sensation. He twisted his neck, studying the rooftops. No one there. Yet a mounting fear hurried his steps. His eyes kept going to windows. He stumbled on a frozen dike of snow and fell to his knees in it. He jumped up quickly, dusted dirty snow and salt from his coat, and moved toward the Thunder Building, almost at a run.

When he had the portico between him and the sky he panted with relief. His kidneys ached. Drive from now on, he thought. No more parading around the streets like Joe Citizen. Joe Target.

Well, John's new boys would take care of Halvorsen. He scowled as he pressed the elevator button. Might be smart, too, to give the cops a call. Get Nolan in Raymondsville and Keaton here in P.C. to alert their men. They could pick him up, when he showed in town for food. Then the boys could drop by and visit him at the jail.

He stood alone in the humming, slowly rising steel box. Was there anything else he should be doing? The old man and the kid were sealed off, or shortly would be. He'd bricked off the EPA and the media. But other agencies might be interested, especially if there was anything messy about Halvorsen's termination.

Was there a better way? What if he talked to the old man once they found him, offered him his pension back if he withdrew the report? Hell, if that worked he wouldn't need John's muscle, wouldn't need Leiter even. But even as he thought this he knew it wasn't really an option. Aside from the personal danger, every day Halvorsen lived, in or out of custody, gave him time to spread tales. Once the Thunder trucks stopped being invisible the dumping business would be over. Most deadly, any news break or even rumor would hammer down the price of T.O. stock.

He couldn't afford to leave those stakes on the table. Putting it to bed now was the minimum-risk, minimum-cost strategy. He straightened his tie in the elevator mirror. For a moment he almost pitied the old man, fleeing through the winter woods, knowing no matter where he came out he'd be taken like a rat.

But Halvorsen and the boy, they'd had their warning. And ignored it.

When he stepped off on the executive floor his secretary was chatting with a refractories salesman. Brad nodded to him, but shook his head at her. Weyandt could see him. Twyla handed him a card but instead of looking at it right away he asked her to call Cherry Hill and have Mr. Jones come into town. Mr. Jones would be accompanying him full time for a while.

He drew coffee, deciding that his fright on the street had been due to the drinks at lunch. Here, five stories up, his fears seemed childish. He took a sip and headed for his office.

She sat in front of his desk. Dark blond, shoulder-length hair, tweed suit, heels. When he cleared his throat she twisted, looking back at him. After a moment he came the rest of the way in. He slid behind his desk, put his hands behind his head, and leaned back.

"Dr. Friedman," he said, his voice flat. "Nice to meet you."

"Hello, Mr. Boulton."

He examined her dispassionately. Intellectual. Thirty-five, thirty-six. A stripped-down model, serviceable, but basics only. "I don't recall having an appointment with you."

"You don't. I found myself in P.C. and thought I'd stop by. I think we're due for a talk."

"Is that so?"

"Yes."

"It wouldn't be about a job, would it? We have several openings for talented, conscientious medical people."

"No, Mr. Boulton. In fact, hell, no."

He made himself relax. Bitch break, he thought. She wouldn't like cigarettes either. He found the pack in the desk, lit one, and leaned back farther. "Talk to me, Doctor."

"I understand you've taken on a new physician. A Dr. Patel."

"That's right. He'll be overseeing our health care division."

"I suppose I know the answer to this one already. But I'll ask it just the same. Is he competent?"

"How would I know? I'm a layman. Vinny's a licensed physician. If he's good enough for you guys he's good enough for me." He waited, but the ball didn't come back. "Can I offer you a drink?"

"No."

"How about a quickie? That door can be locked."

"You're not amusing me, Mr. Boulton. You're not even disgusting me."

"Well, I must be doing something right. You're here."

"I'm here about your antisocial activities in this county."

"What activities are those?"

She held up fingers. "One. Poisoned heating oil. Two. Groundwater contamination. Three. Roadside dumping. Four. Your string of rip-off nursing homes." She rippled her other hand. "I'm sure there's more. But those are all I'm sure of at the moment."

"Do your directors know you're here?"

"Directors?"

He said patiently, "Of Raymondsville Hospital, Doctor. Barnett, Whitecar, Froster, Gerroy, et al. The men who hired you. They know you're up here tossing off casual insults at a major donor?"

"They will when I tell them."

"Or maybe sooner."

She laughed suddenly. "Wait a minute. Is that supposed to scare me? That I may have to take a better-paying job someplace I can hear a symphony or go to a museum? Find another button, Mr. Boulton. That one's not connected."

"Oh, I'm sure there's one." He thought about saying something witty about lesbianism, but instead found himself yawning. It seemed like an effective statement, so he did it again. "Look, did you have something substantive to say? If not, I'll ask you to peddle your bleeding heart on somebody else's carpet."

"Just that I know what's going on, and I intend to stop it. Hemlock County has a board of public health. So far it's dealt with rabies, mainly, but I think you're a bigger threat."

"You could have told me that on the phone."

"True. But I wanted to meet you. It seemed important, somehow, before I took you on."

"I guess that makes sense."

He wondered if he ought to make an effort here. Offer her a new cat-scan machine or something. Then he decided, to hell with her. "Okay, you've seen me, we're enemies. Happy? Now get out."

When she was gone he waited a few minutes, till his pulse rate fell. It was time for a decision, and he didn't want to make it hastily or emotionally. He wanted to do it cold, cold as snow.

For a moment he felt fear again. This time not visceral, like his terror under the open sky, but a deeper disquiet. Word was spreading. How many had *she* told? Would his contacts, Ainslee's influence, the Thunner name be enough this time? He thought of his last trip to Vegas: the roulette table, up to a thousand from pocket change and putting it all on the red. The ball rolling, rolling, in its eye-riveting downward spiral. He had to decide. The shipment, and the payment, were coming in tomorrow.

But then he realized—suddenly, with relief—that he wasn't thinking straight. There was no "decision." This wasn't a choice, like the kind they made in high school plays, between good and evil.

This was business. He was acting for the company. For the stockholders, who'd employed him. For Dan and Ainslee. And indirectly, for Williamina. Thunder would be hers one day. And business sense, hard-headed logic, told him the only way to save it was to seal this whole problem off. Right now. Waffling or delay just meant more people would be hurt.

He thought about it for a few minutes longer, just to make sure. When he was satisfied with it, calm, he reached for the intercom. "Twyla."

"Yes, sir."

"Get me that number I gave you this morning. Over at the Holiday Inn."

"Yes, sir. Sir, how was that coffee this morning? Are you ready for a refill yet?"

"Yeah, that was great, meant to say something—is that the—"

"The Kona blend."

"Yeah, that's great stuff, babe. Get me that number now, will you?"

But before the outside call light came on the intercom beeped again. He pressed the lever, looking out over the town. His, by the grace of God. And his it would stay. "Yeah," he said. "Isn't he there?"

"It's an incoming call. Your wife, sir. She sounds, um, angry."

"What? What does she want now?"

"I'm not sure, sir . . . something about your daughter."

He had to close his eyes before he could force his voice into the empty cheeriness that was the only way, now, he could deal with Ainslee Thunner Boulton. When would it end? When would she be off his back?

Then he thought: You know when. As soon as the new board meets, and you run it. After that she's history, she and her taxidermy specimen of a father, and all her fucking forebears. And then, baby, it's a done deal and a new era.

"Okay, Twyla," he said, the cheerfulness real now. "Put her on."

Twenty-eight

T he rear wheels whined, slickspinning on snow and frozen grass greasier than ice. Phil sweated, fighting the big Plymouth's slide toward the drop. The tires slid, grabbed, slid again.

Yet somehow the cruiser still trundled upward, skating wide around turns where the road canted bodily, as if the hill were trying to buck them off.

He glanced at the old man. Halvorsen sat motionless, one hand braced to the dash. Then pulled his eyes back to see treetops in front of him. He downshifted and jerked right, missing the drop by inches. "Jesus," he mumbled through dry lips. In back the puppy struggled to its feet, moaning.

Finally he couldn't stand it any longer. This was only the fourth time he'd driven a car. He hated to think what would happen if they got stuck, if his father woke to find the squad car missing. He wouldn't have dared take it again, but there was so little time before dark and so much to do. He cleared his throat. "Uh, I don't think we can get much farther, Mr. Halvorsen."

The old man grunted wordlessly and reached for his rifle.

When Halvorsen stepped out of the car his nostrils flared involuntarily. Raw, disquieting, the smell rippled like a danger flag on air that up to now, seeping through the window, had carried only snow and the astringent bite of evergreen. He lifted his head and closed his eyes, trying to decipher it.

The driver's door slammed. When he looked across the hood the boy's questioning gaze was locked on him.

"What is it?" said Phil. Something about the way the old man had hesitated, eyes closed, made him nervous.

Halvorsen grunted and shook his head. He reached his pack out, then narrowed his attention to the road. He studied it for several seconds, then lifted a slow regard to examine the woods, first to one side, then the other.

"What do you see?" Phil said, hearing nervousness in his voice.

Halvorsen silenced him with a downward wave. He shifted the rifle to his left hand and dropped the lever. He fitted a cartridge to the chamber. Then, a technique he'd learned hunting the big browns, he wedged three more rounds ready in his right, gripping them between his fingers, primers to the palm.

Holding the weapon ready, set to pivot instantly for a snapshot, he followed his searching gaze slowly up the last mile of Mortlock Run. Behind him, limping, came the boy.

The smell sharpened as they climbed. Halvorsen felt it seep into him, penetrate him, lodge like a sickness in his bowels. When he came out at last into the clearing he looked around once more, a long, searching examination of the bourn of forest and wind-smoothed snow.

Then sank to his knees, staring into the charred, stinking hole that had been his home.

Phil blinked at the old man's back. The flakes fell casually on it, one here, one there, glistening like diamond-chips on the faded wool. Then he raised his eyes to the woods, searching for whatever Halvorsen had been looking for. The thugs who'd torched his place, he imagined. Though it looked like they'd been gone a long time.

There was something else going on too. Something he didn't understand. And he didn't like the way the old man looked. Drugged, or worse, sort of scared.

That didn't fit his picture of W. T. Halvorsen. If he's scared, Phil thought, what chance have we got?

At last the old man got up, stiffly, using the rifle as a prop, and looked around with a brief blank glance. "What d'ya think?" Phil asked him.

"Ain't been long." Halvorsen's voice was unsteady. Phil heard him take a breath, let it out, to drift rapidly away from them toward the valley.

He looked at the basement carefully, trying to use his senses the way the old hunter did. He smelled burned wood and paper, a faint reek that might be gasoline. There was no smoke. The butts of the beams, where the fire had burned itself out, were frosted with gray ash. But then, concentrating, he felt heat on his face. It was still radiating from the rock walls. When at last he looked up, Halvorsen's nearly colorless eyes had lifted to dwell on his.

He said, the words awkward in his mouth, "Somebody, uh, burned it."

"Right."

"And the other guys, the ones who came after you—"

"That was over there. On the north face. I imagine this second bunch picked up the bodies."

A moment later Halvorsen shook himself and said harshly, "Well. Let's get to work."

"You're going down there? Is it safe?"

"Let's see what we got, anyway."

Halvorsen let himself carefully down the steps, feeling weakness tremble his knees. He knew why. Forget that, he ordered himself. Sure it smells the same. But it's gone, over, years before and done with. So many years this kid beside him hadn't probably even been born.

He shook himself again and narrowed his gaze to the present.

The destruction was uneven. The flames (gasoline, he could smell it plainly) had destroyed the mud room and most of the front. He paused at the bottom of the stairwell, then stepped gingerly through a rectangular hole framed in black char. The smell was choking and to get room in his brain to think with he began breathing through his mouth.

Past that he was confronted by a fallen shatter of joists and floorboards and bridging, the floor-beams of the house. Burned out from below, they'd collapsed in the center and lay now pointed down into a pit from both sides. But their fall, the sudden descent of several tons of old ash, earth, and snow, had snuffed out the fire. Beneath the debris he could make out the blackened smashed frame of his armchair, and near the wall his sofa. The center of the room had suffered most; the stove was completely buried.

Yeah, he thought, right lucky Jez and me was out hunting when that first bunch come up here.

He put the rifle on safe and leaned it in the entrance. Clumsily, barking his knee, he got down in a crouch and crawled in.

The stink of burning, the peculiar sadness of familiar things reduced to ruin and uselessness . . . he tried to close his mind to emotion and memory alike. Moving like a ferret through a tunnel, he crawled over his sofa, circumnavigated the central collapse, and came out in the back. The roof had only sagged there, not fallen, swayed like a nag's spine. He stood again, cautious of his head. Enough of the winter light came through for him to make out his workbench. The descent of the overhead structure had dropped a beam through it. He eyed the timber, remembering how he'd hewed it out of the valley, dragged it up here . . .

No. No more memories.

He touched it, lightly as a cat, then gave it a shove. It didn't move much. Just enough to unsettle the debris above. Dirt came down, and dried grass and a layer of old ash. The ash drifted downward through the cold white light, the old falling onto the new, and both smells mingled and came up to him.

He sank to his knees, covering his face with his hands.

When he saw the old man go down again Phil hesitated, just for a moment, then ran down the stairs.

Stepping into the fire-stink was like entering an overchlorinated pool. It teared his eyes, and he sneezed violently. Then he was on hands and knees, crawling. A rusty spike bit and he hissed.

Halvorsen was squatting in a corner, staring at a pile of trash. Down his gray-whiskered, soot-smutted face ran white tracks of tears.

Phil crouched, puzzled. What was the old man crying about? What had he lost? Nothing in this hole to cry over. Then, all at once, he understood.

He moved forward, and reached out.

Halvorsen smelled of old wool and tobacco and his beard was rough. Phil felt his shoulders jerking under his gloves. "It's okay," he said. He wasn't sure of that, but it was all he could think to say. "It's okay, Mr. Halvorsen. That was a long time ago."

The old man said nothing, but after a moment Phil felt his hand. It clung to his shoulder, surprisingly strong; then pushed him away. He almost fell backward, but remembered the spike and scrambled up before he went down.

Halvorsen dragged a sleeve over his eyes. He blinked a few times, faded-denim eyes staring into the dimness under the collapsed roof. Then hawked his throat, and spat.

He pushed char and dirt off a tin wood-scuttle and began hunting around and throwing things into it. Phil watched him pick through bits of metal and cardboard. "What're we looking for?" he said at last.

"Nothin' . . . ah, here she is." Slow fingers brushed dirt off a little box marked Olin. It went into the scuttle. He unearthed a red can, a pair of pliers. "What are you doing?" Phil said again.

"What we're going to use don't touch off as easy as nitro." Halvorsen jerked his head at the box. "That there's shotgun primers. There's a pellet of azide in each of 'em. Put a bunch together and it ought to do for a cap. Take that up and come on back."

Phil looked at what the old man had gathered. There didn't seem to be much of anything there. Except the red can, and that looked to be barely a pint.

"Is this enough gunpowder to blow up a bridge?"

"No."

"Well, then, how—"

"That's what I sent the girl after," said Halvorsen sharply. "Don't worry about that. Just do what I tell you."

Phil resented the tone, but decided his resentment didn't matter. He crept out, cradling the scuttle. Carefully; the red can made him nervous. He left it on the snow.

When he got back Halvorsen had another rifle in his hands. Abruptly he turned, and Phil found himself holding it.

The old man watched him silently as he turned it over. The wood was scorched near the butt but the working parts looked okay. He stared at the muzzle. It was round and old and deadly-looking.

"Know how to use one of these?"

"No, sir."

"This here's a old Enfield. British, bolt action. See this magazine? Cartridges go in there. Make sure the rims go ahead, not behind. Then"—the old man took it from him and demonstrated, working the action rapidly—"Flip your bolt up and back, then down again like this. Set your sights, aim, squeeze her off."

"What are you going to use?"

"Oh, I'll stay with what I got." Halvorsen shoved aside a section of fallen rock, rubble, and dirt. "But some more ammo might come in useful. Give me a hand, let's see how hard this back door's jammed."

Jaysine shivered suddenly as she swung her legs down to the snow. Her eyes lifted to the cloud-veiled brightness in the west. She didn't know exactly what time it was, but it was getting late.

Well, her shopping was almost done, and her checking account with it. She tucked in her scarf, grabbing for the end as it flickered on the wind, and glanced into the hatchback. Big box of kitchen matches. Flour sifter. Two ten-pound boxes of confectioner's sugar. A length of tin stovepipe. And a twenty-five-pound sack of fertilizer from the Agway, the exact kind he'd told her. She stood now in front of the old Raymondsville Hotel, looking up and down the street. The wind howled down it, channeled by century-old brick walls, storefronts, false fronts.

The door jangled behind her, closed-in air scorched her cheeks. She stamped snow from her boots, glancing quickly around before her glasses fogged.

It was the kind of store her mother loved, packed solid with old junk. She listened to the chiming ticks of a dozen old clocks all going at different rates. There didn't seem to be anyone around, though at the counter a shadeless Art Nouveau lamp glowed candle-dim. She rubbed her glasses with the scarf, leaning to look at old medals, Zippo lighters, folding Kodaks, silver plate. She took a turn around the store. Comic books, old ones she'd never seen before. An antique glass washboard, porcelain, an interesting picture of two naked girls, or was it a girl and a boy, lying on a porch above a mountain lake.

She was peering at it when the door jangled and she started, remembering why she was there. The little man was whistling through his teeth, stripping off mittens. When he noticed her, he smiled shy and quick and dove behind the counter, just like a rabbit. "Hello. Just come in? I was over to Pickard's for some cough drops."

"Got a sore throat?"

"A little. It's the weather." He coughed to demonstrate. "Haven't seen you here before."

"Well, it's going to be Christmas soon."

"Sure is, sure is."

She paused, wondering how she could introduce this. "I wanted something for my brother. He's interested in old oil-field things."

It took a while to get to what she wanted. She had to consider and turn down a rusty oil lamp, a sounding stick, some strange tools. Then Rosen brightened. "I know just the thing! I took it out of the front room, but—just a minute. I'll be right back."

It was a wooden box, old but nicely made, with a wooden handle set into the top. She touched it gingerly. "What is it?" she said, though she knew, at least in general terms, from the old man's explanation that morning.

"It's a dynamite detonator. Old guy in here not long ago called it a 'spark box.' They used to set off charges down in the wells with 'em. You can get a nice shock if you hold those two knobs and push down the plunger."

"No, thank you," she said. "I don't like shocks." They both laughed and she said, "Gosh, I don't know. How much you asking for it?"

She could see him examining her clothing. At last he said, "I guess I could let it go for sixty."

"You have so many nice pieces here, I'm glad I came in. I see several things I like. Like that print of the girls and the mountain. And this dresser, my mother's been looking for one like that. I like this, this old thing too, my brother'd love it. But I can't pay that much."

"Make me an offer."

She hesitated. She'd drawn all her savings, and the other things had cost more than she'd expected. "As a matter of fact, I've only got twenty dollars."

"Twenty." The little man looked, she thought, dreadfully disappointed. She too felt balked.

"Wait a minute. Do you buy things here too?"

"Once in a while."

"Well, I see you have some jewelry in your case. This bracelet—well, a—an old boyfriend gave that to me. I don't want it anymore." She twisted it off. "It's silver and turquoise. Go on, take a look."

"Excuse me," said Rosen. He went into the back room with it. When he came out he said, cautiously, "I guess I could move it. It's not good stones, it's what they call 'male' turquoise, but I could give you . . . twenty dollars for it."

"How about if we trade? That, and—oh, I have a watch here too you can have—plus twenty dollars, for this?"

"Well. I don't know."

"I know my mother would just love that dresser," she mused, moving around it, touching the table lamp too, conscious of the little man's eyes following her.

When she came out, the box heavy under her arm and her wrists feeling light as air, the sun was impaled on the dead trees atop Town Hill. She examined the street again. Mr. Halvorsen had warned her to watch for police. None in sight. She put the box carefully in the back with her other purchases and got in.

She had the key in the ignition when the passenger door opened and a man she didn't know squeezed himself through it. At the same moment another materialized outside her window. It was done so casually that from the sidewalk, if anyone had been watching, nothing would have seemed out of the ordinary. She twisted, too startled to speak. The one next to her—not large, but with a heavy, cruel face she wished she wasn't looking at—said, "Go ahead, start it."

"Get out of my car!"

"You Farmer?"

"It's her," said the outside one. She heard him only faintly, through the window.

"What do you want?"

"Start your car."

She found suddenly she couldn't breathe. It wasn't the sight of the gun. There was something wrong with her chest. She felt dizzy, and put her head down. The man took the keys from her mitten. He looked out at the other one. "Too shit-scared to drive."

"You better take it."

The man outside opened the door. He shoved her over into the passenger seat. The one inside moved to the back. But his left hand lay extended forward, beside her, so that she could see the shine of the gun, chromed like a pair of thinning scissors, where the seat belts buckled.

"Start her up," said the one in back. "Let's go south. There's a lot of woods down that way."

Phil felt doom heavy in him as he rolled backward out of the hills. It was getting late. Odds were his father was awake already. He'd left the old man at the clearing. He had to get the cruiser back, and fast.

He turned it around, sweating bullets, on the first widening, and almost got stuck. But he didn't, and the rest of the way down was straightforward, though his fingers throbbed from clenching the wheel. He thought: Wire, that's all we need now. He'd get home and crash for a few hours. They'd have to watch all day tomorrow, since there was no indication in the notebook of precisely when on the nineteenth of December a truck would rumble across the bridge at Rich Falls and into the empty woods beyond.

Dusk was falling. Across the valleyed road stretched the inchoate shadows of the hills. The cold snap had iced bridges and overpasses and there weren't many cars out. He pulled at knobs on the dash till headlights glowed on.

He was going up the flank of Gerroy Hill when he saw the rust-speckled little white car coming toward him. Its lights were off. He flicked his highs at it approached, recognizing it as he did so as Jaysine's.

It flashed past, and he saw in the transient illumination of his brights her face, not in front of the wheel but to the left. There were two men with her. Just their expressions told him instantly what they were.

Even as his foot slammed down he knew with instantaneous horror he'd done exactly what he shouldn't have. The tires lost all grip on the glare ice and at fifty miles an hour the world began to revolve.

He forgot the Toyota, forgot everything as he threw the wheel first one way and then the other. No response. The woods . . . the rear hatch of the white car, a blur of backturned face . . . the rusty guardrails over the drop to the river . . . woods again. He closed his eyes and bent, wrapping his arms over his head, waiting for death.

The Plymouth, spinning slowly around its center of mass, skated momentum-driven up the hill perhaps two hundred yards. Then, impelled by the crown, sagged off to the right. It crunched into the four-foot snowbank thrown up by the plows. The engine tried briefly to push the bumper deeper, and then stalled.

He sat with his eyes closed, shaking, and then opened them. He stared down into the river. He couldn't move for three or four seconds.

Then, all at once, his muscles unlocked. The engine ground back into life. He threw the Plymouth into reverse, a two-point turn. Then aimed it downhill and slammed the pedal into the firewall.

Two hundred police-duty horsepower polished ice briefly with rubber before he wrenched the wheels up on the crown. The squad car leaped forward, accelerating with a howl. He hit the curve at the bottom at seventy, weaving and fishtailing on and off the berm.

The Toyota was a dot far ahead, visible for a moment around the arc of the river before forest screened it. His engine screamed like a panther and he came into the next turn, still gathering speed, to find himself head to head with a huge green Genesee Beer truck. Its headlights flicked in surprise, then it began spewing snow from under locked wheels. Finally it ran off the road, horn blaring. He hurtled past, pushed back in the seat by rigid arms, eyes blasted wide by speed.

Another turn . . . he eased his foot slightly for this one. He was beginning to get it. When the skid started you eased the wheel toward where the nose was going. The car would straighten with a snap and you were back in control. That is, if you were still on the road. So you took each curve on the inside, and trusted to luck there wasn't anyone coming your way.

Fortunately there wasn't for the next two. When he came out of the second, on a short stretch where the road ahead was visible along the river, the white car wasn't far ahead.

Maybe they hadn't seen him. It seemed odd that they wouldn't have looked back after a police car but then he remembered he'd flicked up his brights. In the dusk it was hard to see behind high beams. And then too, they'd have had no hope of outrunning him in the little Toyota. The grim-looking man driving might have kept his speed down to avoid official interest.

But now he had them. Now, he thought . . . now *what?* He had the rifle in the back seat, but he couldn't drive and shoot too. He had a fast car but only the luck of the stupid had kept him from wrecking it. If he tried to force them over he might kill everybody. He didn't have much time either. This was the last straight stretch between here and Petroleum City. Once in town they could lose him easily.

He was thinking he'd better do something soon when he saw again, turned backward toward him, the oval paleness of her face. He thought: What am I afraid of? The worst that can happen is, we all die.

He tramped the accelerator and mashed his hand against the dash. Sudden scarlet shafts stabbed out into the darkness, and the siren blasted out its two-tone discordance.

The squad car surged up on the Toyota, skidded just before it got to it, and ran up on two wheels onto the snowbank. The Toyota veered left, its rear wheels cutting up white roostertails. He'd expected that, though, and he jammed on his brakes with all his strength as his right wheels slammed down again.

The cruiser bounced, yowling. The small car cut right again as he dropped back toward it and he stabbed the brakes again, hard as he could, trying to do now on purpose what he'd done before by accident.

The squad car torqued instantly into the same sickening spin, plowing along at right angles to the road and to the oncoming sedan. Unfortunately it also slammed his head into the dash. He blinked broken light off his eyeballs and twisted, reaching back for the rifle.

When he poked up his head again both cars had stopped. The Toyota's doors were open, swinging idly. He gaped stupidly for a moment before he saw, on the bank above, two men in overcoats running for the woods.

He thought later that it might have been nice to think he had the presence of mind not to get out just yet. Not to chase them, to take them on two against one. But actually he got the door open, on the far side from the now-vanished thugs, then found himself too busy being sick onto the glassy, tire-planed surface of Route Six.

Jaysine got to him first. She came hesitantly forward, blinking into the red and white flashes of the strobe.

She'd thought the police car was trying to ram them. Obviously her kidnapper thought so too. Fright had been plain in his curses as he yanked the wheel this way and that. Then, when the cruiser stopped dead across both lanes in front of them, they'd been out and running before her car stopped rolling.

She halted, puzzled, when she saw no one in the Plymouth at all. Then heard the retching, like a sick cat she thought, and ran around the hood.

"Phil! God, what was—what were you trying to do?"

"Hurt my head," he mumbled.

"Oh my God, you're bleeding. Here between the eyes—"

"Hit it on that radio thing."

"Hold still. Put your head back. I'll get some clean snow."

He straightened, still inside the car, then realized that blood was running down his face. He could imagine what would happen if his father found it on the upholstery. But he still couldn't walk. So he just sat down on the road.

By then she was back. He put his head back against the fender. The snow clamped down, cold and gritty, stinging for a moment and then numbing like Novocaine. He let her hold him and, after a moment, kiss him on the neck and the cheek and at last, at last, the lips.

Half an hour later they rolled back into town together. Phil, utterly drained, stayed at twenty-five. Like a short cortege the two cars crept beneath the streetlights, paused at the single stoplight, then turned up Sullivan Hill. He found his father's usual spot and cut the engine. He wasn't afraid anymore. He was too exhausted to feel much of anything.

When she rapped on his window he rolled it down. She was standing ankle-deep in snow, hugging herself.

"Why are we stopping here?"

"This's where I live."

"Oh." She glanced up State Street. "Well—I'm scared. Do you think you could, like, come and have a drink with me or something?"

"I don't know."

"Do you got to go home? Is that it? Maybe I could stay there too."

He had to grin at the idea of bringing Jaysine in, telling his mother she was going to sleep over. "I don't think that'd be too swift. Look, I got to get these keys back to my dad. He'll be pissed. It might take a while."

"I'll wait."

"Well, let's see how it works out." He checked his forehead in the mirror, then brushed his hair over the cut. They got the rifle and Halvorsen's scuttle out of the Plymouth and put them in her car.

Then the ascent to Paradise Lane, dragging his carcass up the stairs, heart heavy as his legs. He was late. His dad would have already been down to the car, to start it—he hated to start patrol cold. As Phil came down the alley toward number 11 he limped more and more slowly.

On the drifted-up porch his father's tracks were plain. He sighed, straightened his shoulders, and limped inside.

Joe Romanelli sat on the couch in his uniform. A football program was on. A coach spoke gruffly about determination and pride. As Phil dragged the door closed his father glanced up at him through Camel smoke. Phil placed the keys silently beside him.

"At long goddamn last. Where the hell were you?"

"Noplace."

His father's hand cracked against his cheek, knocking him into the television. "You couldn't have done me the favor. Told your mother you were takin' it. Or left a note."

"I didn't think I'd be gone long—I figured you still got time to get to work—"

"No shit!" His father turned his face away. "The point is, stupid, since you didn't bother to tell me you had it, I called it in stolen."

Phil's mouth opened. "Oh," he said.

"Yeah. 'Oh.' So you tell me, smart-ass, whatta I tell Nolan now? That it wasn't stolen, you was just taking a joyride in it?"

He didn't have any answers for that. He kept his head down, wishing his father would hit him again, but at last he just shook his head. "You poor little bastard," Joe said softly. "What is it? You taking this Ryun girl out on the sly?"

It took him a moment even to recognize her name. His date with Alex seemed like years before. "No."

"You aren't still mixed up with this old guy? This Halvorsen?"

". . . No."

"That's good, 'cause we just got the word to pick him up. Armed and dangerous, they said." Romanelli shook his head again, staring at the TV.

"I don't get it, I just don't. I could understand maybe a girl, you was trying to impress her. Stupid, but I could understand it. This other shit, I don't know. Is it worth licking you anymore? Does it do any good?"

He had the answer to that one, at least. "No."

"Then I guess I got to turn you in. You're a juvenile, they'll probably give you a suspended sentence, remand you to me."

"Dad—"

"Shut up!" The shout echoed in the cold little house. "Don't you get it, it's that or my job! And without a job, this is news to you I bet, we don't fuckin' eat! You got to clean up your act, boy. Your sister's making it out of here, college and all, but you're not going to, no matter how smart you think you are. Not with a record."

"Dad—don't you think . . . you can tell them somebody else took it, kids, you found it down the hill—"

"Shut *up*! Whether I do or not, you're grounded. Total. Permanent. Here or school, that's the only place you go. Understand me?"

He nodded.

When his father left he stood for a while, staring at the moving images of Bears and Redskins. Gradually his pain faded to a deadness within his ribs, as if he'd been cored, like an apple. He didn't really think his father would turn him in. It was just to scare him. But he didn't care. At last he pulled the volume knob off and pocketed it. The set went dead and he went into the kitchen.

His mother was sitting by the stove, eating canned pineapple. He wanted for a moment to touch her, share the misery; she'd heard it all, but he hadn't heard a sound from her, she'd probably been afraid to come out.

But he didn't. White hate was growing in him, not for her, not for his father, but for all the powerful, all those who oppressed and tormented others. It was too big a hatred to spare room for even the smallest love.

In the little room under the eaves he pulled boxes from beneath the bed, rummaged in them, dumped his scavengings into his Scout pack. He found the coil of wire he used for home-built radios and dumped it in too. He went back down carrying it. His mother looked up as he passed her. Then half rose, scattering can and fork to the linoleum.

"Where do you think you're going?"

"Out."

"But your father, he just told you not to. Where are you going with that? Philip, you'll get hurt. Something awful is going to happen, I feel it in my bones."

"I got to, Ma. I got things I have to do. I'll be back."

He was lying, of course. He didn't mean to be back. Ever.

"Oh, God, don't go!"

He was nauseated with her melodrama. He hated it even as he admitted its sadness. *If this is life,* he thought, pulling free from her clutching hands and wrenching open the door, seeing the world dissolve and melt in tears again even as the cold laid its hand across his face, *fuck it. I'm through.*

A hundred yards down the hill, he slid in beside Jaysine and slammed the door. He didn't look at her.

"Did you get what you needed?"

"Yeah. Let's get going," he said. His mother might come down after him. If she did he wanted to be out of there. He wouldn't miss his dad, he thought, if by some weird and perverted whim God made you keep feeling things even after you were dead. But he'd miss her. That was the only thing he regretted. That after this last task was over, he wouldn't pull that trigger without hurting her more than himself.

But he didn't think that would stop him.

"Where to?"

"Well—we could go to your place."

"No!"

"Why?—Oh." He glanced over at her; her face was white. "You can't go back there anymore, can you? Because they'll be watching. Well—how's your heater?"

"What?"

"In your car, here. Does the heat work?"

"Oh. It works all right. It works good. Why?"

"Well, we could just head out toward the Falls, and wait till Racks shows up."

"Is there a place we could hide there?"

"There's some side roads."

"Will you drive?"

"No! I mean, you'd better." Phil shuddered, remembering the beer truck. "I'm never driving again."

He kept looking back as she drove slowly east, into the blowing snow; but they only saw two sets of headlights the whole time. One was a Thunder tanker and as it pulled out around them from behind he caught the bored glance of the driver. He wondered if this might be . . . no. It was headed east, not west. This one carried Thunder products, not poison.

"We getting close yet?"

"Better slow down. Look for a place."

In the end they went up a hollow south of the road, and found a cleared road leading back to a deer camp. He doubted anyone would go in or out before dawn. It would be cold, but they only had a few hours to wait. Four A.M., Halvorsen had said; that's when their vigil would begin.

When she turned the lights and then the motor off dark flooded in like black water. He blinked, unable to see her, the trees, anything. The only photons came from the luminescent hands of his Timex. The only sound was its faint ticking, their breathing, and the wind, sandpapering sheet metal with snowflakes.

"It's gonna get cold in here," she whispered. "I forgot, the heater runs off the engine."

"Uh huh."

She came over to his side and unbuttoned her coat. He took his off and they arranged them in a kind of tent, sitting close together. After a while, as it grew colder, they wriggled around to face each other. It was warmer that way.

Her breath was hot on his neck. Two pendant softnesses pressed against him. He thought about touching her, but only briefly. She'd just laugh. To a woman like this, he was just a child.

But as time passed the steadily deepening cold drove them closer, and with mingled guilt and horror he realized he was getting hard. Close as they were, she couldn't help but feel it. When she shifted again his now rapidly growing bone pressed against her thigh.

Jaysine had felt him stiffen, felt him begin to tremble. It made her smile. It was cute, a boy his age.

Then she remembered how the big Plymouth had roared ahead of her little car, the bloody mask of rage he'd raised when she came up to him being sick on the road. He'd risked his life for her, and saved her, too. She had no illusions about what would have happened once those men got her out into the woods.

She turned her head, searching in absolute darkness for the warmth of his breath. It smelled fresh. Unlike Brad's, sour with coffee and whiskey and something else she'd never been sure of.

"Usually, when two people get this close, they're kissing," she whispered into his ear.

A few minutes later she gasped. His hands were cold.

"What is it? I'm sorry, Jaysine. Did I hurt you?"

"No—wait. Wait, Phil. I didn't know you'd want to do that. I wasn't expectin' to, ever again. With anybody. Really."

"Why not? You're beautiful. I mean, I think you're beautiful."

"But we shouldn't—that's not what I mean. I think you're nice too. But I've got this—" She stopped, unable to finish that sentence. Not yet. "I'd like to make love to you. But we'd need . . . protection. You understand?"

He smiled in the dark. "Sure. No problem. I, uh, carry 'em all the time."

She had to help him when at last he wasn't sure how to do what he'd imagined for so long. When it was over they clung together, close, panting and murmuring, as if the only heat in the winter darkness was between them, folded like sleeping flowers in the night.

Twenty-nine

Halvorsen watched the dawn come that last day, as he had most of the twenty-five thousand mornings of his life. It began with a pearly foreglow not long, by his old Elgin, after five. But then it faded. For a long time none of the three who waited could have said there would be day at all.

Gradually the sky turned gray above Singer Hill. Light came slowly, as if it had to be pumped down through the overcast. Came gradually, creeping with the stealth of an old fox between the still-dark hills.

He remembered words he'd memorized long ago, declaimed aloud in a one-room schoolhouse. Something about the rosy-fingered dawn.

This dawn's fingers were a corpse's, pallid and cold.

When he could see the bridge he stood up. Beside him the boy did too, then the woman.

Halvorsen stretched his legs. When they were a little more limber he moved stiffly down the rise.

They came out of the trees a little above the falls. They were just rapids now, but the name remained. He remembered sawmills here, years before. Then when the forests were finished the dams had been blown up, or left for the Allegheny to destroy more slowly but just as completely.

He remembered the river as it was then. No bigger than a creek in July, but in spring brawny with glass-green snow-melt, a torrent neither horse nor man would dare. Up till the thirties it had flooded the towns along it regularly every few years. Then the WPA had tamed it.

Here, where the river narrowed, you could make out the bones of the old dam under the ice.

He looked northeast, into a rough Y, with himself between the arms. The river flowed toward him, propelled by the land's slope down from Potter County. On his left hand it went west, through Raymondsville, Petroleum City, Bagley Corners; then into McKean County, New York through Olean and Salamanca, then back into Pennsylvania. On his right hand Rich Creek was only a flatness under the snow. Must of froze early, he thought. Didn't matter, the springs that fed it would keep right on flowing. It would be seven, eight feet deep, under the bridge.

In a few days the water that was sliding past them now, deep beneath the ice, would join the Monongahela at Pittsburgh to form the Ohio.

The Rich Creek bridge crossed it about a mile from the newer span that joined the side road to Route Six. It was no great feat of engineering. Just a rusty iron truss, single-lane, with planks to take the weight of tires and feet. The north end sat firm on a New Deal concrete pier; the other, much older, was footed on hand-laid stone.

Halvorsen thought then, slogging across the ice, about tools. He patted his pockets. Pliers, Case knife, camp ax—that should do it.

This wouldn't be a complicated job.

Phil, a few feet behind him, edged out cautiously onto the ice. The old man had said the thing he cradled like a petrified baby was safe. He believed him, but he didn't want to test it.

He'd watched fascinated in the dark, holding the flashlight on a flat rock brushed free of snow, while the old man had assembled it.

It looked insultingly simple. Halvorsen wedged a cap onto one end of the stovepipe, then tore open the sacks. He measured the sugar and fertilizer into the other lid, then combined them with Jaysine's flour sifter. He worked deliberately, but still it wasn't long before the pipe was full, packed to the top with the gray mixture.

This was laid aside, and he held the flashlight closer as Halvorsen slid open the box of primers. Following his directions, Jaysine took each one apart with the needle-noses and threw everything away but the pill inside. These went one after another into an empty cartridge casing Halvorsen produced from a pocket.

That complete, Halvorsen asked for the wire and matches. He stripped a few inches and worked with his knife until one shining copper strand remained. This he carefully wrapped around the heads of two matches. This too went into the case, filling it, and he taped it shut.

He dug a shallow hole in the fertilizer/sugar mixture, poured powder in from the red can, then stuffed the squib in till only the wire was visible. He put the lid on and rocked back on his heels.

"That's all?" Phil said after a moment. It didn't look like his idea of dangerous.

"That's it. You can buy the same stuff from DuPont in pretty cans, but this'll do the job. Got the rest of that wire?"

"Uh, yeah." He held it up: a coil of number sixteen. Halvorsen spliced the squib to it and taped the splices.

"And the box."

"The what?"

"Spark box."

"Oh."

The old man wet two fingers and placed them firmly on the brass posts. He nodded to Jaysine. She leaned her mittens on the plunger, and he jerked his hand back. He rubbed it, saying nothing, and Phil thought: Obviously that works too.

And now dawn was here, and he gripped the tube as his boots wandered across the frozen surface. Snow and below that ice, glass-hard, grease-slick, black as obsidian. He was happy when he was off it and climbing the bank.

Phil smiled, realizing suddenly what he'd just thought. That he was happy. Well, damn it, it was true.

Then they were at the bridge. He looked down it. The parallel lines of trusswork and roadway formed a square at the far end. It was still all but dark, still hard to see.

He realized then he'd lost the others. He turned completely around, pointing the three-foot cylinder like a bazooka. There was no one else in sight in the gray winter dawn.

"Hey," he said.

"Get down here."

It came from beneath him. He shuffled to the edge and peered over. At the crown of Halvorsen's floppy cap, at Jaysine's fur hat. The cap tilted back and the oilman's face appeared.

Halvorsen said, "What're you grinning about? Get off that road."

"Sorry."

When he bent beneath the planking he found they'd already quarried several rocks from the old pier. They were loose, jimmied by decades of frost and flood. He squatted, holding the tube.

"Okay," grunted the old man. "Guess that'll take her all right . . . hand it here."

Halvorsen worked it into the foundations. Then he and Jaysine packed rocks in on top of it.

"Anybody comin' yet?"

"Wait . . . no, all clear."

"Both ways?"

"Yeah, both ways."

Halvorsen came out, unreeling wire like a casual old spider. It disappeared into the snow, cutting a thin wavy slice. He headed for a patch of iced-over brambles thirty yards downstream. He threw the last of the coil over it and disappeared round the far side. After a moment he called, "You see me from there? Either of you?"

"No," Jaysine called back.

"No, but I might from the bridge," said Phil.

"Forget it, driver'll be worrying about those planks."

Gradually, in the slowly blossoming light, Phil made out the old man's standing figure. He was looking down the road. Finally he said, "Well, I guess that'll do her. You two can clear out now."

"Clear out? Hey, no way. I'm staying for the fireworks."

"Don't be stupid, boy. The girl's leaving and so are you."

"I don't have anyplace to go," said Jaysine.

"She doesn't have anyplace to go, Mr. Halvorsen. And neither do I. You might as well get used to having us here, 'cause we're going to stay."

They heard him grumbling. Phil grinned at Jaysine. Then suddenly they were kissing again, there under the bridge.

"What's goin' on under there?"

"Nothing," she called back, giggling a little.

"You two think of bringin' anything to eat?"

"No," they said in unison. This time they both laughed.

"We'll probably be here a while," said Halvorsen. He came out from the bushes and squinted down at them sourly. Kids, he thought, a pair of kids, cuddling and sparking like it was their honeymoon. What am I doing out here with a pair of kids? "I wanted to get set early, but I doubt if anything'll happen till after dark. So if one of you wants to drive back to town, get something for us to eat, I'll set and watch."

"Uh . . . I'm broke," said Phil. Jaysine raised empty mittens and shook her head. Finally the old man, mouth grim, reached into his coat. He produced a pocket watch and pried the back off with the tip of his knife.

"Unfold it careful, that's a old bill."

"I'll go," said Jaysine. "But I don't want to go back to Raymondsville."

"There's a store in Roulette."

"You want anything special, Phil?"

Last meal, he thought. Well, why not? "Potato chips would be nice. New Era, or Wise. And maybe some chocolate, and peanuts."

She smiled, and cold as it was he felt warm again. "Junk City it is."

"Get something that'll keep us warm," said Halvorsen grumpily. "Stew or something."

"We've got enough here for both. And some Bisquick. I can make us some biscuits."

"That's some better," said Halvorsen.

Just then, out in the valley, they heard the whine of a distant car. Halvorsen crouched back into the bushes, and disappeared. "Romanelli, get over here with me," he called. "Jaysine, you go on. We'll be here, just honk."

She waved at them as she bumped across the bridge. The planks clattered under her wheels, but it felt sturdy enough. Only for a moment did she wonder: *What if it doesn't work?*

A few hours later, two hundred feet up the hill, Halvorsen spooned up scrambled eggs and bacon, bit into a hot pan biscuit dripping butter. Not as good as mine, he thought. But darn nice just the same after all morning out here in the cold.

He fed a little to the pup. She wasn't happy, tied to a tree, but she accepted it with only an occasional whine, a complaining bark.

A car droned by out in the valley, and he glanced down the slope. From up here, where he'd built the cook-fire, he could see the boy's stocking cap behind the bushes. Then the curve of the snowy shoreline, marked by the abrupt end of scrub and trees. Beyond that the bridge, a complication of triangles charcoaled above the ribbon flatness of frozen creek.

He kneaded his legs and sighed. He'd hiked near eight miles to get out here. Man my age don't need much sleep, he thought. But I got to be alert tonight. Well, he'd try to catch a few winks later.

He narrowed his eyes, but even farsighted he couldn't see the girl. That was good . . . He'd put her out toward the main road, overlooking the turnoff. That way, with the boy's little radio, she could let them know when the truck was coming.

If the truck was coming.

He groped around in his coat and located his plug. Only one chew left, a short one at that. He put it back.

No, couldn't let himself dwell on that . . . the possibility that Boulton, or those who worked for him, might have gotten skunked by him killing those men at his place, and canceled or postponed the run. He figured it was possible. But not likely. People like that didn't ever think they might fall. And that in the end was generally what brought them down. They'd told him a word for that years ago, in school. Greek word. Couldn't remember it now, too long ago.

He changed his mind and broke out the chew again. The wrapper snapped on the coals, shriveling to a wet-looking black wad before it suddenly popped into flame.

He tried to think of what might go wrong.

The driver should never see the girl. So any discovery or error would take place at this end. If it did go bad he and the boy had the rifles. He could cover them till the young people made it to the woods.

Timing. He'd never used this jury-rigged kind of jack-squib before, but it might take a while to heat up and go off. A truck making any speed would be across the bridge in seven or eight seconds. That didn't leave much room for mistakes.

He thought then, we ought to put something across the road. At this end of the bridge. So the driver would have to stop, get out, and move it out of the way. While he was out of the cab he'd touch it off. That got the driver out of danger too.

Halvorsen stretched, looking up. It looked like it might clear today; a little while before he'd seen a patch of blue in the east.

He decided he had time for another pan of coffee.

Jaysine played with the little radio with a mittened thumb. It looked like a toy. Silver and black plastic. Phil said he'd gotten them for a dollar each at a pawnshop and fixed them. They looked like it.

Still, they seemed to work, for the few hundred yards between her, above the main road, and him, at the bridge. She looked at her watch. She was supposed to check in every hour. Coming up . . . she pulled out the antenna and pressed the button. She whispered, "I'm here. Are you there?"

"Check," came the voice, tiny and crackly, but recognizably Phil's. She smiled and said, "Can you hear me?"

"Yeah. Don't waste the batteries."

"I'm not. Are you cold?"

"Yeah."

"We stayed warm last night. Didn't we?"

"We sure did."

"I like you. You're a good lover, Phil."

"I . . . like you too. Don't waste the batteries! Over and out."

The radio hissed for a moment, and far off on it she could hear someone else talking: interference; but he didn't say anything. Then it went off.

She smiled. How differently this affair was starting out! She'd never had a younger boyfriend. It was funny to be the older woman, the experienced one. She closed her eyes, remembering how he'd tried to please her without knowing what she needed.

Then after a moment, opened them. Something else was nagging at her. What was it? It teased her, but wouldn't come out where she could see it.

Warm and comfortable in Halvorsen's old down bag, she stared down at the empty road, trying to figure out what it was.

They waited all afternoon and on into the night. Toward evening the
weather changed. The clouds that had sealed off the valleys like paraffin
on a jar of preserves slid west. For an hour, just before dark, the sky was
a clear, dimming sapphire.

Phil sat on the hill, watching the day die. He'd made himself a clumsy
flapjack from the last of the flour, and though it tasted burnt he made
himself eat it all. It was all they had left, and there was no more money.

He hoped something happened soon. They couldn't stay out here
much longer. He was slowly freezing, and he could see the wear on the
old man. In a few more hours even Halvorsen would have to give up, go
back. That would be too bad. He'd hoped to make a difference.

But even if he couldn't, the funny thing was, it didn't seem so all-
important anymore.

He glanced at the rifle beside him. Short, ugly-muzzled, when the old
man had handed it to him, he'd thought it would be the last thing he'd
ever need. He'd planned to strike one blow as he went down, a blow
against lies, and greed, and power abused. Then finish what Halvorsen
had interrupted, up on the hill behind Paradise Lane.

But since then . . .

Could he have been wrong? Could it be possible for him to make contact with another human being? She'd said, what had she said—oh, yeah.
That he was a good lover.

An unaccustomed thrill of joy made him tremble. Hugging himself with
his good arm, he watched the inexorable approach of night.

Jaysine sat alone above the faintly glowing ribbon of road, snug and drowsy
in the bag, her back against a log, looking up at the stars. It seemed so
long since she'd seen them. So long she couldn't say when the last time
had been.

It seemed like a long time since she'd been alone, too. Always there
were people around. Too many people. And always she'd worried about
pleasing them. Her parents, her teachers, Marybelle, her customers, Brad.

She was still lying there, looking up, when a funny thing happened.

She seemed, though she was still half-sitting in the snow, to be gradually
rising.

Below in the starlight the trees fell away, and her sight seemed to expand. She could see now that the hills in all their folds were dark. Dark,
but at the same time light, as if they were made of light. Dark light, folded
and crumpled on itself into what looked like lifelessness, but to her eye
now filled with a dancing, burning radiance.

She blinked slowly and lifted her hand. Rising in front of her, white
and frail in starlight reflected from snow, it too was made of the same

stuff as the hills and the trees: the same changeless star-stuff, cold to the mortal touch, but filled with immortal, living fire.

She saw for an endless moment that what she'd been puzzling over for so long was an illusion. There was nothing in the world but God.

She remembered now what she hadn't been able to remember before. It was summer and she was looking in through the curtains of the dining room. The cat, Thomas, had been beside her, polishing himself against her jeans. She'd been looking past her mother's shoulder at the widow, Mrs. Rogers, from down the road. All the kids knew her. She'd been harrowing her field, getting ready to plant potatoes, gotten down to open a gate, and the tractor had slipped into gear and ran over her. For years she'd walked twisted, as if her bones had been heated and bent, then cooled like that.

But she'd been watching that afternoon with the crickets going and the cat's little motor running against her ankle when her mother finished the reading and leaned forward, holding the widow woman's hand in hers. There'd been a long silence, so long she'd been about to turn away. Then without another word or remark the old woman got up, nodded to her mother, and walked out of the room.

And Jaysine, her legs suddenly belonging to some other child, had run to the front porch and watched as old Mrs. Rogers walked slow but straight up the walk and under the rose arbor and got into her car and drove off.

Now why didn't I remember that, she thought, the breath of stars hot on her eyelids. Why didn't I remember? Why did I deny?

She knew the answer, if she was honest. Because it was easier to deny than believe. Easier to be like others than bear witness to the Truth.

Guilt and terror shook her. Who could forgive such a betrayal? Yet in the next moment she knew, and was at peace again, with the stars glittering around her.

She'd been wrong about so much. About Brad. She'd thought him good, and he wasn't; then thought him evil. She'd cursed, hated, feared him. But she'd forgotten the single fact that made sense of life.

Evil didn't exist. Nothing existed save Him, and she was in Him, and He in her; and the same was true of every other being on this vast silent world, so dark in seeming, but in reality the white-hot heart of light. Her sin and sickness were only shadows cast by her error. She'd thought she needed the love of a man. But she'd always had something greater, more precious, eternal and inexhaustible.

Without knowing how or why, as if she'd just been handed a present, she believed again.

But if she believed, what was she doing here? This lurking, this scheming—it was hollow. Revenge only dealt more pain. *Be not overcome with evil, but overcome evil with good.* The only way to conquer was with perfect love.

She was thinking this, motionless against the log, when she saw some-thing out on the road.

Not headlights; they were too dim. It took her a while watching them—not interested, just faintly curious, or perhaps it was only that the shadows were the only things in the world that moved—even to decide there was anything there. She blinked. Wasn't there something she ought to do? Something she ought to remember . . .

Without thought, her fingers closed on the radio. A moment later a faint voice asked her something. She didn't reply, only set it aside and began struggling out of the warmth. She got up clumsily, balancing on numb feet.

Whatever it was, it was coming toward her. She could make out the purr of engines, given back from the looming blackness of the hills.

Like walking in a dream. Her legs moved, but she couldn't feel them. Couldn't see the snow, as if all the world, hills, rock, snow, sky, gave back only the faint light infused in them at Creation. As if it all had been fashioned from the same pure silver, forged and tooled into the manifold shapes that tricked the eye. Surrounded by an immense comforting hum, she heard only distantly the squeak and crunch of snow beneath her felt-pack boots, the crackle of her breath as it drifted off.

She reached the bottom of her sentry-hill, hesitated, then began climb-ing toward the road. When she hit level she stopped, mittened hands tucked into her coat. She shivered, but didn't feel cold. She felt warm and happy.

There were no lights now. But she knew someone was coming. He meant to be invisible, but she saw. She was part of something now that knew everything, knew it and still loved it, no matter how misshapen or ugly, how sick or mired in error.

She waited. There was no one with her. But she knew she was not alone.

The first shadow came out of the black of the trees. She heard the mutter of exhaust and the cry of the snow as the tires crushed it down. There was the faintest glimmer, someone lighting a cigarette. She stood motionless, hands in her pockets.

For a moment she wondered: Will they see me? Then she knew they would. There was the world as men perceived it: blind matter, moved by mindless chance. Beyond that lay another. She belonged to that world now.

The lead shadow slowed, and its engine dropped to idle. Then light blinded her. It lasted only a moment, then became two hot-red spots that faded through orange back into blackness.

She couldn't see now, dazzled, but she heard the grind of tires again. Someone called out. An electric window hummed, coming down.

Her outstretched mitten found the car. The voice was the one she'd been expecting.

"Who's that?"

"Hello, Brad," she said softly. "It's me."

Phil tried several times to get her to answer. At last he turned the walkie-talkie off. He sat silently for several minutes, turning his head from side to side, focusing all his being on the far end of the road.

He heard the motors then.

Oh, shit, he thought. To come all this way, risk everything, to have *them* win—

Jumping to his feet, he limped as fast as he could along the bank. The icy air whipped at his face, but he was past caring. His low hoarse shout, meant to carry but not far, preceded him. He saw the old man suddenly unfold.

"They're coming! I can hear 'em—Jaysine called, she didn't say anything but I think she must of tried to—"

"Shut up," came Halvorsen's voice, cold as the stars. "What're you doing, boy? Get where you belong!"

Phil realized he was right. He'd lost it, he'd deserted his post, and he was instantly shamed. He wheeled in his tracks, headed now back down the hill. Toward the river, toward the bridge.

He saw then that he would be too late.

She waited, knowing with mysterious certainty he'd recognized her voice. He didn't say anything right away. Then, sounding astonished: "Jay. *Jay?* What the hell are you doing out here?"

"Waiting."

"What for?"

"To warn you."

Someone else was in the car with him. She sensed a movement in back. But there wasn't enough light to see. She felt larger shadows behind his car. Then heard the crunch of boots, many of them, and voices. But she wasn't listening to that. She didn't care who they were.

"What are you doing out here?" he said again, and there was annoyance in his voice, and fear.

"I told you. Don't go on. There's people waiting for you down this road."

"What the hell are you talking about?"

"They know everything, Brad. It's your decision, to go on or not. But I have to tell you what God wants you to do."

"Oh, he told you, did he?"

He honed the question with contempt. She took a deep breath. Her fear of him tried to creep back, but she knew now how foolish it was.

Conquer evil with love.

"Give up, Brad. You've already lost. All you can do now is lose more."

He said swiftly, "To who? You say there's cops up there?"

"Not police. Just people."

The shadow that had come up behind her said, hoarse and lisping a little, "Who's this, Mr. Boulton?"

"This? This is the crazy bitch you let escape."

"What's she doin' out here?"

"I'm not sure. She says there's some locals waiting for us up ahead."

"That so? I'll tell everybody, get set for them."

"Good."

"We'll take care of her now too, if you want, Mr. Boulton."

"Do it," said his voice. She stood in the snow, hearing the mechanical whir again. She reached out, before they seized her. But her hands met only the smooth coldness of sealed glass.

They were pushing her into another car when she remembered Phil and Halvorsen. That she was supposed to warn them. But then she smiled, even as they twisted her arms behind her. There was no need for her to worry. God would take care of everything.

Down the road high beams came on suddenly, paling the stars. The road, the trees, the bridge leaped from nothingness to sudden bright relief. Phil tried to run faster and slipped. He screamed as his hip smashed into ice unyielding as concrete.

The lights reached the bridge. He heard the hollow clatter of planks, like machine-gun fire, then a sudden scarlet flare: brakes. He fought gasping through the bushes, their ice-cased arches cracking and tinkling around him. Thorns tore his face. He reached the detonator, crouched, and searched the darkness at the end of the road.

For just a moment, he saw something moving behind it.

There was a flash then at the near end of the bridge, where he and the old man had dragged the stump. Weeping with pain and rage, he fumbled for the wires. Halvorsen had warned him not to connect them till the last minute.

They slipped from his shaking fingers, and vanished into the snow.

He looked up through cold tears to see a car rolling off the bridge. Its brakes flashed again briefly before it accelerated up the hollow and disappeared into the woods.

He stood up, looking for the rifle. He didn't know what he was going to do with it. He was reaching for it when hands shoved him from behind and he pitched face-forward into the snow.

"Stay down." The old man's scratchy whisper. "That was just the advance man. There's something else comin'."

They lay in the snow, listening. Then Phil felt it in the ground, vibrating through frozen earth into his hands and arms and skull until he heard it not with his ears but with his bones.

Something heavy was coming up the road.

A rumble, a blackness against the stars. He trembled to the hollow roar of its exhaust, the clatter and mesh of gears, the yellow stack-flare above. Then saw faces, green-lit, hellish, high above, in the cab.

"Okay, I got them wires on. Get ready," Halvorsen hissed.

He scrambled to a crouch again, feeling wooden and detached. He couldn't take his eyes from the truck. His fingers grabbed for the plunger and drew it up.

"Not now! Wait'll I say. Remember, not just one push, that won't give her enough juice. Got to stroke it like a water-pump, fast, five or six times till she—"

The old man went quiet then. Phil looked up. His mouth came open, and his hands froze on the handle.

Two more cars came out of the trees, following the truck.

"Steady," said the old man then, and to the boy the voice sounded tired. Or maybe only resigned.

Halvorsen watched the truck edge out onto the trusswork. Moving slowly, as he'd hoped. But he hadn't planned on the cars. The first one he didn't worry too much about. It was on his side of the creek now, but as long as he could dump the tanker he didn't care that much about it.

But he knew what was in the others. More of Boulton's blacklegs, more of his hired thugs.

He wondered dully if he should go ahead. Or if it was too late. From what the boy said they'd gotten the girl. He was sorry about that. She'd seemed right spunky.

But since they had her, alive or dead, it meant there wasn't any choice about what he did. Whether he blew the bridge or not, they'd know about him and the boy. And be coming after them.

He decided this was their only chance. From here on it was up to luck, or Fate, if you believed in Fate.

The truck loomed over the concrete piering. Old bolted iron groaned as it took the weight.

"You ready?" he asked the boy.

"Any time," Phil said. He'd turned his head, and though Halvorsen couldn't see, dark as it was, it sounded like he was smiling.

Kid's crazy, he thought. He switched his gaze back to the bridge. At last he judged it looked about right.

"Okay, let her rip," he muttered.

In front of him the boy straightened, then his shoulder dropped. Halvorsen heard the generator whir, then stop as the plunger hit bottom. He put out his hand but the boy was already hauling it back up. And pushing down again.

Halvorsen watched the bridge, head bent as if he was praying. The stars shone above it aloof and undisturbed as the black truck moved on, a little faster now, gears shifting upward as if its driver understood what they were trying to do.

Phil was racking the handle upward for the third time, his arms crying out, when he saw a faint red spark under the bridge. He thought for a moment it was a failed connection. Then the sound reached them and he knew it wasn't.

A heavy, muffled thud, not much louder than a shot, but deeper. Then blackness took the place of the stars. In it there was a rumble, and through choking smoke rocks started hailing down around them, whacking down into the ice like meteorites.

"Stay down," shouted the old man, behind him; but he didn't listen, didn't obey. Instead he stood up. A rock whacked down a few feet away, but he didn't care, he wanted to see.

The cloud swept past, and dimly he made out the trusswork down and a black whaleshape lying half on and half under the surface. Sharp cracks came to his ears, and the hiss of hot metal meeting icy water.

"Come on," Phil screamed.

"What?"

"We better get out of this smoke."

Halvorsen had to admit, the boy had a point. He reached for his rifle and followed him up the bank.

They were standing on it, looking across, when there was a flash and bang across the creek. A bullet sighed with expiring sadness over their heads. Then came a roar of motors. Headlights flicked on, wheeling into position, dazzling and revealing them as they stood surprised.

"Get down," said Halvorsen, shoving him. "Be with you in a second."

"What you want me to do?"

"Hold 'em off." Halvorsen bent and jogged stiffly into the darkness.

Another shot cracked from across the river. Phil bent double, slipped, and fell down the bank. The rifle jumped out of his hand and he grabbed frantically after it. The headlights lit everything around him, snow, rifle, sliding for the creek, the gracefully curved branches of the blackberry bushes. The ice a few feet out cracked suddenly and flew upward; bits of it stung his face.

Something moved in front of the lights, and he realized it was men, running toward the creek. Toward him.

He found a hollow at the shore, and threw himself gasping behind it. He lay there, hugging the rifle, and then remembered and turned and thrust it over the frozen earth, supporting the barrel against snow, rather than with his weak left arm. He tugged at the trigger blindly, then remembered the safety.

The muzzle-blast was deafening, and he yelped at the blow to his shoulder. His ears rang and a glow wavered over the darkness even when he blinked. Bullets smacked around him. But though he could see his own hands, lit by the headlights, he couldn't see anything to shoot at. He sobbed, working the bolt desperately, and got another shot off, aimed at darkness because that was all he could see.

Suddenly he realized that he no longer wanted to die. Not even heroically. He wanted to live. Not just with Jaysine, though he wanted her. He might love her. He wasn't sure yet. But through her, or in some mysterious way freed by her, he knew now that there were others out there to reach out to. Other hands, that would welcome his. Like a charm in a fairy tale, her kiss had toppled some prison wall he'd never realized existed in his heart. And if it was in his own heart, that meant he had built it. He wanted to destroy it, level it, and welcome in the crowd. How mysterious life was! How much he had to learn!

Christ, he thought, *Just let me live through this. That's all I want. I don't want to be a hero. Just get me home. That's all I want.*

From above and behind him came a sudden crack like a giant whip.

The corners of Halvorsen's lips twitched when he moved far enough out onto the stump of pier to look down.

No one would clear this without heavy equipment. The tanker lay with its back broken amid smashed and floating ice, half submerged. A nauseating stink welled up from it. The trusswork lay collapsed around it, the riveted box-beams crumpled, cables snapped and twisted like a net around a fallen elephant.

He nodded, and turned back toward the growing crackle of gunfire.

When he came out on the bank again things weren't looking any too good. The men on the far side had moved the cars to shine their lights in the boy's eyes. From time to time he was letting off a round, the old .303 making an impressive boom, but Halvorsen doubted he could see a thing.

He unslung the single-shot and knelt down on a bare spot on the road, wrapping the sling around his forearm. A moment later he lay forward and steadied the sights. During the long forenoon he'd paced off the far bank at near about a hundred yards. Downhill, but not enough to matter.

His first bullet smashed through a headlight. He dropped the block, thrust in another cartridge, and fired again without taking his eye from the scope. The second light went out in a drifting fizz of sparks.

Working with the slow deliberation of long practice, Halvorsen shot out the lights on the other car. He shook the last four cartridges from the box in his pocket. Then paused, sweeping the now dark creek-bed with the old Fecker.

If they were smart they'd be hugging ice down there. If they weren't they'd be looking his way, trying to make him out. He'd see a pale blur, a face—

The little rifle cracked and jumped in his hands. He sighed. After a while there was another crack, and then the sudden deep boom of the old British rifle, down on the creek bank, followed by a shout and the clatter of metal on ice.

Then for a long time silence grew along Rich Creek, silence and the glitter of stars. Then, gradually, a new sound crept into the valley. Halvorsen lifted his head. It came faintly against the wind, but it was there. The high sad keen of sirens.

"You boys hear me?"

A pistol-shot, far wide of him, he judged.

He raised his voice. "Better put them guns up! I got one of them night scopes up here. I can see all you bastards plain as day. Crawl this way, you're dead. Crawl back, I'll leave you for the cops."

When he heard them discussing this he called down to the boy, "Hold your fire, men, let 'em think it over."

It didn't take them long. He hadn't figured it would. It would be cold as hell on their bellies on the ice. Plus they knew what kind of stuff they were breathing. Gradually a slow scraping rose from the pit of lightlessness that was the creek.

One of the cars started up. Its backup lights glowed suddenly, then cut off. The other started too. They pulled out, shifted, then howled, gathering speed down the hollow.

When they were gone the silence and darkness seemed twice as deep. Halvorsen began feeling his way down the bank. "Boy?" he called. Then, a little later, "Phil?"

He found him down by the shore. He knelt by him for a long time, till his knees turned to stone in the snow.

Halvorsen went over it all, kneeling there. What he'd tried to do, and what he'd ended up doing. What they'd tried to stop, and the price they'd paid.

How the boy had wanted to die, then found something to live for. But then had died anyway.

Only at least, Halvorsen thought, he'd died fighting for something he believed in. Something that would help the others. That had to count, didn't it? If anything counted at all.

He was wondering if there was anything he could have done different when the hum of a powerful motor came down the hollow.

He left the boy as he lay and scrambled back up to the road.

It had to be Boulton. Waited till the shooting stopped, then come back to find out who won. Get over in them bushes—no, closer would be better. Next to that twisty chunk of bridge.

The hum grew louder, pushing amber foglights ahead of it.

The Jaguar came out of the treeline at high speed. Its brights snapped on, sweeping across the bridge, then steadying on its entrance. Then dipped, suddenly, as the brakes locked and the tires squalled, the car still tracking straight down the road, not skidding at all, aimed right for iron-framed emptiness.

It halted a dozen feet from where shattered asphalt hung like an extended tongue over black water and ice. It crouched there idling for a minute or so. Then the door opened.

It was the same man he'd met at Cherry Hill, big as he remembered him, in a tan car coat. Halvorsen saw him clearly by the courtesy light. He stood by the edge for a minute, looking down at the tanker. Then came back to the car and stood beside it, looking around. He seemed to be waiting for something.

At last Halvorsen got up. He went a couple of steps toward him before he said, "Hello, Mr. Boulton."

When the man turned he had something in his hand. "Who's that? Stay there. I'll shoot."

"It's W. T. Halvorsen."

"What've you done, Halvorsen?"

"Just an old man's foolishness," he said. "Blew up the bridge. Dumped your truck o' poison in the river. Won't be so easy to cover things up this time.

"Oh, yeah, and we chased your boys off. Once we evened the odds a little they lost their taste for a fight."

"Who's 'we'?"

"Me and some friends," he said. "A couple of which got their guns on you right now. If you care to try me out one on one, though, you're more than welcome. After what you done to me, and my county, and my company, I don't mind seein' which of us is the better shot."

He could see now what the other man held. It was a little gun, aimed at him.

Boulton laughed. "You're a fool. You really think this'll do any good?"

"I figure it will."

"It won't. You might stop me, but you can't stop what's happening. It's business. Somebody else will take my place, that's all."

"Not in this county they won't," said Halvorsen.

It sounded okay as a comeback. But he wished the boy was behind him.

His back felt naked. "Anyway," he said, "you better put the gun away. Cops'll be here soon."

"And if I'm not? If I deny everything—say the drivers were doing it on their own—"

" 'Fraid not. We can prove you done it. Knowed about it, planned it, and took the money."

Boulton bent, glanced into the car, then turned back. His free hand went into his coat. It came out with an envelope.

"You mean this."

"Whatever," said Halvorsen.

Boulton looked across the blackness to where the lights and sirens were turning into the hollow. He tore open the envelope with his teeth. The old man saw what was inside.

"I guess this's where I ask you what your price is."

"Good a time as any."

"Well?"

"There ain't enough money in the world, Mr. Boulton."

Boulton fired. The shot missed Halvorsen, but before he could react the big man had slid back into the car. The door slammed and he caught the click of electric locks. But by then he had the rifle up. The sight framed the silhouette of a head.

Halvorsen pulled the trigger with the most complete and savage sense of justice he had ever felt.

The engine roared and the car leaped back, jerked around, and came at him, lights blazing. Halvorsen stood his ground, aiming at the windshield. An instant later he threw himself back, down the bank, just in time for the fender to graze him.

The Jag swerved, tires spitting snow over him, squealed the rest of the way around and accelerated up the hollow again.

He got up slowly, feeling a numbness in his shoulder. He realized the other man hadn't missed, as he'd thought. He was glad he hadn't waited, taken that second shot. Some kind of armored glass on that car.

He thought quickly, sketching out the country to the south in his head. There was no other way out. Not in a car. A man could walk out, though, go to the end of the road and take to the woods. It'd be the devil of a trip at night, but a desperate man might make it.

The lights were drawing away rapidly, dwindling away uphill.

Let's see if we can't slow him down, anyway, he thought.

He thrust his last round into the action and fitted the butt to his wounded shoulder. In the scope he saw the taillights, the license plate light, the way the tires were kicking up snow. Must be doing eighty, he thought. He corrected upward, to where the snow was coming up lit red, and took a breath and let half of it out and squeezed off.

The lights staggered and slid off to the side. They jerked up and down, blinked, and stopped. Then they seemed, not to go out, but to be slowly eclipsed.

"Holy hell," he muttered.

As fast as he could, which was not very fast, he began running up the hollow.

When he got to the edge he stopped and looked down. The car was already sunken up to the doorhandles. He looked around. He felt like he ought to do something, but he didn't rightly know what. He'd go down too, if he got in that pit with it.

It was a slime pit, full of muck and old oil and the runoffs from the sand-pumpings. No telling how deep it was. Halvorsen looked down at it. I was just trying to stop him, he thought. I didn't mean to send him into this.

The hood disappeared. The muck moved steadily up over the wind-shield, not fast, not slow, just steady, like a blacksnake swallowing its prey.

He could see something moving inside. The door had unlocked, come open an inch, then stopped, held closed by the pressure of the slime. Someone was hammering at the windshield with a gun. But only a faint tapping came through the thick armored glass.

Halvorsen felt suddenly weak. He's not going to make it out of there, he thought. Not unless somebody helps him.

A stand of tamarack stood not far away. He found himself under them, snapping off boughs as fast as he could reach. His shoulder hurt like a grease-scald now but he ignored it. Running back to the pit, he threw an armload between the dike and the door.

Something in his head, maybe the boy's voice, said *Forget it. Let him drown.*

"No," he panted aloud, back at the pines.

Leave him to die, said the boy. *It's what he deserves.*

"Ain't his goddamn judge," muttered the old man. "Shouldn't have shot anyway. Just got mad. Knew who he was. Just turn 'im in." He felt weak and dizzy.

"Let me help," said a deep voice from the darkness. Halvorsen spun, groping where he'd propped the empty rifle.

The man seemed made out of night itself; dark coat, dark hair, dark face. "Let me give it a try," said Lark Jones, holding out big empty hands.

After a moment Halvorsen said, "All right. But let's get us some more brows down first. I don't want that pit to eat nobody else."

The car slid deeper. The faintly glistening slime, viscid and greasy un-derneath a frosting of snow, was halfway up the door before they had enough branches down for the black man to move out cautiously onto them. The needled surface sank under his weight. Halvorsen tore more boughs from the evergreens. There were lights moving down by the bridge, but whoever was carrying them was too far away to help.

Jones got his fingers around the door and pulled. His shoulders bunched. Cloth tore beneath his coat. It yielded a little, with a sucking sound, but as soon as he slacked off it closed again; he was pulling against the direction of descent. "Throw me a piece of wood," he shouted.

Halvorsen couldn't find any that weren't rotten from lying on the ground. At last he passed him the rifle. Jones wedged it in and levered it. The stock snapped and his ankles disappeared.

But the door had yielded a little more, and he wedged the broken gun in it and folded his body over it and reached in.

The sinking car belched softly and started to turn over in his direction.

Something black and glistening slid out, looking like part of the slime. "Watch out, he had a gun," Halvorsen said.

"He's not moving."

"Clean out his mouth," he said, putting a boot on the boughs and reaching for the feet. "Get him up here where we can work on him. Looks like he hurt himself when he went off the road . . . Yeah, lay him down there."

The lights came closer. "Hold up," said Halvorsen, glancing down the hill to where several men on foot were approaching, spread warily across the road. "Seems like I know them fellas . . . Hey! You there!"

"Who's that? Racks?"

"Up here, Bill. It's all right."

Bill Sealey was the sergeant from the Beaver Fork barracks. Halvorsen told him quickly what was going on. A couple of troopers set down their lights and bent to work on the body that lay, covered with the oily slime, on the dike.

"Where'd you fellas come from?" Halvorsen asked Sealey.

"Got a tip something was going on down here."

"Who was it?"

"Don't know. Anonymous call. Woman's voice. Real cold-sounding bitch."

"Did you get them others?"

"Five guys, three of 'em shot, and a girl."

"Kind of a short blonde? How is she?"

"In okay shape. Beat up a little, is all. She one of yours?"

"You might say that. Yeah."

Sealey asked him, "What the hell happened down there? At the bridge?"

"You better call the state water people," said Halvorsen evenly. "They're going to have a little cleanup problem on their hands."

Halfway through the explanation Sealey nodded, as if he guessed the rest. He looked down at the man, who was beginning to cough. "His trucks?"

"That's right."

Boulton moved an arm. It waved in the air over the pit. The car belched, shifted, lurched, pointing more markedly downward. All but the back window and trunk was out of sight now. The silver letters XJ glittered against the flashlights.

The hands grasped nothing, then came up to lie on his chest. Then, quite suddenly, he pushed off the man who was bent over him and sat up. He coughed savagely, as if trying to speak.

"What the hell's the matter with him?"

"Hold him! He's tryin' to go back in!"

Three of the troopers grabbed him, pulling him back from the edge. A low, animal moan came from the struggling man's blackened lips. His hands clawed the air. His eyes were startlingly clear, open and agonized, staring toward the car. His mouth gaped again. This time it made words, slurred, but clear enough to understand. "Get her out—she's still in there—"

Halvorsen turned. In the wavering glow of the focused flashlights they could see clearly, in the rear window, flattened against the heavy glass by the pressure of the inflooding muck, the gay stitched smile of a child's rag doll.

The Afterimage

Could be the last snow this winter, that little bit last night, Barry Fox thought. He hoped so. This hadn't been a hard winter. Nothing like last year's. But he was ready for spring.

As the big plow snorted through a turn he lifted his fingers from the wheel, working each one separately, then returning each to its job. Though the cab was warm he could still feel the sting of frost, a tingling afterbite that came whenever it got cold. The doctor had said he might always feel that, on and off.

He didn't mind a little stinging. At least he had his fingers. Hell, he was glad just to be here.

The blade clattered suddenly and the snowplow rocked. Damn, he thought, when're they going to get this stretch fixed? The damn state never spent a dollar till they had to spend a hundred.

He was meditating angrily on this when he saw the figure ahead. Old red-barred coat, tan pants, flop-eared cap, lace-up boots . . . he downshifted, and tons of salt and sand brought the plow rumbling to a reluctant halt. Cranking down the window, he leaned out. "Yo! Racks!"

The old man stopped, half-turned. He stared up, eyes blue and distant as winter sky, then nodded slowly.

Halvorsen hauled himself stiffly up into the cab, shoving a box in ahead of him onto the seat. He looked out the windshield. Then, a little reluctantly, said, "Hullo, Barry. Good to see you."

Fox let the clutch back in. The plow reaccelerated slowly, rumbling like an empty oil drum rolling down the road. He dropped the blade and sparks danced under the skids. "Heard you got out. Figured I'd be seein' you along here, one of these days. How you been doin'?"

"I'm okay."

"You headed home? How long you been back?"

"Couple of weeks," Halvorsen said.

"Let's see," said Fox. "I don't really remember . . . We was reading about the trials and all, but I was sick, then when they let me out of the hospital we went down to visit my wife's sister that spring . . . it's kind of fuzzy . . . what exactly did they give you finally, there in the end?"

"It was pretty long drawn out," said Halvorsen. He stared out the window, remembering the months. The federal grand jury had indicted him even after he'd explained everything. Probably wanted to find out if he was telling the truth, though he'd told them right out that he was. Then after the federal trial there'd been the state one, just as long, and then after that they'd kept calling him as a witness to this and a witness to that; till toward the end he'd started to think he'd never go anywhere else; he'd spend what was left of his life in courtrooms, or huddled with Quintero going over what he was going to say.

"Well, it took 'em long enough," he said slowly. "But they finally got everything figured out, I guess."

"Pulled some jail time, didn't you?"

"Oh, they give me five years on the state charges. Judge said, blowin' up the truck while it was dumpin', he could of overlooked that. And the manslaughter charge they dismissed. But blowin' up state property, he meant the bridge, that wasn't something they could let you go scot free. Even if they did get a new bridge out of it . . . anyway my lawyer, she got me out early on what was left, account of how old I was." Halvorsen shrugged. "How're you?"

"About back to normal. But it took a while." The younger man scowled. "Doc Friedman says I got to get checkups the rest of my life, though. In case a' cancer. Christ!"

"Same here," said Halvorsen. "Well, you got your bills paid, anyway."

"Yeah, and *he* paid too. Though I wish—well, his kid wasn't to blame. She shouldn't have suffered because of what he done."

"Nobody should of. The ones he hurt, I mean. Trouble is, once you start doing things like that, can't tell where it's goin' to end."

"He won't be putting it to nobody else for a long time. Conspiracy, dumping, accessory to murder—what was it, twenty to twenty-five years? Must have been a clever guy, do all that without them knowing about it at Thunder."

"What's that?"

"That's what the paper said. Thunder had lawyers there, proved nobody knew about it but him. I don't think it's all settled yet, but looks like the company's going to come out of it okay. Hey, you tried that—no, you don't have a car. Anyway, I got me a tank of that new Thunder Green. Burns clean, with all the zip of premium, like they say on the radio. Gonna sell a lot of that, I bet."

"That so? That's good. That'll bring some jobs back."

"Oh, they're already hiring again, down at the refinery. Told my brother that, he come back from Buffalo. He's goin' down, try to sign on."

Halvorsen nodded slowly, but didn't say anything. Fox looked at the seat between them. "Whatcha got in the box?"

"Chain saw."

"Firewood?"

"Roof beams."

"Oh, yeah, right. They burned you out, didn't they."

"About halfway," said Halvorsen, looking out the window at the passing hills.

"That reminds me." Fox reached across him to the glove compartment. "Got some things of yours here. Been holdin' on to them, figured you'd be back sooner or later."

"Thanks," said Halvorsen, looking down at the gloves and scarf. There was a black smear on the scarf. He folded it carefully, not touching the smear, and put it in his pocket.

"Say, what ever happened to them kids that was with you? Wasn't there two other people?"

"Boy and a girl," said Halvorsen. He looked out the window, to where the moosewoods were starting to bud. "The boy got shot. Put up a good fight, though. They had his picture in the paper. All his buddies from the football team carryin' the casket. His dad wrote me he's some kind of a hero to a lot of the kids."

"And the girl?"

"Oh, she testified, but they let her off. She moved on. Said she didn't want to stay. Got religion, I think. Went on down south someplace, to live with her brother. Virginia or Florida or some such. Got a card from her. Says she's happy."

"Be warmer, either place," said Fox, peering out into the rearview as he adjusted the spinner. "Not like this. Snow, snow, all the goddamn time. I'll tell you one good thing come out of it all, though."

"What's that?"

"Me and the wife. Remember, I told you we were havin' problems? Getting along a lot better. Ain't till you really need a woman, you find out how much she loves you."

"That's true," said Halvorsen after a while.

He didn't say anything more and for a long time the other man was silent too.

Rolling along high above the road, the old man thought how sometimes it all seemed to stem from the hunting. Men had come to be what they were fighting the other beasts for dominion. When the animals were conquered, gone, they'd channeled that drive into war.

And when war got too expensive and too dangerous, not just to the warriors but to everybody, that need to kill and win had become business. Just like the old human sacrifices had become animal sacrifices and then just to offering bread and grape juice, till people forgot even what it meant. They'd finally outgrown their terror of God.

But in a few that drive and need still went too far. When that happened the rest, the men and women who stayed sane, had to step in and stop them.

He leaned his head back, watching the sky as the truck rumbled along. Clearing snow. Seemed it didn't matter how often you plowed, it would come back, falling from the sky as it always had, inevitable and remorseless, without mercy or pity or regret.

But it could be cleared. And would be. Again and again. Till it was spring.

It's awful slow, Halvorsen thought. Terrible slow, and it ain't easy. But seems to me we might be making some headway.

Fox said, "Saw that old buck again. He must live out near you, you know?"

"Think I know the one you mean."

"Guess he's made it through the season again. Some of them deer, smarter'n you'd think. Hey, getting close to the Run. You want, I can maybe get you up pretty close to your place. Save you some walking, anyway."

And the old man said, his eyes narrowing in what might almost have been a smile, "That'd be just fine by me."

AS THE
WOLF
LOVES
WINTER

For Tony and Mary

Acknowledgments

Ex nihilo nihil fit. For this book I owe much to James Allen, Rich Andrews, Natalia Aponte, David Burlin, Arden Bush, Tom Doherty, Stan Folks, Lee Forker, Bob Fort, Cassie Gallup, Robert Gleason, Frank Green, Fran Goodrich, Greta Goszinski, Becky Harris, Lenore Hart, Steven de las Heras, Cindy Hervatin, M. Frances Holmes, Bud Kiehl, Doug King, Ruth Mason, Barb Needham, Minh Lien Nguyen, Alan Poyer, Spider Race, Scott Reitz, Al Sherman, Paul Sorokes, Burdett West, J.M. Zias, and others who gave generously of their time. Thanks to the Bradford Public Library, the Friends Library in Kane, the Eastern Shore Public Library, and the U.S. Immigration and Naturalization Service. All errors and deficiencies are my own.

If thou wert the wolf, thy greediness
Would afflict thee, and oft thou
Shouldst hazard thy life for thy dinner.

—Shakespeare, *Timon of Athens*

Prologue

The man in the rust-colored parka had almost reached the crest of the mountain, after a long, wearying climb, when he first suspected he wasn't alone.

He stopped, thrusting thumbs under pack straps as he frowned around at the monotonous gray trees. The blowing snow made them wavering and grainy, like an old film. Something had moved out there. But what? He'd left the last house, the last road miles back. The only trails up here were deer trails. Hunters? But the season was over, and few hunters came back this far anyway.

Around the listening figure the hills rose steep as the waves of a frozen storm at sea. Till now in his march he'd looked up at them. Now he stood on the ridgeline, knowing there was only a little way yet to the summit. The long crests shouldered forward under snow that hissed steadily down from clouds the color of a worn spoon. In the afternoon light no road or building, no human artifice or habitation was visible on the deserted land.

Finally he decided it must have been a deer. But cold and fatigue had stiffened his muscles during the pause, and he winced as he forced them into motion again. The deep unbroken snow dragged at his boots. Dropping his head, he bulled along through heavier drifts where the woods opened, then into a stand of white pines. Their resinous smell stung his nose pleasantly.

Yeah, getting tired . . . he was still in good shape, though. Not like the other guys at work. He couldn't think of one who could have kept up with him out here. He smiled faintly, planting one foot ahead of the other as the ridgeline lifted toward the clouds. New snow creaked and popped under his boots. From time to time he looked up.

At last he glimpsed a wedge of sky between the stripped boles. He stopped again, blowing out with relief, and shrugged the pack higher on his shoulders. Light when he'd left the car, it had gained an astonishing amount of weight as he'd humped it across miles of forest and up nearly a thousand feet to this deserted height.

His eyes searched the trees, the hundreds of stark vertical lines with snow sifting and whirling between them. No wonder they called it the Wild Area. The vacant, wind-ringing woods, the mist-wreathed hollows didn't feel empty. They felt haunted. He didn't believe in ghosts or spirits. But it was spooky out here. Wild, like the forest of fairy tales, or of nightmare.

The Kinningmahontawany, they called it.

He shifted the pack again, then bent for the last time to the slope. Around him the oaks stretched skeletal limbs in impotent entreaty to an indifferent heaven, the colorlessness broken only occasionally on the misty hill flanks by the bluegreen of pine. That might have been what I saw, he thought. An evergreen bough collapsing, giving way at last under its icy and ever-increasing burden.

A labyrinthine writhe of blown-down trunks and shattered limbs opened above him. Years before a wind had swept up from the hollow, or a tornado had touched down. Beneath the fallen trees holes opened like black mouths ringed with jagged teeth. The snow supported his weight at first, then gave way with a sullen, treacherous crackle, plunging him thigh-deep, filling his boots and pockets with icy powder.

When he emerged from the blowdown, soaked with sweat under the parka, the ground leveled out. It wasn't easy to know when you were at the top. There was no open vista to look out from. But as he slogged on, the land started to drop. He stopped, resting, then backtracked.

At last he judged he was as near the summit of Colley Hill as he was likely to get without surveyor's instruments. He didn't have to find the exact apex, but the closer he got the more even the repeater's coverage would be. Coughing white breath like cigarette smoke into the icy wind, he unslung the pack. Digging a gloved hand into his aching neck, he peered up into dully glowing clouds, murky and turbulent, but at their hearts the same dead gray as the motionless trunks around him.

Finally he decided on a huge old black cherry. Like an ancient column, it towered straight-trunked up at the crown of the hill. Its upper limbs were twisted, lightning-shattered, but it looked like it would be here for years to come. He knelt to the pack and unzipped it, revealing a coil of insulated wire, a foot-square panel, and a plastic case sealed with epoxy. He set these aside and pulled out a set of climbing spikes and a lineman's belt.

Straightening, he peered around once again, still wondering what that movement had been. Like a ghost slipping through the empty woods, among the winterstripped trees . . .

He clamped the spikes onto his boots, shrugged off the parka—this would be warm work—and draped it over ice-brittled laurel. Tucking box and wire inside his sweater, he pulled on heavy leather gloves, looking up.

A few minutes later he was sixty feet up, stapled and strapped to the black pillar of the ancient cherry. Even through the gloves he felt the dead, sapless cold of the sleeping wood. The wind was much worse up here. Unslowed by underbrush or second growth, it scraped the hilltops like a knife across a cutting board, laying icy steel against his cheeks and ears.

He climbed rapidly, setting the spikes with his toes, then levering himself upward against the huge rough cylinder that narrowed as he rose. From time to time he came to branches, massive outstretched shoulders, and had to unbuckle the belt and work his way over them. Some were cracked from ice load and lightning storm. At these moments, with only the strength of his arms holding him, he couldn't help thinking all he had to do was open his hands . . . and some obscure part of him that stepped out of the shadows only at times like these urged him to: to let go, fall, and die. The only way he could keep going was to close his mind against it, as a man looks away from fear, or madness, or unpermitted desire; things that once acknowledged are half surrendered to.

Twenty feet from the crown of the tree he paused for a rest. He tugged at the belt, making sure it was locked, then leaned back and clamped a glove over his face. As his breath warmed his cheeks, wasp-stinging them back to life, he looked out over an immense and lifeless solitude.

From up here, high above the summit, hundreds of square miles of hills stretched out like sleeping cats beneath the falling snow. The bellies of the clouds dragged on the prickly tops of the ridges, the dead-looking branches snagging tufts of white fog like wool and combing it out to lie in opaque drifts in the benches and hollows. Everything was black, and gray, and white; a world possessed by winter so profoundly it seemed impossible that anything could ever change.

White, and gray, and black . . . and a furtive stir at the periphery of vision.

He whipped his head around, peering down through the treetops like a bird of prey. But his eyes were not a hawk's eyes, and again his focused sight found nothing. Nothing but the snow, and the slowly vanishing connect-the-dots of his own trail, ending far below.

Puffing out a stream of frost-smoke, he set his spikes again and hoisted himself to where he could wrap one arm around the narrowed trunk. The great tree soared upward still. But this was as high as he could force himself. Anchoring his weight with a locked elbow, stripping a glove off the other hand with his teeth, he reached inside his sweater.

Checking the lay of the hills, he set the panel so that it would face south and pressed its spiked back into the black bark. He spun the wire out, then swung the box in an arc and let go. It landed on the next branch up. He tensed, clinging to the tree. The box rocked, then dropped over the branch and hung from its antenna.

He smiled, as much as his cold-stiffened face would permit.

He was a radio ham, and the box was an FM relay. Dotted through the countryside, these boxes let hobbyists communicate outside the crowded and sometimes undependable shortwave bands. Powered by the sun, they would serve for years before they had to be replaced.

Huge as it was, the cherry swayed as a gust drove through it. He quickly fumbled his glove back on, afflicted by a shiver both of cold and anxiety. He'd raised four daughters on nursery rhymes, and the repetitive verses played themselves back at odd moments. Rock-a-bye baby, he thought. Daddy better get the hell out of this treetop. If the bough broke, it could be days, maybe weeks, before anybody found him.

He was setting his spikes for the descent when a throaty rumble came from below him.

When he looked down his lips parted in astonishment. What was a German shepherd doing out here? It stood at the base of the tree, staring up at him. He let go with one hand and waved. "Hey, boy," he called, but his voice sounded weak and tremulous against the enormous empty chant of the wind.

The dog went silent for a moment after he spoke. Then the low growl built again, like the sound of a distant battle.

He felt suddenly apprehensive. He tightened his grip on the belt, twisting his spurs into the rough bark, then looked down again, studying the animal.

The first thing he noticed was how long its legs were. The second, the pinkish-red tongue hanging from a black-rimmed mouth. Then, one by one, other details. The brindled coat was the color of wood-smoke, the shoulders and head outlined in charcoal. The pointed ears were forward-focused on him. He was too high to see its eyes. The big splayed paws rested easily on the snow. The fluffed-out tail was carried half lifted as the animal circled the tree, nosing at his pack, then the parka. It had narrow shoulders and a smallish head, and wasn't as big as he'd first thought. Not large for a shepherd, certainly not as big as a Saint Bernard or a rottweiler.

His eyes darted hopefully around, but he saw no sign of its owner. Nor could he make out a collar. It was probably feral. People thought they were being merciful, abandoning their pets in the country. They told themselves they'd make it on their own, but what happened was they starved, or farmers shot them.

Giving the relay a last glance, he began working his way back down the trunk. This occupied his attention for some minutes. Going down was harder than going up. He was shuddering now. The wind's icicle teeth gripped his bunched, straining biceps and thighs. He got to the last branch, twenty feet up, and perched on it to readjust the belt for the final descent. He glanced curiously down again as he did so.

The dog was sitting on its haunches now, still looking at him. A frosting of fresh snow had gathered on its back. He could see its eyes now. Flat, expressionless golden orbs that did not look away but stayed locked on his.

Suddenly it lifted its muzzle, opening its mouth in a tremulous, high-pitched wail that echoed and re-echoed, first from the trees, then from the bare, far-off flanks of the hills.

A shiver ran across his shoulders as he heard the answering howls. He clung to the branch and made no further move to come down.

Presently three more forms materialized from the forest. They came one by one, gliding with an easy lope across snow he'd slogged through laboriously. From different directions, as if each had been hunting on its own. As they trotted up each new arrival touched noses with the first, or gave a short, whining bark. They examined the parka, then sniffed and snapped at the pack, pulling it around until the contents lay scattered on the snow. Then they circled restlessly for quite some time, looking up at him with the same speculative stare as the first, before curling themselves into the snow as if it were a down quilt. One shifted several times, unable to find a comfortable spot, till settling on a patch of open snow.

The man clung to the tree, watching them. His arms were shaking now, muscles cramping. The wind came through the cableknit sweater as if it were made of lace. When he lifted his eyes to scan the ice-scoured woods, the snow drove needles into them. When he lowered them to the animals again their gazes met his, unconcerned, opaque, intent, and unafraid.

They can't be, he thought. There aren't any of *those* left around here. Not for a hundred, two hundred years.

He clapped his arms awkwardly against his chest, sitting crouched over on the icy limb. At the movement heads rose, ears cocked. He explored his pockets. A jackknife, nothing to face four wolves with. A stripping tool. A pair of needlenosed pliers.

He poised the pliers like a pub dart and threw them at the first wolf, still sitting below him. It leapt aside and they missed. It sniffed at the hole in the snow, then followed its tail around and lay down again in the same expectant position as before. He threw the stripping tool too, but it went so wide the animal didn't bother to move. It just sat there, tongue lapping out, looking up at him with what almost seemed to be a grin.

During the next hour he passed from shuddering through numbness to a frozen immobility. Sitting on the limb, buckled to the trunk by the lineman's belt, he didn't need to worry about falling. But he understood now that unless he could build a fire soon, or at least recover the parka, he would die.

He thought of his .22 rifle, at home in the hall closet . . . If he'd brought something to eat, he could toss it to one of the wolves, make them fight over it, maybe get to his parka while they were distracted. But the only food he'd brought was a Hershey bar, and it lay now below him, nosed but undisturbed by the wolves. He thought of cutting off a branch, wiring the knife to it to make a spear. But he couldn't get out to a limb that would break, and when he tried to unbend his fingers from the belt they were frozen to it, like iron clamped to leather. He might uncrimp them, but then he might not be able to close them again.

If he went down, the wolves might kill him. But there was no question about what the cold would do.

Meanwhile the day dimmed toward darkness, and the snow whispered to him with the tongues of dead leaves. *Soon*, it sounded like. *Soon, soon.*

Finally he decided he had no choice but to try. If he could wound or kill the pack leader, maybe the others would run.

He pried his fingers apart clumsily. His hands still bent, but not as individual fingers. He lobster-clawed the knife open and gripped it in his palm like a Neolithic hand ax. He shifted his feet around toward the tree, dug the spikes in, and reached round to unsnap the belt.

The wolves rose, leaving their comfortable positions and trotting forward to gather beneath him. His heart thudded. Warmth touched his face again, throbbed in his hands. He fixed his eyes on the russet nylon of the parka, judging the number of strides to it. Okay, big bad wolves, he thought with resigned dread. Here I come, ready or not.

Instead he heard a crack, felt a sudden, sagging drop. He whipped around, grabbing for the trunk, but his frozen, scrabbling fingers slipped off. His kicking feet gouged off spinning clods of bark but gained no purchase.

The rotten branch gave another rifle-crack and disintegrated into wood-meal and ice, peeling off a long, splitting strip of bark as it came apart under his weight. The woods spun above his head. The last thing he saw was a gray patchwork of sky.

The wolves stood in a rough circle around the motionless figure sprawled in the snow. Then, into the gathering night, rose a haunting, ululating chorus that the gusting wind carried far out over the darkening hills.

One

W. T. Halvorsen

The next morning a gaunt old man with gray-stubbled cheeks stood blinking at the sky from a clearing in the woods. He sniffed the wind, hands shoved deep into the pockets of a red-barred hunting coat. Only when a white-and-brown hound whined, nuzzling the laces of his boots, did he clear his throat, then turn from the leaden sky to empty his cheek into the snow.

About time it started warming up some, Halvorsen thought, kneeling stiffly. Been cold as hell for the last couple weeks. His hand smoothed the dog's head, and she bored her muzzle into his glove.

He didn't want to go into town. He didn't care to have that much to do with people anymore. You got a bellyful of them in prison. But his battered tin canisters were empty of sugar and coffee and beans. He needed a washer for the pump; it had leaked all over the floor and the water had frozen, and yesterday he'd slipped, gone down next to the sink. Miracle he hadn't busted a rib.

It was time to go, whether he wanted to or not.

The bitch pulled away and bounded gracelessly through the snow toward the trees. "Come on back, Jess," he called sharply. "Ain't no time to play."

Pulling his old green cap down, he turned abruptly from the hilltop, the shimmering air above his makeshift chimney. Back straight, head erect, he started down the road, eyes following the ridgeline as if unwilling to lower themselves to the snow-obliterated track.

He looked out along the dark, rising masses of Town Hill and Groundhog Hill, Gerroy and Lookout Tower and Sullivan Hill and Raymonds Hill. Below them, out of view though he knew it was there, the Allegheny River slept in black silence beneath white snow. Halvorsen shivered. Not a hundred yards gone and he missed home already. It wasn't much, just a basement. But it was warm, the stove red-hot with good, seasoned birch he'd cut the fall before.

Forcing reluctance from his mind, he marched stiffly along, keeping to the right-hand side, where it was more or less level and the ruts under the snow weren't as deep. When he was a boy he'd put his tongue on the train tracks once, just to see what the bare steel tasted like. The freezing air tasted like that now. Behind him the dog hesitated, looking off into the woods. Then, as he dropped out of sight, she bounded after him, whining anxiously.

Halvorsen strode along, feeling pain in his bruised side but figuring it would work itself out after a mile or two. Powder snow a foot and a half deep, crunching at each step like sand between your teeth. Under it gravel and clay were frozen to a bone-jarring hardness. The road dipped steadily at first, walled in on either side by stands of beech and birch and an occasional oak, black and ominous against the luminescent, shadowless white of the snow.

Half an hour later the road turned left for its shallower descent along the frozen creek at the bottom of the run. He felt warmer now, almost comfortable. His muscles were limbering up and he felt pretty good for as old a son of a bitch as he was getting to be. His old Maine boots crunched steadily. The hound whined behind him, but he didn't look back.

He couldn't help thinking what he thought every time he walked this road, that in summer there was no lovelier place on earth than Mortlock Hollow. Then it was filled with the chatter of chipmunks and the cries of birds, the vampire whine of mosquitoes and the milling clouds of midges that rose like smoke from the ferny spots where the water pooled in shadow. Among the branches silver webs shimmered on an intangible wind. The creek sang beneath leaning pines, and down in the gorge groundhogs scurried from rock to rock. Life was everywhere, frogs and mud wasps in the puddled ruts of the road, rabbits in the brambles, the heartstopping racket of quail bursting from cover. As if they understood how little time they had before the chill white silence of winter erased them.

And now it was here. The wind gusted between the bare beeches, sucking the freezing air out of his lungs, numbing his cheeks where they emerged from the turned-up collar. And shivering suddenly in its chill breath he felt the half-revealed teeth of the ultimate destroyer, enemy of all life, all warmth, all light, remorseless nemesis of all that existed in Time.

The road leveled and turned right and he paused to rest. The hound plunged away on the path of a hare. He waited for her, leaning against the rusty iron of an abandoned pump jack, panting out clouds of frost-smoke, eyes blinking with cold tears as he looked out at the stark and brittle universe of winter. At hillsides stripped to rock and harsh planes of snow. Crisscrossed, beneath the naked trees, with furrows and seams like a weathered, ancient face.

The old man sank back into the past like a rock into the cold, dark water of a dammed lake. Seeing not what was before his eyes, but what was sixty years gone.

They'd been bumping southward along a rutted track in old Amos McKittrack's Model T, when the road dropped, the scrub oak fell away, and Billy Halvorsen had gone to stone in his seat.

Before them had been desolation to the blue horizon, fold on fold of hills stripped like battlefield dead. Their slopes were littered with stumps and briars, slashed and gouged with the Shay engines' right-of-way. The trapper, cursing, had told him how the timber companies had bought politicians, lied and cheated the Indians and smallholders off their land, then whipsawed, toppled, and stripped for tanbark twenty-eight million acres of virgin forest.

Eyes narrowed, mouth set like a frozen mask, Halvorsen stood staring out. Then the past gave way again beneath him, and under the snow, under the trees, far beneath the ancient, glacier-planed mountains themselves he saw the form and structure of the land.

Once it had been an immense shallow sea. Over millions of years its buried marshes had turned to petroleum and natural gas, accumulating in traps and fractures as the land twisted and compressed. So that now, thousands of feet beneath where he stood, lay the great sands that had supplied the finest oil in the world for a hundred years. Enough, once, to dazzle the world, and lay the foundations of a thousand fortunes. Once . . . but now it was almost gone.

The wind gusted up from the valley, drawing with it an icy curtain of wind-whipped snow, and he shuddered, standing motionless deep in the woods. Lost in thought, lost in time . . . *useless, daydreaming old bastard . . .* but for a moment it had been as if he could see it all, like God himself, all that was past and yet present, all that had happened and was still to come.

He shivered again, and looked blankly around for the hound. She was investigating some deer tracks. He whistled her in and forced himself back into a walk.

The road came to another switchback and plunged steeply. This was where Alma had trouble when she came out to see him. Damn near straight up and down, broken and gullied by a spring that perked out of the hillside. He slid his boots along, searching beneath the snow for the treacherous slickness of hidden ice. He rolled the plug in his cheek and spat bitter juice. Out of tobacco too, he had to remember to stock up at the store.

His tongue was exploring a sore spot on his gum when he heard a voice. He hesitated, looking off between the naked black trees. It came again, a distant shout, almost a scream. Hard to tell, but it sounded like whoever was yelling was down in the hollow below him.

"C'mere, Jess," he muttered, and the dog followed as he left the road, handing himself from tree to tree down the bank.

Below that were rocks, and then, a few hundred feet down, the creek. Halvorsen traversed the rocks carefully. Big as cars, flat-topped juts out of the hillside, if you slipped you could break a leg easy. He hesitated, almost turned back. Then another scream echoed from below.

The creek came down the run like a ladder. Its slightly turbid water chattered over mossy rocks, making a rounded coating over the submerged stones, curling clear claws around the ones that broke the surface. It ran so fast it didn't freeze, except in the coldest winters.

The old man stopped at the edge, searching for a way across. There, upstream, a few stones showed shallow under the rushing black water.

"Come on, Jess," he said again. "Let's see what's goin' on down here."

A few minutes later he crouched in a stand of pines above a lease road, looking down on what seemed to be a murder in progress.

An ice-and-salt-caked Ford pickup was parked square in the middle of the narrow road. Not far from it two men were beating a third. One was using his fists, the other, a length of what looked to Halvorsen like wire rope. He could hear the blows, hear the choked whimpers of the man being beaten. As he watched, the smaller man collapsed into the snow. His face was a bloody mask, but through it Halvorsen caught something else.

He's a Chink or a Jap or something, the old man thought. But the two guys beating him, they're white.

He squatted amid the pines, muzzling the dog with gloved hands. He didn't like to see two big men on one little one. He wished he had a rifle. He'd feel more confident stepping into trouble. But he couldn't own a gun anymore. They'd made that clear at the parole hearing. Anyway, this wasn't his fight. Whatever it was about, it didn't have anything to do with him.

One of the white men, tall, with a jutting jaw, started kicking the guy in the snow.

You shouldn't get involved, Halvorsen told himself. Just ought to let things alone. Like you shouldn't have got involved in that strike, in '36. Or with the trucks dumping that poison. Last time you stuck your neck out, you lost almost two years out of your life.

But he couldn't let them beat a defenseless man to death. He just plain couldn't do it. He let go the bitch's muzzle, and her barking pealed startlingly loud in the confined bottom of the hollow. "Hey," Halvorsen yelled. "Hey! You men!"

They snapped around, searching the woods above them. But just like he figured, they couldn't see him or tell how many there were. For the first time he got a clear look at the tall one's face, and squinted. He'd seen this guy somewhere before.

"Shit. Somebody up there."

"Who is it? You see 'em?"

"No. Let's get the hell out of here." The tall one jerked the driver's door open and was halfway in when he jumped out again. "Grab his ass," he yelled to the other.

They picked up the Asian and threw him into the bed, tossed a tarp over the sagging body, then scrambled into the cab. The starter snarled and the truck jerked, bounded forward like a startled deer, and disappeared down the hollow, leaving only a fading growl, gravel-spattered ruts in the snow, and a white cloud that drifted downwind, slowly rising, till it vanished into the silent trees.

Halvorsen dusted snow off his pants and stood, frowning. He'd looked for a number as the truck moved off. Pennsy plates, blue and yellow, but so caked with salt-ice he couldn't make them out. All he had was an insignia on the door. It wasn't any he knew: Penelec, the lightning bolt of Thunder Oil, the two raised fingers of Kendall, or the state logo the game protectors' vehicles carried. It was a gray pyramid, with letters inside. Maybe a word, he couldn't tell.

At last he whistled to the dog, who was sniffing at blood-drops in the snow, a twisted snow-angel where the man had fallen. Together they swung off again down the hollow, toward the town.

The blue flames fluttered with a hollow roar, and the gas heat hit him like a blow in the face, drying his eyeballs so his lids grated when he blinked. It was so stifling after the crisp winter air he couldn't breathe for a few seconds after the door swung closed. Taking off his hat, he stood immobile, ignoring the dog's scratching on the outer door. Then reached up a hand. His outstretched fingers groped for ragged fur, a gaping muzzle, teeth. Instead they fanned through empty space.

"Lookin' for your bear, Racks? Ain't there no more."

"That you, Stan?"

"No. It's Lucky."

Halvorsen blinked again, remembering Stanley Rezk had been dead for years. Getting old, he thought, angry at himself. But he didn't recall anything about them getting rid of the bear . . . "It ain't?"

"Took it in to Sonny's for repairs. It was getting kind of moth-eaten. Don't worry, I'll pick up the tab, it's a good draw for the bar."

Halvorsen felt annoyed. What did he care what they did with the damn bear? He didn't hunt anymore. He cleared his throat and unbuttoned his coat, stamped snow from his boots, and headed back past mahogany-stained pine booths with new green plastic cushions, the bar, the swinging door to the kitchen. Four men glanced up from a nook behind the cigarette machine.

"Racks! What you doing down out of the hills?"

"Welcome to Sin City, W. T."

"Hullo, boys," he said, suppressing a smile as he fumbled his hat onto the rack. Didn't make a damn bit of difference what time of day he ran into them, they were hardly ever sober. Jack McKee had been a tool dresser for the Gerroy outfit, a gambler, a fighter. Now he was bald and his hands shook with Parkinson's. Mase Wilson had jobbed for the White Timber Company, cutting and peeling from when he turned fourteen till the day he lost an arm to one of the big band-saws. Fatso DeSantis had played Two Old Cat with Halvorsen through the long dusk after their first day of school, a slim shadow with sneakers flashing beneath the street-lights. Now he was so heavy the only place that could weigh him was the post office; he had to go to the loading dock and get on the bulk-mail scale. Charlie Prouper was the oldest man in town, an emaciated ghost who couldn't speak without putting his finger over a silver tube like a second mouth in his throat.

"They say it's been jammed up for two weeks now. If that don't clear before warm weather sets in, we're gonna see major flooding."

"What's that, Mase?"

"Damn Allegheny's froze up solid over at Roulette. They're talking blasting. Hey, might be up your alley. You used to handle the nitro, didn't you?"

"Ain't touched it for years. Figure I got out alive back then, I'm ahead of the game."

A thin girl Halvorsen didn't know came back with shots of White Seal and bottles of Straub's and Black Label. She started to put one down in front of him, but he said quickly, "Coffee for me, please. With the cream." She set a paper cup down instead and he stared at it before he realized it was for his chew. He spat carefully and folded the top and set it down by his side on the scuffed patterned linoleum. "So, what else's new?"

"Nothing."

"Ain't seen you in a while, Charlie. Weren't you sick, over in that home?"

Prouper looked up slowly from his untouched beer. A low, hoarse, vibrating whisper said, "Had me the pneumonia."

"I was over to see him," said McKee. He sounded angry, but that was how he'd always talked. "Shit, they had him on the damn breathing machine, they didn't think he was gonna make it. But damn if he ain't out here again borrowing my money."

Prouper fumbled for his neck. "Ever tell you boys about . . ."

They leaned back, waiting, knowing it took him time to get breath for words. "When I was with the marines in France—'fore I got gassed—the captain kept sending me out to scout the Hun lines—every night. Finally I ast him, Captain—why do you keep sending me out to scout, why don't you give some of the other boys a chance. Captain said—because you keep coming back." He took his finger off his neck and looked around at them.

"And you come back again," Wilson grunted.

"That's right. But I tell you one thing. I ain't—going back to that there hospital ever again," whispered Prouper. He leaned slowly back, nodding to give his words weight, and returned to the somber, detached contemplation of his Straub's.

Halvorsen sat back too, feeling the hot air nipping his ears back to life with sharp kitten-bites. His coffee came and he counted out change, looking up at the menu in pressed-in white plastic letters over the counter. Might be nice to have something he didn't fix out of a can. The pork chops and potatoes, maybe . . .

Talking about the nitro made him remember the oilfields. How in the winter, long before sunup, the men would start getting ready for the day's operations. With guttering torches, rags wrapped on sticks and dipped in the crude, they'd begin thawing out the rod lines to the jacks. Building fires under the storage tanks, heating the inflammable crude to the seventy degrees it needed to flow. The oil came out of the ground mixed with natural gas but they just let that evaporate, or it howled out of the well pure and colorless and they flared it off. They built the refineries on the creeks so they could dump whatever they didn't want. In those days the creeks had floated inches thick with oil scum. Sometimes it would catch fire, sending a black cloud up behind the hills, and everywhere the air reeked sweet with crude petroleum. It was a smell W. T. Halvorsen had always liked.

Someone pushed by him toward the rest room and his mind recurred unwillingly to the hot noisy interior of the tavern. McKee was talking about some kind of insect. "They're sprayin' for 'em over in the state forest right now. They had it bad down in the Shenandoah, sucked all the sap right out of the hemlocks. Say they can kill a hemlock in a couple of years."

Halvorsen relaxed, the heat making him drowsy, listening as the conversation wandered. A school bus accident out by Beaver Fork. Some farmers had been complaining about dog killings. Finally Wilson turned to him. "You gettin' any of them cherry poachers out your way?"

"The what?"

"Cherry poachers. You know how since they done all that clearcutting they had a lot of black cherry grow back. That and the beech and maple. Well, it's getting to the size they're cutting it, selling it to Kane Hardwood."

"Seen the trucks on Route Six."

"Uh huh. They sell a lot overseas, or down to Carolina, make furniture out of it. Well, now there's guys poaching it. They'll pull in some night with chainsaws and skidders and next day, the people own the land, they'll go out and look and there's nothing left but stumps."

"I heard somebody got the stained glass out of the church over at Four Holes," said the girl, who had come back without Halvorsen noticing. "Right out of the church. They just come out and looked one morning and it was gone."

A man in uniform came out of the rest room. "Hey, Pat," said DeSantis. "You know all these guys, don't you?"

Pat Nolan was the local police chief, a big man, blond around a balding crown. "Hullo, Mase, Charlie, Fatso. Racks, how you getting along out there?"

"Hello, Pat. All right."

"Keeping out of trouble?"

"Tryin' to."

"Good . . . Fatso, if I have to pull that Willys of yours over one more time, you're gonna be walking it."

"Now, Pat, I don't drive her over twenty-five."

"And you're all over the road like paint. You want to have a drink, fine, but get somebody else to drive you home. I'm not kidding, that kind of stuff don't go anymore."

Halvorsen said, "What's happening, Pat?"

"Not too much. I was going out the Derris road and I saw a station wagon stopped. I went up to it, said, 'Can I help you, ma'am?' The lady makes these big round eyes and says, 'Turn around and look behind you.' I think yeah, I heard this one before, so I kind of back up and put my hand on my holster and half turn my head. And there's the biggest fucking bear I ever seen in my life, right up on top of the embankment. I'm the trained observer, right? I saw the station wagon but not the bear. I thought, Ma, sell the shithouse, I just lost my ass. He would have had me."

"What was you doing out Derris?"

"Guy was stealing gas. Property owners get free gas off the wells, you know? Well, this guy had lines led to two other houses he owned, and was stealing electricity from the company, too. Then National Fuel offered to meter and reduced it from a criminal to a civil suit." Nolan looked toward the front of the tavern. "Nice to see you fellows," he called back.

Wilson said, "All this goddamned crime. People don't have no respect for property anymore. And I'll tell you why, it's because they ain't teaching them when they're little. When I was a kid nobody ever stole anything. They never even locked their doors. Now you see it on the television, why—"

"What do you mean, they never stole anything?" Halvorsen said.

"Just what I said. When you and me were kids—"

Halvorsen said, "Shit, Mase, what the hell are you talking about? The first guys out here stole all this land from the damn Indians. Then White and Gerroy and them stole all the timber. Rockefeller tried to steal all the damn oil. What's the damn difference?"

They regarded him with dull astonishment. "Jesus. What's got into you?" McKee said.

"Nothing. I just don't figure what he was saying was right, sayin' nobody ever used to steal anything in the old days. The bastards I used to work with, they'd of stole your goddamned ass if it hadn't of been nailed on." He jammed an elbow into DeSantis's flabby side, shoved past Wilson, put his hand on Prouper's shoulder as he stared into his beer. "Take it easy, boys."

"Goin' already?"

"Things to do, people to see."

"So long, W. T."

"Stop by before you head home."

"And you take care of yourself, Charlie," Halvorsen said, grappling his fingers into the older man's shoulder. It felt slack and bony, and Prouper shook his head without looking up.

He caught up to the officer as he glanced at the empty space by the door. "What happened to your bear?" Nolan asked him.

"Lucky sent it in to the taxidermist, get it cleaned up. I have a word with you?"

"Sure."

He couldn't help it, something made him feel self-conscious about being seen talking to a cop. He muttered, "Let's go outside."

In the street the snow swirled in cyclones down the shoveled sidewalk. The sky was like gray wrapping paper taped down over the double row of brick and frame two-story and false-front buildings that was Main Street, Raymondsville, Pennsylvania. Down the block was the little gazebo and the bronze tablets set into rocks, Veterans Square, and beyond that the black iron arch of the bridge. Above them the hills peered down like squatting boys examining the skitterings of ants.

"What you got, Racks?"

"I was walkin' into town this morning. Seven, eight o'clock. I hear somebody yelling down at the bottom of Mortlock Run. I went down to look and there was two guys beating up on a little fella. I made some noise and Jess, she barked, and they skedaddled in a white Ford pickup. Couldn't get no number."

"What happened to the victim?"

"They threw him in the bed of the truck. He didn't look in any too good shape, but I think he was still breathing."

Nolan had a notebook out, was bent into the doorway of the Salvation Army Thrift Shop as the cold wind shouldered past. "Describe any of 'em?"

"The ones doing the beating, two guys about thirty, forty, wearing work clothes. The tall one had on a Bills hat. Kind of lean-lookin' face, like that Basil Rathbone in the Sherlock Holmes movies. Jaw out to here. Big ears. Kind of bad skin, a red face. Leather jacket. Thought I knew him for a second, but I must of been mistaken. The other guy was heavyset. No, fat. A big gut on him. Had on one of them orange stocking caps and a mule-colored field jacket. I didn't get a good look at his face."

"The victim?"

"Young. Maybe twenty. Thing is, he was some kind of foreigner, looked like to me. Oriental, or maybe Mexican, but he wasn't Negro or white."

"That's a pretty good description."

"Uh huh . . . the truck, it had an insignia on it." He described it as best he could.

Nolan snapped his notebook shut and tucked it into his overcoat. "Okay, I'll file it. Too late to get anybody out there, get tracks or anything, they'd all be covered up. But I'll keep an eye open for a truck meeting that description."

"Maybe the state cops could help. Bill Sealey—"

Nolan moved his head slightly, managing to give an impression of impatience or annoyance, but all he said was "Uh huh. I'll give Bill a call, see if he knows anything."

As Nolan headed for his cruiser, Halvorsen stood with his hands in his pockets, looking after him. At the shabby buildings sagging on their foundations, the peeling signs creaking in the wind, the deserted heart of a bereft, forgotten town. Goddamn it, he thought, turning his head slowly to look up the street, checking his back trail. But seeing nothing except the bridge, the looming hills, the frozen writhe of the river.

It was crazy, he knew that, but he still couldn't shake the feeling that something was following him.

Two

Becky Benning

Biting her lips, she tried to concentrate on the sliver of steel Mr. Cash had given her team after warning them twice how dangerous it was. To either side of her Anne and Jonathan pressed close, all three looking down at the splayed-out creature pinned to the Styrofoam backboard on the gray scrubbed stone of the lab bench.

She closed her eyes, wishing her hands weren't so numb. If she cut herself instead of the frog, it'd feel just the same. Like nothing. So maybe there wasn't really any difference at all between the frog and herself.

She opened her eyes and said out loud to the teacher's frown: "I can't do it, Mr. Cash. I'm sorry." Beside her Jonathan and Anne sighed wordlessly.

"You have to, Becky. It's part of the lab work."

"I can't cut it apart. I'm sorry, but I can't."

"You'll take an *F*, then."

Another voice, at the next bench. "Sir, she doesn't want to. Can't she just watch us do it?"

"This is between Becky and me, Robert. Just let her alone for a minute to think about it. Anne, Johnny, that *F* will be a team grade. Talk to her, okay? The other teams, you can get started on your dissections."

The kids murmured around her, then went gradually quiet until all there was to hear was the click and whisper of blades through dead flesh, the occasional mutter of "Gross" and "Yuk." Across the room Margory Gourley said, "This is fun. Look at how wet its guts look."

"Becky, you scummer," Anne hissed. "If you think I'm going to fail science because you're too damn chicken to cut up a dead frog—"

Becky looked at the frog again. Sagging, eye bulges closed, it looked asleep. It had come in a plastic bag, drifting in some colorless, smell-less fluid, as if it were still swimming in the water. It looked green and fresh and shiny, as if in another second it would open its eyes and croak. She'd been able to slit the bag open and get it out, clammy and bumpy, like a piece of uncooked chicken with the skin still on. Jonathan, her geeky lab partner, had promptly dropped it. But they finally got it pinned to the board. Then they'd watched the videotape, how to identify the stomach and backbone and lungs and brain. How if you slit its leg and tickled it with a battery, the leg would jerk, just as if it were alive.

That was when she'd started to feel sick.

Abruptly Anne stopped whispering threats. It was Mr. Cash again. "Becky? Come out into the hall, please."

In the hall the science teacher's bulk seemed smaller than it did in the classroom. Mr. Cash was huge and he sweated so hard you could smell him across the lab bench. He didn't look at you when he talked and you could tell he thought all the kids were stupid. Now he looked at the wall and said, "Becky, the dissection subject is dead. It is now just like a machine, one that you're going to take apart to see how it works. Think of it just like carving your food, all right? Only, you're not going to eat it because it's not cooked yet."

"I'm a vegetarian, Mr. Cash. We don't eat meat at our house."

"Really?" He seemed more interested in something on her chest than in what she was saying. He was sweating although it wasn't very hot in the hall of the Raymondsville middle school. "Well, you'll have to get over it. You elected to take science. You can't pass the course without doing the dissections. Do you need to go to the bathroom first?"

"If I have to go, I can go myself, Mr. Cash. And I don't need the nurse, either."

"Okay, good, you're feeling better. Your partners are waiting; let's get in there and find out what makes that frog work."

"I'm not going to cut it up, Mr. Cash. I love animals and I'm not going to cut one apart. Even a dead one."

Cash halted with the door halfway open. The interested faces of eleven- and twelve-year-olds looked up from tiny flayed bodies. For a moment he looked baffled, resentful, like a child himself. Then his face hardened. "All right," he said. "But we can't let one crybaby hold up the whole class. I'm afraid you're going to have to explain this to Mrs. Kim."

When their real dad left, Becky was six and Jammy was two. That was the year they moved from Port Allegany to the blue house in Johnsonburg, at 638 Market Street. There was an upstairs and downstairs and they could do anything they wanted in that house, but the smell from the paper mill made everybody sick till they got used to it. And some people never did. After the blue house they moved to an apartment over a store. That was where they'd had her brother's third birthday party. Their dad showed up with all sorts of presents and that made her mad because he hadn't even sent a card on her birthdays since he left and went to California.

She was scared at Johnsonburg because she didn't know anybody. It was a new school and there was a lot of noise and loud kids there. But it turned out not to matter because they moved again. They'd moved a lot then, when their mom was looking for a job and couldn't find one. For a while they lived with their Uncle Will in St. Mary's. Some of their stuff stayed there and some of it stayed with Grammy in Port Allegany. Becky hated moving, the trucks with the furniture and the mattresses in them. She'd pack her stuffed animals and her Barbies. Her mom always told her not to take anything she didn't need, and she and Jammy would stuff as many of their toys as they could hide into the box of old purses Mom took wherever she went. On one move she lost her oldest toy, a stuffed dog with big floppy ears.

But then her mom had met Charlie and they got married and they all moved to his house, out in the woods, and she started going to school in Raymondsville. And again it was new kids, new teachers.

But she had her brother and her mom and, of course, her Barbies.

She had fifteen Barbies. They were all different. Some were old ones they got from the Salvation Army on Christmas when they were living in Johnsonburg. They were pretty new and not worn out, but they had old-fashioned clothes. The fashion dresses were long and the dolls had short curly hair. The new ones she'd got since they'd lived with Charlie had long straight hair down the middle of their backs and midriff shirt tops with long sleeves. Her Rollerblade Barbie had skates that flickered when she rolled. She usually played with the new dolls, her Hollywood Hair, her Tanya Hair, and her Rollerblade Barbie. The new Barbies had long hair and you could braid it or topsy tail it or put it in a ponytail. She liked to wear her own hair like the dolls, up on the side or in ponytails or sometimes in braids. For a topsy tail she put it up like a ponytail but parted her hair and put the ponytail through the loop.

She sat in the hall outside Mrs. Kim's office for almost an hour, feeling sick and afraid. Then she started making up a story about her Rollerblade Barbie. But in the middle of it the door opened and the principal stood there waiting, glasses flashing so you couldn't see her eyes at all. Mrs. Kim was from Korea and hard to understand when she talked on the PA system. The boys said she was mean as hell.

Becky stood up, her legs shaking, and followed her back into her office.

———

"Did you see that?" She leaned forward breathlessly, clutching the hard pipe edge of the seat in front of her in the bus.

"What did you say, Becky?" The driver turned her head.

"I thought I saw something. Out there in the woods."

"I didn't see anything," said Mrs. Schuler. "Is it still there?"

"No, it's gone now. You missed it." She sank back into the seat.

The Piccirillos—her mother and Charlie were Piccirillos but she and her brother were still Bennings—lived out in Crawford Run, east of Derris. If she was little she'd be going to school in Derris, but since she was in sixth grade she had to ride the bus all the way to Raymondsville. It took over an hour and her house was the last stop. It was long after dark when the doors hissed open on moonlit snow. "Good night, Becky," said the driver.

"Good night, Mrs. Schuler."

She stood by the mailbox as the bus grunted through a three-point turn on the narrow road, and waved as the headlights blinded her and moved past. Blinking away fuzzy green afterimages, she looked across the yard to the lighted windows. Started toward them, then stopped. It was a game she played sometimes, pretending she'd never been here before, that this wasn't her home at all, that strangers lived here, people she didn't know and would never see again.

The house was on the edge of the woods, and the trees hugged it like dark arms. Charlie had left five huge spruces in front when he built it, and now their massive pyramids of shadow loomed above the smooth silver of the yard. In the moonlight, the snow caught in their branches glowed as if the light came from inside it. Charlie's boat was a snowy lump in the driveway. The bare bushes scribbled ballpoint traceries on the snow. In the black sky the stars glittered like the fierce eyes of laughing children.

At last she shivered, clutched her book bag tighter, and went up the driveway, picking her way along in the blown-in wheel ruts from Charlie's Jeep. As she got closer she could see into the great room, the big triangular glass windows, the spotlights shining down from up in the loft where the kids slept. It looked deserted and spooky.

She stopped again by the garage, looking back over the road and the woods on the far side. Wondering if there was something there. Something like she thought she'd seen as the bus came up the hill, like eyes shining in the dark.

Finally she decided there wasn't. She ran up on the porch, stamped her boots clean, and let herself in.

———

It was warm inside, the pellet-fed woodstove roaring as the blower blasted hot air into the house. Leo was curled in front of it, eyes squinched closed, kinked tail switching as he dreamed. He was Charlie's Siamese, seventeen years old. He never ran or jumped anymore, just lay curled wherever it was warmest and howled endlessly when he wanted to be fed. Her stepdad was sitting where he always did, in his office, in front of the computer, his back to the door and to them. Books and foldouts were scattered around him and diagrams were taped to the wall. She went back into the kitchen. "Hi, Mom."

Her mother turned a heat-flushed, disapproving face to her. "Mrs. Kim called about you."

"I figured she would. Can I do something to help?"

"I haven't told Charlie yet."

She didn't answer, just pushed the button for the light and peered into the oven. A casserole of some kind. "Okay. Where's Jammy P. Wetmore?"

"Don't call him that. It's not his fault he can't hold it all the time. He's in his room. He's not feeling very good."

"Can I go up and see him?"

"Okay, but you know to be careful."

She didn't answer, just ran up the steps to the loft.

There were three rooms on the second floor, little rooms with low slanted ceilings because they were right under the roof. One was hers and one was Jammy's and there was a bathroom between them they both used to use, but since her brother had come back from the hospital she wasn't supposed to now. Especially she couldn't touch his things, like his toothbrush and washcloth. Sometimes now he couldn't get up when he had to go and she had to help him. She turned the knob quietly and looked in.

Her brother was a huddle under the blankets. His toy airplanes and his posters of the Toxic Avengers and the Ninja Turtles were almost invisible in the dark. Only the glowing numbers of his clock shone red light into the room. "Jammy," she murmured.

"Who is it? Becky?"

"Yeah. How you doing?"

"My throat hurts."

"Are you having supper with us?"

"I don't think so. No."

"Want me to bring you some? I'll bring it up and help you eat it."

He didn't answer, so she closed the door quietly again and went downstairs.

"Is he okay?" her mother asked, rattling dishes as if angry. Becky said, "Uh huh," and got the silverware and started to set the table. She saw Charlie's back outlined by the green glare of the computer screen, his motionless head intent.

Dinner was quiet. She kept waiting for somebody to say something about the call from school but no one did. Until her stepdad shoved back from the table and said, "Hallie, want some decaf?"

"The chocolate caramel's good," her mother said. Becky sat dividing her Jell-O into little squares with her fork, resting her head on her other hand. The green quivering pieces made her think of the frog. Then the coffee grinder whined and above it Charlie said, in his false-hearty Dad voice, "So, how'd school go today?"

"Becky had a little problem," her mother said. "Go on, tell him."

"What kind of problem did you have, beautiful?"

She cut the squares into triangles as her mother told Charlie she'd refused to do an experiment, that she'd been to the principal's office, that she was down for an *F.* "An *F*," said her stepfather. "For the whole course or just that lesson?"

"I don't know. Becky?"

"I don't know," she said sullenly.

"You didn't ask?" She shook her head. Charlie said, "Becky, look at me. Why didn't you do the experiment?"

"I didn't want to. It made me sick."

"But you wanted to take science. You specifically said."

She shrugged. They didn't understand. Mr. Cash and Mrs. Kim didn't understand. Even Robert didn't, he was the boy who acted like he liked her sometimes; at least he didn't laugh at her like Margory.

"Okay, so what happens now? Can you retake the lab? Can you make up the work? What did Mrs. Kim say?"

"She said I had to drop the course if I couldn't do the work."

"That's pretty harsh. Hallie, you say she called? What'd she say to you?"

"That we should talk to her. That she'd arrange for her to do a makeup lab."

"Are you going to change your mind?" her stepfather asked her. She shook her head, looking down at the dissected dessert. "I guess she fails science, then."

"Charles, we can't just say that, that she fails," said her mother. "That's not going to look very good when the college looks at her record."

"That she failed biology in sixth grade? That's going to cost her getting into college?"

"It might if she wants to take pre-med."

"That's right. You said you wanted to be a doctor. What about that?" her stepfather asked her.

She said to the ruined dessert, "You always think you're right."

"What did you say?"

"I said, you always think you're right. You don't like TV, so I can't watch it. You don't like meat, so I can't eat it, either. You always told me not to hurt animals. They're getting extinct and all. Then when I don't want to cut one up, you tell me I have to."

Her mother got up and started taking the plates into the kitchen. Becky could tell just by the way she walked that she was mad. From the kitchen she said, "I think you'd better think about what you just said and whether you need to tell Charlie you're sorry."

She didn't say anything. Just sat there.

"Becky, you have any homework?" her stepfather asked her in that voice she hated, that *I'm older and know better so I forgive you* voice. She knew they had to act nice because he owned the house and he put up with her and Jammy even though they weren't his kids, but sometimes she didn't like him very much.

"No. Sir."

"Don't they give you any?"

"I did it on the bus."

"It's dark on the bus," said her stepfather, but a warning glance from her mother, who had come back in again, made him sit back in his chair. She could hear her little brother coughing up in his room.

Her stepfather got up and went into the kitchen again. He came back out with coffee and set a cup in front of her too. He meant it as a treat, she supposed, but something angry and contrary inside her made her say, "I don't want any. I'm tired, I want to lie down." And finally they let her go, looking up after her as she climbed the stairs.

She sighed, looking around her room. The backyard security light made green patterns on the ceiling, coming through the blinds. There was her bed, still unmade; her desk; her bureau, with folded clothes on top. Her mother was always after her to put them away but she didn't see why she couldn't just leave them out instead of having to put them in drawers first and then take them right out again.

And on the shelf, waiting for her, the Barbies. She clicked the desk lamp on and took Rollerblade Barbie down. Her long hair glowed. She was so beautiful. Thin and tall, with big blue eyes. Becky put on her red satiny skating outfit and raced her along the carpet. When she pressed the blades to the rug, lights flashed and flickered along the runners. And all at once she was in a huge arena, everybody was watching, it was the Olympics, and she stretched out her arms and whirled so fast on the tips of her toes that everyone gasped and the judges held up cards with "10-10-10" all in a row.

Playing alone in the darkened room, Becky Benning forgot about the frog and the day and her parents, for a while, for a long time.

Till the dry coughing came through the wall. Then a moan.

She put the doll aside and reached for another, started to dress its hair, but a frown furrowed her forehead. The dolls danced, but then they collided. They started arguing. Finally they slapped each other and said "Ugly bitch" and "Fuck." She shook them angrily, then put them away, each doll into her own box, racked neatly on the shelf above the cluttered, messy, garment-strewn room.

Her brother was lying in the half darkness with his head propped up on the pillows. His breathing sounded hoarse, like there was sandpaper in his throat. A stick-on moon and stars glowed on the ceiling. She thought they looked spooky but Jammy liked them. He wasn't looking at them now, though.

Jammy had a transfusion when they lived in Johnsonburg. She remembered him going into the hospital. Then he came out, better, and they thought everything was okay. They didn't know there was something bad in the blood he got. For a long time he'd been okay. Then he got sick. That was after they were living with Charlie. Jammy had to go to the hospital, looking so little in a room all his own, and they had to wear masks when they went to visit him. They gave him the test and found out what he really had. Charlie had explained all about it, how it ate up the cells in his blood that killed germs, so now he could get sick from almost everything. She knew she shouldn't touch his blood or spit or vomit or blisters without gloves on. She couldn't kiss him. But she could touch him and she could hug him. She hugged him now, feeling the thin body through the sheets, and felt his sharp bones as he pushed her away. "Lemme go. That hurts."

"Are you hot? It's hot in here."

"My head hurts. I can't get to sleep."

"Did you take your methoprim?"

"Yeah."

"Do you want a cookie or some M&M's? Do you have to go to the bathroom?"

"Yeah. The bathroom."

She helped him up and held him while he sat on the toilet. In the light his face looked terrible, hollow and gaunt above his swollen neck. She didn't touch the blisters.

When he was done and cleaned up she helped him back to his room. He sank back into bed and turned his face away and she heard his breathing again, shallow and fast, like when you're hurt.

"Jammy."

"What?"

"Look, it's Becky. Talk to me, okay?"

"Go away."

She sat on his bed, staring down at his wasted face. He closed his eyes, then opened them again, quickly, as if afraid to face the blackness. "I'm scared," he whispered.

She felt the heat coming off his body. Over their heads the stars glowed, the moon glowed from the ceiling. She looked out the window to see it glowing off the snow too, outside, where the creek ran past the back of the house and then there was nothing but woods. She realized he'd been lying here looking out the window, staring down on the silver snow.

"Don't worry, Jammy. Don't be scared. I'll keep you safe."

"You will?"

"I promise. Whatever I have to do."

"Tell me a story," he whispered. His hand crept into hers, hot and small. And held it, tight, tight.

"About the leprechaun, or the little red tractor, or the baby fishy—"

"No," the little boy said, eyelids drifting closed. "Tell me the story about the wolf."

Three

The Wolf

They stood at the first bench of the mountain, watching the lights move beneath the riding moon. They looked down into the valley for a long time, waiting motionless in the shadows of the trees, of the night, the shadow of the wind, which blew directly into their muzzles. It brought not only scent but sound. Moving into it, they couldn't be surprised.

There were two wolves, almost side by side; the younger, slightly larger, was stationed a step back from the elder.

The old wolf was lean and long, silvery gray with black markings around his ears and muzzle, on his back, and at the very tip of his limply hanging bushy tail. His legs and underbelly were pale, almost white, blending with the snow in the disappearing dim. His deep-set eyes peered out calmly from a huge head, alert and steady.

He had been born far to the north, in a country of spruce on the open plains and alder and beech deep in the folded valleys. In the summer the air was filled with mosquitoes and the birds that fed on them, and the clear icy streams trembled with fish. In the autumn there were berries to feast on, and tiny hot-blooded animals, voles and mice and hares. And in the winter, snow, endless and deep. There were many deer there, and elk, but there were also many wolves. Too many, and at last the pack had to split up. He'd left it with a female, but on the way south a hunter glimpsed them as they drank from a stream.

Her death had made him wary and cunning. He'd followed the faint scent trails of other wolves, lone like himself, and at last had come into a country where no packs howled. For a time he lived alone, traveling his own territory, sending his lorn howl toward the moon, listening always for a reply but hearing only the occasional soprano keening of a coyote.

Then one day a trap had closed on his leg, and darkness had descended. And when he woke everything was strange and new.

But all that was past and the wolf never thought much about the past. Now the snow spread like a blinding desert across the forest and the hills, and all of it up to this mountain the wolf knew. It was his and his pack's. There were no words in his mind so he did not think in words. But he heard, and he felt, and he knew, though not in the way human beings did; so that now as he watched the valley he was aware of the other presence behind him, at his shoulder.

The second wolf was only two years old, but already it was larger than the leader. Its muzzle was narrower and its legs longer, and there was more black on its back. Now, staring nearsightedly down at the strange lights, it stepped forward and gave a questioning cry, half-bark, half-moan.

The silver wolf turned his head instantly and snarled into the larger animal's startled face. It tried for a second to stare him down, then whined faintly. Turning its head, it dropped and groveled. The older wolf seized its muzzle and shook it violently, biting down till the younger whined. He smelled urine as the other voided in submission, cowering to its belly as its muzzle was held in the tightening, crushing grip.

Finally he released it. The other lay crouched for a moment more, then straightened and busied itself for a few seconds licking its mouth. The silver turned his head away, looking into the wind again, and both their attentions returned to the valley.

A train wailed far away, the sound echoing eerily along the range of hills. Their ears twitched, followed it till it vanished; then their heads turned from side to side, scanning the scattered points of motionless light that glittered coldly below them. They sucked cold through their noses, opening their mouths to pant out the thin, used air.

From far below came a faint howl, then a bark.

The barking got louder, floating out over the dark hills. The wolves looked fixedly down toward it, ears cocked forward.

In the old wolf's consciousness, a scent rose faintly to memory, then to recognition.

He swung suddenly into a lope, heading at zigzag angles downhill between the trees. The other animal fell in line after him. They traveled over the powder with a tireless, gliding gait, leaving behind spread-toed tracks almost five inches across, taking trails or cuts when they could find them, but dropping steadily down into the valley. Once, not far from a stand of birch around a frozen spring, the silver wolf detected something on the snow beneath his feet. He swerved instantly and cast around, bending his nose to within an inch of the cold pristine surface, sucking up scent, eyes probing through shadow and inchoate form.

The rabbit leapt suddenly from behind a rock, making desperately for its hole. There was a quick lunge, a snap of powerful jaws, a shearing of razored teeth. A frenzied flopping in the moonlight and a spurting of black blood that steamed for an instant on the snow.

The wolves fed. First the older one, then, when he was finished, the younger. The rabbit disappeared, hide, fur, bones, guts. All that was left was a stain, obliterated even as they ate by the icy drift. When all was gone the wolves sat back on their haunches for a few minutes, cleansing their muzzles and paws with long mobile tongues.

Then they ran on.

When the forest ended they stopped again, shielded by icy, brittle undergrowth. They peered through it, panting, pinkish tongues lolling, lifting their muzzles to read the cold fresh air.

Presently they moved out from the woods and down a shallow slope that in the summer was grass, a field. Beneath the snow the silver wolf smelled the presence of cattle, the mingled smells of feed and ordure and fertilizer. A barn loomed up silently, black and angular, then melted back into darkness as a cloud obscured the moon. The wolves did not falter as they lost the sense of sight. They trotted on in a straight line downhill that ended at the stone foundations of the barn.

Here the old wolf stopped, meditating on the warm, rich, heavy scent of live animals, sensing the crowded warmth within. His muzzle searched along the rough stone. He nosed out the trail where they went in and out, followed it to a ramp and up the ramp to a door. Then stopped, puzzled, as solid planks barred his entry.

Stymied, they left the barn behind after a time and trotted on downhill. They passed a house whose only light glowed faintly from an upstairs window, made a circuit around a parked car, and went down the driveway. Then, very cautiously, the old wolf picked his way out onto the cleared surface of the road.

Here he stopped, sweeping his nose across the powdery, slippery snow, packed and patterned by the passage of tires. His brain mulled the strange sharp odors of machines, oil, rubber, the vibrating stinks of human beings fainter behind them but there like warning signals at the edge of his consciousness. He could smell them all around and they meant *danger, danger.* He sensed other odors too, fainter in concentration, in time. Standing there, he knew the road not as a vacancy in the snowy night but thronged with ghostly apparitions, creatures and presences that had passed hours or even days ago. He stood there for almost a minute, pulling air through his long muzzle and looking nearsightedly about.

Turning so abruptly his tail brushed his raised ruff, he began running full tilt down the road. The other wolf reacted instantly, bursting into a dead sprint after him. Snow and salt crystals spurted up behind the two racing animals. They sprinted past silent driveways leading to silent houses, past mailboxes with caps of snow, past the wooden shelter with DRINK MAOLA MILK THE PERFECT FOOD where the children gathered every morning before dawn to wait for the buses. Past cut banks covered with steep ridges of broken, dirty snow the snowplows had heaved up through a long winter.

Behind them a distant growl grew, a distant roar.

The leader tucked his head and redoubled his efforts till he resembled a silver torpedo moving silently and at great speed down the empty space of the road. The wolves seemed to elongate as they sped, paws kicking up instantaneous crystalline puffs that hung like glittering wakes in the resurgent moonlight. Trees grew ahead, dark and still. The silver quested to and fro as he ran, searching for a way through the heaped ramparts, still curved from the shaping blade. Till at last he sprang, sailing over the obstacle in a breathtaking leap. He landed rolling and scrambled into the shelter of a copse of dead-looking scrub, where he flopped to his belly, panting madly, crouching down into the snow.

The truck's high beams rose like brilliant searchlights scouring the road, slicing black shadows from the mailboxes and the wooden shelter and the barn and the stunted trees. The wolves blinked, flattened, motionless as gray stones.

The snarl of pistons, the whine of tires rose to a roar that shook the ground. The exhaust stack belched blue fire. The truck rose from the road like a vengeful giant, looming above the cowering animals. Then, with a squeal, the wheels ground into the powdery snow, tearing it apart into two plumes that blew outward, hung in the dark air for long seconds, then fell, collapsing, churned into a blowing maelstrom tinted scarlet by the taillights, sucked along in whirling curtains behind the tractor-trailer as it barreled onward down the dark valley.

When it was only a faraway rumble the wolves crept out again. This time they avoided the highway, rocking along through the deeper snow beside it. They reached a side road and hesitated, sniffing the ground. The lead wolf cocked his leg against a telephone pole. Then caution tightened his sphincter. He hesitated, reasoning dimly.

During the night's hunt they'd traveled almost twenty miles from the den, and coming down from the mountain they'd left the outer limits of the territory they knew. Here on the rim of the world the silver wolf was even more cautious. He had seen many wolves die around him, by bullet, by snare, by poison, by starvation, and in battles with prey and with other wolves, but caution had never failed him. This was as far north in the new land as he'd gone, exploring and marking his pack's territory. Till now it had been mountains and streams, forest and meadow, deer in plenty and all the living things of the forest. Not till tonight, when he saw the lights from the mountain, had he encountered the habitations of man.

He hesitated again, then lowered his leg. Stepping into a trot, he led the way around a low retaining wall and up the opposite hill.

This house had great yellow eyes that cast distorted squares of light across the snow. The wolf couldn't see what was inside. But his keen nose told him more than sight could. He knew about the dog long before it leapt at him from the darkness.

The huge rottweiler came out of the night snarling, ready to lock on, hang on, kill. The wolves separated at its charge but wheeled back instantly, darting in to exchange snapping growls as it rushed past. The dog was heavier, but its shorter muzzle was weaker than the long, powerful jaws of the wolves. It was too confident. It expected them to retreat when it threatened. But the wolves did not retreat. They dodged and wove, leaping and snapping, and the dog's attention flickered back and forth between them, distracted from one sliding shadow to the other.

Suddenly snow flew in the darkness, and howls and savage growls alternated within it like thunder from the shrouded heart of a storm. The rottweiler screamed as fangs closed savagely on its head and testicles. The wolves snapped and tore with blind rage. To them the dog was unnatural, neither prey nor wolf, and its strangeness inspired in them a murderous horror. The dog screamed again, then caught a moonlit glimpse of flank and lunged. Its teeth snapped shut, but without penetrating the wolf's heavy, matted winter coat. The dark one slipped from beneath the dog's jaws, wheeled, and lunged in again. This time its teeth closed in the dog's belly at the same moment that the silver wolf darted in from the side, his jaws locking on the soft surprised flesh of the throat, which turned instantly under his puncturing, tearing fangs into a hot mass of salty spraying blood.

When they were done gorging their bellies, all but stripping the carcass, the wolves trotted off across the highway, not looking back. The silver one quested this way and that until he picked up their backtrail. They loped up the hillside till they reached the shelter of the woods again, vanishing among the trees as the pallid moon slid again behind a shutter of cloud. And the night once more covered the sleeping land, like a dark quilt patched with houses, trees, roads, all growing fainter and fainter, more and more remote in distance and memory, till far behind the steady lope of the running wolves they disappeared under the whispering drift of the snow.

Four

Ainslee Thunner

From the second-story window the land looked white and clean under the morning light. The last clouds had cleared off during the night and the new sky stretched pale and clear above the snow-laden hilltops.

Letting the curtain drop back, Ainslee took another bite of the whole-wheat bagel. She was sitting in her dressing-gown in the bedroom, and the German maid was brushing out her long dark hair. Her shoulders ached pleasantly from her workout. She swam every morning, forty laps in the heated pool. Just now, leaning back as Erika finished brushing and started pinning up her hair, she was thinking about how she was going to save a 120-year-old, $344-million-a-year corporation from takeover, ruin, and destruction.

Three years before, the Thunder Oil Company had gone public. Thunder had been only weeks from bankruptcy when she took it into the stock issue. She'd mortgaged their lease lands and even the family estates to keep going. But in the end, she'd had to give in and go public.

The stock offering had given her a breathing space. With the new capital, she'd retooled the refinery to produce Thunder Green, a new, clean-air gasoline. The downside was that although she was still chairman of the board, president, and chief executive officer, she no longer owned The Thunder Group. She'd hoped that the more efficient refinery would let Thunder hold on until oil prices rebounded. But prices had kept sliding, eating away at the bottom line. Bled white by cheap foreign oil and the ruthless competition of the majors, the small refiners—Wolf's Head, Quaker State, Kendall, Pennzoil, and Thunder—were circling one another in a dance of death. Sooner or later, one of them was going to go under.

"All done, ma'am," said the maid, and Ainslee flinched, pulled back from her thoughts. She got up, checked herself in the mirror—God, she needed to see Marty again already, she was starting to look like a sheep-dog—and went into the closet. Erika followed her, and after several minutes' deliberation she pointed out a Kenzo and a pair of black Maud Frizon pumps. As Erika brought them out she tossed the dressing-gown on the bed. "Thanks, that will be all."

"Yes, ma'am."

"Where's my father? Do you know?"

The maid turned in the doorway, blond and stolid. "I think he is in the library, Ms. Thunner."

Dan Thunner slumped in his wheelchair, back to the door, as if staring intently at something. She hesitated, looking past him at the fire crackling in the fieldstone hearth, the burled walnut paneling, the portraits that lined the room.

Cherry Hill wasn't as formal as the house in town. Her father had built it in the thirties as a hunting camp; only later had it become a residence. It still suggested the camp, with huge fieldstone fireplaces, timber beams, walls decorated with the trophies he'd brought back from Africa, Asia, Alaska, and South America. In the hallways the glass eyes of mounted jaguars burned down, interspersed with gun cases, antlers, carved water-fowl from Chincoteague, wildlife bronzes by Remington and Russell and Turner, English hunting prints, art by Frank Benson and Roland Clark and Richard Bishop. She spared them no glance as she went in, feet noise-less on the carpet, because she saw now that he was looking at her mother.

He'd commissioned the portrait after she died, and the artist had done it from photographs and old jewelry and dresses. Ainslee had been four-teen then, and she remembered posing. For her hands, the artist had said. Those were her own fourteen-year-old fingers and wrists in the por-trait. Her mother's smile, her mother's face, but her hands. Maybe that was why they didn't quite belong. She bent and kissed the ancient man in the chair. "Dad."

"About time you got up."

"Don't start that again. I don't want to hear it, how you had to get up at four to fire up the furnaces or whatever. I run an office. There's no point in getting there before nine, as long as I crack the whip when things get started."

Dan Thunner snorted, but didn't argue with her. His face was ruined, and his legs were little more than suggestions beneath the blanket. She remembered climbing the hills with him, following him up the ladders of the cat towers. Bit by bit the years had stolen everything he was and could do, leaving only a shell, like the husk of a cicada. Yet somehow he remained. "What are you doing today?" she asked him.

"Same's ever. Sitting here waitin' to die."

"Enjoying absolute leisure."

"It ain't leisure when you can't move."

She gave him a quick hug. "That gives you more time to think. We all know who still runs this outfit."

"The goddamn gover'ment, that's who. That and the goddamn lawyers." He raised his eyes, all he could still move. "Hear it ain't goin' too well."

"We'll cope, Dad. Don't worry about it."

"Just hang on, Ainslee. Hard times don't last forever."

"Excuse me. Miss Thunner? The car's ready."

She turned to a huge black man filling the doorway that led to the hall beyond. Under a gray car coat, unbuttoned, he wore a dark gray suit. "Did you want me to drive you in today?"

"Thanks, no. I'll manage." She bent again and pecked the dry, soft cheek. "Okay, on my way. I'll be back late, got the producers' meeting tonight at the club. Lark will be here with you, and Miss Erfurt will look in to see what you want for lunch."

"That cold-hearted Nazi'll poison me, more likely."

She paused for a moment in the hall, then put her head back in. "Lark?"

Jones came out silently and stood waiting. "Take good care of him," she said. "I know you will. You do so much for us, sometimes I wonder why."

"Your family's been good to me, Miss Thunner," Jones said, face broad and hard and unsmiling. "I believe in helping the people who help me. If you ever need something—anything—I want you to think of me first."

She patted his arm. "I know, and I appreciate it. Well, try to keep my father out of trouble."

"I hope that doesn't mean playing stud poker with him all day."

"Just be careful. He cheats."

"I know," said the black man, and he didn't smile at all.

The Land Rover was idling at the coach entrance. She stood on the steps pulling on her gloves, looking out at the trees and sky. The cold air felt good at first but when she pulled it deep into her lungs it made her cough. Finally she got in and released the brake. At the bottom of the hill the iron gate unlocked and she nudged it with the bumper, rolled through, and turned onto the road to town.

And slipped back as she drove into thought, planning, strategy. The board meeting was a week away. No longer the undisputed master of Thunder, she'd have to defend herself to the representatives of the shareholders. And certain things were becoming very clear. For one thing, she was going to have to fire between fifty and sixty people.

Her downsizing goal was $9 million less layout in salaries and general personnel expenses for the upcoming year. For each person shaved off the rolls, the company saved the equivalent of two salaries, since personnel overhead, pension, medical insurance, liability, workman's comp, and Social Security went down too. But where could she cut this time? She'd offered a voluntary severance package already and had only four takers. The new subsidiaries were lean. She'd gone over every new hire. But the parent company still had old retainers, staff personnel who were less than essential. This time they had to go. Between fifty and sixty people . . . Who should they be?

She thought all the way into town, and finally decided it would have to be staff. Start with industrial relations, all they did was push paper and make trouble with the unions. That would be six positions . . . She found herself one of a string of cars behind a mud-spewing triaxle logging truck. She followed its swaying mudguards for a while, then picked the phone up and pushed "*1" for the office. She was telling Twyla she'd be late when the truck turned off and gave her a clear run into town.

The Thunder Building dominated the west end of Petroleum City, bigger than the city hall, bigger than the hospital. It was brown brick with diamond-shaped Art Deco inserts of colored glass at each story. The lobby was Art Deco too, Krupp stainless steel and glass brick and mirrors. The guard came to attention as she swung in. She nodded to him as he opened the gilded doors of the elevator. When it stopped at the fifth floor she glanced in the mirror, straightened her hair, and tossed her coat onto a rack. Then, without looking back, walked quickly down the hallway to her office.

"Good morning, Miss Thunner."

"Good morning, Twyla. What have we got today?"

"Weekly management meeting at nine. Meeting with the ad agency at ten, approve the campaign for the Beaver Fork Retirement Living Center. Mr. Eliason needs your approval to settle that accidental-death case, the man who died of steam burns last year. Meeting with the auditors for the quarterly report at eleven. Eleven-thirty to one, lunch with Dr. Patel."

"Why am I having lunch with him?"

"He wants to talk to you about a hospice. Is that—yes, ma'am. Tonight you have the producers' meeting at the Petroleum Club. Your remarks are on your desk for review."

"What's the status on those internal cracks in number two? Did anybody call about those?"

"No, ma'am."

"Put in a call to Ron, I need to talk to him about hydrogen corrosion. Any mail?"

"A letter from the Committee to Reelect Jack Mulholland. They want you on the board for this November."

"I'll have to think about that one. Do we have time for Mrs. Bridger to come in after the staff meeting? Ask her to bring the records for all of the department heads and all staff and line personnel above pay grade five."

"Good morning, Ainslee."

Rudolf Weyandt, her executive vice president, leaned against the doorway, tapping round spectacles against his vest. He'd helped her ram through the reorganization after her ex-husband's spectacular self-destruction. He shoved off the doorframe and came in. "You look great. Been skiing?"

"Not this weekend. I've got a full morning, Rudy, what's on your mind?"

"I heard something about a personnel review. Anything I can help with?"

"I need some time on it alone. I may call you with questions later."

"Anytime. Oh, and we have to talk about Jack."

"Jack who?"

"Jack Mulholland. The indications are he's not going to be reelected."

She looked at her watch, seeing that the weekly meeting was about to start. "I don't do much poll-following, Rudy. He wasn't even challenged two years ago. Why shouldn't he be reelected?"

"The House post office scandal. The challenger's making a lot of noise about it."

"I don't think a woman can win in this district. Anyway, they want me to be on his committee. How can I approach his opponent?"

"You're not approaching her. You're just getting acquainted. About her getting elected, you might be right, might be wrong. We'll find out come November. All I'm saying is, it's not too soon to make a friendly gesture."

"How much?"

"Not a donation. Not yet. I want to set up a meeting. Dinner or something. Me, you, her aide, and Mrs. Kit Cleveland."

"I'll think about it."

"Don't think too long."

Ainslee Thunner sat at her desk, placed her fingertips together, and looked levelly at him across its empty polished surface. "I said I'd think about it, Rudy. Having you around to advise me is nice, but it doesn't relieve me of that obligation."

"Message received," said Weyandt pleasantly. He looked behind him, but the secretary had gone down the hall. "Look, something I've been thinking about. I'd like to take you up to the city next week. Have dinner. See the new Webber musical. Just the two of us."

"I don't know, Rudy, I'd have to make some arrangement for Dad. And we've got the board meeting coming up. I'll have to get back to you on that."

When he left she sat at the desk for a few minutes, staring at nothing in particular, then got up and looked out the window.

Below was the long straight main street of the largest town in Hemlock County. A few cars and pickups engraved the muddy slush. Far down at the other end of the street heavily dressed men moved purposefully about a muddy patch of ground; the yellow claw of a backhoe rooted busily in the earth. A McDonald's was going up, the first in the county. She looked down, fingernails tapping the glass. Her reflection looked cool, unfathomable, but inside she was boiling.

Telling her not to think too long. Telling her to abandon Mulholland and get into bed with that bitch Cleveland. She knew Kit Cleveland. And one thing she was certain of, she'd jam any wrenches she could into Thunder's waste treatment operations. The bonds had been sold, land purchased, the bioremediation plant in Chapman was ready to start operations. They had a federal contract to begin treating soil from a closed-down air force base. But Cleveland had voted against it as a state senator, and if she won a congressional seat, she'd be in a position to deliver trouble and lots of it. Weyandt wanted to insure them with both camps. But you couldn't always do that. They had to stay with Jack Mulholland, and they had to make sure he won.

Now, looking down, she debated how necessary Rudy Weyandt was. If she had to cut staff . . . of course he was irreplaceable. But just for that reason he was dangerous. When her husband had run the company, Rudy had gone through the motions of cooperating. But she suspected he'd actually made things harder for Brad, given him bad advice and watched him destroy himself. Weyandt was a relic of her father's time. Officially he was nothing more than her executive vice president and legal adviser. But over the years at her father's side he'd exercised several stock options. His holdings were nearly equal to hers now, and he knew the old-line producers and investors who held the rest of the core vote her control depended on. If she fired him he'd be out a paycheck, but then he'd be free to oppose her openly.

She smiled grimly, looking down. It was all too obvious what *he* thought. *He* thought they'd run the company together after her father died. Which couldn't be far off.

Well, she had no intention of sharing control with Rudolf Weyandt. And once her father was gone, she'd never be sure he wouldn't challenge her. She'd always feel his presence behind her, always be tensed for the prick of his blade. She had no intention of living like that. Thunder Oil had always belonged to Thunners, since the legendary Beacham Berwick Thunner and the hunchbacked gambler Napoleon O'Connor had punched the first producing well into the Seneca Sands in 1869. It was hers not by vote but by right, and though she had once dreamed of other fates she understood now this was hers. To receive into her hands what her forefathers had built, and to carry it into a new century.

She pressed her forehead to the glass, looking down as behind her the secretary waited in the doorway. Outside, in the bright morning, the sun warmed the air to a certain critical point, and the snow began to melt.

"Twyla? Oh, is it time? Thanks. Hold my calls. I'll be back here as soon as the meeting's over."

The weekly staff meeting was held in the fifth-floor meeting room. It was a smaller version of the big boardroom on the sixth floor, but in a decor so neutral it was hard to visualize when she wasn't actually sitting in it. She stood by the door as people filed in, mentally ticking them off. Herself, Rudy, and Harold Gerarge, the general counsel and secretary. Then the chief operating officers of the subsidiaries: Rogers McGehee, First Raymondsville Financial Services; Jack Coleman, TBC Industrial Chemicals; Dr. V. Chandreshar Patel, Hemlock HealthCare; Bernie Detering, Thunder Petroleum Specialties; Jason Van Etten, VanStar CeraMagnet; Mark Burgeson, TBC Environmental Services. Ranking with them were the vice presidents of Thunder Oil, the core company: Fankhauser, Aldrow, Brosius, Fronapel, Sobel, Chodrow, and Montecalvo. The last man off the elevator was Ron Frontino.

Frontino was a squat, rather immobile man with a broad face and large hands. Born in San Francisco, he was the first outsider ever to be president of Thunder Oil. He had worked for Ashland, Chevron, and as a vice president of sales at Union Texas before being hired by The Thunder Group during the reorganization. Ainslee had found him knowledgeable, tough, a hard-driving manager, just what Thunder needed at this critical point. But at times she felt a certain . . . arrogance. As if sometimes he thought she'd come by her position simply by being Daniel Thunner's daughter. This didn't bother her, since she knew it wasn't true, and if he thought it was, well, sometimes it was useful to be underestimated.

She checked the wall clock. Time to start. She took her seat and the buzz of conversation immediately stopped, and all the faces came round to center on her.

When the meeting was over she said to the two men at the top of the U, "Rudy, Ron, can I see you for a moment?" Frontino nodded without saying anything.

They sat together in her office, just the three of them. The executive committee, she thought. Only it wasn't really, not anymore.

Everything they decided, the board could undo.

Across from her Frontino shook his head at Twyla's silent offer of the coffee urn. He looked at his watch, not ostentatiously, but the message was there. She cleared her throat. "Ron, what's the resolution on number two? Are those cracks in the shell from hydrogen corrosion?"

"We cut a window in the refractory lining over the weekend and got a close look at them. The engineers agree those are rolling cracks, they've been there since we put number two in operation. We welded it up again and it's back in operation."

"Good, I was worried we'd have to shut down and replace the lining. Okay, next item. I wanted to talk briefly about the upcoming board meeting. I will make the presentation, as usual, but I thought it might be useful to have a little talk about our strategy." Frontino and Weyandt nodded, eyes alert, and she took a breath, looking out the window to gather her thoughts.

"You both know this has not been a good year to date. We were starting to come back on profits two quarters ago, but then crude prices went down again and our refinery margins went to hell. We're just holding market share on Thunderbolt Premium, and that's with discounts and the consumer rebate. Well, you both know all that. This is a lean year but things have to turn around. We have our goals and plans in place. I'm going to ask you to look into another downsizing in your operation, Ron—"

"We're cutting personnel again?"

"Unless you come up with nine million from somewhere else, I don't have a choice. Have you got that in your pocket?"

"No."

"Have you met this quarter's sales goal?"

"No, and you know why. That goal was set back when—"

"I can't absorb the loss, Ron," she said crisply but not unsympathetically. "There's no forgiveness in the marketplace. I don't like to fire people but if it's a question of the survival of the company I'd cut my own legs off, you know that. Do you disagree with the figures I'm working with?"

Frontino shook his head silently, and she went on. "Then we have to cut. I will suggest one guideline: the positions should not come from production. I want you to come up with a recommended list.

"But I didn't mean to get sidetracked onto that. Ron, Rudy, Thunder is facing some real problems and we need to stick together and stay the course. I mean by that we have to withstand any tendency by the board to panic when they meet next week."

Weyandt said, "There's one way we can take the pressure off."

"How?"

"Jiggle our depreciation rates. I can talk to the controller. That will put us into the black, for this quarter, anyway."

She looked steadily at him for a moment. "Will it really put us into the black?"

"No."

"Then I don't think much of the idea, Rudy. I'm not going to try to con these people. Especially Fred Blair. Plus, if we start messing with the accounting, how are we going to know how we're doing? We'll have to maintain two different systems. We can't afford that."

"Just a suggestion."

"I know, Rudy. Sorry, didn't mean to snap. Your ideas are always welcome, even if I don't put them all into operation."

Frontino said, "What kind of action are you expecting from the board? A request for my resignation? An attack on Larry Fankhauser?"

Fankhauser was sales. She turned to face Frontino. "I'm not sure, Ron. I'm just reading the tea leaves, okay? We have a relatively new board. Besarcon and Wilsonia and Blair want to earn out on their investment. I think both you and Larry are doing everything anyone could do. But the company's obviously in trouble. In a situation like that, I want to make sure we're all singing from the same sheet of music."

"Which is?"

"Which is that the current downturn can't last. Oil is far below historic values. The value of our reserves in the ground, and any reserves we can acquire at reduced prices during this slump, are bound to go up again. Long-term, our best strategy is to use this as a period of opportunity to strengthen our core business. Tighten our belts, but stay in the ring. We market the best Pennsylvania grade motor oil in the world, the best clean-air oxygenated gasoline, the best specialty lubricants. Quality will always be in demand." She regarded them. "Or are we not in basic agreement about that?"

"I think that's true," said Weyandt. And after a moment, Frontino nodded too.

"All right, then, thanks for your time. Let's get some work done."

When they left she sat alone, looking out the window. Then she told Twyla to send in her first appointment.

Five

_____

Dr. Leah Friedman

. . . sat in her car for a time after she turned the engine off, looking around the clearing. The sky was blue today, the warming air almost comfortable. Compared with where she'd grown up, it was icy, but after years in Hemlock County her blood had thickened. As they say, she thought, lips curving as she visualized a nearly congealed fluid inching through capillaries.

She unlocked the door—even now she still locked car doors, double-locked the door of her apartment—and swung down, boots sinking into the wet snow almost to her knees. She slogged across the field, shading her eyes as she searched for a wavy unevenness, a soft hump not far from the forest . . . There, the old man's footprints, and beside them the tracks of a dog. She paused, looking around.

Like most people in Raymondsville, she knew Halvorsen's story. Once he'd had a name for himself, both in the oilfields and in the big-game records, and once he'd lived in town. Now he lived deep in the woods, alone except for the dog. He gave up both hunting and drinking after his wife died. Then he'd gone to prison, not for long but he'd been there. Since then she saw him occasionally in town buying groceries, or having coffee at Mama DeLucci's, or looking into the window of Rosen's, face closed, as if he was thinking about something far out in the blue hills and didn't want to be interrupted or disturbed. He was supposed to stop at the clinic twice a year, but he hadn't been in for a while, and she'd finally decided to drive out and check on him.

A shimmer of heat, the smell of a wood fire above a little pipe set into the earth. She stepped around a heap of snow and almost fell into a pit that went down into the frozen ground. She went carefully down splintered, scorched railroad-tie steps and rapped on the plank door.

"Yeah?" Halvorsen's face was bristly, eyes watery-red and hostile. Taken aback by his glare, she backed off a step.

"It's me, Dr. Friedman."

"Oh. You want to wait a minute, let me get dressed—"

"Please, don't bother. I've seen worse."

But he kept her waiting outside while she heard rooting around and banging, and finally he came back in pants and an old-fashioned red union suit and felt slippers so worn through she could see his stockings at the heels, and let her in. "Sit down," he said, nodding to a kitchen chair beside the potbellied stove. She sank onto it, unbuttoning her coat. He knelt, surprising her so that she didn't even object as he gently worked her boots off her feet and propped them on a wooden holder to dry. "Get you some tea," he said, and she looked around the underground room while he went off into the dim.

The basement was about twenty by thirty, cramped and cluttered and the air so hot it burned her cheeks. A narrow line of daylight glowed near what once must have been the floor of the vanished house. Now it was the ceiling, held up by massive timbers, some blackened, others new, fresh-cut. Two plank doors led into other rooms. Aside from the narrow windows the only light was an orange flicker from the old-fashioned wood stove. A table was covered with used dishes and cans of beans and tuna and stew; stacks of catalogs and retirement magazines, a few paperback westerns with lurid torn covers.

Halvorsen came back and put a big old graniteware coffeepot on the stove, then bent to rattle the grate. "Be ready in a couple minutes," he said, and sat down, hitching his pants up, in a worn easy chair across from her. Somewhere in puttering around the basement he had picked up his spectacles, and now he peered at her over the glass half-moons. "Nice of you to come out, visit me."

"I need to get away from the clinic sometimes. Get out and see people instead of diseases."

"Makes sense to me."

"I haven't seen you in a while. You're overdue for a checkup."

"Ain't nothing wrong with me, why I didn't come in."

"The point of a checkup, Mr. Halvorsen, is to let the doctor make that decision."

"What decision?"

"Whether anything's wrong with you." She took out the stethoscope. "Now, if you'll unbutton your shirt, we'll get this over with."

By the time she was done the tea was too, and he went into the pantry again for mugs and a can of condensed Borden's. Friedman relaxed, putting her notes into her coat pocket. "Lot of traffic out now the weather's let up a bit. I was stuck behind a log truck all the way down Route Forty-nine."

"Yeah, about their last chance to skid 'em out before the mud puts a stop to it."

"Did you hear about the ice jam? They say it might flood some people out, if they don't do something."

"I seen floods before," said Halvorsen. He pondered, then got up and went back somewhere she couldn't see. When he came back he had a cigar box. She noticed that the edges were scorched. He rooted through it, then handed her a picture.

She held it up to the window light. "Where is this? Oh, wait. There's the old city hall. There's the Odd Fellows—and the hotel—it's Main Street. When was this taken?"

"Thirty-one."

"These are the tops of trucks sticking up above the water!"

Halvorsen nodded. Remembering the way he remembered things now, not just seeing it but so clear it might have been yesterday, because, hell, he could remember the rotten smell of the mud when the water went down, the fish-slippery way it felt under your shoes, and how people had looked, angry and helpless. He said, "It used to flood like that every spring, seemed like. You never could tell once it started to thaw. The river would tear through town, it'd take away the bridges, take houses, cows, horses, trees, cars. Just sweep them right away. Tell you, it was a roarer."

"It doesn't do that anymore."

"No, not since the WPA built the flood control."

She handed the print back. "You know, we had a strange thing happen this week. At the clinic. The kind of thing I thought I ought to ask Mr. Halvorsen about next time I see him."

Halvorsen took a slug of tea, waiting.

"The paramedics brought a man in Wednesday. They were going to the hospital, but they thought he was dying en route so they stopped at the clinic instead. Good thing they did."

"That was a pretty raw deal, them firin' you from out of the hospital."

"I helped you with that dumping case, and I paid the price. And so did you. What can I say? But it worked out. The clinic, I can do pretty much what I like. The only problem now is the rural health administration. But to get back to this man they brought in—"

"What was wrong with him?"

"Exposure, broken leg . . . maybe I better start at the beginning. His name was Zias, Michael Zias. An engineer at the power supply company. Some hunters—I know it's not the season, but I guess they were out just looking over the territory—some hunters found him, unconscious, not far from a lease road south of Deep Pit, down on the Driftwood Branch."

"West of the Wild Area."

"When I saw him he was close to freezing. Internal body temperature way down, almost eighty degrees. He was delirious. He was saying something about wolves."

Halvorsen lifted his head. "Wolves?"

"That's right. He kept talking on and on, over and over, about being surrounded by wolves."

He rubbed his mouth, no longer looking at or thinking about the woman across from him. He appreciated her coming out but at the same time he resented it. Leave you alone, didn't seem like people could do that anymore. They had to keep poking and prying till they knew everything that wasn't their business. While their own responsibilities, well, they didn't seem to bother about that at all. Come to think of it, there was something he wanted to ask her. Couldn't remember it just now. Maybe it would come. But this she was telling him, it was something he had to think about . . . but what was it . . . wolves, yeah. Some guy crawled out of the woods, said he'd been attacked by wolves.

"Anyone else see these wolves?"

"No."

"Tracks?"

"No. The people who brought him in said he'd apparently crawled quite a distance. His knees were worn through, on his pants. Later they went back and looked and found his car. He was only half a mile from it."

"Why couldn't he walk?"

"He had a compound fracture."

Halvorsen thought about this too. He could see why they'd think the fella was delirious. Hell, he probably *was* delirious. Crawling through deep snow with a busted leg was no joke. But that about wolves, that was striking a note way back in his head.

He remembered a track he'd come across recently in his rambles through the woods. He'd stopped, frowning down at it, then knelt, waving Jessie off before she spoiled it. At first he'd thought, a dog. A big dog. And he still thought that's what it was. But a pack of dogs . . . If they were hungry, a fellow was helpless, they'd like as not eat him.

"Wolf wouldn't break a man's leg," he murmured tentatively. "What was he doing out there?"

"His wife says putting some kind of ham radio transmitter up in trees. It's his hobby."

"What, he was up there putting it in the tree, and he fell out?"

"That's what I concluded. He has numerous small scrapes and cuts on his hands and face that would be consistent with a fall. But no bites or puncture wounds."

"What else did he say about them? About these wolves?"

"Said they had big faces. He keeps saying, 'Their faces . . . their eyes.' 'Golden eyes,' he says."

"Huh."

"So I thought I'd ask you, because I didn't think there were actually wolves in these woods—"

"There ain't."

"Then what did he see?"

He said slowly, "Well, could have been several things. First off, he could have made the whole thing up. Not like a story, but like you said, he was kind of nuts. Or, could a' been dogs. Farm dogs, they roam, and some people dump their pets in the woods when they got no more use for them. They pack up, live off rabbits and deer. He could have run into a pack of them."

"What else?"

"Coyotes."

"I thought they lived out west."

"Used to, but they been filtering out here the last few years. An' then there's what they call coy-dogs, when they interbreed. But they're solitary, they don't seem to pack up the way dogs do."

Halvorsen sat unmoving for a while, savoring the bitter herb tea. Remembering.

He'd spent his whole life in the woods. And sitting here he could call to mind as vivid as being there crisp autumn days waiting for gobblers, the chill dawns of doe season. Could remember catching a glimpse early one foggy morning of a bobcat, holding those wild eyes for a long moment before it loped off into the mist. Could recall the heart-hammering thrill of catching a big buck for the first time in the sights of his dad's old Krag. Could chuckle at the time he and Mase Wilson had pelted the bear with snowballs, back near where Hantzen Lake was now. And he'd saved up and gone after bigger, more exotic game: mule deer and blacktail out west, pronghorn in Wyoming, elk and moose and goat in the Cassiars, and the one big trip to Alaska.

Till he'd looked down at a dead buck one day and known suddenly it was over. He'd always loved the woods, but that love had changed, he couldn't say how or why. Now it was the kind of love that no longer needed to kill.

"What are you thinking?"

He started. Shoot, he was getting absentminded. Even forgot when he had company. He said testily, "I was thinkin' about what you said. Was going to answer you in a minute."

"I'm sorry. I thought you might know something about—"

"I'll tell you what I know, but it ain't much." He waited but she didn't say anything, so he shifted on the chair and leaned forward. Clanged the iron door open and spat onto the coals and clanged the door shut on the sizzle and leaned back, trying to whip his thoughts into some sort of shape to where he could speak them out.

"They used to have 'em out here. I remember my aunt saying how when they was kids their parents wouldn't let them go in the woods without a grown-up man along. Then the country got settled, and it was like they all disappeared, or moved west like the Indians; I don't know, don't know if anybody knows. An old fellow I knew when I was a boy, he remembered trapping wolves . . . you sure you want to hear this?"

Friedman put her feet on the stove and stretched. God, she was about that far from falling asleep. "If you want to tell me."

"Well then. He used to say they'd find them early in May along the stream heads, up among the rocks. They'd look for tracks the she-wolves made on the way to their den. If they didn't see any, the hunters'd make a howling, and generally the wolves would answer. He said you'd almost always find them at the head of a stream, or within a mile of one. Like people, they like to be near water.

"If he found the pups and no full-grown wolves around, he'd be careful not to disturb the den. He'd climb a tree and wait for the wolves to come back. The best time to bait with meat was the first of December. That's when they was weaning, so the pups was hungry.

"Another way he'd trap them was to build what he called a wolf house. He'd dig a hole into the side of a hill, where he knew the pack would use the trail, near a stream, or between the stream and the den. Then he'd build a house out of heavy logs, and on top of it a log roof. Then on the top he'd put a trapdoor with a spring on it, and he'd tie the bait on to that. The first wolf to come along would jump up on the roof to get the bait, or just to sniff at it, and down he'd go. It wouldn't hurt it, just drop it down into where it couldn't get out. But then it would yell, and the other wolves would come and try to figure out what happened, and they'd run back and forth across the top, and pretty soon you had the whole pack. Then you dropped in your poison and there you were."

Friedman shuddered. "*Poisoned* them?"

"Poisoned, shot, trapped—however was the easiest way to kill them. It was the bounty they were after, so they didn't have to worry about the pelt like if it was a fox or a beaver."

"Why did they hate the wolves so much?"

"*Hate* 'em? I don't know as Amos hated 'em, or Ben Yeager or Bill Long or the Vastbinders—they was the big hunters in this part of the country back then. But the state had the bounty on to them, and so they trapped them, and shot them, till there wasn't any more to kill."

"When was that?"

"What, when they was all gone? I don't know—wait a minute, I do." Halvorsen rubbed his mouth again, realized he hadn't shaved. Why did people always show up when he wasn't presentable? Hadn't even had his goddamn pants on. "Gimme a minute. Something about a black wolf . . . okay, I got it. Shoot, I ain't thought of this for years." He leaned forward, and again the spittle sizzled, melting into the wavering red-hot heart of the embers.

"Fella called Shoemaker, old guy, he knew just about everybody in the woods. One night me and him and Amos was sitting on the porch out at his cabin, and a fellow named Black-Headed Bill Williams. Anyway, we was sitting there looking out over the valley, and Williams, he says, 'The last time I heard a wolf call out here on the mountain, it was in the fall of sixty-three, when I was home on furlough from the army.' "

"Sixty-three—did he mean eighteen sixty-three?"

"Yeah. But then Shoemaker says he heard about a black wolf they killed over in Oak Valley fifteen, twenty years after that. And he says he always thought it was more of a devil than a wolf."

"Is this a ghost story?"

"Are you going to interrupt me every sentence, or are you going to listen?"

"I'm sorry. I'm listening."

"So Mr. Shoemaker, he goes on and tells this story, and here it is, way I remember it, anyway.

"He said there was this fella in the east end of Oak Valley named Silas Werninger, a lazy fella who never cut a cord of wood in his life. And one Saturday night he was at old Tommy Mertz's hotel at Youngmanstown and he got into a fight with a couple of farmers and before anybody could stop him he shot 'em both—one died—and he got on his horse and off into the mountains.

"Well, after a couple weeks he got tired of playing catamount and started visiting his wife and children at night. They lived in a log cabin outside of Jacobsberg. And that leaked out, and one morning the posse surrounded the house just before daybreak. But his dog started barking and Silas started shooting. He got two of the posse from the upstairs window as they was battering down the door. By then Mrs. Werninger and the little ones, they had ran out to safety, so the deputy, he threw some burning rags through the window and then backed off to see what Silas would do. But he didn't come out, and when they went in they found he'd cut his throat with a razor.

"After that the question come up of a funeral. The Lutherans had a graveyard and so did the Evangelicals, but neither of them wanted Silas, him being a murderer and a suicide both, and some said Jewish to boot . . . no offense. But anyway nobody'd take him. So they ended up burying him after dark in the middle of a white-oak grove.

"Well, everything was fine till the cold weather came on, and some kids said they saw a big black shaggy dog hanging around the grove. Later some men who were looking for chestnuts saw it and said it wasn't a dog, it was a black wolf. The old men at the hotel said it couldn't be, there hadn't been a wolf in those parts for years, and they were gray and never black. Finally old Ira Sloppey saw it. He'd killed a lot of them in Clearfield, and he said it was a wolf, all right. So he got up a hunting party and they went after it.

"Well, they found it there in the grove. And Ira said, 'It's there to dig up the murderer's body and eat it.' They surrounded it, but just then it made right for Ira himself. About twenty muskets and rifles went off. But when the smoke cleared they found the only one shot was old Ira. He got a ball in the ankle and was a cripple till the day he died.

"That broke up the hunt, but people kept seeing that black wolf. The women were scared to use the road. Then one day Sam Himes chased a deer clear over to Spring Run, and found himself near Granny Myers's, the witch woman who used to live there. And he stopped in and told her the story.

" 'Goshens,' she says, 'that ain't no wolf, you foolish. That's poor Silas Werninger's spook, and it ain't happy at being planted in them lonesome woods. You go back and put him in the cemetery, and you won't see nary more wolf.' And Sam went back and told everybody that at the hotel, and that night him and Ira and the rest went and dug up what was left of Silas and buried him beside his mother at the Lutheran cemetery. The next day Sam said he'd shot the wolf at the edge of the grove. But old Ira used to say in his knowing way, 'When are you going to show us that wolf's scalp? And, remember, you got to give me half the bounty.' "

"And, don't tell me—they never saw the wolf again." Friedman studied him. "So what are you saying? You're sending a message, but I don't think I'm getting it. The wolves Zias saw—they were ghosts? Spooks?"

He raised his eyebrows. "Wasn't tryin' to tell you nothing. Just an old story," he said mildly.

"But what about it? Do you think they were real wolves?"

Halvorsen didn't answer, just stared into the fire. That fuguelike state worried her. She didn't think it was a seizure, but sometimes it resembled one. She saw a lot of burns and falls, old people living alone. She shook her head and got up, felt in the dimness for her boots. They were warm and dry. "Thanks for the tea."

"Leavin' already?"

"I'd better be getting on. Got to see the Greggs. See how their daughter's doing. And the little Benning boy. Oh—and there's something else I wanted to bring up. Again."

Halvorsen stirred, and his head came up and faded blue eyes glared through the spectacles. "I know what it is. And the answer's still no."

"Your daughter wants you in town. I know she's asked you several times."

"I'd just be a burden to her. I can still take care of myself."

"There are places you can do that, places where it's easier and there are other people your age. Central Towers is a beautiful facility. How about if I set you up for a visit?"

"I ain't going in no old folks' home. Either that one or that one in Beaver Falls. Besides, I can't afford it."

"For the tenth time, it's a state service. It's free. Don't you realize, at some point you're going to have to come in from the woods. From playing—what did you call it?—playing catamount."

"I ain't playing nothing. Just tryin' to finish out my life—"

"Well, you can't take care of yourself forever. It's not all that different from what you do right here, except—"

"Except there ain't no woods, and somebody'll be always telling me what to do. And what about her?" He kicked the hound lightly, and she whined. He hoisted himself out of the chair, crossed to the door, held it open for her with rigid dignity.

As she brushed by him, he suddenly remembered it, what he'd been cudgeling his brain for since she showed up. "Oh. Wanted to ask you something, long as you're here."

"What?"

"You seen any Japs or Chinese or anything? Some foreign kid. He got beat up a couple days ago, I wondered if he'd come in to the clinic."

"I haven't seen anyone like that. They'd probably go to the hospital if they weren't from around here. Is it someone you know?"

"No, no, nothin' like that." She asked him several more questions, but he only shook his head and mumbled. At last she lost her patience and left.

Halvorsen looked after her, sucking at the sore spot in his mouth and thinking. Wasn't any of his business, any of it. Just like it wasn't any of hers, where he finished up his goddamned life. He cursed himself for a fool. Then, as she backed her car up, getting set to head down the hill, he grabbed his coat, grabbed the newspaper, climbed laboriously up out of the pit, mumbling angrily to himself, and flagged her down.

Six

Halvorsen kept the paper folded under his arm as she drove him west down Route 6. He stayed in the car when she stopped in Racker Hollow. While she was inside the double-wide talking to the family he unfolded it again, squinting at page four.

The two-column ad was for Beliejvak's Auto Body and Towing, "Your Auto Body Professionals." In the "before" photo, a crumpled Chevy hung from a wrecker like a trophy buck from a gutting rack, then "after" was the glittering centerpiece of an admiring family. He took out his spectacles and examined the "after" picture again, holding the glasses away from his eyes to magnify it. A light-colored truck was half hidden by the corner of the body shop building. On its door, barely visible as a pattern of halftone dots, was a triangle inside a circle.

"Something interesting?" He flinched and shook his head, refolding the page as Friedman got in and started the car again.

She dropped him in Gasport, east of Petroleum City. "Sure this is where you want to go?" she said through the rolled-down window as he stood on the slushy, muddied roadside.

"This is it. Thanks."

"How will you get home?"

"Don't worry. I'll get there."

"All right," she said, her voice falling, the message that he wasn't acting reasonably coming through. He didn't like it but didn't argue, just stood there in front of the Dairy Freez's SEE YOU NEXT SPRING sign till she cranked the window closed again. As she drove off he lifted his glove casually, then turned to look down the street.

He'd been to Gasport when he was little. His dad had taken him in for fodder and supplies in the buckboard when they lived on the farm. But mainly he remembered it from when he'd been a roustabout here for Victor O'Kennedy and the gang at Evans Cresson before he went to work for Thunder Oil. Shoving his hands into his coat pockets, he squinted around. Yeah, the same . . . same shabby buildings, not as many and not as close together, that was all. You could still look down Evans Street and see the steel bridge with the tank farm back of it, and then the white level surface of the frozen-over Allegheny. He'd seen Evans occasionally in the shop, a big old open-handed booming man who'd lost and won millions in oil in the eighties and nineties. His eighteen-room house was the county children's home now. But there were vacancies too. The empty space that stretched down to the tracks had been the machine shops and shed of the Gasport Motor Works, smoky sparkspewing ironclanging blocks that made everything you needed to drill and pump a well. During the war Jenny had worked there, making fuses and adaptors and bomb racks. Now it was an empty field, with a few scattered remains of concrete foundations, rusty bolts sticking up where the prime movers had been mounted.

He swiveled as a truck barreled through the intersection, noise and diesel exhaust battering his senses, mudguards swinging ponderously with their shiny cutouts of a naked girl. Across the street a building looked familiar yet strange, some windows bricked closed, others dusty and blank.

Then his eye caught the tracing of faded paint and he remembered Tracy's. Remembered Harry Tracy, bald and bluff with the cigar-juice stain down the front of his shirt. He'd bought a car here after the war, cashing in all his war bonds and blowing nearly two thousand dollars on the best auto he'd ever owned, a big, dark green Hudson Super Six with a gray pinstripe interior. He'd driven it for ten years and practically cried when he traded it in, knowing he'd never own another like it, they'd never build anything with such pride and craftsmanship again.

And beyond and above it up Knaller Hill, where the Foster Run Company's huge iron pressure tank still stood unused and full of bulletholes, there were a few of the old row houses left, clinging to the shale cliffs. He remembered when the hillside was solid with them, paintless one-story frame cribs, wood-floored shacks so straight you could fire a shotgun through every room and built so close together you had to turn sideways to walk between them. "Irish Hill," they'd called it, and nothing but brambles above that till the hill flattened out. Now it was a mass of woods again.

Then his mind fell through another layer and he remembered even before he worked for O'Kennedy, back when he was fifteen, working slush-boy for Don Ekdahl. His first payday the men on the crew had taken him in to Gasport on the truck. Carl Garvey, "Teabag" Salada, Mike Otto, and the other guys, pumpers and drillers whose names had gone forever from memory. They'd walked him up the wooden steps caked with frozen mud to a house with heavy drapes and they'd had to take off their muddy bighole boots and leave them inside the door. An old guy with a Bismarck mustache took their money and brought up the bottles of beer from under the house, where it was cool. They drank it sitting around a table with a checked tablecloth and bread and pretzels in thick creamware bowls. He remembered it all perfectly because he'd been so scared he couldn't swallow the pretzels, had to wash them down with the yeasty-tasting bootleg beer as the men joked about drilling in a gusher.

Then after he'd had a few, so that he wasn't scared anymore, he'd gone around back to a house with a Liberty bond poster in the window, and a girl in a flowered wrap let him in. Her hair tumbled down past her shoulders red as red and her name was Mary Shaughnessy. He remembered like it was yesterday the crucifix on the bare board wall and how she'd lain back on the bed and curled her legs up against her white belly and let him do anything he wanted. When he went back to the house the men had looked at him and then Carl Garvey had bought him a ten-cent shot of whiskey, the first he'd ever had.

He'd gone back to Irish Hill every payday after that. A buck a tumble and you could stay as long as there wasn't anybody else waiting on the porch. Then Ekdahl put him on the crew to build a rig at a new lease at Red Rock. It took them five days to throw up a seventy-two-foot rig, and in a week of fourteen-hour days after that they'd drilled to two thousand feet and hit a ten-foot sand so dusty dry the only thing they could do with the well was dig it up and sell it by the foot for postholes. When he got back Mary was gone and there was a Hunky girl instead, Pauline something, some Slovak name—Poleshuk, that was it. But he hadn't liked her as much, he'd been crazy about Mary, and he'd never gone back to Irish Hill after that, hardly even thought of it again till now.

Standing there he thought how funny it was, memory; how every time you visited a place it laid down a layer, like sandstone. Remembering was like drilling down and finding it all still there, only concentrated by time, so sometimes you hit pressure and up would shoot something you hadn't thought of for years, the rattling go-devil driven by a blast of mingled sweetness and pain that made your eyes fill in the cold wind as you stood shifting from foot to foot on the street. He blinked, dragging a glove across his face. That was the worst part about getting old. You got so goddamned sentimental. Nobody cared about the stuff he remembered. It wasn't important, just people who worked and had kids and got old and died. So why did it feel important, precious and irreplaceable, and as if somehow it must mean something?

Shit, he thought. I never expected to get this goddamned old.

Blowing his nose in his fingers, he spat into the pile of dirty slush heaped along the road, waited for the light, and crossed the street.

A bell jangled as he let himself into a dirty room with litter and boxes but nobody in it, smelling of old oil and mildew and burnt coffee. He went through it into a cavernous sheet-steel back shed, where an oil stove driven by an electric fan roared like endless thunder. A bearlike man crouched like a feeding wolf over the rusty skeleton of a truck. An air grinder whined and whitehot sparks shot out in a fan, bounding off the concrete floor, displacing the coffee smell with the hot, metallic stench of oxidizing iron. Halvorsen yelled, "You Beliejvak?"

The grinder whirred to a halt and the man tossed back a protective hood, revealing a heavy black beard and small blue eyes with a penetrating, wary expression. "Yeah," he said. "Who're you? I know you?"

"Name's Halvorsen. W. T. Halvorsen." He looked around. "This used to be a car dealer's."

"I heard, a lumber mill."

"Before my time."

"It's an old building, all right."

"I used to work oil around here, years ago," said Halvorsen. "Ever hear of a guy named Don Ekdahl?"

"No."

"Carl Garvey? Otto? Shaughnessy?"

The bearded guy said, "My mother's family was from here. Poleshuk. Know any of 'em?"

Halvorsen carefully shook his head no, and decided to get off the subject of local history. He unfolded the paper, told the fellow what he wanted. Beliejvak thought about it, then said, "Why ya want to know?"

"I got a beef with one of the sons a' bitches that drive their trucks."

"What kind of beef?"

"It's personal."

"Oh," said Beliejvak. "Well, okay. Let me look it up. I remember the job, not the company. Come on in the office. Want some coffee? You sure you didn't know the Poleshuks? They come from here in Gasport."

"No, I didn't know any of them," said Halvorsen. "I'll take some coffee, though. It's still pretty goddamned cold out there."

After he had what he wanted he left and stood outside, spitting to get the taste of the burnt coffee out of his mouth. He looked around for Jessie, then remembered he'd left her at home. He groped in his outer coat pocket, found the plug, hard with cold, and nipped off a chunk the size of a Brazil nut. Put it in his mouth and winced as it came to rest against the sore spot. Shoot, he thought, I should of mentioned that to Dr. Friedman when she was looking at me. He didn't chew for a couple minutes, just let it soften as he looked down the street, thinking.

According to the mechanic's records the truck belonged to the Medina Transportation Company. He didn't recognize the name. From the tools he'd seen in the bed, though, he figured they were in the natural gas business, either a producer or more likely a pipeline company, that was what "transportation" meant around here. The Medina Sands were gas sands, so that fit too. But it had to be a new outfit, because he knew all the producers in this part of the country. But what were they doing up in Mortlock Hollow? There wasn't any gas around Raymondsville, wasn't really any till you got over toward Potter County. So that left another question, not only why they'd been beating up the Chinese guy, but what they were doing up in his neck of the woods in the first place.

Beliejvak said he was sorry but he didn't have a billing address or a phone number. He didn't keep up his records the way he should. Halvorsen stood there thinking about it for a while, stumped, then all of a sudden remembered he knew a guy who might be able to help. Last he'd heard he was in the brokerage business, specializing in oil and gas stocks, out of an office in downtown Petroleum City, which wasn't but two or three miles from where he stood.

Sitting in the Merrill, Paine & Wheat office up over the bank on Main Street, feeling tired from the walk and out of place in his wet boots and old coat and hat, he fitted his glasses on and looked closely at Joe Culley. The boy he'd carried in his mind was twenty years old, a kid working summers for Halvorsen during his last years with Thunder. But Culley was in spitting distance of middle age now, with a tie and suit and polished wingtips. A computer on his desk. Sales awards on his walls and gut spilling over his belt.

"Looks like you're doing okay," Halvorsen told him.

"It's not like working for you. You know, there are times I miss it, being out in the fields." Culley sat hunched forward, his face and hands, Halvorsen thought with pity, the same dead ivory white of fungus on a fallen tree. It didn't seem to him like a good trade either, but he just said, "Well, I bet it pays better."

"You got to think about things like that when you've got a family. Hey, I got pictures."

Halvorsen looked at the pictures of kids and a wife and searched his head for something to say. Finally he just said again, "Yeah, looks like you're doing okay. I always knew you would, Joe."

Culley grinned and put them away and stretched back in his leather chair. "What can I help you with? Let's see, you used to own some shares of Thunder, didn't you? Lot of changes there in the last few years."

"Since Dan got out of running it."

"Uh huh. And his daughter took over."

Halvorsen remembered meeting her once. A good-looking woman, but as hard a piece of goods as he'd ever seen.

"You still got those?" Culley prompted him.

"Oh, the stock? I sold that years ago. Maybe I should of hung on, but I needed the money."

"Always a good reason to sell. But that's not what you're here about."

"No. Wanted to ask you about a company, name of Medina Transportation."

"Thinking of buying?"

"Just want to know something about it."

"Idle curiosity?"

"I seen their trucks up around where I live. Figured to find out what was going on, drilling or what."

Culley didn't seem to find that out of line. He said, "I know the name. It's not traded over the counter. I couldn't call it a hot company because of the lack of a market, but I know they've done better since prices firmed up. We're seeing wellhead spot-sale levels over two dollars per MBtu for the first time in ten years."

"What's that in MCF's?" said Halvorsen.

"An MCF, a thousand cubic feet, that's about a thousand BTU's. You can compare natural gas prices better to oil values that way. Just a minute, let me look it up. See what I can tell you." Keys clicked and Halvorsen half got up so he could see the screen. Lots of numbers but nothing he could make sense of. He sat down again and Culley said, "There it is. Incorporated two years ago. Yeah, privately held."

"Who by?"

"There's no requirement for listing that."

"Got any address or anything on it?"

"Just a box number, in Coudersport. If you want I can look into it for you, maybe find out a little more about it."

"No, that's all right." Halvorsen felt suddenly weak, dizzy. He struggled to his feet, gripping the back of the chair, fighting not to show it to the younger man.

He'd found out what he wanted to know. Who owned the truck. He'd tell Nolan that and then wash his hands of it. No reason he should be doing the cops' jobs for them. He couldn't complain about other people poking their noses in his business and then spend his time doing the same thing to them. It was time to go home, or maybe stop and see Alma and Fred, see if there was any cake or cookies to be had.

"Maybe I'll come out to see you sometime, we'll take a little hike in the woods," said Culley. Halvorsen muttered, "Sure, come on by"; only he knew it would never happen. You could see it in his eyes, the same look you got from a trapped animal. The office had Joe Culley, it had tied a tie around his neck like a colored noose, and he'd die in a leather chair.

He stuck his thumb out and got a ride back to Raymondsville with Warner Fetzeck, who had six hundred acres along Todds Creek, north of town. Fetzeck had a load of bagged fertilizer in the back, and whiffs of it surged up into the cab as they drove along the river. Halvorsen said it was getting warm, everything was melting. Fetzeck said yeah, but he wasn't going to put any vegetables in yet. "It's been that kind of winter. I figure we're good for two, three more storms. I just hope the snow cover don't hang on too long. I like to get my oats in middle of March or they don't hardly have time to grow."

"What you doing with the fertilizer?" Halvorsen asked him.

"I like to top-dress the wheat some, I get a warm window like this. Field crops're like everything else; they like to feel somebody up there gives a shit about 'em. And sometimes you can work a better deal than you can in the spring, everybody wants five loads." Fetzeck steered carefully around a rusted-out Omni waiting to make a lefthand turn up Date Hollow. "Get your deer this year?"

"I quit hunting a while back."

"That's right, I forgot. I got me a nice buck. A little, fat five-point with a twelve-inch spread. Right after that big snowfall."

"Where'd you get it?"

"I just go up the hill behind my place. There's a place the power lines come down, I stand-hunt there and I generally get one."

Halvorsen remembered Friedman's story about the guy who thought he saw wolves. "Ever see any dogs out there? Wild dogs?"

"No."

"How about those what-do-you-call-'em, those coy-dogs? See any of those?"

"Shit, you know they ain't going to let you see 'em. Hear 'em once in a while, howling. Never seen one," said the farmer. "Tell you one thing, they *better* stay out of sight. I see one, I've got a thirty-thirty in my hand, I'm gonna put him down."

"Think that's the thing to do, huh?"

"Well, I'll tell you. I got as much respect for life or whatever as the next guy. But I got sheep, I got pigs, the next thing they're gonna do after they run out of deer is come down and start eating my livestock."

They drove the rest of the way in silence, and Halvorsen tipped his hat when they got into town and climbed stiffly down in front of the post office. He checked his box and found two pension checks and a lot of contest envelopes, catalogs, and political flyers. He dumped those into the bin in the lobby and took the checks across to the First Raymondsville.

Then he walked up the back street to the police station. Nolan wasn't in but the dispatcher gave him a note pad and pencil. Halvorsen waited till his glasses unfogged, then laboriously inscribed, THAT TRUCK I TOLD YOU ABOUT BELONGS TO THE MEDINA TRANSPORTATION COMPANY. GAS CO OUT OF COUDERSPORT. W. T. HALVORSEN.

He left it with the dispatcher and headed down the street, noting the shadows of the hills lengthening across the valley. He stopped again at Les Rosen's to warm up, then kept on. At the Texaco station he hesitated, looking at the house behind it, then went round the back. A brown and black dog flung itself wheezing at the end of a chain till it recognized him and licked his outstretched hand. He went heavily up the steps, carefully, because they were going rotten, and knocked twice at the storm door.

His daughter sat across the table, looking at him as if she hadn't seen him for years. Alma was a heavy, sad-looking woman, and today she had a red nose and weepy eyes. Halvorsen bit into the brownie and took a slug of the hot chocolate, wishing for a second it could have had brandy in it. "Sorry you ain't feeling so good," he said when he came up for air.

"Fred's got it too, everybody's got it at the service station. I was flat on my back all last week."

Halvorsen reflected gloomily that now he'd probably get it too. One thing about living alone, you didn't catch colds. "How's the station doing?"

"The fuckin' Sheetz is cutting the ground from under me," her husband, Fred Pankow, said from the doorway. "Aw, don't get up, Racks. I just come back for a second to get the mail. The fuckin' Quik Stop's underselling us by six cents. I see people over there been going to me for twenty years. They got milk, pop, beer, chips, and their gas is cheaper too. It's not quality, but do they give a shit? Far as most people think, gas is gas. If it wasn't for the muffler business . . . How you doing?"

"Okay."

"Are you taking care of yourself, Dad?" his daughter asked him.

"Uh huh. Had a doctor visit just today."

"That's good. I'm glad you're taking care of your health. Are you taking those vitamins I got you?"

He hadn't, but he'd meant to. He took another bite of brownie and didn't answer. Pankow kept complaining and Halvorsen's mind drifted while he talked. Not really thinking about anything else, just not listening to Pankow. His son-in-law had a mouth and loved running it. But he felt tired. A long day, and a lot of it walking. So when Alma asked him if he'd stay for supper he said yes, and when she asked him after supper if he wouldn't like to stay for the night, have a hot bath and sleep in the spare room, he said he would. Hoping that they wouldn't have to have the same discussion she brought up every time he stayed here.

But sure enough, as soon as the electric heater was whining, taking the edge off the chill in the little second-floor room, and he'd turned the light out and laid back, sighing, into the fresh clean sheets, listening to Pankow's dog coughing in the back yard, he heard the steps creaking. Then the hesitant tap at his door. "Dad?"

"What?"

"Are you okay? Did you find the washcloth?"

"Yeah. Thanks."

"Dad, we need to talk about what you're going to do. Where you're going to live. When you get to where you can't—"

"Going to live out Mortlock. Like I always done."

"I know you keep saying that, but you don't look good. Sometimes I don't think you're listening. I asked you twice if you wanted more chicken and you just looked out the window and never answered me—"

"I was thinkin' about something else."

"Do you feel all right?"

"I'm okay. I can shift for myself."

"I wish you'd move into town. Where I can take care of you."

"Don't need nobody to take care of me, Alma. Not you, and not nobody in no nursing home, either. When it's time for somebody to do that, I got no business being here anymore."

"That's an awful thing to say."

"How I feel. Don't want to be a burden on you, Alma."

"It wouldn't be no burden, Pop."

He didn't answer, just stared grimly into the dark, and after a while he heard her sigh, and sniffle, and then, making him blink, the faint and oddly final click of the closing door.

Seven

T he silver wolf stopped in his tracks, right paw raised, staring uphill toward where he'd heard the faint click. Blunt ears cocked, jaw hanging open as the cold air silently ebbed from his lungs, he gazed fixedly into the gray trees.

Around the motionless animal the hill slanted upward in a great slow rising from a broad valley below. The valley was wooded, covered with the stark black lacework of oak and the pale striped trunks of white birch. A wide, shallow creek was visible through the denuded trees as a white blankness broken here and there by the upward heave of huge rocks and the tortured roots of an erosion-toppled oak. The only sign of man stood at a ripple of black water and white ice where the river dropped: the shattered, roofless remains of an old mill, timber walls weathered silver under the gray sky.

The wolf had covered ten miles since leaving the den at dawn. He'd crossed two ranges of hills, rocking along in a distance-eating gait where the melting snow lay thin on the south slopes and cut banks, picking his way cautiously across the dissolving ice that bordered the rock-floored streams. Once he had to plunge in, muzzle thrust upward, eyes rolling, lips drawn back while he swam furiously against the icy current. All that time he had examined every movement and scent and sound with fierce and total concentration. He'd found nothing to eat and seen nothing living except an occasional raven soaring above the hills. These he eyed closely—ravens sometimes led the way to prey, or at any rate to carrion, which the wolf would eat if nothing better showed up—but the distant shapes only circled aimlessly. So he trotted on, alertly inspecting every shadow, every trace of scent on snow or wind, every sound that carried in the windfilled woods.

Till now.

The old wolf shifted his weight, still staring uphill. His trap-injured leg had healed years before, but it still ached on a long traverse. His pricked-up ears searched in short arcs, and his deep-set eyes peered into the brightening, waning, ever-shifting patterns the trees traced over the snow as clouds passed silently between them and the hidden sun.

Suddenly he burst into a leaping, bounding progress through the eroded boulders that littered the hillside. Here on the north slope the snow was deep and still dry, sheltered from the destroying sun by the great curved shadow of the hill, and with each leap the wolf came up out of it, chest scattering a burst of white, then plunging back till the pale fur of his belly smacked down into it. After moving in this way a hundred yards he paused again, tail hanging down, and lifted his black-marked muzzle to probe and search the wind.

The wolf was hungry. Since killing the rottweiler his only meal had been the desiccated body of a dead owl, rank and leathery, but he'd grimly crunched and gulped down bones and feathers nonetheless. But his own hunger was not his greatest concern. He ground his teeth as he peered into the wind. There, the suspicion of motion in a clump of snow-covered laurel . . . He pounced with all four feet and burrowed into the brush with his forepaws, tossing snow behind to stream out on the wind, grunting and blinking as twigs stung his eye and blurred his vision. But nothing emerged, his probing paws came up empty. He sat back on his haunches, then up on all fours again.

Suddenly he stiffened. He wheeled slowly, pointing his round black nose uphill. His tail switched.

Casting back and forth, he bounded quartering across the invisible trail, leaving the scattered boulders behind for a dip surrounded by slim young beeches, then climbing a steeper slope, tacking his way into the flow of cold air that tided over the top of the hill. He moved in careful stages, loping a few yards, then pausing to lift his nose again into the wind. That invisible river carried messages, mysterious scents, innumerable knowl-edges that hovered at the edges of understandability. He loped a few more meters, then froze again, a white and gray and black shape melting with immobility back into the immense white wilderness, the racing gray clouds, the racing wind that ruffled the hairs on the tips of his ears as he waited. Waited . . .

The buck stepped slowly out, dark protruding eyes searching the woods. It lifted its hooves delicately, probing through the snow to firm ground. Its antlers, lost that December, had not yet begun to grow back, but its gray flanks were solid muscle, its chest round as a barrel. Its lifted head and long, pricked-up ears mirrored the wolf's. Instantly the wolf crouched, pressing his belly to the snow. His ears flattened back. His pupils dilated, fixed with tremendous intensity on the prey. Motionless, barely breathing, he trembled with eagerness. Air pumped through his muzzle as he concentrated all his attention on the animal that stood twenty yards above, searching between the surrounding trees with rapt caution.

The deer went suddenly tense. The wolf was so close he could hear it breathing. Its hot smell came down to him on the wind, nearly driving him mad as he watched the huge ears turning uneasily, listened to the snuffle of air through its widened nostrils.

The buck's searching, dilated eyes locked on the wolf's. It gave a prancing sideways jump and a startled, whistling snort, staring down at the crouching predator as if aggrieved and somehow outraged by his presence. But then it stopped, stock still, and the two stared at each other for a time that stretched out, tauter and tauter, till it seemed the whole waiting woods beat with a thudding thunder of prisoned blood. The wolf crouched even lower, and a vibration grew in his throat, faint at first, then rising to a snarl.

Suddenly both animals burst into furious motion, as if all the tense energy with which they had charged themselves in their immobile regard had been instantaneously transformed into velocity. The buck took four leaps and bounded into the air, legs flashing out like swords being drawn as it hurdled a fallen tangle of rotten wood, black splintered boughs thrust up from under the covering white like claws. It seemed to float in the air, on the verge of taking flight among the iron-gray trunks, about to soar upward, past their spidery bare crowns, to disappear into the clouds like the ravens that floated there now, drawn by some mysterious instinct. But then it drifted earthward like dandelion down, lightly touching on delicate hooves, only to race ahead for five or six bounds before projecting itself into another breathtaking jeté, snowy tail bobbing, turning its head slightly to track its pursuer.

After it bounded the wolf, driving his chest through the snow with a leaping, thrusting gather-and-stretch of powerful legs. The huge spread paw pads sank into the yielding white, then flung the silver-and-black body forward in tremendous fifteen-foot bounds. The harsh rhythm of his breath accompanied the crunch of the snow and the crackle of brush. Driving himself with every ounce of his strength, the wolf gained on the buck. As he bored inward his eyes fixed on the bounding deer's outstretched neck. But then the buck turned downhill, into heavier cover, and the wolf swerved to follow. Now his progress slowed as he had to weave around other, larger obstacles, the convex humps of snow over bushes, tangles of blackberry brambles, dry and brown but still barb-tipped. The deer did not hesitate. It floated over the uneven terrain while the wolf, beginning to tire, struggled to keep up. The wet snow dragged at his body. His paws sank in, and occasionally he stumbled, misjudging his footing.

The deer turned once more, zigging down a steep gully into an aspen thicket, and the wolf's pace slackened. At each bound now he dropped farther behind. His tongue dragged out, and he stared despairingly after the crazily bobbing white flag. At last it faded to a flicker in the forest, and the wolf quit and flopped down in his tracks. He lay panting, tongue touching the snow, for about fifteen minutes. Staring off into the woods with nearsighted, blank, golden eyes. Then he got to his feet and shook himself like a Labrador emerging from a lake. Turning away from where the buck had disappeared, he trotted off downhill.

The silver got back to the den two hours later, belly still empty except for a long, muzzle-numbing drink from the clear spring that surged from the ground a half-mile back. In all that time he had seen only one other sign of life, a busy gray squirrel high in an oak. He'd waited, looking up, then after a time understood hope was vain and trotted on again. Now he stood in the center of a tramped-down space of snow, panting from the trek, tail drooping as his nose told his disappointed belly there was no fresh meat here, none of the others had found food either.

The den was invisible from the clearing. The entrance was behind a blown-down tree, screened by a black tangle of laurel brush, tucked back beneath an overhanging chunk of blackened stone shaped like a flattened loaf of bread. Close to water, sheltered and yet near the intersection of several game trails, the narrow cave had been a wolf den many times before, though the last had been so many decades ago no trace or trail of old scent remained.

The silver wolf leapt over the dead tree, wriggled through the blow-down and snow, and slid beneath the rock. Inside the walls opened out, though the ceiling was still so low it pressed his tail downward. It was dark and dry and warm, deep beneath rock and earth, and he stood blinking and sniffing before giving a short whine.

The female whined back from the darkness, and he yipped softly and slithered through a narrow tunnel toward her. Then he felt her tongue lapping over his muzzle. In a moment they were tussling and biting like two pups, kissing and licking each other in the chamber that, in a few weeks, would be the home of the cubs. Then he sensed from the smell of her breath she was hungry. He whined anxiously and the pleasure went out of the play. He backed out of the den, turned in a circle, and lay down in the dark, intending to rest for a time, close his eyes, then go out again that night. But rest did not come. The wolf did not reason that his mate needed nourishment. He knew it another way, a deep unease, and a moment later he was up again and creeping out into the afternoon brightness with one thought in his brain: he had to find food.

He was standing in the clearing, debating which way to go, when his ears pricked. A faint high whine was drifting down to him across the valleys and ridges. He did not respond to the howl. Only waited, listening, till he was sure of the direction, and then burst into a run.

He found the bobtailed wolf standing stiff-legged with its tongue hanging out in a stand of hemlock. It was the fourth member of the pack, after the silver and the dark wolf and the female; it had lost all but a stump of its tail as a pup and seemingly all its confidence along with it. Under the snowladen, dense cover the shadows were quiet and gloomy. Neither wolf could see very far, but neither could they be seen. As the older trotted in both animals wagged their tails, and there was a brief, perfunctory face-licking before the younger wolf gave several muffled yips and frowned, directing its attention downhill. Then it ran a few steps. The old wolf followed, tail lifted like a flag, and they bobbed silently down the slope, one in the broken trail of the other. Then the bobtail dropped to its belly.

Two unwavering pairs of yellow eyes peered out through the screening evergreens at a clearing below a crumbling cut bank, not far from a jumble of rusting gears and wheels and bogies intertwined with dense brambles and jacketed with snow.

The elk stood in the center of a clearing, antlerless and sway-backed, dull brown with a lighter rump patch and darker legs and neck and head. It looked huge against the small evergreens and aspens, a full five feet high at the shoulder, dwarfing the buck the silver wolf had chased that morning. The old wolf stared at it dumbfounded. He hadn't seen an elk since he'd left the north. But here one was, nibbling at the bark of an aspen. He swung his head, testing the air for scent. A snatch of memory: many elk, traveling together through deep snow. But he didn't sense any others here. This female was alone.

When the wolves trotted out into the clearing the elk wheeled to face them. It lowered its head, then tossed it, snorting and stamping its feet. The silver wolf eyed those heavy, sharp hooves. He hadn't been afraid of the rottweiler, but he respected the elk. Apprehension and hunger battled in his heart. He looked swiftly around, noting the cut bank behind the big animal, guessing which way it would run. Something this huge and powerful could not be taken from the front. If it stood its ground in front of the bank they might not be able to get close enough to attack. He sat back on his haunches and yawned ostentatiously, anticipating a period of mutual testing, mutual confrontation before giving battle. The bobtailed wolf hung back, its gaze flicking from its packmate to the elk.

But instead of making a stand the elk bolted, with no warning whatsoever. Its sudden lunge took the wolves by surprise. They sprang after it with such a single mind they collided in midair and fell rolling and yelping to the snow. But a moment later they were up again, bounding hard through white powder and pine needles. The old wolf leapt over the gears and gained a few feet; the younger one kept doggedly behind the elk, pushing it along.

At first they gained as the immense hooves only slowly pushed the great animal's heavy body into motion. It didn't leap and bound like a deer. It galloped, crashing through light underbrush. But then, like a locomotive building steam, the elk began to draw ahead. The old wolf redoubled his efforts desperately, remembering how the buck had escaped that morning. Not again! But then, not fifty paces into its stride, the elk made an error. Stepped into some hole or depression under the snow, or turned its hoof on a stone. The wolf didn't know what caused it, but he saw with grim joy the collapse of the animal's off leg, its forequarters buckling. It recovered almost at once, but by then the wolves had caught up.

The silver struck first, from behind, darting in and snapping at the elk's hind leg. Tendons and muscle tore between his teeth, and he scrambled back as a hoof sliced down, spraying snow and dirt where his head had been. One of those slashing blows could break a wolf's back. The elk turned, facing the wolf, but now there was no bank to screen its rear. The old wolf's black lips drew back as he saw that the younger had already guessed this and was flinging itself through the flying snow to gain a position of attack. The elk charged a few feet, and the silver loped backward, suckering it toward him as the other completed the circle.

The bobtailed wolf leapt, and its jaws met in the elk's haunch with a sound like a meat cleaver hitting flesh. The powerful teeth sheared through hair and tough hide and met in meat. The elk screamed, dragging the younger wolf around in a half-circle, but it held grimly as hot blood streamed down over its muzzle. It growled savagely, releasing its teeth only to bite again, shearing through flesh and fat and muscle. Then one of the hooves found its mark, and the wolf rolled away as the elk reared and struck again.

Around the circle of their combat the silver wolf stalked, muzzle wrinkled in excitement and rage. His yellowed teeth glowed in the dimming light. He leapt, snapped at the elk's muzzle but missed. It turned to face him again, snorting heavily, and lowered its head to charge.

The old wolf leapt again, a great flying spring, and this time his teeth met savagely in the cow's lowered nose. The great jaw muscles drove them through rubbery flesh into cartilage and bone, and he moaned with fierce pleasure, snapping and tearing, coughing to clear his throat as his mouth filled with the hot upwelling of salty blood.

The elk pivoted, trumpeting hoarsely, and smashed him off against a rock. He tumbled into the snow. He lay still for a moment, blinking through a dazzle in his brain, looking up into the treetops. Then struggled up again.

Screaming and snarling echoed from the dimming flanks of the hollow. The bobtailed wolf still clung to the cow's rump, biting and growling, gradually shifting its grip from the haunches closer and closer to its belly. The cow screamed and bucked and stamped, rear hooves pistoning downward with enormous force into the churned-up, bloody ruck of soil and leaves and snow that was gradually surrounding the struggling animals. The wolves snarled and snapped and tore, darting in and out and in again, bushy tails flickering like gray flames. At last the silver wolf, limping, nearly exhausted, threw himself in recklessly and hit the hind leg again. The elk went down with a crash that shook the woods.

It stayed down only seconds before it struggled up again. The night was coming and it cast a last, despairing look past its tormentors, searching the darkening ridges and hollows. Blood streamed from its muzzle, its face, its savagely mauled rump. But its sight met nothing but the coming darkness.

The silver was drained now, wheezing for air, and his side throbbed where it had slammed into the rock. He backed off and sat. The stump-tailed one hesitated, then joined him, both watching with lolling tongues as the elk staggered to all fours and propped itself once more to face them. One of its eyeballs had been punctured and it kept its remaining eye toward them. The younger wolf whined impatiently, then dipped its head to the snow and began eagerly lapping up the blood.

The woods kept getting darker and darker, till it was hard to make out much beyond shapes against snow, the vertical shadows of the trees, the dark pools of scattered blood and leaves. But the old wolf just sat. Now that the elk was wounded, bleeding, they could afford to wait.

Finally he got up again and approached the elk warily. It kicked at him when he tried to approach, and the other wolf got up too and circled in the opposite direction. The elk tried to follow them both with its single eye. Blood dripped slowly down its face.

The elk lurched into motion, heading stiffly uphill. This time the tactic didn't surprise the wolves and they followed, in no hurry now, dropping back to let the elk lead the way through the evergreens. The woods were more open beyond the copse, with deep snow lying between larger trees. The wolves plunged along in the broad, deep trail the elk plowed out, weaving among the tree trunks, till it came to the top of another bank. The wolves slowed, but the elk didn't. It kept on going as if it didn't see the eight-foot drop, and suddenly plunged over. The wolves surged forward at this and leapt over too, landing on the elk's broad back as it struggled to its feet at the bottom. As they rolled off the bobtailed wolf grabbed for the muzzle this time, and dragged it down as the old wolf scrambled in through a flurry of snow and pounding hooves to tear the elk's belly open.

The cow screamed and sprayed out liquid brown feces onto the snow as it went down on its side. The old wolf leapt in again past the younger one and bit savagely down on either side of the elk's eyes. The skull crunched as his blunt teeth drove inward. This he knew was the end and he bit down again and again, driving bone splinters and teeth deep into the brain, and at last the elk stopped struggling and the two wolves, snarling and snapping, began to feed.

The old wolf gouged out a mouthful of meat, swallowed it down hungrily, then rolled on the bloody snow, whining and panting, before squirming in again, a savage imitation of a puppy nosing in to nurse. On the other side of the still-twitching carcass he heard ripping and grunting as the other wolf fed. Blood was still pumping out onto the snow, melting it, sinking into shallow depressed pools of darkness.

The old wolf seized the bloody skin of the belly and began tugging with short, powerful jerks. The legs kicked in dying reflex as the hide tore off. He slashed his teeth into the hole and growled in meat-lust, eagerly licking up the rich juices, the soft, gushy tumblings of half-digested browse. Then he felt something else. He set his teeth into it and pulled.

The fawn slid out onto the snow, still folded, in a rushing tumble of blood and amniotic fluid. It struggled weakly, eyes still closed. Tiny hooves jabbed through yielding membranes like penknives. The wolf growled deep in its throat, and with one snap bit through its neck, the soft tissue yielding in salty cracklings. Without a sound, without ever opening its eyes to the immense and snowy woods, the fawn died in his jaws.

The wolves fed. The bloody snow steamed. Ravens fluttered down from the cold sky and hopped about, waiting for the initial fever of devouring to pass. One hopped too close and the bobtailed wolf left off gulping to snap at it. It fluttered off a few feet before landing again, cawing reproachfully.

Finally the old wolf could not choke down another mouthful. He sat back on his haunches and yawned in exhausted, meat-drunken satiation. Juices soaked his pelt, dripped from his muzzle, his teeth. The huge carcass lay motionless and silent except for the excited hopping and scratching of the ravens. Even all the wolves' gorging had barely diminished it. It would last for days. He would bring his mate here, and the dark wolf, and they would all feast together again and again, until nothing was left. The silver wolf yawned again, looking with wide pupils up into the black sky, then staggered to his feet.

And stopped, suddenly rigid.

Some strange vibration or sound had come to him, as much through the ground as through the air, a faint quiver sensed through the pads of his feet. The old wolf lifted them, put them down again, feeling the tremble with wonder, as if the great earth itself had begun the throes of death. He whined, and the other wolf lifted its head too, ears laid back, staring into the darkness.

The sound ebbed, was gone. He kept listening, looking out into the trees, then up at the looming hill, as if waiting to see or smell whatever lay beyond. But nothing else happened. Presently he relaxed, yawned, and began grooming his fur. When he was clean he picked up the torn remains of the fawn in his jaws, carefully, almost gently. Then, carrying it with his head cocked, trotted off into the darkness, heading downhill.

Eight

Sitting with her hands twisted together in the front seat of the car, looking out at the snow-covered fields and then the night lights in the gas station and the tire store and the Sears as they got closer to town, Becky thought she'd never forget the smell of bleach and vomit.

She didn't know what time it was when she woke up. Just that she'd been asleep when she heard a funny noise from Jammy's room. A thudding bump, almost like a door closing, except it went on and on. She listened for a while, staring up at the ceiling and feeling her heart beating hard, too, like an echo of the strange noise.

Finally she threw back the covers and got up, shivering as the cold night air slid under her nightgown. A dark comma uncoiled at the foot of her bed; Leo, the Siamese; it jumped down reluctantly, paws pattering on the floor. She got her old Dumbo flashlight from under the bed and went out into the hallway. The carpet felt sticky and cold under her bare feet. Below in the darkened great room the stove clanked and hummed to itself, sooty windows flickering as she hesitated outside her brother's door. The noise was coming from inside, violent and irregular, as if something were struggling to escape. She pushed the door open suddenly and aimed the light at the floor.

Then she was screaming "Mom! Mom!" and bending over her brother. She heard her mother pounding up the stairs.

A moment later she was slammed into the chest of drawers, and her ears were ringing and her cheek stung. "*Don't* touch that," her mother hissed, standing over Jammy like an avenging angel as Becky touched the side of her own face gingerly. "Get the bleach. In the bathroom. No, wait—first hand me that plastic thing. The yellow thing. The fish. Now go call Charlie. Tell him we've got to go to the hospital."

No, she'd never forget. Clorox was supposed to kill the viruses, but the smell made her sick to her stomach. She knew after tonight it would always make her remember her brother's room and being so afraid she could hardly breathe.

When Charlie was carrying Jammy down the stairs, her little brother's shuddering body wrapped in a blanket and the yellow plastic fish clamped in his teeth, her mother came back and found her curled in the corner. She squatted beside her. "Becky."

She turned her face away.

"Becky, listen. I'm sorry I hit you. But I told you never to touch vomit or blood or—anyway, I'm sorry. Now listen. We're taking your brother to the hospital. I want you to go back to bed. If we're not back by morning, you'll have to get up and make yourself cereal and go out and catch the bus by yourself. You're a big girl, I know you can do that. And remember to turn the lights off and the toaster oven if you use it. All right?"

"I'm not staying here alone. I want to go to the hospital with you."

Her mother hadn't bothered to argue, just patted her head and got up. Becky huddled there in the corner, the bleach fumes making her eyes water.

She was so scared. She couldn't stop thinking about her brother's body thrashing and flopping around on the floor amid his animals and blocks, banging into the bed and the dresser.

She could hear them talking downstairs, running back and forth and getting things. Charlie's voice, deep and logical sounding. Her mother's, higher, explaining, pleading. At last she got up, uncurling herself into the cold air again, her throat so dry it clicked and hurt when she swallowed. She went down the hallway to her room and started getting her school clothes on.

When she got downstairs Charlie had the car running and they all got in, her in front with Charlie, and Mom in back holding Jammy. Her mother had looked at her, started to say something, then didn't. And now they were driving through town, passing the houses that didn't look much better than the ones in Johnsonburg but at least Raymondsville never smelled as bad. There was the blue *H* sign and they turned onto Maple and there was the parking lot and the overhang that said EMERGENCY and she could hear Jammy still breathing hoarsely, so now it was all right, the doctors and nurses would take care of him and everything would be all right. She leaned back, feeling a great wave of relief, as if only her watchfulness had kept him alive till now and at last she could leave it to the people at the hospital.

"It's some kind of convulsion, some kind of seizure," her mother said to the man who came out and looked into the car. And Charlie, leaning over Becky toward the window, added, "He's HIV positive."

Becky saw the man's face change, saw him take his hand off the car door. His voice got different too as he said, "Can you bring him in, please?"

The emergency room made her squint and put a hand over her eyes after the night outside. It smelled scary, like alcohol and something else she imagined was blood. Carts banged through doors that flipped closed behind them. An announcement came over a speaker she couldn't see, but the words were all garbled. They wouldn't let her stay with Jammy. She looked back as the nurse shepherded her and Charlie on, seeing her little brother so small and his face looking weird, withered and old, more like that of a monkey than a little boy, writhing under the blanket as her mom held his feet and the doctor clipped something to his ear. White stuff stained the plastic fish in his teeth. Then the curtain slid closed, and she couldn't help wondering if, when she saw him again, he'd still be alive.

She and Charlie had to wait on blue plastic chairs in a little room with a shut-off television. They were the only ones there. Charlie didn't say anything so neither did she, just sat there feeling scared and unhappy and then finally sleepy. Tomorrow was Saturday, not a school day, anyway. She remembered that now. Her mom had thought it was a school day but it wasn't.

She looked at the TV but knew she shouldn't even ask to turn it on. So she looked at the tile floor, the clock, the picture of some deer coming down to drink at a stream. It looked like the woods in back of their house, except that the hills weren't as high.

They sat there for a long time. And gradually she started to get uneasy, not just about Jammy, but about her stepfather. He sat so grim and un-smiling and hadn't said anything at all in the car, or since they got here, just "He's HIV positive" to the man when they first pulled in. So that finally she said timidly, "Charlie?"

"Yeah?"

"Is it going to . . . is it going to cost a lot, bringing Jammy here?"

"I don't know, Becky. Don't worry about it, okay?"

"I'm sorry he's sick. I know it costs a lot, for his medicine, I mean."

"Don't worry about it," he said again. She couldn't tell if he really didn't care, or if he was doing that grown-up thing where they pretended you were too little to know anything, or if he was mad. If he was mad, that wasn't good. She remembered how it had been in Port Allegany and in Johnsonburg. People would come and want the rent, and they didn't have it, and she had to go with her mom and borrow money from Uncle Will. Then he couldn't give them any more and they had to move. Sneak out in the middle of the night so the people who owned the house wouldn't know they were going. How they had Kraft Dinner and jelly sandwiches all the time, and had to shop at the thrift store, till finally Mom had to go and see the lady at the county office, and for a while they'd been on relief. She didn't mind that kind of stuff, actually she liked Kraft Dinner and fish sticks, but she could tell it made her mom feel bad. Living with Charlie wasn't always that great either. Sometimes it was like he wasn't even there, just in his room with his computer, but other times he said things. He didn't exactly yell, and he never hit her mom that Becky saw, but once she'd heard her crying in the kitchen when she didn't think anybody could hear. And once she said something about doing it for the kids. Becky wished she was older and had a job, and a place of her own. Then Mom and Jammy could come and live with her.

She wanted to ask some other things, but the way Charlie had said "Don't worry about it" she was afraid to. So she didn't, just sat there for another long time till her behind went to sleep. Finally she reached into her coat pocket, where it hung on the chair, and got out her Barbie she'd stuffed in it before running down the steps. She held it in her lap for a while, then got down on the floor and started rolling it on the carpet. The wheels lit up and she whispered to herself. She was on television and everybody was watching her, it was ice dancing. Till Charlie said sharply, "Becky."

"Huh?"

"Don't say 'huh.' Say, 'what' or 'excuse me.' "

She said, looking at the floor. "Excuse me, Charlie."

"Could you stop playing with that doll? How old are you?"

"Twelve."

"For a twelve-year-old you spend a lot of time playing. And fixing your hair. Why didn't you bring your homework along? Or a book you could read?"

"I didn't think of it," she said, looking at the doll in her hands. It wasn't a champion skater now, it was just a toy.

After a while she had to go to the bathroom. She told Charlie and he nodded, not looking up from his magazine. She went around the corner, trying to be quiet, looking for a toilet. Then down the hall, and all of a sudden she felt herself starting to cry. She couldn't help it, she was just crying, and she put her hands to her face and leaned against the wall and let the tears come out. It was very quiet, all the doors were dark, and then she thought she heard her mother's voice. She sniffled and crept a little farther down the corridor and heard talking from around the corner. It was a woman's voice, but it wasn't her mother's. She heard the woman say "pneumonia," then murmur, and then "not expected this soon after a PCP infection. But it's not uncommon either . . . meningitis. That's the proximate cause of the convulsions."

"What should we do?" There, that was her mother, and then suddenly she knew who the other woman was: Dr. Friedman, the one who'd taken care of Jammy last time he was sick. She must have come in, because she hadn't been in the emergency room, at least Becky hadn't seen her there. She wiped her nose with the back of her hand, listening.

"They've given him rectal Diazepam, Mrs. Piccirillo. That's an anticonvulsant, which is what he needs right now. It's working and he's resting quietly. It will wear off pretty soon, though. He'll have to take something else for a while, along with the antipyretics and antibiotics to take care of the fever and the infection itself."

A pause, while her mother murmured something she couldn't hear. Then, "No, he'd better stay for a few days. To make sure . . . I don't believe they're exactly pleased to have him here. You know how it is. There are precautions to take, extra work. But we don't have beds at the clinic or certification to keep patients overnight. He'll be well taken care of here. I'll have a talk with the head nurse, make sure everyone understands."

Another murmur, then, "Some of it should be covered. Charles has insurance, doesn't he? Oh, self-employed . . . I don't know. You'll have to discuss it with them, with the business office."

Becky stood on one leg, leaning against the wall. Then a door must have opened or something, because she heard her mother say, really clear, "Then what happens?"

"What do you mean?"

"He stays here a few days, they release him—then what?"

A space of silence and the whisper of paper. "You mean a prognosis," the doctor said.

"Please."

"Long term." Friedman cleared her throat. "He pulled through the pneumonia but this is not so good. I've seen this before, where I used to practice. There can be intervals of stability. They can last for months. But I believe in telling people the truth, Mrs. Piccirillo. He's already past the median survival time. All we can do is try to fight the infections as they come along, and try to keep him as comfortable as we can."

Becky strained her ears, but her mother didn't cry out, didn't gasp. It was as if she already knew. She didn't even sound different when she said, "What about my daughter? I've been thinking, it might be better to send her to live with my sister in Erie."

"That's not necessary. She should be safe around him as long as there's no body-fluid contact. Emotionally—it's not going to be easy, but from what I've seen of her she—"

Suddenly she heard footsteps. She ducked into the bathroom as the folding door rattled back. A moment later the doctor called, "Mr. Piccirillo? Could I see you for a moment?"

She couldn't hear what they said after that. She sat on the cold toilet seat, holding her stomach in the dark and not wanting to turn on the light. Trying to make sense of what the doctor had said. She didn't understand all the words. But no matter how she thought about it, she could come up with only the one meaning. That pretty soon, no matter what the doctors or anybody did, her little brother was going to die.

Nine

The Petroleum Club had been built toward the end of the great Pennsylvania oil rush, more than a hundred years before. Hardly anything, Ainslee thought as she let the doorman take her coat, had changed since. The decor was Victorian, so old it was back in style: balustrades carved into spirals, patterned damask wall hangings, crystal chandeliers dropped from the high ceilings. Age-spotted photographs leaned out above the walnut wainscoting: as hundreds of timber derricks porcupined the hills, tiny figures posed in stovepipe hats and worker's caps. Sepia gushers leapt skyward, Governor Hoyt clipped the ribbon to an opera house, Adah Isaacs Mencken posed nude on a white stallion, and Company I, Sixteenth Regiment, marched in puttees and slouch caps down Main Street to entrain for the invasion of Cuba. This early in the morning the smoking room was empty. As she passed the bar a white-jacketed waiter said, "Good morning, Miss Thunner."

Tonic and orange juice in hand, she went through into the meeting room. A dozen captain's chairs surrounded a library table. Men stood as she came in and she shook hands, quickly, firmly. This was a tradition, this informal gathering of the clan before the official meeting. Something her father had always done when he held board meetings. It was a tradition worth preserving. Not because traditions were necessarily good—it hadn't been that long ago no woman was allowed into the sacred precincts of the club—but because it reminded everyone here exactly who she was and what she represented.

Which was four generations of the Thunner family. Their portraits lined the wall behind the table. Left to right: 1869, Beacham Berwick Thunner, a legend in frock coat and stovepipe hat with his partner, Napoleon O'Connor, in front of number sixteen, the first producing well to reach the Seneca Sands. Colonel Charles Thunner, who had led Company I up San Juan Hill, in front of the old city hall with his brother Philander, a powerful figure in the company and the General Assembly for decades, and their wives, Lutetia and Frances. Ainslee remembered Great-Aunt Frances, a tall, thin woman with velvety cheeks who loved children but never had any of her own. And Daniel Thunner, tall and straight and spare, shaking hands with Herbert Hoover in 1931, and looking about sixteen times as presidential as the pudgy Iowan. A pale patch showed to the right of that, where a family portrait had hung.

"Good morning, how are you, Luke? Rogers?"

"Good morning, Ainslee, you're looking beautiful as ever."

Luke Fleming owned thousands of acres of oil leases; his crude flow constituted from a quarter to a third of the Thunder refinery's intake. He wasn't a Pennsylvanian, but a Texan who'd taken a flyer, buying up old leases for pennies an acre just before tertiary recovery unlocked millions of barrels from the retentive sands. After his positions in Texas had crumbled he'd retired here. She noted dispassionately that he was already three-quarters drunk. Rogers McGehee was the chairman of the First Raymondsville Bank, another member of The Thunder Group. They both dated from before her time at the helm; McGehee had worked with her father, and Fleming had been brought to the board by her ex-husband.

She took the seat at the head of the table as more people drifted in, carrying the *WSJ* or *Business Week* or the Petroleum City *Deputy-Republican*: Conrad Kleiner, Peter Gerroy, and the only other woman on the board, Hilda Van Etten. Ainslee had recruited Hilda, a bright young MBA graduate, from one of the oldest families in town. The Van Ettens had built the first glass furnace in the county, built the Lantzy Airport, built an electric motor production facility, and then a resistor plant. Now VanStar CeraMagnet was one of the biggest employers in the county, producing ceramic magnets, laminated cores, and printed circuit boards. Lately the component business had fallen off, but VanStar had won a contract for army ceramic helicopter turbine rotors and was building an addition. Peter Gerroy's family owned the local media, newspapers and radio; and "Connie" Kleiner was another oilman.

The barman put his head in. Fleming waved his empty glass. Van Etten quietly requested coffee. Frontino came in, big and unsmiling, and Weyandt. Rudy smiled at Ainslee, nodded around the table, and sat down. Then he got up again and bent over her shoulder to murmur in her ear, "You look great."

"Thanks."

"Have you thought about New York?"

"Thought about it, Rudy. But first things first."

When the refills came it was five past. She pointed to the door and the barman closed it as he withdrew. The others quieted. "Good morning," she said, pleasant, casual, bright. "Thanks for joining me for a little morning strategy session—"

"Your dad always used to call it foreplay," Kleiner said.

She smiled frostily. The first time the old man said this it had amused her, the second annoyed her, but by now it was just part of the ritual that was Thunder Oil and her life. "Yes, Connie. The difference is, after foreplay somebody gets screwed. But after our little strategy meetings, everybody wins."

They all chuckled except Hilda, who looked shocked. Ainslee resisted the temptation to wink at her. Business ain't exactly like they told you at Columbia, Hilda, she thought.

"I'm going to bring up three items at today's meeting. I don't expect any major disagreement, but it's better to go in with our minds made up. Especially since we have outside stockholders now.

"The first is political. Jack Mulholland's in trouble. He's fighting this ethics charge and he'll face a challenger this fall. You know who I'm talking about. She built the new library when nobody thought it could be built. She has grassroots appeal. We need to show our support for Jack. I will recommend a ten-thousand-dollar PAC contribution to his reelection campaign. Although I will not bring this up at the board meeting proper, we can also contribute up to two thousand dollars apiece personally. That can add up to a sizeable addition to his war chest. Some of us can do more." She looked at Gerroy, who said, "The *Century*, the *Record*, and the *Deputy-Republican* have always been Mulholland boosters, Ainslee. But if he's actually indicted, I reserve judgment."

"Fair enough."

Hilda said, unexpectedly, "Are we just—writing off Kit Cleveland? I mean, I know her. She has a lot of good ideas, ideas that would be good for the district."

"Yes, Hilda, I agree. It would be nice—in some ways—to have Kit. But realistically, we must stay with the Republicans. Not only is he pro-business, Jack has seniority. He was helpful getting that helicopter contract for VanStar, wasn't he?"

"That's true." The girl's face went quizzical.

"Kit would start out as a freshman, with no significant committee assignments and very little budgetary clout. Are we all paddling in the same direction now? Good. The second point I will raise is refinancing. Very briefly, we have a window of opportunity to significantly reduce our debt costs. We refinanced half our obligations last year. I believe we can turn over the rest, about eighteen million dollars, at a rate that will have a major impact on our debt service. Rogers, would you like to say anything about that?"

"I'll vote in favor."

"Right, that's a no-brainer," said Weyandt. "Let's go on."

Ainslee felt her hand tighten on the glass. Was he saying *she* was wasting their time bringing up a pat issue? But it wasn't. They were betting the bond market wouldn't keep falling. Plus, every time you refinanced you faced the risk that regulators would find something they didn't like and disapprove the issue. Once that hit the street a stock as weak as Thunder's would go into free fall. And finally, what she really had in mind was not simply a refinancing of existing debt, but roughly a doubling of it. But that would wait. She smoothed her tone and went on. "The third point is that we need to go through another round of right-sizing."

"In production?" said Kleiner doubtfully.

"No, Connie, we've cut production about as far as is safe. This time we're proposing a bottom-up review for all positions pay level five and above, with a target savings of nine million." She looked at Frontino. "Ron, I'm going to call on you during the meeting about this."

He started talking, also without notes, about the procedure for review and what the downstream costs would be in early retirement and possible legal costs. She let him run for four minutes, then caught his eye. He closed and she said, "Well, it's getting to be time. Those are the major issues I'm going to present this morning. I would greatly appreciate your support on those points, and of course on anything else that comes up in the course of the meeting."

"What about the contract renegotiations?"

"An important point, but they're not till next year, Luke."

"Oh." Fleming submerged himself in his whiskey again, and Ainslee looked around the table. "Any other questions? Then thanks for coming by, and I'll see you at the board meeting."

The boardroom was an immense walnut-paneled space on the sixth floor of the Thunder Building. The great oval table gleamed like polished amber. Twelve high-backed leather chairs were carefully spaced around it. Its air of hushed solemnity, she thought, made it seem like the soul of the company, the seat of power and responsibility. The heart of the tempest. But one entire wall was glass, and looking out and down she glimpsed past the grimy sprawl of downtown the real heart of the company: the three twelve-story catalytic cracking towers, and below them a maze and boil of tanks and pipes and steam and smoke and fire.

From a thousand wells scattered through these hills, the raw Pennsylvania crude, finest in the world, throbbed down to refinery number one;

from it, by truck and rail, refined products flowed out to the world. All America knew Thunder Gasoline, Thunderbolt Premium Racing Oil, Magick Penetrating Oil, Linette Paraffin. Less celebrated steady sellers were "#1" home heating oil and the gamut of TBC Brand industrial chemicals, high-quality feedstocks for the dye, plastic, and drug industries of the U.S., Europe, and Japan.

Number one and the company had taken a century to build, passed down from Beacham Berwick to his son Charles, and thence to his son Daniel. And from Dad, she thought, to me.

Hers to preserve and build on anew.

At the far end of the room was a lectern and projection screen. But it was not yet time to begin. She circulated, shaking hands, chatting but never smiling. Weyandt stood by the door, welcoming the vice president and board members. When a director came in, he discreetly handed him a sealed envelope that contained his fee.

The open bar and the heavy free lunch were starting to take effect, she saw. Fleming was already glazed, a couple of the other members were close behind. That was fine with her, a tranquilized board was a harmless board.

Then she saw Quentin Kemick.

When Thunder went public she'd expected to keep control through the buyer profile that Merrill, Paine & Wheat had predicted. The split of ownership between institutional, pensions and mutual funds, and small investors would make her holdings, combined with those of the other local owners she'd met with at the club, the controlling ownership.

But the market hadn't seen it that way. There'd been three major buyers. The first was Wilsonia Bank and Trust of Quincy, Massachusetts. Nominally a bank, it was actually an investment management firm for pensions and mutual funds. The face it showed Thunder was Bernard N. Parseghian, a relatively young man whose agreeableness masked what she'd quickly discovered was a ruthless focus on the bottom line. The second was the Besarcon Corporation, a Swiss-based conglomerate with interests in agriculture, data management, electrical devices, and car-rental agencies. Quentin Kemick was on the Besarcon board and usually attended Thunder meetings. Last was Frederick Blair, one of the semiretired principals in an asset-rich partnership out of Dallas. Together the three owned enough stock to threaten her position, but not enough, as she calculated it, actually to challenge her. Still, they had to be kept happy. It wasn't always pleasant but it had to be done, and she had no doubt of her ability to do it.

If only the company were making money.

"Well, shall we sit down?" she said, and began moving toward the lectern. Time, she thought, to perform.

She checked her notes as Weyandt dimmed the lights. She felt charged, alive, the way she did just before skiing a challenging slope. Watching the last members take their seats, she noted that the three outsiders sat together, while Peter, Hilda, Connie, and Luke grouped opposite them. Against the walls in an outer ring sat the vice presidents of Thunder Oil and the chief operating officers of the subsidiaries. They were there to listen, to answer questions, but never to speak out. The officer-directors—Frontino and McGehee—were together too, on the far end of the table from her. Significant? She dismissed it from her mind, cleared her throat, and began.

She started as always with the treasurer's report and the minutes of the last meeting, got them approved, then went on to discuss current activities, concentrating on her plans for a balanced restructuring. She called on Rogers to discuss the details of the refinancing and then on Frontino to talk about the new round of downsizing. By then she could hear snores from Luke Fleming. Blair was older than Fleming, but he wasn't sleeping. He was wide awake, staring at her and taking notes.

After Frontino, she introduced Gerald Rinaldi, the chief engineer for TBC Environmental Services. Rinaldi had come from New Jersey on the recommendation of friends. He was a hard charger from the word go and had built the bioremediation plant in Chapman under budget and on schedule. He made a short presentation, complete with a computer-generated animation of the slurry-phase bioreactor system, and giving five-year throughput projections. She could see, looking around the room, that she wasn't the only one who was impressed.

When he was done she opened the floor to comments. The first pencil up, and she nodded. "The chair recognizes Mr. Kemick."

"Ms. Thunner, I don't want to be too blunt, but do you have any plans to turn the P&L picture around?"

"Yes, we do. I've already talked about our cost-cutting initiatives. But that's only half the equation." She outlined the new sales program and showed them slides of the new packaging for Thunder Premium. She discussed the expansion of the Lightning Lube quick-oil-change outlet chain into Ohio. She had a five-year revenue projection for the Chapman plant to match Rinaldi's report. McGehee caught her eye and she gave him the floor for a report on First Raymondsville's uptick in loan placement. Kemick listened politely, but when they were done said, "Perhaps I put the question wrong. I meant to ask, do you have any long-term plan for returning the company's core business from loss to profitability?"

She decided it was time to squash this issue. "Mr. Kemick, the distinguishing characteristic of the fossil fuel industry is and always has been volatility. Except for the limited amount of local crude we actually produce, the basic costs of our raw materials are out of our hands. The market fluctuates with every coup in the Mideast and every new discovery in Turkmenistan. We are in the midst of an extended downturn, but that downturn will not last forever. We are having a lean year, but so is everyone else in the industry. I believe this presents not only a challenge but an opportunity. I understand your concern, but our core business is sound. I must caution you not to pull up the flowers to see how the roots are growing."

"Besarcon comprises thirty-seven different corporate entities, and through thick and thin we're maintaining a ten percent growth rate. We expect Thunder to stay with the pack."

"Mr. Kemick, I agree that growth is good. But the Thunder name is a promise to our consumers. I'm not going to break that promise in the name of one or two quarters' growth. We produce a premium product. Once we lose that reputation for quality, once we become just another producer of a commodity, the cheaper oils and gasolines will undersell us and we will be gone."

"You misread me," said Kemick gently. "I see the possibility for growth primarily in your subsidiaries. Environmental services, industrial chemicals, and health care—these are all growth sectors. Your investment should go into these areas. I agree, you put out a fine oil. But the refinery's too small to be economical much longer. I don't want to see you waste your efforts fighting for a lost cause."

Ainslee said, "Thunder Oil is not a lost cause. It's how we define ourselves: the company that produces the best motor oil in the world. Too many companies today try to do a little bit of everything, whatever pays. I don't want the core to be carried along by the subsidiaries. I want them all to be strong, with Thunder strongest."

The young man from Wilsonia, Parseghian, said, "I understand what you're saying about volatility. But I don't think we can just sit and wait for a turnaround. At Wilsonia we recommend that when a company's not doing well in a given environment, we need to either restructure it so it does better, or else change to another environment. What Mr. Kemick is saying is in line with that."

"It's not an either-or choice," said Ainslee. "We are moving ahead deliberately to develop all our profit centers. This is what I mean by a balanced restructuring. The downsizing is part of that. It will leave us slimmer and meaner when the market heads up again. At the same time, we are growing our subsidiaries as fast as we see business for them."

Now Blair, the oldest man there, lifted his white head, and she said, "Mr. Blair. What does Texas have to say? You're not going to tell me to get out of oil, are you?"

"You mentioned additional debt in your initial presentation," Blair said quietly, and she thought, yeah, he saw it. "How much are you thinking of taking on, and what will you use it for?"

"Right now we're at a twenty percent debt to equity. Our credit rating is double A. With the Fed dropping the prime rate again we can refinance and take on an additional twenty percent of debt, total forty percent, and maintain the same rating."

"Where will the new investment go?"

This was the nut, and she didn't pull the punch or soften it in any way. She said, "I'm going to aggressively purchase gas and oil leases, prospects, and smaller production companies. I want to acquire enough reserves so that when the upturn comes, Thunder—Thunder *Oil*—will be in a stronger long-term position."

Silence around the table. She didn't let it stretch out too long. "Are there any other questions?" There weren't, and she said, "Thank you, everyone," and stepped away from the lectern. The men all rose and she nodded to them and permitted herself a tiny smile.

She didn't get away till after the follow-on round of obligatory hors d'oeuvres and drinks, but finally the elevator closed on the last director. She went back down to her office, closed her door, and sat pretending to read several letters Twyla had prepared. Actually she was going over the meeting again, analyzing each remark and response and comparing it with what she'd planned.

She gradually became aware that she wasn't happy with it. Everyone had been perfectly courteous. But there had been too many questions. A strain afterward, as they held martinis and scotches and talked about golf and skiing. They don't like what I'm doing, she thought. Well, that's okay, it's their job to protect their investments. But it's my job to save this company and the six thousand people who work here.

It might be worthwhile, though, to try to build more support. Just in case push came to shove. Build some bridges to the outsiders, Blair, Kemick, and Parseghian. Another possibility might be to outflank them. Add more people to the board. Ten was a little low. Who? Titus White came immediately to mind. White Timber and Real Estate. A solid man who understood what the Thunners meant to the area. Who else? Another officer-director? Or somebody quite different? Suddenly she remembered Rinaldi's crisp, dispassionate presentation. She didn't mind strong people on the board—as long as they could be counted on never to challenge her leadership. White was too old to take over, and Hemlock County would never accept a Rinaldi at Thunder's helm. She had to think about things like that now. Especially since she'd never had the son everyone expected of her.

She turned her mind away from that and went back to work.

Late that afternoon she was standing beside the Land Rover, looking at the sky and wondering at how warm it was, when a car pulled up beside her in the lot. "Where you headed?" Rudy asked her, and she noted the fine lines around his eyes, the hint of gray.

"Home. Cherry Hill."

"You looked good this afternoon. You cracked the whip and they fell into line."

"You're exaggerating, but don't stop, it feels good."

"I've set up that trip. Hey, you got any idea how tough it is finding a hotel with an indoor pool, midtown Manhattan? I finally found one. The Parker Meridian."

"East side or west?"

"Kind of central. Between Sixth and Seventh, Fifty-sixth Street."

"That's actually—that's actually very thoughtful of you, Rudy. But I don't think I'm going to have time to go."

"We could see Kemick while we're there. His home office is in New York. He could use some stroking, some person-to-person contact."

"I was thinking the same thing," she said, looking at him with new interest.

"But you didn't think of combining it with a show, did you?"

"I'd need to pack. Set somebody up to watch Dad."

"Erika and Lark can watch your father. I'll set up the appointment with Kemick. All you have to do is go. All right?"

"Maybe." She looked down the drab, colorless streets, the gritty wet pavement, and looming over it, like ramparts penning it in, the hills. Suddenly she decided he was right, she needed a break. "Okay, let's do it. Next week?"

"Good," said Weyandt. They smiled at each other, and then she got into the car.

Ten

Halvorsen stood at the north cliff of Town Hill, where it dropped away in a clearcut. From here you could see across the valley all the way to the blue clustering of pine forest around the Pringle Creek reservoirs. He could see Beaver Fork, too, and the abandoned lookout tower away off on Allen Hill. The pale shadows behind it were New York State. Such a crisp, clear day; he felt like taking another walk. That was the way it was once you started gallivanting around, he thought. It put an itch under your hide.

Instead he turned his back and went on through the woods, slogging his way through the half-melted, slushy snow, and after a few hundred yards came out on the bare southern crest. He looked back for the dog. Nowhere in sight. He was opening his mouth to call her in when he remembered he'd left her in the basement. That seemed to be happening a lot these days, and every time it happened he felt silly, absentminded, old. He hated it . . . He shook the feeling off impatiently and examined the sky. This warm spell wouldn't last long; if he wanted to go anywhere he'd better take advantage of it. Finally he spat into the mush and dead grass and went down the steps, scraped the mud off his boots, and went on into the warm.

Don't know what the hey is going on, he said to himself, sitting in the worn chair with his stockinged feet resting on the stove bumper and the hound snuffling and crunching at her dry chow in the corner. The fire glowed with radiant heat. Every time he saw the paper it was worse. Well, he wouldn't have to live through the bad times. Come to think of it, the thirties hadn't been the height of comfort. The Depression, strikes, floods. Then the war. He still felt a shiver of gratitude they'd won. The stories the guys coming back told about Dachau and China, well, you had to be thankful Hitler and Tojo hadn't had their way.

He got up restlessly and opened a can of soup and put it on the stove. He wasn't hungry but he tried to eat three meals a day. That was another trouble with getting old; once your health started to slip it was hard as hell to build yourself up again. And he'd slipped pretty far in prison. He picked up a Max Brand and then had to hunt around for his spectacles. He tried to read but lost the thread and sat just staring at the blurry print on the yellowed pulp page. He put it down and noticed the soup bubbling. He got up, shuffling around in stocking feet, got a spoon, and ate it from the pan. Then cranked the pump and washed the spoon and put it away and put the empty can in the paper bag out in the cold room so it wouldn't smell.

What now? he asked himself.

As if in answer something thudded at the outer door, making him jump. Hardly anyone came out here all year but Alma, he thought, then all of a sudden it's Grand Central. He passed a hand over his hair, adjusted his glasses, and checked his fly. Least I got pants on this time, he thought, and jerked the door open.

"W. T. Halvorsen?"

He stared out at an apparition: a fiftyish man in a camel's hair coat, a tweed hat, green scarf. Rubbers on his shoes. Even a tie. "Yeah," Halvorsen grunted.

"I'd like a word with you. May I come in?"

He hesitated, then stood aside. The other stepped in, admitting a blast of wind that made the flames whip and quiver in the stove. He put his shoulder to the plank door and shoved it closed. The man took off his hat and unwound the scarf, looking around the basement. "Pass inspection?" Halvorsen grunted.

"Excuse me?"

"You're giving her the once-over, figured I'd ask."

"It looks comfortable."

"It's a goddamn hole in the ground."

"Well, I see what you mean," the man said. "But it could be worse. That your dog there? Nice-looking hound. At least you're warm . . . My name's Youndt. John Youndt, go by Jack. Y-O-U-N-D-T." He held out his hand and after a moment Halvorsen took it, not very eagerly. Some kind of salesman, what he figured the guy for.

"What can I do for you, Mr. Youndt?"

"Call me Jack." Youndt felt in his coat and extracted a brown-paper parcel. When he pulled the bottle out of the damp, wrinkled bag Halvorsen saw it was a pint of Seagrams. "Join me in a drink?"

"I'm off the stuff."

"Oh. They told me in town . . . never mind. All right if I—"

"Go right ahead," Halvorsen told him. He got him a clean cup. Then he got another chair, this one straight-backed with lathe-turned rungs, chipped and paint-stained now, but once it had been part of a dining room suite, and put it by the stove for himself and motioned to the easy chair. "Thanks," said Youndt, pouring a small one, tossing it off, and grimacing companionably. "Sure you won't join me?"

"No. What's on your mind, Mister Call-Me-Jack Youndt?"

Youndt tipped one more splash and capped the bottle. He set it on the floor as he let himself down into the easy chair. Jess headed for him and Halvorsen grabbed her tail. When he was down and settled he said, "I wanted to come out and talk to you concerning some inquiries you made about the Medina Transportation Company."

"Oh. Oh, yeah," Halvorsen said, relaxing now that he knew what this was about. He turned the spare chair around and perched himself stiffly on it, propping his arms on the back as the dog turned around twice and settled herself again on the worn spot in front of the stove. "That whiskey's not going to warm you up. People say that, it don't. I can make us some coffee—"

"Not for me, thanks." Youndt unbuttoned his coat and grunted comfortably. "That fire sure feels good. They say it's gonna get cold again next week."

"So, did you find out who was beating on that Chinaman?"

"I'm sorry?"

"Who was beating on the kid. Whatever he was."

"Sorry, I don't really know what you're talking about."

Halvorsen sat motionless. "All right," he said, alert again. "You don't know what I'm talking about. I figured you for a detective, lookin' into a report I made. But you don't know nothing about that. So why don't you tell me just exactly who you're with, and what you come all the way out here to see me about."

Youndt cleared his throat and sat forward. "Mr. Halvorsen, I'm an attorney. I practice over in Coudersport, the Potter County seat."

"I know where Coudersport is."

"Uh huh. Well, I understand—maybe we're talking about the same thing—that you reported seeing something in the woods."

"I see a lot in the woods."

"Something you reported to the police. Is that what you meant, about the 'Chinaman'?"

"You're an attorney?"

"That's right."

"Who you represent?"

Youndt cleared his throat again. "As I said, I do civil practice in Coudersport. Occasionally I represent the Medina Transportation Company. That's a natural gas producer active down south of here, down around the Hefner River."

Halvorsen was absentmindedly reaching for a chew when his thoughts tripped over something. "Down around where?" he said.

"The Hefner. It's a tributary of the Allegheny, comes down to meet the river through Derris—"

"I know where it is. But you said the company's active there. You mean what, pumping stations? Reservoirs?"

"No. Gas wells. Way south of Derris."

"You sure about that? I thought you said they was out of Coudersport."

"Not exactly, Mr. Halvorsen. I said *I* was out of Coudersport. But it's the closest town of any size to their operations—you know how small Derris is—so they do most of their business out of there. The leases themselves are down to the south, on national forest land. Floyd Hollow? You might know that."

"I heard of it. You work for them, you were saying."

"Well, the company's asked me to come out here and find out more about these allegations. Stories like that drifting around can be a source of concern."

"Everybody tells stories," said Halvorsen. He was hunched forward, studying the man in front of him with the intensity of a wild animal that, confronted by something new, feels both fascinated and threatened. "Still a free country, ain't it?"

"Sure is. But there are laws about false accusations, libel, slander."

"I'm feeling a little slow today, Mr. Youndt. What are you sayin'? Spell it out for me."

"That means spreading rumors like that, it's against the law," said Youndt.

"An' if I keep on?"

"The company could prosecute."

Halvorsen's cheeks contracted in a stubbled smile. He leaned to the stove and spat, and it spat back, hissing-hot. "What, send me to jail? I don't hardly think so. They don't have room for every geezer shoots his mouth off. Hell, they let me out two years early, and that was for blowing up a bridge."

"That's a good point," said Youndt. "I made a couple of calls before I came out here. Some interesting things. First, that you've got a reputation as a troublemaker that goes way back. Back to the nineteen-thirties, in fact. And right now you're on parole. Any trouble with the law, you go back to prison. No trial necessary. Just a hearing. You know Judge Mixson?"

"I know him," said Halvorsen, feeling his arms going tense.

"I know him too." And the way Youndt said it told Halvorsen clearly and exactly that what he meant was: if Youndt, or whoever had sent him, had a word with Mixson, then Halvorsen would walk out of that hearing in shackles again. The lawyer reached down again and Halvorsen noticed the red mottle of his cheeks and nose and wondered how much of a practice he really had and how much he'd drunk away.

"But I really did not want to go to any talk of things like that. If I myself had seen something like you describe, I'd report it too. But the company looked into it. There was a fight, a disagreement between two of the workers. They've expressed their regrets and shaken hands. So it's been settled, and we don't see any point taking it any farther. This has been explained to the police. But the company's asked me to go the extra distance, to come out and put your mind at ease."

"I appreciate that," said Halvorsen dryly. He got up and searched around in a gloomy corner. Something fell with a clatter and Youndt started, craning around to see what he was doing.

Halvorsen came back out into the light carrying a piece of heavy, thick wire rope. Youndt frowned at it. "That's what they were using on him," Halvorsen said. "Not this long, but the same size as this sucker rod line. I seen men fight before. Mixed it up myself more than once, when I was younger. This wasn't no scrap, two guys getting an understanding between 'em. If that little fella wasn't dead when they threw him in the truck he wasn't far from it. I could hear his bones breaking."

"I see you're a man who makes up his own mind. What will it take to convince you?"

"Show him to me," said Halvorsen. "That little fella who's well enough to shake hands and make up." He stalked away and the cable clattered back into its corner and then he came back into the light. "Bring him here, or take me there, and let him tell me how he wasn't really hurt. Then I'll shut up. Till then, I'm gonna ask Nolan about it every time I run into him. Threatenin' me won't do you no good. Or bringin' me liquor, either."

"You're a stubborn man, Mr. Halvorsen."

"I ain't blaming you. I figure that's how you make your living. People hand you sacks of their mess and say, go clean it up."

"In this case, I happen to believe them."

"Have you seen this guy? The one that they said wasn't hurt that bad?"

"Matter of fact, I have."

"An' now you're lyin' about it." Youndt's eyes slipped away and Halvorsen said harshly, "Or you would of known what I was talkin' about at first, about him being a Chinaman, without my havin' to explain it to you. You warmed up now? Good. Now get to hell off my property."

When the lawyer was bundled up again and gone, Halvorsen stood in front of the stove, angrier than he'd been in many a day. He'd told Youndt he wasn't mad at him, but that was a lie. He was mad at every son of a bitch who took money to kick dirt over other people's mess. At every bastard who held his hand out to let the law go by. He'd worked for everything he ever got, and seen too many good men bleed to make another dollar for people who had more than they needed already. It just wasn't right and never had been, and if some smooth-talking son of a bitch thought he could scare him off or trick him, well, they were setting themselves up for a fall, that was all.

He crossed the floor and his stockinged foot hit something hard. He bent and groped and felt smooth curved glass. Without looking at it he jerked the stove door open and threw it in, not uncapping it, just chucking the bottle in. A second later there was a thump inside the heavy iron, like something was fighting to get out, and the flames danced blue and the biting smell of hot alcohol crept into the basement.

He stood in the center of the underground room and stared at the flames. His nostrils twitched. His hands began to shake.

It hadn't been that different a day from any other, till the end, but he remembered it all. There was no picture of his wife here, but that wasn't because he didn't remember her. It was because he remembered her all too well; even after all these years it wasn't a minute didn't go by without him remembering her.

She'd hit him in the face once with a potato. Yeah . . . when she was pregnant with Alma she'd gone into the utility room one day and picked up a sack of potatoes. Unnoticed, they'd gone rotten, and the bottom of the bag too; and when she lifted it the whole thing had suddenly disintegrated, and the rotten, stinking potatoes had made a sound like mushy thunder and rolled all over the floor, under the washer, brown slime everywhere. When he'd come in to see what was going on she was on her knees, crying. He'd made some kind of joke and she'd flown into a rage and snatched up a potato and let him have it, right in the kisser. Well, every marriage had its low points . . . but all in all they'd had it good. They'd been happy. Up till the end.

Halvorsen reached out slowly, bracing himself against the hot chimney pipe. In the dark basement he stood trembling, seeing again things and people lost forever, years gone, decades vanished.

It had happened on a Sunday. As usual he started the day with one or two and kept the fire lit all day long with an occasional shot or a beer in front of the television. So that later, getting the chainsaw ready, he happened to spill some gas while he was filling it. Not a lot, but enough to make a puddle on the linoleum floor of that same utility room. He didn't bother to wipe it up, or think about what might happen. Just picked up the saw and went on out to the woodpile.

While he was out there the fumes must have gotten to the water heater. When he heard the explosion he ran for the house, yelling for her to get out. When she didn't answer, or he couldn't hear her over the flames, he tried to get up the stairs but the smoke drove him back, seared his lungs so bad he must have blacked out.

Because the next thing he remembered was waking up outside, lying with his face pressed against the grass and beneath it the dead cold of the earth. Jenny had been so proud of that lawn. The way it opened out the woods, letting her look out the big window to see the hills and valleys, never the same, always changing; the blue shadows that lay across them in the winter, and in the summer the soft green of thousands of treetops; and what she liked best of all, autumn, when the forest exploded into a million shades of orange and yellow and scarlet, tangerine and brilliant siennas. And he'd turned his head and saw her lying in her flowerbed, below the second-story window she'd pried open. Her head was twisted sideways, and a little later she'd stopped breathing, just him and her alone when she died, their home and everything they owned burning behind them.

And since then, the old man thought savagely, you just been waiting to die yourself. Minding your own business, not because you're better than any of them, because you ain't and anytime you pretend you are you're lying to yourself. Because you are waiting for judgment for what you did by your own hand. He clutched his face, digging his fingers into his eyes. "Son of a bitch," he whispered, trying to stop thinking about it, trying to think about something else, about anything else.

So what was he going to do? Because the fact Youndt had come out to see him meant nothing was going to happen as far as Chief Nolan was concerned. More than that: meant Nolan had told them he, Halvorsen, had been asking questions. Just that they'd paid a lawyer to come out and warn him off meant something was as stinking rotten as those potatoes. He didn't know much about lawyers, just always figured an honest man didn't need one. You either did something or you didn't, and the more you complicated that the farther you got from the truth.

Not that he figured they had anything to worry about from him. What harm could he do jerking his jaws in the Brown Bear? Nobody listened to him anymore. When you got old that happened; people pretended to, but you could see their eyes sliding past, eager to get to something important. As if you weren't really there, or as if nothing you'd seen and learned mattered anymore. While the one thing you did learn after sixty or seventy years was that nothing was new, just the same damn stuff happening over and over. . . . He could keep bothering Nolan, but he didn't think it would do any good. He could tell Bill Sealey, down at the state police barracks. He'd always figured Bill for straight. But odds were he'd just say there wasn't anything he could do. Unless there was something more he could give him, something solid to work with.

He came dully back to where he was, staring at the stove. The blue flames had burned out. The fire had sunk to a weak red glow. He banged the latch open with the heel of his hand and swung it out to reveal a bed of coals. He grabbed a chunk of beech and threw it in and banged the latch closed again and bent and worked the grate. A mist of hot ash filled the room and he sneezed twice, quickly, and wiped his nose on his sleeve.

He started to sit down and then stopped, hunched over, struck by a new thought. Something off center about what Youndt had said.

Halvorsen let himself down into the easy chair. He felt for a chew and bit off a piece and leaned back and the dog came up and thrust her head under his hand. And sitting all alone in the dim silent basement, scratching her ears, he slowly started trying to work it all together. What he'd seen in the woods, and what people said. What Joe Culley had told him about the company, and what he knew himself from too goddamn many years working and hunting this godforsaken corner of Penn's Woods. A long time went by, and every once in a while he leaned over and picked up a coffee can and spat black juice into it and then set it carefully back down.

Finally he had it. What had struck him as wrong.

If what Youndt said was true, that Medina had wells south of the Hefner River, well, then, somebody had made a mistake. Or something was screwy. Because there wasn't any gas in Floyd Hollow any more than there were diamonds or gold.

Sitting there in his worn easy chair he opened his memory, like a box he'd put something in once and hadn't opened in forty years or more.

To find that he remembered it clear as clear. Working for Thunder then, forty-eight, the big push after the war. They'd taken five light cable-tool rigs up the Hefner on sledges. That was the year Dick Myers had died clutching his chest, face white as paper as he tried to drag a tree off a rod line. Halvorsen always figured the pace old Dan Thunner set helped kill Dick, though it wasn't really anybody's fault he had a bad heart.

Anyway, they'd gone out after the seis work, after the geologists had set off their charges and haggled over their graphs, and Halvorsen's and four other teams had started hammering down well after well. As he recalled they'd hit bottom of water around four hundred, four hundred and fifty feet, and drop the water string and go on with a $7\frac{7}{8}$" hole down to the top of the target formation, whatever that was. You could tell when you hit the Oriskany. The cores came up looking like granulated sugar, white, or a little yellow if there was iron in it. They'd drilled well after well, in formations the geo boys swore were three-sided traps, and came up with nothing. They hit one small pocket of oil, and a faint sniff of the unmistakable sweet Oriskany gas came up with it, but not enough to do anything with but cap it and move on.

And finally he worked his way down through the years to what he wanted: the one they'd put down in Floyd Hollow itself. They'd chewed their way down through the sand and gravel and small stones near the surface down into the rock. Sixteen hundred feet to the Bradford Sand, five thousand to the Oriskany, six thousand to the Medina, all the way eight thousand feet plus to granite basement and nothing but a whiff of carbon monoxide, dry as the sands of Mars in those Edgar Rice Burroughs books with the almost-naked ladies on the covers.

The kicker was that ten years later he'd opened the *Century* and read about Consolidated lucking into a huge trap not twelve miles east of where they'd drilled. The Lorana had flowed at five million cubic feet a day. But that too, Christ, big as it was, the Lorana had played out in the 1970s; it was a storage field now, full of pipeline gas pumped up from Louisiana and Texas.

So there was something that just could not be explained, at least not by sitting here and thinking about it: that certain people were acting like there was gas where there wasn't. True, Youndt had said south of Floyd, not Floyd itself. But south of there was nothing, just empty hills and wild country, a huge tract of wasteland: the Wild Area.

He got up and stalked around the narrow basement, and suddenly it was no longer home but what he'd told the lawyer it was, a hole in the ground, narrow as a grave. He looked at the high slits of windows and thought: I got to get out of here. Been cooped up too long. One thing Alma and them were right about, it was getting harder to get around. If he didn't keep limber, pretty soon he'd be fit for a nursing home and nothing but.

He began moving about the dim underground rooms, pulling together as much by habit as conscious thought the things he'd need. His old down-filled mummy bag. The army surplus pack he'd carried on some of the toughest hunts of his career. A mess kit. The basics: salt, coffee, lard and flour for biscuits, dried beans, bacon. A coil of light cord, a ground sheet, a light hatchet. He tested his old Case on his thumb and decided it could stand a sharpening. When it was razor-keen he dropped it and his Zippo into the pocket of his old red-barred hunting coat.

He didn't have to think about what to wear. The same long johns he had on; two light wool shirts, one over the other; heavy melton pants with suspenders and a wide leather belt. A patch pocket wool shirt and a down underjacket. Cotton socks under heavy wool. He perched himself on the chair and started pulling his boots on; considered for a moment, holding one to the light; got down a can of strong-smelling grease from a shelf.

He didn't bother with a compass or a map. But he looked longingly up at the empty line of pegs. No gun, that'd be eight or nine pounds less to carry. But he sure would feel more comfortable taking one along.

Pack slung, he paused by the door, glancing around the room. The lamp was out. The fire would die by itself. He was ready to go, except for one thing. And that was in town.

"Forget it. It ain't anything I can take you along on," he told the dog.

She whined, peering up at him, and he started to close the door on her, then thought, what if he didn't come back? What would she do then, all alone out here? Finally he opened the door, letting her out. Pulling the door closed behind them, he climbed heavily up into the light.

The interior of his son-in-law's garage was so hot, with the doors pulled down and the oil burner roaring in the corner, that sweat popped out on his face the minute he stepped inside. The shining barrel of the hydraulic lift gleamed. Steel clattered as Pankow and his assistant stripped the nuts off a rusting Taurus wagon perched over their heads. Halvorsen stood in the doorway till Fred noticed him. He let go a final burst and hung the air wrench from the chassis. When he put his hands to his back and stretched they left black greasy prints over his kidneys. "Racks," he grunted. "What you doin' back here again? Forget somethin'?"

"Come by to pick up some things. How's your cold?"

"Shitty." A bell rang and Pankow said, looking out the glass, "Frank, get the pump."

"Business?"

"The fuckin' Sheetz is cutting the ground out from under me. I can't get my supplier to go any lower. It's gotta be bootleg gas. You know they can't be paying taxes on that stuff, not at that price . . . How you doing?"

"Okay."

"Too bad about your buddy," Pankow said, going back under the car. His head disappeared, his voice echoed, as if he himself were inside the muffler he was taking off.

"What buddy?"

"Din't you hear? One of your old pals died. That Charlie Prouper."

"He what? He died?"

"You know the parking garage over the Star Lanes? The one backs on the river? He had his old car up there, had it in storage. An old green Club Coupe. They took his license away years ago but he had it up there and every month or so he'd go up and start it to keep the engine oiled. Sometimes drive around the garage real slow. Yesterday he rammed it through the back of the building. You can see the hole. It went right through the wall and flipped over in the air. Mrs. Schoch, used to teach at the high school, she was standing on the bridge and saw it all. It turned over in the air and landed in the river. They got him out but he never had a chance. Car's still there, sitting there upside down."

"They think he done it on purpose?" Halvorsen said slowly, remembering the last time in the Brown Bear; remembering Prouper, air hissing through the silver hole in his throat: *But I tell you one thing. I ain't going back to that there hospital ever again.*

"No, Nolan figures he was up there playing around and it just got away from him. Got in gear and went right through that old rotten part of the back wall."

Halvorsen stood silent for a moment more, horrified. But then he thought. It ain't so different from what you always figured to plan for yourself. Is it?

Pankow was looking at him expectantly, as if he'd asked him something he hadn't answered. He said, "Sorry, what'd you say?"

"Said, you thought about what Alma said? About movin' in to town?"

Halvorsen didn't answer. He looked out through the grimy dirty glass to where Frank was bent over a pickup's open hood. He said, "Fred, I come by to get me one of my rifles back."

Pankow coughed and spat. Rusty steel rasped as a length of pipe subsided into his hands. He tossed it on the scrap heap in the corner and slid shiny curved metal from a box. "C'mere, hold this while I bolt her in," he said, and Halvorsen obediently lifted his arms and held it while Pankow positioned the power wrench.

"Son of a bitch, that's loud. Like to make you deaf."

"Tell your daughter that. She just thinks I don't listen to her."

"How about it, Fred? I think the lightest one, the .218. The little single-shot."

"Them ain't yours no more, Racks," said Pankow, squinting up at the muffler.

"I know, but I need one of 'em back."

"Law says you can't carry one no more."

"Them's my guns, Fred. I just gave 'em to you for safe keeping. And now I'm going out for a little hike, so how about loaning me one back for a couple of days. Oh, and I tied Jess up in the back yard with your dog. Maybe Alma can feed her for a couple days, till I get back."

"Why? Where you going?"

"Told you, out for a hike."

"Well, I ain't got all them guns of yours no more," said Pankow, suddenly loud, suddenly angry. "You gave 'em to me, they're mine to do with, ain't they? A guy come in, we were talking, he said he'd like to pick him up a hunting rifle long as it didn't cost an arm an' a leg."

Halvorsen said quietly, "How many of 'em did you sell, Fred?"

"You don't need them no more. You're too old to be out in the woods anyway. Alma's right, you need takin' care of."

Too angry to speak, Halvorsen left him standing there and picked up his pack in the office and went out by the pumps. He walked out into a sudden light flurry of snow.

Okay, he thought, I'd feel better taking a rifle along on this but it looks like I ain't going to. Am I still going? But even as he asked himself he knew he was.

There wasn't anything else he could do. The cops wouldn't bother. Nobody else cared. All he could do was satisfy himself.

Head bent, he trudged down the street until he was lost in the dancing snow.

Eleven

Jammy was coming home that day, and Becky wanted to stay home from school and help. She told her mom she could read to him, or play games on the bed. But her mom said no, she had to go. So she got dressed in the cold and went out to the bus stop. Sitting on the ripped vinyl, she worried about him for the whole long ride as the seats slowly filled with kids from Derris and Carrier Creek and Triple Band Run. The sun was up when they got to Raymondsville but it didn't bring much light with it. Everything looked dingy and cold, the snow on the lawn, the halls, even the kids shouting and fighting. She sat through class after class, hardly listening to the teachers. In science, though, they had a video called *Our Bodies, Part III: Blood.* She watched it with total concentration, alert for anything that might help Jammy. It talked about white corpuscles and red blood cells, but it didn't say anything about what was making her brother sick.

The bell rang, but Mr. Cash stopped her as she was leaving. "Becky? See you a minute?"

He sat sweating at his desk, white-shirted stomach pressing over the pulled-out drawer like the dough inside an undercooked bun. His black grade book was under his hand. "Becky, your dad called me. He said you want to be a doctor. That right?"

She didn't answer. Just looked down at her feet.

"Do you really think you can handle being a doctor? Because you're not looking very good in our biology module so far. Are you?"

He must have seen she wasn't going to answer that either, because he sighed. She could smell him, aftershave and chalk dust and the stuff they kept the frogs and fetal pigs in. The boys said he drank it, back in his trailer, but she didn't think so, it was just that he was around it all day so the smell got in his clothes. He lowered his head and she could see through his hair down to the pink skin on top. There were hairs growing out of his ears too. Then she remembered to pay attention to what he was saying. "Anyway, I want to give you another chance with the frog. Okay? Individualized attention. So you don't have to carry that *F* around for life. You pick a day, I'll stay late, we'll do the lab together."

"Will I still have to cut it up?"

"Well, that's the point of the lab, Becky. To teach dissection techniques, as much as the location and appearance of the various organs."

"Then I won't do it. You'll just have to fail me again."

Cash heaved another sigh. "Okay. Let's try it again. Why won't you do the dissection?"

"I just think anything that's alive is special."

"So do I, that's the whole point of this course, isn't it?"

"Yes, sir. But I don't need to kill things to prove it."

"You are *not* killing it. The frog is *already dead*," Cash said between clenched teeth, his cheeks turning an interesting shade of purplish-red. It was a little scary.

"But that's just letting somebody else do it for me."

"Do you like hamburgers, Becky?"

"We don't eat meat at our house."

"We have it in the cafeteria."

"But I don't eat it."

"Well at least you're consistent." Looking at the grade book, Cash blew out heavily, making his stomach yearn against the desk. "All right, here's how we'll handle it. I will do the dissection. You will observe and take careful notes. It's not in accordance with our teaching guidelines, though, so you have to promise me you won't tell anybody else about it."

Becky really didn't want the *F*, and she felt a lightening of her heart at the possibility of still passing. "Thank you," she murmured.

"So, when do you want to make up the grade?"

"Wednesday?"

"This Wednesday. Back in the storeroom. Do you know where that is? Out back, the mobile classroom, by the fence?" She nodded and he made a note. "Okay, then. Better go or you'll be late for your next class."

She grabbed her books and ran through the halls, already empty, the doors slamming shut like traps as she flew past. She pounded into the echoing gleam of the gym and into the side, slamming her locker open beside Margory Gourley just as the bell rang.

"You're late," said Margory.

"No, I'm not." She dialed her combination and snapped the lock open. The next moment Margory was reeling back, arm pressed against her face.

"Oh, *gross*. Your locker stinks like shit. Don't you ever wash your gym clothes?"

Becky didn't answer, ashamed. She couldn't say Margory was wrong; the smell had hit her so hard when she opened the metal door that she'd gasped. She'd forgotten to take them home again. Margory turned away, said loudly to the other girls pulling on sneakers and T-shirts and shorts, "I can't stand a pig. She hasn't had her stuff washed since we were in fifth grade."

"Shut up, Margory."

Anne Masters said, "*You* shut up, Becky. She's right, I can smell it way over here."

Margory said, "She's such a pig and so dumb. She's going to flunk a whole grade because of a *frog*. And her family's atheist and her germy little brother has AIDS. I don't know why they let her keep coming to our school—"

Her back was to Becky and her hair was swinging right next to Becky's hand. She didn't think or anything, just grabbed it and pulled. Margory shrieked and fell backward across the bench and her head slammed into the sharp edge of Becky's open locker door. The next minute she was crying and there was blood everywhere, on the tile floor and the bench and all over Margory's white Raymondsville Ravens T-shirt.

"What's going on in here?"

Mrs. Fieler stood like a bad cop at the door to the basketball court. "Gourley, what's wrong with you? Are you hurt?"

"I fell," Margory said, giving Becky a hate-filled look through her bloody hair. She whispered, "I'm going to kill you, me and my friends, you scummer bitch."

"Wash it out under the shower with cold water. Scalp cuts bleed a lot, but it'll stop in a minute," the coach said. She came in another step and jerked her thumb over her back and they ran out shouting onto the shining wooden floor. She gave Becky a close look as she ran past. "You need a bra," she yelled into the auditorium after her. "Tell your mother to get you one, Benning. I want to see one on you next week. Understand?"

She stood on the road in the dark, the doors hissing shut behind her. The bus rumbled up the road a few hundred feet to the turnaround, then ground into reverse. The motor grumbled and roared, then its headlights came back, growing stark black shadows from every stone and stick and furrow around her. She waved to Mrs. Schuler and heard her tap the horn.

The bus loomed past, tires crackling. The horn wailed back from the hills and the trees and then it was gone, a red glow shrinking off down the run, a fading, faraway growl moving away down the mountain.

"How was school?" her stepfather asked when she let herself into the great room. The stove was humming and the house felt stuffy after outside. He was sitting on the sofa reading one of his computer magazines.

"Okay."

"What did you learn today?"

"Oh, a lot of stuff. Is dinner ready?" She looked at the stairs but didn't move toward them yet.

"Just a little while," said her mother, from back in the kitchen. "It would be ready sooner if you'd offer to help."

She went into the kitchen and started cleaning carrots. "Where's Jammy?"

"Upstairs."

"What did they say when they let him out? Is he . . . okay now?"

"He's better," said her mother. "Don't put those peelings down the drain! Put them in the compost container."

"Mom, I brought my gym stuff home to wash. And Mrs. Fieler said I got to get a bra."

"You don't need one yet."

"She said I *have* to have one by next week."

"Well, we'll see."

A little while later they sat down to eat. She wasn't very hungry. Charlie asked her if Mr. Cash had talked to her and she said yes, she was going to do a special makeup lab with him. Charlie smiled. When they were done she said, "Has Jammy had anything to eat? Can I take him some of this pudding?"

"I guess so. But don't wake him up if he's asleep."

She wanted to ask more questions. Was he really better? Could the doctors do anything? Would he have to go back? But one look at her mom's lips, pressed into a thin line like a scalpel cut, told her not to bother asking. They'd just lie to her to make her feel better. To make them all feel better. Except that Jammy wouldn't, would he?

Her brother's room was dark except for the stars and planets shining on the ceiling. She couldn't hear him breathing or making any sound at all, and for a second she was afraid. Then she saw his eyes were open, looking toward where she stood. "Jammy?" she whispered. "You up?"

"Yeah."

"Can I come in? Are you feeling better?"

"I don't know. I don't feel real good."

She sat down and after a moment turned on the little light on his dresser. He blinked and said, "Shut it off, Becky," but she'd already seen how bad he looked. His face was all broken out. She felt sad, then mad. That damn Margory.

"Did they treat you okay at the hospital?"

"Uh-huh."

"I brought you some pudding."

"I don't want any. You eat it."

"You should try to eat some."

"I don't want any," he repeated, and stirred under the tousled covers as if the bed was too narrow and couldn't give him any rest.

"Did you take your methoprim yet?"

He shook his head, and she went and got it and a plastic cup of water. She held his head and he took the pill, then lay back again with his wrist over his eyes. She was about to tiptoe out when he said something. "What?" she said.

"Tell me a story."

"All right. Sure. You want the one about the little red tractor, or the Doughnut Princess, or the leprechaun—"

"No," said her brother. "Tell me the Wolf Prince."

Becky hesitated. It was his favorite story but she didn't want to tell it again. It was from an old book they'd found under the stairs in the house on Market Street. It was so old the pictures were like old postcards, glued on the pages, and somebody had colored them by hand. At first they seemed pretty but the longer you looked at them the creepier they got. And the book had been in Johnsonburg so long it smelled when you opened it, like something dead. She'd read it to him once and then he wanted to hear it again every night. But one day Charlie found the book and threw it away. He said it was sexist and too scary for kids. He did that to a lot of their things; like he wouldn't let them read *Green Eggs and Ham* anymore because he thought it was about drugs. She didn't know about the sex part but he was right, some of the stories in the old book were so scary she could hardly stand to read them. But by then she didn't need it anymore, she knew it by heart from reading it to Jammy so many times, and he remembered every word, so she had to tell it the exact same way every time. She was sick of it. But he was watching her, his dark-hollowed eyes so intense and eager that she sat down again on the bed and looked out the window at the moon shining on the snow and the trees and said, reluctantly, "The Wolf Prince." Her hand smoothed the covers.

"Once upon a time a poor woodcutter and his wife lived deep in the forest. They had one little child, named John, who they loved dearly. But they were so poor that often they did not have enough food for him, much less for themselves. So the little boy grew up sickly and then one winter, despite all they could do, he died.

"One winter evening soon after, the old woman was walking through

the woods, when she saw ahead of her a handsome young man lying in
the snow. His hair was long and silver and his mustache was black, and
he was dressed in a long silver cape. She was afraid at first, but as she
drew closer he did not move at all or answer her when she bade him good
day. So she hurried to her house and told her husband. Together they
carried the young man home and laid him by the fire and gave him hot
water to drink, for that was all they had. And by and by he woke, and said,
'Do you know who I am?'

" 'No,' they said.

"He said, 'I am the prince of these woods, and you have saved my life.
Therefore ask of me anything you wish.'

"The two old people were puzzled, for they knew the king of that country had no son but only a daughter. They did not know of any prince who
lived in the woods. But being polite, the old woman just said, 'Alas, we
are old, and riches can do us no good. All that we truly loved was our
child, our little son. Even if we had as much gold as there is wood in the
mountains, it could bring us no happiness, for now he is gone.'

" 'Where is your little boy?' said the young man; and when they told
him where they had buried him, he said, 'What was he worth to you?'

"The old people shook their heads, shocked. They had no answer to
such a question. The prince said, 'I ask this for a reason. I can bring him
back, but if I do, you must give me what you cherish most.' The woodcutter and his wife smiled sadly, for they owned nothing of value. But the
young man persisted, and at last they agreed.

"Then the prince went out with them to the little mound where they
had buried their son, and he held out his hands, and called him forth,
and their boy rose up from beneath the icy ground, and shook off the
snow like a shirt, and greeted his father and mother with tears of joy on
both sides. But after some time the prince reminded the old people of
their promise, and said that in exchange for returning him to life, he
would demand what they cherished most: their son. 'He will be well
treated, and he will be my godson; but you shall never see him again.'
The old people sobbed and wrung their hands; but at last they bowed
their heads and agreed that they must be content with their bargain. So
they told the boy to follow the man with the silver hair. With that the
prince threw a purse full of gold on the table, and with many kisses the
old parents and their son bade each other a fond farewell.

"No sooner were they out of sight of the cottage than the two old
people heard a wolf howling in the woods. But that was not so strange in
those days and they thought nothing more of it. So they went to bed,
marveling at all that day had brought.

"Now little John was alone in the forest with the prince. He was afraid
and lagged behind, and the young man kept looking back and urging
him to follow. 'For you must trust in me before I can show you my magic,'

he said. At last John assented. The prince bent and picked him up and the next moment they were whirling through the air on an icy gust of snow. They rode the wind over the mountains, and the boy shouted in wonder. At last they descended and came to a great palace deep in the woods. The walls were of gold and the roof was of diamonds, and the furniture was of silver studded with precious stones. There, the prince told him, he would live always. Little John was afraid again, but when other children came running and the prince hugged them and tossed them laughing in the air he felt better. Then they all went in to a great banquet and the little boy forgot his fear as he ate all he wanted for the first time in his life. The prince stood watching the children, smiling, and then he went to a door and unlocked it with a golden key and went inside. And they did not see him again that night.

"John lived there very happily, playing with the other children and dancing to the music that came from deep inside the palace, until he forgot what it was to be hungry or sick or cold.

"But at last the day came when he was tired of singing and playing all the day long. Also he had noticed that occasionally one of the children would disappear and never be seen again. So one day when the prince was playing with the littler children, and had laid his silver cloak across a chair, John went and searched it and found a secret pocket. He put his hand in and when he took it out there was the prince's key, of bright gold and set with blood-red rubies. The boy's first thought was to put it back, but then his curiosity got the better of him and he decided to keep it a little while. So he tied it on a string and hid it around his neck.

"That night the prince, who was very fond of him, sent for him. 'My boy,' he said, 'I have lost something that was very dear to me, and I wondered if you had seen it about.' But John said that he had not seen anything of the prince's.

"The prince said that what he had lost was a golden key, and that if one of the children found it, they must quickly return it. 'Everything else I have is yours for the asking, but the golden key you must never use,' he told John. But the boy thought only of what wondrous thing he might find that the prince had to put under lock and key.

"That night, when everyone else was asleep and the palace was dark, John crept to the great door and opened it with the golden key. He passed through three rooms, each of greater beauty than the one before. For the first was of copper, and the second of silver, and the third of gold. At last he found himself in the prince's bedchamber. It was lit by a single candle of red wax. Very quietly he stole near and picked up the candle, raising it to light the bed.

"But when the candlelight fell on the form sleeping beneath velvet covers, John saw not a man but a huge silver wolf, with great pointed black ears and huge cruel teeth of curved ivory. And his hands shook so that a drop of the hot wax ran down, burning his hand and dripping onto the wolf's pillow.

"The next morning the prince called John to him, and said, 'John, did you steal my golden key?'

" 'No,' John answered, holding his injured hand behind him.

"Then the prince took his hand, and saw the burn, and knew that the boy had lied to him.

" 'Are you quite sure?' he said again. 'You did not unlock the great door?'

" 'No, I didn't.'

"The prince looked sadly at John, and said: 'I know you have stolen the key and opened the door to my chamber. I cannot let you stay with the good children any longer, but you will always be my godson.'

"As he spoke he laid his hand on John's head, and suddenly they were whirled up out of the palace on a blast of snowy wind. John sobbed and clung to the prince, terrified, but the prince did not relent. Over the mountains and forests they flew on the icy blast. The next thing he knew he was alone in the midst of a dark forest. He ran back and forth searching for a way out, for a house, a light, or a path back to the palace; but all was in vain. Seeing this at last, he crept into an old hollow oak tree for shelter, weary and cold, and cried himself to sleep.

"For ten years John lived in the dark wood, eating roots and berries and often going hungry. His silken clothes became faded rags. Then one day the king's hunt rode through the forest. The king himself was chasing a stag through the underbrush when his horse stumbled at the lip of a crag. But at the last moment John leapt out and stopped the horse and saved him from the fall. The king, grateful to this ragged hermit, dressed him in new clothes and hung him with jewels and brought him home to his castle.

"As soon as they rode through the gate his daughter, the princess, saw John. Her father had often tried to find a husband to please her, but she had refused them every one. Yet she fell in love with John the moment her eyes fell on him, and so happy was the king that she had finally found someone she loved that he gave his permission for the princess and the poor hermit to marry.

"A year later a little son was born to the royal pair, and the whole kingdom rejoiced. But that night John looked out the window, onto the snow, and there in a ray of moonlight stood the Wolf Prince. Great and silver and terrible, with eyes like fiery rubies and huge curved ivory teeth. The wolf growled, 'Will you confess now that you stole from me? For if you persist in denying it, I must take from you what you cherish most.' But John clung to his falsehood, and denied it. And so the wolf took the child and vanished with it.

"The king found John standing at the window with the baby's swaddling clothes in his hand, and the cradle empty, and the tracks of an immense wolf in the snow. And all the kingdom mourned, believing he had thrown the child to hungry wolves so he could reign himself when the old king died. John was brought before three judges, and though he told the truth, no one believed his story, and they condemned him to be burned in the marketplace. At last the day came for him to be burned, and John was tied to a stake, and the fire set alight.

"When John felt the heat of the flames, and knew he was to die, he was filled with remorse. He remembered how good the prince had always been to him and how he had rewarded his generosity with treachery and falsehood. And he cried aloud, 'Oh, Wolf Prince, I confess my theft! Here, here is your key, which I have carried ever since around my neck, cursing its weight, but too proud to repent of my sin! If I am still your godson, forgive me my lie. Let me die for my wickedness, but return my innocent child to his mother!'

"Suddenly a swirl of snow filled the square, and blanketed the flames, so that they hissed and went out. And there in the midst of the people stood a beautiful young man in a great silver cape, and in his arms laughing and smiling, the baby. Too happy to speak, John took the infant and held him up, and all the people cheered. And a great feast was held in the castle, which the Wolf Prince attended. John lived with his princess and their children in happiness and plenty for the rest of their days, and if I am not mistaken, they live there still."

She thought her brother was asleep when she was done because he didn't move. So she tried to get up quietly, without shaking the bed. But his hand crept out. "You still awake?" she whispered.

"I was scared in the hospital," he whispered.

"I guess it wasn't any fun, huh?"

"Mom don't want me to say that. And Charlie just says I got to be brave. I ain't so brave, Becky. I'm really scared." He sniffled. "Will you sleep with me?"

"Sure, Jammy. I'll sleep right here with you. You go to sleep now, okay? It's gonna be all right."

She lay there until his breathing smoothed out and his thin little arms and legs stopped twitching. Then she had to pee, so she got up softly and went out onto the loft landing.

Down in the great room the stove rumbled and hummed, feeding the flickering flames. She looked down at her parents sitting across the room from each other, her mom with her *Prevention*, Charlie with his *Compuserve* magazine. They looked lonely, and worse, they looked helpless.

Her brother was dying. They didn't want her to know but she did. They didn't want to admit it to themselves, even, but it was true. Unless somebody did something, he was going to die. Who would save Jammy? Not the hospital or the doctors. They didn't know how. Not her mom or her stepdad.

She understood then, trembling in the dark at the top of the stairs, that if anybody was going to save her little brother, it would have to be her.

Twelve

L eah looked down at the mangled, frozen body on the examining table, struggling to stay detached. It helped to bite down on the inside of her cheek. The pain brought tears to her eyes but distracted her enough to keep on with the examination. She held the sheet turned down for a long time, exposing the body from ice-clotted black hair to the bottom of the torn belly, as the two men in fluorescent orange cleared their throats and shifted their weight.

She asked them, "Were her clothes like this when you found her?"

The older man said unwillingly, both anger and guilt in his voice, "Yeah. Just like that. All we did was carry her down the hill and put her in the back of the car. What, we should have just left her there?"

"I didn't mean that. Where exactly did you find her?"

"Up on Gould Run, back up the long hill there—I don't know what its name is. Not far from the road to Derris. We weren't hunting, but Will here got a new Marlin for Christmas. We was up there sighting it in."

"This is your son?"

"No, just a buddy from work."

"How did you find her?"

The younger one, Will, said, "We was plinking at some crows on the snow. Then when we got up closer we saw what they were pecking at."

Friedman reached up and turned the lamp to "high," making the men blink and shield their eyes. Grasping the left shoulder—she could feel the resistant coldness even through the rubber gloves, like a roast just taken from the freezer—she braced herself and half-rolled the slight, small body to the left, exposing the back. Mangled and shredded too. But all shallow wounds. The deep tears and bites on face, breasts, and neck were the most likely cause of death. The throat in particular was badly torn. The arms were too rigidly frozen against the chest for her to make a more thorough examination, but she bent to examine the hands. Though they were crimped into claws, she saw what she expected: jagged punctures in the soft flesh of the thumb root. A black rime under the broken nails would turn out, she had no doubt, to be blood. Both were typical defensive wounds.

"Looks to me like some kind of animal got her," the older man muttered. "Something big and mean."

"Maybe. But what?"

"I been wondering that myself. She's been dead a while, hasn't she?"

"It will be hard to determine, frozen like this."

"What I'm getting at, we couldn't have—"

"Oh, I don't think there'll be any question about that. And I'm sorry you misunderstood about—about her clothes. Okay? But I'd like you to stay a little while longer. I've called the coroner and the state police. You'll have to tell them what you just told me." She looked down again and sighed. "You can wait in the other room if you want."

They thanked her and left, looking relieved. Leaving her alone in the brightly lit examining room, staring down at the bare small feet. They looked cold. She knew it was silly, but still she felt better when she'd covered them with a towel.

She'd have to check the depth of the puncture wounds. But it looked to her as if what had killed this young Asian woman, perhaps twenty-five years old, five three, one hundred pounds, with the marks of a previous pregnancy on her belly and the pinch of early starvation in the curve of her ribs, had been several sets of sharp teeth.

She picked up a metal probe and bent forward, eyes narrowed against the burning light.

When Charlie Whitecar cleared his throat at the door she straightened and dropped the probe rattling onto a stainless steel tray.

The Hemlock County coroner stood in his black car coat and gray fedora rubbing at warmth-fogged glasses with a wadded scrap of tissue. Like most country coroners he was a mortician by trade, a thin, bent, sober man. His name was Whitecar, like the creek; his family had been in Hemlock County for a long time. Now he finished polishing his wire rims and put them on one ear at a time, like an old man, though he was only middle-aged.

"Hi, Charlie."

"Leah."

"The two guys in the waiting room brought her in. Have you talked to them?"

"Those two outside, yes. We probably ought to have Sergeant Sealey in on this."

"I had Martha call Bill at the barracks. He's on his way over." She stood back. He didn't speak, just looked down.

"Oriental," he said at last. "Or—possibly Indian?"

"Good point, Charlie, I didn't consider Indian. Indian is a possibility. My guess was Chinese."

"Uh huh. Then she's not from around here."

"There wasn't any ID with her. And I kind of doubt if there will be. Look at those clothes."

"Ragged," said Whitecar, disapproval shading his regret.

"Yeah, ragged cotton and no underwear. The buttons were missing but that could have happened in the struggle, whatever killed her tearing at her clothes. Short fingernails. No polish. No jewelry, ears not pierced, no wristwatch marks or ring marks. This one may be on the county. You want to sign the death cert or shall I?"

"You saw her first."

"Okay, but how do you do names? When you have an unknown, I mean? In New York we used Jane Doe."

"However you want to do it. Jane Doe is fine."

"How do you usually do it?"

"We've never had one here before."

"Oh. Never had an unknown body? Okay . . . let me tell you what I'm thinking. Cause of death: animal attack. But what kind of animal would do this kind of damage? How do bears kill, Charlie?"

"Black bears? Well, there's some biting. We had a boy bit by a bear five or six years ago. It was bear season, he shot it and thought it was dead till he got close enough for it to grab him. But mainly they bat and crush. Looking at this deceased, I would say that this is probably not the work of a bear. Besides, they're all in hibernation."

"Are they? Oh. Well, what else?"

"Could be dogs," said Whitecar.

"Wild dogs?" She thought immediately of Zias, the engineer. Funny, she hadn't heard anything else about him since he went to Maple Street.

"Feral dogs, yes."

"How about wolves?" she said, watching for his reaction.

There wasn't any; Whitecar's face stayed somberly placid. "There haven't been any of those around here for a hundred years."

"Could a wolf do this? Hypothetically?"

"A big dog, a wolf, a coyote—it's all a guess, isn't it?"

"Maybe we'd better stay with 'unknown animal.' I see lacerations, bite marks, tears about the face and neck. Proximate cause of death would be loss of blood and hypothermia."

"You're the doctor."

"Would you add anything to those findings?"

"Whatever you want to put down, that's fine with me."

"The funny thing is—the question I'm asking myself—Charlie, you with me?"

"I'm listening."

"What stops me is, the only actual feeding marks are on the back, and from what our noble riflemen say, those were ravens. Why didn't whatever killed her eat her too?"

"Maybe they frightened it off."

"I don't think so. I think it was gone and she was frozen long before she was discovered. Days, maybe weeks. No, we had that warm spell—it could still be there, four days she was out there. Next question: Who was she? Where was she from? Why was she wandering around out in the winter woods in the first place?"

The coroner said, "My vehicle is outside. Can you arrange for someone to take the deceased out to it?"

"Not till Bill gets here."

"Well, I can't stay any longer. I have another call to make. When he's done, please arrange for the deceased to be taken to the chapel. It is possible that a relative may turn up from out of the area."

"Okay, Charlie, thanks for coming by." She looked after him, then stuck her head into the waiting room. The two hunters were looking through *People* magazines. Through the window she saw the patrol car slide in, and said, "Here's Bill."

Sealey did his investigation, talked to the men, looked the body over, and took fingerprints. He asked the hunters if they'd noticed any tracks around it. They said no. Then he asked them if they minded taking him up to the site, and they said they would.

The door opened just then and a man with a mustache and thick glasses came in accompanied by a blast of snow. Two cameras hung from around his neck. The sergeant sighed. "Jerry. How'd you find out so fast?"

"These two lads stopped for gas on the way in."

"And?"

"The clerk called us. Everybody else is out, so I ran over here myself." The editor wouldn't let them leave until the older man described again his finding of the woman. Then he looked at Leah. "What about the body, Dr. Friedman? Can we get a picture?"

"It's pretty grim, Jerry. I don't think you'd want to run it in a family paper."

"Well, how about just a shot of the face? Maybe somebody will recognize it. Bill, that could help you guys out, couldn't it?"

"It might," said the trooper. Friedman thought that over, and finally let him go in. She covered everything from the neck down with the pale green sheet. The strobe flashed and whined three times before she said, annoyed, "All right. That's enough."

"Just trying to get the exposure right. What do you think, Japanese?"

"I think Asian of some kind. Charlie suggested Indian."

"I'll check with the Seneca tribal police," said Sealey.

"What do you think killed her? Polly down at Sheetz's said she thought it looked like a wolf got her. What do you think?"

"At this point we're still entertaining possibilities. Some sort of large canid is one."

"That guy who fell out of the tree, the engineer, he kept talking about wolves. I never ran that because it sounded crazy. But what about it?" He looked at Sealey, who shrugged, then turned back to her. "Doc?"

"Look, Jerry, I grew up in Manhattan and then I lived in Miami. You start talking animals, I don't know from whatever. Whitecar says it wasn't a bear. What else would attack a human being out there? Everybody keeps telling me there aren't any wolves. Well, maybe not, but we keep getting hints of something that looks a hell of a lot like them."

"Nice." Jerry Newton scribbled a last line and stood. "Thanks, Doc. Who says nothing ever happens around here? Bill, where are you going? Are you going out there where they found her? Well, there probably won't be much to see. If somebody ID's the body, will one of you call me at the *Century*? Thanks."

She watched them troop out, still talking, and wondered what the speechless and anonymous body behind her had set in motion. *Wolves*... the word carried both a shadowy threat and a sense of mysterious wonder. She turned back to the torn, sightless face that stared up into the humming light. Only then did Leah notice the muddy boot prints all over the clean tile of the examining room, and mingled with the mud, the pink of melting blood.

Thirteen

When her mother called, "Becky, time to get up," the first thing she noticed was that it was snowing. She stood in the pocket of shivery air between her bed and the window, looking out at the back yard, at the hillside. Under the greenish glow of the security light fluffy fat flakes were drifting down out of the dark. In the rippling green light everything looked like it was underwater, and the snow was dead stuff falling from far above to lie on the silent floor of the ocean, unchanging, forever.

"Beck-y!" her mom yelled again from downstairs.

"I'm *up*, Ma. Don't yell, you'll wake Jammy." She pulled on her stuff quickly, jeans and pink hightops and pink sweater with the standup lace collar. Too impatient to wait for hot water, she washed her face quickly in the cold and brushed her hair and flipped it into a topsy tail. Then she ran down the stairs.

"There's your gym clothes, I washed them. The bag too. It smelled terrible." She was getting herself cereal and didn't answer and after a moment her mother said, "You're welcome."

"Thanks a bunch, Ma. Where's Charlie?"

"Still sleeping, he was up late working on the Beta programming."

She was on her way out the door when she remembered and came back in again. "I almost forgot. Mom, I'm going to be at school late today. I have to make up a lab. Can you drive in and get me?"

"I guess so. Let's see, I can go to Bells, we need some groceries. What time?"

She said she guessed around four-fifteen, that would give her an hour to do the lab. Then she ran out, seeing the headlights of the bus shimmering like early dawn, coming up the run.

School was like always, boring, despite the incident in gym. Margory was very quiet. When they had to sit across from each other Gourley didn't even look at her. That was weird, but okay with Becky. Robert whispered her name in geometry, and she smiled, leaning toward him, but all he said was, "What answer did you get to fourteen?"

When the last class let out she put her afternoon books in her hall locker and waded back against a tide of bodies through the emptying halls to the back of the building. Honks, bleats, and crashes, the lame sounds of the school band practicing. From somewhere else, the hesitant notes of a piano. She was a bus student, so she hardly ever stayed after school. The shadowy corridors felt haunted. The echoing discordant music reminded her of the soundtrack to a horror movie, and she couldn't help glancing back over her shoulder as she pushed open the back fire door.

Outside the snow was still coming down, not hard or fast, just spiraling down as if it had all the time in the world. Still, there was an inch of new powder on top of the old. She shivered and pulled her coat tight as she crunched her way across it into the evening.

There were two trailers out back, "mobile classrooms," the teachers called them, like school was a show you could take on the road. They'd held classes in them years before, when the town had more kids, but now they were just for storage. Rust ran down the huge white boxes' corrugated sides like old blood, making them look like a giant's grisly takeout. They were perched on concrete blocks along the back fence, where the casket factory property started. The factory had been abandoned for years and brambles poked through the fence like skeletal fingers reaching for the kids on the softball field. Behind her the music lurched uneasily from bar to bar, carried on a chill wind. An old ladder was propped against the fence, reaching upward toward the darkening sky. She hurried across the last few feet of snow, seeing no other footsteps going that way except the big dragging ones she figured were Mr. Cash's. Under the trailers the shadows looked menacing, like someplace monsters would hide.

She tapped on the door, then jumped at the sudden yell of "Come in." She stamped her boots off on the mat, looking around.

The inside smelled of formaldehyde and other chemicals and something else, a sweet reek she didn't recognize. The window was dirty and smeared and not much light came in. Dusty towers of boxes marked "Edmund Scientific" and "United School Supply" were stacked around the walls, and metal shelves held cartons of glass beakers and tubes and things with lenses and black rubber plugs. She didn't see anybody and said hesitantly, "Mr. Cash?"

"Back here, Becky."

She slid through a narrow aisle between the boxes and through a door, and there was a little office and Mr. Cash sitting in a swivel chair with his coat off. An electric heater was whining away on the floor and the air was close and hot. "Take your coat off and stay awhile," he said. She unzipped her jacket, looking around, and finally hung it on a hook behind the door. The science teacher got up to close it, and she suddenly felt bad, remembering what she was there for.

It was on his desk, already pinned to its board. She knew it was dead but it was hard to believe having pins through you like that wouldn't hurt. The frog was so still he seemed to be waiting. Waiting for her.

"So how was your day?"

"All right."

"Ready to make up your lab?"

"Uh-huh," she said, forcing herself to look directly at the frog. It peered back questioningly with dead eyes. "Uh, is that it?"

"That's it." Mr. Cash sat heavily, creaking down into the chair, and picked up the scalpel. He sliced the little body open so suddenly and deeply she couldn't help making a faint squeal. "Take careful notes, now," he said, and she opened her workbook numbly as he started picking things out and pointing to them.

"There, this is the heart. Are you all right? If you're going to be a doctor, you need to get used to seeing things like this. And worse."

"Mr. Cash, that was my stepfather telling you about me being a doctor."

"You don't want to be a doctor?"

"I'm not maybe . . . smart enough. What I told Charlie, that's my stepdad. I said I wanted to be a nurse, and he said, why be a nurse, why not be a doctor. He said girls can be doctors, too. I mean, I *know* that. But it would be okay to be a nurse, as long as I get to take care of people."

To her surprise, her confession didn't make Mr. Cash angry. He seemed almost pleased by it, and smiled as he continued the dissection.

Finally it was over. She sighed as he dropped the remains into a trash bag and said gravely, "Good-bye, Mister Frog, and thanks." He pulled a wipe from a plastic container of Chubbs and cleaned his fingers, though he really hadn't touched anything, and threw that in the trash too. Then held his hand out. "Let's see your notes. You can sit over here, on the desk."

She perched, hightops dangling, as he squeaked his chair around toward her and opened her workbook. She looked at the top of his head for a while, then around the trailer again. It was so hot it made her head swim. When she looked back at him she noticed that now he was sweating, looking not at her book, but at her legs. She crossed her arms over her chest and hunched her shoulders a little, so her sweater didn't cling.

"Are those okay?"

"What's that?"

"My notes, are they okay?"

"Oh, yeah. They'll do. You know . . . Becky, a nurse or a doctor, whichever you decide to be, they have to cope with all kind of things," Mr. Cash
said. "Like, they have to know a lot about people. They see things not
everybody sees. Things they have to keep secret. Like, they have to know
about how women and men are different, and not be embarrassed or
afraid of that. Do you think you could handle that?"

What was he talking about? She shrugged. "Uh, I know about my
brother."

"You have a brother? So you know he's different, then. From you.
That's a start. But men are different from little boys, too."

"Uh-huh," she said, looking at the window, wishing he'd hurry up and
let her go. It was dark outside now and the glass was a grimy mirror. It
reflected her perched on the desk and the racks of stuff behind them and
Mr. Cash sitting at his desk. His hand was down in his lap, and in the
window she suddenly noticed that he was rubbing himself, behind the
desk.

"I can show you, if you want," he said, and his voice sounded funny
now, like he'd been running or exercising hard.

She didn't want to know or see whatever it was he wanted to show her.
She was afraid she knew what he was doing with his hand, behind the
desk. But she was starting to feel strange, faraway, like she wasn't really
there in the little hot room with the metal walls. She'd recognized the
sweet smell at last. It was cologne. *Mr. Cash had put on cologne for her.* She
didn't want to be here anymore and she didn't like this, her stomach was
squirming, she wanted to jump down off the hard edge of the desk digging into the back of her legs and run out knocking down boxes and
smashing glassware until she was back in the cold clean air. But somehow
she couldn't. She didn't know how to without hurting the feelings of the
fat red-faced man whose pleading eyes were fixed on hers.

She kicked her feet, face heating, starting to feel panic. Her mother
had said not to let strangers touch her. But a teacher wasn't a stranger,
and he wasn't touching her, either. What should she do? Maybe the best
thing was to pretend she didn't notice anything, then get out as soon as
she could. She cleared her throat and slid down off the desk, out of his
reach. "Uh, I guess I—"

"Do you want to?" he asked her again, urgently now. And again she
didn't answer, because she didn't know what to say. She kept staring down
at the floor. Worn-out speckled tile, a dead cricket squashed and dried on
it. But he must have taken her silence to mean yes, because suddenly he
stood up and she couldn't help looking, just for a second, at what he was
showing her. Under his belly, from a nest of black hair . . . she looked back
down at the squashed bug and said, not very loud, "Um, Mr. Cash," and

then, suddenly, from outside, came a yell and then a clatter, a bumping scrape against the outside of the trailer, and then more shrill screaming, going on and on as if it would never stop.

Mr. Cash gasped something she didn't understand, and stood there tugging at his pants. His face mottled and seemed to swell up before her eyes, as if it was going to explode. He said, in a harsh voice, "Get out. *Get out of here.*" She grabbed her workbook and ran through the trailer, hitting her leg on an overhead projector on the floor, but not stopping, she just wanted out.

When she jerked the door open there they were, Margory and Anne and Jenna Dusenberry, all standing in a circle. The ladder had fallen down in the snow from where someone had propped it against the trailer, and now running out from the school building, her sleeve clutched in Cathy Zaleski's fist, was Mrs. Fieler, mouth already set with the certainty of trouble.

Her mother didn't speak the entire drive home. It felt like they would just keep driving forever, never getting anywhere, like on the old *Twilight Zone* reruns they used to watch before they came to live with Charlie and couldn't watch TV anymore. Finally, as they turned up the run toward home, she said, "What exactly did he do to you, Becky?"

"He didn't *do* anything, Ma. Just talked to me, then stood up and showed me his, uh, penis."

She saw her flinch at the word. "Did he touch you?" her mother asked. Her voice sounded muffled.

"No. Huh-uh."

"Those girls said he did. They said you were . . ." Her mother didn't finish her sentence. That was not a good sign.

"They were *lying*, Ma. Those girls all hate me and they're lying."

"Why would they lie about a thing like that? What were you doing back there in that dirty place with him anyway?"

"I told you this morning, I had to make up a lab, that's why I missed the bus—"

"You know better than to go back into some . . . trailer with a man. Have you been back there with him before?"

"Ma, I told you I was going to, remember? But I didn't know he was going to do anything like that. I just wanted to get my grade raised so then Charlie would be happy. But he never tried to do anything to me. Mr. Cash, I mean."

"Exposing himself to a twelve-year-old is doing *nothing*?"

"No, Ma. That's not what—I mean, I just said that *they* said he was doing something else to me, like having sex or something, and we *weren't*. That was what Margory said and that's a lie."

"I can't believe they could let this happen. You don't seem to understand how serious this is. If he's done it to you, he's done it to other girls. And gotten away with it, till now. Exposing himself, that's only the first step. Thank God someone was there to see—"

"Mom, cool it," she said, "*please*," but she saw from the way her mother's knuckles were white on the wheel that her mom was not going to cool it in any way, shape, or form. She wanted to say that maybe it wasn't as bad as everybody thought, at least she wasn't hurt. That she knew what had happened *was* bad but it hadn't been nearly as horrible as everybody was making it out to be; and that she was afraid that if they made a huge deal out of it, like it sounded like they were going to do, it wasn't going to be just Mr. Cash that would be sorry, it would be her too.

But then she thought maybe her mom was right. Maybe it was worse than she knew and everything was ruined, now she'd never be a nurse or finish school or have a boyfriend . . . She started to cry, which was weird, she hadn't felt like crying up till now, just mad as hell at Margory and her lousy clique for being peepers and tattletales, for telling lies about her and calling her a scummer and a whore. She didn't want to ever go back to that school. She felt her mother's hand around her shoulders, heard her murmuring, "It's okay, darling, it's over now, he's never going to touch you again," but she didn't feel comforted, she just wanted to scream, everybody and everything was so screwed up.

At home everything was just as bad, worse, because she had to explain it all over again to her stepfather. And behind his pale expressionless face she had to guess what he was thinking, which made her so nervous she started crying again. Then he and her mom had a big argument. By the time she crawled between the cold sheets in her room she felt limp as her brother's floppy bear. She had meant to lie there in the dark and just wait, but she felt so wrung out she knew she'd fall asleep. So she turned the light on again and set her Little Mermaid clock, then closed her eyes and lay back.

And then, wouldn't you know it, she *couldn't* sleep. Just lay there, her body exhausted, but her hands kept making fists and things kept running through her head one after the other in a jerky blur like the videos in school when you fast-forwarded them. She felt dread at the thought of going back to Raymondsville. If only there was a way never to go back. But there probably wasn't. Her mind skipped back and forth. Mr. Cash's penis, like a fat thumb poking out from a snarly patch of black hair. Margory's face pressed to the window. Mrs. Fieler, mouth an *O* of horror as the girls screamed out the lies they'd made up. Mrs. Kim's stern black eyes. Mr. Cash standing outside the trailer in the snow, looking down at the trampled muddy slush, his shirttail hanging out and his lip quivering just like Jammy about to cry . . .

The alarm went off. She didn't recognize the noise for a long time, and when she did she yawned and groaned. It kept peeping and finally she stuck her arm out into the cold air, groping for it. She stared astonished at the glowing hands. It was only two o'clock.

Then she remembered. She started to turn over for a couple more minutes in the warm bed. But she made herself get up instead.

It was like getting up inside a refrigerator. The furnace didn't send much heat upstairs. She hunted around for her clothes, groping around in the clammy, still blackness, then under the bed for her flashlight.

Jammy looked so sound asleep that her hand hovered above his shoulder. As long as he was asleep, he wasn't hurting. She reminded herself grimly that this was for his own good.

"Ouch. Quit it. What are you doin'?"

"Shh, not so loud. It's me. Get up, come on. You got to get up and get dressed."

He was so sleepy he didn't protest as she pulled his pants and shirt and socks on. Only when she started to pull him out of the bed did he wail, startlingly loud, reaching back toward his bear, "Sleepyhead. I want to take Sleepyhead."

"All right, all right," she hissed. "Take him, but be quiet. You'll wake everybody up."

Her little brother moaned, head drooping as he held up his arms for his sweatshirt, then his coat. She didn't know how long they'd be out, so she dressed him extra warm. When he was ready he looked like the teddy bear, a round ball of coats and sweaters and snowboots and mittens and hat. She went quietly out onto the landing and looked down into the great room. The fire made jumping frog shadows on the wall. The only sounds were the subterranean rumble of the blower, the ticking of the clock, and far back in the house Charlie snoring.

"Okay, come on," she whispered.

She held his hand as they went down the stairs. Like always, Charlie had left a bunch of mail and stuff on the steps at the bottom, and she steered Jammy around it grimly. Still his snowsuit caught the corner of a box, and it tipped over before she could catch it. Some electronic thing fell out and clattered away. She held her breath, waiting for her stepfather to come out and ask coldly what was going on, but the snoring kept on.

"Where we going, Becky?" Now Jammy was awake, whispering too, eyes wide.

"Out back. Come on."

"It's dark. It's the middle to the night."

"That's right. Come on, come on. The dark won't hurt you."

"No, it won't hurt me," he repeated in a doubtful murmur.

As she eased the back door closed the cold hit her in the face, making her gasp. The security light was a green vibrating star. Bright close to the house, it made the blackness beyond it more immense and more threatening.

"What are we doin', Becky?" he murmured again.

"We're going up the hill, Jim-Jam, that's where."

"Won't hurt you," he murmured, but he didn't say anything else as she tugged him forward by the hand.

Last winter when Jammy had felt better they'd played on the hill. Charlie had built a log bridge across the creek and past that was a field slanting up and then came the woods. They slid down the field on a red plastic toboggan. You had to drag your feet at the bottom or you'd keep going right through the winterberry bushes and down the rocks into the creek. So she knew her way at first. The green star faded and their shadows stretched out farther and farther against the snow. She crunched along, dragging Jammy by his mittened hand.

By the time she reached the trees it was too dark to see. She took out her flashlight and turned it on. The beam seemed thinner, weaker out here than it did in her room, as if something was soaking up the light. There was a way up through the woods, a path, and she pulled Jammy along, taking it real slow so he could keep up, fitting his smaller boots into her footsteps. The snow was up almost to his middle.

"Where we going, Becky? What are we gonna do?" he said again. She searched for words to tell him. The trouble was, she wasn't sure. Why were they climbing in the dark till the windows of their house were only pale squares far below, till the green star flickered, whipped by the bare black branches of the trees, till the forest surrounded them, and the wind was roaring in the treetops and invisible snowflakes stung their faces? The truth was, she didn't really know. But she knew it was important, special, and the only way it could be done. So she just muttered, "Come *on*, Jammy," and tugged him on up the path.

Till they came to the Rock.

The Rock was the farthest she'd ever been up into the woods. It jutted out of the hillside huge and jagged like a giant's clenched fist. When you stood on top, where the knuckles would be, you could see all the way down the valley. In the summer they'd built a fire below it. Roasted marshmallows till they bubbled black at the edge and their guts turned gooey and ran down the stick. Now that summer friendliness was gone. The Rock loomed up in the falling snow immense and dark and the shadow of it made a shiver run down her back like she was facing something alive and powerful and maybe evil too. She felt her cheeks freezing and her toes too, and Jammy was sobbing now as he stumbled after her, but she kept on till she got to the clearing under the Rock. That felt like a good place to stop, so she did.

But now that she was here, what was she supposed to do?

She turned the flashlight off. Standing very still, holding her brother's hand, looking into the dark. She murmured, not very loud, "Is anybody there?"

Only the wind answered, hunting restlessly through the treetops, rattling the hard branches like brittle, clattering bones.

"We came to see you," she tried again. "We came to . . . ask you something."

The nervous click of dark limbs, the sigh of the wind. But no answer she could understand. It took all her determination to pull Jammy's hand again, climbing a few feet higher. It was even blacker there, but she resisted the impulse to turn on the flashlight again. "Who you talkin' to, Becky?" her little brother whispered, and she jerked his hand with a fierce insistence and hissed, "Keep quiet."

Because she heard it now.

She had called and it was coming. From back in the woods, moving through the dark between the trees. She could hear the soft crackle as it set down its huge paws. She could hear its breathing. She knew what it was now, what she was calling *Here boy, here boy* to.

It was what you saw when you had a fever. The thing that comes in nightmares, when you're so scared you can't move to get out of bed and turn on the light. She trembled, listening. Above her head the sky was black as if the sun had never been made.

Jammy whimpered. She glanced down and saw he had one thumb of his mitten in his mouth. That was when she knew it wasn't just something she was imagining, because his eyes, filled with terror, were fixed on the same place as hers. She shook his arm to make him quiet and tried again, hearing her voice quiver and break. "I can hear you out there. Come out, come out, wherever you are."

The clash and clatter of dead branches answered her, and the wind. Then, from far away, a long, abrupt, eerie cry: three long, mournful falling notes that echoed till she couldn't tell where the sound came from. Jammy cried, "What's that, Becky? What's that?" She stood trembling and said, "I don't know. Maybe just an owl."

But she didn't think it was just an owl. There was something else out here watching them through the falling snow, something that didn't call or cry out, that hardly breathed. She was so scared she had to go to the bathroom. It was just like a nightmare, only worse, because she knew she was awake. Her hand came up slowly, pointing the flashlight, feeling for the button on the back of Dumbo's head. If she pressed she'd see it, just for a minute. But her thumb wouldn't work right, it slipped. Her heart was going bang, bang, bang. Her hand started to shake. Somehow the flashlight slipped out of it, and fell, and she heard it hit the snow.

"No, *no*," she said.

It must have heard her. Because, very slowly, as she stood trembling, the woods became empty again. Silent except for the clattering branches, the hiss of falling snow. Everything looked the same, but it wasn't. It had been there. But now it was gone.

She'd failed. She murmured to herself in horror and relief and self-reproach, "*Damn, hell, you stupid bitch.*"

Her brother whined, "I'm cold, can we go back now?"

That was the last straw. She spun him around and hissed, "Shut up, I'm tired of you crying. Look, you scared it off." She bent and felt around in the snow. Her stiff fingers found the hard cold cylinder of the flashlight. She turned it on to light their way back.

That was when she saw it, there in the snow.

She started, then dropped to her knees, examining the mark in the round ring of light. Jammy started to walk over it, and she pushed him back.

It was a footprint. There were more, beyond it. No, that wasn't what it was called, it was a *track*. Like a dog track but bigger. A lot bigger.

Was it a sign?

She looked at it a while, then back at the woods. Finally she decided it was all she was going to get, at least tonight. She gave Jammy the light and told him to hold it steady. As if lifting a newborn kitten, she scooped her hand gently under the print. The first crumbled apart but she tried again and at last got one up all in one piece. The snow was wet and packed together but finally she held it in her hand. A whole huge track. *His footprint.*

"Okay, Jammy, we can go home now. You first. Be careful on the bridge."

They got back to the house okay and she held the snow-print awkwardly with one hand while she fumbled the door open with the other. Then she had to figure out how to get Jammy undressed and back into bed. Finally she put the piece of snow in the refrigerator, in the kitchen, and took him upstairs. She got him undressed and tucked in and then went back down. She got some Saran Wrap out of the pantry and slid it under the snow and carried it back carefully up the stairs, holding the two ends of the plastic wrap, and took it into Jammy's room.

"Okay, now. Hold still," she said, and lowered it till it rested on his forehead. He lay quietly, eyes closed, not complaining about the cold, and she held it in place as the wind-driven snow skittered at the window.

She realized then, looking down at his closed eyes, something she'd never thought of before: that love didn't always make you feel good. Sure, there was happy love, parties and friends and hugging, but there was other love too. Sad love, angry love, wrong love—like Mr. Cash's, was that some weird kind of love? There were all kinds, all different. But all parts of caring. Some just about themselves, others about people who could be hurt, who could hurt you, who could make mistakes. Who could die . . . she sat half-comprehending, not really understanding but feeling it trickle down inside her. Making her not any happier but older, somehow.

Sitting there beside her sleeping brother, she suspected for the first time that maybe growing up was not going to be so great after all.

Fourteen

Her knees trembled as the little jet jerked and creaked, climbing into the turbulence. Ainslee didn't like flying in small planes. The curved ceiling walled her in, reminding her she couldn't get out, till her heart raced and her mouth went dry. Rudy passed her a glass and she sipped gratefully. Poligny-Montrachet. "Sorry, no peanuts," he said and she laughed. The hills fell away, the clouds blotted the windows with white. The air smoothed and she leaned back and relaxed and even, God help her, felt grateful to Rudy. This was what she needed, a little time off. Between worrying about Dad, about the company, trying to anticipate every threat and see to every detail—sometimes she got so wound up she felt frantic. Too stressed out even to sleep.

"Everything calm at Cherry Hill?"

"I think so. Erika's staying there, and Dr. Patel will be looking in daily; and of course Lark will take care of anything special Dad needs, and more or less be at his beck and call."

"He's a treasure, your Lark."

"I don't know what I'd do without him."

"He's been with your family a while."

"Dad just picked him up by the side of the road one day, outside Philadelphia. He was fifteen. No family. No money at all, today they'd call him a runaway. Dad talked to him a little while, liked what he heard, gave him a job, and looked out for him. And he's grateful."

"Mark Twain," said Weyandt.

"What?"

" 'If you pick up a starving dog and feed him and make him prosperous, he will not bite you. That is the difference between a dog and a man.' I may not have the quotation exactly right, but that's close."

"That's a pretty cynical way to look at it," said Ainslee.

"Maybe you're right."

"So, where are we headed?"

"Straight to town. We'll check in first, relax a little. See Kemick at three. I don't know how long that will go so I didn't schedule anything behind it. Dinner at six, a new Thai place. Then the play." Weyandt took his glasses off and put them away. Leaned back.

"This is really very nice of you, Rudy."

"I want you to enjoy yourself," he said quietly, and for a moment she almost liked him. Before she remembered that was exactly what he wanted. But now he was talking again, they had a two-bedroom tower suite, Central Park view. She said that sounded fine.

They landed at Teterboro in fog and blowing snow after a forty-minute flight. The limo was waiting but there was a six-car pileup in the Lincoln Tunnel and they didn't get to the hotel until one. That didn't leave much time till the appointment so they checked in, had a quick lunch at Shin's, in the hotel, then headed downtown to the World Trade Center.

Besarcon was in the west tower. The lobby of the great building was high-ceilinged, corporate-sterile. They checked in with security and got badges, then headed for the massive elevator banks. Ainslee felt her ears crackle as they soared relentlessly into the sky. She felt dizzy, as if the steel-girdered fabric was moving slightly beneath her feet.

When they stepped off on the fiftieth floor the corridors were being ripped up, cables were being replaced under the floors. A young man showed them past the workmen to Quentin Kemick's office.

Kemick had his coat off and sleeves rolled. He looked rumpled and tired, as if he'd been there all night. He welcomed them in and showed them to an L-shaped couch in the glassed-in corner of his office. At least, she thought, he had a good view. Beyond the Battery the Upper Bay blazed silver so far below it made her skin crawl, and Liberty lifted her lamp with her back turned to America. Kemick offered them drinks, asked how their flight had been, how long they'd be in town. Then segued seamlessly into Thunder's financials.

"When I first looked you folks over, it was obvious you had problems, but the kind we could help you turn around. We don't buy junk at Besarcon. We almost always keep the original management. That way we get an experienced team, good business systems, an established position in the market. The value we add is capital investment, financial controls, and a much broader view of the long-term movement of the economy.

"Now, Ainslee, you know I have serious concerns with the way Thunder's performed over the last few years, and where industry fundamentals say you're likely to go. None of this is new to you, if you're as sharp as I think you are. In fact, I'd guess that's why you're here, to try to persuade me your approach is the right one."

"Go on," she said, unable to stop smiling. Not that his message was fun to hear, but the man himself had that knack of somehow making you like whatever he said. As long as you were listening to him, at least.

"All right, I will. We can't stay with yesterday's industries. Pennsylvania grade was the best there was—once. Today synthetics are as good if not better. So there's no real advantage in paying more for Thunder Premium."

"Synthetics are more than twice as expensive."

"The price differential's not enough of a penalty to turn off the people who buy top of the line. The drivers who bought Thunder Premium are going to buy Amzoil or Mobil 1, and the rest will reach for Cheap Willy's in the cardboard can. Your future lies in diversification."

Ainslee said, keeping the joking tone, "But you can say exactly the same thing about anything else we can do. Nursing homes. Bioremediation. Electrical components. We try to grow out of our regional niche, we're going to be just another little company competing with Tenneco and General Dynamics. *That's* risk. The country will always need oil and gas. I'm cutting costs and increasing productivity. But I'm not going to diversify away from our region and our expertise."

Kemick looked out the window, watching a tug and a string of barges making their way slowly out to sea. He said, "You really feel that strongly that sticking with your traditional core is the proper strategy?"

"Yes."

"Rudy, how about you? Any thoughts?"

"I agree with Ainslee, of course," said Weyandt quietly.

"Well, you're president and CEO, Ainslee. It's your call," said Kemick. "Taking on more debt, though—are you sure you've milked all the cash from everywhere else?"

"Yes."

"Who owns the Thunder Building?"

"I do."

"I take it you mean the company. If I was in your shoes, first thing I'd do would be sell it. Then lease it back. Put the equity into productive assets rather than brick and mortar. Do the same with every piece of land you own, except the one under the refinery."

She had to grit her teeth to swallow her first response, that her dad had built that building, she'd helped lay the cornerstone. "That's worth considering."

"I've thought about your product line too. To grow in a static market, you've got to expand product range. Correct?"

"That's one strategy."

"How about this: a low-priced Thunder motor oil. You buy a bulk generic, maybe a recycled oil, repackage it, and position it on the low end of your line."

Ainslee wondered if the old man was trying to provoke her. Beside her Weyandt said, "It might be worth doing some research, see how low we could come in on the shelf."

"Good. I'll say one thing more. Your man Frontino—have you given any thought to his successor? Who'll step into his shoes?"

"Ron's only been with us for three years."

"My benchmark is six. After a man's been in charge for six years, he's ready for a change. Either retire him or if he's still young, give him more challenge somewhere else. If you're interested, I can start looking for a place for him at one of our other companies."

"We're very happy with him."

"Then there's no need to look into that. Was there anything else I can help you with?"

"I don't think so. We just wanted to drop in."

"I'm glad you did." Kemick hoisted himself up and accompanied them out to the lobby, apologizing for the torn-up floors and asking them to stop back the next time they were in town, he'd set up an evening at the Met. "I'm something of an opera buff," he said, ducking his head and grinning like a bad boy.

They had dinner, then walked to the show. The air was chill but bracing, and she felt that lift of the heart she always felt in the city; the sense of limitless possibilities. The canyons of buildings were like yet so different from the Hemlock hills. After the show Rudy insisted they try a new club. Two cocktails, a hailed taxi, and when he put his arm around her shoulders in the hotel elevator she found herself thinking: Perhaps . . . perhaps. It wasn't good business. But it had been so long. Maybe it would be wise to find out, once, what she'd be missing. She was still thinking about it when he asked quietly if he might come in for a few minutes. She said of course, to help himself to the bar, she'd be right back. He poured himself a Johnny Walker straight and one for her, then occupied the couch.

"What did you think of Kemick?" he called through the open door to the bedroom. "What he was saying?"

She looked at her naked shoulders in the mirror. Everyone said she had shoulders like a man. She took the shoulderpads out of dresses when she bought them. It was the swimming. She brushed out her hair, then searched her suitcase for the green silk dressing gown. She called, "He's got a lot of experience. But so do we. I think we're right."

"Maybe."

"You sounded pretty sure about it when he asked for your opinion."

"What was I supposed to do? Disagree with you in front of one of our investors?"

She came out, tightening her robe, a frown starting between her eyes. "You mean you *don't* agree?"

Weyandt took a reflective sip. "Sure I do. I just think he might have a point, too."

"We should abandon oil? Sell the Thunder Building?"

"No. But he's right, we can't hang onto the past forever. That was what your dad tried to do. And we damn near went under."

"I know, Rudy. That was the whole point of the reorganization. To broaden our base. But now we need to dig in and get the core healthy again."

"Can we stay afloat that long?"

"If we can keep a positive cash flow from the Medina operation."

"And what if we can't? If something happens to that—"

"Nothing's going to happen," she cut him off. "Prices have got to rebound. When they do Parseghian and Blair and Kemick will tell us how right they were all along to let us have our head. Watch."

She looked down at his head. Gray, now, but still attractive. She'd known him a long time, from way before her marriage. Long enough to know if there was a first move, she'd have to make it. But there would be complications. Was it worth it? Was it a diversion from what she owed her every waking thought to, which was the revival and preservation of her company? Hell, she thought then. I'm an executive, not a nun.

She bent slightly and kissed his hair. Then, quite naturally, she was in his arms.

"You know something," he said, holding her, "I've loved you for a long time. Since you were, oh, at least twelve. Know that?"

"I suspected it."

"Did you think this might happen someday?"

"I thought it might."

"I have something I need to tell you."

"What?"

"I love you, but not in the way you probably think. Wait, wait." His arms tightened as she settled back again. "I admire you, Ainslee. You're a wonderful woman and a fine executive."

She smiled, smelling his hair. It was all so relaxed. So different from the fumbling excited groping when you were young. "What are you trying to say?"

"I just don't happen to find . . . women very exciting."

She tilted her head back and stared at him for what felt like a very long time. He nodded sadly. "Oh, my God," she said, suddenly sitting up. "I never suspected."

"I don't exactly advertise it."

"But if that's true . . . then why did you—"

"Believe me, it wasn't to embarrass you. It was to make you a slightly different proposal. I don't know if you realize it, but you're in trouble. Kemick's not the only one who thinks you're heading Thunder down a blind alley."

"Who else?"

"Oh, no. I know you. If I tell you you'll start plotting revenge. But if we were married, that would end it."

She laughed incredulously. "You're not seriously suggesting that I marry you?"

"I'm doing more than suggesting it," said Weyandt. Then, to her astonishment, she found herself looking down at a green velvet jewelry box.

"Open it."

"Forget it." She pushed it back into his hands and got up. Her robe fell open and she snatched it shut, tightened the sash with a jerk, suddenly conscious that she was totally furious. "You want to marry me, to play husband, and you're *gay*?"

"But I love you. I explained—"

"You're a—a—you're something else, do you know that? Why on God's earth would I want to marry you?"

"Because we'd have something on each other then."

She waited, rooted, balancing between outrage and intrigue and even in a way amusement; because it *was* kind of comic, even though the joke was on her. "Okay, Rudy. Explain."

Weyandt leaned forward, palms together, and said earnestly, "You've never trusted me, Ainslee. Oh, as your executive vice president, you're happy to let me help run Thunder. But you've never seen me as a friend. More as a minor threat, I'd guess. I don't think I've ever given you any reason to see things that way. I serve you just the way I did your dad, sort of the family retainer. Like Lark, but with a juris doctor degree. But trust? I never felt it from you."

"I trust you, Rudy."

"Then why haven't you ever proposed me for the board? I have the holdings. I have the experience. But you never did. Why? Because you think I'm the one person who could supersede you. The one person who goes back far enough with Thunder to be a credible threat. You're exactly like Dan! That is *exactly* how your father thinks! Why not admit it?"

"Because you're wrong."

"And I know everything. I know who blew the whistle on your ex-husband. I know about the gas operations in the Wild Area. I know where all the dirty laundry's buried. If I'm allowed to mix my metaphors."

"Get to the point."

"I just did. You've always seen me as a threat? Well, now you have something on me. Now you're a threat to me. Maybe not in New York, but in Petroleum City—definitely. My—orientation is not exactly smiled on. So maybe now you can trust me. And if you do, we're natural allies. Aside from the physical aspect, and we can agree to make our own arrangements for that. Together nobody could ever challenge us."

She still couldn't overcome the shock. She stood at the window and felt a probing finger of cold air seeping in around the seal. Looking down at the lighted empty streets, the endless city like the endless hills. The wailing of invisible sirens was like the faraway howl of wolves.

She hated to admit it, but his proposal made sense. "What about the direction of the company?"

"Put me and Titus White on the board. We'll form a voting bloc the outsiders can hammer at as long as they like. Meanwhile we publicize the deadlock and let share prices drop. Eventually they'll get tired and sell out."

"But am I right?"

"What, about strategy? Christ, who knows? Either way you go it's a gamble. I think your plan's got as good a chance as theirs. At least we can go to hell our own way."

"You really think it could work?"

"You know it'll work, Ainslee. That's why you're still standing here listening to it."

She stood immobile, struggling with the idea. With her emotions . . . she still didn't trust him, but he was absolutely right, she distrusted him not for himself but as a threat to her control. Could she live with him? It was so lonely at Cherry Hill at night. Her father wouldn't live forever. Then she'd really be alone, all alone, forever.

She drew a deep breath. "I can't make a decision like that so quickly. I've got to sleep on it."

"All right," he said. "That's fair." He got up and after a moment put out his hand. She started to take it, then hugged him instead. He hugged her back, staring past her at their locked reflections in the darkness of the window.

———

Standing on the street the next morning she told him she'd thought about it, appreciated his offer, but had decided to decline. She would propose him for the board but she didn't think marriage was a good idea. Not for two people like them. He nodded, face unreadable, and raised his hand for a taxi.

Fifteen

Halvorsen was sitting on a log when the morning came, looking across a field at four deer that stood stock-still, examining him.

The old man sat hunched over, careful not to move. Like most prey animals, deer couldn't see you if you held still. A smile quivered at the corners of his lips. No matter what happened, the woods didn't change, the deer didn't change. But then he remembered they had. They were nocturnal now, feeding only in the dawn and late dusk, when they were safest from hunters. But in the old days, deer had been a daylight animal. They had to be able to spot the predators then—wolves, panthers, bear— far enough away that they could flee.

But the deer still looked the same, smooth swelling flanks the same bark color as the trees, their rump-heavy bodies tensed. Their deceptively thin, graceful limbs planted deep in the snow.

With a sudden motion, he flirted coffee grounds from the tin cup onto the snow. Muzzles jerked around. Brown eyes widened. A moment later only their tails were visible, flicking like white scarves in the drifting fog. Then were gone, vanished silently into the vast forest gray with misty dawn. He smiled and reached for the smoking pot again.

He'd camped here after an all-day hike out of Mortlock Hollow. He figured he'd made about twelve miles yesterday, not bad for a man his age. Not that he'd been trying to set any records. He just wanted to see the land again, see if it had changed as he himself had changed. And not for the better, he thought, sipping morosely at the hot, bitter brew.

But he wouldn't think about that. Not on a dawn like this, crisp and cold, with the reproaches of ravens echoing down the backside of Storm Hill. Not with the memory still fresh of the gaze of deer, their startled snort as they'd wheeled all together, like one of those flag teams, and then suddenly were gone, melted magically back into the winter woods. It didn't matter how old or young you were when you looked out on something that close to pure beauty. He'd been a lucky son of a bitch, spending his life out here. Could have been stuck in a factory all those years. Or some office. He'd worked hard, but a man needed work to do. Without it he had too much time to think up devilment.

After hiking down from Mortlock he'd paused at the side of Route 6. Traffic was light but steady, a couple of cars every minute, an occasional truck. He knew if he waited and looked expectant one would stop. Instead he'd hitched the pack higher on his back, crossed the road, and left it behind, trudging up a one-lane blacktop that led up into Pretrick Hollow. Knowing he'd see the highway again in a couple miles, and if by then he felt tired he'd know this was a bad idea. Then he could stick out his thumb to get home. But he'd gone swinging on, not fast, and it hadn't felt bad. In fact it felt good, and when he'd come out on the road again where the Allegheny bent west in a big loop he was warmed up and going along so good he'd had to remind himself, Better take it slow, boy, you got a long way to go if you're headed where I think you are.

Now he waited, squatting by the coals. Sometimes deer would drift back once they got over their fright. They were curious, like kids. But they didn't this time. At last he gave up on them and started cleaning up, getting his gear stowed again for the trail. He scraped his pan off, the one he'd made biscuits in, rubbed it with snow, and put it back in his pack. He cleaned his spoon and cup and stowed them too after emptying out the pot. Started to get up, then leaned back again to enjoy the morning for another minute before he got going.

He'd left Route 6 again, this time for good, for an old lease road. He hiked south along a little frozen-over stream that didn't have a name he knew of. It trickled into Whitecar Creek, which lay a few miles ahead downhill, and Whitecar ran into the Allegheny. Which in turn, he'd thought, striding along a level stretch of snow-covered road bordered by pine and tulip poplar, the poplar's naked, kinky branches pointing toward the sky, joins the Monongahela at Pittsburgh to form the Ohio, which flowed into the Mississippi, and so on and so forth. He wondered if they still taught kids stuff like that. His thoughts drifted and dissolved like the frost-smoke he puffed out as he hiked along. He was glad he wasn't dressed any warmer, he was starting to sweat. He pushed his hat back, the old floppy green cap he'd worn in the oilfields, and the fresh air rubbed his cheeks and neck with cold hands.

No, he couldn't regret it, except for one thing. The kind that happens in one thoughtless minute but that you could never change or escape or forget your whole life long. He thought about that for a while, about her, as he pushed down to Whitecar, and back onto a snowplowed one-laner. Till there below him was the old covered bridge they put on the cover of the brochure that said, "Welcome to Hemlock County, Land of Pleasant Living." He followed his echoing footsteps through its shadowed tunnel and left that road past the T, heading up an unmarked, untrafficked dirt lease track that after a few hundred yards turned abruptly into a narrow, rocky foot trail winding through low scrub forest up into Grafton Run.

It wasn't till the middle of the afternoon he'd started to feel tired. The trees were quiet and pretty in their powder-white dresses and it wasn't really that cold. But when the land angled up and the trail got steep and the rocks turned his boots under the snow he just slowed down and slowed down and when he was halfway up it, the looming bulk of Harrison Hill to his left and Storm Hill to the right, really the first uphill he'd come to even though he'd gone almost ten miles by then, his legs felt like rusty junk iron and he was wheezing like a sand pump with the packings gone rotten. He stopped to rest, squatting on a stump and blowing it out, but he felt like a tire with a slow leak, just kept getting weaker and the pack kept getting heavier until he wasn't sure he was going to make it to the top. But he gritted his teeth and kept pushing, resting when he had to but making himself get up after he had his breath back and going on a few more yards. Till at last he'd reached the saddle and looked down into the valley beyond, had inspected the dusking sky, and listened to his pounding heart, and thought, Hell, I'm played out, it's time to call it a day.

So he walked downhill with his eyes probing between the trees till he saw a likely spot. Sheltered from the wind, not too level, not too slanting, with spruce and deadwood handy. He'd started making camp as dusk fell. Everything was damp, but he'd stripped some birch bark earlier in the day and dried it inside his jacket. With that and dry branches from under the spruces, he had a good little fire going soon enough. He'd had a bite to eat, sitting exhausted by the campfire, and recovered enough to scrape a hole in the snow and cut down some low-hanging boughs to sleep on. He thought about heating some rocks. That would keep you warm as a cat on a wood-stove, burying hot rocks under where you slept. But his bag was good down till zero or thereabouts and he didn't think it was going that low tonight.

His last thought before sleep, smelling the sticky perfume of cut spruce and listening to the flames crackle and spit and watching the firelight make the trees dance in the darkness, was that he'd probably lie awake till two or three. Like he did at home. But then night had covered him with a soft black blanket and he hadn't opened his eyes until dawn.

Now he felt alive as he hadn't in months. So he was old, what did that mean? Just that he had to take it a little slower, that was all. He felt stiff, sore, but it was a good soreness. And if he overdid it, pushed too hard on one of these uphills—well, it wouldn't be a bad way to go, under the rolling majesty of clouds, in the shadow and glory of the omnipresent hills.

Finally he hoisted himself to his feet and kicked snow over the fire, then scattered the coals till they gave up hissing and died. He didn't really need to, it wasn't going to wildfire under inches of soggy snow, but once you had a good habit going you didn't want to break it. Not at his age. He unbuttoned a few feet away and nursed out a feeble trickle. Then bent and strapped his snowshoes on. He thrust his shoulders through the pack straps and looked downhill.

An hour later he was two miles farther on.

He took it slow and rested before he got winded and didn't actually get to the Wild Area until that afternoon. He spent the day in the long valley that still carried names from when people had lived here. Mitchell Hollow. Jonathan Run. Reeds Still. Now he hiked through scruffy orchards long gone to seed, past the gray shingles of a pitched roof resting in the undergrowth like a mushroom without the stem. They'd tried to farm here after the forest had been cut down. Then one day a far-seeing president had decided that if people couldn't make a living on a piece of land, however hard they tried, then maybe that land ought not to be farmed; and the government ought to buy them out, and resettle them and help them make a living somewhere else. And over the years the worn-out land returned to forest, and instead of dust bowls and subsistence farms the country was dotted with parks and game lands and forestry preserves. Halvorsen had never seen that president, but he'd seen his wife once, and the memory had always stayed with him of a plain, determined woman who cared more for the common people than for her own country club set.

At a little before noon by the sun he stopped and ate a can of cold beans and drank cold coffee from his canteen. He sat for a time looking down into the icy clear tumble of the west branch of Reeds Still Creek. The stream gurgled and sang, polishing its pebbles till they glowed like a miser's hoard in the shallows. On either side the pines were green spears holding back a cloudy sky. He peered thoughtfully down from an overhang of bluff into a black depth of pool that looked like it might be worth investigating for brooks or browns. He hadn't brought a rod, but there were other ways to catch fish. Then he recollected where he was going and pushed on up the run.

Around one he stopped and put his hands on his hips. He hadn't been following a road, or a trail, either. He'd just been slogging along the bank of the creek, detouring out into it from time to time when the woods crowded close. When he did the water tugged at his boots, flowing fast and dark. But there must have been a road here once, because somebody had heaped a pile of dirt and rocks high enough to stop a jeep. A few yards past it a turnstile of welded pipe barred his path. A stamped tin sign read KINNINGMAHONTAWANY WILDERNESS PRESERVE. KINNINGMAHONTAWANY RANGER DISTRICT, ALLEGHENY NATIONAL FOREST. NO OFF-ROAD VEHICLES. DISTRICT RANGER, A. C. RANDALL.

He looked around at the silent woods, at the sleeping hills. Then ducked stiffly under the padlocked gate and went on up the run, his boots slipping on the loose, water-rounded stones.

The Wild Area, they called it around Potter and Hemlock and McKean and the other counties in the northern tier. Hundreds of square miles of wilderness, one of the largest wild preserves in the country.

There were other great forests in Pennsylvania: the Tiadaghton, the Susquehannock, the Wyoming. But the Kinningmahontawany was different. You could hunt and drive around the others and in the winter run snowmobiles, and now and then there was a timber auction. But the Kinningmahontawany was as close to closed as public land could get. There were no roads in, and damn near no trails; no campgrounds, no visitors' centers, no cabins, no gift shops, no family campsites, no swimming sites or snack bars or environmental interpretation centers. It had always been tough to get into this part of the high Alleghenies. The valleys were steeper, the hills rougher, and the land more savage than anywhere else Halvorsen had ever seen east of the Mississippi. There were even patches of virgin forest still, too high and difficult for the timber companies to get to. They would have, given time; but in 1923 Governor Gifford Pinchot had decided from his castle in Milford that one corner of the land should be wild forever, held in trust, primeval and inviolable. His magisterial finger had placed itself on the Kinningmahontawany, and ten years later Congress had accepted the gift as a public trust. Since then it had lain untouched, and gradually the marks of man had faded from its face, till it seemed he had forgotten it as it had forgotten him.

But Halvorsen remembered.

He remembered taking this same trail, only it was a road then, when he was a boy. Twelve years old but big for his age, he'd kept at his father till he nodded a reluctant assent to go trapping over the winter with Amos McKittrack. Halvorsen had a sudden flash of the old man, blue eyes crinkled to weatherproof slits, lips pursed, white beard rusty with tobacco juice. Sixty some years since they'd wintered together.

Yeah, sixty years . . . and he still could see it plain as day. They'd cut down pines for the cabin. Split out puncheons and clapboards and built the chimney out of river stones chinked with spring moss and plastered with mud. They'd trapped what people called the Wilderness then all that winter, running a line of two hundred Oneida Jumps, Victors, Blakes, and Newhouses.

Halvorsen stalked along, a silent, bent old man, taking out the memories again to finger and test like coins of a metal that never tarnished or lost its value. Remembering how the hemlocks in the deep hollows had stood shadowy and tall as the nave of a cathedral. Remembering the endless hours of skinning and stretching, working the soft pelts till they lost any resemblance to part of an animal and became just something to sell. The powerful smell of the curing shed, and the battle with weasels and blowflies to keep your pelts in good enough shape for market.

He remembered McKittrack's hands, so tanned from decades of salt and acid it looked like he was wearing leather gloves. Remembered days on the line, the old man heading east as the boy headed west in the long double loop that centered on the cabin on the Blue. Nights when he lay alone under a silvery dust of stars and dreamed of what his life would be like. And the hunting, for food and bait more than for sport, but he'd never forget laying the bead of the old man's ancient Colt .44-40 on the chest of his first black bear.

And when they couldn't trap or hunt, when the wind howled and the creek froze like translucent iron solid to the bottom and the snow covered the door and froze it shut, they lay up in the cabin and Amos would begin to yarn. And the listening boy heard tales that had come down hundreds of years from the Seneca and Iroquois; the legend of Noshaken, who'd been kept captive at Punxsutawney, where the spring boiled; how the Indians had made everything they needed from the land and forest, from bark and sinew and flint, and used the oil they found floating on the creeks to mix their war paint. The tale of the first whites to come to this land, the French, who'd buried a golden plate at Indian God Rock to claim forest and mountain for King Louis. Stories of the trappers and wolfers, Philip Tome, Bill Long, the Vastbinders, and Ben Yeager, king of them all, who Amos had trapped with when he was a boy. How the Seneca, defending their land, had fought for the British during the Revolution, and for picking the wrong set of white men lost the land known to them as Sinnontouan.

And since then, destruction; logging, oil, strip mines, the abomination
of desolation. For from that moment no one had looked at a tree or rock
or stream of the new land without wondering how to turn it into gold.

Lips set, snowshoes sliding over the white, the old man hiked on.

Late that afternoon he hit the headwaters of the Hefner River at last, and
turned southwest, trekking gradually uphill between two steep ranges of
hills. He traveled through empty woods and bubbling creeks, the snow
crisscrossed with animal trails. Halvorsen slogged across it in patient silence, occasionally bending to read a sign or examine a dropping. Lots
of deer, he thought. They were safe here . . . He spotted the pigeon-toed
track of a porcupine, the shallow channel where its belly dragged, and at
the bottom the prints of its paws like little toy snowshoes. Another time
he squatted quickly behind a bush and cupped his hands to his mouth.
A moment later the cry of a bobcat echoed over the snow. The old man
listened, but heard no reply.

Hiking along, he thought now, remembered now, the days when he'd
drilled out in this country.

The vanished sea, now six thousand, eight thousand feet below his
slowly advancing boots, had been shaped like a huge butter dish. The
Appalachian Basin ran from western Virginia northeast under the high
cold Allegheny Plateau, rising forty feet to the mile as it slanted north-
ward. The sandstone layers of its ancient beaches were named for where
they finally reached the surface, in Oriskany or Medina; the underlying
granite cropped out north of Buffalo. As sea and plain became mountain
and valley, the formations had cracked and buckled. The fractures became
traps, and over ages the enormous pressure of underground water forced
the lighter oil and gas into them. If the rock above it was porous, the gas
gradually escaped into springs and then into the air. If it wasn't, it stayed
where it was till a drill came down.

Hiking along, Halvorsen suddenly caught a thread of memory. There'd
been a gas spring around here. Where had he heard that? Not from
McKittrack, it had been . . . Denson, that was it, a crusty old bastard tough
as a spudding bit and with a plunger pump's capacity for Monongahela
whiskey. Every noon as they opened brown bags and lunch boxes at Evans
Cresson, "Bull Head" would tell the younger men contemptuously how
tough it had been in the old days. God, he'd hated Denson, but to his
surprise he still remembered his stories.

Like the one about the boiling spring. Denson had called it "Vernus,"
said it was always bubbling like a pot on boil, not from heat but from the
constant eruption of gas. Every day at four o'clock it would overflow. If
you threw in a match then the spring would burn with a dancing blue
flame. Denson said some brothers from Emlenton had drilled there and

made a big strike. All over this part of the state were towns named Burning Well or Roaring Spring, but this particular well had been somewhere on the upper reaches of Coal Run Creek, west of the valley he now slogged through.

And now that he'd remembered Denson, called his blustering, blasphemous shade back from the grave, his cracked hoarse whiskey whisper came back too, telling about the great Fairview that blew out thirteen hundred feet of casing and tools in 1873. You could hear it roaring five miles away, and the salt water in the gas made it look like a column of blue smoke rising out of the valley. The East Sandy, that burned for a year, a pillar of fire that lit the countryside at night for ten miles around before the pressure fell to where the drillers could cap it.

So there *had* been gas hereabouts once. But not for a long time. He knew that, because he'd tried to find it back in '48. And he had enough confidence in himself and his crew and the way Thunder did things back then that he just couldn't believe anybody else could have found it if they hadn't.

Hiking along, he asked himself: Was that sinful pride, was he just being a self-important old man? But after reflecting on it he was still sure as sure that if there was anything south of the Hefner they'd have found it all those years ago, he and Dick Myers and that stuffed-shirt Jew Marty Rothenburg.

Another funny thing. If somebody was pulling gas out of this valley, he'd have seen some sign of it by now. You didn't just pump gas out of the ground and sell it from a spigot. You needed roads, tool shops, field processing to take out the contaminants and dry it with triethylene glycol or Zentrite before you sold it to the utility, North Penn or National Fuel Gas or Columbia. They owned the pipeline and pumping stations that got it to the end user, the glass plant or brickworks or the distribution network that snaked beneath the streets home to home. Yet so far he hadn't seen a sign of it—well, processing, pipeline, *anything*. He was beginning to wonder if there was really a Medina Company at all.

Frowning, he set his feet for a climb.

Not long before dark he found himself on a flat bounded by steep hills. He gazed around, a mittened hand grating at the bristle of his chin. As he plodded on again the very contours of the ground took on a tantalizing familiarity. The poplars grew spaced about, almost as if they'd been planted. And then he came to a place in the woods where they opened out, and under the decaying snow patches of earth showed bare dirt and dried grass and here and there a strangely regular shadow under the snow. He shifted his pack and ambled toward one, lifted his snowshoe, and with the bent-up toe scraped the snow off.

To reveal the rich red brown of weathered brick, the charcoal gray of weathered mortar. He kicked it and the old foundation crumbled apart. He stood there, and this time as he looked searchingly around his eye picked out beneath the scrubby growth and scattered debris an old railroad grade, the half-circle remains of collapsed receiving tanks, a frozen-over creek.

He knew where he was now.

Cibola had been the most famous city in all the history of oil. And it had all happened because of a hazel twig.

He squatted on the crumbling brick and looked around at the silent poplars. Remembering hearing the story as McKittrack's Tin Lizzie bounced and churned her way through the center of a town that even then had been dead and abandoned for almost sixty years.

In 1865 John Syracuse Babbitt had leased the mineral rights to the 110-acre farm of Thomas Borbrown, and with a group of Philadelphia friends formed the Western Rock Oil Company. They hired Hiram Derris, a well-known "oil witcher," to find a place to drill. Derris had gone down to the creek-trickle and cut himself a hazel withe. The dowser had stopped on the far side of the creek, and that was where the drill went down. A month later the first oil well in Hemlock County blew in a gusher. When they finally capped it Babbitt Number One was producing eight hundred barrels of high-grade Pennsylvania crude a day.

The news of the great strike pulled speculators and drillers from Bradford and Titusville over the hills into the place Babbitt named Cibola. With the oil men came ex-soldiers from both sides of the war, German laborers, Irish teamsters, monte throwers and thimble-riggers, toughs, dive-keepers, hookers, and other ornaments of the underworld put out of business by Appomattox. In June 1865 there were four buildings in the valley. By November there were twenty thousand people in Cibola and four outlying towns, with forty bars, three banks, eleven hotels, five churches, two hundred brothels, and the second busiest telegraph office in the United States after New York.

When the new wells around the Borbrown proved in, suddenly the forests disappeared, replaced by a jungle of wooden derricks, and hundreds of drills and steam engines thudded and smoked as the ground was churned to mud. In the back rooms you could dance the two-backed jig or play faro, craps, poker, three-card monte, thimble rig or chuck-a-luck twenty-four hours a day. There was an Irish quarter, a German quarter, an Italian quarter, a Rebel quarter, and on Band Rock on Independence Day the Irish played Irish tunes and the Germans played oompah-pah from the opposite bank until the two sides met in the middle of the creek with knife and shillelagh, revolver and whiskey bottle.

And there for a while this little valley had been the wickedest city in the world, until a Confederate ex-captain of the Richmond Artillery named J. D. Puckett organized the Committee of Vigilance in January of 1866. It hanged five men and a woman the first night, but the result was not peace but war. Not until Puckett and six other citizens faced down the most desperate bad men in a local OK Corral did public opinion swing their way.

But if Cibola grew with dizzying speed, its crash came just as abruptly. In 1867 the great Babbitt suddenly stopped flowing, and not long after the others dried up too. They tried the new Roberts torpedo in the greatest detonation yet seen on the planet, setting off five hundred gallons of nitroglycerine and shattering every window for a mile. But when nothing came up but an oily smell the whole vast structure of speculation and credit collapsed in a paper avalanche. Vice and greed moved west to the new silver strikes in Nevada, and then one April evening a fire started and the oil-soaked timbers and sidewalks went up like fat pine tinder. So often from Cibola's pulpits the preachers had thundered about the fate of Gomorrah, and the valley was lit all night as their warning came true. Leaving, the next morning, only cooling ashes.

And a few hardscrabble remnants. Halvorsen remembered seeing one when he was here in—he and McKittrack on their way in for the winter season—could it have been 1920, 1922? Anyway he recalled the shaggy, bristle-chinned woman who had called out something the boy Halvorsen hadn't understood at the time to the old trapper as they chugged slowly past her hovel, the narrow high wheels of the Ford churning the fall mud like a paddlewheel steamer moving up the Mississippi. When they were past McKittrack had spat over the mudguard. "The most beautiful woman in town, once. And, you know what? She still is." And Billy Halvorsen had laughed and said, "She's the only one?" and been answered with a twitch of the old man's tobacco-streaked beard, so slight you had to winter over with him to know it was a smile at all.

Halvorsen looked at the creek, at the birches, and nodded slowly. It was as good a place as any to camp.

He was deep in sleep when something jerked him awake. He stared up at the flickering evergreens, wondering what it had been. A quaking, as if something huge was abroad. Jack hearing the Giant coming home. *Fee, fi, fo, fum.* Deep in the earth, a detonation, a landslide, a hungry growl. A falling tree, a huge old black cherry shaking the earth as it collapsed? A collapsing mineshaft, back in the hills? It sounded almost like the torpedoes he used to set off in the oilfields, but no one had used those in years. He listened, but when it faded silence succeeded it. He lay wondering, then turned over. Snuggled back into the warmth, into the sheltering snow.

If anything was out here, he'd find it. Till then, he just had to keep on looking.

Sixteen

The phone rang at the clinic while Leah was discussing cervical cancer with a frightened young woman who was neither poor nor rich enough to afford an operation. "Excuse me," she said gently and picked it up. The receptionist had left at five, but the woman across from her needed someone tonight. "Dr. Friedman," she said, hearing her voice brittle and impatient and tired.

"Leah? Jerry Newton here."

"Hi, Jer. That was quite a front page this morning."

"Thanks. Now there's some people asking why I ran it, was I trying to hurt business, you know. The usual routine. Look, there's going to be a meeting at city hall tonight. Can you make it?"

"What time?"

"Eightish."

"Is this an official invitation?"

"No. I just think you ought to be there."

She sighed and slipped her shoes off under the desk. Across from her the patient took a shuddering breath, looking out the window. Her hands twisted in her lap like desperate snakes. "I'll be there," she murmured. "Look, got to go, I'm with someone—'bye, Jerry." She hung up while he was still talking and leaned back, reconcentrating her tired mind on the problem of how a divorced single mother with a minimum-wage job was going to pay for the surgery she needed to save her life.

Seven-thirty, long after sunset, and the snow-paved streets of Raymondsville were almost empty. Main was a desert of smooth-rolled white glistening under her headlights. The powdered air seethed beneath the sulfur-yellow arcs of the streetlights. Icy crystals scratched at her windshield like ground glass. Gusts shuddered the Isuzu as she passed the Brown Bear, the Moose lodge, the flashing time-and-temperature sign of the First Raymondsville Bank, the lighted lobby of the Raymondsville Hotel, boarded up for years before the Patels reopened it. The *Century* office, McCrory's, Mama DeLucci's, M & M Office Supplies were dark storefronts. Two kids stood at the counter of the Pizza Den, an island of fluorescent light and racks of Herr's potato chips and the red-and-blue glow of Pepsi coolers. They were so heavily bundled she could not tell if they were male or female. Then as she rolled slowly by they turned their heads, and she saw it was a boy and a girl; and as she continued to stare, the boy bared his teeth, bent, and began mock-biting the girl's neck.

She jerked her eyes back to the snow-writhing road and turned onto Jefferson. There was the little brick city building, several cars already in the ice-glistening lot. The blinds were closed but the lights inside shone through in bladelike slices.

She braked for the turn, but too quickly. The wheels locked, the slick surface released them, and the steel box around her leaned sickeningly as she planed sideways. The tires whined. She pumped the brake, fingers digging like cold iron hooks into the wheel as the cars ahead loomed closer and closer. She got traction back just in time to avoid crashing into a green game commission pickup. She breathed out and parked in the last space. She left her hat and gloves in the car, reasoning it was only twenty yards, but regretted it the moment the night air attacked. It was icy, Arctic, like breathing in some scorching fluid. By the time she got to the door her cheeks felt dead.

"Dr. Friedman." George Froster looked up from the head of the table. The mayor didn't look pleased to see her. She nodded to Vince Barnett, the chairman of Hemlock County Recreation, Inc., the shopkeepers' association; Chief Nolan; Robert Witchen, the green-uniformed district game warden, though now they called themselves "wildlife conservation officers"; Lois Herzog, who owned a real estate agency on Main Street; Greg Pickard, Pickard's Drug; Marybelle Acolino, who owned the Style Shoppe on Pine Street. Small-town movers and shakers, she thought. People who had never liked her New York accent and her New York ways, who'd looked the other way when she was asked to leave the hospital. Who hadn't helped at all to establish or support the clinic, as if people who couldn't afford a doctor didn't really deserve to live.

Yes, she thought, it all looked so egalitarian in a small town, everybody knew everybody else and the accents were the same, but under that yawned fissures generations deep and the gap between the haves and the nobodies was as deep as anywhere else she'd ever worked. She knew she shouldn't judge people, but when she was tired and her guard was down she hated these: so selfish and self-satisfied and instinctively hostile to anything that might stir up the ant heap so that maybe they wouldn't be on top anymore. But still she was a doctor, and in their cast-concrete minds that counted for something even if they didn't like her, and they shoved over to make room and she threw her coat onto the pile on an empty desk and sat down.

The mayor said, "Leah, we were discussing this situation concerning the—whatever killed the woman whose body they brought you yesterday. We've got to have some kind of policy on this. We can't let Jerry just stir people up without taking some kind of action. We just heard the Pittsburgh paper's got something about it in the evening edition. Vince has pointed out that in a way we're lucky, it's not hunting season. But people have memories. They start associating Hemlock County with anything negative, and they'll go someplace else next fall. Can you help us out with the medical facts? What did her in?"

"I'm no forensics expert, George. But I measured the bite marks, what clear ones I could find. It looked to me like a large canid. Something in the dog family, with pointed sharp teeth. Charlie Whitecar's seen bear maulings, and he says this wasn't a bear."

"No bears this time of year anyway," said Barnett.

"Right, Vince. Uh, do we know who she is yet? Did you turn up anything, Pat?"

"No, sir," said Nolan. "I put the picture and description out on the wire but we haven't had any replies."

"Robbie, how about you? You're the closest thing we got to a wildlife expert."

"I don't know too much about wild dogs, sir. Or wolves, either."

The first time the dread word had been mentioned. The others sat silent, frowning at the table. Finally the mayor cleared his throat again.

"All right, let's summarize . . . We've had two animal attacks, one fatal. Robbie says he's heard howling occasionally. And you guys tell me you've heard other stories, people seeing things crossing the road at night, watchdogs getting killed. Let's think about what we do if it's really a—wolf. Who would we talk to, to get it taken care of? Robbie, isn't there a state predator control program?"

"Not for wolves, far as I know," said the warden. "I can check."

"I can put together a private group," said Barnett. "From down at the Rod and Gun."

One of the council members said, "Are you talking about shooting them?"

"Well—yeah. What else?"

"Better check the federal regulations before you do. I think they're a protected species."

"Oh, God," somebody said.

"That's exactly why we better do something now," said Barnett. "We start going to outside experts, asking for government help, pretty soon we're going to be knee-deep in tree-huggers and owl-lovers and we can kiss next hunting season good-bye. I think me and Robbie ought to put our heads together and get a couple of local hunters or maybe trappers and go out and see what we can do before this goes ballistic."

"Wait a minute, Vince," Leah said. "You're going to do this before you even know if that's what killed her?"

"What else should we do? Wait for another body? Let's not get misty-eyed, Doc. You're the one made out the death certificate, right? If there's really a pack of wolves, dogs, coyotes, *whatever* loose out there, we need to take care of them. Before they get somebody else."

She opened her mouth, then closed it again. He was right: she'd seen what they could do. Her fatigued brain was all too ready to yield up again the image of the torn body, the broken fingernails that had tried, and failed, to ward off whatever had attacked her. There was still too much she had no explanation for. But it was all too obvious something vicious was loose in the dark hills.

"So, we got some kind of agreement here?" said the mayor.

"May I say something?" said a middle-aged woman. "Because, frankly, I don't think it was wolves."

"Mrs. Skinner?" said Froster, his face giving no clue to how he felt.

"Mr. Mayor, before I came over I went through the card file, pulled several references off the shelf. In the first place, it's not impossible to coexist with wolves. People live with them around in Minnesota and Canada. But I don't think what we have here are wolves."

"Then what *are* they?"

"Werewolves," somebody murmured, and nervous chuckles rippled the overheated air.

"You see, wolves don't attack people," the librarian went on, ignoring the laughter. "There's not a single record of any substantiated attack on a person in North America by healthy wild wolves. Pure-bred wolves are very shy of humans. So I think these are either feral dogs, or first-generation dog-wolf hybrids. There was a case in France. The notorious Wolves of Gevaudan, which killed and ate more than a hundred people in the seventeen sixties."

"Oh, my God," somebody moaned. The mayor said, "Mrs. Skinner, please. Don't say things like that, even as a joke. Don't you have anything serious to contribute?"

"I *am* being serious, George. We need to step back and look where we're going before you start talking about what Vince is talking about—which is basically an extermination program. Or we may all find ourselves in very serious trouble. Also, a procedural question? I wonder what kind of meeting we're having here. Is this a special council meeting, or what? I don't see anyone keeping minutes, and it wasn't advertised to the public."

As she spoke the murmuring had increased, and the moment she paused everyone began talking at once. People began jumping up, shouting at each other. Barnett banged the table and quiet returned. The mayor glared at him, but didn't object. Barnett said, "This isn't an official council meeting, so there aren't going to be any minutes. But a woman's been killed and we need to get off our butts and do something before it happens again. George, Robbie, you guys just stand fast. I'll take care of it. Nothing on the record, and if we find anything, well, we'll just have shot some wild dogs. Jerry, all you got to do is not pour any more gasoline on the damn fire, all right? Just write about something else for a couple days, okay? Like how many deer there are going to be next year. We would very much appreciate that, in the recreation association."

Pickard, the druggist, said, "Vince, it might be better to wait. Notify the state. Let them take it from there."

"No, Greg. The longer we wait, the more assholes—sorry, ladies, the more *people* get involved in this, the less control we're gonna have over the situation. Us, the ones who have to live here."

Leah said, "But we still don't even know who this woman is. Whatever the engineer saw, they didn't harm him. You can't just start killing things, hoping they're the right ones."

"We know something's out there. We can't just wait for the next time—"

Friedman pushed herself to her feet. "No! Your reasoning's off, Vince. Just because we're afraid, we don't start forming posses and shooting anything with fur and teeth. This is neither the proper venue nor the proper way to reach a decision. We have to involve the people who live here. *All* the people. I propose a public meeting here, tomorrow at seven."

"I second," said the librarian, and so did several others. The mayor, face reddening, shouted above the din, "There are no motions and rules of order! This is not a council meeting! And if it was, Doctor, you aren't a member. I know what you're after, Leah. Publicity. Just publicity. Please leave. Everyone who's not a council member, please leave."

"Tomorrow night at seven," Leah yelled again, picking through the pile for her coat. Someone bumped her from behind, just hard enough to make her stumble, and she heard Barnett's growl: "Look, Doc. We don't need your advice. You don't know us and you don't know the woods. Why don't you go back to your deadbeat clinic? We can take care of this ourselves."

"Thanks for your input, Vince. I'll keep it in mind. See you tomorrow." She bared her teeth in something as close to a smile as she could muster, and slammed her way through the door, out into the black wall of icy night.

Seventeen

The ambulance stood in the driveway, its rotating flashers making the spruces on the lawn flicker and jerk so that it seemed odd to Becky that their burden of snow should still cling to their branches. She stood on the porch with her arms wrapped around herself, cold wind whirling where her stomach used to be.

They were taking Jammy away again.

She'd thought he was getting better after that night at the Rock. His fever went down and Mom had let him come downstairs and play on the rug in front of the stove. She hadn't gone back to school yet. Charlie was talking to a lawyer about Mr. Cash. So she played with her brother, building towers and roads and whole cities and then knocking them down. He'd topple them with screaming glee, then glance at her; and she'd laugh too, just to see him standing there looking strong again.

But a few days later he got worse. He stayed in bed and said he felt sick again. Then last night her mom had to call the hospital, and now he was going back.

She hugged tighter to stop the shivering and watched two men in blue smocks and rubber gloves slide the stretcher basket into the back. He looked so small in it, a pale doll. Then her mom got in, not looking back or waving or anything. The doors closed with a hollow metal sound. The woman at the wheel smiled at her in the mirror, then headed down the driveway. Becky expected her to turn on the siren but she didn't. Then the road was empty, the burning flicker was gone, the spruces stood still. Nothing remained but tracks in the snow, and Jammy was gone.

Charlie came back up the driveway, dragging a shovel. "You left this down by the mailbox," he said. "Don't stay out here too long without your coat." And went inside, leaving her standing in the cold.

She thought numbly: What did I do wrong?

She felt lost and guilty and above all she didn't understand. She thought she'd done it right. Talking to the thing in the woods, and getting the paw print, and putting it on her brother's head until it melted. And after that, yeah, he'd gotten better. But now he was sick again, really sick, or Mom would have driven him to the hospital herself and saved ambulance money.

When she finally let herself in her stepfather was sitting in front of the stove reading a magazine. He said, "It's not shut all the way," and she went back to the door and closed it. Then she threw herself into the other chair, where her mom usually sat, hating the strange emptiness in the house. The old Siamese lay in front of the stove, watching the fire fighting and twisting behind the heavy glass as if it were a trapped animal that wanted out.

"Charlie," she said.

"What, Becky?"

"What's gonna happen to Jammy?"

Silence behind the magazine. Then, "What do you mean?"

"I mean if he doesn't . . . come home again."

The pages sagged to show her stepfather's face. He looked embarrassed, or maybe disgusted; it was always hard to tell what he was thinking. He cleared his throat so harshly she thought for a moment the stove had made the sound.

"You mean, if he dies?"

"Yeah," she said, relieved he at least understood what she was asking. But then the next minute she knew he didn't, because he said, "Well, it's something we have to face, Becky."

"But what's going to *happen* to him?"

"I'm not sure what you mean."

"I mean, what happens if you—if *he* dies?"

"Well, he won't be here with us anymore, Becky. That's really about all you can say about the situation."

"Uh-huh. I meant like after that."

"After that. Well, you'll always remember him, won't you?"

"Sure. He's my brother."

"And we all will. He's a good little kid and we all loved him. So as long as we remember him, he'll still be with us."

He said "loved him," as if Jammy was already gone, and she suddenly understood, with a really bad feeling, what he was actually saying. It was the way adults always told you something real bad, they told you the opposite, like it was something good instead. "But what'll *happen*? To *him*?"

"He'll be gone, Becky. That's really all I can tell you." Her stepfather looked up toward the faraway beams of the ceiling. "Some people would tell you different things. Like, that he'll go to heaven or someplace else nice and we'll see him again when we die."

"That's what they said at church, when we used to go when we lived in Johnsonburg—"

"I wish it was that easy and that nice," said her stepfather. "I know it's a hard thing to face, that we'll never see the people we love again. But we have to learn that lesson sometime."

"Then, where *will* he go?"

"Sugar, there's nothing left to *go* anywhere. Once a person's dead, they're dead. Like one of your dolls, okay? Suppose we burn it up. Where would you say it went?"

"It just burned. There's just the ashes."

"That's right, sweetheart. And that's what happens to people too. So we have to make our lives as meaningful as we can, be as nice to each other as we can every day. Because there isn't going to be any second chance."

She slid down and sat on the rug where the stove breathed out hot air, where it was real warm, where Leo lifted his head and stared at her with black, depthless eyes. She ran her hand along the old cat's thin bumpy spine, thinking about it. And tried again. "But won't he—come back? Someday? Like if another baby gets born, just like him—"

"No, honey. There's only one of each of us, and when it's over, it's over."

He sounded so sure of himself that she felt something inside her falter. "How do you know all that?" she whispered. "I mean, for sure."

"Becky, remember when we talked about Santa Claus and the Easter Bunny and all? There are nice things we wish would happen. So we talk about them as if they were like that. Only, some people actually start believing in their wishes." He opened the magazine again and she knew he was tired of talking to her. He looked at her over it. "Do you understand what I mean?"

"Uh-huh," she said, running her finger along the pattern in the carpet.

But actually she didn't.

Oh, she understood what he was saying. That people were the same as his computers: that after you got turned off there wasn't anything else there. Like taking a battery out of a toy. But she couldn't imagine herself seeing nothing, feeling nothing, being nothing at all.

But then, what would happen? The only thing she could think of was that you *went* someplace else. She thought she knew where, too. The same place you went in dreams. She didn't know if it would be a good place or a bad one. Margory was always saying so-and-so was going to hell, but if heaven was going to be full of Margory Gourleys, she sure didn't want to go there. But she didn't think Charlie was right either. Or maybe that was what happened to adults—they didn't have any dreams anymore and forgot how to get to the place kids knew where to go.

It was all confused and weird, but sitting there in front of the stove running her hand over the cat's silky warm back, she decided she liked the way it was in the old book better. Where a fairy could bring a puppet to life, and animals could talk, and there were elves and fairies and trolls, and magic could make a difference.

That night she stood outside again, gripping the flashlight inside her pocket but not taking it out. Maybe it was the flashlight that had scared it off before. But now she'd figured out what she hadn't done the last time. This time she'd get it right.

She patted the lump under her coat, not sure she *could* do it. But she had to try. For Jammy.

The snow had stopped falling but there still weren't any stars. No wind, either, and the cold air was so calm that as she climbed her boots crunched like eating dry Cheerios and squeaked like Jammy's toy whale. The only light after she left the yard was from the west, a pinkish glow. As she climbed that faded too, blotted out by the hill, till she had to feel her way along the cold pipe handrails of the bridge. The scent of woodsmoke reached her on the chill air.

Past the creek she stumbled blindly uphill. Her outstretched hands scraped over the rough boles of the trees, and the dead branches of the bushes went *zip, zip* over her coat like goblin claws. She slipped and fell, but each time got up and went on. Till at last she sensed the loom of the great rock, poised above her like a black fist about to fall.

Far away, above the clouds, an airplane droned. When it faded the silence was twice as still. She stood listening to the hiss of her breathing and the thud of her heart and the faint creak of the snow as it sank under her weight.

With cold-stiffened fingers, she unzipped her coat and pulled out the bundle.

She'd figured out what she'd done wrong before. It was simple. She hadn't brought what the stories said you had to bring: a present, a gift, a sacrifice. *The thing you cherish most.* She unwrapped the towel slowly. When she ran her hand over them the wheels sparkled like miniature fireworks. She held the doll tight, remembering how beautiful she was; her long wavy hair, her pretty blue eyes. She was so lovely and she was hers and she loved her best of anything she'd ever owned.

Sighing, she laid Rollerblade Barbie down in the snow.

She took out the can of charcoal lighter and closed her fist around the cap. The childproof circle slipped, until she bore down as hard as she could. Then the threads caught and she unscrewed it, trying not to spill any on herself in the dark.

When she touched the doll's feet with the lighter-flame the kerosene burst up in a wavering yellow tongue that pulled out of the darkness astonished trees, the wire skeletons of bushes, the cruel ancient bulk of the Rock glittering with ice. She backed off and stared, as beneath the hungry glare Barbie's golden hair and eyelashes grew a blue halo of delicate fire. Her fair skin wrinkled and softened, as if fifty years were passing in a second, then suddenly burst into flame, erupting into black blisters that swelled and burst. Her pretty dress withered like a dead rosebud. Smoking, it contracted itself around her tapered limbs with an embrace that passed in seconds into burning. The lighter fluid had pooled in her joints, her neck, her arms, her tiny waist, and the yellow, hungry flame ate most hungrily at these, gnawing until the doll's whole trunk was bubbling and burning. Her eyes stared up unblinking, tragic but resigned, then suddenly sagged and sank backward into a gaping emptiness. And without knowing why, because she'd loved the doll, Becky could not look away as it destroyed itself, as the plastic melted and fell apart into little black bubbling scraps that dropped away hissing into the snow. The stink of burning filled the air. Then the flames dropped and died, and around them the startled dark crept slowly back.

Till the last flame guttered out, and only a snapping hiss came from where the doll had been.

She dropped to her knees, staring into the dark woods.

Only now it wasn't all dark. A faint silver glow outlined the trees and the snow. Showed her the Rock, looming like a thundercloud. Though she couldn't see it yet, the moon was rising. Enough of its light seeped through the clouds that she could make out the faint, vibrating outlines of things, like ghosts of themselves. A mist lay like a silver cloak over the hillside, creeping through the trees. Cold seeped through the knees of her jeans, but still she knelt, no longer breathing, staring up the hill.

It was back.

She could feel it. It was watching her right now from the mist, from the silver dark. Her breath was coming crazy and fast and she couldn't make it slow down. She wanted to turn and run downhill, back to the circle of safe green light, her own backyard, back inside the walls of her house. But through the fear and dizziness she reminded herself *she* had summoned it, whatever it was. She had to ask it for the—what did they call it in the stories—the boon. Or sometimes, a wish. One wish, that was all she needed. Only, what was out there, *what* had she called? Her gaze roved among the trees. Then she stopped breathing as sudden terror closed her throat.

It stood at the edge of the woods, head lowered, its eyes empty sockets. It didn't move, and though it seemed to have just appeared magically, congealing from the mist, she knew it had been standing there watching her for a long time. Huge, silver gray in the moonlight. Then with a thrill of understanding she recognized it.

It was all right; she'd done everything right.

But then she made out another shape, behind it, loping between the trees. That one ran swiftly along to her right and disappeared behind a fold in the hill. She lost sight of it, but simultaneously her eye caught yet another moving shadow. Now her mouth was dry with fear and the thick smoky taste of burned plastic. Wasn't there only supposed to be one? The story hadn't mentioned any other wolves. What if they were real? But there weren't any real ones in the woods anymore. So these had to be magical wolves. Didn't they? And the great silver one who lifted his head to stare at her—there was only one thing *he* could be.

She heard a crackle or snap behind her and whipped her head around so quickly a muscle shrieked in her neck. The brush along the creek was a black wall across the silver blankness of the field. Across that flat frosted space something coursed with an easy rocking motion, and the *pant, pant* of its breath came to her in the stillness.

She turned back to find that the first wolf had moved. No longer among the trees, it had advanced, standing now between her and the forest. Scraps of mist blew past him, glowing like his own silver fur. Now she could make out black ears, pricked up, great furred paws planted motionless in the snow. A gray plume of tail like a puff of woodsmoke. But still she could not see his eyes.

Her thighs were trembling, her hands shaking. She couldn't stand up even if she wanted to. And she wondered: Could this be a dream? The mist, the invisible moon, the ghostlike impossibility of the thing that watched . . . But her sickly, lurching heart insisted it was all really happening. She'd made the sacrifice, called him, and he'd come.

The Wolf Prince.

Another brittle crackling to her right. She turned her head slowly to see that one of the other wolves had come out of the woods too. It stood motionless, just like the first. A faint white stream drifted from its muzzle.

Above their heads the moon showed itself at last. Not all the way, just a sliver, as if a patch of cloud had slid partway back between it and the earth. Now in the brighter light she looked into the prince's eyes. They were deepset, questioning, intent only on her. The tips of curved teeth gleamed in his half-parted jaws. His tail moved slowly. Pale fur glistened, fair as her doll's, only a little darker than the snow. The slowly increasing light showed every detail now: the silver-tipped hairs on his back; the black claws; the fractured, sparkling surface of the Rock; the crouching shadow that was the second wolf.

A sharp popping startled her, and she cowered instinctively, arms cradling her head. But when it came again, not as loud, she realized it was

only the remains of the fire, the plastic cracking as it cooled. The reek
was choking, making it hard to breathe. Then movement drew her eye
again, and she saw the third wolf emerge from the brush below her on
the hill, looking from her to the prince as if waiting for his order.

She lurched clumsily to her feet, terrified at how weak her legs were.
She couldn't run even if she had to. Again she felt the dreadful prickle
of doubt, and stood hugging her hands to her chest. Was the great silver
shape in front of her the prince or a ravenous beast? The magical bene-
factor of the fairy tales or a dangerous wild animal? There was only one
way to find out. She swallowed, choking down fear, and called out:
"Prince?"

The silver form did not stir. It seemed to be listening.

"I need your help. I need to ask you for something."

She paused, breath sobbing, cold burning her throat. It was hard to
speak. But she had to. She took as much of the icy air as she could hold
and lifted her head and whispered: "Please, please, I need you to save my
brother."

There, she'd said it, and she knew he heard. The clouds were moving,
the light fading, and the prince was becoming part of the shadows once
again, a black cutout against the vertical strokes of the trees. A picture in
a storybook, black crayon on black paper. He neither moved nor made a
sound. But straining her eyes, she thought he turned his head toward the
woods behind. Was that a sign? A muffled whine came from behind her
and she spun, searching the darkness. She couldn't see the others but
they were there, because the low, eerie whine came again, making the
hairs prickle on the back of her neck.

She turned back to the great wolf, but he had moved into the forest.
Not retreating, just looking back at her. Was he beckoning her on? Was
that her answer, that she was to go with him like the boy from the story?
She hesitated, then took a step. Then another.

The wolf kept moving ahead of her. She could hear the *pad, pad, crunch*
of his paws on the snow. His outline faded into the forest shadow, returning to night and mist. She hesitated again, looking back to where her
bedroom window glowed. She wished there was somebody with her, Charlie or her mom or even Dr. Friedman. But maybe it had to be her, alone.
Because when people grew up all they could see was what Charlie called
logic, and everything was ordinary, nothing could be strange or magic.
The prince looked like a wolf, so that was all he could be; they'd never
see that under that form he was the Prince of the Woods, powerful and
good, and he could save children who were dying, even children who were
dead.

She followed the silent retreating shadow up and on through the deepening gloom to the top of the hill and then downward again. He led her
on, never running, moving no faster than she did. At times he seemed to

be waiting for her to catch up, standing in an open patch of forest so she could make him out in the wavering moonlight, looking back with head lifted and the night filling his eyes.

It wasn't till late that night, deep, deep in the woods, that Becky Benning realized she was lost.

Eighteen

Good morning, Ms. Thunner—"

"Good morning, Twyla." She snapped her coat off and bent to slip off her boots, taking her business pumps from her bag. After hearing the morning news, she wasn't in a good mood. Bodies in the woods, meetings, media attention to the Wild Area were not pleasant things to think about. Just then she felt a tickle, an insect-crawl along her shin, and realized too late it was her stocking. The boot zipper had caught in it and now she had a run, right in front. "Shit," she muttered. Then she noticed several staff people standing in the corridor, and snapped, "What are you staring at?"

"Uh, Mr. Blair is here to see you, Ms. Thunner."

"Frederick Blair? Here?"

"That's right, Ms. Thunner."

"How long has he been here? I didn't know he was coming." She clattered down the hall, then paused, looking over her shoulder. The staff was grouped together in the lobby, still staring after her. When they caught her glare they scattered. Shaking her head, she strode into her office. Old Mr. Blair rose from the settee. "Good morning, Ainslee."

"Fred, what on earth are you doing here? Sit down, sit down! Did someone forget to tell me something?"

"No, no, I just dropped in." The old oilman seemed embarrassed. His hand felt soft and frail in hers, his fine white hair shone in the cold light from the window, and his sagging cheeks were like waxed paper over a fine reticulation of scarlet veins. "We need to talk for a minute or two, honey. In private, before the meeting."

From him, the Southern familiarity of "honey" pleased her, but she was at a loss as to what he was talking about. "What meeting? Fred, what's got you so upset?" She sat at her desk, glancing surreptitiously at the calendar Twyla had left out; no, nothing scheduled today that would involve any of the directors.

"Ainslee, a special board meeting's been called for ten today."

She went suddenly still inside. "The chairman schedules those, Fred. And I haven't called any."

"This is a special meeting, like I said. I hope you'll chair it." The old man still seemed at a loss, standing slightly bent and looking off to her left. Finally he let himself down slowly onto the settee. "Can we close the door?"

She punched the intercom. "Twyla, close my door, hold my calls. Till I tell you otherwise. Oh, and send somebody down to La Femme. Get me a pair of taupe, sheer, size B or medium. Donna Karan if they have them." Then clicked off and leaned back. "Now let's talk. First off, Fred, there's no meeting today."

"Everyone's here, Ainslee. Several of the members requested it and they called around and arranged for everyone to be here at ten o'clock. It pains me to bring this kind of news. It's unpleasant for everyone concerned." Blair cleared his throat. "But we can still carry it off without anyone's having to suffer any—embarrassment. This is a special directors' meeting to vote on your request to step down as chief executive officer."

She didn't laugh, though for a moment she wanted to. Instead she said, "Don't be an ass, Fred—I can talk to you like that, you know Dad from way back. Let me assure you, I have no intention of making any such request."

"Hear me out, darlin'. Please," said the old man, and she forced herself into silence, into listening.

"Ainslee, we've known each other a good long while, and I have great respect for you. As an executive, and as a person. When this issue came up I said we should give you full support for two years, wait and see if things turned around. Give your strategy a chance. I flattered myself I was persuasive. But the votes said otherwise."

"Ah," she said. "Secret meetings, secret ballots. How exciting. Go on, please. Give it to me straight, at least."

Blair's face flushed. "All right. Besarcon has a management team ready to come in and get the company reoriented in a more profitable direction. They want an interim CEO in charge, pending their recommendations. They very much want you to continue as president, but they want to relieve you of the day-to-day responsibilities of chief executive.

"This is very difficult for me to say, Ainslee, but the bottom line is you've jumped in the river with too much chain to swim with. You've lost the confidence of the board. Right or wrong, that's how it stands. I'm here right now to try to persuade you that the best thing you can do for the company is to open the meeting today with the announcement that due to the demands of business you would like to have someone else take on the position of CEO. The board members will be suitably surprised and not altogether in agreement, but they will reluctantly accept your resignation."

Through her shock and anger she was surprised to hear how calm her voice sounded as she said, "Who thought up that little charade, Fred?"

The old oilman bent his head. "Me."

"To spare my delicate feelings? How thoughtful. Who do you want in my seat? Frontino?"

"We don't want anybody else 'in your seat,' Ainslee. We want you to stay on as president and chairman. As for CEO, we truly need your advice on that. Maybe you could suggest two or three names. Good people you trust."

"And you expect me to go along with this—coup? This rather shabby stab in the back?"

"It really isn't that, Ainslee. Please don't take it personally. Quentin and Bernard and several other people have tried to warn you your strategy was not popular with the more income-oriented investors. You think they're wrong and you're right. Total self-confidence? That's great in a wildcatter. It's something Dan had in spades. But what worked in the field in thirty-two is not what works in a modern boardroom. They can't hang on for the long haul. They've got to show quarterly results. They've carried us for over a year. It's the best thing for the company."

Now she leaned forward and let go, just a little. "Bullshit, Fred. It's a takeover. Once they have their men in place they can take us apart. Strip out the equity, sell off the profitable parts, and close what they don't like or don't have the guts to run. You know that! Thunder Oil will be history and thousands of our people will be out on the streets. I won't do it. I will not go in there and lay my head on the block for my executioners."

"Then there'll be a vote."

"And I'll win it."

"Oh, honey, I don't think so. Believe me, if they didn't know they'd win, they wouldn't even try."

But she wasn't listening anymore. Because while the old man had been talking she'd been counting votes in her head. The way she called it she had Luke, Ron, Rogers, Connie, Hilda, and Pete. That, with her own vote, was seven to three against the outsiders, and she might even be able, once he saw how strong she was, to peel off Quentin Kemick. Blair was bluffing.

But more than that, he was making a major mistake. He was handing her the opportunity to destroy her opposition utterly and forever.

If you strike at the king, strike to kill. Her lips drew back in a wolf-like smile as she said, "All right, Fred. Thank you for—offering me the option of stepping down gracefully. I'm sure you meant well and I appreciate your thoughtfulness.

"But here is what is going to happen this morning. I'll announce this emergency meeting you want me to call. We'll have our vote. And the minute I step out of there after winning it, my PR department will fax a press release to every financial paper, magazine, and newsletter in the Northeast outlining how you assholes tried to railroad me out of the management of my own company, and how miserably you failed."

"That wouldn't help our stock value, Ainslee—"

"It'll send it straight to the basement, Fred, and I want to see how Parseghian and Kemick explain that to their pension-fund managers, a fifty percent drop in a stable market. Let them explain how they personally brought it on by trying to rape the sitting CEO of a profitable corporation." She got up and jerked the door open, ignoring Blair's spluttering explanations. She yelled, "Twyla! Rudy! Get the boardroom open! Call Judy Bisker and get her up there, on the double. I want videotape for Channel Four. And now, Fred, if you'll excuse me, I have some calls to make before we convene."

Blair must have passed the word to his co-conspirators, because when she stepped off the elevator into the sixth-floor lobby she found herself confronted by a circle of stony faces. Parseghian and Kemick and Blair, and a stranger she frowned at. Parseghian said, "Ms. Thunner, this is Jack Whiteways, from our legal staff."

"Bringing in the attorneys so early, Bernie?"

"This is a closed meeting, Ainslee. All our board meetings are closed," he said, his eyes narrowing as Judy Bisker stepped off the elevator with a handheld camcorder.

"The chairman determines whether it's open or closed. I want this abortion open, I want it all on the record."

"Technically she's right," said the attorney, and Parseghian winced. But then the lawyer added, "*So long as no damage to the corporation results.* Otherwise, she can be liable in negligence."

"Hear that, Ainslee? You try to make this some kind of Dreyfus case and—"

"Fuck you, Bernard," she said sweetly. "Hi, Judy, nice to see you. Go on in and get set up. We're going to have some fun this morning."

The chill in the boardroom felt appropriate. She shivered; the wall heaters had only just been cut on. Icy fingers had drawn frosty arabesques on the inside of the great window, and only at the bottom, closest to the warmth, were they beginning to melt. She crossed the room and paused in front of it, looking out and down.

Below her the snowbanked streets, the brick and stone buildings streamed out like arteries radiating from this pumping heart. The trucks and cars and snowplows crept along the sanded pavement like busy corpuscles drawn in and out. Beacham Thunner had sketched those streets on a hand-drawn map when this valley was a smoky wilderness of black mud and wooden derricks. Through the low-hanging mist loomed the pink brick geometry of the new Lutetia Thunner Auditorium at the University of Pittsburgh at Petroleum City. And past and beyond that the tripled steel keep of refinery number one loomed up behind its omnipresent veil of steam and smoke, glittering with a thousand lights and crowned with the twenty-foot-high flareoff flame. Beyond it across the river were huddled masses of low roofs; the homes of people who depended on Thunder, and on her. The sight gave her strength.

We've been here since the beginning, she thought. And here's where we'll stay.

"Ainslee," said a male voice behind her, and she spun to see Rudy Weyandt by the door.

"Are we ready?"

"I think so."

"Okay, let's get started."

She stood at the lectern, surveying the directors as they filed in. No buzz of idle chat this morning. The local contingent took the left side of the table, as usual. Only then did she realize why the meeting felt strange, felt wrong. She'd had no time for the traditional council at the club. Her side was going to take the field without a game plan. For the first time she felt a stab of doubt.

But she had something up her sleeve too. The chairman of the board controlled the procedure and sequence of discussion. If they wanted a vote on her executive position, they'd get it, but not before they had it out on another matter. She stood still, scanning the table as the directors adjusted chairs and cleared their throats. Counting and evaluating the strength of her own forces, and estimating those of the other side.

On her right was Luke Fleming, heavy face somber. Thank God he didn't look as if he'd been at the bottle yet. Or maybe that was not to her favor, she couldn't be sure since she'd never seen him sober before. Pete Gerroy looked relaxed this morning in a tattersall shirt and tweed jacket, no tie. The editorial look. Hilda gave her a smile and Ainslee winked back. She could count on that young woman. Beside her, Connie Kleiner's chair was empty. But she'd made her dispositions to cover that hole in her front . . . all in due time . . . At the far end of the table sat Ron Frontino, heavy-lidded and even a little sleepy looking. The chief operating officer of Thunder Oil nodded as she noted him. Frontino's loyalty? She'd hired him, but he wasn't from Hemlock County. His first concern would be whether a change at the top would threaten his position. As long as she looked like a winner, he'd support her. If she betrayed weakness, though, it was perfectly possible for him to flip. Beside him sat the other officer-director, Rogers McGehee, short, balding, and fussy in a three-piece banker's uniform. An old family friend, a regular at the Christmas parties at the house in town. He too would back her initially, but she knew Rogers needed his salary from First Raymondsville.

So far, that was three votes firmly for her, and two lukewarm allies.

Ranked along the polished wood on her left, the enemy. Never really her friends, but only now revealed for what they truly were. Blair and Kemick sat close together, murmuring in low voices. Blair debriefing the other on her response to his offer, no doubt. Parseghian looked youthful in a European-cut suit and one of the two-hundred-dollar silk ties that seemed to be his only vice. He gave her an unsmiling half-bow before seating himself. She nodded coldly and adjusted the lectern. Time to start, and she knew now how she was going to approach the coming test of strength. Compromise meant defeat. Once they saw she would permit no retreat and take no prisoners, the waverers would fall into line. She flicked a finger to Weyandt and he closed the doors. Instead of taking his usual seat against the wall, though, he remained standing.

"Good morning, ladies and gentlemen. This special meeting of the board of directors of The Thunder Group is called to order. We have a quorum. Thanks, Hilda, Pete, Luke, for coming in at such short notice. However, Mr. Conrad Kleiner will not be with us today. Connie is down with the flu. But he has faxed me"—she held it up, not concealing a grim smile—"his proxy. He has requested that Mr. Rudolf Weyandt will take his seat today and vote in his place. I ask you to welcome Mr. Weyandt." She paused as he came forward, sat, as Pete leaned over to shake his hand. Then went on, "It is my intention to propose Mr. Weyandt, as an executive vice president of the corporation and a sizable stockholder in his own right, as an additional member of the board at our annual meeting in April."

Parseghian and Kemick sat immobile, expressions betraying neither regret nor anger, nor any emotion at all. Blair looked tired, resigned. All right, she thought, you people want to play poker? You lost the first hand. Let's see how you like the next one.

After all, she was the dealer.

"Let's see . . . treasurer's report . . . minutes . . . well, those are not yet ready, given that this meeting seems to have been scheduled without notifying the secretary or the treasurer. So unless there are objections we will skip over that part of the procedure and proceed to the business at hand." She looked around, meeting each set of eyes in turn. She felt electric, charged. It was time to begin.

"The floor is open for motions."

Blair lifted his hand. "Madame Chairman."

"The chair recognizes Mr. Blair."

"I would like at this point to adjourn for a few minutes. Mr. Kemick and I would like to consult with you privately."

She shook her head. "No, Mr. Blair. I'll put adjournment to a vote, if you want to move the question, but we all know what we're here for. And we'll have it all out in the open so the stockholders and public can see exactly what is happening. If you have a motion to make, let's get to it. If you don't, then say so and we will adjourn without further action."

Blair shook his head, subsiding, and Kemick said, "May I have the floor?"

"You have the floor, Quentin."

Kemick began his speech by praising her for the progress the company had made since the reorganization. She sat blank-faced, letting herself show neither pleasure nor displeasure. The red light of Bisker's video camera burned at the corner of her sight, as she knew it burned in his. From his encomium he went into his little talk about turning over management every five or six years. It was the same spiel he'd given her in New York about Frontino; the message, she now realized, had been aimed at her. Okay, she'd been with Thunder a long time. Since she was born. But when your family owned the company, *was* the company, what better motivation to keep you alert every minute, scheming to gain any advantage or toehold? She tuned back in for his closing. "I therefore move that Ainslee Thunner be tendered the thanks of this board, and be permitted to vacate the position of chief executive officer, while retaining the positions of president and chairman, as long as she shall wish to so serve."

She said crisply, "Any discussion?" and Hilda, bless her, leaned forward and said, "But does Ainslee *want* to go?"

"I'll answer that, Hilda. I most definitely do not feel it is in the interests of the company, the employees, or the shareholders of The Thunder Group that I should step down as chief executive officer at this critical time. This resolution has been introduced without my concurrence and I disagree with its premises. As Mr. Kemick has so kindly pointed out, Thunder has weathered a difficult period, but we are not yet safe. Our strategy of investing in oil and gas assets and modernizing our production capacity during a weak market period will position us for increased profitability and value when prices rebound.

"This motion is an attempt by outside interests, I suspect without the knowledge of the institutions they represent, to unseat me and impose an imported management team. I don't believe their ultimate goal is the welfare of Thunder or even its continued existence." She reflected, then decided that should be it; keep it brief, it could play well as a sound bite on the evening news. "Any other remarks?"

"I can't believe they want to replace you, Ainslee."

"Thanks, Luke." She waited for the others to speak: Frontino, Mc-Gehee, Gerroy. But they didn't. They didn't look happy, but they didn't look angry, either. They seemed to be thinking it over. Was delay in her interest or in theirs? She decided they were looking to her for leadership. She also decided to start the voting with the hostile side of the table, to draw the line in the sand, locals versus outsiders. So she said, "Okay, shall we vote? Let's start on my left."

"In favor," said Blair, his face hardened now. Yes, he could see he was in trouble. But how could he ever have thought they'd win?

"Aye," Parseghian said.

"Aye," said Kemick.

That brought it down to Frontino. The chief operating officer of Thunder Oil sat robot-immobile. She held his gaze, making sure he understood what would happen to him if he voted against her and she won.

Then he too said, "Aye."

Her hands tightened on the lectern. They'd co-opted him, there was no other possibility. Who else had they suborned? But McGehee, good old Rogers, bristling like an enraged porcupine, said, "Certainly not. This is a power grab! I vote in the negative!"

"Thank you, Rogers," she said quietly. Four to one. But now her side was coming to bat. "Pete?"

"Nay."

"Hilda?"

"Nay."

"Rudy?"

And Rudy Weyandt, looking across the table at Kemick, said in a strong, confident voice, "I respect Ainslee's abilities. But I think we need to re-orient the company to the future. We need a new direction for Thunder. I vote aye."

She stood thunderstruck, unable for a moment to speak. Then fury surged, but she tamped it down, kept her expression steady. Said in a level voice, "Luke?"

Fleming looked across the table, glanced at Weyandt, beside him, then up at her. "Well?" she prompted him.

"Uh, I abstain," said Fleming.

She couldn't believe her ears. "Luke, what—you're an oilman, you understand how important it is to us to invest—"

"I abstain," he said stubbornly. "You heard me."

"All right, what's that make it?" said Kemick. "That's five in favor, one abstention, three against. The motion carries."

"*Four* against," Ainslee snapped. "I most definitely am not voting in favor."

From his seat by the window the lawyer, Whiteways, whom she had forgotten, said, "You can't do that, Madame Chairman. I've studied Thunder's bylaws. It's there in black and white: no director may vote in any question concerning his status or salary as an officer in the corporation."

She stood frozen, remembering now. It was true.

"You lost, Ainslee," Kemick said softly. "Would you mind leaving us for a moment?"

"What for?"

"A compensation matter."

"I have no intention of leaving this room."

"Ainslee," said Blair. "Please. We are going to discuss a matter relating to your compensation, and you are required to leave. We will call you back in no more than five minutes."

But still she stood frozen. Her eyes were locked on the window, on the plume of smoke and steam and fire rising as it always rose from the great refinery. White steam against the gray hills.

But she was really seeing her father, holding her hand as they walked through the acre-sprawling pipe-ceilinged maze of the process area. She remembered looking up in awe at the great stacks of the powerhouse and the receiving tanks and the chemical treatment building and, mysterious and wonderful, the soaring towers her father told her "cracked" the raw crude to yield gasoline, diesel, kerosene, heavy fractions, and, most valuable of all, the golden-green Pennsylvania grade motor oil the world demanded as rapidly as they could produce it. Enfolding them as they walked was a cocoon of sound that never ebbed or eased: the hollow roar of compressors and boilers, the echoing clank of switches, the *clickety-creak* of railcars, tank cars rolling slowly down the spur lines, and the eerie flicker of the flareoffs; and she breathed in to become part of her childhood and her very self the sweet petrol smells so thick you could taste them and the wet mildew stink of steam and the scorching smell of welding as above them tiny men climbed like ants amid the intricate, interlocking spiderweb of stairs and pipes and tanks and pumps and towers.

She stood frozen, hearing and seeing it all again. Then finally understanding, with a physical shock that felt like her own heart was being cracked apart, that it was over.

For the first time in a hundred and twenty years, a Thunner was no longer in charge.

She left the lectern and drifted dreamlike across the room. The men rose as she left, and the door closed behind her without a sound.

———

She stood in the hallway, fists doubled, as feeling and rage returned. Alone in the carpeted corridor, outside the oaken doors, she panted rapidly as a runner who has just been defeated, and who yearns for another race.

The door opened—Weyandt, not meeting her eyes. "You can come back in now."

She braced herself at the head of the table, feeling like a convicted criminal awaiting sentence. McGehee, Hilda, and Gerroy gazed at her fiercely, as if expecting her still to rally them and triumph somehow. The others doodled or examined the ceiling as Kemick said with lubricious ponderousness, "Ms. Thunner, in recognition of your importance to The Thunder Group as president, the board has decided that an additional eighty thousand dollars per annum shall be added to your current salary of nine hundred and twenty thousand, along with an upgraded package of executive benefits."

"Thank you," she murmured. Waited a moment, then moved to the lectern again. Before she could speak Parseghian raised his hand. She recognized him with a nod.

"For the post of interim chief executive officer, pending a thorough management review, I propose Mr. Rudolf Weyandt."

She opened her mouth to protest, then forced herself to close it. Forced herself back into presiding over what felt like her own liquidation. She could not fight this new outrage. Two defeats in a row would finish her. She said through numb lips, "Are there any other nominations?"

"I nominate Ainslee Thunner," said McGehee, glaring at Weyandt. "This is a very shabby business. I intend to hold this new, this new management to very strict standards of accountability."

"How many shares do you own in Thunder, McGehee?" Parseghian asked, and suddenly the polite veneer tore, and through it thrust the ruthless muzzle of a hungry animal. "You and the other old-line directors have kept this company moribund for years. Thunder has got to change or die. I do not intend to let sentiment, friendship, personalities, outworn tradition, *anything* stand in the way of a fair return to my stockholders. Wilsonia, Besarcon, and Blair Partners agree that we have to move toward the future."

Ainslee waited him out. They'd raised her salary as president, there were compliments and testimonials, but she was not mollified. She knew stripping her of that title too was only a little distance away, and that at the next annual meeting there would be a new slate for the board and an alternate nominee for chairman, too.

The motion to make Weyandt chief executive officer passed.

There was no other business and she closed the meeting abruptly. The directors filed out in silence. Hilda came over and took her hand. "We'll fight it," she whispered, and Ainslee nodded. Suddenly she felt tired. She wasn't old, but she felt ancient, exhausted.

Then, incredibly, Weyandt was standing in front of her. He said, "Ainslee, a word?"

"What more do you want, Rudy? There's not much left."

"I want to explain. I know how you expected me to vote. But it just wasn't in the best interest of the company."

"Really?"

"Yes, really, and in a year or two you'll agree. Once they have our sails trimmed to their satisfaction, I have a feeling Bernard and Quentin will be more open to additional investment. Then we can do all the things you planned—but with their money instead of ours."

She stilled the first words that rose to her lips. She wanted to lash out, to say, "How clever. And to think I actually thought you were selling me out for a prearranged promotion." But she didn't. Looking carefully into his eyes, she understood she had both underestimated and misjudged Rudolf Weyandt. He could not have betrayed her had she not trusted him off the leash. Now that he was in position as CEO, though, he would be nearly impossible to dislodge. As he'd so carefully pointed out to her in New York, he was her only credible successor. He'd spent his career with Thunder; the Van Ettens, the Gerroys, the Whites knew and accepted him. But he was flexible enough to do the bidding of outsiders. Would he really sell out, destroy, strip, and loot the company he'd spent his life with? She had to admit that it wouldn't surprise her. After all, it had never had his name on it.

It would be very difficult to retrieve the battle she'd just lost. But already she was planning how it could be done. So now, looking into his eyes, she was careful to give no clue to what was in her heart. Instead she said, tone neutral, "I see. Well, I won't pretend I'm happy about it right now, but maybe it will all work out."

"We've got to work together, Ainslee. This is just how business goes sometimes. You know that better than anyone."

"I understand, Rudy," she said. "But I don't want to discuss it right now, all right? Let's cool off a little, then we'll talk about it before the Besarcon team gets here."

She saw his relief, and made herself take his hand as he held it out. "I'll come up tomorrow," he said. "See if we can work out an orderly turnover."

"Ms. Thunner? What did you want me to do with this tape?"

Parseghian had lingered in the doorway. She caught his smirk as she told the PR director, "Leave it on my desk, Judy. Don't release it, don't make any copies." And past Parseghian she saw Kemick and Blair, heads together again by the elevator.

Yes, gloat, you bastards, she thought. You beat me today. To them all, even to Weyandt, she had returned a soft reply. She did not yet know how she would win it. But in her heart she knew the war for Thunder had only begun.

Nineteen

loyd C. Froster Middle School was out at the east end of town, on a flat plain above the river. The hills behind it were black backdrops in the blue evening as Dr. Friedman, driving more cautiously since her near-accident the day before, turned off Finney Parkway. As her car growled upward the lot came into view. Dozens of headlights were wheeling in, and she saw she was going to have to park along the road. Fortunately she had her boots on and a heavy coat. A lot of people, she thought. And no wonder, after the news that afternoon. News that had moved the public meeting she'd proposed to a more capacious location.

The news about the Benning girl.

The corridors were brightly lit and she felt a rush of chronological vertigo. The school she'd gone to in Queens had looked like this, smelled like this, and each open door she passed, each momentary vista of empty chairs and footscuffed floors seemed to taunt *you're late, and you haven't studied.* The other adults streaming in must have felt it too. Gray-haired ladies giggled like sophomores. A stout man punched a locker door with a tentative fist. Then the glass expanse of a trophy case reflected tired eyes and lank dry hair, and she knew she wasn't fifteen or even twice that age.

The auditorium was already filled and people were sitting on the floor along the aisles. On the stage behind a folding table sat the mayor; Rob Witchen, the game protector; a man she didn't know; and Bill Sealey. The state cop sat stolidly, hands on his thighs. Froster looked nervous; beneath the table his leg jittered. Leah climbed the steps and stood waiting until

Sealey cleared his throat and said, "George, the doctor needs a chair." She settled in to his left, crossed her ankles demurely, and folded her hands in her lap. There.

Froster glanced at his watch and stood. Raised his hands. "Good evening . . . let's quiet down . . . Thank you all for coming. Neighbors facing problems together, that's what makes me feel great about this town."

"No campaign speeches, George."

The assembly murmured like a rising wind and he added quickly, "No speeches, I hear you. Okay, what we're here for tonight. First, the attack on the engineer from Petroleum City. Then the body, the woman they found south of Derris. We've sent fingerprints to the FBI, but there's still no ID on that victim, by the way. And now and most—uh—well, they're all unfortunate, but now we have little Becky Piccirillo, who by the way attends this very school. You all know she's missing and we're all very worried about her.

"Okay, we're here tonight to discuss these events, especially Becky's disappearance, listen to some experts, and get some sense of where the community wants us to go. Then your elected officials can go on out and take action. Now, it's important we allow each person the chance to speak without interruptions or heckling. Oh, I also want to say Pat Nolan couldn't be here because he's coordinating the search for Becky. Okay, now please listen and let's observe our courtesies. First, let's hear from Sergeant Bill Sealey, station commander, Pennsylvania State Police."

Sealey stood heavily. "By now you've all heard about Becky. Her parents found her bed empty this morning and called me. The trooper we sent found her footprints leading up into the woods behind her house on Crawford Run. He also found and photographed tracks that indicate we have on our hands a pack of either large dogs or wolves—the tracks are too large for coyotes. However, there was no sign of violence or injury to the missing child at that point. Now, as far as the search. Forestry's lead agency on search and rescue, but we've got everyone at our barracks out, and the Game people are helping too. We'll have a helicopter coming in to Lantzy Airport at first light. I don't know if it'll be much use, actually, till the weather lifts. But everything we can possibly do to find Becky will be done.

"Now let's talk about these animals. Bob, want to introduce your friend?"

The game warden said, "Thanks, Bill. This fella sitting up here with us is Scott Ostrander, the game commission wildlife biologist from over in Kane. He's an elk specialist but he's seen wolves in action up on Isle Royale. I asked him to come over and look at the tracks. He'll brief us on his conclusions."

The biologist stood slowly, looked around, put his hands into his pockets. He sounded like he had a bad cold. "I want to say first off that I'm no expert on wolf behavior. But I examined the tracks up at the Piccirillo place. They were pretty well snowed over, and when we got to the upwind side of the hill we lost them. So we can't be sure which direction she went in after that. There were three individual animals. All were the size of mature adult gray or timber wolves. *Canis lupus.* Five-inch pads. Judging by the length of the strides, they weren't moving very fast. The girl was also walking."

"So they're definitely wolves?" someone asked from the audience.

"That's my opinion." Ostrander took out a handkerchief and blew his nose.

"Where did they come from?"

"Hard to say. The closest known free-ranging wolves are in Michigan, the Upper Peninsula. It's hard for me to accept that any could filter this far south and east with no sightings in between. We're talking about all of southern Michigan, then Ohio in order to get here. Still"—he paused—"I won't say it's impossible. That they came from there, I mean. There are instances on record in Canada and Minnesota where individuals have turned up hundreds of miles from their parent packs."

Someone called up, "Are we sure the tracks were made at the same time? That they're not independent of each other?"

"The way I read them, the wolves were following the girl as she went into the woods." The biologist paused, but aside from a general murmur no one interrupted him; he went on. "The good news is that there was no sign at any point of any attack on her or of any blood. The only odd thing we found was a burnt spot, bits of burnt plastic. We're not sure what it was." He cleared his throat. "That's about all I can contribute from a scientific viewpoint. Once we break from here, I'm going to rejoin the search."

"All right, maybe it's time for public input," said Froster. "If you want to speak, stand up. State your name and then go on and say whatever you got to say. You there, sir, in the Agway hat."

"My name is Warner Fetzeck and I'm a farmer, got a place north of here on Todds Creek. I been hearing howling at night and I seen tracks too. I thought they were coy-dogs but now I guess I was wrong. This about the little girl, this is just terrible. What I want to say is, I got sheep, I got pigs, I got milk cows. If there's wolves out there I want them taken care of. Killed, or took back to wherever they come from. That's what I pay taxes for and I want it done." He sat down to a good deal of applause.

"Next, you over here in front."

"Name's Ernie Bauer and I agree with Warner. I'm a farmer too. And I got a daughter. My granddad used to tell me stories about how you couldn't walk in the woods in the old days without a rifle. I don't want to go back to that, but I got a twelve-gauge. I see a wolf, I'll kill it."

A hunter spoke next. He said quietly that he didn't have anything against wolves, but that they had been replaced as predators. "We've already got bears and coyotes out there. Those and the human hunters are enough to regulate the deer population. There just isn't room anymore in the ecosystem for every animal that's historically been there. Point two: deer are our major crop in Hemlock County. I'm not just some bowhunter, I pay taxes here too. If we start letting wolves compete, we're going to be cutting our throats in terms of the people who come here to hunt, who support local businesses and keep a lot of us off the welfare rolls." He sat down to scattered clapping.

The next to stand was a young woman, thin, her face placid. She held a baby in her arms. When the mayor pointed to her she said, "My name is Mary Bryner, and I think you're all wrong."

"Go ahead, Mary," said Froster.

"I think you're all being very selfish. Wolves were here a long time before we were. The Indians got along with them. Then we came here and killed them all. Now there's a few of them coming back. Well, I don't see why we can't live with them. I saw on the television about a man who even lived with the wolves. If you're a farmer, all you got to do is put up a fence. I think everybody around here is too concerned with the money. They advertise and get the hunters in here and it's all a business. Well, I'm not very smart but I don't see why it's okay for people to kill deer but the wolves can't." She sat down, and Froster said, "Thank you for your viewpoint, Mrs. Bryner. Who's next?"

Leah cleared her throat, but Froster seemed not to hear or see her. She leaned over into his field of view but he kept calling on people in the crowd. More hunters spoke, and people who lived near the woods, most with children. They all called for extermination. Then a pale man struggled up on crutches. Froster recognized him.

"My name's Zias. I met the animals you're talking about."

The murmurs rose, accompanied by hisses to keep quiet and listen. The man straightened. "I was putting a radio relay up in a tree on Colley Hill when I looked down and there they were. There was no way I could get away. They were wolves, all right. I've looked at pictures since then, and that's exactly what they were.

"What I want to say is—I don't know exactly how—but I got to say it. A branch broke under me and I fell right into the middle of them. When I come to I had a busted leg. But they didn't hurt me. The tracks were all around but I was alive. I crawled downhill and some people found me before I froze to death. I don't know anything about this Chinese woman and I don't know about this little girl that got lost. But they had the chance to get me and they didn't take it. That's all I got to say." He sagged slowly down and a dark-haired woman put her arm around his shoulders.

A stir in the back, heads turning as three people made their way down the aisle. One was a minister. Froster stood, motioning for silence.

"I believe—Mrs. Piccirillo?" he said.

"Yes, I'm Hallie Piccirillo. I just wanted to come down and say thank you for being concerned about Becky. Thank you for your help, and your prayers. I know the people who are out looking will find her. I just hope they're not too late, that when they do she's not . . ." She put her head down and didn't continue.

So the man beside her did. "My wife's grateful and so am I. But I don't think we should assume that the animals are to blame. Or even associated with her leaving. Becky's been under some emotional strain. It's possible she wandered out there on her own, and—"

"Stop. Stop it!"

He turned a shocked face to his wife. She said, "They took her and you're saying don't kill them? I don't—I don't believe this. I don't believe it!" Her voice rose and the clergyman put his hand on her arm and she turned away from both of them and ran back up the aisle.

Leah stood, taking advantage of the hush that followed. "Dr. Leah Friedman. Look, I originally proposed this meeting to discuss what we need to do. There are some other disturbing aspects. Not just Becky, though she's in all our thoughts right now. We need to talk this out at length. I propose we form a committee—"

"Committee, hell!" Other shouts broke out and she halted, surprised.

"No more discussion!" Vince Barnett yelled. "Now hear this! I want every man with a gun and a pair of snowshoes at home to join me out in the hall. I've got a topo map. We'll divide the whole county south of Route Six into sections, and starting at sunrise we'll hit the woods and stay there till we find Becky."

"Just a moment. Mayor. Mayor!"

A woman in a pale green uniform stood with head lifted, waiting to be recognized.

"Uh, Vince, hold on a second, okay? Abby's got something to say. Just quiet down, folks. We got the federal government here wants to say something."

Leah watched the petite woman as she climbed the steps to the platform. Abby Randall was a new face in the county, the first female forest service ranger Hemlock had seen. Not only that, she was the district ranger, overseer of the hundreds of square miles of the Kinningmahontawany district of the Allegheny National Forest. The bronze badge shone above her uniform pocket as she slipped a card out into her hand and stood square in the center of the stage.

"Good evening, and I want to make an announcement. It's something we had planned a full report on later this year, but based on recent events, maybe that was a mistake. To wait, I mean.

"So, this will be the official announcement. One year ago, the U.S. Fish and Wildlife Service, in consultation with the U.S. Forest Service, implemented the reintroduction of an experimental population of *Canis lupus* by means of a hard release of six adult individuals within the boundaries of the Kinningmahontawany Wild Area."

"No," Leah breathed. Then, she was on her feet, with the rest of the audience, shouting and screaming, many shaking their fists. Randall stood waiting it out as Froster struggled to get the crowd pacified to where she could be heard again. Behind her the men from the state game commission were on their feet too, staring incredulously at her erect back.

Finally the ranger was able to resume. "We implemented the experimental project in response to direction from Congress in the form of the Endangered Species Act. As part of our long-term plan red wolves have already been successfully reintroduced in North Carolina. The western wolf is reestablishing in Glacier Park and we're looking at the Adirondacks and the Great Smokies. Kinningmahontawany is the largest vacant wolf habitat in the Eastern states. Reintroducing the eastern timber wolf here is the next step for the wolf recovery program."

"And now they've killed a child," someone yelled.

"I very much doubt if the wolves had anything to do with harming Becky Piccirillo," said Randall calmly. "The girl probably wandered into the woods on her own, and the presence of wolf tracks was purely coincidental. I'm sure we'll find her, and all the personnel I have available will join in the search."

Leah finally got Froster to nod her way. She said, "How could you do this? I'm not against wolves, not necessarily, but how could you release them without consulting the local population?"

"We learned from Yellowstone not to get bogged down in public hearings and politics. That project could have been done very simply and quietly. Instead it's become a—"

She couldn't believe what she was hearing. "So now you just sneak them in without telling anyone?"

"No, we execute a low-public-impact reintroduction strategy. Remember, this is only an experiment. If it's a failure—"

"It's already a failure," someone shouted from the floor.

"Now, let the Forest Service have its say," said Froster. Leah saw the glitter of sweat on his brow.

The game warden said, raising his voice above the tumult, "I want to make it clear to everyone here that the state game commission is not involved in this. We were not consulted and I think it's safe to say there's going to be a strong reaction from Harrisburg."

Randall waited, hands on her hips. "If you really think we've put something over on you, I'm sorry. But all our studies show the reintroduction will turn out to be a net benefit, economically."

"Packs of wolves roaming the woods, that's going to make us money?"

"Increased tourism will. You don't seem to realize what a boon this can be as a natural attraction."

"And meanwhile they're eating our kids?"

Randall said imperturbably, "If, and I emphasize that *if*, they do turn out to be a threat, there are several possible approaches. One is to live with the problem, compensating for livestock losses and other damage as necessary. There are control strategies that can be implemented, including relocation or elimination of problem wolves. Our studies show that a small population of perhaps two to four breeding pairs could be supported solely by the land currently contained within the Wild Area. Let me emphasize again, none of this is engraved in stone. There'll be time for everyone to discuss and comment on it during the development of the environmental impact statement."

"And then what? Then there's no hunting there?"

"You may have a point," said Randall.

"Good, I'm glad you—"

She said calmly, "Maybe you're right, and these animals are more dangerous than the experts think. As the ranger in charge, I have to bear public safety in mind. So, effective immediately, with the exception of properly authorized state and federal personnel, I hereby declare the Wild Area closed. Maybe that's the best solution, until we all have time to think it over."

For a moment they all sat silent, and Leah saw the dark zeros of open mouths. Then men rose, shaking their fists, shouting obscenities and threats in a sudden din. Randall faced it all, and Leah had to admire how cool she was.

Finally she could make out Froster's voice. He'd found a gavel somewhere and was whanging it on the back of his metal chair. "Quiet, please. Quiet! Uh, thank you, ranger, for being so—up front with us. We may need, we may need a little time to consider this whole matter. And we'd like to see any figures you have on the economic impact you mentioned. Ms. Randall, anything else?"

"No, I think that's about all I want to say right now."

The audience seemed stunned. A buzzing rose here and there. But the district ranger had demonstrated her power beyond any possibility of doubt. With the federal lands closed to lumbering and hunting, the county was effectively under blockade. So that when Froster declared the meeting closed and people stood and began shoving out they still hadn't come up with anything they all agreed on. Even Leah's idea of a study committee had just died.

She saw Vince Barnett standing in the back of the hall. Men clamored around him, but he wasn't responding. His eyes passed over her without seeing her. He looked dazed. Join the club, Vince, she thought as she pushed past. For the first time since she'd come to the county she felt like they were on the same side. Against the forest service, they were helpless. There wasn't a thing the few thousand inhabitants of Hemlock County could do faced with the federal government.

She'd hoped a meeting would let everyone discover they wanted the same thing, get them to find their common direction. But now, as she joined the throng outside, it seemed to her that they were all lost, and that the dark was gathering all around.

Twenty

W. T. Halvorsen looked up through the skeletal treetops for the tenth time that morning, sucking air through aching teeth, then turned his head and spat. He looked passionlessly down at the black clot of blood on the snow.

The whirling, driving darkness above the hills told him all he needed to know: that there'd be more snow soon, and that it would get colder. Much colder.

Halvorsen had walked a long way in the last two days, and he was tired. His snowshoes dragged in the deepening powder. When they caught in nooses of blackberry bramble he lay for long minutes, mind nearly blank, till he levered himself up wearily again amid the towering ravines, the great shadowy boles of the old forest.

He stood now at the crest of a long hill deep, deep in the Wild Area. The vanished city of Cibola lay miles behind, the last half-erased traces of man. He had left the Hefner and struck south, into a blank area on the map. Trudging on mile after mile, he had passed gradually from the land he knew to a land he did not recognize; from a land with names to one with none; to hills that were more rugged than he remembered, to remote and savage valleys that had slept from the beginning of time without hearing the ax of the white man.

Somewhere down here was Floyd Creek.

Later he limped slowly down a short grade from the crest. He emerged from the woods, the scattered trees along this rocky and infertile crown. And stopped, his body going tense as he stared down.

He stood at the edge of a drop so steep he couldn't see the bottom, only a sheer falling-away to a jumble of white-frosted rocks a hundred feet below; and a step out from them, a white nothingness. He backed slowly, confronting the abyss as if outstaring an enemy. Not till he was a few steps distant, anchored against the furrowed gray-black solidity of a huge maple, did he feel braced against the terrible absence that gazed unblinkingly back at him.

The hill dropped away below him as if sheared off by a gigantic blade. Whatever had done it, glacier or long-vanished river, it fell so starkly that here and there great rocks thrust out from the frozen soil like black rounded thumbs. At the steepest points the trees themselves had given up clinging to the bare rock. Long stretches of scree lay naked, too steep for even the snow to stick to.

Lifting the straps off his shoulders, swinging his pack down to the snow, he peered out into white nothingness. Into a mist, a fog as opaque as if the created universe itself ended a few feet out from the toes of his snowshoes. His mind told him there had to be ground down there, but he couldn't see any. He couldn't even see treetops. So it was a hell of a long ways down. His numbed searching fingers found the coil of rope at the bottom of the pack. But then he just stood with it dangling in his hands.

Finally he sighed. Even with the rope, he wasn't going to make it down this cliff. Not here. He coiled the rope slowly again and then slipped off his snowshoes, used the line to lash them to the pack frame. He stamped circulation back into his feet and began slogging east toward the gradually dropping crest that he dimly sensed through the gray-silver curtain of the snow.

Yeah, he was tired. For five days he'd been slogging, uphill and down, first along road and lease road, then abandoned trail and after that, for the last couple days, breaking his own way through deep snow. At first it had been a joy, to see again the land he loved. He was surrounded again by the forest he'd spent his life in, and its minutest details were familiar and dear to him. The way birch roots gripped a boulder like the tentacles of a slow octopus; the bluish lichens that spelled north on a maple trunk sure as any compass; the huge old wild grapevines, big around as his thigh, that hung in great loops from a fungus-spotted beech. The faraway crash and splinter of a falling tree, echoing in the stillness, startling a deer into flight.

But gradually his body had informed him, with steadily growing insistence, that he was old. It took hours now to fight his way up a hard slope. His joints ached and after that first night he hadn't slept well. He went under, but only to a dogged, exhausted unconsciousness that when morning came left him nearly as tired as when he'd laid down his head. The steadily dropping temperature hadn't helped either. He had what he needed. His old mummy bag, coat, earflapped hat, good boots. A fire every night. But still the cold was creeping in. Curling itself around his bones. Jelling his blood. Till he had to stop every few steps and rest, clinging to a tree as if trying to suck energy out of thickened sap and steel-cold bark. Till he felt as if he too was sinking to the temperature of the immense emptiness all around, returning step by step to the silent, cold quiescence of the unliving rock.

At midmorning he made out a ravine ahead, cutting into the steep fall of the hill. Over the eons a spring, a stream, had sawed out a rock-walled gorge. He could make out the white flatness of frozen pools at intervals down it. Pines sagged where the undercut bank was crumbling away. Their comblike branches formed an interlocking ladder that he could maybe work his way down, if he was careful and took his time. He didn't like to think about falling. All he had to do was break a leg and he'd be dead. They'd never find him out here. He hadn't seen so much as a footprint since leaving the Hefner. He slogged up to the edge and stared down, trying to extract a navigable path from the jumble of white and gray and black that faded as it fell into the mist. There. A shallower descent gave onto a knit jumble of evergreen, some fallen, some still growing slanted out over the abyss. Below that, boulders, then what looked like scree. The scree would be tricky. Beyond that the land fell away so that he couldn't see.

Uncoiling the rope, he slid downward into the jaws of the ravine.

Half an hour later he reached the evergreens. Scrawny, low, they were more shrubs than trees, huddled in a triangle over a jutting shelf of ground like, he thought, a woman's pubic hair. Beneath their stubby branches, loaded so solid with rounded white it was nearly dark under them, the ground was covered with a mattress of short needles many inches thick, soft and spicy-smelling. He collapsed panting on it, looking up at the interlocking green. He pinched off a branchlet and held it to his eyes, then his nose. The underside of the needles was almost white and it smelled like gin. Juniper, all right. For some strange reason just having the cover of the branches between him and the curling blank whiteness made him feel safer.

He lay there for a long time, and gradually his eyes sank closed. His ragged breathing slowed. His fingers moved spasmodically, grasping at the soft ground.

He woke to the distant bark of a fox, echoing and reechoing far below, rising with a weird buoyant clarity through the mist. He stared up. For a time his mind floated, as imprintless and formless as white fog. What'm I doing here? he asked himself. Where the hey am I?

When it finally came back to him he shook his head, then got stiffly to his feet. His hands moved in shuddering jerks, brushing dried needles from where they clung to wool. Then his fingers paused. Reached up to pluck off a dead twig.

A few minutes later a tiny fire was crackling inside a stone ring barely a foot across. Halvorsen reached his pan up through the branches for snow. When it bubbled above the unwavering yellow flame he snapped his old Case closed and tilted in the handful of aromatic bark. Let it steep for a few minutes, then strained the bark out with his teeth, working his lips as he sucked in the hot resinous infusion.

The last curl of smoke hung above the stamped-out fire. The ring of stones lay scattered. Below it he slid downward, sending flat gray rocks spinning and clattering away below him, braking himself at each step as his fingers gnarled around the dwarfed and twisted trunks.

He was picking his way along the bottom of the ravine, through fallen, half-decayed trunks and a clutter of stones the size and shape of severed heads, when it began to snow again. A few random crystals fell first, like scouts. Then, suddenly, a dizzying mesh of twisting, whirling flakes crowded the narrow air, clinging together as they dropped, heavy and dense. Around him the agonized shapes of the cliff-clinging trees loomed dark as graphite and rigid as cast iron through the heatless incandescence of the falling snow. He pushed on grimly, stopping to lean against the mossy flank of a boulder when he felt too weak to stand. And gradually, through the thronged air, he sensed as much as saw the floor of the valley below gradually emerging from the white formlessness.

Now and then as he rested, his staring eyes fixed for long seconds on a white flatness between the banks. The snicker of flowing water teased his hearing.

At last it occurred to him that he ought to refill his canteen. He snapped off a dead branch and broomed it cautiously across the snow. Beneath was black ice. His stiff fingers wrestled a rock from frozen soil. Lifted it above his head, smashed it down again and again. Till finally the black mirror cracked, then shattered into flakes fine and sharp as obsidian. Kneeling, he plunged his canteen in, letting it gurgle its fill of icy-cold spring water. Then he took a mouthful. The icy fluid chilled his gums instantly to numb insensibility.

Not long after that he came out of the ravine at the bottom of the valley. He still couldn't see much. The wavering circular curtain of falling snow was drawn close all around him. Down here the ground cover was deep, two or three feet, and he strapped on his Hurons again. But as he shuffled forward he found the land rising again, then dropping, in a series of broken low ridges.

Gradually the knowledge came to him that it was time to turn back. He felt dispirited, weak, and worst of all, old. There was no more food in his pack. He sighed, reading the skittering shorthand in a tight thicketing of hobblebush and trillium and elderberry. Snowshoe hare, turkey, grouse. He looked for the tracks of the fox he'd heard barking from up above but didn't see any.

He'd penetrated to the heart of the Wild Area and found it empty. Well, that too meant something. Maybe the last long hike he'd ever take, if he got out. He thought he could, though. If he could find or catch something to eat . . . strike east, and after maybe a day he'd come out on Elk Creek. Downhill from there would take him into Potter County, somewhere south of Fox Mountain. He'd hit the First Fork sooner or later. He could pick up the road again there, take the easy way back.

But all this time he was still moving forward. Very slowly, but still trudging on. His snowshoes creaked as they took his weight, imprinting themselves down into the fluffy blank surface of virgin snow. The Floyd Valley . . . long as he'd gotten himself here, he really ought to go all the way to the far side. Make absolutely sure.

He decided to go one more mile south before heading out. Should be one range of hills, two at the most, before he hit Elk Creek. He could last that long. Just rest up tonight, maybe trap something for dinner. His mouth watered at the thought of rabbit stew, roasted rabbit.

He pushed on, a warm trickle of breath bleeding from his lips and drifting away in ghost-vapor on an almost unnoticeable wind. Above his bent head the snow whirled down heavier now, muffling, spiraling out of white mist to the white ground. He couldn't see more than fifty yards now. Only the black traceries of the catbrier and blackberries had reality. That and the hoarse sawing of his breath, the dragging weight of the pack, the nagging sharp aches in his knees and ankles and back.

Beneath his feet the land leveled again. The broad laced flats of the snowshoes crunched as they trod down crisp vegetation beneath the heavy coat of snow, springy, rebounding as he lifted his feet once more. In summer this must be some kind of meadow.

Then he saw the stream.

It was fast and deep, built of all the springs that came down all the ravines
in this remote valley. The transparent water looked somehow thicker than
water ought to look, like some heavier yet still crystalline fluid. It flowed
so swiftly around the boulders that bulged up from the basement of the
valley that instead of freezing it had built half-moon-shaped helmets of
ice over them.

Halvorsen stood on the bank, examining the stream. The mist hung
close, hugging it like a white shawl, and now he saw that it came from the
creek itself, curling up in pale evanescent tufts that wove themselves into
the overlying shroud of fog.

And down through it came the eternal snow. Each individual flake fell
steadily and without haste until it seemed to hesitate, hold its breath for
a moment, before plunging into the swiftly flowing blackness. The effect
was eerie, unsettling, like watching living beings plunging silently to their
deaths.

He jerked his eyes away and looked at the pattern the boulders made.
Upstream a near-bridge zagged across, but it was loaded with slick-looking
ice. He needed a ford, not stepping stones.

Or did he need to cross at all?

Maybe this was the end of his journey. The end of his penetration of
the unknown. If he crossed this creek, he'd have to come back over it to
strike east. If he fell in . . . at his age, that could be a death sentence. He
could save himself a lot of risk by just turning away.

On the other hand . . . he'd come so far. Youndt, the lawyer who'd
come out to his place, this was where he'd said Medina's operations were.
He really ought to make double-damn sure there was nothing here. Then
he could head back with a clear conscience and decide what to do after
that on the way.

Compacted brush crackled beneath the snow as he trudged upstream.
The river roared steadily below. He inhaled its dank icy breath, felt the
fog's clammy fingertips explore his face. There, a widening ahead; a possible ford. As he pushed closer he saw that once there'd been a dam here.
Maybe an old log pond years ago. Nothing now but scattered rocks in the
shallows. The ice had crept out from the banks and locked them in a
white embrace. Only through two narrow gaps did the water pour with a
hollow curving roar. Caught sticks bobbed, glazed with a transparent
sheath. The gaps looked just narrow enough he might be able to jump
them. If he slipped, though . . .

His guts cramped. He didn't want to go out on those rocks. He didn't
want to cross this river, so dark and swift-flowing, the only moving thing
in all the frozen valley. He shuddered, looking upward into the falling
snow. Why did this all seem so familiar?

Then he knew. It was the kind of place he'd always figured he'd die in.

He stood beside the ford for a long time, looking at the water. Finally he bent, hands shaking, and unlaced the harness on the snowshoes.

The first rock was flattish and jutted out from a four-foot bank. He approached it cautiously. The snow could be an overhang. He didn't want to step through it right down into the river. Two feet of snow on the rock. Solid under his feet. The iron-cold smell of water, the curling fog blowing toward him. The icy lips of the snowflakes on his eyelids. He edged out and studied the first gap. The water bawled endlessly, clear fingers of air prying up under it as it churned on and on over the rocks. Was there any other way across? He didn't see any. Hoped the far side wasn't slippery. Well, he could stand here long as he wanted, he didn't think any bridges were going to grow.

He landed hard, and one boot skidded off the turtlebacked rock into the water. He jerked it out, flailed his arms and almost fell backward before he dropped to all fours on the rock. His belly cramped again on fear and hunger as he crouched there, staring at the next gap. Farther across than he'd thought. Shoot, he didn't know if he could make this one. He straightened, arms outstretched for balance.

Then he stopped, blinking. Trembling at the edge of the leap, he stared down, into the depths of the stream.

A moment later he was on the far bank, scrambling through wet snow. Then he had a snowshoe in his hands. He grunted as he dug it in again and again, shovel-fashion, flinging huge clumps into the water to bob and capsize and slowly spin downstream like miniature icebergs.

The flash of yellow again. He dropped the snowshoe and dug with mittened hands. Then stood up, breathing hard but filled with triumph.

The plastic tube emerged from the stream and burrowed on across the meadow, invisible under the snow. If he hadn't glanced down as he crossed the creek he'd never have seen it.

It was standard polyethylene gas line, six inches in diameter, smooth and unmarked except for printing every few feet that identified the manufacturer. He couldn't hear anything over the roar of the river, but when he put his hand on it he could feel a faint, singing vibration. He jammed a heel down on it, brought all his weight to bear. It didn't yield or even indent. Close to five hundred pounds, then, average transportation pressure for a full-production field.

He looked up the valley, smiling faintly to himself behind the ice crystals clinging to face, whiskers, eyelashes. Bending again, he slipped his snowshoes back on.

———

An hour later he squatted at the edge of a copse of black birch, looking through a nearly impenetrable heath thicket of mountain laurel and wild rhododendron down at the camp.

It wasn't in Floyd Valley, but in one of the tributary ravines that opened into it from the south. Four small buildings were tucked into a stand of old-growth pine. A smokeless haze eddied above tin pipes. Barking came from behind them. Halvorsen couldn't see the dogs, but since he'd come in from crosswind they didn't worry him. And he was pretty confident he could pick cover well enough that nobody down there would see him. So he felt secure squatting there, watching.

After following the pipeline from the ford to the first well, he'd cut up onto the hill that formed the south wall of the valley. He'd stayed alert, moving one cautious, sliding step at a time, pale blue eyes examining each inch of tree and fold of land ahead. The first sign of the camp had been the muffled thudding of an engine. By the time he'd worked his way around the perimeter, staying above it on the hillside, he had things pretty well figured out.

He was looking at a bootleg production outfit.

Somebody was drilling gas wells in the Wild Area and using light lines to lead the gas out and sell it. Using the gas for heat, too, that was why there was no smoke above the stovepipes, no stacks of cordwood like you'd expect. One long unpainted building looked like a bunkhouse. Not exactly new, the wood was weathered gray, but it hadn't been there long. A stamped-out trail led between it and the other buildings, and a side branch descended to the little creek that laddered its way down the ravine from where he crouched. There wasn't much equipment in sight, but then you didn't need much once you had your wells drilled. Far away as the nearest power line was, he figured the engine throb was a diesel compressor.

When he figured he'd seen enough he stood cautiously, brushing snow off his pants. There were still things he didn't get. Such as where the gas was coming from. And who was running this show. But none of that was as important as just knowing it was here. He rubbed his face. Back along the creek, then two ranges of hills and out along the Elk. He could do that. Then talk to Bill Sealey. Let him straighten it all out. That's what the law was paid to do.

He was still standing there, looking down, when he heard the *snick-click* of a cartridge going into a lever action.

He didn't turn, didn't move. He hadn't made any mistakes. That meant whoever was behind him had been standing guard. Far enough away Halvorsen hadn't seen him, but close enough to make him out against the snow. He stood waiting as the *crunch squeak* of steps drew closer.

"You lost, Grampaw?"

He half-turned his head. There he was, gut testing the zipper of his mule-colored coat. He had a blue cap on now, but it was one of the men he'd seen two weeks before in Mortlock Run. He remembered the big square hands in front of him holding not a rifle but a length of wire rope. Beating a smaller man who didn't resist, till he no longer moved . . . Halvorsen didn't say anything, just returned his look. Till at last the other snorted, and the barrel of the .30-30 swung toward the camp.

"Go on, get on down there," the fat man said, eyes narrowed against the falling snow. "And we'll find out just who you are."

───────────────

As they picked their way down the hill the fat man called something Halvorsen couldn't make out, something in another language. An excited voice answered from down by the creek. Then he saw its owner, running up the path from the ravine. A Chinese, with a hard flat face and eyes that looked as if they'd been spray-painted on. He was in a loose white parka with a fur-trimmed hood and heavy wool pants and he carried a semiautomatic shotgun.

"Don't stop, Grampaw. Keep going," said the white man, giving Halvorsen a shove. "No, hold on. Let's see what you got in that pack . . . okay, take it back. Go on, get down there."

Carrying the pack by one strap, Halvorsen plodded on. The buildings grew slowly before his eyes. Behind him the other floundered and cursed as his boots punched holes through the snow. But when he glanced around the rifle was still pointed at his back.

Three of the plywood-sided sheds were huddled together, the paths between them trampled to frozen bare earth. They looked even shabbier close up. The fat man shoved him with the rifle and Halvorsen fell. He tensed for a kick or blow but the two men just waited as he picked himself up and got going again. The bass thud of the diesel grew louder.

"No, past there, keep going," grunted the fat man. "Drop the pack. Gimme it. Anything else in your pockets, put it in the pack."

"Am I goin' to get these back—"

"Just put 'em in the pack, Gramps."

The engine shed was off to the left. Behind the long building, the one he thought of as a bunkhouse although it didn't have any windows—funny, only one had any windows at all—was a little shack he hadn't seen from above. The fat man shepherded him up to it. His breath puffed out a lingering cloud as he worked at a padlock and chain. It clicked, and the door creaked open on blackness.

"Inside," he said, but Halvorsen didn't have to step in. The Chinese in the parka grabbed his shoulders from behind and the next thing he knew he was on an oily-smelling floor and the chain was rattling. Then he was listening to the retreating crunch of steps, fading away, until all his ears gave him was the whisper of snowflakes against wood and the strained rapid thump of his own frightened heart.

He'd hit his head when he fell and it took a few minutes before he felt like sitting up and looking around. When he did only the faintest outline of light was seeping in around the door. When he put out a hand his fingers brushed something hard and rounded. Then he stopped. Cocked his head, held his breath, listening.

He wasn't alone.

Someone else was breathing the same dark air.

"Who's there," he grunted. "I can hear you. Who's *there?*"

"Just me," somebody said from the dark.

It was the voice of a child.

Becky sat all scrunched over in the corner behind the barrels. There wasn't really any place to hide. But it made her feel safer to be wedged in, the splintery wall against her back. As if when they came to get her they wouldn't be able to find her, if she held still enough. They'd look and look, like in hide-and-seek, but they wouldn't find her.

Only, she knew they would.

She stared into the dark, where the other person was. The man who'd said in that gruff voice, *Who's there, I can hear you.* She was afraid to say any more. Why would they lock somebody else in with her? If they wanted to hurt her, do anything to her, wouldn't they take her out, into the light?

Halvorsen lay still. He said, trying to make his voice kind, "Hey there. What are you doing in here?"

"They found me," Becky said. He didn't sound like one of *them.* He sounded pretty old. But old men could still be mean.

"Who are you? Where you from, what you doing here?"

She opened her mouth to answer but found herself starting to cry instead. Then, through the dark, felt the brush of a hand. She jerked back, gasping. "Don't touch me," she said.

"Sorry. Didn't mean to . . . look, my name's Halvorsen. William T. Halvorsen."

"What are you doing in here? Are you going to hurt me?"

Halvorsen didn't answer right away, considering the possibility this was some kind of put-up job. Have a kid in here, or somebody who sounded like one, get you to spill your guts. But, hell, they had no warning he was coming. They couldn't keep people in a freezing shack full-time just on the off chance somebody would stumble by. And he didn't think anybody could fake sounding so scared. "Uh, I come back here looking for something like this. Guess I found it. How about you? You from around here?"

"I'm Becky Benning, from Crawford Run."

"That's up near Derris. How'd you get way down here? Must be fifteen, twenty miles, no roads."

"I walked."

"Walked? Shoot, that's a hell—that's a pretty long way."

"I didn't *want* to. I was lost."

Becky stopped. She couldn't believe she'd done it now. It seemed like something a little kid would do, somebody who didn't know any better. She'd had time to think about it. A lot of time.

To remember the night she'd walked out of her house and up the hill with the moonlight shining between the moving clouds. The weird windy murmur of the woods, the shadow of the great rock looming through scraps of mist. The gross burning-plastic stink. Then the great silver shadow with the yellow eyes, and how scared she'd been.

She'd talked to him though, asked what she'd come to ask for.

And she'd thought he understood. He'd trotted off through the dappled shadows, melting into the night. Not retreating, but waiting, beckoning her on, as if he wanted her to come with him. And like a fool, she'd gone! Followed him on and on through the deepening gloom. Sometimes she lost him, then she'd see him ahead, standing in an open patch of forest, glowing in the moonlight, staring back at her.

Then one moment he'd been there and the next he hadn't, and she'd called and called. Only then had she realized she had no idea where she was. She'd tried to find her way home, but somehow she must have got turned around. So she'd just kept going, all night long, her legs so sore she cried like a little baby; and when daylight came she was in a valley with no houses or roads anywhere. She'd really been scared then, started screaming for help. But no matter how loud she yelled no one answered. It just got colder and colder, and kept snowing. She kind of didn't remember all of that day or the next night.

Then the men had found her.

"What's the matter?" said the old man's voice from the darkness. "Why you cryin'? Hey."

Halvorsen had never felt comfortable around kids. But he knew one thing, if you could get them talking they always felt better. So now he kept asking questions until he got it out of her, or most of it.

It was pretty strange. About dolls, and her little brother being sick, and some favor she wanted from the wolves. He wasn't sure he understood that part. But then she'd got lost and ended up down here. He tried again when she clammed up. "You say you ran into the men then? Or did they find you?"

"I ran into five of them. Out in the woods."

"Then what?"

She didn't say anything more but he heard her sob. So finally he said, "Oh," feeling like a bastard. There was a silence in the shed.

Becky sat with her hands wrapped around her knees. She was shivering. After a while she whispered, "You hungry?"

"Yeah."

"They'll feed us tonight. Rice. In the morning and at night. In the daytime everybody's out working."

He ruminated in the dark, wondering what they'd done to her, then decided not to ask just then. He stood and started to explore the interior of the shed.

His sight had sharpened in the gloom and he could see, now, the joints where the roof met the walls, and gaps in the floor. The walls felt like plywood. Couldn't reach the roof even when he jumped, which God knew wasn't very high. He ran his fingers around the inside of the door, tugged on the jamb. Solid, locked from outside, hinges on the outside too. He stamped on the floor. Heavy boards, sounded like. Shoot, he thought. They built this thing solid.

As if she was listening to his thoughts the girl said, "I tried all that. There isn't any way out."

"How long they had you in here?"

"Two days."

"Found you two days ago?"

"Yeah, I guess." A pause. "What are you doing here, Mr. Hal—Hal—"

"Halvorsen. Well, I saw some things going on I didn't much like, and the sign seemed to point out here. So I come out to see for myself." He looked at the invisible ceiling. "Lookin' for different things, but we both ended up in the same place, huh?"

She didn't answer and he tried again. "Whereabouts in Crawford Run you from? I done some work out there now and then."

She told him but he didn't recognize the house. He asked her about her dad and her mom and she gave him some short answers. After that he couldn't think of anything else to talk about. So he just said, "It's pretty cold in here."

"It gets a lot colder at night."

"I guess it would."

"They gave me a blanket." A pause, then, "I guess if you want to we can share."

Halvorsen shivered. The floor was icy cold under his rump, even through wool pants and long johns. He wanted warmth, but he made himself say, "That's all right. You better hold on to it."

And after that, for a long time, neither of them spoke at all.

Later, he couldn't see his watch but the light had faded from the chinks and it was as dark as the inside of a mine. Dark as the inside of a well casing, the time he'd been fool enough to go down one. He'd been in some close places before and got out okay.

That didn't mean he was going to get out of this one, though.

Five feet away Becky was wrapped in the threadbare blanket, thinking, How could I be so dumb? The Wolf Prince. Oh my God.

But she'd believed it, and followed him. And now she was in the worst trouble of her life. Not only was she missing school, and probably her mom was worried sick, but . . . Her mind stopped then, not willing to go any farther. Because there were just so many bad things that could happen she was afraid even to think about them.

She heard the whine of a motor and, not long after, the voices.

When the door jerked open Halvorsen was startled out of a half-sleep. He squinted up into a brilliance that probed his eyes, then flicked back into the shed. "Where's the girl?" said a taut voice from behind it. Not the fat man's, or the Chinese's. A new voice.

"I'm back here."

The light pinned him again. "So, who are you, buddy?"

"My name's W. T. Halvorsen."

"What brings you to Floyd Valley, Mr. Halvorsen?"

"Nothing. Just out for a hike."

"Ain't you a little old for the Boy Scouts? Jer here says he caught you up on the hill, spying on us. How about that?"

"Wasn't spyin'. Just surprised to see people back here."

"About as surprised as we are to see you. But we been getting a lot of visitors, all of a sudden."

The light went out suddenly and he blinked at green moving blotches that weren't really there. "Look, I don't know what you're doing back here, and I don't care, either. How about you let me and the girl go, and I walk us on out of here."

"I'll think about it," said the voice. Another light came on, and for the first time Halvorsen was able to make out the man he'd been talking to.

It wasn't Fat Gut. Wasn't the foreigner, either. This guy was tall, with a Buffalo Bills hat and a short work jacket that didn't look warm enough for this weather. Lean and lantern-jawed, with narrow hostile eyes and pitted cheeks. Halvorsen frowned. Once before, in the hollow, something about him had seemed familiar. Now the sense he knew him was even stronger. Trouble was, when you thought that you never allowed for the years. What would this fellow have looked like ten years, twenty years ago . . .

"Roddy," he said.

The man lifted his chin sharply and showed some not-so-great-looking front teeth. "I know you?"

"Sure do. An' I know you. Roddy . . . Eisen. That's it. Eisen."

He stared down at Halvorsen, suspicion working in his face. Then something eased. "Shit a brick, if it ain't old Racks. Jerry! I used to work for this old bastard."

"That so?"

"Yeah," said Eisen, drawling out the sentence. "At least till he fired my ass."

Halvorsen remembered the rest of it then, too late. How one of the men in his crew had caught the tall kid, yeah, just a kid then, on his first job, stealing tools out of his box. How all the guys had missed tools since he hired on, and when they opened up his box there they were. So he hadn't had any choice about sending him for his pink slip. No crew would tolerate a thief. As he recalled, Roddy Eisen hadn't been dumb. Quite the opposite.

And now Halvorsen recognized him, he remembered hearing other things about him later, stories men traded over a beer in smoky bars after work, word passed with a thermos of coffee while a rig ground its way down into the earth; about how he'd gone to work for Ashland, then somebody said he ran into him down in West Virginia with Alamco. And after that he didn't remember hearing anything about him at all.

He came back to find them all standing in a dangerous silence. So, just to take the sting off the memory for the other man, he said, "Uh, somebody told me you was working down south."

"Yeah, I was down there. Then went out on my own. Made something of myself. Remember what you told me?"

"What's that?" said Halvorsen, afraid to ask but having to, because he plain didn't remember.

"You took me off in the woods before you sent me down to the head office. Gave me this little daddy-son talk. Remember that?"

"Can't say as I do."

"It was real uplifting," Eisen told the fat man, who was standing back, carbine pointing at the ground. "Racks here told me how the name of a thief wasn't gonna do me no good in life. How he had to let me go, but 'cause I was so young he wasn't going to put down why on the paper. Told me to get smart, turn over a new leaf. Remember now?"

"I guess so. Did you?"

"For a while. Anyways I didn't steal no more socket wrenches." He looked past him into the shed. "Becky, how you doing today?"

"All right."

"You going to come out for dinner?"

"I want it in here."

"You hungry?" Eisen asked him. Halvorsen said he was. They turned away, motioning him to follow, and he noticed they didn't lock the shed behind him, just left it open.

He stopped inside the mess hall, mouth dropping open. Staring around. He couldn't help it.

It was filled with small, thin men whose black eyes flicked up to his, then back to tin plates. Chopsticks clattered like dice in a game room. The air was hazy with grease and smoke and the smell of wet clothes drying over a gas stove. "Who are these guys?" he shouted over the din of talk and eating. Eisen didn't answer, just pointed to a table set apart, with spoons and forks. A bald fellow in the dirtiest apron Halvorsen had ever seen came over and put rice and some kind of stew in front of them.

The fat man slid in on the other side, boxing him in. "So, you and Rod are old pals."

"We ain't pals," said Eisen. Brown sauce ran down his jaw. "Knew him before, that's all. Racks, this here's Jerry Olen. Try some a' this. It's better than it looks."

"Where all the Chinamen come from?"

Olen said, "They ain't Chinese. They're Vietnamese. And what they're doin' here is none of your goddamned business. People come sneaking around here, we bury them up on the hill."

"Shut up, Jer," said Eisen, but he sounded resigned instead of angry.

Halvorsen's spoon paused halfway to his mouth. He made himself take a bite anyway. Then coughed it out. "This is—this stuff is *hot*."

"It's all you're gonna get, so you better like it. Like I say, I was figuring to kill you till I saw who you were. And I still might." Eisen yelled something in the other language to the cook, who went into another room and came back with three cans of beer. Eisen popped Halvorsen's and then his own. The fat man drained his in one long draft.

"How about the little girl?"

"Just worry about yourself, Gramps," said Olen. "Hey, really, why we keeping this guy, Rod?"

"Shut up, I'm trying to think," said Eisen. So for a while they just ate. Halvorsen got about half the plate down with the help of the beer. He hadn't had a drink in so long it made him dizzy. The men kept shouting and rattling plates. After the silence of the hills the noise was deafening.

"Somebody said they seen one of these Vietnamese up at Mortlock, couple of weeks back," said Halvorsen.

"Where?"

"West of Raymondsville."

"Oh yeah. That was Vo."

"What was he doin' up there?"

Eisen frowned but didn't say anything. Olen said, "Oh, don't worry about him. Fact, he went the same place you're going."

"Knock it off, Jer."

"Hey, I don't care if he's your dear old dad, we can't let him go. And we can't keep him around. You know what we got to do with him."

"Shut up."

"Wandering around in the woods, nobody'd be surprised if something got him. Something with big teeth."

Halvorsen quit eating. His mouth was too dry. "Shut up, I said," muttered Eisen, and Halvorsen started to see how it was between the two men.

"I see you've got production going," he said, to get off the subject.

"How you know that?"

"Come across your line crossing the river. Lot of gas going out of here."

"See, what this old fart don't know about gas, oil, anything to do with drilling, it ain't worth knowing," Eisen told Olen.

"So what?"

"So we got a problem, he maybe could be the guy to help."

Jer looked at him, sucking his lip. "He's awful goddamn old."

"We got the gooks, we want muscle. Hey, another Bud?"

"No, thanks, but I could use some water or something."

Eisen yelled out in what Halvorsen figured was Vietnamese, and the cook brought out a can of Royal Crown. He gulped it, noticing the workmen were leaving. Each time the door opened icy air blasted in from the dark, till the roaring heater drove it back again.

"So, what you doing out here, anyway? I don't see no license. And he didn't have a rifle, you said."

"No, ain't hunting. Ain't been hunting in a good many years."

"So what you doing out here?"

"Just stretching my legs. You get to be my age, you got to keep moving or you stiffen right up."

"Way in the middle of the Wild Area? I don't think so. Here's what I think. It was you saw us beating Vo up, and you got curious. Right? Level with me, I'll treat you fair as I can."

"I asked some questions," said Halvorsen. "I found Medina."

"An' ended up here." Eisen popped another beer, then abruptly set it down. "Anybody else with you? On your trail? Cops?"

"Just me."

"How I know you're tellin' the truth?"

" 'Cause if I wanted to lie, I'd tell you somebody knew I was here."

"He's got a point," said Olen.

"Okay, look. Maybe I appreciated what you done for me way back. But we got a going operation here and we don't need people poking around. That's what we got the wolves for."

"What wolves?"

"We paid some people to bring in some wolves. Figured once the word got out they were out here, there wouldn't be as many hunters and shit coming around."

"But it didn't work out exactly that way," said Olen.

"Right, the fucking wolves didn't want to hurt anybody! They see you, they run the other way! Then I ran into Jer. He runs these big, mean fucking attack dogs."

"Yeah, I heard 'em barking," said Halvorsen, swallowing.

"They're a piece of work. You don't want to dick with them pups. Anyway, if we keep you on, you got to justify your existence. Clear so far?"

He nodded, and Eisen went on. "What we got here is a gas field. But you figured that already."

"Why you using the Viet Cong?"

They laughed. "They keep their mouths shut," said Olen. "Can't talk English, most of them. Don't have papers, they're illegals. So they stay here and work."

"How many wells you got?"

"Eighteen."

"Pressure?"

"Most of 'em, around two thousand pounds."

"How much you pumping?"

"Hundred million cubic foot a day."

"That's a hell of a lot of gas," said Halvorsen. "Considering there ain't any in this valley."

"Why you say there ain't no gas here?" demanded Olen, but Halvorsen saw that gave him a jolt.

" 'Cause there ain't. I drilled here years ago and come up bone dry. So all I got to say, you ain't getting it from here. And that's why you got Vietnamese and guard dogs and all. Either you ain't got no gas, and this is all a blind for somethin' else, or if you got it—well, I'm kind of at a dead end there."

"Shee-it," said Olen.

"Told you he was smart. Okay, you figured it out that far," Eisen told him. "Don't stop now."

"That's all, except I got two questions. If it's gas, where's it coming from, and who you're selling it to? And if it ain't gas, then what is it?"

"Well, you think about it and maybe it'll come to you. Meanwhile we got a problem. Think you could help us out? Take a look, see if you got any professional advice?"

"What kind of problem?"

"A production problem."

"What about the girl?" Halvorsen asked them.

"Nguyen thinks the crew should have her," said Olen. "Seeing as they lost their previous entertainment."

Halvorsen sat staring at them. Eisen examined the low ceiling, expression distant. "We done shit worse than that out here," Olen said. "So don't think we won't kill you. In spite of you being best buds with the Rodster."

"Come on," said Eisen, swinging long legs down with the air of a man making a decision. "Finish that up, let's get going."

"Where we headed?"

"Got something to show you."

There wasn't any opportunity to talk on the way. He was on the back of a snowmobile, behind the stocky Vietnamese they called Noo-yen. Eisen led the way on the other, his rifle—apparently it never left his sight—thrust into a boot on the side. Halvorsen hung on grimly, absorbing bumps and hoping they didn't have far to go. He didn't like snowmobiles. After a while he heard something over the sound of the engine. He couldn't tell what, but it was loud. Then the engine faltered, and they slowed, and the godawful bumping stopped, and he opened his eyes.

The pillar of fire filled the ravine with noise and light so deafening and blinding that even three hundred yards away he cowered, shielding his eyes as if staring into the sun. The gas blasted up out of the pit so fast and strong the flame didn't even start till twenty feet up. Then it caught in an eighty-foot-high explosion that went on and on, churning with internal turbulence. The flare wasn't blue but yellow, ragged orange at the edges, and a roiling mushroom of fire hovered above the central flare. It lit the whole hollow with a yellow glare, making their shadows leap madly on the sooty snow. It was so loud he couldn't make out what Eisen was yelling until he bent and cupped his hands right over his ear and yelled, "Let's get in there, take a look-see."

Halvorsen put his hands over his face and followed him into the heat. Eisen kept going, kept going, till he thought they were just going to walk on into the flame. The wind leaned on his back, pressing him in toward the immense torch. The continuous roar hammered his lungs like drums, made it hard to get his breath.

When he got to within a hundred yards his feet wouldn't go any farther. The radiant heat from the fireball seared his face. Like standing outside a burning house, fighting to get closer, but knowing it wasn't any good . . . Shoving that memory back, shielding his eyes, he peered into the pit.

A conical, ragged crater of dirt and rocks blown up from below. Twelve, fifteen feet across. No sign of pipe, no flange or valve, just a hole straight to hell. The gas rushed up endlessly, a clear but still visible column that suddenly flashed into dancing, writhing flame. No snow around it for a quarter mile, just trampled bare mud pocked with boot marks and tire treads, chunks of scorched wood and twisted metal lying around as if a bomb had gone off. Opposite him a wrecked vehicle lay on its side, metal skin blackened and torn like a gutted carcass.

Eisen stood with him, shoulder to shoulder, for four or five minutes. Then jerked his thumb. Bending into the icy wind, they followed their writhing shadows back to the snowmobiles. They went about a hundred yards past them before they could talk, even in a shout.

"How long's it been burning?" Halvorsen yelled.

"Three days now."

"How'd it happen?"

"Had a blowout. You know how it chills when the pressure reduces to atmospheric. Makes the metal brittle. Well, this here's a new well. The guys put a two-thousand-pound valve on it. Figured it'd be the same as the others, down in the valley."

Halvorsen knew then where the gas was coming from, and how, and why they had to keep the wells' exact location secret. But all he said was, "That ain't no two-thousand-pound flare."

"No, it ain't. So it blew the valve off and burst the pipe, then the whole wellhead went. A spark—*kaboom.*"

"You mean the casing's cracked?"

"I figure there's a fracture down there, ten, twenty feet."

"This is about as bad a gas fire as I ever seen," said Halvorsen.

"I lost three guys so far trying to put it out," said Eisen. He didn't look unconcerned now, or distant. He looked scared. "How'd you use to take care of a bitch like this?"

Halvorsen rubbed the stubble on his jaw as he considered the flare. The ravine flickered like the entrance to an immense furnace.

It was a tough one, all right. You couldn't get in close enough to work, and even if you could, there wasn't anything left in the hole to clamp or bolt a valve or a flange to. The gas came out with such power it would blow away anything they put into the stream. No way in the world to reduce the pressure short of drilling another slant hole and pumping in mud or concrete, and it didn't sound like they had either the gear or the expertise to do that. He asked Eisen, "What you tried so far?"

"First we tried to get a reducer on it. Couldn't get close enough. Tried to drive a truck over it, cut the flame off, but it didn't work."

"Yeah, I saw it. What kind of pipe you got down there?"

"Seven-inch."

"You need to make you up a tee. Maybe a foot diameter on the bottom leg, two foot on the sides, valves on the side legs. Drop that over it with both your valves open and screw it into the ground. Pump her full of bentonite through a two and seven-eighths till she stops flowing. Then put a head back on to it and flange it up. How you fixed for welders?"

"We got welders," said Eisen. "But how do we get in to the well-head? It's kind of a catch-22. We can't get to the jet to cap it while it's burning. But we can't stop it burning till we can cut the gas off."

Halvorsen studied the storm of fire, eyes narrowed. A flare wasn't anything to mess around with. "Don't suppose you want to drill relief wells around it," he said.

"Take too long. Sooner or later somebody's gonna notice this. And there's smoke—"

"Yeah. Only thing left to do's blow it. Snuff it out."

"You know how?" said Eisen. In the heat of the torch his long face was sheened with sweat. "Done it before, maybe?"

"I done it," said Halvorsen. "Not for years and years, but . . . it ain't something you want to try off the top of your head. You don't set it right, all your flame'll do is waver and keep right on burning. Or it'll snuff out, the gas keeps flowing—then she reflashes. They lost a whole crew in a reflash over in Wellsville in fifty-eight. That was in a ravine too, just like this. Anyway, you'd need nitro—"

"You got to have nitro? How about dynamite?"

"Dynamite would work," he said, still looking at the monstrous torch. He was afraid of it. He'd never seen one this hot before. But just for that reason, that it was a real bastard and they didn't have the right equipment to take it on, fire pumps and a boom and tractors, he found himself wondering if he could do it. "What kind you got?"

"Red Cross Extra."

"Something slower would be better. Say a forty percent straight dynamite, or a nitrate-and-diesel mix."

"All we got's what I said."

"Need more of it, then. Nitro, that'd be a two-gallon shot. Say, dynamite, forty pounds, be on the safe side. Worst thing is to not use enough. Best thing's to hit it hard, snuff it out, then get your tee down over it."

He heard the revving engine only when it was on him. He turned to see the Vietnamese, Nguyen, sitting on the snowmobile. His eye snagged on the butt of the shotgun, sticking up out of the boot. He carefully looked away.

"So you'll give it a try?" Eisen asked him.

"Guess I got no choice. Do I?" Halvorsen turned slowly to face the roaring light again. His left hand was seven feet from the gun. If the Vietnamese turned away, if he could reach it before Eisen got to his rifle . . .

"Not much," said Eisen.

506 WINTER LIGHT

Halvorsen licked flame-parched lips. "One other thing."

"What?"

"The girl. You let her go first. Then I set up the shoot." He glanced over again. The Vietnamese was looking away, toward the woods.

"You don't get the picture, Racks. We ain't inviting you to bargain with us. You cap that flame, or we throw you to Jerry's dogs. That's the only choice you got."

Just then, startling Halvorsen, the Vietnamese swung himself off the snowmobile. He walked five paces off and turned the back of his white parka to them. Halvorsen realized he was urinating. He glanced at the shotgun again.

All at once his heart accelerated with the imminence of risk. The waterfall roar of flame faded. The smooth curved wood seemed to grow, to fill his sight. His hands opened slightly, and his head came up. Taking a casual step forward, looking away from the weapon toward the fire, he said: "The girl goes. Or I don't turn a hand."

He waited, balanced knife-edged between the bargain and the lunge. He figured the other had to go for his deal. Either that or beat him up, try to make him do it by force, and he didn't figure they had much chance of that. Eisen must not have figured he did either because at last he turned his head and spat into the snow.

"I ain't lettin' her go. But I'll do this much: she stays with you. All right?"

He was digging his boots in for the spring when the Vietnamese suddenly finished and turned round. As he slogged back to them Halvorsen sagged. Well, there'd be another chance. If he stayed alert.

"Nguyen, your boys are gonna have to wait for the girl. I had to promise her to Pops here."

The Vietnamese glanced at Halvorsen, then spoke for the first time. He had an accent, but his English was perfectly clear. "They aren't going to like that."

"You get paid to keep those monkeys in line. So earn it. Okay, Racks, you got a deal."

"Good," said Halvorsen, taking the hand he held out, looking calmly and carefully into the eyes of a man he knew he could trust only a little, and only until his usefulness to him was at an end.

Twenty-two

Becky lay trembling in the iron cold, eyes wide on darkness. Her leg and side were cramped, but she didn't move. Images of home burned her vision like pictures made of fire. Her eyes were hot with tears she couldn't let go of.

She kept seeing her brother asleep in bed, face innocent and happy. Her mom in the kitchen baking something good and the dryer thumping away in the basement. Her room, the bed she'd slept in since she was a baby, with the scary face in the wood grain. Her Barbies. Her tapes on the rack Charlie had made for her. Her desk, and her books . . . she was getting so far behind. What would they do about science. Maybe since they found out about Mr. Cash they'd give her a passing grade. . . . Her mom probably thought she was dead. And Jammy, who was taking care of him? She hugged herself. She'd been so *stupid*, going off into the woods. How incredibly *retarded*. The night she'd thought she was going to freeze to death, she'd been almost glad. Glad it was over at last and she didn't have to walk anymore through the snow. Or have to explain it all to anyone.

But then *they'd* found her.

And now she was in the worst trouble of her whole life.

She stopped sniffling instantly when she heard the lock rattle and the door grate open. The glow of a flashlight explored the floor. She stared at the door with eyes wide and mouth open like a small, cornered animal.

"Becky, you in here?" *His* voice, the one who looked like a Halloween skeleton. The one she hated most of all.

"I'm here."

"Where? Speak up, I can't hear you!"

"Back here!"

"Okay, take 'em off," she heard him say to somebody else. "Boots, yeah. Leave y'socks on. And your coat."

"It gets cold in that shed, Rod. I need that coat."

A pause, then, "Let him keep the damn coat. But search him, pat him down good, understand, Nguyen? Look in all his pockets."

The muffled sound of hands slapping cloth. "He's clean."

"Okay, get in there. Get yourself some sleep, we're gonna turn to real early tomorrow."

The grate of the hinges, the chain rattle, and darkness again. Her fingers explored smooth plastic in her pocket, but she didn't move. She didn't even breathe.

She just listened.

Halvorsen stood motionless in the center of the dark. He could sense how close it was, how tight, with things stacked to above his head on either side. When he extended his arms they moved two feet before hitting hard, cold surfaces. He dropped to his knees on the planks.

Tomorrow, he thought. Tomorrow they're gonna want me to blow that flare. If I don't—they kill me. If I do—well, they're going to kill me then too. And here he was, locked up in a damn toolshed without even anything to chew.

Becky listened, head cocked. She heard breathing, a ragged sound that ended in a cough. It was just the old man. She murmured, "Hey. You all right?"

"Yeah. Yeah, I'm all right."

"I thought they were . . . taking you away."

"They brung me back, though. Fed me an' brung me back. This time, anyway." Halvorsen took a deep breath, trying to make his voice less shaky. He didn't feel too confident. But he had to act it. That was the trouble, being around people. You always had to be what they wanted. At least kids, though . . .

"Did they hurt you?" she whispered.

"No. No, they didn't hurt me."

"That's good."

"Yeah. Listen, we got to talk. Where are you, anyway? Hard to tell where you are back there."

Becky sat crouched, listening to the old man's mutter. She was jammed into a space so narrow it was hard to take a deep breath. Sometimes her legs made themselves into knots and hurt so much it was hard not to yell.

And it was starting to smell. But she felt safe back here, like a holed-up mouse with cats outside.

She didn't want to come out. But he asked her again and she felt so lonely and afraid that she finally turned sideways and inchwormed a couple of feet and reached out her hand. It was gripped immediately by a rough, hard, large one.

"Okay, listen to me, girl. First off, we got to get you out of here. They want me to do somethin' for them, but after that they won't need me no more. These fellas don't have anything good planned for either of us. I'm old, it don't matter to me either way, but we got to figure some way to get you out of here."

"I can get out anytime. They leave the door open during the day so the men can come in and get stuff." She swallowed. "Mr. Halvorsen, you don't get it, do you? I can walk out just about anytime. But if I do, I'll probably . . . die in the woods. I was just about dead when they found me. It's way below zero and there's nothing to eat out there and I don't even know which way to go."

Halvorsen sat thinking about that. Her hand felt so small in his. Hell, he thought. I didn't ask for nothing like this. He said gruffly, "How old are you, again?"

"Twelve. And a half."

The trouble was, she was probably right. Even if he could get her a compass somehow, matches, she wouldn't even get to Elk Creek. And if she turned the wrong way, or got her valleys mixed up, she'd freeze to death one of these bitter nights.

"We got to go together, Mr. Halvorsen. You too. Not just me."

He didn't answer and Becky squeezed her eyes shut. But the fear, like a terrible pressure in her chest, kept forcing the words out. "Sometimes they try to . . . get to me. When they come in the shed. They laugh, like it's a game. I don't know what they're saying but I know they're talking about me."

"Good thing you got these barrels to hide behind."

"Uh-huh."

"Say, what is this stuff, anyway?" Halvorsen reached out with his free hand to rap one. It felt hard but sounded hollow.

"You want to see? I got a light."

"You got a light?"

"It's just a little flashlight," she said. "A little toy flashlight."

"Let's see it," he said. Yeah, it was time to check out all this stuff. Maybe there was something here they could use.

He was a little startled when Dumbo's head lit up. He'd have to work fast, the bulb was already fading. He ran the orange glow over rounded surfaces, tilting his head back. He wished he had his glasses, but they'd been in his pack, the fat man had them now. He wished he had a lot of things. Finally he grunted, "Can you read a couple of these for me?"

He saw her face for the first time as she read out the labels on drums, coils, boxes. She was even younger than he'd pictured from her voice. But she's got sand, he thought, she ain't a whiner. He nodded, listening as she read the shipping bills. It sounded to be production supplies. Pipe fittings, wire rope, drums of bentonite mud, silica gel, electrical wire. Some came wrapped in gray plastic tarps. A thought occurred to him then and he said, a little sharper than he meant to: "Wait. Look on the top of that last one. Up where it says something like 'Bill To.' There anything typed in there?"

"This one's blank. No, wait, it says something but it looks real faint. Like a copy."

"Look at the others. Here, take the light." He squatted as she pushed her eyes close to the paper, squinting in the dimming illumination.

"Here's one."

"What's it say?"

"Starting at the top, it says, 'M-I Drilling Fluids, a Dresser/Halliburton Company'—"

"That's who sold it. Keep going."

" 'Shipped by: P-I-E'—funny, that spells *pie*—"

"Go on, go on."

" 'Ship to: Medina Transportation Company, Dutchman Hill, Coudersport, PA 16915.' "

Halverson sucked on the sore spot on his gum. Finally he said, "How about 'Bill To'?"

" 'Bill to: Department MT, The Thunder Corporation, Petroleum City.' Do you want the address?"

Halvorsen sat motionless in the dark. His mind touched it tentatively, lightly, like a spider exploring something strange that has just landed in its web.

"Do you want the address?" Becky asked him again.

"Huh-uh. Know it already."

"What's the matter?" she asked him, thinking, He sounds funny. Like somebody just told him something he didn't really want to know. She turned the light off to save the battery while she waited.

"Nothin' . . . but, can you peel that off there? Without tearing it? Fold it up small and put it in your pocket. Or, no—have you got someplace you can hide it, where they won't find it if they search you?"

"I got a little inside pocket on my pants."

"Put it in there."

"What is it? What's it mean?"

"Maybe nothing. Maybe a lot. Look—I don't see anything in here we can use. I was hoping for tools, something we could maybe saw our way out with, but all this stuff is just drillin' supplies. Mud and pipe and stuff. But we got to get out of here. You're right, ain't no point just springing you. We got to go together. How, that's the problem. These guys keep real close tabs on me."

"I can get out in the daytime, like I said. Only, I can't go anyplace. And you probably know your way around the woods. Don't you?"

"Good as anybody, I guess."

"Only, they won't let you out."

"About the size of it," he said dryly.

"If we could, like, put the two of us together, then maybe we could do it. Get out, and keep going."

"They'd come after us."

"At least we'd be out," she told him. "And there's got to be people out looking for me. Maybe they'd find us before *they* did."

They were both quiet. The dark pressed closer, and the cold. After a time a wailing came from outside. Dogs baying, far away, yet all too near.

"Wonder what that wolf of yours is doing," he whispered.

"Oh, that. I don't know."

"You sure it was a wolf? Well, how would you know. But you say it didn't ever try to hurt you?"

"No," she said quietly. "I don't think it's a prince or anything like that, not anymore. But it never tried to hurt me."

The wind whispered over the roof, and he listened to the grinding whisper of drift snow against the outer walls. Better try to get some sleep, he thought. Blowing a flare wasn't a cookbook operation. Dynamite was more forgiving than nitro, but there were still a lot of things that could go wrong. He pillowed his head on his arm and lay down on the planks. Cold, but not as icy solid cold as you might expect. When he rapped them with his knuckles they sounded like there was an air space between them and the ground. When he put his cheek to them he felt cold air bleeding up between them, through the cracks.

He said, very quietly, "Come on over here, Becky. Bring your blanket."

"What?"

So close to her ear she could feel the warmth of his breath, he whispered, "I don't know if it'ud work. But I think there just might be a way to try and do it."

Twenty-three

He was already awake the next morning when he heard the voices, the heavy deliberate steps grinding toward the shed. He'd been awake most of the night, going over everything in his mind. When the door grated open he stood and stretched. He felt clear and empty. His boots flew in with a thud, and he bent to pull them on.

The overseer, Nguyen, stood waiting, shotgun cradled in one arm. The sky was still dark. The only light came from a battery-powered lantern the Vietnamese had set down beside him. The snow glowed a cold white around it, as if lit from underneath.

Halvorsen finished lacing his boots. He stepped out and turned his face to the sky.

Snow. It fell out of the darkness into the sphere of buzzing light, touching his face like long-dead fingers, gentle with love but cold, cold. He sucked in the crisp air of what could be his last day.

"Ready?" said the Vietnamese.

He nodded and the other jerked his head toward the mess shack. Halvorsen started toward it. Then another form took shape from the dark. It was the fat cook, with a covered plate. Halvorsen stopped. "Where's my snowshoes? I want my snowshoes."

"We got them inside. Keep going, we'll give them to you when you need them."

The cook peered into the shed. He called, "Bec-kee!"

"She's in there," Halvorsen told him. The man glanced at him blankly, then called her name again. Faintly he heard the girl replying. The cook set the pan on the floor, then reached up and pulled the door closed. But he didn't touch the lock and it swung idly on the hasp, tapping against the jamb.

Halvorsen turned and headed toward the light again. As they plodded after the rolling shadow of the cook he asked the man in the parka, "How'd you get into this, mister? Ain't this a long ways from where you grew up?"

"It's a long story," said the Vietnamese, but he didn't tell it. Just added, "Keep going."

The mess shed was full of men eating, talking all at once. He headed for where Olen and Eisen were attacking eggs and bacon. Good, something a man could eat. He slid into a chair and they gave him hooded glances. He applied himself to the food and then the coffee.

Eisen sat back at last, rubbing his cheeks. Dark eyes burned deep in his long face. He lit a cigarette and sucked smoke. Then dropped his look to Halvorsen. "So what you been doing all these years, Racks?"

"Not much. Finished out my time with Thunder, then retired."

"Wasn't you married? I seen your wife once. She come out to bring you your lunch once, you forgot to take it."

"She died. A while ago."

"So you all alone now? Or what?"

"Got a daughter in town." Halvorsen got up and their eyes followed him as he went to the stove and poured himself more coffee. "How about you?"

"Married, divorced, married again, divorced again. Two kids. They live with their mom outside of Parkersburg. Anyway." He shifted irritably in his chair. "You ready to blow this motherfucker?"

"Guess I'm ready to try."

"You done this before, you said?" Olen asked him.

"Yeah. I done it before."

"Big ones?"

"Big enough."

"An' you always put them out?"

"Sometimes it took a few tries," Halvorsen told him. "But you know, there's been gas flares they never were able to put out. Just had to let them burn out, let the pressure drop to where they could cap it."

"This one ain't going to burn out," said Eisen. "Is it, Racks?"

"How should I know?"

"You mean you ain't figured it out yet?"

Halvorsen went quiet inside. "Figured what out, Rod?"

"Don't give me that innocent look. You know where this gas is comin' from. Don't you?"

Halvorsen kept his eyes on his cup. "I ain't given it much thought, Rod, to be honest with ya. Got other stuff on my mind."

The door slammed open and three small dark men came in. Halvorsen caught the ozone smell of burnt metal. They spoke at length to Nguyen, who said to Eisen, "They're done with the tee."

Eisen shoved his chair back. "Let's go look at it," he told Halvorsen.

He stood under a gray dawn, inspecting the huge metal weldment that lay blocked up on split lengths of log. Thirty feet of two-foot-diameter pipe capped with flanges. Halfway down its length a ten-foot length of one-foot tubing, ream-sharpened at the bottom. Opposite that, a three-inch opening, capped. He picked up a wrench and tapped each weld, listening for flaws. Stuck his head inside and looked for light. Finally he grunted, "Looks solid. How you gonna set it?"

"Twenty-five strong backs."

"I guess that should work. Way we used to do it before we had tractors and such. Okay, where you keep your fireworks?"

The dynamite shed was set off from the rest of the camp. As they neared it Halvorsen heard the dogs start to bark. Then he saw them through the trees, and they went crazy. They were leaping against a wire pen, mad eyes riveted on his. German shepherds, barking and growling and slavering. He shivered. "Them dogs sure sounds wild."

"Them pups would love to tear you apart. Olen don't feed them too good. Keeps them mean. Hey! Jerry! Call off your hounds."

Olen kicked and cursed the dogs back into a smaller run and latched it as they filed in through a gate in the wire. The dynamite shed was inside it, actually inside the dog run. Halvorsen saw how terrified the Vietnamese were of the dogs. He didn't like their looks much himself. When they reached the shed he felt relieved. Eisen unlocked it and stood back. "Go on in."

He smelled the dynamite as soon as he stepped inside. It made his pulse speed up, the way it always had before a shoot. Dynamite was nothing but nitro with padding, something to soak it up and tame it a little. All of a sudden he was twenty again and Pete Riddick was telling him, "Now, one thing you never want to forget around this shit. You fuck up and you'll never know it. It won't hurt. So there ain't no point in being scared. Just take your goddamn time and make sure you don't never let anything slip."

Eisen was pulling a fiberboard crate off a stack in the far corner. He hurried forward and got his hands on it too. They carried it to the door and he grabbed the tape tab and pulled it off.

"Good old Red Cross Extra," said Halvorsen, looking down at fifty pounds of explosive. "What you been using this for?"

"Ditching. Boulders. Grade work, to get our access road in here. This do the job?"

"I'd rather had a straight dynamite. But this here'll do her." He took out one of the waxy, heavy sticks. Examined it, checked the date, then laid it gently as a raw egg back among its fellows. "That a fresh tin of caps? Got a crimper? I'll put that fuse inside my coat, get it warmed up so it don't crack."

"What else you gonna need?"

Halvorsen told him, and Eisen yelled orders. The dogs snarled and chewed wire mesh as they crossed the churned-up yard. Halvorsen saw a dark, bloody spot where he figured Olen fed them. He glanced back to see one of the Vietnamese shift his grip on the case of explosive. "For Christ's sake, tell him to be careful with that stuff."

"Take it easy. How long you want this steel boom?"

"Fifty feet. Unless you want to write off another Jeep."

"Fifty feet of three-inch do it?"

"Make it seventy, and hang something heavy on the back, pipe clamps or something, balance it." He'd thought it out during the night and now he listed the things he needed. "Blankets, a dozen if you can spare 'em. Water, a lot of it. Pliers. Rope. Got any fire extinguishers?"

"A couple. In the compressor shack."

"Bring those. We're gonna have to cool things down, keep it from re-flashing."

They reached the main camp and Eisen started shouting. Men came running from the bunkhouse. Motors started. Halvorsen swung himself up into a jeep as Eisen turned the key. They bumped and wallowed along what he now saw was a bulldozed road under the snow.

They heard the flare a mile away. It was after dawn now, but he could see the hellish flicker of it on the hillside. He felt his hands trembling. No point in being scared, Riddick had said. Pete had been about the most safety-minded guy he ever knew. But it hadn't kept the nitro from getting him. They'd never found a thing, except for a key that had been in his pocket. Halvorsen still had it, in a cigar box back home. They'd found it embedded in a timber derrick, half a mile away from the blast.

They worked through that morning getting everything carted out to the site and set up. Halvorsen moved among them on his snowshoes, checking the work. He didn't see Olen the rest of the morning. Apparently the fat man was back at the camp, with his dogs.

The flare roared steadily, leaning on their eardrums with a continuous avalanche bellow that made his head hurt.

Or maybe it was handling dynamite that gave him the headache. When it came time for that he didn't have too much trouble persuading the others to back off, leave him alone for a while. He looked down at the blanket spread on the snow, making sure he had everything he needed: cap crimper, coil of copper wire, caps, dynamite, fuse, pliers, knife. Should be it. He slipped off his snowshoes and put them beside the blanket and squatted down. So that he was pretty much out of sight, out from under their incessant observation, when he opened up the box again to reveal the neat rows of stacked sticks.

A hundred and ten of them, fifty pounds of dynamite.

He licked his lips, took a few deep breaths, forcing himself into calm. The flame light flickered at the edge of his sight as he selected a stick and laid it aside. He bent over the box, concealing his next movements. Then leaned back, took his cap off, and dragged his sleeve across his forehead. Despite the cold wind, he was starting to sweat.

He fumbled at his coat and slid out the tin. Time fuse was better for blowing a well. Simpler than electric, less to go wrong. He opened the little round can and there it was, an old friend, Clover brand safety fuse. He unreeled the waxy orange cord, measuring with his arms. Safety fuse burned at two minutes a yard. He wanted enough time to get clear, but the longer the fuse, the more time the charge had to heat up. After some consideration, sitting in the snow with his lips pressed together, he cut a four-yard length and set the tin aside.

Next, the cap. He held a Number Six in his teeth while he stripped his gloves off. It tasted metallic bitter when he touched it with his tongue.

Squinting, he trimmed the end of the fuse square across with the old Case knife he'd begged back from Olen. Then, holding the dull silver cylinder hollow end down, making sure the powder core of the fuse showed, he inserted it gently into the cap. He clicked the knife closed, then crimped the cap onto the fuse with the cap tool, slow, even pressure, working all the way around until he was satisfied it wouldn't pull free.

Now the dynamite. He looked around and saw a fallen branch not far away. He got up clumsily, broke a stick off it, and whittled the end to a point with his blade.

Kneeling again, he uncrimped the paper at one end of the cartridge, exposing the gray paste of explosive. Holding it between his knees, he pressed the sharpened stick down slowly into it. The dynamite was stiff from the cold and he leaned forward, putting his weight behind it. Finally he pulled it out and examined the hole. He took off his hat and wiped his wet hair back.

Using both hands, he fitted the cap into the cartridge until only the fuse was visible, emerging from the end. Then he rewrapped the waxed paper cover around the orange cord, snipped off a bit of wire, and tied it closed. There, that was his primer.

Now for the main charge. During the long night he'd decided the simplest thing was to leave the dynamite in the box, just unpack enough to put the primer cartridge in, then lay the rest back on top of it. So that was what he did. He closed the flaps and cut off twenty yards of wire and wrapped it tight all over, and twisted the ends together till they locked.

He stood up and yelled, beckoning: "Could use a hand over here."

A reluctant-looking young Vietnamese trotted forward. He gave Halvorsen a frightened smile. Halvorsen pointed to the dynamite, then to the jeep. The boy hoisted the box with a grunt and held it in place while Halvorsen wired it securely to the end of the boom.

Okay, done. He pointed back down the ravine, and the boy, throwing a last glance at the dynamite, sprinted away.

Next came the blankets. He wrapped these around the charge, swaddling it in a rough ball of wool, then backed off and examined his work with a critical eye.

The jeep sat with the steel pipe extended like a knight's lance. Lashed along the driver's side, the boom hung out over the hood, drooping slightly, to a point fifty feet forward of the radiator. On the end, wired to a welded-on steel plate to focus the explosion, was the charge. The fuse led back from it along the boom, hanging in arcs from wire loops. He made sure it wasn't kinked or bent, and measured it again to be sure. Four yards. That gave them eight minutes to set the charge in place and get back to safety before it blew.

All in all it looked like it should do. So he turned and waved, and after a while the others got up from where they'd been sitting and came slowly up to him.

Eisen looked it over. Finally he said, "That gonna work?"

"It should."

"What's the blankets for?"

"We wet those down before we go in, keep the dynamite cool. It's gonna be hell-hot in there and we don't want no volunteer explosions. We want it all to go off at once, the right way, in the right place."

"I guess it looks all right."

Halvorsen watched his face but he couldn't tell if he was pleased or not. Finally he said tentatively, "Uh, Rod—"

"What?"

He worked his lips. "You know, I really could use a chew."

"Oh yeah? Well, we ain't got any."

"How about a butt, then? I'm gettin' a nicotine fit."

Eisen pulled out a pack of Winstons and shook one out. Then he shrugged and gave him the pack. Halvorsen said, "Thanks. Got a match?"

"Some in the cellophane there. On the side. . . . Hey! Got that done yet? Let's get some lunch while they finish up." Halvorsen started away, but something must have looked wrong. Because suddenly the boss said, "Wait a minute. Nguyen—search him."

"The old man?"

"Yeah. All over, under his coat, pockets, boots. That hat too. Make sure he's not holding out on us."

The Vietnamese found the dynamite cartridge he'd hidden inside his coat. When he held it up, showing it to the boss, Halvorsen grinned shamefacedly.

Eisen slapped him, so hard he staggered back. He raised a hand to his mouth. It came away spotted with blood.

"You didn't need to do that, Rod."

"Hold out on me again, you'll get worse. Nguyen, he's lost his chow privileges. Lock him up."

Back at the camp Nguyen pushed him off the snowmobile, but not roughly. Halvorsen wondered if it was his age. He'd always heard Orientals respected old people. He trudged up to the shed, then stopped. Bent down. The overseer waited as he unlaced his snowshoes and left them flat on the snow.

"Becky," the Vietnamese called.

"Here." Her voice floated out of the shadows, from behind the barrels and coils and crates. Nguyen grunted and shoved the door closed behind Halvorsen. He heard the padlock click shut.

He dropped to his knees in the suddenly enclosed dark. Whispered hoarsely, mouth next to the planks, "Hey. You there?"

She lay on the bare hard dirt under the shed, shivering, lips still pressed to the gap in the planks she'd just shouted through. On Halvorsen's advice she'd taken along one of the gray plastic tarps, wrapped herself in it, but it was still freezing cold. There wasn't much room under the rough board floor, but at least there was light. It came in from the sides, a cold whiteness strained through the snow shoaled against the foundation blocks.

After the old man had left that morning she'd crept out hesitantly from her retreat. Crouched, wolfing down the rice the cook had left for her, then gathered her courage and slid out the unlocked door.

She'd hesitated there in the open dark, feeling exposed, vulnerable. But no one else was out in the predawn stillness. The only sounds were the wind in the trees and the breakfast clatter of pans from the direction of the camp. She'd quickly run around to the back of the shed, dragging the heavy plastic to smooth the snow behind her, then dropped to her knees. She'd dug quickly through the drifted-up snow, till it fell away into empty space and she was able to squirm in under the corner of the wall.

She'd stayed there all morning. Once someone came out, looking for something in the shed. She lay breathless, still, watching the boards sag and creak above her, till at last he left. Probably just the cook, getting her empty dish.

Now, hearing the old man whisper, she put her face to the gap again. "Yeah," she murmured. "I'm down here."

"Sounds good. Sounds like you're still back there behind the barrels. Everything go okay?"

"Yeah, except I'm freezing."

"You got the plastic?"

"It helps, but it's still cold. I wish I had a warmer jacket."

"Shouldn't be too much longer. I got the stuff."

"Where is it?"

Halvorsen put his face right down to the floor. Was it his imagination, or could he feel the warmth of her breath between the warped boards? He whispered, "My snowshoes are out front. Beside the door. Wait till we leave, then pull them in under the shack."

He kept on whispering, making sure she understood everything. He just hoped she could do it when the time came.

Nguyen didn't linger over lunch. It seemed like he was back almost at once. Halvorsen said grumpily, "Where's my dinner?"

"You gave it up," the Vietnamese said. "Trying to steal that dynamite. Get on. No, not there, here, behind me."

He clung to the overseer's back as they gunned eastward along the valley. It was still snowing, but he could make out smoke, a long streamer of black reaching off to the south. They churned uphill and there was the Jeep. The snow had built a coating of white on everything, the hood, the boom, the blanket-wrapped bundle at its end. Halvorsen hoped it didn't get to the fuse. He should have covered it with something. Damp fuse was bad news.

Eisen came up, rifle slanted casually over his shoulder. He yelled, "Ready to do her?"

"Guess so. Got your men in position?"

"Nguyen?"

"They're ready."

"You're on, Racks."

He nodded. "I'm gonna need some matches—"

"Thought I just gave you some." Eisen fumbled in his pockets impatiently, finally handed over a box of wooden matches. Halvorsen trudged toward the jeep, then turned. "Who's drivin'?"

"You."

"Wait a minute. I thought somebody else'd be driving. I was going to—"

"No, you do it," yelled Eisen over the bellow of the flare. "You're the expert."

Halvorsen blew out and turned to face the jeep again. Then wheeled back once more. "Where's the water? I got to have water."

Nguyen shouted and two men ran up with buckets. Halvorsen pointed and they dumped them over the blanketed charge. He made sure they wet it down thoroughly, till water ran down onto the snow. Dynamite wasn't waterproof, but it should resist the wet for a little while. "I want more," he yelled above the chest-shaking rumble. "Two more buckets, put 'em on the passenger side, on the floor."

When the buckets were in place he checked the fuse with his fingers. It felt damp and he cut two inches off the end and slit it carefully so that the powder fuse-train inside was exposed. Then he got in, climbing laboriously in over the door, which couldn't be opened because the boom was tied over it. He settled himself into the driver's seat. And finally looked ahead at what he'd avoided facing all that morning.

The flame loomed into the sky, the red-orange milling fireball just like the movies he'd seen of atomic bombs going off. He felt the heat on his cheeks a quarter-mile down the hollow. It would be a barbecue close in. For a moment he couldn't move, thinking, Maybe it'ud be better just to let Eisen shoot me.

Then he remembered the girl, and Nguyen's plans for her.

He took a deep breath and shoved the clutch in, reached down for the key. He hadn't driven for years and it felt strange, like doing it again the first time. The engine started. He got the parking brake off and headed up the ravine, the boom springing and waving out in front of him as the jeep jolted over frozen ground. Take it slow, he thought, and eased his boot off the gas. The motor shuddered and he hit the clutch. Too late; it stalled and bucked to a stop. When he got it started again he couldn't get the wheels to grip. They whined and spun and he sweated, jerked it into reverse, forward again.

Finally he found traction and rolled on, directly uphill, toward the huge hovering balloon of fire. It kept growing, getting steadily more terrifying. It took every ounce of guts he had to keep heading for it.

As it loomed up he remembered the last big flare he'd blown, out in Shinglehouse in '62. A huge, violent son of a bitch. Took three tries to put that one out. And that was with reflective suits, a trained crew, the works. Not stuff thrown together out of odds and ends, welded up by guys who didn't even speak English.

He muttered into the all-obliterating roar, "Shit, I thought I was done with this when I retired."

When heat seared his exposed skin past enduring he ducked beneath the dash, racked the gearshift into neutral, and set the parking brake. The continuous thunder made it hard even to think. The ground shook, the vibration transmitted through tires and suspension till it jiggled him in his seat. When he was sure the brake would hold, he leaned over, grabbed the first bucket, and upended it over his cap and his head. The icy water slammed his breath to a stop in his throat. He unzipped his coat and poured the second bucket down his undervest and shirt, soaking himself to the skin.

He folded the wet earflaps down and pulled the wet scarf up over his face. Beneath the roaring air the vehicle shivered, walking the empty buckets across the floor. He swallowed, looking up at the flare.

Like an aged crab, he scuttled stiffly over the seat, kicking the empty buckets out to bounce and roll soundlessly on the bare ground. He jumped down after them and crouched, eyes slitted against the heat. The snow on the hood was melting, running down in streams. He jerked his eyes away from it and fixed them on the end of the fuse. It fluttered and swayed in the wind that sucked endlessly in to sweep upward into the turbulent combustion of the fireball.

He fumbled the matches out and got two ready in his hand.

Turtling his head, he jerked the scarf up again and walked quickly out from the shelter of the vehicle, directly into the inferno.

With each step the heat increased, roasting the backs of his bare hands. The ground, muddy a few yards back, was suddenly dry, dusty earth baked hard as pottery clay.

He reached the fuse and turned his back on the flare. He got the matches set and struck them. The phosphorous ignited and he was touching it to the fuse when the wind, blowing always toward the flare, snuffed it out.

He dropped it instantly, grabbed the box, and struck another. It blew out too.

Crap, Halvorsen thought, feeling the heat growing steadily on his back. I didn't figure on this wind. Now steam was curling up off his sleeves like white smoke. He risked a quick glance over his shoulder.

It was like looking into the open door of a blast furnace, so bright he couldn't see detail. The charge, even closer to the flare, was steaming like a marshmallow on a stick. When all the water evaporated the wool would burst into flame. Not long after that the dynamite would cook off. More than enough dynamite to take care of a skinny old fool, crouched over desperately striking his third match spitting distance away from living hell and protected by absolutely nothing. His hands were shaking now and the matchhead crumbled in a red smear without striking a spark.

Mustering all his resolution, Halvorsen turned around to face the flare.

The backs of his hands were bright red, felt like rare steaks on their way to medium. His eyelids scraped helplessly over dry eyeballs. He bent his back against the wind, set his teeth, and struck the fourth match. It flared in the shelter of his body and he applied it quickly to the exposed powder of the fuse.

A two-inch spurt of sparkly fire leapt out of the slit end. He dropped the matches and ran clumsily back toward the jeep. He clambered over the gearshift and twisted the key. Too late, he remembered he'd left it running. He couldn't hear the starter grind but he felt it scream through the gearshift.

Bending his head, which felt like a matchtip about to burst into flame, he put the jeep into first and let up on the clutch. Driving forward again, now with the fuse sputtering and flaring ahead of him, jouncing like a crazy candle out at the end of the boom.

Now the hellish glare outlined every rock and charred stick. The paint was blistering on the hood, coming up in soft pimples that burst and gave off puffs of vapor like little volcanoes. The huge bloom of flame writhed and bellowed above him as if it knew he was coming to kill it, like some superannuated Saint George. The long boom swayed and sprung wildly as the wheels ground over dirt and rocks. He peered through the windshield, grateful for its shelter, till suddenly a crack zagged white at the edge of the glass.

When he dragged his attention back to the wheel the hood had drifted off track to the left. He corrected back, aiming for the center of the invisible column that rushed up out of the pit and climbed into white fire twenty feet up. His foot itched to go faster, get it over with, but he forced it to let up on the pedal. Couldn't hurry this. He couldn't get the charge actually in the gas column or it would tear off, flinging up into the fireball, where it would explode without effect. But if he stopped short it wouldn't blow the fire out, and he'd have it all to do over again. Four yards, that was where he wanted the charge. Four yards from the flame.

Putting him right beneath the fireball.

The myriad little volcanoes on the hood suddenly caught fire. The whole hood was smoking now, so bad he could barely see. He caught a glimpse of the charge, the wool wrapped in a white ball of smoke that streamed in toward the pit. The flare was sucking it in, sucking everything in like some immense open mouth. He slowed down even more, creeping now. Another ten yards—another five—

The windshield shattered, and a fist of heat struck through it straight into his face. Blinded, he clamped his hand over his eyes, then screamed as it too blistered.

But the jeep kept going, and only when he saw that the charge wore a coat of fire did he set the brake and collapse down under the dash.

Instead of getting out he crouched there, sucking the hot fumes of scorched wool and clutching his hand, eyes clamped closed, teeth grinding so hard he could hear it through his skull even over the roar. He couldn't get out into that hell. He'd catch like an oil-soaked rag. But he couldn't stay here either.

Eight minutes. How many had already ticked away?

Gagging on the plastic stink of scorching upholstery, he raised his head enough to look up into the reversed backup mirror. Looking for the fuse.

He couldn't make it out against the glare, but he saw that the main charge was catching fire. Flames danced along its top, leaping yellow and writhing white. The wind fluttered them, but unlike his matches they sprang up again, each time reaching higher. The gray blankets were charring black.

I got to get out of here, he thought, body and nerves and brain all shrieking together. But still he couldn't move, staring, held by the flame like a motionless moth.

The charge burst into flame all at once, all over, and pure terror booted him out of the jeep. The heat clamped down like a hot iron pressed to his back. He screamed soundlessly, stumbling into a blind run. His eyes were slitted closed but he had to keep them open. If he tripped he'd never get up again. His sleeves burst into flame and he knew this was the end. He was a dead man.

He staggered a few more steps and toppled forward weakly.

The explosion caught him halfway to the ground and blew him forward like a scrap of paper in an enormous wind. He sailed tumbling, lungs empty, as an immense soundless sound shook the world. Upside down, he glimpsed a blue-white flash, succeeded by an orange-white bloom of fire and then dirty smoke.

He crashed into the ground and lay unknowing for some time he couldn't count. Then shook himself and raised his head weakly.

The pit was obliterated, blotted out by a great tornado plume of dust and black smoke that pillared up into the gray sky. The ringing aftermath of the explosion sang on and on in his ears. But the dust kept streaming upward, and as it spread out over the valley he saw that the heart of it, where the fire had been, was vacant, empty, snuffed out.

He grunted and let his head sink into the cooling embrace of the snow. He turned his burning hands over, letting its icy kiss numb the blistered skin.

The growl of a motor came from down the valley. He raised his head again to see a truck rolling forward. Heads and arms poked from it like a wheeled centipede. It reached the edge of the pit, braked, and backed around. Dozens of men jumped off.

"The extinguishers," his cracked lips formed, but without breath or sound.

As if in answer two white jets leapt out, licked around the base of the pit, were sucked in and blown upward. Eisen pushed the men who held the CO_2 bottles closer, down into the pit, forcing the white icy plumes down toward where hot metal might still glow ignition-hot. At last he gestured angrily.

Halvorsen saw the tee then. Dozens of hands seized it and slid it off the truckbed. Men struggled with the massive pipe, falling, getting up again, staggering under the weight, gradually working it closer to the pit. Suddenly it all seemed apocalyptic, weird, filled with a meaning beyond his capacity to understand, with the low-hanging smoke writhing above the scorched and blasted hill, where dozens of antlike men struggled to erect a naked steel cross on the wrecked and trampled ground.

Halvorsen rolled himself over and sat up. He felt dizzy and weak. He looked around and saw his hat a few feet away. He got up and limped over to where it lay smoking. He beat it against his leg a couple of times, then jammed it on his head.

When he looked up again the crew had the tee lifted, almost erect. It wavered, nearly fell to crush them; but backs bent, men grunted and yelled, ropes came taut, and finally it stood upright, balanced by out-stretched arms. The roar went hollow. Dust erupted as the gas, divided now into two streams of lessened pressure, rushed out horizontal to the ground. Someone ran a rope to the truck, and it grunted into motion, twisting the lower leg of the weldment down into the soil. The crewmen's shouts came faintly to him as he trudged up the hill, limping. Then he felt dizzy again, and staggered over to a hemlock stump.

Half an hour later it was over. The heavy steel tee squatted in the pit, screwed deep into the ground. Nguyen was checking the blind flanges that, bolted onto the legs, had cut off the last of the gas stream. The sky was cloudy and smelled of burning, and the snow fell unhindered, already laying a thin, impossibly delicate frosting of white over the cooling ground. The well was tamed. Halvorsen had watched from his perch on the stump. Now he got up, still weak but feeling better, less shaky, and trudged up to the pit edge, where Eisen stood by the jeep, frowning at burned-away paint and melted plastic and bare springs.

"Your crew done good work," Halvorsen told him in the unearthly sing-ing quiet.

Eisen turned. "Racks! Thought you was a goner. We saw that dynamite catch fire and I said to Nguyen, 'Forget it, we ain't seein' him again this side of hell.' But damn if you didn't do it. Snuffed it right out, like the candles on a birthday cake."

"So I done what you wanted."

"You sure did. Thanks."

"You don't got to thank me," Halvorsen said. "We had a deal. Now, how about your side of it?"

Eisen looked around. Yelled, "Nguyen!"

"Yeah."

"C'mon over here. You know, I didn't think you could pull it off, Racks. I really didn't. But here you are, so now I got to think what to do with you. Let you go? Knowing all you know? Can't do that."

Halvorsen felt his shoulders slump. The bastard was going to welsh on the girl too. He could feel it coming.

"Well, can I keep you around? Have to have somebody watchin' you twenty-four hours a day if I do. I ain't got that kind of spare manpower. Besides, I never said I'd let you go if you helped me out. Just that I'd keep you around till then.

"So, only thing I can figure is—Nguyen!"

The Vietnamese stood waiting, squat and unreadable, shotgun dangling from his hand.

"Take Mr. Halvorsen over to Jerry. Tell him we feel bad about it, wish there was somethin' else we could do. But there it is. After that, the girl— just remember, I don't want to see her after your guys are done."

Halvorsen cleared his throat. "Rod—that ain't right. I never done you no harm."

"I don't feel too good about it myself." Eisen turned away, started toward the truck.

He raised his voice, called after him. "Hey. How about this. Let me an' the girl go. We'll walk out of here and you won't never hear anything about it. We can keep our mouths shut. Rod!"

"Wish I could believe that. Me, I'd be on the phone to the cops the first house I came to. No, I don't got any choice in the matter, W. T., so there ain't no point in begging."

Halvorsen looked at the Vietnamese. He didn't see any mercy in those dark eyes either. Maybe a little pity. But no sign of anything but resolve. He straightened. "Then do me one favor. For the time I gave you a break. Don't throw me to the damn dogs. Come on, Rod. Shoot me in the woods."

"What difference does it make? You're gonna be just as dead."

"That's right. What difference? But it makes a difference to me. I always tried to live like a man. Let me die like one, instead of some dog's dinner. For Christ's sake."

"All right," said Eisen reluctantly. "Goddamn it. Take him up the goddamn hill and shoot him."

"*Tôi sẽ làm,*" said the Vietnamese. He lifted the shotgun, checked it, then motioned Halvorsen up the hill.

Twenty-four

The hill sloped away below them into a mass of prickly treetops crowded along the frozen writhe of the creek. From up here the activity around the well was invisible, screened by the white folds of the hill and the steady fall of snow.

Halvorsen stood motionless, looking out and down at the valley, and above it the great wall of flat-topped hills, all the same height, the surface of the immense plateau that had once been the bottom of a life-brimming sea. Raising his eyes he saw dimly through the curtaining snow range after range, each fainter, bluer, stretching off into infinite distance as if there was no end to them and no end to the world or time.

Behind him the Vietnamese waited. He felt the man's eyes on his shoulders as his hands had been there before, shoving him on. He took a deep breath and let it out, trying to master his fear. His mouth tasted hot and coppery, as if he'd been sucking pennies.

After Eisen had told the Vietnamese to kill him they'd left the valley by climbing straight up the side of the ravine. For a time Halvorsen could look back to the brown patch the flare had left, a muddy, trampled fairy ring on the rocky soil. Then they'd descended a fold in the hill and it was gone.

Now they were in the woods again, the woods he'd loved all his life.

The trees surrounded him, familiar but impotent, able to witness but not to help. He remembered the years he'd spent in these forests, playing out by the old farm, then working, hunting, living.

And now, dying.

"Go on," said the man behind him, not roughly, but with an edge of impatience or annoyance. Halvorsen took another breath, rubbing his quivering thigh muscles, and began climbing again.

As they ascended into the sheltering trees, he remembered how it had been each year.

How into each ironbound and rigid winter, the first sigh of spring breathed like a whispered word to wake a sleeping land. Pale light, the warmth of a lingering sun, and everywhere suddenly the hidden murmur of water. It chuckled and rushed beneath the stubborn snow as the trees burst into buds tiny as chipmunk ears and the air, still cool at this altitude, sang in the lungs with the promise of renewed life. Then summer, hot and drowsy on open meadows filled with wildflowers and timothy but cool and shadowy where the ferns nodded on the wet north slopes. The rumble of a thunderstorm rolling through the valleys. The fresh sharp scent of rain . . . Then the fall. Frost splashing the hills with harvest yellows and ochers, startling purples and brushfire scarlets, till the woods were a bouquet arranged by a master artist. And in rainy autumns the milky mists hung between the hilltops like curtains.

And then again came winter . . .

As winter had to come.

Behind him the Vietnamese grunted: "This is far enough."

Halvorsen didn't turn or make any other sign he'd heard. He just kept climbing, lifting his boots and putting one in front of the other through the deep new snow. His underclothes were icy clammy against his skin. He was still wet through. Only his muscle heat, the shivering and the relentless piston-push of climbing, kept him at all warm. Around him he noticed the birches were giving way to beech, the gray iron trunks straight and cylindrical as elephant legs except that they writhed slowly as they rose into the gray sky. And ahead, at the top of the mountain, the pyramidal blue of an old stand of hemlock. He rested his eyes on them like a man looking at heaven.

"Stop," the Vietnamese said again, louder, and this time Halvorsen turned his head.

"Just a little farther. I want to look down on the valley."

The other hesitated, shotgun halfway to his shoulder; then lowered it. "Another hundred meters. That's all. I got to get back."

"Thanks." Halvorsen spat into the snow, noting the rusty stain of blood. He didn't want a chew anymore. That was one thing about taking your last walk, going to your death. He didn't seem to want a chew anymore.

He lifted his eyes as the valley came into view. In the falling snow it was mysterious, distant, curtained like a sanctuary from the gaze of the profane. The snow fell without haste, slanting as it dropped, filling the air with a multitudinous whisper like thousands of fingers stroking velvet. He looked down the long hill to the white rumpled blanket of the valley.

Impossible to believe that beneath that sterile blank lay all the sleeping summer. So that you had to wonder if somehow there mightn't be summer again for men too, if they died as the fern died, their deepest roots never perishing but only sleeping, so that when light returned to the world so would life to them, world without end. The words of a hymn they'd sung when he was a boy, the old clapboard church on the hill, the face of his mother bent over the *Lutheran Hymnary* held above his head. And right now he couldn't call to mind another thing out of the terrible sterile blankness that was his mind, as whitewrapped and featureless as the shrouded valley below. You wouldn't think old as he was he'd be so scared. But all he could think of was standing in Sunday school singing the children's service: and the words, the words came back he used to sing, knowing he'd never get old enough to die:

Jesus, who called the little ones to Thee, to Thee I come;
O take my hand in Thine, and speak to me, and lead me home.

Staring steadily down, he blinked cold tears away as the wind rode over the crest of the hill. The blowing snow brushed his face with a cold, melting caress. His legs quivered. He didn't have his snowshoes, had left them at the shed, and now each step plunged almost three feet into the deepening drift.

A little later Nguyen said, behind him, "That's far enough."

He stopped, then turned. He looked out over the tops of the trees and up at the undersides of the clouds. The snowflakes slowly kissed his cheeks, his lips, his eyelids. He lowered his eyes to see the Vietnamese raising the gun.

He was trying to cup Jenny's face in his memory, looking up at the sky, when he heard the girl calling. He couldn't tell what she was yelling, but it was her voice, drifting up, then faraway in a gust, high and thin. He jerked his eyes down, searching the trees. Above them on the hill or below? For a moment he couldn't tell. The Vietnamese was doing the same thing, eyes flicking around the boundaries of their sight. Then the long gun barrel swung down to cover the beeches that fell away into the gray blur of forest.

He saw the hurled cylinder at the same time the Vietnamese did. Falling through the snowy air, trailing a blue ribbon of fine smoke. From above them, not below. The fuse drew a tracer of sparks across the air. Nguyen reacted instantly, jerking the gun up and around.

The cupped-hands clap of the twelve-gauge bounced off the trees and rattled away. But he must have missed because the dynamite finished its arc and punched a neat hole in the snow six feet short of where the executioner stood.

Halvorsen hurled himself down, as deep as he could burrow, into the white hug of a drift.

It went off with a hollow bang not much louder than the shot had been. A sphere of dirty gray ballooned for a second where the Vietnamese had stood. From inside it came a second detonation, oddly muffled. Then it collapsed, snow and dirt dropping back to the ground, and chunks of rock and wire pattered away through the branches around them.

Becky hugged the cold trunk, its rough bark skin tattooing her cheek. She squeezed her eyes tight against what she'd just done. Whether it worked or not, she just didn't want to see.

When the last echo died, she opened them slowly. She was breathing in little hitches, she couldn't get enough air. Not just from climbing the hill, practically running up it through the deep snow and around the bushes and rocks, trying to get out in front of the two climbing men. But from knowing she'd just tried to kill somebody.

"Becky." The old man. "Becky!"

Still shaking, she peered around the tree.

Mr. Halvorsen stood below her, brushing snow off himself and looking around. Behind him lay a fallen, misshapen rag doll in a coat the color of the snow, arms outstretched. She stared at it, unable to move. Till she heard her name again, and at last something heard inside her head and pried her fingers off the bark and sent her stumbling and sliding down the bank to see what she had done.

The little girl came slowly down the bank. She was pale as ice and she was shaking. She slipped and fell but picked herself up with a sort of awkward curtsey and kept coming. Halvorsen waited, then trudged forward to meet her, taking slow, deep breaths to calm down himself.

"Nice throw," he said. "Where'd you learn to throw like that? When I was a boy, you couldn't have found a girl could throw worth a darn."

She didn't answer, just stood looking down at the wadded-up remnant of a man. Halvorsen looked too. There was blood on the snow, but not much. Some of it was leaking out of a puncture in the parka. The punctures, he figured, came from the heavy wire he'd wrapped the dynamite with, to make a crude grenade.

After he'd finished making up the charge that morning he'd stood still while they searched his coat, his boots, his hat. They'd found the stick inside his coat and punished him for it. As he'd figured they would.

But they'd missed the one lashed under his snowshoe.

He cleared his throat, not liking the way she looked. Blank eyes too wide. Arms hugging herself. She was about to go round the bend. "For a while there I thought you weren't going to show," he said.

"I was there. It was hard to get ahead of you without letting him see me."

"Went as slow as I could without makin' him suspicious. Well, you done great, girl. But we ain't out of the woods yet by a long shot. First thing, let's get you something warmer to wear."

She didn't help as he stripped the body, but she let him put the parka on her, holding her arms out for the sleeves like a toddler. He worked fast. Eisen would miss his overseer, send somebody to see what was holding him up. They had to be gone by then. He rolled the body over and found a wallet, found shotgun shells in a trouser pocket. He left the wallet but the shells reminded him to look for the gun. He spotted the butt sticking up from where it had been crushed into the snow as the Vietnamese fell.

When he picked it up it felt good to be holding a gun again. Then he noticed the barrel. He turned it over and looked at it disbelievingly. Then hefted it, and swung it around, and let go. Spinning, it dropped down the hill and disappeared into the treetops.

"It isn't any good?"

"Need a gunsmith, a new barrel. He must of had the muzzle jammed down in the dirt when he pulled the trigger that last time. How's that parka? Any warmer?"

"Yeah." She looked at the body again. "Is he really—"

"Dead? Uh huh. Come on, we got to get moving."

"We can't help him?"

"Come on." He reached back impatiently and shook her shoulder. Forced her eyes away from the body. "Look at me! He didn't care about you. He wanted to give you to his men. You just did what I told you to do. Come *on*!" He turned and started stamping uphill, and when he looked back a few seconds later, she was climbing after him, head down.

He gave all his attention to the hill and their escape. Losing the gun had taken some of the wind out of his sails, but now he felt keen, eager as he glanced around. He hadn't really figured any of it to work. He'd known what Eisen would do, though, all right. Once he got the flare put out he didn't have any use for him anymore. He'd had to depend on the girl to stay hid in the woods, keep her eye on where they took him to finish him off. But she'd done good. She'd pitched that dynamite like a Molly Maguire. He opened his mouth to compliment her again but her face, when he turned his head, made him clamp his lips shut and concentrate on climbing.

He'd decided last night that if by any miracle they got free, he'd head west. True, the Elk Valley was the closest populated area. But Eisen knew that too, and he had enough people that he could deploy them right across their trail. Heading west, they'd be swallowed by the fastnesses of the central Kinningmahontawany. Back where he'd trapped all those years ago. He knew the lay of the land. If he could shake them off their trail, he and the girl could go to ground in there for a couple of days, then find a way out to the north or northwest. The important thing right now was to put as much distance as they could between them and Eisen. And make it as hard as he could for the other to track them. . . .

He became suddenly aware of that, of their track. He looked back to see a long straight ditch plowed deep by himself and then the girl, her walking where he'd broken trail. It was still snowing but it would take a lot of snow to cover that. Still an hour to dark, too. If they came after them in those ski machines of theirs—

"Mr. Halvorsen."

"Yeah?" He stopped, blowing out fatigue. His legs felt like used pipe cleaners, wobbled like old bent coathangers.

"I can't climb much farther. I'm tired."

"We got to keep going."

"I can't. I'm sorry, but I can't. This snow's so deep."

"You didn't bring my snowshoes."

A shamed face, a quick glance. "I'm sorry. I forgot."

He said slowly, figuring he knew the answer already: "And the matches. The ones you used for the dynamite?"

"I must have dropped them after I threw it. I was . . . I just . . ." She looked stricken, close to crying.

He sucked a tooth, wanting to tell her, You forget things like that out here, you ain't going to make it far. But he judged she felt bad enough already, killing the fellow and all that. And criticizing her wasn't going to bring back anything they needed. So finally he clapped his hand to his pocket. Clambered upslope, to the lower boughs of a gigantic hemlock.

"Come on up here," he said.

Becky looked down in awed wonder as he fitted the second makeshift snowshoe to her boot. She couldn't really believe what he'd just done. He'd stared at the big tree for a few minutes, muttering in his whiskers, touching this branch and then that. It was like a pine tree, but bigger than any pine she'd ever seen, with rough dark bark. Then the knife had clicked open, and he'd slashed off two flexible boughs. Bowed them, his hands molding them into a rough oval, with the ends parallel, then binding them on with wire. A minute or two later he was boosting her to her feet. She teetered uncertainly. Tried a step, then another.

"How's that feel? The needles interlock there. That put you on top of the snow?"

"Yeah. Thanks. Are you going to make yourself some?" But he already was, knitting more needle-laden branches together, then wrapping them with more short lengths of wire. He lifted his red coat and pulled off his belt. Cut the leather in half. The straps went over his boots and he tightened them and knotted them firmly. Then he stood too, balancing on the feathery surface of the fresh deep snow.

"Let's go," he said, then seemed to recollect something. He reached far back under the tree, hacked off a longer bough, and broomed it over the snow. The wide round indentations of the snowshoes were much shallower than their bootprints. When he whisked the heavy green needles over them they vanished almost entirely. The snow obliterated what marks remained, as if eager to help, blurring them minute by minute into invisibility, as if she and the old man had never been here at all.

"Neat," she told him. "Where'd you learn to do that?"

"When I was your age an old man showed me that. An old cuss name of Amos. Okay, come on, we got to get into some rough country, or—"

"What's that?" she said, lifting her head.

"What?"

"I thought I heard a motor."

He stood silent, head cocked, and she listened too. "One of them snowmobiles," he said at last.

"It's coming this way."

"Let's go. Fast as we can, and keep brushing out your trail."

She headed after him up between the trees. The old man moved in a glide, hardly lifting his snowshoes, and after she tripped a couple of times she tried to figure out how he was doing it. Just lifting her feet a little bit, like skating, letting the tail of the snowshoe drag. It was easier, at least until the backs of her legs started to hurt.

The motor sound was getting louder. For a little while, when she first realized they were free, she hadn't been scared. But now she was frightened again. The old man was almost at the top of the hill now. He started left, around a huge flat rock that had paused in its slide down the steep face of the hill, but then changed his mind and took the steeper way up it. She dug her hands into the snow, feeling its cold teeth bite like snakes, and yanked herself up after him.

Ahead Halvorsen paused, looking back between the trees. He couldn't see much. The snow was coming down too heavy, and it was getting dark. But he could hear the machine, like a chainsaw whining and *brrruup-up-up*ing along the valley.

He'd hoped they could slip away. Stay ahead till darkness fell, then travel all night while the snow covered their trail and be untrackable miles away by dawn. But Eisen must have heard the explosion. They had a head start, but the machines could travel much faster.

But they couldn't come out of the valleys. Up here the slopes were too steep, covered with loose scree and boulders, close-set trees, fallen timber and blowdowns and blackberry hells. Up here, if they could keep going, they could still escape. Get far enough west, then come down along one of the creek valleys and find help. Find a phone, or somebody with a car.

They got to the top of the hill, to where there was still some hemlock but more birch and maple. The woods were dense but there wasn't much undergrowth. Here and there along the crest lightning or storms had toppled the biggest trees. They lay like fallen giants cloaked with white. No, anybody who got up here would have to come on foot. He'd of felt better with the shotgun, but if they came, he knew some things he could do to make it interesting for them.

But now he couldn't hear the motor anymore. And presently, trekking on along the crest, it occurred to him to wonder why. A spark of hope started to glow down in his belly and he thought, If we can just make it to nightfall . . . He listened, but he didn't hear anything. Not for a long time. Just the creak of the hemlock branches under his boots, the crunch and pant of the girl behind him, the dragging whisper of boughs raking through the snow.

Behind and below them, standing by the idling snowmobiles, the tall man and the fat one stood looking up at where the incline ended in a sheer rockfall. "That's where they went, all right," Eisen said.

"How'd they get Nguyen? He's torn up from hell to breakfast."

"Dynamite, sounded like."

"They went right up this cliff. Should we go after 'em?"

"Not tonight. That's rough country, top of this hill." The tall man rubbed his chin. "Can't use the Yamahas up there. And he'll know that, he'll stick to the up and downs."

"You're not gonna let him get away?"

"No," said Eisen. "One of the gooks, I'd figure let 'em go, let 'em freeze theirselves to death. But old Racks . . . the son of a bitch just might make it. If he does, this whole operation folds and we're out in the cold. Here's what we'll do. We'll let 'em run tonight. They can't get far in the dark. When it gets light again we'll send your dogs after 'em. Think they can track 'em down?"

"I don't think they'll have too much trouble," said Olen. "Where you think he's headed?"

"East makes the most sense, so he won't go that way. He's a cunning bastard, forgot more about these woods than you or me'll ever know. But he's old, and he's dragging the kid with him. I figure he'll head west. Push up above Coal Run, stick to the rough patches we can't get the machines up into. Can you get the dogs up there? Run 'em up onto the ridges?"

"Oh yeah. No problem."

"But if that don't work, he's got to come down sometime. If he's headed west, he'll have to come down Cook Creek or else cross Fischer, farther west. Up above the falls. When he does, we'll be there waiting."

"We'll get 'em," said Olen. "Don't worry about that. Them doggies love to chase things through the woods. They done a good job on the woman, didn't they?"

"Too good," said Eisen. "They weren't supposed to kill her. Just catch her."

"Hate to try to stop 'em, once they get started. Anyhow, you want these two put down, don't you?"

Eisen lifted his face to the falling snow. He said, "Yeah, Jerry. I want 'em killed."

It was almost dark when Halvorsen lifted his head again. To hear the faraway baying, echoing from the glooming hills.

Tomorrow they'd send the dogs after them.

He waited in the falling snow, legs shaking, dizzy, for the girl to catch up. His heart felt like chunk ice. Dogs; and they were unarmed, except for the knife and two shotgun shells. No tools, no weapons, no compass, no matches, no map. The girl was brave but she wasn't going to be much help out here. It was all going to be up to him. But he was tired. So tired. And so damned old.

He turned his head and spat. A dark bloom stenciled the snow. Then they slogged on, into the gathering night.

Twenty-five

The gathering night kept trapping her gaze, as if trying to draw her out through the windows into it. Ainslee didn't want to be here, on the sixth floor of the Thunder Building. Her head pounded with the blood-throb of a tension headache. But she had the feeling it was nothing compared with the one the presentation she was about to receive would give her.

She sat with eleven other Thunder corporate officers around the table, and not one high-backed leather chair was tilted back. The bar was closed tonight. There was no chat, no conversation. Stony faces sat waiting. Now Judy Bisker moved along the windows closing the blinds. Cutting off pane by pane their view of the falling snow, the sparkling glitter of the refinery, the firefly glimmer of the town beyond. Ranged around the table to hear their fates sat the vice presidents of Thunder Oil and the chief operating officers of The Thunder Group subsidiaries. The officer-directors—Frontino and McGehee, Ainslee as president, and beside her Rudy Weyandt—sat at the foot of the table, with the best view of the computer-driven projection screen the Besarcon team had brought with them from New York.

Now a huddle of men and women at the door broke apart, taking seats around the perimeter of the room, leaving one balding man in a gray suit and gold-rimmed bifocals. He cleared his throat, bent his head for a moment, then stepped to the lectern.

"Good evening, gentlemen, Ms. Thunner. I'm Fredric Jacobs, head of Besarcon Corporation's management assistance team. My background is corporate finance and I've worked with Norfolk Southern, PepsiCo, and ITT before coming to Besarcon four years ago. Can everyone hear me? In back?"

As Ainslee nodded she thought how swiftly events had moved since she'd been voted out as chief executive officer three days before. As she'd been warned, Kemick had his hatchet people in Petroleum City the morning after the surprise board meeting. The team consisted of two women and three men, counting Jacobs. After a short meeting with Ainslee and Weyandt they fanned out to the nerve centers: sales, marketing, finance, human resources, data processing, the refinery, purchasing, and the headquarters of the various operating divisions.

They did not discuss their findings with the men and women they interviewed. For the last two days Ainslee had been fielding worried calls from the division chiefs. All she could do was advise them to cooperate, use their common sense, and stay alert. But not till now had there been a whisper of the victors' intentions toward what was now effectively their company.

Jacobs adjusted his glasses and said, "Welcome to the Besarcon family. We're proud to have Thunder as the thirty-eighth corporate partner in the most progressive organization in America. Hm? Now, I personally want to testify that we've met with the fullest cooperation and we appreciate that. Also, I have to say I've never visited a company with more esprit de corps than Thunder. Hm? Its personnel are proud of their long tradition. And justly so.

"At the same time, segments of the company have fallen behind current standards of efficiency, productivity, and profitability. Hm? Those are the areas we will address tonight with our quick-look recommendations. Neil?"

Ainslee looked down reluctantly at a laser-printed ten-page document. The cover read, *THUNDER: Blueprint for a New Century*. She didn't want to open it. But all around her pages rustled, and finally she did.

"Our goals were to find ways The Thunder Group can streamline operations, restructure assets, and increase profitability. Our recommendations include decentralizing, rightsizing, shedding certain noncore businesses, refocusing, and setting new goals.

"Restructuring a company is never easy. For anyone involved. But let me tell you, as a guy who's done both, it's a lot easier than trying to resuscitate a Chapter Fourteen. And that's what we're here to prevent.

"One further thing. I know we come in as 'outside experts,' which means we automatically get handed the black hats. Well, we're not here to humiliate anyone, or to shake things up for the sake of shaking things up. We are simply pointing out actions management can implement to create a significantly trimmer, more efficient organization.

"Now let me introduce our management team, for those who haven't yet met them. Seraphaea Jones is our financial specialist; Michael Jerram, production; Fran Salazar, pensions; Greg Morein and Neil Hanoway, my own staff assistants. We'll give you a few moments to look over the report before we begin. Please hold your questions until the formal presentation is complete, as I think most of them will be answered in the course of our remarks."

She was only half-listening now. No one spoke as they all leafed slowly through the document. Paragraphs and phrases leapt up to snare her eye, each making her heart sink farther.

> . . . *The divestiture of assets that do not meet the company's long-term objectives is a vital part of strategic refocus to revitalize long-term prospects.* . . .
>
> . . . *In view of the poor outlook for U.S.-based electronic component manufacture and reduced military budgets, we recommend all operations of VanStar CeraMagnet be terminated and land, facilities, and equipment be sold. A limited number of selected engineers and production personnel will be offered the opportunity to relocate to Irvine, California, where VanStar's current contracts with the U.S. Army for helicopter components will be filled by Besarcon's Aeromarine Technologies Division. Current contracts for electronic and ceramic-magnet components will be filled by the Compania Metallurgica Industrial Cabrera of Tecate, Mexico.*

Poor Hilda, Ainslee thought. And Jason's face had gone stark white as he read. But she could spare them only a moment's compassion as she saw that the next page was headed.

PETROLEUM OPERATIONS

> *For Thunder Oil, we have identified four actions that will enable this core division to achieve earnings growth:*
>
> - *Streamlining the process plant*
> - *Adding outsourced options to the product line*
> - *Cost reduction*
> - *Expanding gasoline margins.*
>
> *As presently structured, the core refinery is too small to operate economically across the spectrum of the product stream. Increased investment is contraindicated in view of long-term trends in the energy market, declining local crude production, and the distance of the refinery from offload points for foreign oil.*
>
> *We therefore recommend streamlining operations by discontinuing production of solvents and intermediates, closing the ethylene and propylene crackers, and discontinuing other specialty production as shown in Figure 2. This permits shutting down a significant portion of the process plant and means 1,055 positions can be eliminated.*
>
> *We recommend disposition by sale of the Thunder Building, the Adminis-*

*tration Building, Railyards #1 and #2, the Truck Repair Facility, the Truck
Park, Research Laboratory Building and associated parking and test stands,
the Cafeteria, the Medical Center, the Precision Machining Facility, the Pipe
Shop, the Fire Station, and the Plastics Division. Approximately 385 staff and
maintenance positions can be eliminated from overhead simultaneously. Some
laboratory and operations personnel may be offered relocation to other areas of
the country.*

*Additional cost reductions are available in the following areas: renegotiate
supplier contracts. Reduce raw materials expenditures. Eliminate redundant
inspection operations in the production of Thunder Premium and Thunder
Green.*

Her hands were shaking now, but she forced herself to keep reading
through the sense of doom and ruin and disbelief. Above all, she had to
maintain control of herself.

*Rightsizing requires consolidation of unnecessary layers of management. Sig-
nificant research functions, financial planning, and strategic decisions in the
petrochemical market can be more efficiently managed from New York than
Petroleum City. We thus recommend shedding 145 positions from management
and administrative overhead.*

*Significant sales gains can be achieved at the low end of the motor oil
market by introducing a Thunder economy line of repackaged bulk motor oil
stock purchased from a Gulf Coast refinery. . . .*

*. . . In view of the reduced production of specialty products, we recommend
combining TBC Industrial Chemicals and Thunder Petroleum Specialties into
one operating division. This will permit consolidation of management and
result in the saving of another 92 positions . . .*

They were decapitating the company, selling off what would bring in
cash, reducing the rump to an appendage run from New York. She caught
Frontino's mouth tightening as he worked his way down the page. In
anger? Regret? It was impossible to tell. The air in the room had turned
to some heavy, hot fluid that choked her even as she panted it in and out.
She forced her eyes back to the print as her head throbbed, the pain
doubling at each page.

*The growth will come in environmental services, industrial chemicals, natural
gas development, and health care. We recommend targeting investment as
follows:*

*Double the throughput of the bioremediation plant in Chapman and add
sales staff to focus on obtaining trash disposal contracts.*

In view of the growing demand for environmentally friendly laundry prod-

*ucts, invest $2.7 million in TBC Industrial Chemicals to increase capacity
for oleochemicals and specialty surfactants.*

*Accelerate development of deep gas reserves in the Floyd Valley/Hefner River
region.*

*Implement a Phase II expansion plan for Hemlock HealthCare Corporation,
adding 350 beds to existing facilities and franchising new facilities in Erie,
Williamsport, Lock Haven, and Lewistown.*

The last section of the report was a discussion and analysis of financial
conditions, pension funding, and accounting policies. She breathed deep
and slow, forcing her mind back into its traces, absorbing the recommendations and relating them to current-year projections.

When she reached the last page the overall plan was quite clear. There
was no way the refinery, already trembling at the lower edge of profitability, could be made more efficient by downsizing it. Quite the reverse.
So though it was not set forth as such, she understood quite clearly that
Besarcon's long-range intention was the shutdown of all refining operations, followed by exploitation of the Thunder brand name to sell low-
quality bulk products bought on the spot market.

Through her own shock she found the presence of mind to examine
the other faces around the table. Even Weyandt looked shaken. The silence was like that moment at an interment when the words are all said
and it remains only to turn over the first shovelful of dirt. Someone
coughed; there was an uneasy creak as someone else shifted in his chair.
Then Jacobs's smooth voice spoke again, the lights dimmed, and a seven-
color display came on. "The new Thunder," he intoned. "A new strategy,
a new Thunder for a new century. Let's begin with analysis of current
earnings. . . ."

The Petroleum Club loomed up from the darkness, through the falling
snow, like an old and opulent manor house. Rogers McGehee held the
heavy oak door as she bent in out of an astonishingly bitter wind. She
glanced around as she stripped her gloves off, let the attendant take her
coat. With the lamps turned low the age-darkened carved wainscoting
sucked all light from the room and spewed back seeping shadow. The
marble statues of Commerce and The Arts that flanked the sweeping stairs
glowed in the dimness like ghosts, and the immense chandelier, unlit, was
only a web of faint gleams above their heads. The cool air smelled of
lemon oil and old dust, with a lingering memory of long-dead cigar
smokers.

Nine P.M. The club seldom opened this late anymore, but a phone call
to Joan Brinberg as soon as the meeting at Thunder broke had kept a

skeleton staff on duty. Ainslee nodded to the barman and asked quietly for a sherry. She carried it into the little room past the empty lounge chairs.

The gathering of the clan, she thought as they rose, some with the ease of youth, others the creaky deliberation of age. Above them the hooded, predatory eyes of her ancestors stared down. Beacham Berwick . . . Colonel Charles . . . Philander . . . Lutetia and Frances . . . Daniel. And the blank space where a family portrait had once hung. Had she been altogether fair to her ex-husband? She wasn't as sure now as she'd once been. She recollected herself and placed her glass at the head of the table. "Good evening, everyone."

"Evening, Ainslee, you're lookin' beautiful as ever."

"Thank you, Luke." Ice in her reply; she hadn't forgotten Fleming's abstention. She could smell his bourbon breath from where she sat. Rogers sat next to him, nursing coffee. Past him was Peter Gerroy and then Hilda Van Etten. And then, sitting with them but in some indefinable way separate, Ron Frontino, Thunder Oil's president, stocky and expressionless with hands lying flat in front of him on the table.

A sneeze from the doorway; Connie Kleiner. "Sorry, 'm I late?" he muttered into a handkerchief.

"You're just in time, Connie. Glad to have you here." Pleasant, casual, bright, she told herself. "Thanks for joining us for this little strategy session—"

"Your dad always used to call it foreplay," Kleiner said.

Hilda snickered and before Ainslee could answer said, "Yeah, but the difference is, this time we're the ones who got screwed."

Gerroy pulled a copy of the report from inside his jacket. "The messenger service got this to me as I was getting into the car. Is this for real?"

"Genuine as they come, Pete."

"They can't be serious about implementing this. Closing VanStar? Selling off half Thunder's facilities? Moving headquarters functions to Manhattan?"

"I didn't get a copy of that, whatever it is," Fleming grunted.

"Here's a spare, Luke. Rogers, you were there. Were they kidding us?"

"Oh, they're serious," said the banker.

She leaned forward and took the helm with a three-minute summary of Besarcon's plans for The Thunder Group. She finished, "It's obvious to me that destructive as this is, it's only the first step in looting us of assets, equity, contracts—anything that could be of value to them or sold elsewhere for cash. There are gestures at reinvestment, but even if they're implemented, they'll account for only about thirty percent of the liquidity generated. Everything else is blood being sucked out of the company. Now, I called this meeting to get two things: one, a consensus that we have to fight; and two, some ideas as to how we can do that effectively. Hilda?"

Van Etten dropped her hand. The smile was gone now. "Ainslee, everybody—my father is devastated. They want to close everything he's worked to build. We're not leaving him alone tonight. I think whoever didn't vote for Ainslee the other day realizes now what a terrible mistake they made. So I think we ought to say to Luke and Ron that we all have got to stand together now."

Frontino spoke for the first time. "Where's Rudy? Did you ask him to this meeting, Ainslee?"

"No."

"Why not? He's the CEO."

"It's an unofficial meeting. I invited whom I wished."

"I see."

"All right, then. How do we oppose this takeover and dismemberment and regain control? Any ideas?"

McGehee: "We need to present an alternate slate at the next shareholders' meeting. Spend the time in between getting the word out. It's certainly not going to be popular locally. Pete, you can help. The papers and radio stations have got to take a strong editorial stand."

"Now, I voted in favor of Ainslee, Rogers. But that doesn't mean our interests are automatically against any restructuring. Let's face it, the area as a whole could probably benefit from some of these recommendations."

"Like closing VanStar?" Van Etten snapped.

"Of course not, Hilda, but some of the other initiatives . . . what I'm saying is, these are only recommendations. Maybe we can work out a compromise acceptable to both sides, instead of stonewalling any change and maybe going down in flames." The publisher hesitated, then added, "Anyway, a lot of the stock is held outside our readership and listener area now."

She went around the table, but one after the other, except for Hilda, each director offered not support but temporizations, rationalizations, half-hearted regrets. She saw in the lowered eyes and averted faces that she had lost them. Luke was drunkenly stubborn, defensive, and greedily curious about the new program's increased investment in gas drilling. Frontino said little even when pressed; he was going to attach his loyalty to the new leadership. Connie Kleiner seemed confused, unable to bite down on what was going on. Even Rogers admitted to anxiety over whether, if he came out in opposition, he would lose his position at First Raymondsville.

These were not the faces of people ready to risk their investments, status, and jobs in a revolt. With a bitter knowledge she realized that her father's policy of choosing followers for his board, not leaders, pliant tools rather than the strong, was working against her now. As long as she'd been unchallengeable they'd backed her a thousand percent. But now that her tower was tottering, she found not concrete but sand under its foundations.

From the walls her ancestors stared at her in accusing unanimity.

"It's me," she said into the cellular. The Land Rover ticked over almost silently, heat blasting out the vents, tightening the skin around her tired eyes. She was parked as close as she could get to the snow-buried curb at the corner of Main and O'Connor, out in the West End.

Weyandt's voice, surprised: "Who's this—Ainslee?"

"That's right."

"Where are you?"

"Down on the street in front of your apartment. May I come up?"

A pause, then, "Sure. Just a minute, I'll be right down."

"I can come up."

"No, no, I'll meet you in the lobby. Just let me get a shirt on."

The lobby of Weyandt's building was so brightly lit she blinked. She'd only been here once before, a dinner party he'd held years ago to introduce his niece. Rudy's hair was slicked back, shower-wet, and his shirt was open at the throat. He blinked and she wondered if he was as nervous as she was. They rode up to his floor in silence, each staring at the line of buttons on the panel. He took her down the hall and closed the door behind them. "Scotch?"

"Thanks."

She looked around the living room as he busied himself in the kitchen nook. It was immaculate. Surely he didn't do his own cleaning? Queen Anne furniture, beige upholstery. Bach playing on the PBS station from Buffalo. Ice clinked and he called, "Understand there was a meeting tonight at the club."

"There was."

"I didn't hear about it till it was too late to go. Anything interesting?"

She didn't answer. Just sipped the drink he handed her, and crossed the room to a long window with a view of the town. The snow, falling ever more heavily, had built up two feet deep on the balcony outside. The suburbs were a patchwork of light spreading far to the south of the Allegheny.

"Well," she said, feeling uncertain now she was here. It had made sense when she was driving over, when she was sitting in the car.

He said, behind her, "Pretty radical changes in that strategy paper they put out today."

She turned but he was bent over, adjusting something in the corner; a gas log. "Why don't you sit down?" he said.

She hesitated, then took the easy chair in front of the fire. "Yeah. It's a shocker."

"Ainslee, I want you to know there are some things in there I'm going to fight. Closing the lab, for example."

"That would be a major loss." She took a deep breath and plunged in. "*Any* divestiture would be a major loss. Rudy, I'm ready to declare peace. We've got to figure out a way to work together."

"Great. I couldn't agree more."

"I was hoping you'd say that. We've got to find a way to stop this—"

"Whoa, there," Weyandt added. He took the chair beside her and shoved a stool over to her with his foot. He was still in slippers, she noticed. "I told you in New York, I thought a lot of what Kemick was saying made sense. I'm aboard with the basic thrust of the recommendations. Not all, but most of them."

"You can't be serious. They'll scuttle VanStar, butcher our production force, people we've spent years training, dump half Thunder Oil's facilities on the market—"

"Those facilities have been costing us money a long, long time, Ainslee," Weyandt said quietly.

"We won't be a player without them."

"Face it, Ainslee. Thunder hasn't been a major player in the petroleum industry since the mid-fifties."

"Not true. Thunder Green—"

"Was a disaster. We went public to re-engineer our production facilities for clean-air gas. But now the majors are announcing their own high-oxygen fuels. By next year we'll be straining to keep up with the pack again. Only, burdened with debt this time."

"We kept afloat. With the cash flow from the Medina operations—"

"Exactly." He sighed, running his hand through graying hair. "By the way, I need the files on that. That should have been part of the turnover as CEO. I'll need them soon—that's going to be a very delicate matter to explain to Kemick. But has it ever occurred to you, Ainslee, that if the only way we could stay solvent was by doing things like Medina, that in essence we were bankrupt already? Did that ever occur to you?"

"I never heard any objection from you before."

"I try to support my boss."

She bit off the reply that rose to her lips: that if his behavior at the last board meeting had been loyalty, she'd hate to see his idea of treachery. Instead she said again, putting every gram of conviction she could muster into her voice, "Rudy, we have to put that all behind us. This is too big to let anything that was, or is, between us prevent us from standing shoulder to shoulder against these people. They're going to tear us apart and eat us piece by piece. If you don't understand that now, you will when next year's plan comes down the pike."

"Your meeting—let me guess. You were trying to rally your loyal knights to battle. Did you succeed?"

She looked at the flickering flames instead of his eyes. "There's a lot of resentment there, Rudy. I'm afraid much of it's directed against you."

"I'm sorry to hear that. That'll make it tougher to do what has to be done."

All right, he wasn't going to move on the loyalty point. Not without some overwhelming reason. She had a sickening feeling that she didn't have many more cards to play. In fact, really only one. She rubbed at the back of her neck. "Are you all right?" he said, sounding suddenly concerned.

"A headache. It hasn't been a good day."

"Did you take anything?"

"Yes, but it doesn't seem to be working."

"I have a trick I do for headaches. It might help."

"It can't hurt any worse." She turned her back to him in the chair and a moment later felt his hands on her shoulders, on her neck. A knuckle dug into her spine, applied pressure that slowly increased, then held for five seconds, ten seconds, fifteen. When he finally released her, blood fizzed in her ears and her skull felt light as Styrofoam. To her surprise the pain really did seem to retreat. "Thanks," she said. Then added in a low voice, "I've been thinking about your—proposal."

"What proposal was—oh. *That* proposal. You have?"

"I have. And it looks to me as if you'll need me even more now than you did then."

"That could be." He was leaning back, and now it was his turn to study the fire. The blue gas flames that flickered endlessly, never charring or changing the ashless and perfect logs.

She said quietly, "What I'm saying, Rudy, is, I think you were right. Together you and I could be stronger than any other bloc. This week's events have had one positive effect: to convince me of that beyond any possibility of doubt."

She waited but he didn't answer, just kept staring at the flames. Finally he raised the glass and took a sip. Murmured, so low she had to lean closer to hear: "In New York I was ready. Right now—I'm not so sure it would be a good idea. It might look contrived, if you see what I mean."

She waited. He did too and the silence stretched out. Finally he added, "It's kind of a thrill, being in charge. I've been sawing second fiddle for so long. First to Dan, then to your ex, then to you. I'm a little reluctant to give up being the boss, I guess."

"But how long will it last? How long before they decide they want their own man in the driver's seat?"

"That's always a risk," he said. Then another silence, the gas jets hissing, the quiet recorded violins in the background like the rhythmic passage of time itself. Then he said, "Okay."

"Okay, you agree—"

"No; okay, I've decided. I appreciate your offer, Ainslee, but I think I'll decline. I'll support your continued presence on the board but I don't think marriage is a good idea. Not for two people like us."

She sat motionless, recognizing her own words to him on a windswept street in Manhattan. "There's no need to be vicious, Rudy."

"I don't like being manipulated, Ainslee. I know, we all do it sometimes. But that's all I've ever been to you. A tool, a threat, a puppet—never just another person. Well, that's all over." He smiled. "The Blue Fairy came. I'm a real boy at last. Now I can dance without the strings."

She stood, shaking with anger. "I think I'll be going now."

"I'll walk you down," he said. And he did, and when she looked back, shivering in the bitter wind as her key clattered searching for the lock in her car door, he was still standing in the pool of light in the lobby, looking out at her from the warm.

Twenty-six

───────────

Becky opened her eyes on a mass of tans and yellows interlocked so close above her they were just a blur in the dimness. She felt warm and drowsy and for a moment she thought she was at home in her room, and somehow she'd gotten her head under the blankets. Only when she stirred and things crackled all around her did she remember how far from home she was.

She sat up suddenly and her head crunched softly into the mass of dead leaves and branches. It yielded reluctantly, weighed down by snow. Combing stuff out of her hair with her fingers, she recalled where she was and how she'd gotten here.

The night before she and the old man had hiked till long after nightfall, climbing the hill on their makeshift snowshoes as fast as they could go. She was already tired and it was hard to keep up. But he kept saying they had to go as far as they could before it was too dark to travel. That was why her legs were so sore. She turned over in the warm tunnel, suddenly realizing she was alone. All through the night he'd been there, and though sometimes his snore woke her she was so tired it hadn't mattered. She'd just rolled over and gone to sleep again.

Now, suddenly apprehensive, she felt around for her boots. Crawling to the end of the narrow space, pushing out a plug of leaves and snow, she let in the cold silver light of early morning.

She stood shivering in the center of an endless army of trees. Huge and gray, they marched away to vanish into a haze like the inside of a cloud. Beside her the snow pit was invisible, just like a drift except for the dark wipe of leaves and green pine boughs she'd pushed through to get out. Like a butterfly from a chrysalis . . . science class . . . Mr. Cash's reddened face. She shuddered. It seemed so far away, so long ago. Would she ever see the noisy, familiar corridors of the Raymondsville middle school again, the jeering face of Margory Gourley?

The night before she'd thought they were going to freeze. Asked the old man when they could stop and build a fire. He'd just given her a look like she'd said something really stupid. But she was freezing, she couldn't feel her face or hands or feet. So finally he'd stopped beside one of the big evergreens. Told her to open her jacket and thrust handfuls of dry needles in between that and her shirt. It prickled but it felt warmer, and they'd gone on. Till at last it was too dark to see, and she just stumbled after the sounds he made with her hands out, like when she and Jammy played what her little brother called "come-find-me."

Ages later he stopped again and said, "Gimme your light, there."

She sank to the snow as he scuffled around. Dumbo glowed on a couple of times, but never for long. She heard him grunt, then the crash of something falling.

"Gimme a hand here."

She got up stiffly and went to see what he wanted. He shined the light down into a pit he'd kicked out beside a big fallen tree. It was full of leaves and pine needles he'd thrown down into it.

"What's that for?" she said, staring down.

"That's where we're goin' to sleep tonight. Now, I'm goin' to lay these branches across over it. Then that piece of tarp you brought. And on that we're gonna pile on snow, lots of it. The snow, that's what's going to keep us warm tonight."

She'd been so frozen and exhausted she hadn't even argued, just done what he said. And then when it was done crawled in. At first it had been bitter cold, and then not so bad; then, suddenly, without warning, she'd fallen asleep.

Now she stood in the silent light and looked around at the empty woods. For a second she was so scared she could hardly swallow. Then she saw his tracks. They led away between the trees. She saw her snowshoes hanging from a branch. She got them strapped on and started after him, bending to peer at his tracks in the shadowless light. Then remembered the tarp, went back and got it and started out again.

"Oh," she said a few minutes later, looking down at the blood, then at the limp, floppy thing he was working at with his knife. "What was that?"

"Rabbit." Halvorsen finished dressing it and started quartering it, slipping the blade through muscle and joints. He stripped out the two white cords from alongside the spine, and the long ones from the rear legs, and laid them aside on the snow.

"Tendons," she said, remembering the frog.

"What's that?"

"Those are its tendons. They transfer the energy of the muscles."

"That's right. Or sinew, when you're using it for something else." The old man's bushy eyebrows lifted, he studied her for a second, then returned to his work.

"How'd you catch it?"

"Snare."

"What's a snare?"

He glanced to where a wire loop dangled from a sapling.

"I don't understand."

"It's a kind of trap. You look where the rabbit tracks go. Figure where their hole is. Then set her right outside. Like this." He showed her how the whittled peg held the loop down till something disturbed it. "They pop out and catch a foot in it. Then the bent tree, see, it whips them right up into the air. You come along later and there they are."

"Did you think of that?"

The old man seemed to think that was funny. He shook his head, smiling. "No, not me. Sleep all right? You was kind of restless toward morning."

"My mom says I always kick in my sleep. It was warm, once we got in."

"You know to build a pit, you'll never freeze in these woods. How's your legs? Sore? That'll work out after breakfast."

"Breakfast?" she repeated, looking distastefully at the mess, at his bloody hands.

Halvorsen calmly wiped them on the snow. "That's right."

"I don't eat meat."

"You'll eat 'er this morning," he said shortly.

"No, I won't."

"You're not hungry?"

She felt her belly cramp just at the thought of food. "Well . . . yeah."

"Then you'll eat it."

"I don't like to kill animals," she said automatically, her mind pushing far away the memory of the man-doll splayed out in the red snow.

"Neither do I," he said. "That's good, you don't like to kill things. Killing ain't never good. But if it comes to where you won't kill to keep yourself alive, it's time for you to lie down and die. 'Cause you're too good for this world. You're way too young for that. So give me that stick there by your hand."

She didn't say anything, just handed it to him. Thinking about what he'd said.

———

Halvorsen studied her across the bloodied snow. She looked so damn thin. Nothing but pipestems for legs. But she'd kept up last night till he was ready to drop. Whining about being cold, but hell, she'd kept going.

Okay, he thought, we got to do some real traveling today. But we better get some hot food in us or we're not going to go much farther.

The only trouble was, he still hadn't figured out what they were going to do if the dogs caught up to them.

He sharpened the end of the stick with his old Case, then drilled out a little pit with the point in the piece of flat bark he'd pried off the dry underside of a fallen tree. He looked around, then got up and plodded over to a birch and reached up and sawed off a flexible branch about the size of his little finger. He notched it, took off a bootlace, and strung a fire bow. Then squatted again. "This might take a while," he muttered to the girl. "Ain't done it for a long time."

But to his surprise he found it had stayed with him. Leaning on the top block with his left hand, he sawed the bow rapidly back and forth. The spindle whirred. A couple of minutes went by and he was starting to get winded, starting to sweat, when a wisp of smoke crept up from the milkweed-down he'd used for tinder. He bent quickly, blowing into cupped hands, and a red glow brightened and suddenly a tiny flame twined itself through the dry twigs propped around it.

When he was sure it was going to hold he built the fire up, propping more twigs teepee-style around the brightening flame. Finally he leaned back. It grew up through the bigger branches and started crackling and hissing, the fire song he never tired of listening to.

He looked up to her fascinated eyes. "See how I done that?"

"That was neat! But that's not a very big fire. Aren't you going to put more wood on?"

"Longer you spend in the woods, smaller the fire you need. You can start a fire like that just about anytime, long as you make sure you get dry twigs. That ain't hard in winter, but it can be rough when it's been raining awhile." He worked as he talked, spitting the quartered rabbit and propping it over the fire. He dug down under the snow and fumbled around and found a flat rock. Laid it canted toward the flame and dealt out a double handful of acorns he'd picked up from under a stand of white oak. Most acorns you couldn't eat without soaking, they'd pucker you good, but white oak was different.

Becky went self-consciously away, into the woods. She didn't like to be out of sight of the old man, but she didn't feel like peeing right in front of him, either. When she came back he said, "Okay, should be done by now. Here's your piece."

She looked down at the roasted rabbit. Almost bit into it. It *did* smell good. But she just couldn't help seeing the bunny, the sad, floppy way it had lain in his lap. She remembered the blood, so much of it in one little body. She lowered the smoking meat slowly. "I can't eat this."

"You better."

"I *won't*," she said, suddenly sick of him telling her stuff, of everybody telling her what she should do and think and feel. They all said they did it to help her, but she didn't need it anymore, she was sick of it, she was old enough to make up her own mind.

"You're a stubborn one, ain't you?"

"If I am it's my own business. Here, you eat mine. I'll trade it for your half of the acorns."

"Suit yourself," said Halvorsen. And for a while there was an angry silence. The old man gnawed his portion and then hers, eating it all, fat and gristle, right down to the bone. Becky thought the acorns were like roasted almonds, but bitterer. She ate till there weren't any more. Then said, "Those were good. But they sure make you thirsty, don't they?"

"Don't eat that snow," said Halvorsen sharply.

"But I'm thirsty."

He picked up the flat rock with two sticks and dropped it into clean snow. It hissed, melting its way down, and to her surprise when she looked down the hole was filled with liquid water. He handed her a hollow dried stalk. "Drink it through this elderberry stem. Drink all you can, then I'll have some."

While she was sipping the cool, flat-tasting liquid he got up and went away and came back with two more long, thick, straight sticks. He squatted and whittled, then laid them carefully over the fire. He got up stiffly and dusted snow off his knees. "Set to travel?" he asked her.

"I guess."

"They're gonna be after us today. We got to be ready for 'em."

"How?"

Halvorsen didn't answer. Instead he pulled the sticks out of the fire and kicked snow over it till it died in a spitting hiss like an angry snake. When he handed one to her she saw the point was sharp now, blackened, hardened by the heat. It was a spear.

Gliding side by side on their makeshift snowshoes, they moved off into the woods.

They left camp along a long ridge furrowed with occasional deep folds of the land. Halvorsen moved along at a slow trot. He stopped once to dig the toe of his snowshoe under the snow. A delicate lace of dried ferns lay preserved beneath it. Wet up here, despite being at the top of a ridge that had to be 2,500 feet up. He saw birch, beech, hickory, a lot of maple. Only an occasional hemlock now. The snow lay deep and undisturbed between the black trunks.

A half-mile on he paused again. "Look at that," he said.

Becky stared at the heavy tracks, punched down through the snow cover into leaf mold. "What's that? Deer?"

"Bigger than deer."

"What's bigger than deer? Moose?"

"Close, it's elk. See how big and round the prints are. And look there—"

"Yuk. Elk poop."

Halvorsen almost smiled, but managed not to; it hurt his cracked lips too much. "Uh-huh. Follow these tracks back to the downwind side, I bet you find you a wallow. Where they bed down for the night. Look at all these tracks. I bet there's twenty of them."

"What do elk eat?"

"That's probably where they are right now. That there's fresh tracks. Headed down into the valley. Probably a good stand of aspen down there. They eat the bark in the winter. And they like to eat old hemlock logs, the soft bark, I guess, and the rotten parts."

"Oh my God. They eat *rotten wood?*"

"You'd be surprised what some animals will eat," said Halvorsen. "And what you can eat too, if you know about it and ain't too squeamish. There's a lot more in the summer and fall, berries and such, but see those beech? There's nuts under 'em, under the snow, turkey and deer love them. You know what cattails look like? We find a patch of those, you'll fill your belly. Cattail roots. And Indian cucumber, that's got a nice root to it too. There ought to be some of that around here if we can spot it."

She said, "I wouldn't want to—unless we were, you know, starving—but could you kill an elk with these spears?"

He frowned. "You can make a call that'll bring them in, you do it right. But it'd be tough to get one of these spears into 'em."

"I didn't mean I wanted to."

"I know."

She lifted her head suddenly, just like a deer. Halvorsen stopped too, watching her. He couldn't hear anything. But he felt his heart sink as the pink disappeared from her cheeks.

"It's the dogs," she said at last.

"Which way?"

She pointed. Downhill, to their right.

He nodded grimly, figuring what Eisen had done: gone down Archer Hollow to the old mill, then sicced the dogs up the hill after them. He heard them now too. The distant baying echoed eerily through the vast winter silence.

He stood unmoving, not knowing what to do. There was no way he and the girl could outrun them. The crude spears wouldn't keep a determined shepherd off for more than a few seconds. He and the girl could climb, but Olen and Eisen would just shoot them like treed bears. Same with going to ground in some hole or covert.

No, he had to fox them somehow.

His slowly traveling gaze came to rest on a snaky vine twisting up into the treetops. Set a trap? He could probably get one dog, maybe a couple. But the belling, ever closer below them, told him there were more than that. There'd been eight of the crazed animals in Olen's pen. Too many to trap and fight no matter what he did.

Still something nagged him. Some prickly thing his mind couldn't shake. Some shred of memory, annoying as gristle caught between your teeth. Something about . . . the aspens? He squinted around, surveying from long habit the lay of the land, the drift of the wind. From the north, maybe a trifle northeast. The dogs were coming downwind and uphill.

Aspens liked dry ground, not like this up here but ground that had been cleared or burned. Then they came back with their quick-growing, graceful thin trunks. But why in hell was he thinking about them?

Then, suddenly, he understood.

Becky stood shivering, feeling her skin trying to crawl up the back of her neck. . . . She lifted the spear, inspecting the blackened point. It didn't look like anything she could kill a big dog with.

So when he finally said, "Come on, we got to run," she was almost glad. But then he started running, not away from the steadily growing clamor of barking but almost *toward* it. Downhill, off to the left. She hung back, then her heart lurched and she stumbled after him. Her legs felt numb and clumsy and the snowshoes were coming apart under her feet. Why hadn't she noticed before? He could have fixed them. Now she had to run, through the trees, down a bank. Suddenly one snowshoe disintegrated under her and her foot went through and she pitched forward into the snow. She struggled up and fell again, this time rolling till she hit a tree so hard it knocked the breath out of her.

The barking, furious now, steadily closer.

Something loud bawled out ahead. She stiffened, then saw him standing alone in the middle of a clearing. A cone of bark held to his mouth. As she watched Halvorsen called again, a high, frantic-sounding bawl.

An answering call, deeper, startled sounding, trumpeted back from down the valley.

He motioned her up to him, eyes squinted tense. "Hurry up," he called. "Bend over, 'case they see us. Come on, *run!*"

And she ran again after him for what seemed like forever, hunched over, downhill and along what looked like an old road and then down a bank into a frozen stream and then through the woods again till her back screamed and her throat ached and her breath couldn't keep up. The last branches came apart under her boots but she kept going, floundering through the deep new snow, sobbing with effort. Her spear rattled against branches, raining snow on her head. Her feet were so heavy she could hardly lift them out of the snow.

At last the old man dropped to his belly behind a fallen tree, motioning her down with one hand. She dropped beside him, hearing him wheeze and cough, his face pressed into the snow to muffle it. When he could talk he pointed off to their right. Didn't say anything, just pointed. She lifted her head above the log and saw something out there. Like a deer, but far bigger, shaggy-brown, with huge spreading horns. Then her eye picked out more shapes behind it.

Her sight had barely registered them before a frenzied burst of barking exploded. Yelps and growls rang through the woods. The big animals wheeled suddenly, in unison, like a four-legged drill team. Raising her head a little more, she saw they were facing the approaching dogs.

Then the biggest one trotted forward, bounding easily through the snow, and disappeared. She waited, teeth chattering, and then flinched and caught her breath at the sudden roaring and bellowing, the screams and clatter of battle.

Halvorsen stood still, listening to the struggle. Sharp cracks and thuds echoed up through the woods, furious snorting, howling and snarling, and the heavy steam-hammer thud of huge hooves.

A bull elk weighed out at seven or eight hundred pounds, with huge, towering racks. The females weren't much smaller; no antlers but they fought viciously with their hooves. A herd of twenty—no, he didn't think those dogs would be bothering the girl or him anytime soon. By the time they got themselves sorted out from the angry elk they'd be in no mood to chase anything another step.

The baying grew fainter, and the bellowing followed it. Becky whispered, "They're getting farther away."

"Heading down into the valley. Elk, they'll go for a ways. They won't double back like your whitetails. We won't see them dogs for a long time."

"Won't they find our tracks?"

"Dog don't pay no attention to tracks," Halvorsen said. "I ain't never seen Jess—that's my hound—even look at a track. Dogs go by scent, and this snow—once it gets a chance to cool, I don't think these shepherds he's running got the nose to find us again. See, the dogs don't know they're supposed to be after us anyway. Olen just sent them up the hill, and if the first thing they hit's elk, why, that's what they're going to chase."

He felt relieved but still tense. The immediate danger was past, but he couldn't believe Eisen wasn't going to try for them himself. He felt so helpless without a weapon.

A weapon. A gun, or maybe—maybe something else.

He started west again, the girl swinging into file behind him. The fear had reinvigorated him and he felt stronger, though he knew it wouldn't last. So he kept his eyes aloft, looking for a maple low enough he could get at the branches.

Behind him Becky was hugging herself, trying to warm up again after lying in the snow. She still couldn't believe the dogs weren't coming. She'd been ready to fight them with her spear. But she was glad she didn't have to. She wished she could have seen the elk and the dogs fighting, that would have been so cool. She hoped the elk killed them all.

"Hold up," Halvorsen said. She stopped, then went forward obediently when he motioned her up.

"What?"

"See that maple? If I boost you up in it, can you hack off some branches for me? I'll tell you which ones. No, leave the blade closed, don't open it till you get up there."

She took the knife gingerly and stepped into his cupped hands. He lifted her with a grunt and she grabbed the lowest branch, got her leg over and perched on it. Then hauled herself up.

"Now what?" she called down.

"Get a couple of the long switches. Pick ones with nice curves in 'em, without big knots or twigs. I want a couple about as thick as both your thumbs put together. And two more bigger than that."

She looked around from time to time as she sawed. From up here you could see a long way along the hill and down into the valley. But she couldn't see anything moving, just bare snow and treetops. The cold wind made her cheeks numb, like a shot at the dentist's. She had to stop and put her mittens over them and breathe into the damp wool till her face stung and hurt again. It took a long time to cut through the branches. The knife kept slipping in her hand. She almost cut herself. But the old man didn't yell at her or say anything. He just stood there waiting, looking off down the hill. The tree swayed under her each time she leaned out to drop a branch to him.

"That enough?"

"Yeah, that's good. Throw me the knife and come on down."

She tossed him the closed knife, then hung by her hands and dropped lightly into the snow. He was already at work. He had one thick limb trimmed to a stick four feet long and a thinner one a little shorter. They looked like curved sticks, that was all. So what, she thought. Then, as she watched, he shaved the back of them, in the middle, to a flat surface.

"What are you making?"

"You tell me. See this flat part here? And this one here? Put them together. Wrap your wire here—or twine, or hide strips, whatever you happen to have."

She looked puzzledly at two C-shaped staves wired together, a smaller and a larger, like two thin curves of new moon back to back. "I don't know. Another kind of trap?"

Halvorsen didn't answer. He cut notches at the ends of each of the sticks. Then, starting with the smaller, he strung wire from notch to notch. Halfway done she recognized it—sort of. "It's a bow, isn't it? But not like any kind I ever saw."

"Don't mean it won't work." He finished wrapping the last bit of wire, not permanently, but in a loop. He lifted the bow and drew and she saw how both sticks bent as he pulled. He unsnapped the loop and laid it aside. "Now we'll make one for you. Stand up straight while I measure, we want a custom job here."

"How did you learn this?" she asked him. "Not in school, that's for sure. You said somebody taught you when you were a kid."

"That's right. Old fella I used to trap with. He learned it from a fella name of Ben Yeager; and Yeager, he learnt it from the Indians when he was a youngster. The Senecas adopted him."

"They adopted him? What happened to his mom and dad?"

Halvorsen stalled, already into the story in his mind; he'd never asked himself that. He said grumpily, "I don't know. You want to hear this or not?"

"Yeah. I'm sorry."

"Anyway, there's a lot of stories about Ben. Like, one winter he was hunting down along Falkiner Creek. That's where we're headed, west of here. And he shot a deer with his last pinch of powder. Now, in them days all they took was the pelts, they left the meat except what they wanted right then. Well, he had the hide dressed out and was ready to head home when it commenced to snow.

"It snowed so heavy he couldn't see. So he tore down some boughs and bedded himself down under a hemlock, there's always a dry place there, covered up with the hide like a bed quilt, and went to sleep.

"Well, he woke up about midnight, and first thing he noticed was something had smelled up the place awful. He felt around and found sticks and leaves all over him, and that rawhide he was under stunk of cat. Some mama panther had claimed him and was gone to get her cubs for dinner."

"Oh. Wow! So what did he do then?"

"He just pulled that hide back over himself and got ready for her. Took some of those dry needles under the tree and struck him his steel and got a little fire going. And he hid that and waited.

"Pretty soon, sure enough, he hears her comin' over the snow, pad-pad-paddin' toward him. He waits till he feels her hot breath in his face,

she's sniffin' the hide. Then suddenly he throws it aside and pushes the
fire into her eyes. She gave a scream, her whiskers caught like broom-
straws, an' she was gone, cubs squallin' after her. He nursed that fire till
dawn, but she never came back."

Becky said, a little nervously, "Are there panthers out here now?"

"Not no more. They're all gone, just like the wolves is . . . or was." Halvorsen held up her bow and made her try it to make sure it was the right
size and draw. "So that's where I learned it. An' I'll tell you more when
we get out of this. That is, if you want."

"Sure," she said. She was glad he knew all this stuff, about what to eat
and how to trap things and what the animals were doing. Why didn't they
teach this in school, instead of cutting open dead frogs in smelly labora-
tories and writing dumb papers about old books?

Halvorsen heaved himself up and glanced at the sky, then forced his
stiffened legs into motion again. There wasn't any sun, but he had a pretty
good feel for the way the terrain ran. Where this hill ended they had to
come down, cross a little steep valley, then go up another hill. On the
down side of that was Cook Creek, which they'd follow down past the fork
of the Blue to Fischer Creek. So he didn't really need a compass. And
now he started looking for pines.

Becky plodded along behind him, bow slung over her shoulder, so tired
she couldn't really think. It seemed like they'd been out in the woods
forever. Her feet were so blistered it was hard to walk. She tried not to
complain but it was impossible not to, at least inside her head. But she
never stopped moving. She knew if she did she'd die. And if she died, she
didn't think the old man would make it out either.

Because he looked weaker and sicker than she felt. He had to stop
every couple hundred yards, even on level ground, and she saw that when
he pointed to some interesting tracks or peered at the sky or stopped to
snip off some pine needles, he was actually just resting. He was spitting
blood. He couldn't have made the bows without her, and she'd saved him
from being shot. Yesterday she'd just been numb, but now she felt a shiver
of satisfaction at what she'd done. Followed by a stab of guilt: what would
Charlie say, what would her mom think? Then she felt resentful at feeling
guilty; Nguyen had been evil, a real crook; he was going to kill Mr. Halvorsen; he'd probably killed lots of other people. Why should she feel bad
about him?

It was too confusing. But it was all she had to think about other than
being afraid or exhausted, so she kept turning it over and over in her
mind, like a strange-looking rock, while they hiked along the ridge.

Finally Halvorsen stopped. He looked around at a wilderness of frozen-over bushes. She didn't notice until she ran into him, almost knocking him down. "Sorry," she muttered.

"Let's take a break."

Without a word she sank down into the snow. Halvorsen looked down at her closed eyes and felt bad. Girl couldn't take much more of this. And it was all up to him, she was a baby in the woods. She needed food, warmth. Not much spare meat on those thin bones. He unclasped the knife and waded into the mass of frozen, snowed-over brush.

"Here. Open up."

Becky lifted her eyelids to a blurry hand hovering above her face. She opened her mouth and something hard and round and cold as a frozen gumball dropped into it. She bit down and it was icy-sweet.

She blinked in the cold light of afternoon. "What's that?"

"Hobbleberries. Deer got most of 'em, but there's some left if you look." He dropped a purple hail of them into her cupped mittens.

"They're good. Did you get some?"

"Ain't hungry," he said shortly, and she knew he was just saying that. But when she sat up she saw instead of looking for more he was whittling again, this time on some long stalks. She figured it out right away: arrows. She watched him sharpen one end carefully, then wrap wire around it. Then he laid the shaft down and pulled some sprigs of pine needles out of his pocket. He lined them up on the shaft, then fished something out of his mouth. When he started wrapping it around the pine tuft like thick white twine, she saw it was the sinew from the rabbit.

"What are you going to use for an arrowhead?"

"I'm just goin' to point it for now. Might whittle one out of that rabbit bone later."

"Do you think they'll come back?"

"Who?" Halvorsen held the shaft up and squinted along it. He bowed it carefully, pressing with his thumbs, then sighted along it again.

"Those dogs."

"They might. Take a while to sort 'em out from the elks, but they could be back." He didn't tell her he figured it would be when they crossed the valley that afternoon. No sense getting her scared now. He balanced the arrow on one finger, then hoisted himself and unslung the bow from his back. Fitted the wire cord and set the arrow's notched butt to it. Glanced around, to see Becky putting the finishing touches on a miniature snowman. She stood back. "Try him," she said.

He figured it for ten yards. Lifted the bow, and for a vertiginous moment had a weird sense he was twelve again in these same woods. He started to blink it away, then decided to stay with it. Sure, okay, he was twelve, and old Amos was drunk again, down in the cabin. Maybe he could bring back a fat raccoon for dinner. Surprise him.

The bow made a dead-sounding twang and the arrow flew too high but not that far off in windage. She ran and brought it back. He tried it again and the bow snapped in his hands.

When he examined it he found the notch had broken at the bow tip. That was always the weakest point. He recut it and wrapped it with wire to strengthen it. Damn glad he'd taken that spool of wire along. There, that was better. A couple more tries and he figured out where to hold. At his last shot the arrow went *chuff* through the snowman's chest.

"Let me try," she said, and he handed her the arrow and showed her how to string her bow. While she practiced he made three more arrows. Then built a little fire, keeping it small.

Halvorsen made her drink all the pine-needle tea, though she said she hated it. A lot of vitamins in pine tea. They needed the water too. He wished they had something more substantial to eat than hobbleberries. That made an awful thin stew. But they'd been moving too fast to set any more snares. Maybe now he had the bow he could get a shot at something. There ought to be grouse around these berry hells. He'd seen turkey tracks up the hill, but he wasn't going to get any close-in shots at a wild turkey. They were smart as the devil and twice as wary.

When she said, "I'm done, that's all there is," he said, "Just a minute." Then tossed her the new set of snowshoes. "All right, we better get going. I want to get across this valley and up on the other side fast as we can, hear?"

He led them down as the hill's curve gentled under a ghostly, heavy snowfall that blotted out the afternoon light, dropping dense and heavy as pellets of cattle feed. Halvorsen both liked and didn't like all this snow. It would help them scent-wise, but he couldn't see spit. A hunted animal needed to see. He tried to remember if there was a creek ahead. He was pretty sure there was but he couldn't come up with any picture of one. He hoped that meant it wasn't deep. That could really put them into a fix, a big stretch of rushing water they couldn't cross.

Behind them Becky tottered along like a sleepwalker. The hot tea made her head nod, and the wild berries churned uneasily in her near-empty stomach. She carried the spear, the bow, two of the arrows. They weren't heavy but she was so weak. Her mouth hurt, and her feet. Her toes felt like ice cubes. But the old man had made it clear complaining wouldn't help. So she didn't, just kept going, lips clamped tight.

Halvorsen pushed along the gently undulating valley floor, eager for the uphill cover of the far side. He felt exposed and vulnerable with only the falling snow to screen them. If it just kept up . . . He strained his ears but still couldn't hear the dogs. The elk must have taken them miles away. Or better yet, killed a couple. That would be a break.

They needed every break they could get, if they were going to get out of this alive.

Then, muffled but still distinct, he heard an uneven drone. At first he hoped it was a plane. Then he knew it wasn't. His first impulse was to turn away, try to cross the valley on a slant away from the ominous whine. He turned left and started trotting, the girl dogging along behind, for a quarter mile. Then another thought hit him.

Halvorsen stopped without warning, so abruptly she bumped into him again. "He's tryin' to drive us," he muttered.

"What?"

"He knows we can hear them engines. He's tryin' to drive us, like deer. See, there's a rise up ahead. Bet you a silver dollar there's somebody on it with a gun."

"So which way do we go? Toward the motors?"

"That wouldn't be so good either."

She looked around. It had seemed to be going better, there for a little while. But now she was scared again.

Halvorsen eyed the field, looking for cover. There wasn't any. They were caught in the open. The snowmobiles were getting closer. Running slow between the trees. Keeping a sharp eye out for them, no doubt. He yearned for fir, spruce, something nice and thick, where the brows came down to the snow. But there weren't any, and sweat prickled under his coat. He forced himself to think. The snow was deep enough they could burrow under it, but that'd still leave sign. He'd do it if there wasn't anything else, but he didn't think it would fool anybody.

Then he saw the opening ahead, the gray light reaching through the treetops. The creek, if he wasn't mistaken.

He hiked out onto the bank and shaded his eyes, head hunched as if the open sky oppressed him.

The creek was shallow and broad but his heart sank. There was no bank, nowhere to hide. Just a fifty-foot-wide expanse of snow-covered ice, dotted here and there with rounded rocks. A big scraggly-looking willow leaned sadly downriver. Past it a goshawk was circling in the winter sky above where he figured the snowmobiles were coming. Scaring out the rabbits, he thought. He knew just how they felt. Searching for somewhere to hide, trembling in their burrows as the hawk's shadow neared.

But there weren't any burrows big enough for a man and a girl.

He turned to see her watching him. She said, "What are we going to do?"

"I'm still thinking."

"How about if we go out on the ice?"

"Out on the *ice*?" He looked out over the boulder-dotted flatness. "What are you talkin' about? We'd stand out like—like—"

"Not if we had that old tarp over us. It's the same color as the rocks."

He squinted at her, then at the creek again. Not a great idea, but he didn't have any better. Maybe they wouldn't expect them out in the open. They'd check cover, trees, blowdowns, but with luck maybe they'd just sweep through the fields and the creek. "Okay," he grunted. "Let's give her a try."

Becky ran out onto the snow after him, dragging the branch. Halvorsen eyed the boulders and picked a likely spot. Then knelt. As the motor roar built they unfolded gray plastic and tossed handfuls of snow into it, digging till they hit black flat ice. "Go on, get underneath," he growled, watching the hawk tilt a wing practically right above them.

She squirmed under it into a place of dim light and stark cold. The bare ice was rough as chilled concrete beneath her knees. The snow sat on her back and she shifted uncomfortably. "Lie still," he grunted. "Don't move a hair." Then she felt him burrow in beside her.

They lay in a frozen huddle, shivering. Halvorsen hoped the snow didn't shake right off the top. Already the falling flakes would be joining the whiteness over them. He'd smoothed it quickly flat with his glove to the same contour as the other boulders. Up close it wouldn't fool anybody, but from a moving machine, a quick glance . . . He made himself go limp, trying not to let his bladder relax too much.

The tall man with the pitted face stood up on the slowly moving machine. It growled as the track thrust it through the drifts. The rifle was slung loaded-heavy across his back, ready for a quick shot.

But he didn't see anything to shoot at.

He ran down toward the river, and the other black machine, fifty yards behind and echeloned off to his right, swung to follow. Out onto a field dotted with saplings and stippled with the tracks of animals. He kept his eyes peeled but caught no sign of an old man and a girl.

"Where the fuck did they go now?" Eisen muttered.

Pulling a small pair of binoculars from an outside pocket, he ran them over the long bulk of the nameless hill that ran along with him, moving as he moved, as if it would accompany him wherever he went for the rest of his life. The magnification jumped the treetops closer but couldn't penetrate them.

The dogs had limped back hours before, one missing and another torn up with what looked like sword cuts. Olen had moaned over the hurt one, fondling and hugging its bloody head till he'd said, "For Christ's sake, Jerry. Either stitch him up or shoot the son of a bitch and quit crying over it."

The fat man had wiped his nose on his coat sleeve. "What'd he use on them? Dakota's hurt bad."

"Hell if I know. But he's got to come down off that mountain some-time. There's nothing to eat up there but snow. I'm betting it's today. I want all our guys out. Give 'em clubs and axes and line 'em up across the valley. We'll run the Yamahas up along the creek and make 'em run the gauntlet."

But now he didn't think he had them figured at all. He hadn't seen a track or a trail. Maybe they were still up here. Or maybe they'd already crossed the valley somehow. He frowned through the falling snow at the great three-cornered mountain, shamrock-shaped, that barred the way north. Could they have moved that fast, an old goat and a shit-faced kid?

He was glaring across at it when something caught his eye. He blinked, peering into the falling white. All he saw was the creek. The flat white carpet of snow, the white-black humps of rocks. And beyond it the woods, gray and motionless and bleak. But hadn't he caught one swift, furtive movement past the creek, among the trees? He stared through narrowed lids for long seconds. Then the machine hit a dip and jolted his gaze off the spot, and he decided he hadn't seen anything after all.

Well, if he didn't get them on this sweep, that wasn't the end. More like just the beginning. Maybe the best thing to do was figure they'd gone north already. Set a trap. Use the dogs again. Cat and mouse, but he didn't mind a little fun before he put a bullet into the old bastard. It would be repayment for losing Nguyen.

He couldn't shake a creepy feeling, though, that the old man wasn't far away. Maybe closer than he thought, maybe Halvorsen was pissing in his pants listening to his engines right now. Thinking that, he twisted the throttle hard, as if he was sending him a message. Like, *I'm after you, Racks. Here I am. Come on, let's get it on.* And the roar rolled out over the creek and the field, filling the narrow valley till the echoes thundered back from the confining hills.

Twenty-seven

At the first hint of dawn on what he knew would be the last day, one way or the other, the old man fell to his knees. Staring up at the barely visible black lace that stark, contorted branches snipped from a sky the color of hemlock bark.

He couldn't move another step.

The girl sank too, then slowly toppled into the powdery snow. Her closed lids looked bruised. A loop of wild grapevine led from her waist to his.

Behind them, shallow dragging tracks plowed an unsteady wavering down from the still-dark forest, from the heights of the great tripled mountain.

Halvorsen laid his cheek against the smooth white, feeling its cold as if by telephone. As if someone else lay here empty and useless as a fired cartridge. He shouldn't stop. They might never get up. Flakes patted his face, coming down still steady and thick, the way they'd fallen all night. The night they'd spent blundering through the darkness, their sharpened stakes pointed out ahead of them like the antennae of a blind slug.

Behind him Becky lay hardly thinking at all. She'd talked and talked, then gone silent. Twice during the night she'd cried, begging him to stop. It was so cold the tears had frozen to her cheeks. They kept falling and running into things. And then he'd tied them together, so she couldn't stop if she wanted to.

She didn't want to go any farther. She just wanted to lie here. If that meant she died, well fine, that was okay. As long as she didn't have to walk another step.

Ten feet away, Halvorsen had slipped seamlessly into sleep.

In the dream he was a kid again. Not as old as when he'd gone off with McKittrack, just a child. Too little to be without his ma. He wanted his ma. He kept looking for her and calling but she wasn't anywhere in the woods.

Then he came out on the top of a hill and looked down. The sun was shining but it was faraway and cool. The steep slopes of the hollow were studded green with pine. On the left the trees petered out uphill, and down the center of the run twisted a river. It didn't seem to have a beginning or any end, just came out of the fog and disappeared into it again. He couldn't see the far end, only white churning mist.

Then he saw the pool. Still yet slowly roiling beneath, with pallid fog boiling silent and ghostly off green depths. When he looked down into it he saw the faces.

He recognized them without surprise or fear. There was his mother, her hair up in braids like she wore it for church. Her dress rippled in the slow current. His father in starched shirt and black coat. His older brother, James, who'd died in the war. There was Jenny, hand linked with, oh, a girl beside her in a flowered wrapper and her drifting hair was red as red and he thought, Strange, Jenny never knew about Mary, but here they were sleeping together peaceful as twins under the watery mist . . . Now through the wavering he made out somebody else deep under the green, separate from the rest. He shaded his eyes. It was an old man with an ugly lined face and gray whiskers like algae grown beneath the cold clear water. His eyes sealed. Lying alone, but slowly drifting toward the others in the cold clear current of the river.

The child recognized without surprise or apprehension that the old man was himself years and years from now. It didn't bother or scare him. Who could cry for anyone that old?

Lifting his gaze, he looked down the valley. He knew what waited behind the obliterating fog, the featureless mask of mist. It had always been there but it had always seemed faraway, though every time he had ever looked up it was closer. Now it was almost on him, and he had no one to protect him. Not his mom or his dad or his brother, or anybody, least of all the old man under the water.

He shivered, waiting helplessly for it to appear.

He woke some unascertainable time later to find the sky burning lethal and warmthless as radium above the treetops. He jerked himself to a stiff sitting-up. Mumbled, "Guess I drifted off a minute."

The girl didn't answer. He crawled over to her. Shook her. She didn't move. He pulled his hand away, stared at the rise and fall of her chest. Then he grabbed her nose and pinched it closed.

She reared up, shaking off his hand and the snow that had settled on her. "You didn't—you didn't have to do that."

"Come on. We got to keep moving."

"We went all night." Her voice was a pleading whine.

"And we only got a little more to go. We're on the downhill now. We'll hit the creek pretty soon today. Then we just follow her till we get to the Gasport road, there's houses there."

"How far's that?"

"Just a couple more miles," he lied. It was more like six, but two sounded better. You could always go two more miles.

She got up slowly and tottered to a tree. Leaned against it, eyelids sagging again. He got up too and felt around under the snow for his spear. There it was. And the bow.

Leaning on their staffs like pilgrims, they limped slowly downhill.

An apocalyptic sky glowed with a pale opalescent turbulence beyond the myriad descending flakes into which they blinked. When the snow whirled in solid-laden gusts they lost sight of the upper limbs of the trees. Between the flakes the air tasted like cold glass. They staggered in white wrappings, buffeted by the wind. Halvorsen kept putting one boot in front of the other. His legs had long since ceased to hurt. They were just wooden accessories moved by his thighs. After a while he closed his eyes again.

He'd learned to do without sight during the long night. At first he'd known the way. Just a long slogging climb up out of the valley as the light failed. Later, after dark, he'd felt the saddle of the triple hill as a cupped hand that tilted up if he strayed too far either way. But on the long plateau at the crest, he'd slowly become aware he couldn't tell which way to go.

Afraid to stop moving through the darkness, like an airplane that if it pauses must plummet to destruction, he knew he had to make the right choice. Too far to the left and he'd come out not into Cook Hollow but way the hell west, on the Driftwood Branch. That led south, not north, and a killing long way it was to anywhere. Longer than they could last to walk, that was for sure. Too far right and they'd come down off the mountain into Coal Run. He knew that part of the country, but it was so rough he'd almost died there once, tracking a man when he was younger. So there wasn't any margin on this job. He had to head just right, or they wouldn't make it. Only how to tell, sightless, compassless, mapless, starless?

Finally the numbing wind whispered the answer. And he'd walked through the night like that, feeling its steady freezing breath on face and forehead like a compass needle pointing the way to home.

The funny thing was that now and then during that endless march he could have sworn there was something else out there with them. Not following them, exactly. Not leading, either. But never far away. He couldn't guess what it might be. Never heard anything but the wind, and now and then the faraway shriek of an old bough rubbing. It was just a feeling. The kind a hunter got. Or maybe he was just getting shaky, going around the bend at last.

And in all that bitter night he doubted they'd actually covered more than five miles.

He rubbed snow from his eyebrows and shifted the bow uneasily. The trouble was, he didn't recognize a single landmark now it was light. He was in a valley, but which one? It slanted north, he could tell north, now he could see the tree trunks, so it couldn't be the Driftwood. Didn't look like Coal Run. But it didn't look like Cook, either. Cook ran into the Blue, where he and Amos had wintered. He should recognize something at least of their old trapping grounds. If it was Cook Creek below he should have crossed the old railroad grade by now, the one that seventy years before had carried puffing engines from the Selwyn & Evans mine. But he hadn't seen a thing. Maybe he'd crossed it already, in the dark. There were no rails anymore, just the grade, and trees pushing up between the rotting ties. He could have crossed it and never noticed. But uncertainty gnawed at him. Were they lost? Had he descended to a hollow or run he didn't know? Or was his memory failing him at last?

If it did, they'd die out here, whatever Eisen and his pals did.

Something slammed into his head and he fought it furiously with his hands before his sluggish brain recognized it as a tree. Resignation and anger struggled, and he chose rage. Bent to its mounting him like a rider an exhausted horse. This far below zero, resignation was a receipt for death. Wrath was the only goad that could spur him now. All he had left to kindle heat inside a body free of any other passion. He cursed softly between frozen lips, blinking snow-choked lashes. Then lifted his head, suddenly alert, waiting for the sound to come again.

"Mr. Halvorsen," Becky said again, behind him.

He turned, and he looked not only exhausted and old but sick and full of hate, and in that moment she feared him. "What," he snapped.

"I can't." She couldn't even finish the sentence. Her mouth wouldn't move to do it.

"Don't tell me that again."

"Told you."

"Know it's hard. But ain't much farther." He took her chin, hand clumsy as a lobster claw, and searched her face. Two white spots glowed on her cheeks. Her nose was white and lifeless as a porcelain doll's. He stripped off his gloves and put his hands to her. Giving her the poor remnants of his warmth.

"Your hands are ice cold," she murmured.

"You got frostbite."

"I can't feel my f-feet."

"What?"

"I haven't been able to feel them for a long time. Can't we—you built a fire before—"

"Can't stop. We got to keep moving."

"But why? I don't care anymore if we—"

"Justice," said Halvorsen. The word floated between them, hollow and weightless, cold and light as a snowflake. She stared uncomprehending into age-folded eyes blue as shadow on snow.

"These people killed a young fella. I saw it happen. Beat him to death. You heard 'em, they been killing them poor damn Vietnamese right along. Tried to murder us, too. Racks Halvorsen don't lie down and die before he gets them for that."

He turned away, and without words left to plead again she stood silent, watching him move slowly away, till he was just a silhouette behind the snow. She started to sit down again. Let him go. She'd stay here and rest. Then she remembered: he needed her. Too stubborn to admit it, but without her he'd never make it. She had to stay with him.

Still tied together, falling now and then to lie like exhausted children before they struggled up again, they made their way slowly down into the last valley.

Below them Eisen checked his carbine, easing the bolt silently back just enough to reveal the chambered case, brass-shining, ready to fire.

He sat shivering under a crude tent made of a tarp thrown over the snowmobile. He'd driven up the valley from Coal Run at 3 A.M., engine muffled, turning the lights on only when he had to, then snapping them off again. Not far away, on the other side of the creek, he'd stationed two of the Vietnamese, Pham and Xuan. He didn't like to trust them with guns, but he didn't have a choice, did he? Damn Halvorsen, losing Nguyen was already crippling the operation.

Now all he had to do was wait.

The way he figured it the old man had to come this way. Every other trail would take too long. Halvorsen knew that too. So he'd also know, foresee, that *he* would be waiting somewhere along this last descent before the great open valley, steadily broadening, that led outward and downward to the lands and homes of men.

Sitting there, forcing himself to patience, he thought again it was a shame, in a way, that he had to kill them. Because he admired Halvorsen. He himself, thirty, forty years younger, he wasn't sure he could have made it as far as the old man had. Not in this blizzard, without a tent or sleeping bag, on foot. The old bastard was tough as they came.

But he didn't have any choice. Eisen lifted the flap and snow detached itself and fell soundlessly to the soft white that blanketed the earth. That covered everything, living and dead. He smiled into the chill wind. He didn't care how good he was, not even Halvorsen could see this ambush till it was too late.

On the far side of the creek Xuan sat clutching the gun the Boss had given him, back jammed against a tree, shivering as if the malaria had come back. He coughed querulously. He hated the American cold. It hurt his lungs. He wasn't watching the trail. He wasn't thinking about the old man and the girl he was supposed to be waiting for. He was thinking about Tranh. He'd liked her. Nguyen had too. But that was the third time she'd tried to run away. So Mr. Olen had given the dogs the special whistle. Xuan had been there. He helped Mr. Olen with the dogs sometimes.

That didn't mean he liked them. He hadn't known, until they were all over the young woman, tearing at her—he blinked, shook his head to clear it of the horrible sounds. If he thought he could make it he'd run away himself.

He sat freezing on the snow, dreaming of the heat.

Where he'd grown up. In the South, in a hamlet on a river. Paddies around it to the horizon, flat as the river and in the growing season even more startling green, and in the dry season burned black as if all the earth were charred ash. Once banyan and bamboo had grown along the water, but when he was small the planes had sprayed them and they'd never grown again. There was an old burial ground where the older boys said demons lurked at night, evil beings with white beards who could kill with their flaming eyes. Far away curved the red roof of what had once been a famous monastery. Then it was a club for the French, then for the Americans, and finally headquarters for the plantation the government had established, after the Northerners won the war.

That was where he'd worked, slaved, at the banana plantation. Till one night he and four others had slipped down the river and out to sea. After that days of drifting, and then the rescue, but not really a rescue but a new slave-taking. From there they passed from hand to hand and at last were smuggled ashore in America and sold to Nguyen, who had sold them again, to the tall American with the angry red face.

He shivered in the falling snow and wished again he'd never left. Harsh as it had been, he missed the slow moist heat, the live smells of growing rice and the river and the sweet, rotting stench of crushed bananas where

they loaded the trucks. Now he was a slave to the dogs. That was a dis-
honor for a Vietnamese. But he had no right to honor. Now he had to
kill an old man and a helpless child. Well, he had to obey the Americans.
Or at least pretend to. But if there was any way he could manage not to
see these two who tried so desperately to escape . . .

He checked his shotgun again, then sat staring blindly out into the
everlasting white, the color of mourning and death, spread like a winding
sheet over a dead land.

Two hundred yards away Halvorsen stopped, looking down at the mess in
the snow. He slumped against a hickory, bare hands thrust into his coat.
The tattered hanging bark grated his cheek. He ground his face into it
till the pain arrived. Even that was tardy and somnolent. He was walking
in a delirium. He seemed to see things moving between the trees, stalking
them, but when he jerked his chin up and squinted to sharpen sight the
woods stood ringing empty, echoing with the endless hiss of a cupped
seashell as the snowflakes dissolved between his quivering lids.

Behind him the girl stood trembling, gaze fixed on distance. His glove
was cut open and laced across her face, so that all he could see was her
eyes.

She lowered them slowly to the deer's savaged head.

Halvorsen sagged to his knees and turned over the scraps of hide with
the tip of an arrow. Nothing left but fur and bone, a gnawed fragment of
antler. Beneath the fresh fall he could make out faint, shadowed indentations for many yards around it. The buck had fought hard, but it hadn't
been enough.

"What killed it?" she murmured.

"Can't tell. Thought we might find some meat, but it's been chewed
up pretty good." He straightened and stared searchingly off downhill.
"Better look sharp from here on."

"What?"

He reached out and gripped her shoulder. "Seems like I recall—if we're
where I think—should be a falls up ahead, not far. A falls, and a little
lake. If they're waiting for us, that's where they'll be. Where the valley's
still narrow, but they can get to it with those machines."

Behind the glove her voice was muffled, shapeless. "What can we do?"

"We better just see them first," he told her. She didn't respond, just
gazed past him dully. The snow had built white shoulders on her coat. He
shook her, the freezing air biting his bare fingers. Her head snapped back
and forth and she blinked at him. "Listen! You done great up to now.
Now's the last we got to go through before you see your folks again. Your
little brother. Jammy, that his name? *Hear me?* So get that thing off your

back and get ready to use it. That's right." He stepped back as she fumbled the bow into position. "Where's your spear?"

"I—I guess I dropped it. Back there someplace. Sorry—"

"That's all right." He considered, then let his go too. It toppled slowly and dug a narrow long grave in the snow. Christ, he thought, must be four foot deep. Could they run their ski machines in this? He didn't know. But for the next mile or so he'd better take it a step at a time. He blinked wearily into the blur of forest downhill. If he was where he thought, it wouldn't be far now and they'd hit the creek.

Moving out to point, he slipped into the wavering white curtain, bow ready in his left hand, the first arrow notched in his right.

Pham's feet were freezing. His shoes were torn and the snow leaked in even though he'd tied rags around them. He'd asked again and again for boots, but he'd never gotten any.

He yawned and rubbed his sleeve across his face. You couldn't see far in this snow. He wished he had some tea. He fingered the metal button on the gun Eisen had given him. What did it do, this button? His sight flicked to the can hanging on the bush, downhill toward the creek.

He called softly to Xuan in Vietnamese, "How long are we going to stay out here?"

"Be quiet. Till the American says we can go back."

"I'm cold."

"*Tôi lanh.* Be quiet."

He yawned again, fingering the button. He'd smiled as the American had explained how to operate the gun. He didn't understand half of what he heard, but he knew what happened when someone made the Boss angry. So he'd just smiled and nodded, and accepted the length of icy wood and metal.

Halvorsen heard the falls a little later. The distant water roar restored his confidence. Hell, it had been fifty, sixty years ago, no wonder he was a little uncertain. The rushing clamor grew steadily ahead as they descended a steep bank, picking their way down, grabbing saplings to brake themselves. The thin trunks were brittle-cold as filigree iron. Peering ahead he caught one glimpse through the falling snow of a flat expanse, smooth and white as planed poplar.

As if that was the last piece snapped into a puzzle, he suddenly knew where they were. He remembered the creek, and the falls, and the tumbled rapids below them, and then the pond, the pool, almost big enough to call a lake. He'd pulled a lot of muskrat out of that pond. Above it on the slopes lived fat raccoon, leaving prints like babies' hands in the mud where they came down to wash their meals. He'd stood on the bank watching a deep wavering shadow and pulled six five-pound brookies out one after the other to panfry for breakfast. Jesus, he thought, mouth springing water just with the recollection. And how pretty they were, wedges of rainbow flashing in the noon sun.

Whirling white devils closed in again and he lost the creek. But now he had his bearings and he could steer by the sound and the sure map of his memory engraved harder and more lasting in his brain than on steel. He came down out of the woods, leaving the shelter of the trees behind but comforted still by the white protective anonymity of the snow, and angled to the left. He figured to cross above the falls and take the west bank down the valley. Then short-cut across Tory Hill. Only six or seven miles now to the road. His stomach cramped suddenly, retrieved from starved numbness by the memory of food. Yeah, them brookies was sure good. He was tempted to stop, cut a rod, do some ice-fishing.

He was thinking this, a smile cracking stiffened lips, when something caught at his foot.

Halvorsen blinked down at the thing that had just snagged his boot. He half-lifted his snowshoe. The strand of fishing line tugged up, white-invisible against white. Strung from bush to bush, rock to rock, six inches above the snow.

Foxed, the old man thought in that dread frozen second. He foxed me with a snare. I knew he'd be waiting here. Even told the girl to watch out. But I was walking along dreaming, not paying any attention. Dreaming over fried fish.

The rifle blast split the snow apart with a white flash. He dove for the ground, hearing the hiss of a bullet over his back. Part of his mind jabbered that from that whiplash crack it was a high-velocity load, smaller than a .30 caliber but with plenty of muzzle energy. A good load for hunting medium-sized game.

Like people. He lay stunned, then twisted his neck to look for the girl as another shot cracked out. Couldn't see—no, there she was, hugging the ground too. Smart girl. Whoever was firing was probably sighted in along the tripline. But if there was somebody else on the other side—

Another, deeper report shook the valley. He made that out as a shotgun. Off to his left, above the creek. So there were two of them. Maybe more, but two for sure.

"Mr. Halvorsen!"

"Just a minute," he growled back over the rolling afterthunder of the guns, over the river roar. "Keep down. Let me think."

That was how he'd of set it up. One guy east of the creek on Selwyn's, the other west, on the opposite side of the valley. Eisen favored a rifle. So

that was probably him to his right. Nguyen was dead, so the one across
the creek with the shotgun was probably the fat ass, Olen. But he didn't
hear any dogs. The scattergun boomed again, closer, forty or fifty yards,
but he still couldn't see anyone. The snow hissed down opaque and impenetrable as a china cup inverted over him. Lying flat, he figured they
hadn't actually seen him either. Probably a tin can or something hung on
the line, to rattle warning.

Then he heard an engine start, from the right. Eisen'd be coming down
the line in a second, closing the trap.

He didn't have much of a chance. But if he could get to Olen first—

"You clear out," he grunted to the girl. Her scared eyes peered back at
him from just above the ground.

"Where are you going?"

"Goin' to circle down toward the falls. See if I can get one of 'em. Or
at least pull 'em off. You go on uphill to the right, there, into the woods—
no, wait, go the other way. You can get across the creek but I bet they
won't risk takin' that there snow machine out on the ice. Then if you can
shake 'em, keep on traveling. Go half a mile, then come down to the
creek again. Follow it all the way, five, six miles, till you see a road. You'll
cross a couple little streams but *don't leave the creek* till you see the road;
then flag a car down. Tell the state cops. And don't forget to give them
that receipt in your pocket."

Her eyes, blown wide and frightened, were still determined. Her head
shook back and forth. "I'm not going to leave you here."

"Yes, you are. Now git!" He waved her up angrily and yelled, again,
"Keep low!"

As her running shadow melted into the storm he scrambled stiffly to
his feet and limped as fast as he could the other way, gripping the bow.
The engine sound grew louder. It was coming in slow, deliberate, but it
was getting nearer. Still shambling along, he stripped off his red-and-black
coat and paused to drape it on a small pine. Then struggled on, shivering
as the wind sliced under his vest and shirt. Freeze for sure without his
coat, but in a couple minutes he'd either get it back or he wouldn't need
it, wouldn't feel the cold ever again.

He was almost to the treeline when he saw a vibrating blue-white light
probing toward him out of the falling snow. With the last two steps left to
him he reached a rock and crouched behind it. It wasn't big enough to
hide behind, but it gave him a little cover.

Fumbling with clumsy, frozen hands, he renotched the arrow.

The light bounced around in the snow and suddenly turned, heading
across his line of vision. An outline took shape: skis angled up in front,
louvered cowling, and astride it the thin shadow of a tall man, like the
head and shoulders of a mechanical centaur. Halvorsen calculated where

it would pass, and stood. He finished drawing the bow with all the strength that remained in him and sighted along the shaft. Then increased his lead and let fly.

The arrow left the bow with a thud, flew out, and disappeared into the blowing powder. He stood hoping, but the shadow shrank, bumping and roaring on until it melted out of his sight. "Hell," he muttered. He notched his other arrow and crept out from the rock, then ducked back as someone shouted off to the left, just above him. A high voice, not in English. So there were three of them out there, not two. And him with one goddamn arrow left.

Another rifle blast behind the wavering curtain told him somebody had discovered his coat. At least by now the girl had gotten up into the woods. He could fade back up the other hill and probably make his escape too. He crouched behind the rock, trying to slow down his racketing ticker. Felt like it was trying to shake him to pieces, like the old Indian motorcycle he'd been riding back when he met Jenny. The 1929 Powerplus veetwin. A 990-cc sidevalve engine and a suspension like a cement truck. Ride that sucker over a brick road was like riding a jackhammer. That night at the carnival in Hecla Park, the night air chill in September, but Jennie had been wearing a print dress and her hair up and looked like a million dollars, would be all too little . . . He pulled his errant mind back to the here and now. Yeah, that was what he probably ought to do. Go and just keep going, scoot, skedaddle, haul his tail out of here.

The trouble was, he didn't feel like doing what he probably ought to. He might be old but by Christ that didn't mean he was going to roll over for whoever wanted to kick him. Red Halvorsen had never done that and never would, not till the day he laid down and died.

He crouched there a second longer, trying to look at it cold, scared but knowing scared didn't mean you couldn't; angry, but not letting it blunt an old hunter's cunning. Finally he told himself: hell with it. You had a good run. Let's give 'er a shot and see what happens.

Stepping out from behind the rock, he ran stiffly down the hill.

Becky labored panting up between the trees. They stood silent and black and bare. She was gasping and crying. The shot claps cracked off the bark and rumbled away along the hills. Each shot made her flinch. She hadn't wanted to leave him but he'd said she had to, had to make it back to town. She had to tell the police. He said so. The snow scratched her face like a cat and tangled in her eyelashes. *Told you*, it said. The voices of teachers, parents, aunts, adults. *Do what you're told.* She hit at it angrily with her mittens, sucking in the numbing wind.

———

Eisen saw the shadow loom up out of the snowfog too late to think. He didn't slow, couldn't even aim, it was too close. All he had time to do was jerk the rifle up from where it rode by his side and snap-fire three times, the narrow butt of the .223 kicking his shoulder. The Yamaha slewed around as it bumped to a halt five yards from where the bare snow ended at a tumble of huge black rounded rocks, and beyond them, the creek. The shadow hung there, didn't fall, and he steadied his sights and aimed. This time he called the shot right through the body of the man who stood in the snow, red coat frosted with fallen white.

Then he sat openmouthed, unable to understand why Halvorsen hadn't fallen. Pham was shouting something off to his right. Finally, leaving the engine at idle, he threw his leg over it. Holding the rifle on the still-motionless figure, he took a step forward. Another.

Then whispered, "You old *bastard*."

He ran forward, shouting, "Pham! Xuan! Over here!"

Halvorsen stood crouched over in shattered ice and thigh-deep water so cold he wasn't sure he even had legs anymore. Here below the falls the air hung solid with drifting mist. Icicles dripped, cast from fog. Below the jutting overhang, where green water poured curving down, the creek bed was rocky and jagged, with caves and undercuts along the bank, roofed with treacherously cantilevered snow.

He crabbed his way up the chaotic tumble, slipping and belly-crawling over rock and ice and then rock again. His hands had gone dead at the first plunge into the dark, swift-flowing stream. But it was good cover and he kept climbing, peering ahead to the growing rumble of falling water. Till he saw something odd growing out of the snow on a rounded boulder like a tortoise's back. He glanced at it curiously as he moved from cavern to rock, and at last saw it was his first arrow. One for me, he thought, and dashed out to pick it up. It looked unharmed and he thrust it through a beltloop.

Finally he got to the foot of the falls. Cook wasn't Niagara. Just fifteen or twenty vertical feet from the edge down to where the tumble of rocks and ice he'd just traversed extended a hundred yards down-river. But the water poured down furiously, hammering itself apart over the rocks into white foam. Mist thickened the air, clammy and dank-smelling. He spidered slowly up it from rock to rock and finally eased his head up for a look.

Across the creek three men stood in a semicircle, staring at his coat. Two short, one tall. The snowmobile was idling, exhaust mingling with the mist and snow.

About a thirty-yard shot, he judged. A light arrow would get there but he wasn't sure how hard it would hit. Well, he wasn't going to get any closer. He renotched the arrow, sucked in air, let it out. The black water hammered down on his left, on his right, below him. His hands shook. He sucked breath in again, willing his lifeless fingers closed, and hauled back the quivering length to rest for a timeless moment against his whiskered cheek.

Pham was standing beside the Boss looking at the coat on the tree when something whished in toward them out of the snow. Before he could even flinch there was a thud like a fork punched into raw meat. The Boss made a choking sound. Pham backed away a step, then another, rag-wrapped feet dragging in the snow, before his militia training dropped him to the ground. The two Vietnamese, and Eisen himself, looked at the peeled-bark shaft poking out of his chest.

Then he reached up and jerked it out. It came easily and when he held it up there was no arrowhead, just a sharpened point. Eisen panted a couple of times, still looking surprised, exploring the hole between his ribs. Blood oozed out. Pham watched, horrified but fascinated.

"You . . . okay, Boss?"

"Don't know about okay, but I ain't dead. He's over there, down the falls. You got guns. All he's got's these little toy arrows. What the hell are you staring at? Go get him!"

"We can't see in this snow."

"Neither can he, asshole! If he gets away, next time we see him's when he comes back with the cops. Then you get shipped back to Commie Heaven. Get the picture? Hundred dollars bonus to whoever gets him."

They nodded, but despite the offer he didn't see any enthusiasm. Still, they started off. He walked carefully back to the snowmobile and groped in the saddlebag for the radio.

"Jerry, Rod here."

"How's it going, buddy?"

"Not so good. You better come on out, and bring your pets."

"Who's gonna mind the store?"

"Just tell them what'll happen if they're not sitting tight when we get back. Get them out here soon as you can. We got Grandpa cornered, but we're gonna need 'em to find the girl."

As he signed off he caught his breath. He hadn't felt any pain when he was hit, just impact. And nothing much when he pulled the shaft out. But now it was coming. He pressed his hand over the wound. Lucky it hadn't been any deeper. He sat hunched on the snowmobile with the lights off, glaring into the falling snow. Gripping the .223 and waiting for something to show.

———

Halvorsen was shivering, still clinging hunched where he'd launched the arrow from, just beneath the lip of the falls. He'd seen it fly true; must have hit somebody, he'd heard the yell. He risked a quick glimpse between boulders crusted with still-green moss, the preserving ice clear and rounded and magnifying like an expensive crystal paperweight. A head bobbed just above where the creek began its plunge through icy chutes down over the riprap, smashing itself apart into tumbling froth before subsiding at last into the wide pool below.

They had guns. But not only didn't he feel like running anymore, he knew he couldn't. He was at the end of his rope, at last.

Notching the last arrow, he waited. Till the head bobbed up again, right above him.

Xuan coughed nervously. He was still freezing and now he was terrified too. He couldn't believe how the arrow had suddenly grown out of the boss's chest. Like dark magic, sudden and pointed as a flung curse. It hadn't killed him, but a hand higher and it would have been in his heart.

He'd never have believed it. For some reason he'd never really thought the loud-voiced Americans could be hurt, much less killed. . . .

He took one more step, the gun heavy and strange in his hands. He had no liking for any of this. He coughed, the sound faint even to himself in the thunder of leaping foam. Snow needled his face, melting in sweat and the condensation from the thick wet air. The fog squatted on the dark water. Nguyen was dead. The word had passed from mouth to ear in the bunkhouse. And now the Boss was wounded. Before, everything had been clear. The workers had to stay, they owed much money for their passage. The Americans beat them or shot them or let the dogs eat them if they tried to leave. They'd killed Vo as an example. Shown them his beaten body. And set the dogs on Tranh. But now . . . a hundred dollars, the Boss had said. More than he'd ever imagined having. But what good was money in the camp? This wasn't what he'd run away from home for, left the hamlet, sailed out into the China Sea.

Hesitantly, he took one more step. Then stared in horror as a white-bearded, red-eyed apparition rose over the lip of the cliff. A screaming, grimacing demon from the tombs, with a drawn arrow pointed straight at his heart.

Halvorsen waited till he heard the nervous cough again, just above him. Then stood, quickly, all at once, and aimed the drawn bow over the top of the cliff.

Two small, dark men stared at him, mouths open, puffing white astonished breath. One started to raise his weapon. Halvorsen swung to cover him.

Time seemed to turn liquid, spinning itself out in clear, gelatinous drops, as if it too slowed in the cold.

Then, to his astonishment and relief, both abruptly whirled and began running, clumsily, legs plunging down at each step into the moving water and then the deep powdery cover of the bank opposite. They didn't drop their guns, but they didn't use them either. Their shapes receded into the ragged lace that shivered in the air. Sighing, he let the bowstring go slack.

He stood and watched till a racking shudder wrung him. He was freezing. He had to get his coat.

Hauling himself over the edge of the falls, slinging the bow, he started up the slope.

Waiting in absolute silence and motionlessness, Eisen had heard the startled exclamations. He'd seen the two shadows sprinting upvalley at the edge of his vision. And contemplated shooting them. Fucking gooks, he thought. But instead he held still. The old man would come back. He understood now what iron inexorability he had called into being in Halvorsen. This time he would use it, to bring him out of the snow into his sights.

Motionless as a tree, peering into the whispering white, he waited for the old man to come. Waiting, the rifle half-pointed toward the endless clamor of the falls, his finger resting lightly on the trigger, safety off.

Becky stood still, listening more completely than she had ever listened before. The falls rumbled below her like trucks going by at night. The ground slanted away into the white haze. Was it her imagination, or were there dim shapes, indistinct objects ahead? They seemed to be trees, but she couldn't be sure.

But one thing was sure: she wasn't going to run away and leave Mr. Halvorsen to do everything by himself.

Holding the bow out horizontally in front of her, gripping the drawn arrow lightly, she slipped silently downhill, squinting into the snow that breathed silently down all around.

Halvorsen was pulling on his coat when he heard the shot. And the cry, off to his left. *Becky*, he thought.

———————

Eisen lowered the rifle. Take that, you old bastard. The shadow had wavered, then crumpled to the snow.

He was still grinning when the arrow drove through his cheek and out the far side of his face, as if to pin that smile there forever.

She lay stunned on the ground, fingers clutching where something had hit her so hard she couldn't breathe or even think. Her open eyes felt frozen. She looked up at the cloudy sky.

Then she saw the old man's face thrust close above her. It bent toward her, then swung back up toward the trees. He didn't have the bow anymore. Now he was carrying a gun. She saw his mouth moving but she couldn't hear any words. It was like the waterfall was making so much noise she couldn't hear anything at all.

Then the rushing thunder faded, and she realized it wasn't the waterfall at all but something else roaring in her ears. Because now she could hear him. Faintly, but she could make out words. "Becky. Get up. You got to get up."

She didn't want to. She just wanted to lie there. The sky so bright and the snowflakes spiraling down out of it. So pretty. She felt quiet inside, sleepy, like after a long, warm bath.

But he kept talking and finally she tried. But her legs felt very weird. Like they were stuffed with cotton. They couldn't hold her up. She couldn't move her arm at all. It felt heavy and it dangled. The old man got her other arm wrapped around his neck. He was practically dragging her. She thought how funny it must look, and almost laughed. "That's good," he said into her ear. "Try to walk now." She noticed his coat had holes in it. How could he be walking with so many holes in him? He stumbled and she knew it was because of her so she tried harder. They stopped at the waterfall, looking down to where it leapt and crashed endlessly into the rocks. Like it was playing, having fun. On some of the stones there wasn't any snow or ice, just green moss and some kind of weed waving down around the sides. There were deep places between them where she could see nothing but white water, like a crazy outdoor washing machine.

The old man held out the rifle, then dropped it. It fell and one of the deep places swallowed it and she couldn't see it anymore. She twisted her head to look at him, astonished, and he yelled, grizzled cheek close to hers, "No more cartridges. Threw the bow away too. We still got a ways to go."

She nodded vaguely, biting her tongue to fight back a wave of faintness.

Together they staggered drunkenly from rock to rock, first up, then down, circling around the falls. It was steep and they kept slipping. The second time they went down it felt like her arm was tearing off. She couldn't help screaming, and Halvorsen stopped and used her scarf to make a sling. After that he went slower, but it still hurt, and kept on hurting, more and more.

Below the falls were rocks and caves and little rapids all covered with ice and black rocks covered with snow. She coughed and tried to speak. Halvorsen bent. "What?"

"What happened?" Her voice was hoarse, as if the scream had used it all up.

"We made it. Eisen's dead."

"Did you kill him? Or did I?"

"I don't know. We both shot at the same time, I think."

"I think probably you did. Where we going now?"

"Home. All we got to do now is walk six miles."

She laughed. It hurt but she couldn't help it. She whispered, "I'm not gonna make it any six miles."

"Oh, yes we are," Halvorsen said.

Just then, above them, they heard the motor start.

He'd lain there with his eyes closed as the old man stood above him. It wasn't a ploy. He really couldn't move. The rough shaft pressed his tongue into his lower jaw like a horse's bit, pinning his mouth closed. It was filling with blood and he had to breathe shallow, shallow, through his nose or else strangle. He felt the rifle being taken from his arms. Wouldn't do him any good, the clip was empty. So he just lay there.

When he finally cracked his lids the old man was gone.

He lay there for a while, waiting for Xuan and Pham to come back, or for Jerry to arrive. Then the fact he was freezing registered. He could be dead by the time help arrived. He was losing heat. And blood. The taste of it gagged him, creeping down his throat in a thick hot stream he had to keep gulping.

He struggled up and pulled himself onto the machine. Glared around into the snow. It seemed to be letting up some. He could see all the way to the woods' edge now. He squinted dizzily at his watch. To his surprise it was still only a little before nine. Blood kept filling his mouth, dribbling down his chin. He touched the arrow tentatively. It entered to the left of his nose. The peeled stick ran slantwise through his mouth, where he could touch it with his tongue, went through his lower jaw and jutted out the right side. He could work his jaw a little, just enough to open his lips. He bent over and spat and the blood drooled out in half-coagulated stringy clumps, staining the snow.

He felt the pointed tip where it emerged. Like the first arrow, the one that struck his chest. Just sharpened wood.

Quickly, without thinking about it, he grasped the shaft hard and yanked. A great gush of blood filled his mouth, almost choking him, but this time the arrow didn't come out. The bone held it tight. He worked at it, gasping at the dazzling white screens of pain he tuned in each time he tried to move it. At last the shaft snapped and he got the lower part loose. Now he could open his mouth. But he couldn't budge the rest, the part in his cheekbone. The blood kept welling up and running over his tongue, tasting like hot bouillon. He gasped, coughed, searching his pockets. All he came up with was a half-used pack of Kleenex. He fumbled it apart, wadded up three or four tissues, and stuck them up into the roof of his mouth, around where the splintered stick exited the gum. Then he did the same to the hole in his lower jaw, plugging it roughly with impacted paper.

Then he fumbled for the key.

The starter chattered and then the motor whined. The headlight came on. The tach twitched upward and the clutch engaged and he started forward over the snow. He caught his breath as each bump and lurch jabbed at his shattered face, but kept feeding the machine more gas. At first the skis turned away from the creek, scribing an arc on the slanting hillside. Then he hunkered in the seat, cursing, and wrenched the handlebars back. Track whining, tilting and bucking, the snowmobile obeyed.

Till it was pointed back toward the falls.

Gunning her unevenly, rocking from side to side, he raced past the falls and up into the woods. Growled and bumped uphill between the trees at twenty miles an hour, jerking the handlebars from side to side as he blinked through the jagged sheets of light. A bank dropped out from under him, the long-travel suspension bottoming out with a slam that made a choked scream bubble in his throat. But he got control back, heading downhill now, and a minute or two later burst out of the forest, heading down in a long shallow curve.

The rock-strewn tumble below the falls came into view, a hundred yards of white water and whiter ice. Below it was the broad blank-paper expanse of a little lake framed by pines. Across it he saw two locked-together figures, dark against the white, pale faces turning as he squeezed the throttle all the way open, kicking the motor into a scream, aiming straight for them.

Halvorsen stood rigid, looking up as the black machine came down off the hill. Understanding all at once how stupid he'd been. He hadn't taken the snowmobile. Now Eisen had revived, somehow, and was after them again. All he'd had to do was take the keys out of it, throw them into the creek along with the carbine.

But he hadn't thought to.

He stood motionless, and all at once something that had bent farther and farther in him broke at last. His arm dropped from the girl's shoulder. He stared dully at the approaching machine.

"Come on," Becky said. "Come *on!*"

"Where?"

"Out here. Out onto the ice."

He looked apathetically out across the smooth outstretched surface of the great pond. Here, below the falls, the creek spread lazily, as if it had earned a rest after its tumultuous descent. It was a couple of hundred yards long and maybe a hundred yards across, all of it windplaned flat, snowglazed and featureless in the blue shadowed light. On this side the hill fell into it; on the far side the land rose again. Like a pit, and here at the bottom was the pond.

"That ice ain't thick as you think," he mumbled. "This here's moving water, it don't freeze to the bottom. And it's deep. I trapped here, I bet it's thirty feet down. Maybe more."

"So, what, you just gonna give up?" Becky taunted him. Getting hurt had warmed her up. Made her feel crazy. Like she had new batteries or something. Maybe in ten minutes she'd lie down and die, but right now she felt ready to run and run and run. But old Mr. Halvorsen just stood there, looking up at the black machine that grew closer every second, surfing down the slope zigzag toward them. Every time it hit a patch of lumpy snow she prayed for it to turn over, but it didn't. Eisen just kept coming. She could see his face now through the little windshield. It was smeared with blood. God, she thought. He should be dead. Why isn't he dead?

Halvorsen stared too. He'd really thought Eisen was finished. Should of made sure, he thought. His fingers closed around the old Case in his pocket.

"Come *on!*" Becky shouted.

"It ain't safe."

"It ain't safe here either! Come on!" She lurched free of his suddenly grasping claw and reeled out stumbling onto the white surface. Her snowshoes were shreds around her boots and she waded through the snow. It wasn't quite as deep here as it was drifted on the hill. A couple of feet. Her arm swung in the makeshift sling. "Come on! Are you scared?"

"I ain't going out there."

"I dare you. Double dare you!" she screamed, pointing, laughing at him.

"I don't take no dares," growled the old man, stung. He caught his breath and stepped out onto the ice.

His boot plunged down through soft cover and jarred, then his heart jarred too as it broke through. But it was just a crust, and six inches beneath it was the solid ice. He gathered what scraps remained of will and courage and waded out after her onto the level white expanse of the frozen pond.

On the far side the machine roared, bucking and whining as it searched a way toward them through the rocks.

Becky gasped as each step jolted her arm. Glowing fireflies drifted around the edge of her vision. The ice was sidewalk-hard under the snow. She didn't see what he was worried about, it was perfectly safe out here.

Above them Eisen jerked the skis around the last boulder between him and them. The snowmobile bounded over the last uneven ground and then lifted its nose as it found the smooth surface beneath. He squeezed the throttle and the tracks dug in. It squatted, winding up, then suddenly bolted into high gear. Wind pressed his face. The running figures grew swiftly over the cowling.

Looking up, Halvorsen saw the thing spewing up a smoky wake of white snow, heard the chainsaw whine of the engine winding to full power. No bow anymore. No spear. He had the knife. But the way Eisen was coming, he meant to just run them down, not get off and fight. Snow shot up around the points of the skis, sharpened and angled up like a pair of gutting knives. The louvered nose swung as if sniffing them, then steadied. The headlight pinned them, growing rapidly brighter.

Then he felt it. The first faint creaking sag under his boots.

"Run," he yelled to Becky, a few feet ahead. And turned to face the oncoming machine.

Eisen felt it too, the oh-so-slight tilt and tremor under his rocketing weight. It was too late to turn back so he squeezed the throttle tighter, as high as it would go. The tach wound into the red. The engine hit the high note of its song of power. The track screamed like electric mixers set on "whip."

Then he felt the ice give way beneath him.

Halvorsen saw the black curved cowling dip, and didn't understand, expected it to come back up. But it kept nosing down. At the same moment the solidity beneath his own feet suddenly began to quake.

He threw out his arms, staggering as the snowmobile, going at full speed, dug its skis into the ice as if trying to pry it up. Then nosed over and drove itself gracefully as a sounding porpoise beneath the parting surface, into an opening, cracking, suddenly liquid darkness beneath it.

The ice splintered open under him too and Halvorsen fell backward onto a rocking floe, his arms flung wide in instinctive plea for support. The floe tilted and he slid off, hugging two armloads of loose snow after him, down into the blue-black water.

Ahead of him Becky screamed as the ice collapsed beneath her. She plummeted straight down. Only at the last instant before her head went under did her good arm shoot out to snag on a solid edge of still-unbroken ice.

Silence returned to the pond. Silence, the creak of the pines, and the clack and clatter of slowly milling ice in the three interconnected holes. That and the sigh of the wind.

"Becky," Halvorsen yelled. His voice sounded high and breathless and for a moment he was afraid his heart had quit beating. His chest felt tight and he couldn't pull in enough air to fill it.

"Over here."

"Can't see ya."

"Help me!" She struggled, suddenly understanding as icy teeth bit through her coat and jeans to her skin. She tried to pull herself up onto the ice but couldn't do it with just one arm. She sank back slowly into the water's embrace.

Separated by fifteen feet, they bobbed slowly in the half-liquid, half-solid detritus of the pond's surface. Halvorsen smelled gasoline and craned his head back. A slick was forming where the snowmobile had disappeared. He didn't see any sign of its rider.

He turned his attention back to the ice around him. About four inches thick, not as much as you'd think this late in the winter. The moving water beneath had kept it thin. Snow on top of that, except where it had tilted, when he'd gone down and dumped the loose drift off. The shattered chunks rocked as he shifted, edges grating, a floating jigsaw puzzle. The ice seemed higher now. He frowned, then realized he was riding lower. As the trapped air left his clothing, replaced by near-freezing water, he was slowly sinking.

Ahead of him Becky lay with her good arm clamped over the border of solid ice, staring into the lake water between the shattered chunks. It was gruelly, sludgy with snow crystals, like an unflavored sno-cone. At first the cold hurt. Then, gradually, it soothed away her pain. Her eyes fluttered shut. "Help me," she whispered again, who to, she didn't know.

Then she opened them again and clawed out. Her nails dug chips from the smooth, puckered surface of the ice. Her legs kicked and she pulled, digging her fingers in even harder. Her nails bent and snapped but it didn't hurt. She kicked and struggled and got her chest up on the solid part. Like pulling herself out of a swimming pool with one arm, except she'd never felt so weak and so heavy. All these wet clothes. She teetered there, puffing, a jagged corner jabbing into her belly. Then reached out farther and felt something embedded in the ice. A stick or something, frozen in. She seized it eagerly and gave a great frantic pull and her belly slid up over the sharp rim too. She lay all but free, only her legs still dangling, gathering breath and strength for a final effort.

With a sodden, yielding crack, the ice subsided again under her. It sagged and parted and let her down gently as caring arms back into the water. She hammered it with her good fist, gasping and crying.

Behind her Halvorsen saw her fur-fringed parka hood bobbing as she tried to get out. She tried twice more but each time she got her weight up on it the ice gave way, dumping her back into the black liquid cold that was creeping up his own neck too. He was sinking, the relentless, irresistible weight dragging him down. Only his grip on the floe kept him up, and his strength was slipping fast.

He lifted his eyes to the hills.

They towered above the valley in the clearing air, their slanted white capes and gray dresses like a train of great ladies promenading off into the distance. Selwyn's loomed close above, lofty and magnificent, and beyond it Cooks and then Rabbit Hill, where he'd seen the one-eared bobcat years ago. Beyond Rabbit curved Black Hollow and the rutted dirt road that led up to the old lookout tower. It wasn't paved but hunters and kids went up it all the time. They'd almost made it . . . He could have shot that bobcat but he hadn't. He could still see its yellow eyes watching him.

He'd been out after turkey that year carrying his .22 Hornet for the first time and heard the *gobble-gobble* a couple of hundred yards away along the flat crest. He'd edged on over toward it, staying below the line of sight. He'd taken his time stalking and been rewarded every few minutes with the turkey's call. Finally it got so close he looked around for cover. A few yards uphill was a stand of spruce and not far from it a big blown-down oak, the branches clustered like fingers on a hand.

He'd made it to the oak and squatted among the branches, jerking his cap down to hide his face and laying the brand-new Savage Model 23 carefully aside, propped against a limb. Taking a deep breath, he gave three soft hen-yelps on the wooden call.

At first he'd got no answer. But finally when he cackled the bird, an old tom by the sound, gave a deep-throated, eager gobble. He sounded close and Halvorsen crouched, the call clenched in his teeth, and was reaching for the rifle when he heard a crackle behind him, soft, like a stockinged foot coming down in the leaves.

When he'd turned his head the bobcat was looking into his eyes not ten feet away. It had just stepped around the log and stood with one big, tufted paw raised. He'd just stared, not moving. He could have grabbed for the gun but he didn't. And the cat had stared back at him with whiskers quivering, its great amber eyes filled with all the strangeness and mystery of the wild before suddenly, in a scratching scurry of dead leaves, it was gone.

He came back to find the cold water like a proffered cup at his lips. He inhaled, got a mouthful, and coughed it out explosively. The shock inspired him to a final effort, but even as he fought he knew it wasn't going to work. Even as he scrabbled crab-desperate at the ice, he succeeded only in clawing more loose snow in on top of him. He lunged weakly up and the blue-black surface frozen around him crackled like cellophane and fell away in tinkling transparent sheets.

His kicking legs slowed. He sank back. The water touched his lips again, cold and sweet, insistent and encumbering, closing around him with dark enfolding arms. Well, that's it, he thought.

Then his staring eyes noticed something moving, up on the hill.

It came slowly out of the high treeline above where the ravine fell to meet the rockslide that edged the pond. Floated slowly out like a gray shadow. Paused, as if debating turning back, as Halvorsen forgot to take the next breath. Then came on, head up, trotting sideways down the bank.

The wolf came slowly out of the woods above them. It stood staring down, the same wildness in its eyes he remembered from the bobcat's.

Becky's eyes were closed when she heard the old man's soft warning. She opened them and blinked. "Up on the hill," he murmured. She could barely understand him, barely cared, but she looked.

She caught her breath, staring, forgetting her danger. It was the first time she'd seen him clearly, in the light. He was lean and long, silvery gray with black-rimmed ears and muzzle and a black tip to his bushy tail. His legs and underbelly were almost white, blending with the snow. Deep-set yellow eyes peered down at them from a huge high-held head, ears up, alert.

It was him, the great wolf she'd followed and who had followed her. In that moment of recognition she had no doubt and no question. She stretched out her hand, and the wolf started, pranced sideways a few steps, tail erect, then stopped again. It peered down at them, head cocked, then seesawed through the snow a few steps closer.

"Help me," she whispered. "Help me, Prince."

The wolf hesitated, looking back up the hill as if it heard something they couldn't. It danced nervously, then made a short bound away, back toward the forest. She felt her heart constrict in horror. "Don't leave us," she cried.

The wolf hesitated again, and she waited, panting harshly, watching it. The dark muzzle swung toward the falls, then up at the hill opposite. Its tail made a low swipe at the snow.

It burst into sudden motion, a silver-gray blue plunging down into the deep white and erupting out again, plunging and dropping down the hillside. Its head bounced crazily above the snow, tongue lolling red from its open mouth. It came bounding down through the rocks like a Slinky toy and when it reached level didn't stop or pause, just seemed to stretch out over the smooth snow so that each lope covered ten or twelve feet. It came almost out to her and braked, stopping just a few feet away. Now its breath rasped the stillness away. Saliva drooled down from a startlingly long tongue. White smoke drifted from parted jaws, and snow sparkled unmelting on thick winter fur. This close she saw its eyes were not yellow but greenish-golden, glowing as if from a light set just behind them. They stared unblinking straight down at her with such calm power that she could not hold their gaze.

"Help me," she whispered. Turning her head to the side, stretching out her neck, she closed her eyes.

She heard a faint, whining snarl, and felt her extended arm gripped. The teeth dug in but she didn't flinch or open her eyes even as the heat of its breath seared the icy skin of her wrist. She stayed limp as the wolf increased its force. It growled, and the teeth clamped harder. She heard its claws scraping on the ice.

Suddenly her body turned and she kicked hard and came sliding up out of the water and into the snow.

The teeth released her arm, and she heard the scuffle of its pads as it danced back. She lay full length, gasping, body completely numb. As if she was just a head, like in an old horror movie she'd seen on TV one night before they went to live with Charlie. Then she pushed herself up and opened her eyes.

The wolf watched from among the rocks. At the flutter of her lashes it started, bounded a few steps away, then stopped and looked back, watching again.

She still couldn't feel her legs but she got them under her. Staggered up onto the bank. The wolf ran ahead of her up the hillside, gamboling like a big puppy, its eyes turned back, wide and alive with that wisdom but no sadness at all, with something that she couldn't help thinking was . . . delight?

"Thank you," she breathed through immovable lips.

"Becky!"

She remembered Halvorsen with a guilty start, and looked around quickly. Here and there at the edge branches poked up like dead fingers. The first she tried was rotten, the second too ice-embedded for her to move. The third she yanked free and ran stiffly out onto the ice again with it. She tripped and fell over useless blocks of frozen feet and got up again on her knees and inched forward through the snow like a crippled beetle, stretched out to distribute her weight, pushing the branch till its end poked the old man in the chest.

"Get back," Halvorsen murmured. He was drifting away. His mouth wouldn't move right anymore, hands either, but somehow he fumbled the limb toward him. She crawled toward him and he gathered his breath and shouted with expiring fierceness, "Get back!"

She stopped and let go. He pulled the limb the rest of the way to him and shoved it around until it bridged the hole. Then threw an arm over it. The branch bent but he held on grimly and added the weight of his leg, hooking his knee over it.

"More branches, quick," he grunted between his teeth. Becky was already crawling away.

The second limb, spiky with twigs and with a few withered, curled leaves still clinging to it, wasn't quite as large as the first. Still, it distributed his weight even more and with the third he was able to roll out of the water on top of the creaking, bending wood. He rested there, letting the water run off him. He felt warm and sleepy. He started to topple back in but her cry woke him again. He clawed his way along the branches and burrowed into undisturbed snow. He expected the ice to give way again but this time it held and he dragged himself on elbows and knees, floundering and blowing loose snow out of his face until he reached the bank. She got there just after him and they collapsed together and clung, both wringing wet and crackling icy in the chill hushed air, their heatless cheeks rubbing, fumbling close together as if to kindle warmth by friction.

They were still locked like that, face to face, when the baying of the dogs floated down to them bell-clear in the frigid air.

Twenty-eight

The wolf stood rigid still, head up and ears erect. Conscious of his packmates above, waiting in the shelter of the trees. But not concerned with them: simply listening, studying every cadence and note of the high-pitched whines and barks that pulsed between the hills, swelling, waning, but growing steadily closer.

He turned his head once to look back at the pond. The trampled snow and cracked black ice from which he'd just ascended. He whined faintly. His right leg ached from the old injury and the awkward strain of pulling. The taste of the human's hand lingered unpleasantly. He swung his head, then lowered it and snapped, obliterating the taint with a scooping bite of icy drift.

Then lifted his snowy muzzle and howled, a sharply rising single note held for a second or two, then abruptly cut off.

The answer echoed from uphill, a wavering, eerie chorus. It ended but the silver wolf didn't respond, just stood motionless. Seconds later a fainter howl shivered the air, the high-held note falling slowly till it ended in a bark.

The wolf swung suddenly into a bounding lope, plunging uphill till he reached the low brush screening the treeline. The others were waiting there. The black one, rangy, hungry-looking, and the stumpy-tailed wolf, jaws slack, cringed as their leader trotted up. They whined together and pushed noses, the bobtail feinting with a halfhearted attempt to bite; then all muzzles lifted again as the pack bayed.

The old wolf tasted the wind whirling along the surface of the snow with fierce and total concentration. Ears pricked forward, teeth unsheathed as he panted out a warm breath-cloud, he gazed fixedly into the violet shadows between the hills. The wind came from behind them, and he realized it was carrying their scent directly to the dogs that moved closer every minute, whose chaotic eager yaps and yelps rang down the valley.

He wasn't thinking as a man would think. But he knew that to survive he had to make the right decision, and soon. The distant howl was the female, still back at the den. She wouldn't emerge until the pups were born. They'd brought meat back to her the day before, from the deer they'd killed above the fall. The silver lifted his muzzle higher, feeling the dark one's scrutiny but ignoring it. His tail twitched, held out stiff and level with the snow.

He knew the approaching dogs. Knew their pack and where they denned with the humans. Had watched them from cover, studied the pen and smelled what they were fed. He'd howled to them and listened to the frenzied, queer response. He knew too that what came now was only part of the dog pack, and wondered where the others were.

From below came the first flash of motion as the dogs emerged from the head of the hollow. The wolf tensed, registering everything: the no-scent from behind him on the wind; the dim images focused through his nearsighted eyes. But his keen hearing gave the most useful clues just now: the jeering of a raven; the *crunch crunch* of the running dogs' pads; the growl of a motor far behind them; and below it all the dull, unending thunder of the falls. Through the trunks he glimpsed the lead dog, muzzle gaping as it loped. The others were strung out behind it in a loose line. Retreat or face them? Ordinarily he would have withdrawn. Melted back into the bitter forest, knowing dogs could not keep up once wolves set themselves to covering distance. But these trespassers were too close to the den. If the wolves fled, the dogs might pick up their backtrail and follow it straight to the denned and gravid bitch.

The old one snarled and swung his head. The others dipped their muzzles, echoing his rumbling growl.

The silver wolf leapt over a fallen tree, descending into snow so deep-drifted he all but disappeared. He came up bucking like a mustang, flinging white from his fur, thrusting up and out until the broad furred pawpads caught surface again and he lunged lightly over it and through a patch of blackberry bramble and thorn tree.

He cut right and suddenly exploded out onto the sloping bare bank above the running dogs. The other wolves burst out of the woods behind him, loping through the broken drifts, smoke snorting from their gaping muzzles. The bobtail whined, but swallowed, choking off the sound as the silver glanced back.

There were six dogs, all huge German shepherds or part-wolf hybrids that did not look unlike the wolves from a distance. Two were much heavier. But the silver wolf felt no fear, only contempt and horror and an overwhelming determination. With no warning but the chuff as his feet left the snow, he plunged over the hillside, raced thirty yards downslope at blinding speed, and caught the third dog in line in the flank, tumbling it down before it even knew it was being attacked.

This was the largest dog in the pack and it shied sideways as he struck at its neck, and he missed. He lunged again instantly and it gave a frightened snarling yelp as his teeth closed on its short muzzle. A shaking jerk of his powerful neck, a snapping, crunching ripping at a momentarily exposed belly, and the silver whirled with bloodied teeth to face the startled eyes of the others. The dark and the bobtailed were snarling and biting at the smallest dog, a young female. It disappeared beneath them. When they sprang off a moment later it kicked feebly and died, spewing blood and a hot blood-reek into the chill air.

The remaining dogs scattered, yelping and howling, at first not helping the ones that were engaged. The dark wolf wheeled as the silver stood aside, panting. It leapt and another dog went down in a yipping welter of loose snow, sticks, leaves, torn fur, and kicked-up powder. Howling and snapping, they rolled over and over.

The dogs recovered themselves and charged in. The melee spread. The bobtailed wolf gathered its courage again and darted in to grip the leg of a stocky male with floppy ears.

The silver wolf hung back for a moment, looking for an opening, then pounced as another shepherd backed off from the fight, whining in fear. But it unexpectedly turned again to face him rather than fleeing, as he'd expected from its attitude. It outweighed the wolf, and face to face with it the silver's hackles rose. He crouched, showing cruel curved ivory. The shepherd started to retreat, then changed its mind yet again.

Suddenly it lunged, taking him off balance. Their shoulders slammed together and their teeth passed snapping in the air like yard shears. The dog, at least thirty pounds heavier than the wolf, smashed him down into the snow. He rolled, snarling for the first time since the battle began. The dog rushed in again, matching his ferocity and exceeding his power. Its jaws closed savagely at the base of his hind leg.

He doubled himself like an eel, taking the wound in silence. Then a black shadow wedged between them, throwing the shepherd back. The black wolf feinted and the dog jumped to meet it.

From behind it the silver wolf struck. Mercilessly the heavy jaws sheared through fat, muscle, and guts to grate at last into bone. The dog yelped and sank, snapping madly at the air.

With a mechanical snarl the snowmobile appeared at the top of the valley. A man rode it, yelling and waving a shotgun.

The bobtailed wolf kicked free from two dogs and ran with bloody

muzzle to join its packmates. The fighting animals separated like interlocked fingers slowly pulled apart, withdrawing into two groups that faced
each other over the trampled, reddened snow. Two motionless humps lay
tumbled and half-covered. The lead shepherd jerked itself whimpering
toward the oncoming machine, uncoiling ropes of glossy intestine dragging after it.

The old wolf stood shoulder to shoulder with the others, blood running
down his leg, panting but silent. Only three dogs were left standing. They
faced the wolves with the bravado of distance, barking and snarling and
feinting lunges back and forth, but coming no closer.

A puff of white came from the still-distant snowmobile, a clap of sound,
and pellets sang through the air. The wolves, still preserving their eerie
silence, turned as one and loped off into the trees.

The snarls and screams had carried clearly down to where they stood by
the pool. Becky said, "It's the wolves."

"I don't know what they're doing," said Halvorsen. He still couldn't
believe what he'd just seen. It had looked as if the wolf had pulled her
out of the water up onto the ice. Rescued her. But that couldn't be right.
He could understand it helping another wolf. But a human being didn't
look or smell anything like a wolf. Well, he'd seen a lot of things in sixty
years in the woods. Some so strange he'd never told anybody about them.
But this beat them all.

"Come on," he said at last, giving up understanding it for now. "We
better get going, while them dogs is occupied."

They hiked down the creek, staying between the ice and the treeline
as the land gradually gentled. The valley opened ahead of them, broad
and flat between hill lines tapering off into the distance. After a long time
Halvorsen squinted, shading his eyes against the growing light with a stiff-
fingered hand. There, around Hart Hill. Still vague in the distance, but
another half-mile or so and he figured they'd catch a glimpse of the water
tower at Gasport, up at the top of Steep Hollow Road.

Becky, plodding behind him, was astonished how fast the excitement
of still being alive ebbed away. Her clothes were wet and heavy. She felt
encased in ice, except for her shattered arm, which flamed at each step.
She kept falling down and he kept helping her up. Finally she went down
again and when he tried to get her up she didn't help at all.

"Come on, Becky. Not much farther."

"No more. We got to stop. We got to build a f-fire or I'm going to
freeze solid."

Halvorsen started to say again that they had to keep going. Then he
thought, Maybe she's right. The barks and cries had faded behind them
some time back and the wide valley opened ahead.

———

They were huddled around the fire, boots and socks and coats propped on sticks to dry, when the man in a stocking cap came out of the trees. He had a black beard and carried a bolt-action rifle. Halvorsen could only watch helplessly as he came up. If this was another of Eisen's thugs, they were finished. He couldn't fight anymore. They couldn't even run. The bearded man trudged slowly up to the fire on metal snowshoes and looked down at them. Up close he looked weary, as if he'd been in the woods a long time. He held the rifle on Halvorsen for a moment, unsmiling, looking at him and then the girl. Then he lowered it and propped it against a rock.

"I guess you must be the little girl we all been looking for," he said to Becky.

And Becky, trying her best to smile though she felt like bawling like a little baby, said, "I guess I am."

The Afterimage

Halvorsen stood under the carriage entrance after he rang the bell, collar turned up, breath drifting in a frosty streamer out into the shrubbery. He coughed into his fisted glove, shivering.

He'd walked up the hill from the gate, nearly a mile, and he was exhausted all over again. He'd only had one night's sleep since coming in from the woods. Dr. Friedman had stared at him reproachfully when they brought him and the girl in. She'd given him a shot first thing, then a hot bath before she put him to bed. She'd tried to stop him from calling Joe Culley, then Bill Sealey. She'd tried to stop him from coming here, too, but here he stood, looking curiously around. Still a pretty place. And big. Past the mortared fieldstone entranceway the elms were larger than he recalled. Then finally the great stone house had loomed up, outbuildings ranked behind it.

Cherry Hill, old Dan Thunner's country estate.

A woman in a green nurse's uniform opened the door. She looked at him inquiringly. "William T. Halvorsen," he said. "To see Dan."

"Mr. Thunner's not in any condition to see people, sir. Is this a business matter?"

"Sorry to hear he's not doing so good. Used to work for him, back when—"

"Miss Thunner handles business things now. You can contact her at her office in town, sir. This is their home."

"I'll talk to her here, if she's in," said Halvorsen. "She might want to see me. Tell her it's about stealing gas."

The woman frowned and didn't ask him in to wait. When she closed the door he coughed again, shifting from foot to foot and breathing into his gloves to warm his fingers. It didn't help. A chill had sunk into him, during that long walk out from the Kinningmahontawany, that felt like it would never leave. He glanced around. He'd been inside this house once before, years ago, and he remembered there was no place to get rid of a chew. He disposed of his behind a bush and was back when the door opened again.

Ainslee stared dumbfounded at the apparition on her threshold. A very old man exactly her height, with pale blue eyes and shaving cuts on his furrowed face. Green work pants and a red-and-black hunting jacket. White hair stuck out from under a floppy-eared cap with the Thunder Oil lightning bolt insignia. His neck was scrawny and his lips were scabbed. He looked faintly familiar.

"Who are you?"

"Told your girl there. I'm W. T. Halvorsen."

She almost closed the door on him, then suddenly put the face and the name together. This was the one Jack Youndt had called about. The hermit who'd been asking questions about Medina. He'd caused trouble before, she remembered now, back when her ex had been in charge. Still, he seemed respectful enough. And he was so old.

"What do you want, Mr. Halvorsen?"

"Wanted to talk, you've got a minute?"

"What could we possibly have to talk about?"

"Natural gas," said Halvorsen. "The Medina Transportation Company."

She hesitated, then said shortly, "Come in, please."

Halvorsen followed her down a long glassed-in walkway to another building. The air was still chilly even though they were inside the house.

She opened the door to warmth and a modest office. Pointed to a chair and sat behind a desk. As he let himself down a large black man in a gray suit came in and took a position beside the door. Almost like a guard, he thought.

"Thank you for stepping in, Lark. Now, what did you have to say, Mr. Halvorsen?"

"Well, maybe I better talk to Dan."

"My father's in no condition to see you. If you have something to say, say it to me. If you can't, I'll have to ask you to leave." She paused, added, "Sorry, it hasn't exactly been a great week."

"Not for me either," said Halvorsen. He cleared his throat, unsure how to begin, though he'd rehearsed this several times on the way up. And he had to admit it, this well-dressed woman with the air of command intimidated him. Her eyes were just like her dad's . . . At last he said, "I was out hikin' in the Kinningmahontawany. And I ran into some people out there I think might a' worked for you."

"I don't monitor day-to-day operations. We have foremen who—"

"You might know about this one." He cleared his throat again of the coppery taste. Really ought to get his gums looked at, that sore spot wasn't getting any better. He coughed, then jerked his tired, stiff mind back to the matter at hand.

"Anyway I was out there, and I run into some fellas in Floyd Hollow running a gas production operation. But there ain't no gas down there. I know, I drilled lookin' for it when I worked for Dan. There was some over east of there, but it ran out years ago."

He had her attention, but she wasn't giving him any help. She just sat looking at him. Waiting. So he went on. "Two fellas name of Eisen and Olen. Anyway, they got them some Vietnam refugees to do the heavy work, and they kept 'em there with dogs. Killed at least a couple of them; like that woman they found, you might of heard about that. When I stumbled onto 'em they tried to kill me, and a little girl too, keep us quiet. I didn't think that was right."

Ainslee sat back, mastering her first surprise to wonder how much more this strange old man knew and what she would have to do to keep him quiet about it. But first she'd stonewall, test his confidence. "This is very interesting. It sounds like a matter for the police to me. But I don't understand why you came all the way out to Cherry Hill to tell me about it."

"Because the company, that Medina Company, why, it's owned by Thunder," Halvorsen said. He drew the receipt from a pocket and held it out. "There, you can see for y'self."

Ainslee glanced at it—it was some sort of bill of lading—and held it, glancing at a frowning Jones, then back at Halvorsen. "Well, I don't know exactly what to tell you, Mr. Halvorsen. I'm not aware of any subsidiary by this name. But it's possible it could fall under Mr. Frontino, or maybe Mr. Detering. Either division could have subcontractors doing production drilling. But what you were saying about there being no gas there—what did you mean by that?"

"I mean there ain't no gas there," said Halvorsen. "Plain as day."

"I'm sorry, I fail to see what you're obviously trying to tell me."

"There's no gas. Not in that hollow. Never has been. But there's a hell of a lot of it seven miles away. On the far side of Elk Creek." Halvorsen took a deep breath. "I got suspicious first when I smelled it. That there was Oriskany gas. Callin' it 'Medina' was just a cover-up, so if anybody figured to ask they'd think you were drillin' a deep formation. An' when Eisen—you know who I mean? Rod Eisen?"

"I don't recall the name," Ainslee said, but her blink told him all he needed to know.

"—When Eisen said the pressure, two thousand pounds, that told me right away it wasn't no deep gas. But what told me for sure what was going on, was when I seen that easternmost well, the one that blew. Well, you know yourself if your wells are drilled to the same formation, long as they're not that far off north-south they're all going to come in right around the same pressure. But move a couple miles east and you get three thousand pounds? Enough to blow out a two-thousand-psi valve? Gas don't work that way."

"I'm afraid you've lost me now. Really, I don't get involved in production." But under the desk she kicked her shoes off, her mind already three moves ahead of Halvorsen, setting up how to open the dealing.

He said doggedly, "What that meant was, the gas was comin' from someplace else. Percolating over through that porous Oriskany sand. And I finally figured out from where."

She favored him with the same mysterious half-smile as the lady in that painting. He couldn't remember its name. By Leonard somebody. He had to admire her, cool as a cucumber and looking so confident and beautiful that, old as he was, he still felt like he ought to have the urge even if he didn't. He was almost starting to wonder if he were barking up the wrong tree, if she really didn't know anything about this. He heard a creak behind him as the black man shifted his weight, but didn't turn, just kept his eyes on her.

Ainslee said, "All right, Mr. Halvorsen. You're obviously dying to tell me. Where *does* it come from?"

"All that gas is coming from the old Lorana field."

"Lorana's been depleted for years."

"I know, it ran out in nineteen-seventy-some. But then it got converted into a gas storage field. You know most of the gas they burn in Pittsburgh and there, it don't all come from around here. We don't produce near enough. It comes up from Louisiana and Texas on the big Consolidated pipeline."

"Go on," she said, knowing now it couldn't be any worse. Somehow this little nonentity had figured it all out, everything she and Rudy had kept running so smoothly so long. She glanced again at Jones. The bodyguard kept his eyes on the back of Halvorsen's head.

"Like I say, it comes up on the big interstate pipeline. That Texas gas is cheap in the summer, ain't no market. So they store it down there in the ground, in Lorana. Then in the winter, when the transportation lines can't keep up, they sell that stored gas to the utilities, North Penn and Natural Fuel. And that's what them wells in Floyd Hollow's doing."

"What's that, Mr. Halvorsen?"

"They ain't producing one cubic foot of gas," said Halvorsen, half-convinced now despite himself that she really didn't know about any of this and somebody down lower on the ladder was running it on his own hook. "They're just stealing it out of them storage fields on the other side of that range of hills."

"That's ridiculous. For one reason." Ainslee smiled and leaned forward. "Which kind of blows your theory, or accusation, or whatever it is, right out of the water. We own that storage field."

"Who?" said Halvorsen.

"We do. The Lorana field is run by The Thunder Group. TBC Gas Management Associates, as I recall."

"So you do know about this. I was startin' to wonder—"

Her voice sharpened. "Don't be sarcastic with me, Mr. Halvorsen. Just draw the obvious conclusion, and then please leave. If as you say Medina's owned by Thunder—and I repeat, I don't recognize the name as one of our subsidiaries—then why on earth would we want to divert our own gas?"

"Medina's owned by Thunder," said Halvorsen slowly. "Thunder owns the storage field too. They'd be stealin' from themselves. That wouldn't make too much sense, would it?"

"Of course not. Now, if you'll excuse me—"

"Unless somehow there's two kinds of gas, worth different amounts."

Ainslee sat motionless. At first he'd startled her, then amused her. But now this old man was striking her as more dangerous than he had at first seemed. She said quietly, "What do you mean by that?"

"Just this." He coughed, swallowed blood. "Tell me if I'm wrong, but— all gas ain't worth the same, even if it looks the same and smells the same and burns the same. Is it? Something about long-term and spot market—"

"You're thinking of the regulatory impact. The Natural Gas Production Act."

"Maybe . . . anyway, way I understand it, there's a two-tier system, long-term and short-term. The Texas gas, what goes into the storage field, comes in interstate on long-term contract. Five-year, ten-year contracts. Goes out to the utilities the same way. Can't change the price on that. But how about new gas? Stuff you just discovered?"

"The market sets the price," Ainslee said. "That's what we call the spot market."

"Spot price, that's higher or lower than the long-term price?"

"It's higher," said Ainslee unwillingly. She tapped her fingernails on the desk. "It's really a very stupid system. But, what can we do? The politicians set it up."

"So you got to live with it."

"Unfortunately."

"Can't do a thing about it."

"Afraid not."

Halvorsen said, "Unless there was some way you could turn long-term gas into new gas, fresh out of the well. Then pipe it out of the Wild Area and bundle it with your local production and sell it at spot price."

He waited for her response but didn't get one, so he went on. "See, I talked to a friend of mine knows the money side of the gas business. He told me it varies with the season, but right now the difference is something like twenty-five cents a thousand cubic feet. Not a lot, sounds like. But multiply that by a hundred million cubic feet a day. That's what Eisen said he was pumpin'. That's—what—twenty-five thousand dollars. Every day. That's worth committin' some meanness for. As long as you can keep it all quiet, way back there in the Kinningmahontawany."

Ainslee slipped her shoes back on and stood, deciding she'd listened long enough. She had other problems to attend to. A company to win back, Kemick and Parseghian and Blair to fight, Weyandt's treachery to punish. Being shaken down by this . . . senior citizen was a minor annoyance. If he could be kept quiet cheaply, she'd do it; if he wanted too much, another means of assuring his silence would have to be found. She remembered the receipt, still in her hand, glanced across the office at the shredder, then noticed it wasn't an original.

"It's just a copy," he said. "I got the real one safe."

She laid it carefully on her desk. "I admit nothing, Mr. Halvorsen. About Medina or anything else. But let me ask this. You seem to have made up your mind it's all true. What do you intend to do about it?"

"What you think I ought to do?"

"Well, first of all, if you have any loyalty left to Thunder, you should consider keeping it to yourself."

"Loyalty," said Halvorsen, tasting blood in his mouth again. "Meanin' I should keep my mouth shut and help you cover your dirt, because it pays my pension. Right?"

"Yours and a lot of other people's," said Ainslee quietly. "Have you thought about that? If you destroy this company, you're going to hurt a lot of people just like yourself. Employees. Pensioners. People the company owes money to, who loaned it to us in good faith. Not just the—responsible parties, whoever they may be. Have you considered that?"

"Maybe I have. And maybe I thought, if that's what I got to swallow to keep getting that pension, maybe I don't want it."

"I would think then you'd inform the police. If you believe it's all true."

"I guess that'd be the natural thing," said Halvorsen. But instead of getting up and stalking out he still sat there. Looking at her expectantly.

She examined him again, thinking, Don't offer too much. He didn't look like he had expensive tastes. She was opening her mouth to start the bidding when Jones said, suddenly, "Miss Thunner."

"Yes, Lark?"

"Before you say anything else—better let me check him out."

"Check him out?" Then she understood and nodded. "Of course, you're right. Go ahead."

"Stand up," said Jones. Halvorsen sat still a moment, then rose. "Take your coat off. That's right. Arms out. Now that down vest."

"Oh," said Ainslee, looking at the transmitter and antenna wire taped to the old man's chest. Feeling faint, she leaned against the desk, reviewing everything she'd said for any admission of guilt or knowledge. "Who sent you here?" she asked him, trying to keep her voice level.

"State attorney's office," said Halvorsen.

"Listen," said Jones.

Ainslee heard it too. For a moment it sounded like the distant howling of wolves. Then she recognized it. Sirens, coming up Cherry Hill.

"Excuse me," she said, and then, to Jones, "Lark, please call my attorney. Ask him to come at once." She walked rapidly back through the glassed-in walkway to the main house.

Her father was in bed upstairs, leaning back against the pillows with his eyes closed. The nurse sat a few feet away, reading a magazine. Ainslee said, "May I have a moment with him, please," and she got up and left, shoes squeaking across the tile floor. She drew the wicker chair close. "Dad," she murmured.

The ruined, blind eyes flickered open. The desiccated lips parted, but no sound emerged.

"Dad, I need some advice."

The withered lips worked. Finally Dan Thunner said, faintly, "What's your problem?"

She sat by his bed and explained, staring at the carefully ranked medication bottles on the side table, the green tank of oxygen. The hills were visible past it, through the window. When she got to the part about Halvorsen the old man stirred. "Red," he muttered.

"What's that?"

"Old Red Halvorsen. He still alive? Thought we . . . took care of him." Then he fell silent again. She loosened her scarf; the heat in the room was intense.

"Well, he's downstairs now. And now it seems the police know too."

"Pat Nolan . . . take care of us."

"I'm not sure your friend Mr. Nolan will be able to. Halvorsen said the state was involved."

Her father lay still for a long time as she looked out the window. The cars were pulling in, parking in the drive. Then he whispered, "I ever tell you . . . Napoleon O'Connor."

"What?" She wasn't sure she'd heard right.

"My grandfather's partner in Sinnemahoning."

"The one who died." She got to her feet, disappointment mingling with pity; he was drifting, useless, back in the past. He probably hadn't understood a word she'd said.

"That's right." Thunner licked his lips. "Only, he didn't die all by himself."

She sat down again.

"Granddad told me this. This was when the railroad ring was tryin' to break the producers, round them all up into a monopoly. Beacham wanted to fight, but O'Connor wanted to take their profits and sell out. Both of 'em half owners, and no way could he argue O'Connor to go along with him. So there was only one thing left he could do. That boiler, when it blew, wasn't accidental. It was an old boiler, but not that old.

"And in nineteen thirty-six, in the strike—sometimes you got to do things you don't enjoy doing. That strictly speaking you ought not to do. Not for yourself. For the company."

"I understand, Dad."

The old man whispered, "This you're talking about . . . sounds like you got to throw somebody to the wolves."

She said softly, "That's what I was thinking too."

"I figured you was. You were always a smart girl. Only question then is, you got what it takes? I think you do. You're a Thunner, clear through. So your only question is, who goes? Only other advice I got is, if you got any other scores to settle, now's your time. Just make sure there's no trail leadin' back to you."

His eyes sank closed again. His breathing gentled, gentled, became the steady rhythm of sleep.

She was still standing there looking down at him when she heard someone clear his throat. "Yes, Lark?" she murmured. "What is it?"

The black man stood in the doorway. "Miss Thunner. The police are waiting downstairs."

"Thanks. Did you get hold of Mr. Holstown?"

"On his way over, with his partners. He said he wanted to call Senator Buterbaugh first, though. And for you not to speak to anyone until he arrives."

"Thank you. Tell the police I'll see them as soon as counsel arrives. Have Erika offer them coffee. Now." She took a breath and put her hand on his arm. "Lark, you've always been there for our family. You have always been willing to do what had to be done."

"I try to be, Miss Thunner. I owe your dad a lot. I don't hold that lightly. I've told you that before."

"I need your help with a problem. Something you can do for me, and for him, and for all of us."

"Just tell me what it is, Miss Thunner," Jones said, holding her eyes as if he already knew what she was going to ask.

Raymondsville

Becky sat beside Charlie, her aching feet propped up on one of the waiting-room chairs. She was trying not to think where she was or what they were waiting to hear. Her mom had gone in with Jammy. Outside the narrow window of the clinic she could see the sun and the tops of the trees. For a moment, studying them, she thought they were budding. Then she saw it was big drops of melting ice, hanging on the tips of the twigs. But it wouldn't be that long till spring and Easter vacation. So far going back to school hadn't been as bad as she'd expected. If only Jammy—

The door opened and Dr. Friedman came out. Becky stared at her, trying to read her face. She couldn't. The doctor's hands were pushed deep into the pockets of her lab coat. Her blond hair hung down straight and she looked very tired. She took her glasses off and sighed, holding the back of her wrist to her eyes. Then saw them and came over, shoes squeaking on the green tile. "You're still here," she said. "We thought you left."

"We just went out for some coffee," said Becky's stepfather. "So. How is he?"

Friedman smiled wearily. "He's better."

"Better?" said Charlie suspiciously, as if he suspected a lie.

"Yes, he is. And no, I don't know why. There's a lot we don't know about this thing. I've seen this happen before in isolated cases but we have no idea why. If we did we could bottle it and give it to the others. But we don't. All I'm sure of is that the pneumonia's cleared up and his T-cell count has risen. We're out of the woods on the CNS involvement. He still shows a slight fever, so I'm going to continue some of the medications. But on the whole—" she looked away from them, out at the trees—"it's good news. It's what we call a plateau, an interval of stability."

Her stepfather said, "But he's actually better." And looking up at him, Becky saw him brush something out of his eye. A tear. She thought in astonished wonder: He cares. She hadn't thought he did.

"Yes. And that's the important thing."

She asked the doctor, "How long will he feel good this time?"

"I don't know. I can't make any promises. We won't give up. But I want you both to know the truth. It could be anytime. Liver failure, another seizure, another bout of penumonia—it's going to happen eventually. There's not much question about that. I'm sorry, but that's the way it is."

Neither of them said anything. Dr. Friedman turned to Becky, smoothed her hair. "And you, how are you doing, Miss Benning? How's the arm?"

"Okay. Better. I can lift things now."

"And the rest of you?"

"My toes still hurt."

"You're lucky you've still got them all, young lady. You were about that far from losing some of them. How's the counseling coming?"

"All right," she said. She didn't want to admit it, but it was fun talking to Ms. Gallup. She didn't ever say much but it was the way she listened. And sometimes when she did say something, it was funny how things made sense all of a sudden, like how she felt about Mr. Cash, about Jammy, about the nightmares she still had about being lost in the woods.

The door behind Dr. Friedman opened and their mom held it as Jammy toddled out. He was flushed and he had a Band-Aid on the back of his hand but aside from that he looked fine. He ran over to them and buried his face in Becky's lap. She bent to hug him and then all at once she felt her mother's arms around them and then, amazingly, Charlie's too.

For a moment they all clung together, to one another. She thought in wonder, feeling tears sting her eyes: We're a family. She didn't know who or what to thank but her heart had to thank someone. Maybe no one knew how long it or anything else would last, but they were together right now. She held her little brother tight and prayed, to a wolf prince or a dream or God or whoever was listening: Thanks. Please let us stay together as long as we can, and remember to love each other even when things don't go as good as they did today.

THUNDER EXECUTIVE FOUND DEAD AT HIS HOME
by Sarah Baransky

The body of Mr. Rudolf T. Weyandt of Dale Hollow was discovered by neighbors early Thursday at his residence. They were attracted to the closed garage by the continuing sound of an automobile horn.

Mr. Weyandt was a senior executive at The Thunder Group of Petroleum City. His death is being investigated, but the Hemlock County coroner, Dr. Charles Whitecar, stated that it was apparently self-inflicted. The cause of death was listed as carbon monoxide poisoning.

Chief of Police Patrick N. Nolan stated that a note and several documents were found on the seat next to Mr. Weyandt's body. Chief Nolan told the *Century* that the information in the documents may prove instrumental in assigning responsibility in several ongoing investigations. He declined to comment further pending legal advice, but confirmed that they shed light on several recent deaths in the

Hemlock County area. Mr. Weyandt had recently been involved in a business altercation and another Thunder executive, reached by telephone, confirmed that he had seemed despondent in recent days. Mr. Weyandt is survived by a sister, nieces and nephews living out of state. Funeral arrangements are pending.

The Floyd Valley

Pham and Xuan stood uneasily at the end of the line before the tables the Immigration and Naturalization Service had set up outside the bunkhouse. They had discussed in low tones whether it was wise to wait. Whether an unobtrusive slipping away might not be the better choice. But the men in the dark blue jumpsuits carried guns. The woods, too, still surrounded them, the savage forest that had eaten Mr. Eisen, and Mr. Olen's dogs, and into which the fat American, the last of their captors, had disappeared the day after Eisen's death. The day before the helicopter had set down not far from the empty pens. Anyway, where could they flee to? So they stood glumly silent all morning as the queue slowly shortened.

The first surprise came when Pham, shifting uneasily on his freezing feet, saw the woman at the first table they'd reach. The people at the others were white or black, but she was Vietnamese. She wasn't in uniform, but in a nice cloth coat and expensive-looking boots. Several large cardboard boxes sat behind her. While he was goggling she pointed at him. He straightened and stepped up quickly.

"Good morning," she said. Not in English, in Vietnamese, and more politely than anyone had ever spoken to him yet in America. "My name is Minh, and I'd like to have a word with you before you meet with the INS. I'm not with the government. We cooperate with them, but we're a private relief agency, assisting in migration counseling. All right? May I have your name, please?"

He gave his name. She asked him several other questions; his age; profession; place of birth; whether he had a passport or any other papers; date and manner of entry into the United States, how much he'd had to pay, who had arranged it, what had happened since then. She asked him what he thought would happen to him if he was returned to Vietnam. Finally she twisted, reaching down into a briefcase that sat in the snow, and handed him several pieces of paper and a black ballpoint pen. He looked down at them uncomprehendingly.

"Giây này day làm gì?"

"That's an order to show cause. The other papers are applications for asylum and for a temporary work permit. Fill them out today. If you have any questions, come and ask me.

"Now listen. Right now you're going to talk to the INS. After everyone has seen an agent, you'll all be helicoptered out to town and fed. There'll be a place to stay in a local motel tonight. Then tomorrow there'll be a special administrative hearing for everyone who was illegally detained at this camp. No, don't be frightened! I can't make promises for the government, but I wouldn't worry about being sent back, as long as you tell the truth. You've been treated badly enough here."

His eyes grew wide as she reached down again, then began counting out cash into his hesitantly outstretched hands. Fifty, one hundred, two hundred dollars! He stared down at it.

"Welcome to America," said the woman. "This is an emergency loan to tide you over till you can contact relatives or friends. If you have none in this country, we'll help you find a permanent home." She glanced at his rag-wrapped feet then, nodded to one of the cardboard boxes behind her. "And look in there, pick yourself out a pair of boots." She smiled past him at an astonished Xuan. "Next!"

Mortlock Hollow

Halvorsen stood watching the white-and-brown hound cast back and forth along the open clearing beyond his woodpile. It was almost time. Couldn't put it off any longer. But still he stood sniffing the wind, still-numb hands stuffed deep into the pockets of his old red-and-black coat. On the snow beside his boots lay a duffel bag and several cardboard boxes tied with twine.

Alma beeped the horn. He waved her off impatiently, stiff-armed, still staring out over the valley. He shifted his chew and winced, then spat to the side. Still bleeding. The lady doctor had cut a little piece out of his gum, said she wanted to send it to Erie for tests. It had hurt like hell but she said it'd stop in a day or two.

Almost time to go, but he didn't want to. Too many goddamn memories out here. Of Jenny, of Alma when she was little, of all the years he'd lived and hunted and hiked out here in the hollow. But Dr. Friedman and Alma and he had had a talk, and at the end of it, he'd finally agreed to try it a while. Try it in town, staying with Alma and Fred, helping out a little around the pumps. He was still sore at his son-in-law for selling his rifles. But Fred said he had one left, an old one nobody had wanted because it didn't have a bolt. Halvorsen figured that must be his dad's old Krag. Well, a fella didn't really need more than one rifle, long as he knew how to shoot it. And he probably wouldn't have that much call for a gun anyway, now he'd be living in town.

Something caught in his throat. He coughed and coughed and then spat again, sucking in raw chill air that tasted like a knifeblade and smelled like the pines. He gazed like a yearning child at the land he'd known so well, ridge and hollow and river, the moving darkness of the clouds, the eternal hills. Christ, he thought. It is sure beautiful.

And someplace out there still, the wolves.

After the state cops busted up the gas operation and the immigration people took the Vietnamese out, there'd been quite a fuss over what to do with the wolves. They'd fought it out in the papers and had experts in from Minnesota and Canada. There'd been some talk about prosecuting the head ranger, the one who'd brought them in without, apparently, getting the right forms typed up or whatever the government said you had to do before reintroducing a predator species. But in the end they hadn't done anything to her. Some people had wanted them hunted down and wiped out. Others wanted more brought in and the land fenced off so it would be wild forever. But finally they all had sort of fought one another to a standstill, and more or less agreed to just leave the wolves that were there alone, the three or four in that one pack deep in the Kinningma-hontawany, and see what happened. See how they got along with the deer and the elk and the hunters and the farmers at the edges of the Wild Area.

Halvorsen didn't think that was a bad first step. Bring them back a little ways, see how it went. Not rushing anything, but taking it a little at a time. Himself, he kind of liked the idea of maybe bringing the panthers back too someday.

He tilted his head back and looked at the sky. The sun was bright and strong between the clouds. The snow was already soft under his boots. It had been a hell of a winter. He sure couldn't say he was sorry to see it end.

Yeah, the wolves . . . he still didn't understand what he'd seen that day, below the falls. He'd never told anybody about it and far as he knew the girl never had either. It was a secret between them.

He didn't understand, but maybe he'd learned something from it. If only that it was okay to take the hand, or the teeth, or whatever or however it was that somebody tried to help you.

Thinking of the wolves, that they both destroyed and saved, he thought they were a lot like people. Some were like the deer and others were like the wolf. The ones who preyed, and the ones who were eaten. You had to have wolves, or something like them, for the balance of nature to work. So maybe you had to have evil, for the same reason?

He looked down at the hound. She snorted, growled, then suddenly lifted her nose in a barking howl.

But then he thought, No, that's wrong. Man was no longer part of nature. He knew too much. But knowledge brought a burden. The distinction between right and wrong. With dreadful cost, and dreadful slow, he'd learned to respect his fellow man, and woman, and even those who looked different from himself. Now, just as painfully, he was learning to make peace with the land and the sea and the sky. Realizing you couldn't just do what you wanted and to hell with the consequences, like they had when he was young.

Standing there, he felt a sudden compassion for people, for every one, as if he were looking down not from the hill but from somewhere far above. They didn't live very long and all the while they knew they were going to die. So they lived their lives half-crazy with selfishness and fear. And just when they began to figure the real score, the game was over.

The wonder isn't that we make mistakes, he thought. The wonder is we keep on stumbling ahead.

They were all just going to have to grow up. And like any kid, that meant learning to share.

The horn beeped again. "Son of a *bitch*," the old man muttered. Then, aloud, "Come on, Jess! Get your tail in the damn truck."

Sitting stiffly erect in the cab, he did not look back as the truck jolted out of the clearing. Only forward, as the woods fell back and they turned at last onto Route 6; and below the brightening sky, W. T. Halvorsen returned to the haunts of men.

The Kinningmahontawany

Not far from the den, under a stand of old hemlock above a frozen spring, the silver wolf faced the others as the light ebbed toward vanishing.

They ringed him, the familiar faces turned strangers, distorted with horror and hate. As he swung his muzzle from one set of snarling teeth to another his suppurating, useless hindquarters dragged in the snow. The bite at the base of his tail had grown infected, had swollen with pus. The smell and sight of it seemed to infuriate the other wolves, driving them into a growling, snapping frenzy. Facing them, the old wolf understood.

It was the way of the wolves. He too, when he was young, had driven out the old, packmates with worn teeth, the badly wounded; those who could no longer hunt, and who thus threatened the survival of the others. He recalled them only dimly, but he remembered the lesson. Before any individual, the Pack. A choice was given those who were driven out. Vanquished, they could linger solitary and alone at the edges of the territory, and flee from any other wolf. Or they could follow the pack at a distance, and scavenge what they could from the abandoned kills. Feed on their leavings, growing ever more gaunt and spiritless till death came for them some wintry night.

Neither choice appealed to him.

Now from behind the bobtail and the female, the dark wolf stalked out stiff-legged. A long-suppressed hatred gleamed in its eyes, and a long-swallowed growl rumbled in its chest.

The old wolf looked away from it, disdaining to acknowledge the challenge. Aloof, he stared up through the crowns of the ancient trees to the stars, becoming faintly visible beyond. He did not know how old they were, the trees or the stars. Nor did he care. All he knew was that they existed, and they always would, sheltering the pack beneath them.

The dark wolf closed and thrust at him with its chest. The old wolf started to snarl, feeling the familiar joy of battle throb in his chest. Crippled as he was, he might still defeat his challenger. But then he lifted his head again, sheathing his still dangerous teeth lest he be tempted to strike back. He could battle, true. But either his victory or his defeat would only hurt the pack.

He did not care to leave, and he could no longer lead.

For a wolf, only one path remained.

He turned his gaze full into the face of the dark one, and snarled defiance to encourage its rage. But when the blow came, the first sharp scimitar of tearing incisor, he neither flinched nor struck back. Simply stood, head still lifted as they all closed in now, staring up at the stars until the darkness between them swelled and like a charging wolf rushed down toward his own upthrust, gasping muzzle.

When they finally lifted their heads nothing remained but a scrap of hide, a gnawed bone, a clump of fur clinging to the scuffled snow. They gazed at each other, obscurely puzzled. The female whined once, pawing at a small pool of blood. Then dipped her head and licked, greedy for nourishment for the new lives within her.

At last the dark wolf pointed its muzzle at the stars, now shining bright and clear and unblinking down on them all from the everlasting dark. A cry rang out, high and eerie. One by one the others joined in, each choosing a different note, building their wailing, haunting chorus into a long-drawn-out paean to the ancient woods and sky; echoing endlessly out over the dark and empty hills, as if asserting that something lived that time itself could never conquer; until this song, too, sank into silence beneath the gently lofting moon.